THE ISLAND OF LOTE

Emily Kinney

Strategic Book Publishing and Rights Co.

Strategic Book Publishing and Rights Co.
12620 FM 1960, Suite A4-507
Houston, TX 77065
www.sbpra.com

ISBN 978-1-61204-774-4

Dedication

E. K. –
For Jaime, Debra, Jabez,
Mikey, Jona-Lynn, and Jeri.
Thank you for believing in me.

Table of Contents

1
The New Neighborhood

THERE ARE TWO very different types of people in the world:
Individuals and followers. Individuals are their own person, and are
exactly who they want to be. Followers try to take on the image of
the individuals, and do things exactly like them. Individuals don't
follow the crowd, unlike the followers, but create their own image
and don't care what people think of it. Some of the individuals and
the followers are rather rebellious. Some choose to be that way,
while others simply ended up that way, due to pressure. While most
rebellions aren't very much appreciated, there are times when they
can be quite useful. They can help keep people out of trouble, or
help teach them to stand for what they believe in, which you don't
see all that often.

One very good-rebellious person in the world was sitting on a
car seat one warm afternoon, hugging her knees, and was staring
out a window. This person was a fourteen year-old girl, named Milo
Hestler. And she was distraught. At least her stomach was.

Speaking of which, the distraught feeling in Milo Hestler's
stomach increased to an almost unbearable amount as she gazed out
the window of her parent's car. They were driving through a
neighborhood called Shady Ally. Though it seemed to Milo that it
was more like a city than a neighborhood, but her parents declared

it a neighborhood, so it remained that. She also didn't know why it wasn't spelled with an 'e'.

The reason it seemed more like a city was because there were no houses. The only living quarters in Shady Ally were apartment buildings. Dozens of them, all lined up next to each other on each side of the road. That road was the only road there, stretching leisurely onward, making it look more like an actual alleyway. Each apartment building was about thirty to fifty stories high, and they took up most of the sky view. The sun was rarely ever directly over head, but always more to the side, casting shadows from the buildings into the street. So in a way, it really was like a shady alleyway. Why the good people who inhabited the place wanted to use "ally" instead of "alley" was a mystery. An ally is supposed to be someone you trust and rely on. If your ally is shady, it probably isn't a wise idea to continue the relationship.

But that was a very small reason why Milo was feeling nervous. Like any kid moving into a new home, she was worried about adjusting and making friends. The first home she lived in had burned down when she was little, forcing her family to move. She had many friends and relations there and was heartbroken to leave them, especially when she moved into their new house and found that nobody wanted to be friends with her. She moved three times after that, and each time she never made any more friends. She also lost contact with her friends and relations from her first residence.

Continuously finding herself alone, Milo began to fear that she would never have another friend again. She was wrong about that, of course, but for the time being, she begrudgingly sat scrunched in the back seat of a 2002 Camry.

"We're here!" her mother's voice sang out as they braked in front of 711 Shady Ally.

"Ooooh! Goodie!" Milo snapped. "Let's hope we all don't puke with joy!"

Milo occasionally got creative with her words.

Her father turned around in his seat and glared at her.

"Sorry!" she said, lowering her eyes. "It's just that, how do we know that this time we're actually 'here'?"

"Oh, Milo," her mother groaned, grinding the heel of her hand into her forehead. "Can't you just try to be a little happy? I mean, we've been driving around all day, all yesterday, and all of last week. We didn't drive all that way not to be 'here'."

It was Milo's turn to groan.

"Fine!" she mumbled. "I'm a little happy. At least we can get out of this car." She opened her door and got out.

"That's the spirit, hon!" her father said heartily, swinging his door all the way open.

Whenever Milo's father wasn't mad at her, he called her "hon".

"You'll see," he continued. "Things will be different here. You'll make plenty of friends and get used to living here like that." He snapped his fingers. "It'd be impossible not to. You don't even need to leave the building for anything! Your mom and I will have to leave for work of course, but you won't ever have any reason to go outside again, hon!"

Milo stopped in her steps, which were leading to the trunk of the car.

"What do you mean?" she asked, her stomach not settling any.

Both her parents grinned at her.

"We wanted to surprise you," her mother said. "The building we are going to live in, 711, is one of the neighborhood buildings in Shady Ally."

"It's an entire system of living inside one place, hon," her father said. He pulled two suitcases out of the trunk and handed both of them to Milo's mother.

"It's huge!" she exclaimed, obviously sold on the idea long ago. "The building I mean. The idea of an entire neighborhood inside one place isn't very popular at the moment. I don't know why, it seems wonderfully convenient to me. But, as I was saying, the building is gigantic. It has everything you need inside it. First and foremost, a school –"

"A school!" Milo broke in, her eyebrows up. "Right in an apartment building?"

"Yes," her mother said. "Not only that, but also a Wal-Mart and a miniature mall. That's all in the basement. The school is the entire thirty-eighth floor. There are restaurants too, like Burger King and the Olive Garden!"

Milo scrunched up her nose. Despite the fact that she couldn't believe that all this was crammed into one building, she had to sneer at the thought of any restaurant. The family had been on the road for two weeks, eating nothing but fast food. Therefore, just the thought of Burger King made her want to throw-up. She didn't really mind the Olive Garden, but it was still a restaurant and restaurants weren't something that Milo approved of.

Milo preferred to make her own food. She had been interested in cooking ever since she first saw an oven. She kept a large notebook filled with recipes that she had copied from cookbooks. Every time she would find a recipe that she liked, she would copy on a blank page of the notebook, slowly compiling a complete cookbook.

She took this notebook everywhere with her, along with the two other most important things in her life. All three were in the backpack her mother handed to her. The other two were a diary, in which she was writing down her life, and her little radio and headphones.

Without these things, Milo figured she'd die or suffer from some sudden madness. She would write in her diary whenever something interesting in her life happened, such as her house burning down or moving three times. And she would listen to her radio often, in order to relax and momentarily forget about her troubles. She kept extra pens and batteries with her in case one or the other ran out or got lost just when she desperately needed them.

Turning away from the car, with her backpack on her shoulder and a suitcase in each hand, Milo stared up at the building in front of her. Tilting her head back, she could just make out the roof of the building, and much to her surprise, she saw the crowns of trees sticking up from it.

"Uh, Mom," Milo said. "What's that?" She pointed her left suit-case at the roof. Her mother peered upward.

"Oh, right!" she said absently. "There's a garden on the roof."

"Really?" Milo said, perking up. "That sounds cool. It's been a while since I've been able to be alone with nature. This place might not be that bad after all!"

"Not bad?" her father said, striding towards the doors, laden with luggage. "It's the most fantastic place in the world, hon! And the rent's not bad, either. What more could you ask for?"

"Friends?" Milo asked shyly.

Her parents grinned at her. Her mother put her arm around her shoulder and guided her to the doors, her father holding one open with some difficulty.

"You'll see," her mother said confidently. "Things will be different here."

Of course things weren't going to be, but Milo didn't know that. Almost smiling, she and her parents strolled into the lobby, which was decorated with tinsel.

Milo's mother walked up to the tinsel strewn desk and found the bell. Three rings brought a woman in from another room, tottering on heels far too high.

"Hello?" she said, looking around as if blind. She then reached into a skirt pocket and pulled out a pair of eye-glasses. She slid them on and jumped back in surprise, not helping her precarious balance.

"Oh! My! I mean, hello." She smiled broadly. Milo's mother smiled too.

"Hi there," she said. "We are the new tenants. You must be the Lobby Secretary?"

Personally, Milo had never heard of a "lobby secretary" before, but the woman immediately said, "Oh. Yes. I mean yes! Of course I am! I'm Miz Ricca, and you must be the . . ."

Not waiting for a reply, she made her wobbly way past them to the desk, where she began to flip through a registry book.

"Hestlers?" she finished, squinting at a spot on a page.

"That's right!" Milo's father replied robustly, grinning.

"Well, welcome to 711 Shady Ally!" Miz Ricca said, bringing out a set of keys and handing them to him. "Here are your keys, you can make as many copies as you want, and I look forward to getting to know each one of you!"

"Well, thank you!" Milo's mother said sweetly. "Let's start right now, shall we? I'm Sherrill-Jean Hestler, and this is my husband, Earnest, and our daughter, Milolantalita."

"Actually, it's just Milo," Milo piped up, not knowing where on Earth her mother had come up with "Milolantalita".

It most certainly was not on her birth certificate. She had heard the story often enough of how, at her birth, they had wanted to name her Mila, but her father's hand writing had caused the 'a' to look like an 'o', and it got recorded that way. Though they both claimed that they liked it better that way, Milo always had a feeling that her mother was rather miffed that her daughter had a boy's name.

Her mother nudged her hard and said, "Now tell us your name. Surely there's more to it than 'Miz Ricca'."

"Oh! No! I mean, no. I'm sorry, dear," Miz Ricca said apologetically, seemingly startled. "I'm not allowed to tell you or let you use my first name. It's a Lobby Secretary thing, and if I make an exception for you than I'll have to make an exception for everybody! And believe me, there's a fair number of young men in this place who would love to call me Reba! Now then, if you need anything I'll be here, and if you get lost, there are maps all over the building."

"Reba Ricca?" Milo muttered to herself.

"And if you have any questions," she added, "don't hesitate to ask."

"Yeah," Milo said, jumping at the opportunity. "Why is Shady Ally spelled without the 'e'?"

Miz Ricca's lips became a line. "What do you mean?" she said casually.

"I mean," Milo said clearly. "A – l – l – y spells al-i. Alley is spelled a – l – l – e – y."

"Oh," Miz Ricca said, looking away. "That. Well, it does read alley, only they thought it would look nicer without the 'e'. It's still the same thing."

"But," Milo insisted. "It says al-i. Not alley."

"Yes, it does."

"No, it doesn't."

"Yes, it does!"

"Thank you, Miz Ricca!" her father said abruptly, well aware of his daughter's legendary stubbornness, and wanting to actually reach their apartment some time that day. "You've been very helpful. By the way, I like what you have done with the lobby."

Miz Reba Ricca glanced around, distracted and pleased. "Really? You do? Well, thanks. It's one of my own designs."

Milo, deciding to let the issue go, took in her surroundings and couldn't quite see where the word "design" came in. Tinsel was strewn all over the carpeting, all over the furniture, and was glued onto the walls. Milo looked up and saw it dangling from the ceiling in great clusters. The only thing it didn't seem to be covering were the lights, which shone down on it all, making the room look very bright and glittery.

"I think it perks the room up a little," Miz Ricca said.

"*A little?*" Milo thought.

"The elevators are over there," Miz Ricca said, pointing to a hallway on the left side of the desk. "I can see that you have quite a lot of luggage, and elevators are always better than the stairs.

Nobody in the building ever really uses the stairs, so we had to install extra elevators. We might have removed the stairs entirely, except for those pesky building codes. Escaping fire and such. I'd help you with your luggage, but I'm afraid of hurting my back. I've not much practice with large, heavy objects; the most I've carried around is papers, pens, keys, and tinsel."

"That's quite alright, Miz Ricca," Milo's father said, hoisting several bags onto his shoulders. "We'll manage to manage just fine!"

He began to lead the way to the elevators. Milo followed with her mother, but something inside of her told her that it'd be better for her health to take the stairs.

That thing inside her was her conscience, and she was so often arguing with it, that she had personified it and called it Bob the Conscience. That particular day, the argument inside Milo's head, went something like this:

"You know, it'd be better for your health if you took the stairs," Bob the Conscience said.

"I know, but our apartment is on the forty-sixth floor. It'd be too tiring to go all that way with all this luggage," Milo replied as she stepped into the elevator. Sometimes, Milo was so into the conversation that she spoke out loud. But she was careful not to when she was around other people.

"You can handle your luggage," Bob the Conscience retorted. "It'll just make it more challenging. Besides, after being cramped in that car all that time, your legs could use some stretching. It will make you feel energized and happier, too. You should take the stairs."

"No," Milo insisted. "By the time I got to the forty-sixth floor, my parents would have already moved in and started dinner. The elevator is faster; look, we're already on the thirty-sixth floor! And you wanted me to take the stairs! Ha!"

She heard Bob the Conscience sigh.

"Yes, Milo," he said, patiently. "It is faster, and it is useful, if we are on a schedule. But if you keep on riding elevators, you will start to get fat!"

Milo chuckled. "That would do me a world of good," she remarked. She looked into a mirror at herself, which was an easy thing to do because enormous ones lined the walls of the elevator.

She didn't like what she saw.

She could name the things she didn't like about herself from head to toe, starting with her hair. It was a rich, dark brown that hung down past her shoulders. But Milo thought it was too dark and, like all the girls of today, she wanted highlights but didn't have any.

Moving downward, her next complaint was her body. She was very skinny for her age and it showed. Two full weeks of eating fast food, without any exercise, hadn't made her an inch rounder. Milo's arms were spindly and long, and she didn't think she had much muscle on them. Nevertheless, whenever she needed to push bullies away, she always found the strength she needed.

Her legs didn't really matter much to her, but she still found them far too slender for her liking. Indeed, she often referred to them as "tooth picks". Not that anybody could tell, for she often wore baggy jean cargo pants.

Her face didn't contribute much because it was always surrounded by her hair. It was thin, but not pinched. Sure, it wasn't filled with chubby cheeks, but at least she didn't look like she was starving. That wasn't the reason it was normally hidden by hair. The reason was that Milo couldn't find a way to keep her hair at bay. Usually, she would have it up in a ponytail to keep it out of her face, but her mother hated that look, and would always tell her to let it down. Therefore, Milo usually couldn't quite see what was on either side of her.

"It gives you a shy look," her mother had told her when Milo tried to complain about it. She had tried to explain to her mother that the look didn't suit her, because she wasn't a shy person, but her mother wouldn't listen. Milo found that happened a lot.

"It would do me a world of good," Milo repeated softly.

"What's that, dear?" her mother asked.

"Nothing," Milo said quickly.

"No," her mother said. "I'm sure I heard –"

"Here's our floor!" Milo's father sang out as the elevator stopped with a ding. "Our new lives start the minute we walk out of this elevator, ladies."

Of course, for Milo that wasn't true, but she thought it was, as she followed her parents out into the hallway and up to a door that said "B-1107". She didn't know that it would merely be a push in to her real new life.

2
Adjusting

HAVE YOU EVER heard of the saying, "Curiosity killed the cat, but satisfaction brought it back"? That saying is merely implying that sometimes when people, or cats, become so curious that they stick their human nose, or kitty nose, into something they shouldn't, and end up getting in trouble. However, they can get out of that trouble by having whoever they are in trouble with change their minds. That last part does not happen very often, though, and the "cats" usually stay "killed". This is why people usually just say, "Curiosity killed the cat." We have long forgotten about the part, "But satisfaction brought it back."

That saying can be interpreted another way; that's the way it was for Milo. Each time that she let her curiosity overthrow her common sense, she felt a little bit of herself getting killed. Occasionally she did find the satisfaction to bring back those little bits of herself, but it was never much satisfaction.

For instance, when she first stepped into her apartment, a tiny bit of her died when she saw that one of her bedroom windows had a hole in it, like some vengeful individual threw a rock through it. Oddly enough, nothing else in the apartment was harmed. Milo found a little satisfaction though; it was the beginning of June and very hot at night, so the hole in the window was appreciated rather than shunned.

When Milo finally worked up enough curiosity to walk into the school for her first day, a small part of her died when she saw that all the children in her class, and the whole school in fact, wore a snarl and XXL pants. Milo felt like a piece of angel hair spaghetti in a pot of killer meatballs, but she was somewhat satisfied to be back in school. All of the teachers were very nice, the total reverse of their irate pupils, and, also oddly enough, were just about as thin as Milo was.

The reason for this, Milo discovered, was that the entire twenty-seventh floor was a gym. All of the grown-ups in the building visited it regularly and were extremely fit. But children under the age of twenty weren't allowed to go there, it apparently being a safe haven for the adult population, and even if they could Milo had a feeling that they wouldn't.

When Milo's curiosity got the better of her and she travelled to the fourteenth floor, where the restaurants were located, a little bit of her spluttered out when she saw almost every single kid in her class at B.K. She didn't dare go in, especially when a boy with sinister eyebrows close to the entrance growled at her. She did, however, find some satisfaction when she went to O.G. and saw that their prices were half of what they were outside.

And finally, she got *soooo* curious, and bored, that she went down to the basement. Once there, an itty-bitty chunk of her died when she saw nearly all the kids in the building hanging out at the miniature mall, which she quickly learned they did basically every day. The way they glared at her made her so uncomfortable that she couldn't bring herself to enter. But she achieved some satisfaction when she went into the Wal-Mart and saw that very few other kids were there. She was also delighted to find a grocery store attached to it.

She bought ingredients for one of her favorite pasta recipes, and went straight up to her apartment to make it. When she arrived, though, a little bit of her died harshly when she realized they had not installed the oven yet. Frustrated, she put her ingredients in the refrigerator, which thankfully had been install, and grabbed her diary and little radio, deciding to go up to the garden. But when she got into the elevator, she saw that there was no button to take her to the roof. Milo, on the verge of utter exasperation, abandoned the elevator and took the stairs, which were rusty and noticeably neglected.

"She was right when she said that nobody uses these anymore," Milo muttered, referring to Miz Ricca. Every couple of steps or so, she had to wipe flecks of rust and dust off her hand on her jeans.

After stepping out onto the roof, quite a bit of her died woefully as she took in the garden. It was extremely overgrown and a haphazard mess, as if nobody had gardened there in decades.

There were weeds everywhere; in the path, in the flower beds, which had perhaps once held pretty, vibrant flowers, and they took over the grass. The bushes and shrubs looked like someone had stopped pruning them a long time ago. Vines grew all over and constricted the two lovely fountains, which were both cracked and dirt encrusted. The leaves from years of roof top autumns had not been raked, making a thick carpet of matted crumbling, brown leaves and coarse weeds on the ground. A tree that had grown so old and rotted that it had fallen in a swoon had not been removed, or trimmed down, and vines and lichen had claimed it for their own.

Milo, who had always been a lover of nature and well-kept gardens, wanted to cry as she gazed around at everything. There were benches that had barely any paint left on them, the wood shrunken and splitting. Way off in a corner, there was a section of the garden that appeared big enough for a small game of soccer, but was at the second stage of becoming a swamp.

"Great!" Milo muttered dismally, sitting down on one of the benches.

"I wouldn't do that if I were you!" Bob the Conscience said, but he was too late. The bench creaked then cracked, sending Milo crashing through it.

"Ow!" she whined, groping for the iron arm of the bench. "Thanks a lot, Bob!"

Despite a garden full of weeds, which was undoubtedly full of all kinds of insect life, and unstable benches, Milo found satisfaction in the fact that no one else was up there with her. She was at last completely alone. She found a moss covered rock under a tree and sat down. She slipped on her headphones, turned the radio on, and tuned into a good hip-hop station, since that was the music she liked best. She spent about two hours in the garden, scribbling ferociously in her diary. At about 4:45, she decided to go back.

As she stood up, she happened to brush off some moss from the rock and an engraving materialized. Curious, she took a closer look, scraping off more moss with her fingernails. It read:

"This garden is dedicated to the mayor of Shady Ally. Let us hope that when we get one, he will come here."

"Okay?" Milo said, confused. "That's nice, I guess. But . . . heck, if it's in this bad a condition, they probably never did get one!"

She straightened up and trudged back to door to the stairwell, but instead of going to B-1107, she rode the elevator down to the lobby. Once there, she carefully picked her way through the tinsel, finally making it to the desk. Miz Ricca being nowhere in sight, she located the bell and rang it three times. Miz Ricca came hurrying in from the hallway on the right side of the desk.

"Hello?" she said, puzzled, then put on her glasses. "Oh. Hi!" she exclaimed after seeing Milo. Milo gave a little wave.

"Good afternoon," Miz Ricca said cordially, her brow furrowing. "I'm so sorry, but . . . who – I mean, what is your name . . .?"

"Milo," Milo said.

"Oh. Yes," Miz Ricca said, chuckling pleasantly. "Of course, how could I have forgotten? Well, Mila, what can I do for you?"

"Actually it's MILO, trust me, and I was just wondering about the garden on the roof."

"Yes, what about it?" Miz Ricca asked, teetering towards a chair that didn't seem to have enough tinsel on it.

"Well," Milo said slowly, watching her. "It seems a little, let's see, how shall I put it? Un-taken care of."

"You've been up there?" Miz Ricca cried, whisking around in alarm, her ankles almost giving way.

"Yes," Milo said, feeling uneasy. "Why? Is it off limits or something?"

"Oh. No," Miz Ricca admitted, patting gently at her hair, as if worried her sudden movement had disturbed it. "It's just that – well, the reason for it being so unruly is because we haven't really bothered to hire a gardener to keep it well groomed."

"Why not?" Milo asked, hoping she knew that they were talking about a garden and not a dog.

"Because, nobody goes up there," Miz Ricca said carelessly, flicking some tinsel off her sweater. "So it's not worth it. The new elevators don't even have a button that leads up there. I heard that it was once a very popular place in the building. You know; a place where the kids could go and get exercise. But then its splendor wore off, and people didn't care for it anymore. And besides, they were sick of paying the bills for it; so many other worthwhile things to have bills for. It was completely forgotten when the mall and restaurants came. But that's only what I heard."

"Oh," Milo said softly. She felt discouraged. "But it's okay if I go up there, right?"

"Hmm? Oh. Sure. But if I were you, I wouldn't. As you probably guessed, as Lobby Secretary I hear a lot of rumors, and one that I am always hearing is that the garden is full of lice!"

Milo's eyes widened. "Lice?" she croaked.

Miz Ricca nodded amiably. "Yep. Uh-huh. Just chock full."

Milo stiffened and began to walk backwards down the left

hallway.

"Um, thanks, Miz Ricca," she said.

Miz Ricca smiled and waved. "No problem, dear. Take care. See you later!"

"Yeah," Milo muttered, turning around. "Sure you will."

She pressed the button for an elevator then checked to see that she was alone.

"Bob!" she hissed. "Bob! Answer me! I know you're there! You can't be anywhere else!" "Actually," Bob the Conscience whispered ruefully, "I was in the membrane preparing my dinner. Oh, Milo! I'm sorry. How was I supposed to know that it was a lice garden?"

"I don't know!" she hissed back. "You knew that bench was crap and you told me!"

"Well, that one was obvious!"

"And a weed-filled garden isn't?"

Bob the Conscience, for once in his life, was speechless. That's not a good thing for a conscience to be. Bob the Conscience was aware of that, so he spoke anyway.

"Okay! So I didn't see it. But you didn't either. I thought you had more sense than that."

"I do!" she shouted by accident. "I do," she hissed, glancing around hastily, seeing if anyone had heard. The elevator opened and she stepped in. "It's just that you are my conscience and now thanks to you lice may be partying all over me! Now look, boi! If you don't perk up and pull your act together, I'm going to find a new conscience!"

Bob the Conscience gasped in horror. "You wouldn't dare!"

"Oh, yes I would! Get it?"

Bob the Conscience groaned. "Yes, ma'am."

"Good," Milo said tartly, as the elevator stopped at a floor different from the one she had punched in. Somebody else had called it there, and as the doors parted she saw who. Five kids from her class stalked into the elevator and began their habitual glaring.

"Well," one of the boys said loudly as the doors closed. "Look who it is! Otis!"

Milo gulped. "That's Milo," she said, quaking.

The boy growled low in his throat. "Right," he said. "Milo, the little shrimp who decided to die!"

"Actually, no," Milo replied, her voice getting higher. "I don't. Not that it wasn't nice of you to offer!" she added quickly. "It's just that I would prefer *not* to die. Not that I believe that you would actually kill me!"

She chuckled weakly, clutching her diary to her chest, her eyes shifting from one face to another.

The boy leaned forward, leering, and said, "What makes you so sure?"

"She's such a snob!" a girl piped up. "Always eating at the Olive Garden alone and not talking to anyone in class!"

Milo wanted to explain why she was doing such things, but thought it better not to. Right then, accusing them of anything didn't seem like the best way to get out of the situation.

"Well," the boy said, grinning evilly. "We know what to do with snobs!"

"I told you, you should have taken the stairs," Bob the Conscience said grimly.

· · · · · ·

"You could have called for help," Milo's mother said to her some time later back at B-1107.

"I was in an elevator!" Milo cried. She was sitting on a counter, holding an ice pack to her head, while at the same time nursing both a nose-bleed and split lip. Her parents hadn't exactly been thrilled to come home to find their daughter in such a battered state. This was far from the first time, and quite frankly they were getting quite tired of it.

"That's not the point, Milo!" her father said. He had a tone in his voice that was purposely not comforting her. He had taken a wide stance in front of her, arms crossed. "I am sick of you always getting into fights! It seems to happen everywhere we go!"

"Hey, it's not my fault this fight happened!" she said defensively.

"Why do you always do this?" her father asked, ignoring what she said. "Is it because you want attention? I always thought you liked to be alone; to be by yourself. Not that I think it's good for you to always be alone. I would prefer it if you were active in a group or something. You don't get into groups by picking fights. You only get into gangs that way and you certainly are not joining a gang! You also don't make friends this way. I thought you wanted to make friends?"

"I do!" Milo said, fuming. "I told you, this wasn't my fault! I didn't cause it! I don't go around picking fights. They come to me!"

"Nonsense!" her father said dismissively. He raised his chin and looked down his nose at her. "I don't believe you. You know what I heard from your teacher? That you don't 'interact' with the other students! Look, Milo, I am not raising a stuck-up child! For some reason I always thought that you were a shy, sweet little girl. My little girl. My little baby girl! Now what's a father to think when his little baby girl is always coming home with black eyes and broken bones?"

"First of all," Milo said, wincing as she moved her lip. "I only got a black eye once, and I've never had any broken bones!"

"That's not the point," her father shouted at her, his temper flaring up. "The point is that instead of shaking hand, you use yours to make a fist."

"Second of all," Milo continued through her teeth, forcing herself to ignore him. "I was never your shy, sweet little girl. I am not shy or sweet, and you have never considered me your 'baby girl'. I've always been 'hon'! You never have been there to comfort me. It seems like you just blame me to make parenting easier for you!"

"That's enough, Milo!" her mother said sharply. "You have no right to talk to your father that way! I am very disappointed in you!"

"As am I!" her father agreed. "How dare you say such a thing? You ought to be ashamed of yourself! The utter ingratitude! We bring you to this wondrous place, supplied with everything you would ever need. Friends included, but for some reason you seem to think that every person on the planet is against you."

"No," Milo objected, shifting the ice pack on her forehead. "Only anyone who gives me the stink eye."

"Is that so? And exactly what evidence have you seen that proves that any child in this building is a bully?"

"Have you seen the kids in this building?!" Milo asked in astonishment.

"That's not nice, Milo!" her mother said. "Just because the children here are slightly obese, doesn't give you the right to talk so."

"Slightly?" Milo said dubiously, even though she had meant their irate attitudes.

"Milo!"

"Enough!" her father shouted. He ran his fingers through his hair, thoroughly worked up. "Milo, I am disgusted with you! And what's more, you are grounded for a week!"

"What?!" she cried, almost toppling off the counter. "That's not fair. . . . At all!"

"Provoking kids with cruel remarks is what's not fair. When you say things like that to them, of course they are going to release their hurt inappropriately."

"I didn't . . . I – I would never do something like that!"

"No? Then how come you came home absolutely injured?" her mother inquired smartly.

"*Because!*" Milo cried out desperately. "They're all bullies! They growl at me whenever I'm around them for Pete's sake! Like pit bulls! I don't know why they did this to me! Who knows? Maybe they're jealous of me or something. Jealous of how I look."

"Jealous of how you look?" her father said incredulously.

"Well, why not?" her mother asked, briefly siding with her daughter. "I can imagine why they would be. She is a lovely girl."

"That's not what I mean," Milo said, gingerly touching the bump on her lip.

"That still wouldn't be enough to provoke them," her father insisted skeptically.

"Why not?" Milo spat, though she didn't mean to and used her ice pack to wipe it off the counter top. "I always told you, Mom, that some day my looks would get me into trouble! And I guarantee you that this won't be the last time!"

Although Milo didn't actually know this, it was quite true.

"Unbelievable!" her father exclaimed, rubbing one temple and starting to pace. "The excuses you come up with! The ungratefulness! Everything you would want; everything you would need! One place! Nothing but trouble, always!"

"Not everything I need is here," Milo interjected, pointing to the empty corner in the kitchen.

"The oven isn't installed."

Her father glanced at the desolate corner, then back at her. "There are well priced restaurants on one of the floors. You don't need an oven," he stated.

"I need an oven," she insisted.

He rolled his eyes. "Fine!" he said. "If you need one that badly, then you can buy one at the mall in the basement."

"I don't have money for something like that!" Milo cried in protest, sliding off the counter onto her feet.

"Well," her father said, at last looking pleased. "Isn't that your problem?"

"For your needed information," Milo snarled, "cooking happens to be my most favorite thing in the world! But of course you wouldn't know that, because you continuously find short-cuts around parenting!"

"ENOUGH!" both her parents yelled at once.

"Go to your room!" her mother shouted, face flushed from either shame or rage, or both.

"You mean my naturally air-conditioned room?!" Milo asked savagely.

"Yes!" her father snapped. "And you are still grounded for a week!"

Milo grabbed her ice pack, then stormed into her room and slammed the door. This is a very loud and rude gesture, but after all that had occurred, slamming her door made Milo feel quite good.

"Well, look on the bright side," Bob the Conscience said brightly.

"What bright side?" Milo moaned, flopping onto her bed, her head aching for two different reasons.

"You probably gave them all lice!"

And that made Milo feel *very* good.

3
The Summer Camp

HAVE YOU EVER heard of the most-of-the-time-true theory that after a good night's rest everybody is in a better mood, and they take back things they said and punishments they inflicted? This theory did not come to pass for Milo and her parents. When Milo awoke the next day, she was hardly in a better mood; her head and lip still hurt, and she was freezing because it had been an unusually cold night.

Her parents were also not in a better mood because, instead of going to bed and forgetting the fight, they had started a fresh one with each other. This fight had lasted half the night, and therefore they were exhausted and grouchy in the morning, their personal dispute still lingering in their minds.

Since not one of them was in a better mood, nobody took back anything they said, and so Milo remained grounded. Grounded of course means the same thing in an apartment building as it does in a house: She had to go to school, (not that she wanted to), she couldn't go to the mall, (not that she ever intended to), and she had to come straight home to sit dejectedly on the couch with no television, radio, or books.

None of it truly bothered Milo, besides the injustice, but she was now nervous about using the elevators, since they had proved to be an exceptionally dangerous mode of transportation. The danger itself had gotten worse, because Milo's parents had forced her to apologize to her rotund and conspicuously unblemished fellow skirmishers; in front of their parents, no less.

She recited her lines in front many crossed arms and narrowed eyes, the kids smirking menacingly at her from behind their parents. Milo, with sinking spirits, knew that they were thinking that if they ever did it again, they wouldn't get in trouble. All they would have to do was claim that Milo had offended them into passionate retaliation.

Their parents, all roughly the same shape as a tri-athlete and apparently unfamiliar with the hostile side of their children, were nothing short of enraged at Milo. They believed everything her parents described to them; or felt compelled to believe it, much in the way all parents feel they must put faith in their offspring instead of visible evidence. Therefore Milo, standing before them bruised and swollen, was found guilty of all accusations.

This was how the parents of the elevator terrors came to have an unfair and unwarranted grudge against Milo. They, along with their kids, glared at her whenever she happened to be nearby. To avoid this, and any more future beatings, Milo made the decision to take the stairs back and forth between her apartment and school. It was only eight floors, which wasn't nearly as bad as what she was avoiding.

An entire week of sneaking around in a stairwell sounds tiring, but Milo actually benefited from it. Because she was grounded, she also couldn't go to the restaurant floor; therefore, her father, annoyed but left with no choice, bought an oven and installed it. Otherwise she would have starved. Its presence made Milo a little happy, until her parents told her to prepare a special dinner for her adversaries and their parents, as a further apology.

Milo was furious, but powerless and a night of pure tension, but delicious food, at the dinner table occurred. The kids, apparently not only violent but scheming too, were even more convinced to gang up on Milo again. Why not? They wouldn't get in trouble and also get a lovely meal out of it. Milo was therefore reduced to peeking around corners and tiptoeing down hallways if alone or, whenever possible, always standing close to some version of an adult. She was receiving plenty of sidelong glances, but right then she valued her health more than her pride.

The entire week dragged by with excruciating slowness, Milo becoming increasingly frazzled by the day. To boost her morale, she began to pretend that she was the last golden, scarlet-spotted leopard in the rainforest, evading ruthless poachers. This lasted until a few snide comments from Bob the Conscience put an end to it.

After the week went by, her parents, never exactly ones to dwell on anything, had completely forgotten their fight with Milo, and were in terrific moods; partly because they were both having a very good week at work. Milo's mother had been promoted to a higher rank, even though she had only started there a short time ago. And her father, whose company was stationed practically everywhere, had received a large raise.

They both were happy and jolly when they came home for dinner. They chatted cheerfully to each other, not noticing that Milo wasn't making a sound and was just picking at her food. This lasted for a couple of days after the "Week of Horror", until they realized she looked thinner than usual.

"What's the matter, hon?" her father finally asked during one meal. "You aren't eating very much."

"Not very hungry," she replied tonelessly, not looking at him.

"You haven't been very hungry for a few days," her mother pointed out. "Is there anything you want to talk about?"

Milo wearily lifted her head to look at her parent's kind, inviting faces. Her shoulders sagged.

Yes. Sure there were things she wanted to tell them. She wanted to tell them about the way she journeyed to and from school each day; slinking around and hiding until she was in a teacher's sight. She wanted to share how she stayed home on weekends, doing nothing and going crazy. She didn't dare venture out of the apartment in general; too risky. She longed, rather sulkily, to tell them about how she had lice all through the "Week of Horror", and how she had to secretly go to the school nurse for a bottle of medicated shampoo.

There were also the recurring nightmares she had of tinsel turning into a monster and decorating her room; the fact that word of no punishments and lovely dinners had spread to most of the kids in the building; the stairs were exhausting her; the way kids and adults looked at her when she walked by; she hadn't had any peace too long a time; and the only way she got any fresh air was when she went to bed at night, only end up with a cold in the morning.

"No peace," Milo thought sullenly. *"No place where I can think."*

"No," Milo said to her parents, sighing. "There's nothing."

"Are you sure?" her mother pressed.

Milo faced her, shaking her head.

"No, not really," she said. "It's nothing. Really. I'm just a little . . . overwhelmed. I guess it's the whole moving experience. . . . I just wish I could go somewhere to think all this out. Somewhere away from here."

"Is that all?" her father asked in surprise, reaching for a special bottle of wine. From the dark splotches under her eyes, he had expected more. "Well, hon, if you can find a place, you can certainly go there. My goodness, you scared me! I thought it was something else. Like a boy or something."

He saw her shocked face and giggled mischievously.

"Sorry, hon, but it's been on my mind lately. Why *don't* you have a boyfriend? A pretty girl like you should have no problem getting one."

"I'll have one when I get one!" Milo said through gritted teeth.

This was a rather delicate subject for her. She had her own theories about boyfriends and love and so on, and she was determined that nobody was going mess with them. So much in her life was indefinite, she wanted to keep at least one thing consistent.

"It is unusual. That fact," her mother said thoughtfully, taking a sip of wine, acting as if she hadn't heard her. "You know, Milo, there's a women at work who has a boy about your age. If you like, we could hook you two up."

"No!" Milo snapped, jabbing a piece of steak as she did so. "I am too young for dating. At fifteen I can start dating. I only just turned fourteen. I got another whole year to go."

"But don't you want to date, Milo?"

"Yes," she admitted reluctantly. "Of course I do. But not right now, and I want to do it my way. And my way is that I find my own boyfriend; someone that I really like and trust. You know I have my principles about stuff like that. I'm always going to live by them and nobody is going to make me do otherwise!"

That ended the discussion, though Milo, of course, was wrong about that last part. But she was contentedly unaware of this as she lay in bed, trying to think of a place where she could go for a while to clear her head. When she said her prayers, she asked God for a place to go. She didn't care where. Anywhere, really, as long as it was far away. Just a place where she could hear her own thoughts and have maybe even have a little fun.

An answer to her prayers came a few days after school ended. She was walking tentatively through the lobby when, for the first time, she noticed a bulletin board next to the doors. She hadn't seen it before because Miz Ricca had tried to cover it with tinsel. However, all the people who had put up flyers and have-you-seen papers got angry at her, and so she had to remove her special design.

Tacked to the bulletin board that particular day were flyers for a summer camp in Australia, called "Camp Outback". There was a kangaroo in the center of the paper, wearing a khaki vest and giving a cool stare. Milo took a close look at one of those flyers, grabbed it, and dashed into an elevator, scattering all manner of tinsel in her wake.

She rarely saw the lobby these days, not wanting to risk getting trapped in the elevator with any unsavory humans, and the stairs were too long. She was only down there that day because her mother had taken her to the hospital, the only service the building didn't provide. It was only a check-up, since she was very worried about Milo's health. Her appetite hadn't improved yet, and, honestly, Milo could only get so thin before she started to frighten anyone who laid eyes on her. The doctor finding her perfectly healthy, if not underweight, her mother had dropped her off at 711 before going off to work.

Milo, now giddily pressing the down button, prayed that nobody would be on the elevator with her. Once again, God came through for her, and she made it to her apartment safely. It happened to also be her father's day off, so when Milo charged into B-1107 she had a parent to show the flyer to.

"Dad! Dad!" Milo shouted into the kitchen.

"In the living room, hon!" came a voice from another room. Milo redirected herself to the living room and found her father sitting on the couch, browsing through business papers.

"Dad, look at this!" Milo said excitedly, thrusting the flyer in front of his face.

After backing up to see properly, he read, "'Camp Outback: The camp where kids get to have fun, make friends, see amazing sights, and learn the art of boomerang hunting, all in Australia's breathtaking outback. If you are interested in signing up your child, then just call the toll free number below: 1-800-Outback.'"

When he finished reading, he glanced blankly up at Milo.

"Yeah, what about it?" he asked, confused.

"What about it?" Milo repeated. She tapped a finger frantically on the kangaroo. "This is where I can go. The place we were talking about. You said if I found a place then I could go. I did. This place! This is the place! Where's the phone?"

"Whoa!" her father said, holding up his hands. "Slow down, hon! Breathe. Look, I know I said that, but I think before we do anything we should discuss it with your mom."

"Why? Can't you just call?"

"No. We have to talk about it first. You don't go running off to Australia on a whim."

"But –"

"No buts!"

Milo groaned. "Fine," she muttered.

She stuffed the flyer into one of numerous jean pockets and went into her room. She spent the rest of the day in solitude, listening to her radio and telling her diary about the summer camp. When her mother finally came home, Milo immediately whipped out the flyer to show her. Her mother said that they would discuss it after dinner. Again Milo had to wait in the agony of patience while they ate. She could barely swallow her throat was so tight with anticipation.

Afterwards, her mother took a good look at the advertisement, sighed and said, "Oh. I don't know, Milo. It seems *sooooo* far away from home. So far away from us."

"Exactly!" Milo said, grinning.

"Milo."

"Sorry."

"Well . . . I know that we said you could go if you found a place."

"And I found a place," Milo said genially, pointing to the phone-number on the page.

Both her parents had to smile.

"Are you sure you want to do this, hon?" her father asked. "Summer camps are a lot of fun. I know I enjoyed going when I was a kid. But you've never been to one before. You get pretty homesick first time around."

"Look," Milo huffed, rolling her eyes. "I've wanted to go to one for a long time, but we were either moving, or settling in, or we couldn't afford it. Well, this time none of that is holding us back. Not to mention, I would have to be in the Arctic, starving to death, and riddled with frost-bite to ever be homesick for this place!"

Her parents were taken aback a bit by that remark, both of them blissfully well-adjusted to 711, but did agree to call and sign her up.

Milo whooped for joy and danced her way to her room singing, "Joy to the World". Once there, she pulled out her suitcase from her closet. She had hoped a short time ago she wouldn't have to use it for a while, but now she kissed it and gave her backpack a hug. She sorted through her clothes and packed the lucky chosen while belting out, "Hallelujah". She tucked her little radio, headphones, diary, and cookbook into her backpack while crooning, "You're a Lucky Fellow, Mister Smith".

The next morning, she jigged her way to the elevator and rode uninterrupted down to the Wal-Mart. There, she bought four packages of Pilot Point Precise Grip Pens, her favorite type of pen, three pens per package. She also bought five packages of triple a batteries, that being the type her radio used; eight batteries per package. She wiped out most of her money that way, neither item cheap, but she didn't care. Milo considered this camp to be like a vacation, the outback a refuge, and every cent was worth it. She also bought the strongest sunscreen they had.

As she returned to the elevator, bag in hand, and pressed the button, Bob the Conscience suddenly yelled out, "Wait!"

"What!" Milo shrieked in surprise as the doors closed.

"I don't think we should take the elevator this time," he said.

"Why not?" Milo demanded.

"I dunno," Bob the Conscience admitted. "It's just a feeling. A really bad feeling."

Bob, who was a conscience and is supposed to be usually right, was right. For a few moments later the elevator halted at the eleventh floor and opened to reveal the very five kids who had ganged up on Milo the first time, along with three others. Milo stood frozen in fear, her thought process shutting down.

"Well, look who it is!" the lead boy laughed.

The rest began to laugh along with him. A deep, mocking, maniacal laugh. They sneered at poor, scrawny Milo, all alone in the elevator, and took a step forward. In that moment, as each foot landed, Milo made a life changing decision. A decision which would allow her to go to camp, instead of getting into more trouble and thus anchored to 711 Shady Ally. If she hadn't made this decision, there would not be a story to write down. Milo made the decision to run.

She bent her head low, clasped her bag to her chest, and broke into a sudden sprint. Surprising the delinquencies, she managed to worm her small body through the gaps between the bellies before they could grab her. Once past, she made a break for the exit at the end of the corridor that lead to the stairs.

"Hey, you! Get back here!" they yelled after her. "Come on guys! Let's get her!"

They began to chase after her, shouting nasty threats as they ran. Milo had gone through the door and was already in the stairwell, sunshine weakly pouring in through the grimy windows, but the gang closing in. Swallowing hard, she started to climb.

The stairs didn't seem to prove much of an obstacle for her pursuers. At least not for four floors. At five they were panting. At six they were gasping. At seven they were gulping down air. At eight they were moving so slow that they barely moved. They clung to the molting railing and leaned up against the cold concrete walls.

"Just one more floor to go!" Milo whispered encouragingly to herself.

She wasn't exhausted at all. She had been climbing for weeks.

At the forty-sixth floor, she paused to look over the railing at the gasping, furious gang and shouted gaily to them, "Bon Voyage! I'll be seeing you in a month!"

And with that, she sauntered through the doorway into the hallway, headed for B-1107, singing, "This is My Once-a-Year-Day".

4
The Airplane Trip

FOUR DAYS LATER, the Hestlers traveled to the airport. Milo already had a passport, procured years ago to make moving easier, and her ticket had arrived surprisingly quickly. Her backpack and suitcase were crammed with new clothes, her mother having insisted that just because she was going to the outback didn't mean she couldn't look nice. "You are also going to want extra if any get torn or dirty," she had said.

She also had suggested, Milo agreeing wholeheartedly, that they put her radio/headphones, batteries, pens, diary, and cookbook in sealable plastic bags. "It will make it easier if security wants to search your bags," she had said. "Not to mention, you don't want anything to get damaged. I know how much you love all those things, though I'm fairly certain you'll be too busy chasing wallabies to need any of them." Milo strongly disagreed and said that was irrelevant; those objects went with her everywhere, period.

At the airport, her parents waited off to the side while her passport got scrutinized. Once it met the approval of the security personal's shrewd eyes, she was allowed to check her suitcase. Milo had made sure beforehand that her backpack was the right size to carry onto the airplane. She wanted to keep it safe with her until after the trip. Nothing must be lost, or end up in another state.

Before heading down the boarding bridge to the plane, her parents came over to say goodbye.

"I can't believe you're leaving already," her mother said, pulling Milo's scrunchie out of her hair. "I'm going to miss you. We'll be eating out a lot."

"Aw, Mom," Milo groaned, reaching for her scrunchie. "Come on! Just for today?"

"Please, Milo?" her mother asked, holding it behind her back and giving her daughter a hopeful smile. "You look so sweet with your hair down."

"I know," she said. "That's why I want it up. I believe in honest appearances."

"Oh, fine!" her mother said in exasperation, tossing the scrunchie back. "But I give you fair warning. Hot Australian boys are looking for shy, sweet girls."

"Uh-huh?" Milo said, sweeping her hair up into a ponytail. "I'll keep that one in mind, Mom," she lied. "See you later."

"Goodbye, dear," her mother said, giving her a hug and kissing her cheek.

"Bye, hon," her father said, doing the same.

"I'll see you guys in a month," Milo said, other people filing past her into the tunnel.

"Okay and don't forget, you're a Hestler," her father said proudly, beaming at her.

"Um . . . alright. Why?" she asked.

"Well . . . I don't know, hon. Just don't. It wouldn't be fair to us if you did. So don't."

"Right!" Milo mumbled, rolling her eyes at his cryptic words.

"I've always admired your father's satisfying way of answering questions," Bob the Conscience remarked. Milo snickered.

As she entered the grey wormhole, walking to the plane door, her parents called after her. Their voices echoed throughout the terminal, causing several heads to turn.

"Goodbye!"

"Bye, hon!"

"We love you!"

"We what?"

"We love her, Earnest!"

"Oh! Yes! Of course we do! We do!"

"Don't forget us!"

"If you can help it!"

"Keep out of trouble!"

"Keep out of wombat holes!"

"Don't stare at your counselor's butt!"

And just as the door was closing, her father bellowed, "And if he looks at yours slug him!"

"Oy!" Milo moaned, her face burning.

A nearby flight attendant gave her a wan smile, but tactfully didn't say anything.

Milo determinedly tried to forget what her parents had just shouted all over the airport, and found her seat. She didn't put her backpack in the overhead. Instead, she sat down and hugged it tightly, attempting to leech out some comfort from it.

"We're really doing it," she whispered excitedly, glancing out the window at the grey stretch of runway. "We're by ourselves on a plane, going to camp. It's really happening."

"Are you talking to me or your backpack?" Bob the Conscience inquired.

"I don't even know," Milo admitted.

The instructions for such-and-such things came while the plane roared and started to move, but she didn't pay much attention. She had been on airplanes plenty of times before. She knew everything there was to know. While the flight attendants showed everyone how to buckle the seatbelts, Milo gazed up at the white tufts of clouds in the vibrant blue sky, knowing they were about to get significantly larger.

The rest of what happened was regular. The plane sped up and took off, momentarily pressing the passengers to the back of their seats. Milo worked her jaw in circles to get her hearing back once they leveled out. The seatbelt sign eventually turned off, and people began the perpetual shuffling back and forth to the bathroom.

Milo spent the rest of the morning listening to her radio and writing in her diary. When they served lunch, she ate an egg salad sandwich with lettuce and tomatoes. She then recorded the recipe in her cookbook, deciding that the bread had been some sort of sourdough. She had recently come up with a title for her cookbook, writing on the cover in big swirly letters: *Milo's Cookbook of Plagiary*. This is actually a very appropriate title, if you mull it over. Milo adored it.

At two o'clock the plane hit an unusual amount of air pockets, sending drinks, food, items, and people's stomachs everywhere. As the plane was being cleaned, the flight attendants apologizing profusely, several important looking men dashed by Milo's seat and entered the cockpit. The plane didn't settle down for a while, outside or in. When the turbulence finally stopped, they were able to fully clean up. All the spraying and wiping was for naught, though, because there came suddenly a horrid bump. This was followed by an enormous bang.

Everybody inside the plane, all ordinary folks and high strung, flew into a terrified frenzy. Milo, curled up into a ball on her seat, stared unblinkingly at all the yelling, pointing, and pushing. At last the captain himself had to emerge and calm the passengers down.

He composedly explained to them that it was only a small problem and there was nothing to worry about. This seemed to be accepted willingly enough, and everyone sat back down. But even so, Milo felt uneasy. She put all her things away in the bags, making sure each one was sealed. She then hugged her backpack for an hour, telling herself that everything was fine. Another hour later, she was fast asleep.

It's a funny thing, sleep. Deprived of it, you are cranky, tired, and forgetful. Therefore, people ought to get plenty of it. But sleep has one unfortunate stipulation: You must close your eyes, removing yourself from reality, in order to slowly fall into the cycle of sleep that makes you dream. And when you dream, you are in another world, even though you are still in this world, and are oblivious to what is going on around you.

It is therefore good to have an alarm clock, or a reliable mother, to wake you up in the morning. If you didn't, you wouldn't know that morning had come at all, and might miss the bus and have to walk to school. So, even though sleep is usually beneficial and on our side, sometimes it isn't.

It certainly wasn't on Milo's side while she was on the plane. It prevented her from participating in a very important event, thereby putting her life in danger. Nobody bothered to be a reliable mother and wake her up. She what woke her was a loud, blaring alarm. It had been going off for some time, but she had been sleeping deeply, in a very involved dream, and didn't hear it until then. She also woke up because the plane happened to be shifting and rocking violently.

Blearily, she sat up in her seat and looked around, everything dark and blurry at first. Nobody else was with her. Adrenaline shot through her, immediately making her wide awake and alert. Clutching her seat's headrest, she stood up and looked behind her, then in front of her.

The plane was completely empty except for her. Masks were dangling from strings from the ceiling, bopping and dancing wildly as the plane shook. Luggage had been thrown aside and abandoned in the aisle, the arms of seats broken and swinging limply. Milo stared around frantically in confusion, sweat erupting all over her face and neck. A red light was flashing languidly, illuminating the space in an unnerving scarlet glow before fading to darkness. It revealed vacated cushions, rows and rows of them, not a soul to be seen.

Normally any other human being would have panicked, and Milo wasn't looking to be different. She panicked, but only for about two minutes, because when a plane is twisting violently in the air, people have to concentrate on balance more than panicking.

Milo steadied herself and grabbed one of the masks, trying to calm down. She held it to her nose and mouth, taking huge breaths. The jerking and downward, falling motion prevented her from inhaling too long, however. She pushed the mask away, slung on her backpack, and shakily walked into the center aisle.

"Hello?!" she called out, just in case someone was hiding.

There was no answer.

"Hellooo??!" she yelled, taking a wide stance to keep from falling over. "Is aaanybodyyy here?!!"

Once again, no answer came.

"Please!!" she cried miserably.

She looked around frantically, squinting in the meager, red light. She was entirely, one hundred percent alone.

"Oh!" she groaned, clutching her stomach as the plane lurched horribly.

She began to make her way to the back, though the floor was slanting. She caught a glimpse out a window then quickly looked away, gulping. An engine had exploded, and fire was leisurely engulfing the aircraft.

Milo whimpered for a second, then screamed and started to run. She didn't stop until she got to the end of the plane. To her surprise, all the classified, locked doors were flown open, and there was a huge emergency exit open in the back. Night air rushed in at her, chilling her to the bone. She had no idea how long ago she had fallen asleep. She had no idea what time it was. She didn't care. Inching towards the hole, making sure not to get too close, Milo peered out. Stars were sailing by, the moon full and off to the right. It was too dark to see what was below her, though.

The room she was in had been fortified with different supplies for escape, such as instant inflatable rafts, thousands of parachutes, maps, transmitters, first-aid kits and food kits. All the rafts were gone, as well as the kits and transmitters, but there was one more parachute left. Milo crawled over to it and unhooked it from the wall. She shifted her backpack so that it was on her front, and then fastened the parachute to her back.

Suddenly there was an enormous explosion on the left side of the plane that Milo deciphered as the other engine blowing up. It told her that she'd better move it. She clasped her backpack, screwed her eyelids shut, ran, and took a daring leap.

Air whizzed past her, filling her ears with a hollow roar, but she still was able to make out a furious grinding sound. Looking up, she could see underneath the plane and that one of the compartments had broken open.

Suitcases came spilling out, dropping as fast as Milo. A familiar one, perhaps inexplicably able to sense its owner's presence, collided with her head. Blood trickled down her face, getting in her eyes and blinding her slightly. A searing pain raced across her forehead, making her gasp.

Remembering suddenly that she had to open her parachute, she groped behind her for the string that released it. She gripped it and tugged, but it nothing happened. She pulled harder. Still nothing. She yanked with whatever strength she had left and finally heard a click. Cloth came billowing out. The parachute snapped open and caught air, stopping Milo with a jerk.

Her legs swinging loosely below her, she tried to catch her breath, the parachute straps digging into her armpits. At least she was no longer plummeting towards the ground, which was still shrouded in darkness. Yet, she didn't seem to be drifting either. Milo peered upward through the blood and night, trying to figure out why she was still falling rather fast. Her vision hazy, she could just make out a squarish lump amid the stars. She made a strangled noise when she realized that it was the suitcase that had crashed into her head. It was tangled up in the strings of the parachute.

This didn't help her situation very much, but it also didn't hinder it completely. At least she was slowing down a little bit. A good thing too, for a few moments later her legs hit water. Coldness enveloped her as she went under, her body smarting from the impact. Instinctively she began to kick, searching for the surface. Her head suddenly met air, and she pushed hair out of her face.

As she spat water out of her mouth, she noticed it was sickeningly salty. The ocean. She was in the ocean! Salty water splashed into her mouth and seeped into her injury, making her wince. But she didn't have time to fuss about it. The parachute, once her savior, was now filling with water, dragging her down. She detached the belt quickly, letting it slide off her shoulders and sink into the briny depths. Her head was throbbing, making everything pulse blurrily. She worked her arms and legs back and forth, treading water and snorting it out of her nose.

The suitcase floated up, bumping into her fingers. She lunged for it, gripping its handle. She flung her backpack upon it, and floated for a minute, pulling herself together. Gingerly, she touched her forehead, igniting pain. Milo sobbed and whipped her hand away. Tilting her face towards the sky, she saw the plane, all ablaze, barreling downward. She looked to where it was headed and, to her absolute shock and relief, saw an island.

From where she floated, it didn't look extremely big, but at the same time exactly tiny. She couldn't make out any details, but it was solid land and that's what mattered.

As the throbbing increased and her vision got fuzzier, she began to kick her way towards it. Already exhausted and sore, she began to pant. She checked her course every now and then, and soon saw the plane crash down on the other side of the island, creating a mushroom shaped explosion. It surged into the sky and was followed by a deafening boom.

Breathing raspily and heavily, Milo tried to increase her speed. Not only did her head hurt, but her stomach and jaw too. She wished she could throw-up; maybe she had swallowed too much sea juice, or maybe it was panic. But she couldn't stop. In the back of her mind, Milo didn't doubt that she was about to fall unconscious, and she wanted to be on dry land when that occurred.

More blood oozed from her head into her eyes, clogging her nose with a metallic stench. She tried to blink it away, but only succeeded in making it worse. The only good thing in the whole messy ordeal was that the tide was pushing at her, making it easier to move. For what seemed like hours, she kicked away in the water, which had numbed her long ago. On all sides of her, suit cases bobbed and floated aimlessly, headed in the same direction. Now and then she had to pause to push one aside. Nothing was going to get in her way. The island was her goal. Nothing else mattered to her at that moment except getting to that island.

She mumbled dumbly to herself, "Must keep going. Must keep going. Gotta get there! Just gotta."

As the island got closer, her legs got stiff and lazy, until at last she couldn't even move them. Suddenly the water changed climates. It was gradually growing warmer, but that didn't reinvigorate Milo any; she was still too tired to kick. Her consciousness was slowly ebbing away, the lapping sound of the water getting fainter and fainter.

She laid her head down on the suitcase, letting the tide carry her the rest of the way. The shore was growing closer. It looked very foggy and red and was still far off, but she could see it.

"*I'll get there*," she thought weakly.

She had to. Just had to. She would. She had to. Had – to. Just . . . had . . . to. Just – had . . . to. Just . . . had – to. Just had . . .

5
Simon

MILO FELT A cool, wet sensation patter onto her face and arms. It felt good because her skin was unusually hot. More came, droplets of cool, moist heaven peppering her cheeks and forehead, and running down her nose. She moaned softly.

The pain in her head had gone down to a dull ache, and she no longer felt sick to her stomach. She twitched her shoulders and her feet, checking to make sure she still could. She slowly opened her eyes, bright sunshine blinding her for a moment. After cringing and blinking a few times, her vision started to refocus, and she discovered that she was lying under a palm tree on a beach.

Sunlight was sifting through the long, narrow leaves up above her, and white sand lay beneath her, spreading out in all directions. However, she was far more startled by something else. Leaning over her, using a wet cloth to squeeze water onto her, was a boy.

He had straight, dirty-blonde hair, tousled from wind and hanging down an inch past his ears. His skin was a light, golden tan, undoubtedly the result of a life spent on an island, sand granules flecking his hands. He was wearing a pair of swimming shorts and a button down T-shirt, completely unbuttoned, firm abdominal muscles visible. His eyes, easy to inspect because they were less than three inches away from hers, were light brown. By his looks, he was a dream boy, a hot boy; the type of boy you can't help but gape at from afar, but would never dare approach.

Milo noticed this as she opened her eyes and he came into focus. But before she thought about any of that, she first thought, and expressed aloud, "*Aaaaaahhhh!?!*"

The boy, whoever he was, gave a shout of surprise and jumped backwards, toppling over onto the sand. They both sat frozen for a second, breathing heavily and staring at each other. He then smiled at her. Milo tried to move her head and was rewarded with a stab of pain.

"Ow," she groaned and hesitantly reached up to feel her head.

There was a cloth wrapped tightly around it. She ran her fingers over her face her face. All the blood had been washed off. Using her eyes, not wanting to disturb her cranium, she looked around her.

Her backpack, covered in a powdery layer of dried sea salt, was lying next to her. To the left of her was the suitcase that had knocked her out. Squinting, she could see other suitcases lining the shore, all having washed up the night before. Examining the one beside her the best she could at a distance, she gave a gasp of surprise. It was hers.

"Whoa!" she mumbled. "Weird!"

She then angled her gaze towards the boy, who hadn't budged and was still smiling at her.

"Nice teeth!" Bob the Conscience remarked.

"Bob!" Milo cried, flicking her eyes about until she remembered he was in her mind. "Where the heck were you last night?! Huh? I could have died!"

"I was with you last night," Bob the Conscience replied calmly. "You just didn't recognize me because we weren't arguing. I made sure you got out of there safely. I guided you, just like in my job description. I pulled my act together."

"Oh," she said, guilt nudging her uncomfortably. "Right. Sorry. Thanks."

"Uh-huh," Bob the Conscience agreed. "So, who's the piece of beef?" he asked, changing the subject.

Milo, assuming he had meant the boy, admitted, "I don't know."

"Try talking to him."

"Kay?" she said nervously. "Um, hi!" she said to him.

The boy stopped smiling and looked perplexed.

"Hi!" Milo said a bit louder. "HELLO!"

She vigorously waved a hand back and forth. The boy, apparently understanding, smiled and waved back. He stood up quickly, walked over, and plonked himself down next to her, much closer than she would have thought necessary.

"Where am I?" she asked, trying to scoot a few inches away.

The boy once again frowned in confusion.

"WHERE – AM – I?!" Milo repeated slowly and clearly.

The boy's expression didn't change, though he stared at her intensely, so Milo decided to try gesturing. She rotated her arms, which were plenty sore from last night, in a wide arch, pointing all around her. She then shrugged and shook her head, immediately wincing afterwards.

The boy seemed to comprehend and said, "Blatih sa twra ito!"

Milo stared blankly at him.

"Pardon?" she said.

"Creee?" he responded.

"DO," she shouted, as if volume would alter his translation, "you speak English?!"

The boy didn't seem to grasp what she had asked. Milo made a talking motion with one of her hands, pointed to her tongue and then at him. It seemed to dawn on the boy what she meant, and he shook his head.

"Great!" Milo muttered, briefly looking away towards the ocean, it shimmering turquoise under the sun. She turned back to him. "None at all?"

The boy figured it'd be best to shake his head again.

"Oh, great!" Milo sighed. She again tried gesturing to everything around them, hoping he would say a word she recognized.

"Ito!" the boy said helpfully.

"Ito?" Milo repeated. She pointed at him and said, "Ito?"

"Pra, pra, pra!" he laughed, shaking his head. He poked a finger at his chest and said, "Simon!"

"Simon?" Milo repeated, pointing directly at him.

He nodded, grinning and crossing his legs comfortably.

"Huh!" she said. Inspired, she indicated to herself. "Milo!"

"Milo?" he echoed, giving it a slight trill. He put a hand on her shoulder. "Milo?"

She nodded encouragingly, eyeing the position of his hand.

Grinning broadly, he touched a hand to his collar bone. "Simon!"

He squeezed her shoulder. "Milo!"

"Yep!" she confirmed, pleased.

She nodded, for his benefit, and grinned. He grinned back, letting her go. Still, Milo didn't feel all that confident, so she decided to test. She pointed insistently to something behind the boy. He twisted around to look.

When his back was to her, Milo called out, "Simon!" His head whipped around and he stared at her questioningly. She did this several times before she felt satisfied. Suddenly he pointed past her.

"What?" she said, shifting around to look.

"Milo!"

She turned around. "Yeah?" she asked then saw his face.

He was no longer smiling, his arms crossed. Obviously, just because he couldn't speak English, didn't mean he was stupid.

"Oh," she whispered contritely. "Oh, sorry!" Not knowing what sort of gesture could mean "sorry", Milo gave him a tiny, sincere smile.

His grin returned instantly, and he mumbled something incoherent, yet cordial sounding. He stood, putting up one hand to tell her to stay there, not that Milo felt like wandering. He went over to a basket that Milo hadn't noticed earlier. He pulled out a bowl-shaped object and brought it over to her. Falling onto his knees, he showed it to her.

Milo peered in and saw some type of mush that looked like it had been mixed with corn and pepper. He scooped some out with his fingers and brought it to her mouth. She looked at it and then smelled it. It didn't smell too bad, rather fishy, but Milo wasn't about to eat it off his fingers.

She scraped some of the mush off with her own fingers and put it in her mouth. It was actually quite tasty. It reminded her faintly of tuna.

"Mmmm!" she told him, hoping that meant the same thing in any language.

The boy called Simon offered her what remained on his fingers and in the bowl. She accepted the bowl, but passed on the rest. Shrugging, he ate the leftovers on his fingers. Milo didn't realize it until then, but she was starving.

Simon watched her intently while she ate, a type of gleam appearing in his eyes. Briefly he got out a sort of container from his basket and offered it to her. Milo cautiously took a sip from it and was relieved to discover it held fresh water. She guzzled it, not caring if he was watching her. She hadn't drunk anything since last night, when she had swallowed all that ocean water. When the container was empty, she handed back to Simon, who put it away.

Milo was thoroughly enjoying herself. It had been a long time since she had gotten along with anyone close to her age, even though they couldn't verbally communicate, a fact she chose to ignore. While she ate, using one hand to ladle the mush to her mouth, she used the other to open her backpack to see if anything was damaged. Nothing seemed to be. Her clothes were still soggy, but everything else seemed fine.

"Thank Heaven for plastic bags!" Milo whispered, lightly touching her headphones.

She realized her hair was in her face, and felt around in her pack for another scrunchie. Finding one, she tried to pull her hair back, but the other hand was holding the bowl. Before she could set it down on the sand, Simon lean forward, took her hair and drew it back for her. With nimble one-handed dexterity, she put the scrunchie in, and he withdrew his hands.

"Thanks," she muttered, certain her embarrassment was written all over her face.

He smiled kindly at her and abruptly exploded into a frenzy of gibbering in his language. He gestured so fast that Milo couldn't catch a thing he was trying to tell her. Finally he stopped and stared at her expectantly. She stared back.

"What?" she asked, smiling and shaking her head.

He sighed and slowly said something in his language, enunciating each syllable. But of course Milo couldn't understand. She shrugged apologetically. Simon attempted several more times to relay what was on his mind, with no better results. Finally he stood up, turned away from her, and slowly began to walk, with one of his arms erect, like he was holding someone up. After he walked a ways, he turned around and walked back in the same fashion. Once he got back, he looked at her inquiringly, his head tilted to one side.

"Can I walk?" Milo thought. "I don't know. Maybe."

She tried moving one of her legs. It worked perfectly. She tried the other, and it jerked obediently.

"Yep," she said to Simon. She nodded.

Simon's eyes widened, his jaw dropped, and he hesitantly nodded back.

"Uh-huh!" Milo said, nodding faster and giving him a friendly grin.

Simon smiled hugely and laughed softly. The more Milo nodded, the happier he looked. The nodding continued, Milo not sure what else to do, until Simon suddenly let out a cry of joy. He jumped into the air, obviously unable to contain the delight that had overcome him. He flailed his arms and danced up and down the beach, kicking up sand and shouting unintelligibly. The whole time, Milo kept on smiling and nodding her head dumbly. She had no idea what was going on.

At last he stopped and rushed over to her. He bent down and hugged her.

"Uh!" she stuttered. "Um. Thanks. I guess."

Simon straightened up and grabbed one of her hands to pull her up.

"Whoa! Wait!" Milo cried.

She pushed against the ground with her other hand, first putting down the dish. Simon let her go when she was standing upright, leaning against the tree. He then took the bowl back to the basket and picked it up, along with her suitcase. Milo noticed that the basket looked similar to a reed basket she had seen in Hawaii. She had gone there with her parents when she was ten to see if they should live there. It didn't work out though, because while they were on a tour, her mother got bit by a snake and had to be rushed to the hospital. Her mother had had a bias against Hawaii ever since.

Milo was wobbly on her legs at first, and they were incredibly sore, but at least she could stand. She zipped up her backpack and slung it onto her shoulder. Simon grabbed her hand once more, first putting the basket under his other arm, and began to pull her towards the forest. The forest was a harsh entanglement of brush, vines, and trees, but eventually they came to a path. The path wound on and on, Milo not even noticing Simon's hand in hers because she was too busy gawking at everything around her. She saw gigantic leaves, vibrant flowers growing on bark, and different nationalities of ants running drills along tree trunks.

The further they went, occasionally having to pause so that Milo could rest, the more beaten down and worn the path became. Suddenly there was a sharp turn to the left. More turns came after it, and the trees became less dense.

They eventually came to a clearing, the sun creating one enormous patch of yellow on the brown ground, and when Milo looked to the left, she could see the beach. Not the one they had just left, however. This was a different, bigger beach that looked like it ran for miles, with rocks poking out of the water and bunches of boys scattered about.

The only other thing in the clearing, besides a few tropical trees dispersed here and there, was a house. Well, not really a house. It resembled a bungalow, only it was much larger. It was built out of a type of wood that, to Milo, looked like bamboo.

"Only it's not bamboo," she mused. *"Bamboo isn't as big as that. It's not as wide or dark. That wood is very dark and not shiny. Bamboo always seems to look shiny, not dull like that."*

Simon was leading her up to this house. He halted them when they were directly in front of the door, took her backpack from her, and disappeared inside.

"Hey!" she called out.

But he was back in a moment. He didn't have her luggage with him, but he did have something clutched in his hand.

After a few silent moments of them just staring at each other, Milo asked, "So! Whatcha got there?"

She indicated to his clenched fist. Simon, his mouth twitching, inhaled deeply several times before opening his hand to show her. In the center of his palm lay a small, round object topped by a sparkling dot. It was a diamond ring.

"Oh, cool!" Milo commented, taking a closer look at it. She had a keen interest in jewelry, or moreover all things shiny (cd's, silver tea sets, chef's knives, etc.). The only rings she could ever afford to buy were made out of glass, and tended to chip. This ring, however, looked real.

Simon grinned and shoved his hand towards her.

"For . . . me?" she said, dodging out of the way to avoid getting hit.

She pointed from it to herself, and Simon nodded enthusiastically.

"Oh, no! No, no, no!" she chuckled, taking a step backwards. "I can't take that from you. It looks way too expensive."

Simon of course didn't understand what she had said, and tried to put the ring on one of her fingers. Milo pulled her hand away each time, finally stuffing it into a very stiff pocket. But Simon, apparently not one to give up easily, pulled it out again by her wrist. Therefore Milo made a fist, not sure what else she could do, besides run away, which she doubted her legs could handle.

Simon tried to gently unfurl the fist, but she held firm, still shaking her head. However, he was obviously stronger than her, and as his coaxing became more insistent, Milo had to surrender. He opened her hand just wide enough to drop the ring inside, and quickly forced it closed again. Milo continued to shake her head, now trying to get him to take it back. Simon began to look confused and upset. He babbled something in his language, tapping one of her fingers.

"*Oh, dear,*" Milo thought. She wanted to keep things friendly. "*Oh, well. If it makes him happy,*" she thought, though she didn't feel at all comfortable about taking it. But, hey! Who wouldn't want a diamond ring?

"Are you sure about wearing that?" Bob the Conscience asked.

"I wouldn't," she answered. "I don't know where he got it. It might be a family heirloom or something. But he seems to really want me to have it, and I don't want him to get mad. Why? Are you sensing something bad about it?"

"No, not really. It just sort of looks like an engagement ring or something."

Milo laughed. "Yeah! Sure! *Riiight!*"

Oh! If only she had listened!

She slid the ring onto the finger that Simon had tapped, and he resumed his smiling.

"There you go!" she told him, flourishing the hand in front of his face.

Suddenly he reached out and hugged her again, murmuring softly.

"Okay!" Milo squeaked. "*Okay!*" She gave him a hasty pat on the back.

He abruptly put an arm around her shoulders and led her inside the hut. She quickly shrugged him off, though, for she was beginning to feel a little uneasy about the way he was staying so close to her.

The house looked larger on the inside than on the outside. It had dirt floors, packed down hard. The door led into a walkway, a hall extending straight ahead, and on the left was what looked like a sitting room, filled with furniture made from the same wood as the house. To the right of the front door was a kitchen.

Simon walked into the kitchen, not bothering to show Milo the rest of the house. He took a sharp looking knife off one of the counters, which were also made from the strange wood. Milo, who had followed him into the kitchen, now started to rethink her decision. But the only thing Simon did with the knife was cut away the bandages on her head.

He did this so swiftly, the knife just a blur, that Milo's stomach lurched. He unwound the cloth carefully and examined the wound underneath. It seemed to meet his satisfaction, for he did not apply another bandage. Throwing the bloody cloth away in a wooden barrel, which appeared to be the trash can, he turned and headed the door.

Milo, who would have preferred to stay and explore the house, reluctantly followed. It was most definitely his house, and she didn't think it would be polite to wander through it without his company.

Once outside, he again tried to hold her hand. She clasped both her hands securely behind her back and marched straight ahead. Though this puzzled the boy, he decided not to start another argument.

This was wise, considering that Milo was a woman, and you simply can't mess around with women's feelings. Nothing can be more frightening than an angry female, and may no man forget it! Women are warriors of a different breed, and Milo was one of the toughest specimens. Simon could sense this in a small way; if she did not want to hold his hand, then she wouldn't. That was that. No debate. No pushing his luck.

Simon took the lead, striding towards the heart of the island. The ground was becoming as hard as regular cement. The trees were becoming fewer and fewer, and the hot sun beamed down on the two teens. Every now and then they would pass a house, built in the same fashion as Simon's, some smaller, some larger. As they walked on, the trees began to reappear. Very tall, wide trees with broad, green leaves that provided shade. Encircling the bases of those trees were flower beds, where tropical flora had been transplanted.

They trudged onward a short distance until they reached what undeniably had to be their destination. Passing several decorated trees, Milo gasped in amazement. It was a town! An entire town, constructed entirely from that strange type of wood. There were many houses, some sporting porches, several shops, one very large building with a huge doorway, a school house, and a church that she identified by the large cross on its roof. There was another big building, on the far side of town, with a second story and many windows. Milo couldn't tell what it was used for.

All these places were widely spread out from each other. Way off in the outskirts, Milo thought she could see what appeared to be a large, black house. Palm trees speckled the streets, towering over everything. These trees also had flower gardens planted around the bases, and some even had benches nailed around their trunks.

But what most astounded Milo was the abundance of people milling about. They were dressed almost exactly the same as people at home, only more modestly, with no offensive or statement-making clothing. But since it was a tropical island, they were mostly dressed in colorful island attire. Such as what Simon was wearing.

Simon led Milo down the streets, pausing now and then to let her gape in through a window or at a passing person. Nobody was paying them much attention. Simon would occasionally receive a warm greeting, but Milo mostly got bemused stares.

They eventually reached a small store with a window cut into the wall. Attached to the window was a sill, and on the sill was a bell. Not the type of bell found in the lobby of 711 Shady Ally, that you slap and it would ding, but more like an old-fashioned school bell. Simon leaned his elbows on the sill and rang it. Like the bell at 711 Shady Ally, it also had a woman hurrying to answer the call. In complete contrast to Miz Ricca, this woman was a plump little thing, with a pleasant smile and a full bun of brown hair.

She began to gibber happily with Simon, who was very glad to see her. Reaching through the window, they embraced lightly. Milo quietly stood next to him, wondering why Simon had brought her over to meet this particular lady and if they were talking about her. She figured they were, because Simon put his hand on her shoulder while he spoke. As he jabbered away, the woman grew more and more excited. Her gaze kept flicking from Milo and to Simon, her smile growing larger and more animated.

When Simon finished talking, he pointed to the ring on Milo's finger, and the woman clapped her hands together, gleefully bouncing on her toes. She then did something that Milo had not expected at all. The woman spoke English.

"Aw! Wonderful, wonderful, wonderful!" she chirped in a rich Irish accent.

"You speak English?" Milo said, astonished.

"Oh yes, dear!" the woman laughed. "I can understand your

surprise. I'm sure you think that everyone on the island speaks Galo."

"Galo?" Milo repeated breathlessly, bewildered.

"Yes, that's the name of the language."

"Oh!" Milo exclaimed, looking behind her at all the sun soaked houses. "So, are they, like, Galonians? And is this the island of Gal?"

"Oh, no," the lady chuckled, waving the question away. "This island has no name. The people here are just people. They came up with the language many ages ago, and they are allowed to name it. So they named it Galo, just because they wanted to."

"Ah," Milo remarked, wondering why the language deserved a name, but nothing else did.

The woman extended her hand, and Milo politely shook it.

"I am Mrs. Lanslo, dear," she said, introducing herself.

"Hello," Milo said. "My name is –"

"Oh, I know already! Simon here told me. Milo. What a beautiful name! I adore it!"

Milo had to smile. This was not usually what she heard.

"But what is your last?" Mrs. Lanslo asked.

"Last what?" Milo said.

"Name, dear," Mrs. Lanslo clarified. "Simon said he doesn't know it."

"Oh! Right, um, Hestler."

Mrs. Lanslo nodded genially, and, turning to Simon, began to speak to him in the language Galo.

Milo heard her say Hestler, and assumed she was bringing him up to speed. Simon looked pleased, and Mrs. Lanslo again addressed Milo.

"Ah, yes!" she twittered joyfully. "Milo, Simon has told me everything! Absolutely everything! And I am so happy!"

"Did he?" she said nervously. "I didn't know there was that much to tell." What was going on?

"Oh, of course there is! And there's *sooo* much to tell you, as I am sure you have many questions."

"Yeah, I do," she admitted. "First off, we weren't properly introduced. Who exactly is this?"

She nodded to Simon.

Mrs. Lanslo laughed heartily, a hand flying to her chest, and said, "This is Simon Swallow."

"Simon Swallow," Milo repeated, so as not to forget.

Simon, upon hearing his name said twice, gibbered inquiringly to Mrs. Lanslo. She explained what was going on, and he, grinning, offered his hand to Milo. She shook it and afterwards practically had to yank hers out of his grasp.

"Yes, dear," Mrs. Lanslo continued proudly. "A fine boy he is. Understanding and kind. Responsible and polite. Charming and law-abiding. All the girls swoon over him, which makes it a mystery why he has been looking so long for a wife."

"A wife?" Milo gasped, unbelieving. "How old is he?"

"Sixteen, dear. But on this island, when a boy is over fifteen, he can marry any girl over thirteen."

Milo was speechless, her jaw lax and dropping. To her very Western Hemisphere state of mind, this was the most outlandish thing she had ever heard of. "Really?" she stammered.

"Yes," Mrs. Lanslo confirmed carelessly, as if it were a common, reputable practice. "It is an island law. There are many laws here, especially about marriage, and they are always enforced, no matter what."

Milo looked startled.

"But don't worry, dear! The laws are quite reasonable, and as long as you obey them, you have nothing to worry about. All the boys here over fifteen are trying to get married. If a boy is still single when he turns twenty-two, a wife is chosen for him; if he wants to marry, that is. Simon has always wanted to marry, and has been looking for the right bride for some time now. And finally – Oh, I am so happy! – he has found one. Simon is friends with everyone here, and we all will be very happy to see him marry at last!"

"Who is it?" Milo asked Simon.

Even though those laws gave her the creeps, she felt she should at least be happy for him. But instead of translating, Mrs. Lanslo looked confused. She said to her, "Why, dear, it's you."

Milo stood, staring transfixed at them, until she began to laugh.

"Yeah! Sure! *Riiiight!*" She repeated exactly what she had said to Bob the Conscience.

Sometimes the strongest, most provoking words in the world are words of silence, and those very words were being spoken by Mrs. Lanslo and Simon. They said nothing to her. Right to her face. They stared at her, and their looks brought on the horrid truth. The more Milo absorbed these stares of verification, the more she began to lose it.

Slowly she began to shake her head and to utter words such as: "Nuh. Unna. Nuha." She then looked down at the ring on her hand and screamed. Milo wasn't a person to scream at any old thing. When she was on the plane she had a good reason to scream. Sheer terror was coursing through her veins during that time, and this one moment seemed almost worse.

When she finally cut off her screams she looked, panic stricken, at Mrs. Lanslo.

"No!" she cried desperately.

"I don't understand, dear," Mrs. Lanslo said, concerned. "Why are you so upset?"

"Why?!" Milo repeated, breathing hard, her limbs trembling. "Why? Be-*because!* That's why! I don't want to get married! I mean, come on! Married? Are you kidding?"

Mrs. Lanslo, in a tone that implied that she was far from kidding, asked, "If you don't want this, then why did you say yes?"

"Yes?" Milo cried, hitting her forehead with her palm. "I didn't know he was proposing to me! I don't even think he did!"

"Think hard," Mrs. Lanslo said gently.

Suddenly a gesture on the beach flew to Milo's mind, and she gasped in horror. She whirled on the spot and glared at Simon, who knew what was going on thanks to Mrs. Lanslo translating for him.

"You!" she accused under her breath. "You didn't!"

"I'm afraid he did, dear," Mrs. Lanslo interjected. Milo faced her desperately, her brow wrinkled and breaking out in a sweat that wasn't just from the heat.

"Well . . . oh, come on! I didn't know what he was saying! It could have meant anything! I didn't know what I was saying yes to! So . . . technically, I'm not engaged!"

As she thought this over, a small smile of relief curled up on her lips.

"But you have on the ring," Mrs. Lanslo observed, after telling Simon all this. Milo looked back at the ring with new fear.

"Oh. Yeah," she said, without much else to say. She glanced up at the two other people and saw the concerned expressions they had. "Um," Milo mumbled, realizing that she didn't have much of an excuse. "Well. Okay! I don't know why I put on the stupid ring! But I still don't have to marry him!"

With that, she wrenched off the ring and threw it at Simon's feet. He gasped and hurriedly scooped it up. He tried to give it back to her, but she wouldn't take it, instead crossing her arms and narrowing her eyes at him. Finally, he said something to Mrs. Lanslo, who stood in shock at what Milo had done.

"He says," she breathed heavily, "that you have to wear it, and that he wants you to."

"I don't care what he wants!" Milo exploded aggressively. "I don't have to be engaged if I don't want to!"

"Actually, dear," Mrs. Lanslo whispered. "You do."

Milo turned her mutinous glare on the little woman. "What?" she snapped.

"It's one of our laws," she explained patiently. "Once you are engaged, you have to get married. There's no breaking it. Once the girl says yes and puts the ring on, that's that. The deal is sealed."

"B-b-but I didn't know what he was saying!" Milo cried, after finding her voice.

"That would be an arguable case, dear, if you hadn't put on the ring."

Milo, now tapping her fingers on the window sill in an agitated manner, tried to figure this out.

"So," she choked out, "since I put on the ring, I can't get out of it?"

"Yes," Mrs. Lanslo said, nodding sagely. "That's right."

Milo stood gasping, at a loss for words. That is, until she found some.

"I'll just refuse then!" she declared, pounding a fist onto the wood. "You can't force me to marry!"

"Well . . . yes, we can," Mrs. Lanslo said softly.

Milo, her complexion getting more ashen by the minute, said weakly, "What?"

"We can," Mrs. Lanslo repeated, "and we have, and we will. Unless, of course, you do it willingly, dear."

"Never!!!" she shouted, out of control.

At this point, there was a yell for attention behind her, which sounded more like a grunt. Simon and Mrs. Lanslo instantly stiffened with respect. Milo swiveled around to see who was behind her.

There was a group of old – excuse me – older men with pinched faces and impressive beards. They were all wearing long, black and grey robes, and were holding many books. One man especially, whose robe was extra dark and held one exceptionally thick book.

The man in front stepped forward and began to talk to Mrs. Lanslo in a gruff voice. Mrs. Lanslo promptly answered in Galo. She spoke very fast and pointed from Simon to Milo, then from Milo to Simon. The man, whose garb was slightly fancier than the rest, became very angry, the impressive mustache over his impressive beard bristling dangerously. He spoke severely to Simon, who answered him quietly, his gaze reverently downcast. Milo was terrified. Who were these men?

A crowd was beginning to form around the scene, people gibbering to each other out of the corners of their mouths. The man spoke sternly to Mrs. Lanslo, and Mrs. Lanslo spoke to Milo.

"This," she said seriously, indicating to man, "is the President, or Mayor, of the island. Mayor Em-I. He works in the library with these other gentlemen. They make sure everyone abides by the laws."

"I can't see a library," Milo whispered, trying not to look at the mayor. Mrs. Lanslo pointed to a small building on the other side of town. "That doesn't seem big enough to be a library."

"The library's underground," Mrs. Lanslo said dismissively. "Listen, please. Mayor Em-I wants to, first of all, welcome you to our island."

Milo glanced at him dubiously, wondering if this man had ever welcomed anyone to anywhere in his life.

"And second of all," Mrs. Lanslo continued, "to let you know that even though you've just arrived, you still have to obey our laws. He doesn't want you to cause trouble right now, because they are about to investigate a plane that crashed here last night."

"That's my plane," Milo muttered.

"Is there anyone else with you?"

"No, everyone else escaped without me," she mumbled bitterly.

"Oh. Well, the Mayor wants me to read you a few of the other laws, and let you know that you will obey them. No matter what."

More incoherent jabbering ensued between the officials and Mrs. Lanslo, before she added submissively, "This island has been functioning beautifully for generations, and you will not be a disruption."

"Well, we'll see about that!" Milo replied with new vigor, obliged to disrupt no matter where she was. "I'll be rescued anyway."

Mrs. Lanslo began to laugh, holding on to her middle, and relayed to the others what Milo had said. Everyone immediately laughed hard along with her. Milo looked around with wide, troubled eyes. Apparently, this was a humorous topic.

"My dear," Mrs. Lanslo exclaimed, after she got control of herself and caught her breath. "No one knows this island exists! Nobody has ever been rescued from here. I myself crashed here five years ago and haven't been found yet. Now, listen."

The man with the very thick book came forward, flipped to a certain page, and held it open for her.

"'Laws on marriage,'" Mrs. Lanslo read aloud, slipping on a pair of spectacles that were hanging about her neck. "'Once an engagement has been finalized by the female voluntarily donning the traditional ring, said engagement may not be canceled by either party. All fiancées must dwell in the same abode. All engaged couples shall be thrown a wedding, all villagers invited. All married individuals must sleep in the same bed. All those married in their teenage years shall adopt one child and raise it.'"

Mrs. Lanslo, finished reading, lowered her spectacles. The keeper of the volume shut it gingerly and returned to his group. A silence had fallen as the laws were read, even though most of the gathered people probably couldn't understand a bit of English.

"What was that last part?" Milo managed to say, her throat starting to close up. The horror of the laws was biting into her, making her shrivel and shrink as each one was read off.

"You can adopt a child," Mrs. Lanslo said. "Simon will explain it to you later. It's sort of a package deal."

Package deal.

Milo remembered her parents once referring to the apartment building as a package deal. She wasn't in the mood for another one. Mayor Em-I spoke.

"He says," Mrs. Lanslo interpreted dutifully, "that these laws were made by our ancestors, and you will obey them."

Simon tried to give Milo back the engagement ring, but Milo just shook her head. Mostly in disbelief, but she was also saying no. No, no, no. Three no's in a row. No, she didn't want the ring. No, she didn't want to get married. And, no, she wasn't about to follow any unreasonable, unfair, cockamamie laws written up ages ago by a bunch of meddling lunatics.

Mayor Em-I saw only one No, but it was one No too many for him. With a shout, he leapt forward with surprising spryness, pulled a dagger out of his robe and deftly aimed it at Milo's throat. There was a collective intake of breath from everybody, especially Simon, who looked like he wanted to knock the dagger away, but didn't dare.

Milo was too frightened to move. She couldn't even properly see the dagger, but she could feel coldness emanating from its blade. Terrified, her thoughts erased, she let her hand hang limply in the air. Mayor Em-I grunted something sharply, and Simon tentatively came forward to put the ring on her finger. She began to sense that they weren't kidding.

"You never listen to me!" said Bob the Conscience.

6
Ajsha

SIMON HAD LED Milo back to his house with the crowd of villagers trailing after them. Some had come up to Simon and congratulated him, shaking his hand exuberantly. Simon looked extremely happy with it all, and seemed very proud of Milo. He continuously pointed at her while he spoke, but all his friends grew sober and uncomfortable whenever he brought her up. They wouldn't look directly at her, instead giving her hurried, mistrustful glances.

It was as if they didn't like her, but who could blame them! The scene she had made had been incredibly insulting. Every word that Milo had said had eventually been translated and spread around to every Galo-speaking soul. As Simon had guided her out of town, back the way they had come, people ran ahead of them into houses and shops, hastily describing what had just happened and that the trouble maker was headed their way. Soon heads were popping out of windows left and right, and folks crowded their doorways to stare at Milo as she was led by, much like a prisoner. The heads at once began to hiss and whisper in Galo to other heads nearby, until the hot island air was filled with the indistinguishable, yet clearly disapproving, words.

Milo barely noticed any of this, though; she was too angry. Far too angry to pay attention to any of the condemning commotion around her. She kept very quiet, her jaw set and bulging at the joints, her sights on her shoes. The reason was that she was busy complaining to Bob the Conscience. The fury and despair roiling inside her was so immense she simply had to release it in some way, therefore Bob the Conscience suffered.

When they arrived back at the hut, Milo went straight inside, but Simon stayed outside for a while to talk to everyone, undoubtedly explaining how he found her in the first place. When the last person had drifted away, he came inside and closed the door. He sighed in a thoroughly satisfied way and turned around, only to have a pillow hit him *Smack!* in the face. He fell back in surprise. Milo stood in the sitting room, glaring at him, her skin pure white with rage and her fists clenched by her sides.

Simon saw her and grinned, obviously not taking the hint. He picked up the pillow and threw it back at her. Now, Milo wasn't very strong, and when she threw the pillow he had barely felt it. But Simon, the muscles in his arms and legs lean, defined, and tan, threw the pillow and knocked her off her feet.

Furious, she sat up and tossed the pillow onto a couch. Simon, laughing guiltily, trotted over, trying to inquire if she was okay or not. He knelt beside her on the dirt floor and saw her face. He grinned sheepishly and offered his hands to help her up. Milo glared at him scornfully, and gave him a tremendous shove, causing him to tumble over. He sat up and glared at her, all traces of friendliness gone. She glared back.

"I've never seen you this mad before," Bob the Conscience observed. "Perhaps you should calm down. You'll feel better."

"Bob," she said through gritted teeth, "don't talk to me!"

"Right."

She stood up, brushed the dust off her clothes, and stood over Simon.

"Where's my backpack?" she growled.

Simon stopped glaring and stood up. He frowned and shook his head, showing he couldn't understand.

"My backpack!" she shouted, spittle practically flying from her mouth.

She gave an impression of her slinging one onto her shoulder. Recognition sparked Simon's features, and he nodded, walking towards another room. Milo followed behind, seething.

At the back of the house were three doors. Simon went through the one at the far end of the hall. The room they entered had a full-sized bed and two bureaus against opposite walls. Milo's luggage was laid neatly on the bed. Simon pointed to her backpack, and she snatched it up. She stalked back to the sitting room, and found a cozy corner on the floor between a chair and the wall. She took her radio and diary out of their protective plastic.

"Please let me find a station," she thought miserably as she slid her headphones over her ears and clicked on the radio.

Surprisingly, she found a hip-hop station that came in loud and clear. Relieved that one thing was going right on this atrocious day, she began to scribble vehemently in her diary. She wrote about being left to the same fate as the plummeting airplane, and how she wanted just one hour alone with the pilot. She wrote about parachuting into the ocean and blacking out in the water. Then she described the awful situation she was in, and how she got into it, giving the glittering ring on her finger a look of loathing.

Simon at first had hovered by the threshold of the room, straining his neck to see what she was doing. Once or twice he cleared his throat, but to no avail. Eventually he went outside. A couple of hours later, he returned to find Milo in the same spot. Seeing that she still wasn't in the mood to be bothered, he didn't.

This lasted the rest of the day. If Simon had understood and spoken English, he would have asked her why she was so boiling mad about marrying him. And if Milo was able to understand and speak Galo, she would have told him that it was because she didn't love him. Technically, she didn't even like him. She had even recently begun to despise him.

It wasn't that Milo was in complete opposition to marriage. Milo did want to get married someday. Preferably when she was old enough, and she wanted to be in love. That was what bothered her the most. She wasn't in love. Certainly not with him; he wasn't The One. She had only met him that morning. She didn't know anything about him, and he equally didn't know a thing about her. It wasn't at all fair to be forced to marry a complete stranger, just because there had been a case of miscommunication. Yet, Milo was used to things not being fair.

As the sky outside began to darken, Milo's stomach called out to her. A delicious aroma was wafting in from the kitchen, and she got up to investigate. Simon had put two bowls on the table and was spooning food into them. The food looked similar to the mush Milo had eaten earlier. Only this stuff smelled like it had been mixed with lemon zest and basil.

Milo lingered by the door, not sure what to do. She didn't know if it would give him the wrong impression if she ate it. She did not want him to think that she was accepting things. Simon noticed her standing at the threshold and ushered her in. She stepped forward reluctantly, her head bent down.

"Look –" she began, but was interrupted by her stomach crying out for food.

Simon half smiled and beckoned for her to sit down. She did, but mind you, only because she was starving. He sat down too, on the other side of the table. They chewed silently for some time, Milo trying to figure out what type of fish he used.

"This doesn't change anything," she whispered resolutely as they finished, each scraping the bottom of their bowls. "I'll make my own food tomorrow."

She brought her bowl to the sink, which was a huge piece of marble that had been chiseled, polished, and placed in the middle of a counter, under a window. Beside it was a wooden water pump.

"*Hmmm,*" she thought. She decided to try the pump out tomorrow, and left Simon to clean the dishes.

At bedtime, she took a pillow off the bed and a blanket off the chest in front of the bed. She arranged them on the floor.

"I ain't married yet," she muttered defiantly.

She changed into her pajamas, first making certain that the door was securely shut. Feeling a lot better in some fresh clothes, though they were just as salty and still a bit damp, she lay down. Simon came in and paused when he saw her reclining on the floor. He didn't seem too surprised, but his shoulders sagged sadly. He sat on the edge of the bed, on Milo's side. He leaned back on his hands and stared at her. She didn't want to look at him, his face now the face of evil, and so she turned over. She heard him sigh and murmur hesitantly, "Milo?"

When she didn't respond, he rolled over onto the other side of the bed and got under the covers.

"Yoven silten, Milo," she heard him say softly. She figured he was saying goodnight. Groaning, she couldn't think of a single thing that was good about it. Since there was no electricity, the room was lit by candles and oil lamps. Simon snuffed out a candle, and darkness enshrouded them.

Milo tried to fall asleep, but the floor was hard and her mind was full. Too much had happened to her that day, and it kept replaying in her brain. She soon felt like crying, only she felt she didn't have enough of a reason to. She was very tired and finally sleep found her.

When she awoke, she felt sunshine streaming onto her through the windows. She sat up, wincing as her muscles protested. A night on a hard surface hadn't made them anymore agreeable. The bed was made, and Simon wasn't there.

Milo got up, rubbing her back, and dressed. She then went into the kitchen. Simon wasn't there either, but a bowl of breakfast mush was waiting for her on the table, along with a plate of raspberries. Milo looked at it all disdainfully, and would only nibble at it. She suddenly felt eyes watching her, and looked to the window to see three pairs duck out of sight.

"They can't resist you," Bob the Conscience said.

"Shut-up," she growled.

This isn't a nice thing to say, but in Milo's defense it was well used. She didn't need people spying on her, and she certainly didn't need her own conscience making jokes about it. She went into the hallway, where nobody could see her, and spent the rest of the morning meandering through the house. She didn't want Simon's company now, and didn't care if it was impolite.

Besides the sitting room, kitchen, and Simon's bedroom, there was a bathroom and another, smaller bedroom with a narrow, unmade bed. Milo wished she had known about it earlier; she could have slept on it last night.

In the bathroom she saw a large, metal basin in the middle of the floor. On the bottom of the basin was an enormous, flat piece of marble with a hole in its center. A curtain hung from the ceiling on one side of the basin, but the other side was left open to the elements. Craning her neck towards the ceiling, she saw a wooden funnel positioned directly over the basin. Milo took a closer look at the funnel and discovered little, clogged up holes peppering its surface. Arrows had been etched all around the rim, pointing in a continuous circle. Reaching up, she slowly twisted the outer rim, following the arrows. Without warning, water came pouring out of the funnel with reasonable force.

Milo yelped in surprise and quickly tried to turn it off. Afterwards, she nosed around rest of the bathroom. She was thrilled to find the door to the water-closet, which was a room about the size of a broom closet, with a tall wooden chamber pot at its center. This was, as Milo later learned, connected to a series of underground pipes that fed into a subterranean river. Once she finished her business, she examined a similar looking funnel sticking out of the wall. It looked just like the shower funnel, only much smaller and was angled down at a porcelain washbasin. This lay on the ground, a hole also in its bottom. Used to the system, she turned it on. Water trickled out, and she washed her hands. Turning it off, she dried her hands on a clean cloth that hung from the wall on a wooden ring.

As she walked back into the bathroom, she heard the front door open and close. Stiffening, she hurried into the hall and saw Simon disappear into the sitting room. She followed and found him examining her corner from yesterday. He heard her behind him and whisked around. Grinning, he uttered a few sentences in Galo while walking up to her.

In his hand was a tropical flower. It was big and a rich purple, with long graceful petals. He presented it to her with a patch of blush on both cheeks. If it had been any other occasion, and, at this point, from anyone else, Milo would have accepted it graciously. She had never gotten a flower, or flowers, from anyone before. When she had graduated from kindergarten, her father had given her an expired credit card.

Currently, she was disgusted with Simon and his wily, manipulating ways, and a flower wasn't about to tide things over between them. Therefore, when she took it she held it up to his face and began to rip off the petals. One by one, she tore, crumpled, and tossed them all to the floor. She glared at him maliciously, not stopping until all the petals were gone. She then snapped the stem in half and threw it in his face.

At first Simon looked like he was going to cry, but then he marshaled his emotions and brushed past her. Milo couldn't help notice how soft and velvety the petals had felt in her hands. She looked down at the scattered petals on the floor. Using her foot, she began to sweep the little pile of flower parts to the front door. She opened it, and with one mighty *Swoosh!* sent the petals flying.

Though she had used her foot, she wiped her hands together and shut the door.

Turned around, she ran smack into Simon. She stumbled back a few steps, but Simon didn't even break stride. He left the house again and didn't return until eleven o'clock. Milo knew this because of her digital watch, which had also survived the swim in the sea.

When Simon did come back, it was only to drag Milo outside.

"No! Stop!" she demanded, digging her feet into the ground and trying to wrestle her arm free.

But Simon wasn't taking "No!" for an answer. Not that he knew what the word "No!" meant, but he could tell she didn't want to cooperate. He grappled with her until she spotted some island people whacking at vines with machetes. She then grudgingly followed behind. Simon kept glancing back at her, as if expecting her to dart away. Shockingly, he wasn't angry about the rude, hurtful thing she had done, but looked quite happy and excited.

When they entered the town, the people stopped whatever they were doing and watched them pass. This made Milo's blood boil a little, but she determinedly kept her head bent down. She even did something she wouldn't ever do unless she was in a desperate situation, which she was. She pulled her hair tie out and let her hair fall in a curtain over her face, hiding it.

Simon led her up to the two-story building, but instead of bringing her inside with him, he moved her to a nearby tree. He jabbered to her in Galo, gesturing to the tree. Milo figured he was telling her to wait there.

"Fine," she breathed, nodding slightly so that he could understand.

Simon, smiling, gibbered gently and tried to pull her hair back to look at her face. However, as he did this, she tried to bite his hand. He retreated and went over to the building, stationing himself outside the door. Milo could feel people watching her and could hear their whispers. At once her anger was replaced with loneliness.

"Bob?" she called out to her conscience. "Bob, are you there?"

"Of course I am," he replied tartly. "Where else would I be? I can't be anywhere else."

"Sorry," Milo said.

"I thought you wanted me to shut-up."

"Well, now I want to talk to you," she snapped.

"I'm sure," he muttered. "So, what's the boy up to?"

"Beats me," she answered, glancing at him nastily. "Looks like he's waiting for someone."

Truth be told, he was. For a few moments later, small children came streaming through the doors to the playground in the backyard. One particular little girl ran into Simon's arms. Simon picked her up and hugged her tightly, laughing. He set her down, and they held hands for a few seconds before he picked up her traveling bag. They chatted gaily as they ambled up to Milo. Milo was eyeing the little girl curiously.

"Who do you think she is?" she asked Bob the Conscience.

"A law," he answered bleakly.

"What?" she said.

"Milo!" she heard Simon call. She looked up to see they were standing in front of her. Simon, smiling, placed a hand on the girl's shoulder.

"Ajsha," he announced proudly.

Milo's gaze flickered from him to the child.

"Who?" she said blankly.

The girl giggled and said, accompanied by a slight trill, "Ajsha. That is my name."

Milo drew back, astounded. "You speak my language?" she said.

"And Galo," Ajsha answered promptly. "I have been trained as a translator. I will help you talk to Simon, or anyone you want."

Milo looked her over. Her head was level with Simon's waist, her skin a few shades darker than Milo's. Her hair was brown and hung down her back, with wispy bangs delicately sweeping her eyelashes. To Milo's envy, it was filled with golden strands of highlights. Her eyes were dark brown and open, opposed to Milo's whose were green and guarded. She had an adorable smile, which settled just below her cheek bone. Her voice was cute, but unexpectedly wise sounding. She was beaming at Milo, who felt rude just standing there, scrutinizing her. Therefore she put out her hand and Ajsha gently shook it.

"I am so pleased to meet you," she told Milo. "I was so excited that I could barely sleep last night. Simon visited yesterday and told me the wonderful news."

"Wonderful?" Milo scoffed. "Look, I don't know what he told you, but I'm not going to marry him."

Ajsha nodded sadly. "Yes," she sighed. "He told me that the idea of marriage frightens you. But, do not worry. I have known Simon for a long time. We have been friends my whole life and I can assure you that he is . . . What are you laughing at?"

Milo wasn't necessarily laughing, but actually cackling. A verb usually set aside for witches and varying types of villains, not fourteen year old girls. But she was cackling. She had thrown her head back and was cackling away.

"Excuse me!" she gasped. "But I thought you said that I was scared of getting married, or something!"

"Well," Ajsha said cautiously, "that's what Simon –"

"Simon," Milo broke in angrily, "doesn't know crap about me! And neither do you!"

Ajsha lowered her lashes contritely. "I know," she murmured, but then smiled. "But I am going to find out! You and I are going to get along splendidly. I am a very useful person, or at least I try to be. You can say anything to him and I will translate. It is much better than silence."

They began to head back to Simon's house. Milo felt bad about yelling at Ajsha. She seemed like a sweet child.

"I'm sorry," she told her as they walked.

"For what?" Ajsha inquired courteously.

"You know," Milo faltered. "I didn't mean to sound mean or disagreeable."

Ajsha nodded understandingly. "I am sure you didn't. It's okay."

"Thanks," Milo said. "Hey, Ajsha? I have a few questions. Can you answer them?"

"I'll try," she replied eagerly.

"Cool. Okay. First of all . . . sorry, but why are you coming back with us?"

Ajsha smiled, slipping her hand into Simon's. "That," she said, "is an easy question. One of the laws states that if a couple gets married, they are obligated to adopt a child –"

"Right!" Milo said, smacking her forehead. "I forgot. Where do the kids come from? Are you all orphans?"

Ajsha's smile turned sad. "Yes," she said quietly.

"How did you get here?" Milo asked curiously.

"Like everyone else," Ajsha sighed. "By accident. There was a plane, carrying orphan babies six years ago. I believe they were flying to America from England. They got caught in a lightning storm, and crashed upon this island. The place we just left was the orphanage, where they house us and teach us English and Galo. As I said before, I was trained to be an interpreter, in case someone here wants to marry somebody who only speaks English. We are all trained for that, and we study everything about the island, so we will be able to answer any questions people may have."

"That sounds a little demanding for a six year old."

"I am a fast learner," Ajsha said proudly. "The fastest in my class! I was speaking full sentences at two. I could read at four and write at five, in both English and Galo. I can keep up with any conversation."

"Wow!" Milo commented, impressed. "That's incredible."

Ajsha blushed and waved her away. "Ah, no! No. Not incredible."

"Yes, it is!" insisted Milo, who didn't dole out compliments lightly.

"Well," she said modestly. "I work hard. Oh, Milo! I'm sorry, but I'm too excited to keep quiet! Simon and I have been friends for so long. He promised me that when he got married he would adopt me, and we could be together forever!"

"But I told you!" Milo moaned, wiping at the sweat on the nape of her neck. "I'm not marrying him!"

"Oh, but you have to!" Ajsha cried. "It's the law! Everyone here obeys the laws! They make sure of it. You don't want to get on Mayor Em-I's bad side. In the past, people have been executed for breaking laws."

"Marriage laws?!" Milo cried, horrified.

"Well, no," Ajsha admitted thoughtfully. "More serious laws. Murder, maybe. Anyway, no one has ever objected to the marriage laws. Even if people change their minds about being in love, they will fall in love over time. It has worked perfectly over the years, no one minds."

"Well, I do!" Milo declared, suddenly tripping over a stray root and falling to the ground.

Simon jumped to help her, but she wouldn't allow him.

"Get away from me!" she growled at him, shoving away his extended hand. Ajsha watched intently.

"Why do you push him away?" she asked Milo.

"I thought you were an interpreter," Milo responded.

"Yes, but –"

"Then tell him what I said."

"Are you sure that –"

"Yes!" she interrupted again.

Ajsha exhaled and nodded, then turned to Simon and began to jabber, relaying what Milo had said. Simon gibbered something back, and Ajsha translated it for Milo.

"He said, 'Why?'"

"Why?" Milo repeated incredulously, brushing herself off. "I don't want him touching me!"

Ajsha told Simon, and Simon said something in response.

"He said that he didn't know that you don't like to be touched."

"By him," Milo corrected.

"Oh," Ajsha said, and told Simon this. Simon's reply sounded perfectly frustrated. "He said, 'You are being childish. '"

"Childish!" she bellowed, stalking up to Simon. "I am being – being rational!"

Ajsha translated and told Milo, "He says, 'Fine.'"

"Yeah! I bet he does!" Milo nodded in satisfaction.

She was turning away when Ajsha announced, "He says, 'What's that supposed to mean?'"

"What?" Milo snapped. "You told him that?"

"I have to," Ajsha replied resolutely.

"No!" Milo insisted hotly. "That was directed at you. I didn't want you to tell him that."

Ajsha shook her head patiently. "You will have to tell me when you do not want me to translate."

"Be sure I will!" Milo grumbled, striding off under the green tree limbs.

They trudged on till they reached the hut. Simon looked rather dour, and after dropping off Ajsha's luggage he headed towards the beach. Ajsha went straight to the second bedroom to unpack. Milo followed. Along with the twin-sized bed, her bedroom also had a little closet and a mirror. Milo loitered by the doorway, watching her unpack and once more feeling guilty. Before she could summon any courage to say anything, Ajsha abruptly turned to her.

"You treat him so cold," she stated, close to tears.

"Who?" Milo said, alarmed by the sudden quavering in her voice.

"Simon."

"Oh. Yeah, well –"

"He did nothing wrong," Ajsha continued, almost pleadingly.

"He is not acting ill-tempered towards you, and yet you are so cold to him."

"Well, he has put me in a situation that I don't like. At all," Milo said indignantly, folding her arms.

"Why not?" Ajsha said. "Why don't you want to marry him?"

Milo stared across the room at her, the reality of the last forty-eight hours suddenly becoming unbearably clear. She swayed a little, trying to fight off the wave of panic threatening her mind.

"Because!" Milo whispered hoarsely. "I don't love him! . . . He's not even my boyfriend! . . . I'm only fourteen! . . . How can I marry him? I don't love him. I don't even like him. I just met him yesterday!"

She went over to the bed, sat, and buried her face in her hands. Ajsha timidly sat down next to her. She put her little hand on Milo's shoulder.

"Oh," she said softly. "I am so sorry. I suppose I should have figured that. But . . . Simon is such a wonderful person. I guess I thought that everybody automatically loved him."

"I can't even understand what he says!" Milo mumbled into her hands.

"I know," Ajsha said, patting her shoulder comfortingly. "It's hard. But you wouldn't believe how much he has been pressured lately to find a wife. Most of his friends are married. They bother and tease him about it. All the age eligible girls in town are always all over him. He is very polite to them, of course, but none of them appeal to him. Oh, please don't worry, Milo. Simon won't let you down. He didn't let me down. Whenever he could, he would visit me at the orphanage and tell me how someday he would come to take me home. Finally that day came."

Milo sniffed.

"I know you are sad," Ajsha pursued, "but you must understand, I am very happy about this 'situation'. Simon has always been like a father to me, and I always knew he would find me a good mother."

"Mother?" Milo repeated, looking at her in bewilderment.

"Yes."

"Good?"

"Yes."

"But," Milo stammered. "I can't be a good . . . I was so . . . You can't possibly think I'm . . . How can you even stand talking to me?"

Ajsha smiled kindly. "I understand how you feel. Though I just met you, Milo, I must say I like you. You don't mind standing up for what you think. It's hard to find people like that."

"Yeah?" Milo asked doubtfully, and then remembered that Ajsha was used to this place and not America, which had a long history of folks who stood up for what they thought.

Ajsha pulled out a handkerchief from a skirt pocket and handed it to her, as if expecting her to cry. Confused, Milo dabbed at the sweat on her forehead.

"Yes," Ajsha told her. "And as long as you cooperate, nothing bad will happen to you."

"What if I don't?" Milo asked. "Are they really going to force me?"

Ajsha sighed. "I'm afraid so. This island is normally a very peaceful, happy place to live, but they are very adamant about the laws. And I'm also scared for you."

"Why?"

"Well, you see . . . Simon has these friends, and – don't get me wrong! They're great boys, but if you don't do this . . . well . . . they will hurt you."

Milo scoffed. "With what?" she said bitterly.

Ajsha shrugged fretfully. "Whatever they have on hand. Clubs, chains, their fists. They might slit your ears with knives, or burn the palms of your hands with fire."

Milo stared back at her in horror. "And you say they're great?" she gasped.

"They're nice, as long as you don't mess with Simon."

"What are they?" she exclaimed, wringing the handkerchief distractedly. "His posse? His gang? His mafia?!"

"No!" Ajsha said. "And not all his friends are like that. These boys are just . . . protective, I guess. They just want him to be happy, that's all."

"Have they ever actually done any of that stuff?"

"Not exactly. They mostly just talk about it. But please be careful, Milo. I wouldn't want you to get hurt, especially since you're already unhappy. The best thing to do is just go through with it."

"Never!" she declared, standing up.

"But –" Ajsha began.

"I don't care!" Milo told her, feeling herself fill with a fiery passion. "I am *not* going to have anything to do with marriage until I am old enough and in love. Simon's just gonna have to deal with it. I bet his friends wouldn't hit a girl anyway!"

"I wouldn't be so sure," Ajsha said nervously.

"You said that you liked how I stand up for myself."

"Yes, but you have to know where to draw the line. This could be dangerous!"

"We'll see about that," Milo said stubbornly, apparently having forgotten the mayor's dagger.

Ajsha gazed at her solemnly. "Okay," she murmured. "But please! If things go bad, don't fight them. It would be heavy on my heart if you got hurt."

Milo smiled faintly at her. "You should be *my* mother," she said.

Ajsha shook her head. "I am sure you already have a suitable mother."

Milo scowled. "No, not really."

They talked straight through to the afternoon, lounging on Ajsha's unmade bed. They ignored lunch. Ajsha told her that the first people had arrived on the island in 1883. They were sailing on a ship loaded with all sorts of people, supplies, and animals. They most likely were planning to create farms and such once they reached their destination.

("Many of the records from that time were destroyed," Ajsha said. "We aren't certain where they came from, but we think they were possibly heading for America."

"Probably," Milo agreed. "Everyone's always headed for America.")

The ship got caught in a dreadful storm and crashed upon the island. The passengers were marooned, the ship being severely damaged. Since they were of a resourceful breed, instead of griping and moping about the circumstances, they at once got busy. They emptied the demolished ship, and settled onto the island.

Since then other ships and planes had crashed there, in the same area. There was a spot on the other side of the island that was littered with at least nine crashed planes. The people who had survived became apart of the town.

"Wow!" Milo muttered. "And how do they live? I mean, I know they fish, but the first food I ate here looked like it had corn in it. Where did that come from?"

"In the middle of the island," Ajsha replied promptly, as if reciting from a book, "is the farming land. It stretches for thirty acres and is home to a variety of families. They grow much of the food for the island. From corn, to wheat, to oranges, to herbs."

"Where did it all come from?"

"Most of it was on the first boat that crashed. It started out small, but overtime it grew, like the population. More seeds and plants were found on the different wrecks over the years. The farmers deliver the products to the stores, and the stores sell them."

"Sell?" said Milo. "You have money?"

"Of course!" Ajsha said. "We make it out of things we find on the planes. There are Bruns, worth about fifty cents, which are made out of the glass from the windows. Dlos, worth about one dollar, made from the seat material. Enros, worth about one cent, made from the rubber of the tires. And Kons, Gens, and Mors. Worth five, ten, and fifty dollars. Each is made from a different color of the outside of the plane."

"Whoa!" Milo exclaimed. "So then, you have a bank?"

Ajsha nodded.

"Is it the building with the honking big door?"

"No. That is where they store fish. The bank, like the library, is underground."

At that moment, Milo heard the front door opened and closed. Simon's face appeared in the doorway. He appeared much calmer than earlier, and shyly made a gesture, asking for admittance. He gibbered something to Ajsha, who responded cheerfully.

"He wants to know if it's alright if he and I talk," she informed Milo.

Milo nodded and strangely didn't feel that mad at him anymore. Of course, that wouldn't last.

"I'll be in the kitchen," she told Ajsha. Ajsha told Simon.

Milo stood up and edged past Simon. He entered Ajsha's room and sat next to her.

Milo let them be and walked into the kitchen. Immediately she thought, "*Great! I bet they want me to cook! Wonderful! I can't cook!*"

"You liar!" Bob the Conscience accused. "Shame on you!"

"Oh, be quiet!" she shot back, grinning despite herself.

7
Wedding Plans

"ACTIONS SPEAK LOUDER than words", is an old saying that has been passed down through the decades. It still carries a lot of meaning and fits in perfectly with what Milo had done. Of course she decided to cook. It was her passion. She couldn't resist.

In the kitchen she found the replacement for the oven. It was a large, deep, crudely made cauldron with two doors on its side. The top was covered with iron, for pots and pans and any other stove-top activity. The door in the middle of the cauldron opened with a little latch to reveal two levels of grates for baking and cooking things. The door at the bottom opened to show the belly of the cauldron and heaps of ashes. It was where the wood burned that heated the whole cauldron.

Milo had to admit that the contraption was rather clever. A pipe stuck out of the back, connecting it to the wall. If she had gone outside to look, Milo would have seen the pipe running up the side of the hut into the air, allowing smoke to escape.

She scrounged around the rest of the kitchen. She had retrieved *Milo's Cookbook of Plagiary* from her backpack and tried to choose a reasonable recipe. She searched for one that involved fish, because that was mostly what Simon had. She found a recipe for pan-fried tilapia. She had picked it up while she was in Hawaii. It called for tilapia filets (though substitution of any fish was perfectly fine), cornflake crumbs, and pineapple. Milo found plenty of fish, (unidentifiable but already cleaned, so why complain?) but no cornflake crumbs. She decided to replace it with flour and vegetable oil. There were different sized boxes on one of the counters, along with a stone mortar and pestle, and one of them contained flour. As for the vegetable oil, (at least that's what Milo hoped it was) she found a bottle of it in a cupboard.

In another cupboard she found smooth wooden bowls, and in a corner she found a small pile of wood. She stuck a few pieces in the belly of the cauldron and then faced the problem of lighting it. She poked around the cupboards, but couldn't find anything that resembled a match. Wondering how Simon lit the wood every day, she went back and probed at the ashes with a stick. She caught sight of a dusty glow and took a jab at it. Sparks flew out and caught on a twig. A small flame materialized and gradually grew larger.

"That'll do for now," Milo said, encouraging it with gentle blows of air.

She went to the table and mixed a bit of the oil with the flour, making it crumbly. She then breaded three filets of fish. When the oven, which she thought it more appropriate to call a calven, was hot enough to fry, she poured a little oil onto the top and laid the fish down, creating a loud sizzle. She hadn't found a pineapple, but did find a lemon. According to the recipe, while the fish fried, she was to squeeze the juice all over them. She eventually flipped them, using a flattish sort of spoon she had found in a drawer, and did the same to the other side.

While the fish cooked, she cleaned up and tried to make the kitchen look neat, as if she had never been there, which she honestly would have preferred. As the aroma of the fish made her saliva run, she kissed her cookbook, grateful to her semi-bright mind for starting it. She found plates, made from smooth disks of wood, and put them on the table, which she noticed had an extra chair. Simon and Ajsha soon came in, their noses tilted into the air.

Milo served the steaming, crackling fish, and they all sat down to a quiet meal. That action, her making dinner, was speaking much louder than any words she could have had Ajsha translate. The action spoke to Simon as if screaming. It told him things that Milo had never intended to be said. The kind gesture, therefore, became a sign of acceptance. Something Milo did not want to convey.

The evening came to a close as they got ready for bed. Ajsha, in a fluttery white night dress, padded into the "Big Bedroom" and found Milo lying on the floor, her arms stretched leisurely behind her head. She frowned and said, "Why are you not on the bed?"

Milo turned towards her and said, "Are you crazy?"

Ajsha seemed taken aback by this, but then paused to ponder her words.

"I understand," she said finally. "But you can't continue this forever. Once you are married you must sleep on the bed."

"I'm not getting married," Milo replied stoutly, gazing up at the ribbed ceiling.

"I told you," Ajsha said persistently. "They will force you. You will have to –"

"Why make the evening unpleasant with terrible facts?" Milo cut in. "Let's just enjoy one another's company."

She abruptly burst into peals of laughter. Ajsha, mystified, asked, "What's so funny?"

Milo giggled and replied, "What I just said!" She rolled over, shaking with concealed laughs. Ajsha sighed and said, without much laughter, "Well, I came in to say goodnight."

Milo rolled over again. "Goodnight," she chirped.

Ajsha smiled pleasantly and knelt down to her. "Goodnight," she said, and leaned her face towards Milo's.

Milo pulled back, nearly knocking her head on the bedframe, and said, "What are you doing?"

Ajsha's forehead puckered. "Aren't you going to kiss me good night?" she asked innocently.

"Nooo."

"Oh," she said. She fell back, crestfallen. "But didn't your parents kiss you good night?"

"No," Milo replied.

"Not ever?"

"Nope."

"Oh!" Ajsha said sympathetically. "I am so sorry. Here, I will kiss you."

She leaned forward and gave Milo a peck on the forehead. Milo felt a mix of guilt and gratitude surge through her, despite feeling slightly silly. This darling child, who had never had any parents, was concerned for Milo's happiness. Such a small token of kindness brought on such emotions in Milo that she felt the back of her eyeballs sting.

"Thanks," she muttered. She wished she could do more. Why couldn't she give a kiss in return?

Milo had always considered herself a friend to children, but not a mother. She had never given any thought to having kids, or what she would do once she had them. You are either born motherly, or you grow into it. Milo definitely was not born that way. She knew how to be a friend, but a mother was something different. Something Milo couldn't be. Mothers were the type of people who kiss their children good night; friends weren't. Milo just couldn't do it. Kiss her.

Ajsha smiled kindly, just as Simon came in, dressed in a light T-shirt and shorts. Ajsha stood up and rushed into his arms. They gibbered for a moment, exchanging goodnights. Simon kissed her on the cheek, and she on his. Setting her down, he walked her to her room. Curious, Milo tossed off her blanket and crawled out into the hallway. She looked through Ajsha's open door, into her room. The little bed was all made up, and she could see Simon tucking

Ajsha in. She saw him brush her hair out of her face with his fingers, and he was softly singing a lullaby.

Milo couldn't understand the words, for it was a Galo lullaby, but they sounded gentle and soothing. Ajsha slipped quietly off to sleep, and Simon kissed her on the forehead when he finished singing. Milo hurriedly, yet silently, stood up and scurried back to the other bedroom. She had just lain on the floor when Simon entered.

His eyes drifted down to her and he smiled. Though Milo didn't smile in return, he saw that she didn't glare or turn away. This comforted him in a small way. He waved and she lifted one of her hands, not quite in a wave. He snuffed the candle and went to bed.

When Milo awoke in the morning, her hair sticking wetly to her forehead from the heat, the bed was once again made and Simon gone. Milo dressed then paid a visit to the water-closet. After that, she cautiously made her way to the kitchen, glancing left and right, in case Simon was hiding somewhere. She didn't spot him, so apparently he left early every morning. He had again laid out bowls of mush on the kitchen table, an extra one for Ajsha. Milo turned up her nose at the sight of it.

"Is that all he can make?" she thought.

There wasn't a doubt in her mind that it was, and she scraped the mush into the trash/barrel.

"Good morning," said a voice behind her. Turning around, she saw it was Ajsha. She was, much like a child, still in her bedclothes

"Good morning," Milo answered back pleasantly, an empty bowl in each hand. Ajsha walked over to the table. "Sleep well?"

She nodded and asked, "What did you just throw away?"

Milo straightened her back up and said haughtily, "An infernal excuse for a breakfast. Is fish mush all he can make?"

Ajsha giggled and sat down. "We call it 'Finta naldo'. Or in English, 'Fish medley'. It is easy to make and usually tastes very good."

"Usually?" Milo speculated.

"Yes. You see, it can be any kind of fish, a vegetable, and herbs and spices. And sometimes a combination comes out wrong and doesn't taste good at all. Most bachelors, like Simon, eat this all the time. Breakfast, lunch, and supper. The variety is good, and the nutrition meets demands well enough. But they are still happy when their new wives start to cook for them."

"Well, good for them," Milo sniffed indignantly. "I hope Simon does like it, because he's gonna be eating a lot of it! I ain't gonna cook for him. I cook for myself, and since you're here I won't let you starve."

"You cooked for Simon last night," Ajsha pointed out, swinging her legs.

"No, I didn't," Milo said stiffly, putting the bowls in the sink. "He merely ate with us. Quite rude of him, if you ask me."

"You cooked three pieces of fish," Ajsha persisted.

"Yes – well . . ." Milo was stumbling over her words, therefore she changed the subject. "What do you want for breakfast?"

Ajsha looked confused. "Food," she said slowly.

Milo almost laughed. "Any specific type?" she asked

Ajsha shrugged complacently. "Anything you can make."

This time Milo did laugh and said, "Honey, *that* is quite a selection!"

They discussed it until they decided on pancakes. Milo poked around in the ashes of the calven, but they were all cold and devoid of sparks. She grew worried, but she put wood in nevertheless and restlessly flipped through the pages of *Milo's Cookbook of Plagiary* until she found a recipe for pancakes. She found it on the back of a blueberry carton and had changed it around to meet her liking.

"Flour, egg, sugar, baking powder, salt, milk, and any type of fruit to mix in."

Milo, of course, had no baking powder, but she found flour, milk, salt, and oil. She decided to skip the sugar, discovering a stash of raspberries in a cupboard, but couldn't find any eggs. She turned to Ajsha and asked her if there was any.

"Not here," she replied.

"Where?"

"In town. They raise the island birds for eggs. Simon must not have bought any recently. Can you cook without them?"

"I guess so," Milo muttered.

"Shouldn't you light the stove first?"

Milo blushed and said quietly, "Can you tell me how?"

"How did you light it last night?"

"The ashes. They were still on fire."

Ajsha pointed a tiny, slim finger at one of the cupboards. "There should be a flint and stone in there," she said. "Would you like me to show you how to use it?"

"No thanks," Milo responded, reaching for it. She had used one before, and wished she had known about it yesterday.

The breakfast turned out alright, despite the absence of eggs, and afterwards Ajsha showed her how to work the water pump. After dishes were washed and dried, they went into the sitting room.

"Where does Simon go in the morning?" Milo asked as they sat on a couch.

"To work," Ajsha replied.

"He has a job?" Milo said in surprise.

"Oh, yes." Ajsha nodded gravely. "He is a fisherboy."

"Don't you mean fisher-*man*?"

"No. He isn't a man yet, therefore he is a fisherboy, along with all the other boys he works with. They go out to sea with their nets and boats, and bring back fish. It is a good job, for most of the island eats mainly fish."

"Is that all they catch?" Milo asked.

"Oh, no! Whatever they can find. Clams, oysters, crabs, shrimp, even octopus!"

"Octopus!" Milo cried. "People eat that here?"

Ajsha giggled. "Some do. At the orphanage, they used to tell us, 'A rumbling tummy will make anything yummy'."

This pleasant sort of conversation continued for several hours. Milo told her all about 711 Shady Ally and the horrors it contained. Ajsha was an incredible listener, and Milo began to feel like she had found a friend. The happy chit-chat lasted until noon, which was when Simon came home, escorted by two strangers.

One was a woman and the other was a man, both looking like they were in their middle thirties or forties. Simon had the hair of the woman, but the face of the man. Milo didn't need to be introduced to know that they were his parents.

Ajsha, squealing joyfully, scampered over to them, getting a hug from each. Milo hadn't moved, in fact she had halted in mid-sentence. For some odd reason, she had begun to think that Simon didn't have parents. But of course he did! Why shouldn't he? He didn't just get spat out of the sky. And something in her mind was telling her why they were there.

"Come to meet the bride, have they?" Bob the Conscience said.

"N-O! W-A-Y!" Milo screamed, in her mind.

"Oh, yes!" Bob the Conscience countered.

"No, no, no!"

"Yes, yes, yes!"

"Uh-uh!"

"Uh-huh!"

"Oh, Bob, stop!" Milo whimpered, shifting fretfully on the couch. "Help me! I don't know what to do!"

"Okay!" he relented. "Sorry. Really. Sorry."

"Help me!" she shrieked at him.

"Right! Now, calm down. Let's see. Hmmm. Okay, they're probably here to meet you and to discuss the plans for the wedding."

"What makes you say that?" she demanded, her skin going clammy.

"Look at what they're carrying," he said.

She looked and saw that they were carrying pads of paper and charcoal pencils. They also held different sized portfolios, each one labeled differently in Galo.

"Oh, no," she whispered. "What's with these people? I just got engaged two days ago! They could give me a little time to breathe! But, not that it matters," she added hastily. "After all, I am *not* getting married."

"Look at the facts, darling," Bob the Conscience said grimly. "You *are*."

The terrible truth was beginning to sink in. But Milo, tenacity in her veins, refused to give up without a fight. Clenching her hands into fists, she watched as Simon led his parents into the sitting room, where Ajsha promptly began her job.

"Milo," she began, taking her position between the first and second party, "these are Simon's parents."

"I know," Milo said quietly, through her teeth.

"You do?" Ajsha said, surprised. "How?"

"Guessed," she muttered.

"Oh, well, this is Luna and Lennon Pitt," she said, pointing to them in turn.

She then spoke to them in Galo, undoubtedly introducing them, for they smiled at Milo. Milo just stared at them.

"Pitt?" she repeated. "I thought that Simon's last name was Swallow."

"It is," Ajsha explained. "He changed it when he moved out of their house. All the boys are allowed to do that."

"Allowed, or required to?" Milo whispered darkly. But Ajsha didn't hear, because she was busy relaying this confusion to Simon and his parents.

They all chuckled affably, and Simon, grinning, went over to Milo, sat down beside her, and put an arm around her shoulders. Her head snapped towards him and she narrowed her eyes in pure hatred. She was clearly saying, "Oh! You know better, boi!" Quickly, he relinquished his grasp and stared at the floor. His parents sat on the other couch, on the other side of the table, which was an enormous piece of granite. It was about four feet tall and five feet long with flat, polished surface. They laid their things on it, and then jabbered something to Ajsha, who told Milo.

"They said, 'We are simply thrilled about the wedding. We can't wait to get to know you better once you learn Galo.'"

"I can't learn another language!" Milo mouthed, terrified.

One school she had attended had insisted that she try to either learn French or Spanish. She tried, but failed tremendously at both. Not a single verb or pronoun had stuck in her mind. She could barely speak English!

Ajsha continued, not noticing her visible distress. "'The wedding day is in one week, so we thought it best to come now and prepare.'"

"A week!" Milo choked out.

Ajsha translated, waited for the reply, and then interpreted it for Milo.

"Luna says, 'Of course a week. There's no reason to wait. The preparations go quickly because so many people are going to help out. From the food, to the dress, to the flow- '"

"Whoa! Whoa!" Milo spluttered desperately, rubbing her damp palms on her jeans. "Slow down!"

"What's wrong?" Ajsha inquired.

"These preparations!" she said shrilly, starting to shake. "Dress, flowers? Are you kidding me?"

"No," Ajsha said slowly. "That's what all the weddings usually have. Have they changed in America?"

Milo rolled her eyes and shook her head in frustration.

"No! But, look –"

Luna Pitt gibbered briskly in Galo, interrupting her.

"Excuse me, Milo," Ajsha said politely. "Luna says that we have to look at the plans they brought. She first wants you to look at the dresses."

"Food," Milo said tonelessly, staring at her knees.

"Don't worry about the food. They will decide all that; you and Simon won't be eating there anyway."

"Food."

"No," Ajsha insisted patiently. "I told you. You and Simon will be going to a select location right after the wedding. There will be no time to eat."

Milo wanted to roar, "What?!" but could only manage, "Food."

"Listen, Milo –"

"My food!" she gasped.

With that, she clamored to her feet, ran out the front door, and vomited. The Pitts gasped and immediately began jabbering in an incoherent blur, wanting to know what came over her. Simon, shushing his mother and father as he went, hurried outside to help Milo, but only succeeded in getting vomit dribbled onto his feet.

He yelped, springing away. He again tried to help her, gently touching her back, but she shoved him away. She stumbled back into the house, clasping her stomach, and Simon, after shouting something through the window, headed to the beach to wash off his feet. The reason Milo had regurgitated was, when Ajsha had said dresses, the image of being in one made her feel too sick to keep her breakfast in. She slumped into a chair and said breathlessly, "You were saying?"

Nobody really looked at her like she was capable of going on, but, nevertheless, Ajsha persevered. "Um, yes. The dresses."

She gingerly handed Milo a portfolio, then stood looking over her shoulder. Milo, inhaling by the gallon, forced herself to open the cover and look at the hand drawn pictures.

Some of the dresses were completely straight and smooth, while others were smooth down to the waist, then spread out into a puffy skirt. There were some with veils, and some with hats, and then some with both. Some had coats, others had capes, and each one came with a different bouquet to match. There were beautiful designs done with threads and beads, and each page had a tiny square of cloth pinned to it, so you could get an idea what the dress would feel like.

Milo flipped through the pages, feeling like an anvil was sitting on her chest, until a dress involuntarily caught her eye. She didn't mean for it to; she had planned to skim through the entire thing with a bored expression on her face, not pausing on any page. But when her eyes rested on that particular drawing, she just had to murmur, "Oh, wow."

Ajsha was about to translate, when Milo grabbed her arm.

"Don't tell them I said that," she hissed.

"Why not?" Ajsha inquired.

"I don't want them to think I've found a dress I like. I – I just couldn't help it," she explained.

Ajsha shrugged. "It doesn't matter," she said. "They saw the expression on your face already."

Milo felt like swearing, for it was true, but she wasn't one for foul language, so she didn't. The Pitts arose and crossed the room to see the picture.

It was a smooth satin job all the way down, with tiny sparkling beads speckled along the front. The veil trailed down the back and covered the face, and the bouquet was comprised of small wild flowers. Its beauty had caught Milo off guard and caused her to utter those two wretched words, "Oh, wow."

The Pitts gasped when they saw it and began to gabber away appraisingly in Galo. Ajsha grinned, nodding a couple of times, and addressed Milo.

"Luna says that it's a very good choice, and Lennon says that you'll look very pretty in it."

Before Milo could say anything, snotty or otherwise, the portfolio was snatched away from her, and replaced with another one.

"She says that the flowers for the church will match your bouquet," Ajsha translated as Luna Pitt talked and tapped at the cover. "You now have to pick out my dress and the jewelry you'll wear."

"I didn't even agree to wear the dress!" Milo snapped. "Don't start talking to me about jewelry, and . . . you're going to be wearing a dress?"

"Why, yes," she replied softly. "I'm going to be the flower girl. Is that Okay?"

Guilt flooded Milo for the third time, and she said quickly, "Of course. I'm sorry I'm yelling so much, but . . . you've got to understand."

"I do," Ajsha told her soothingly.

Frankly, the simple fact that Ajsha was going to be present at the wedding comforted Milo a good deal. When surrounded by enemies, you must have at least one person on your side to watch your back. Reluctantly, Milo opened the portfolio, but the minute her eyes rested too long on a mother-of-pearl necklace and bracelet set the book was seized from her.

"*Hey*," she snarled. But in seconds her hands were occupied with another. "What's this one?" she groaned wearily, squinting at its unintelligible title.

"Pictures of remote places on the island where you and Simon could go after the wedding" Ajsha explained after an exchange with Luna.

It took Milo a moment to work out just what this meant, and once she did, her nails dug into the paper of the portfolio.

"You mean like a – a – a . . ." Milo couldn't get the word out. She was trembling with rage, her pallid complexion changing color vibrantly. How dare they?

"How dare they!" Bob the Conscience growled.

Milo leapt out of her seat, sending the book crashing to the floor.

"How dare you!" she yelled at Luna Pitt, and at Lennon Pitt, and even at Ajsha, who was quick to interpret.

"They say, 'What do you mean?'"

The two Pitts were exceptionally startled, and moved closer together as Milo went from radish to beet.

"What do I mean?" she shrieked. "You know what I mean! A – a – a – a *honeymoon!*"

Her voice turned hoarse and low as she said it, it clawing at her vocal chords, not wanting to get out.

"You sick, disgusting, revolting, ill-minded people!" she said savagely, thrusting a finger at them. "First you want me to marry him, and what?! Now you want me to have s-"

She was cut off by Simon coming through the front door, calling loudly as he entered. He walked into the sitting room and, instantly registering the tension, spoke to Ajsha, most likely wanting to know what happened. Before she could answer, Milo stormed up to him and gave him an aggressive push. He didn't necessarily go anywhere, but Milo just had to push him. She was ready to maul him, but wasn't sure if she would win.

"You disgusting island boy!" she yelled to his face, her own quite blotchy and spittle flying everywhere. "And I mean disgusting with a capital *D!*"

"Milo, stop!" Ajsha pleaded, tugging on the hem of her shirt. She glanced back at the Pitts, who had no clue why their future daughter-in-law was so outraged.

"Translate!" Milo commanded her.

Ajsha whimpered, but turned to the bewildered Simon and translated. He raised his eyebrows, more concerned than offended, and spoke to Milo.

"He says, 'What are you talking about?'"

"You know!" Milo growled, suddenly realizing that he didn't. "The, the, the *honeymoon.*"

She spat it out of her mouth like it was a nasty taste. She though it was going to strangle her soon. Simon observed her closely before responding.

"He says, 'What about it?'" Ajsha said, her voice quavering.

"What about it?" Milo repeated. "What about it?! The insensitive guts you have, you rotting piece of crap!"

Once interpreted, this certainly drew him into the turbulence. A frown distorted his face as he fired back a retort.

"He says, 'Hey! Be quiet!'" Ajsha said, trying to keep the words steady.

"Are you going to *force* me?!" Milo shouted at Simon, who was now almost as angry as she was.

Almost.

The Pitts had heard everything that Ajsha had translated, and strode over, entering the fray. They yelled at her, along with Simon, and she shouted back with relish.

Ajsha, for a child, was keeping up astoundingly well. She desperately wanted to explain to Milo, and the rest, that it was a mere misunderstanding they were fighting about. She had figured out why Milo was so upset, but couldn't tell her anything. Her training clearly stated that she had to translate when people talked and couldn't interrupt with any of her own thoughts unless it was an emergency. Therefore, she could do nothing but translate for all four people, and they always shot an answer back swiftly. If you have ever tried arguing for four people, then you understand how stressful it is. If you haven't, I wouldn't recommend it.

But it wasn't the difficulty that bothered Ajsha. She had been expertly trained and was able to keep flawlessly, but it was getting to her. Not the fact that she had to speak for four people, back and forth at a monstrous rate. But it was simply because they were arguing at all. It pained her to see them baring their teeth at one another and to hear their hurtful words. They were going to be her family, parents and grandparents.

Have you ever heard your parents argue from another room,

screaming and insulting each other? If it scares you, this author doesn't blame you. But try to imagine *helping* them argue. That was what Ajsha had to do, and tears were beginning to leak out of to her eyes. The pressure was becoming too much for her as she ferried the insults back and forth. Finally she couldn't stand it any longer, and burst out wailing.

"Stop! Why do you have to fight?" she cried, first in English then in Galo. She then ran sobbing into her room.

The four quarreling ones stood in silence and in guilt, letting their thumping pulses quiet down. Simon looked pained and kept running his hands over his hair, pushing it back.

"You should have thought of her," Bob the Conscience said.

"I know," Milo responded, a knot forming in her stomach.

The Pitts gibbered apologetically to Simon as he went after Ajsha, and then gathered their things. As they turned to leave, they glared at Milo.

"What?" she snapped, thinking they were just as much to blame.

They held their heads high and strode disdainfully out the door, leaving Milo alone in the sitting room. She watched them depart, wiping at her mouth and wishing they had never come. Or that she had never come. That she had never got on that doomed plane, or had ever seen that stupid flyer for Camp Outback.

Sighing, and realizing that wishing for something that had happened already to be different was useless, she slowly walked to Ajsha's room. The door was open a crack, and she peeked in to see Ajsha lying on her stomach on the bed, crying into a pillow. Simon was sitting beside her, speaking soft, soothing sentences, trying to calm her down. He spoke gently and lovingly stroked her back. Milo's jaw tightened. She felt guilty for dragging Ajsha into the fight, but she had meant everything she had said. Simon suddenly looked up at the door. Milo quickly ducked out of sight.

She headed to the kitchen, the place where she always thought best, to try to think of a way to apologize to Ajsha. She flipped through *Milo's Cookbook of Plagiary's* dessert section, until she found a simple, yet tasty recipe. It called for apples, honey, and strawberries. After digging around in various cupboards and shelves, she found a banana, honey in a bottle by the oil, and raspberries.

She took out a plate and a small knife, and cut the banana into oblong slices. She then carefully poured a dollop of honey onto each slice. Finally, she nestled a raspberry into the golden stickiness. She made ten, and then cleaned up.

Picking up the plate, she headed towards Ajsha's room. She met Simon in the hallway, and they paused for a moment to glare at each other. Simon's gaze briefly flickered down at the platter she was holding aloft, but mostly his eyes burned into hers. Pretending her pupils were laser beams, Milo burned right back. He was the first to move on. Smirking a bit, she kept walking and finally knocked softly on Ajsha's door.

"Ajsha?" she called out. "It's Milo. Can I come in?"

She heard a snuffle and a, "Yes."

Upon entering, she found Ajsha sitting up on her bed, her face stained with tears. She hiccupped.

Milo sat down beside her and presented her with the plate.

"Thank you," Ajsha hiccupped, selecting one of the slices. "Mmmm," she said while chewing. "It's very good."

"Thanks," Milo muttered. She reached into her pocket for the handkerchief Ajsha had given her yesterday. She handed it to her.

"Thank you," she said, wiping her cheeks.

"I'm sorry," Milo said sincerely.

"For what?" Ajsha asked, blowing her nose.

"You know. For fighting. Getting you caught up in it. That was pretty awful of us."

"Oh, don't apologize!" Ajsha exclaimed. "It's my fault I acted like that."

"I don't blame you," Milo replied earnestly.

"Well," Ajsha mumbled, her head bent low, "interpreters have to keep their cool, no matter the topic of conversation or the vocabulary used. I am ashamed of myself for behaving so unprofessionally. *I* am sorry."

"Please don't say that!" Milo cried. "You're six, for Pete's sake! We should have been more considerate. It's not your fault. I freak out if I even *hear* my parents fighting. I used to get under the covers in bed, plug my ears, and pretend that I wasn't there. It must have been terrible for you, having to be a part of it."

Ajsha nodded, her bottom lip quivering. Milo patted her back.

"I can't say it won't happen again," she warned.

"I know," Ajsha said miserably.

They sat and ate the fruit slices in a dejected sort of silence for a while before Milo said, "I wonder if I made a good impression on the in-laws?"

Ajsha shrugged. "Actions speak louder than words," she said.

8
Simon's Friends

IT'S INCREDIBLE HOW much peace there could be in the world if people just stopped and listened. Most altercations, violent or otherwise, occur because of lack of communication. If the people of the South had stopped and listened to what everybody from the North was trying to tell them, then there would have been no Civil War. If the teenagers in rough cities would stop and listen to their consciences, then the streets would be a lot safer. Even if it is an unexpected moment of chaos, it would usually never happen if people would stop and listen.

If Milo had stopped and listened to Ajsha, the whole fight could have been avoided. Then again, if the island inhabitants had stopped and listened to Milo, she wouldn't be this dilemma in the first place. But, if she had stopped, listened, Ajsha would have explained to her that the "trip to a select location", was not insinuating anything suggestive.

She didn't learn this until after the quarrel, and by then it didn't make much of a difference, but it did soothe her dignity. Ajsha said that the trip had a different purpose for teen couples. It was just a nice way to spend time together, recovering from the stress of the wedding, and, in Milo's case, get to know each other more.

"Get to know each other more?" Milo had ranted upon hearing this. "We can't even speak the same language!"

"I know," Ajsha had replied empathetically. "It will probably be awkward from beginning to end, without me there to help you converse. Of course, it also could be a good opportunity for you to start learning Galo."

"*No,*" was Milo's feral reply.

Milo made dinner again, desperate to release some endorphins. This time baked fish with potatoes, and only enough for her and Ajsha, forcing Simon to make his own dinner. Ajsha felt bad, picking half-heartedly at her food while glancing at Simon, who was bashing things up in a bowl. Milo ignored him completely. Whatever lukewarm truce they'd had going the night before was officially over. She was once again furious at him. She didn't want to make him anything that would contribute to his overall health.

At bedtime, Simon took an extra long time tucking Ajsha in. Milo figured they were discussing the main event of the day, which happened to center around her. She fidgeted uncomfortably on the floor, wondering what Ajsha was telling him. Eventually Simon came in. He looked different somehow. Less angry, more tired. He gazed down at Milo, and gave her a small smile. She snorted at him. Sighing, he murmured imploringly in Galo, but Milo just rolled over.

The next morning, Simon was gone as usual, and Milo wasted no time starting breakfast. She was craving toast, but Simon had no bread in the house. She decided to make a loaf later on. Ajsha came in and sat down. They exchanged good mornings, but no more. They ate in silence, washed dishes in silence, and neither of them speaking until they walked into the hallway. Milo had angled herself towards the "Big Bedroom", but paused when she heard Ajsha's voice.

"I explained everything to Simon last night."

Milo didn't look at her, keeping her back to the child.

"He says he's sorry that he yelled at you," Ajsha said hopefully.

"Hmm."

"He said that since you had made dinner, he thought you were ready to meet his parents and discuss the wedding," Ajsha continued.

"Ha!"

"He deeply regrets the misunderstanding and that things got so out of hand," Ajsha ended. "That was the last thing he wanted."

"Heh."

"Oh, please, Milo!" Ajsha cried. "Say something!"

Milo considered it for a moment then replied, "No."

She stalked into the "Big Bedroom" and emerged carrying her diary and radio. *She* deeply regretted ever cooking that stupid dinner for him.

"Let him eat mush!" she thought viciously. She headed for the door.

"I need a little fresh air," she told Ajsha as she walked past her.

She headed for a palm tree near the beach and sat against its trunk, inhaling the fresh, briny sea breeze. Taking a second to scan her surroundings, Milo had to shake her head. In front of her was looming foliage, to the right of her was bright white sand and crashing blue waves, and directly above her was a blazing sun. It might have all been beautiful, if not for what glittered on her left hand. After glaring at the ring and the scenery for a moment, she mumbled, "It all happens to you, huh, Milo?"

She slid on her headphones, cranking up the radio, and opened her diary. She wrote about Ajsha and her sweet and oddly intelligent ways; then about the meeting of the in-laws and how she had never understood the hype until now. While she was writing, her pen making frantic scratch-scratch sounds, she didn't notice Ajsha hesitantly approach her.

"What are you writing in?" she inquired curiously.

"What?" Milo said, exposing one ear.

"What are you writing in?" Ajsha repeated, trying to peer onto the page.

"My diary."

"Oh. I've never had a diary before. What do you write about?"

"My life," Milo replied, tensing up. She tapped the paper with the end of her pen. "It's all right here. And once I'm done, and rescued, I'm going to have it published. You'd be surprised how many people would be interested in reading a true story about a girl who went from her house being burned down, to being forced to marry after crashing on an island. I'm thinking classic."

Ajsha, who had been nodding ever so slightly, said. "Oh. I'm sorry, but I don't think that your diary will ever be published. I'm sure it's a great story, and I would like to hear it, but you probably will never be rescued."

Milo cringed a little, but managed to wave her away dismissively. "Never underestimate the power of the Lord!" Milo declared.

"He works in mysterious ways," Ajsha responded.

Milo didn't have an answer for that, so she sulkily jammed her headphones back on. Ajsha wandered off, leaving her alone.

She scribbled for a considerably long time. At one point she looked towards the beach and saw Simon. He had just loaded an enormous net full of fish onto a cart. As he finished this task, a group of boys came up to him, greeting him boisterously with half hugs and shoulder shakes. They all began to talk, Simon's face quickly becoming frustrated and sad. His comrades instantly became concerned. Chattering, Simon motioned over to where Milo was sitting, apparently aware that she had been there for a while, and she quickly looked busy. She didn't look to the beach for about twenty minutes and when she did, they all had vanished.

She didn't see the boys again until the next day. She was back in the same place again, not so much writing as enjoying her radio.

Things had not improved between her and Simon over night. In fact, it was almost worse. She had staunchly made only enough food at dinner for her and Ajsha, forcing Simon to scrounge around the kitchen, nibbling whatever he could find. The atmosphere had been quite icy.

Underneath her tree she was doing a sort of sit-and-dance, when Simon and the pack of boys from the beach strode over to her. Ajsha was with them, and she hardly looked happy. Milo, in rather good mood, eyed the small mob with courteous indifference as they came to a stop in front of her. Ajsha shouted that they wanted to talk. Problems arose at once.

Milo was, at the moment, listening to "Hush", one of her favorite songs. And anyone who has ever listened to "Hush" knows that you can't interrupt it. You must listen to the end.

Milo put up a finger, pointer, to ask for patience. But the boys weren't in a mood to wait. They were burly and gnarly, their muscles cut and defined from earning their living in the ocean. One of them grunted loudly and kicked at her foot. She glared up at him, whatever cheerfulness she might have had instantly evaporating.

"Just – a – minute!" she hissed, and readjusted her headphones snugly about her ears.

Ajsha interpreted her request to the boy, and he spat something in Galo. Ajsha winced, but before she could relay anything, he yanked the headphones off Milo's head and threw them to the ground. She sprang with a vengeance. Nobody messed with "Hush"!

"You want something?" she growled, momentarily forgetting that they were a lot larger than her. She caught a glimpse of Simon's face among the throng, looking worried. "What's going on?"

The translating began, the boy who kicked her speaking on behalf of all his friends.

"He says," Ajsha said, stationed between Milo and the mob, "'Simon here says that you're quite the little troublemaker.'"

Milo raised her eyebrows as Simon muttered something that

sounded like a protest, and was shushed by the other boys.

"She said," Ajsha told the boy in Galo, "'*I* am the trouble maker?'"

The boy glared at her. "He said, 'Yeah! Now what's up with that? You don't want to marry him or something?'"

"She said, 'You got that right!'"

"He said, 'Why not? What's wrong with the guy? Not good-looking enough for you?'"

"She says, 'No, nothing like that. I'm just not in love with him.'"

"He says, 'Too bad.'"

"She said,' So I've been told!'"

"He said, 'Well, you've been told right. You're going to marry him, and you'd better stop giving him trouble!'"

Milo, in a state of either overconfidence or disillusion, sauntered up to the boy. "'Oh, yeah? You gonna make me?'"

The boy glowered at her, his lip curling threateningly. "'That's right.'"

"'Uh-huh?'"

"'Yeah!'"

Milo laughed, making all those present bristle wrathfully. "'You can't touch me! I'm *not* going to marry him, I will give him all the trouble I want and *he* will just have to deal with it! You can't do *anything* about it!'"

The boy's skin had turned an angry shade of scarlet. "'Oh, yeah?!'"

Lurching forward, he grabbed her shoulder and punched her in the stomach. Milo gave a squawk of pain and collapsed on the ground, curling up, hedgehog style.

"Pra, pra!" Simon yelled, attempting to shove his way to the front, but his friends held him back.

A few of the boys whipped out weapons from under their shirts. Milo, clutching her stomach, had struggled to her knees, when a boy with a wooden baton came forward and brought it down on her back. She slammed into the dirt, moaning in agony. Ajsha was shouting hysterically along with Simon, but the boys wouldn't stop and listen. Two punks with chains began striking her legs. She screamed as the excruciating pain shot up the rest of her body, then the leader barked a command, and it all ceased.

He gripped Milo's ponytail, jerking her head up, her breath coming in wheezy gasps. He called for Ajsha. She timidly scurried over, trembling. He snarled something at her, and she spoke to Milo, her voice shaking.

"H-he s-s-said, 'This is a w-warning. M-marry him and start m-making nice, or else. This can be a lot better or a lot worse. We'll be checking with Simon at the beach, and he'll tell us if you're cooperating or not. If you aren't, we'll come, and you'll feel pain like you never imagined!'"

His little speech over, the boy pushed her head back to the ground, causing her nose to spout blood. She lifted her head slightly, watching them leave, her sight fuzzy. One brute stomped on her headphones, destroying them. She gave a howl of rage, but it was too late. Tears were begging for release, but Milo had forgotten how to cry, therefore she sobbed quietly, without tears.

Simon and Ajsha were in a frenzy, circling her listless form and yakking incessantly in Galo. Finally Simon gingerly rolled her over and grasped her under the arms. Ajsha got her legs, which were now red and swollen. They gently lifted her up. She had gone completely limp with fright and sorrow. This was getting out of hand; she was an American citizen for Pete's sake!

"But that doesn't matter here," Milo thought numbly, as Simon and Ajsha dragged her into the hut. *"This isn't the United States, it's some barbaric island! No matter how big their town is, no matter how civilized they may be, it is still barbaric to force marriage. It's barbaric to raise a bunch of thugs who beat people. This is so unfair. Why did this happen to me?"*

If Milo hadn't been scared before, she certainly was now. As pain flared with every jostling step that Simon and Ajsha took, Milo realized that she couldn't handle such severe punishment. She would have to marry, if only to stay alive, but maybe there was still a chance. She didn't know what it was, the prospect bleaker than ever, but she would try to find it.

Simon and Ajsha tried to lay her on the bed in the bigger bedroom, but her battered back prevented them from doing so. After some difficult maneuvering, Milo whimpering the whole time, they managed to lay her face down. Simon brought in a dripping, ice-cold cloth. He tried to press it to her nose, but she purposely exhaled through her bloody nostrils, onto his hand. Not very pleased, he gritted his teeth and forced the cloth beneath her nose.

She held it there, laying her face sideways on a pillow. More cold cloths were draped over her neck. Ajsha retrieved Milo's radio and diary from outside. Simon went out as well, but didn't return. Ajsha stowed Milo's things in her backpack and disappeared again.

She returned briefly, and a freezing sensation shot up Milo's legs. She figured they were being washed, but didn't bother to check. When Ajsha left for the third time, Milo tried to sit up. She swallowed screams and sobs, pushing herself up with her hands. The cloths fell from her neck, but her nose had already stopped bleeding. She swung her legs over the side of the bed and sat hunched forward, trying to ignore the throbbing in her legs. She wept tearlessly for several minutes before calling out to Bob the Conscience.

"Bob!" she sniveled, but before she could continue, he broke in.

"Yeah, I know!" he said ruefully. "I messed up! You don't have to tell me, I am perfectly aware."

"I'm not blaming you!" she insisted. "Not this time. This time I'm asking you for advice."

"What?" Bob the Conscience declared, astonished. "You nev-

never asked for advice be-before," he stuttered. "What an honor!"

Milo rolled her eyes.

"I saw that," he muttered.

"How?"

"I just did."

"Listen!" Milo said. "Should . . . should I go through with it? You know . . . marrying him?"

Bob the Conscience sighed. "I know you don't want to, but it looks like you have no choice," he said grimly. "As your conscience, I have to be honest. This whole beating you mercilessly is not something your body can take for very long. The wisest thing to do is – I'm sorry –: Go – Through – With – It."

Milo nodded bleakly. "Did you see that?" she asked.

"Yes," he answered gently.

Milo moaned then scowled. "I knew that Simon was evil! Complaining to his bull-dawgs about me, and then this happens! Instead of handling it like a man, he is now going to report me if I do something unto his liking! I have the right to be a brat! Don't I?"

"Absolutely!" Bob the Conscience agreed robustly. "One hundred percent deserving, but just don't go overboard. The only reason for vengeance is the wedding, nothing else!"

"Yeah, I know," she grumbled. "But it looks like I'll be forced to be a perfect little house wife anyways. Life's not fair."

"This circumstance outweighs the usual unfairness of life."

They complained and comforted each other for a while, Milo using one of the cloths to tidy up her face, until Ajsha came in and saw her sitting up right.

"Milo!" she cried, rushing over. "Are you alright?"

The injured nodded soundlessly. Ajsha lifted up her chin to look into her eyes. They were red and glassy, but no tear streaks were on her cheeks.

"I am so sorry!" Ajsha blubbered, her own cheeks covered with the tell-tale trails. "I didn't mean for this to happen, and neither did Simon."

Milo shrugged. "You tried," she muttered, "but those boys were talking to Simon yesterday. I saw them. I think he mentioned how I've been acting."

Ajsha nodded uncomfortably. "Yes, Simon told me last night."

"Then why didn't you warn me?" Milo demanded.

"I did," Ajsha replied. "The first day I met you, I told you about them. Simon was feeling depressed and worried; therefore, when they asked him 'How are things going?' he told them. He couldn't help it. He asked them not to do anything, but you can't control them. They just want him to be happy."

"And them brutally beating me makes him happy?" snapped Milo.

"No!" Ajsha objected and smiled sadly. "But he'll be happy if you marry him."

"Well, it looks like I got to!" Milo groaned, trying to stand up. Ajsha tried to help, clutching her arm. "And if I do anything to displease his royal tyrant," she continued heatedly, "he'll rat me out to his little mafia, and then what will become of me?"

Ajsha gasped. "Simon would never do that!" she stated reproachfully.

"He did it once, he'll do it again!" Milo snapped, her face twisting as she took a step.

"Never!" Ajsha insisted. "Even if he has to lie! The last thing he wants is for you to get hurt. Please don't be mad at him, Milo. Maybe he shouldn't have told them anything. He should have remembered what they're capable of. But he really does care about you, and won't ever do it again."

Milo stood in an awkward position for a moment then said, "Really?"

Ajsha nodded solemnly. "Of course," she said. "He's not that kind of guy."

Later that evening, after an afternoon of chilling Milo's various limbs, they were in the kitchen. Milo was slicing the bread she had made the day before. She was broodingly silent, lost in thought. Ajsha noticed.

"Are you Okay?" she asked.

Milo shrugged.

"Do your injuries hurt very much?"

Milo shook her head.

"Then what is it?"

"What's what?" Milo asked dismally.

"Why are you so quiet?" Ajsha asked, going over to stand by her side. "I know you've just been through a terrible situation, but you must know, you're quite safe now."

"It isn't that," Milo sighed.

"What?" Ajsha asked curiously.

"It's my headphones," Milo said miserably.

"Your what?"

"Headphones," she repeated.

"Oh! You mean that thing you were wearing?"

"Yeah. That thing. Anyway, some guy stepped on them and broke them."

"Oh, I'm sorry," Ajsha said sympathetically. "You seemed to love them very much."

"Mmm," Milo mumbled. "At least my radio isn't broken. But it's pretty much useless without the headphones."

"Perhaps," suggested Ajsha, "that boy wouldn't have ruined them if you had taken them off to begin with."

"You mean interrupt 'Hush'?" Milo gasped.

"'Hush'?" Ajsha repeated, puzzled.

"Hush," Milo confirmed. "The song. You know? L.L. Cool J.?"

Ajsha continued to stare blankly at her.

"Man!" Milo cried, remembering that she had probably never even heard a radio. "You poor, deprived child," she said, sincerely feeling sorry for her.

"Is it a favorite of yours?" the poor, deprived child asked her.

"Oh, yeah!" Milo said, smiling. "It's one of the best romantic songs ev-ah!"

"Romantic song?" Ajsha repeated in wonder. "Is that like a love song?"

"Not exactly," Milo said reflectively, hobbling around to lean against the counter. "A love song is . . . well, about love. But there are songs that really don't have the word love in them at all. They're really about boyfriend/girlfriend relationships, and some of them really bring down the house! Especially if it's hip-hop. Hip-hop has quite a few good love songs, too. They're always sincere, well worded, and never have any of that mushy crap you hear in other types of music. Some of them are down right beautiful, like 'Let me love you'. Oh! What a great song! I kind of wish that a boy would sing something like that to me –"

Milo realized what she had said far too late, for Ajsha looked extremely excited.

"Don't," Milo warned, sticking a finger in her face. "Don't even think about it."

They didn't have time to argue over whatever Ajsha was not supposes to be thinking about, because Simon walked into the house the next moment. He saw Milo's tilted form and seemed overjoyed. He spoke happily to Ajsha, who conveyed the message to Milo.

"Simon says, 'I'm so glad that you're feeling better!'"

Milo snorted. "Yeah," she muttered. "No thanks to you."

Ajsha translated hesitantly, but Simon merely became sad. He spoke somberly to Milo, Ajsha interpreting. "He said that he is very sorry. It's not what he wanted, and it won't ever happen again."

Milo raised one of her eyebrows. "Can you guarantee that?" she said.

After a minute of translating, Ajsha responded with, "He said, 'Of course! I hate that I couldn't stop them . . . that you got hurt. I'm going to talk to them, ask them not to act so disagreeable.'"

"Disagreeable?" Milo exclaimed. "Stinking mean is what they really are."

Upon hearing this sentence in Galo, Simon winced and gibbered quietly.

"He said, 'I am so sorry. So sorry.'"

"Yeah, yeah!" Milo muttered. "You know," she said thoughtfully, turning to the boy, "if it weren't for you proposing, I wouldn't be in this mess."

Ajsha replied, "He said, 'But I want to marry you.'"

"Really?" Milo said sarcastically. "I couldn't tell!" She then turned serious. "Why?"

"'Why what?'"

"Do you want to marry me?" she finished.

Ajsha jabbered to Simon, who grinned and answered just as incoherently. Ajsha grinned too, and went to stand proudly at his side. He put a hand on her shoulder, and they stood together, beaming at Milo, who stared back warily.

Ajsha announced eagerly, "He said, 'Because I love you!'"

Now, isn't that such a nice thing to say? Notice the word "Love". Ah, Love. A word usually thrown around far too casually and carelessly, and yet is said not nearly enough. Accompanied by the pronouns "I" and "you", it helps to form one of the most sought after statements in the history of the world.

A statement that, if expressed among family members more often, would surely help them all get along better. A statement that, when said, makes people silent with joy and inner thoughts. It might make them cry or throw their arms around the person who said it. One thing is certain: The confession "I love you" has been cherished and

appreciated by human beings for centuries; ever since the first man
of the dust looked into the eyes of the first woman of the dust and
realized just what those feelings were. Even if it is uttered to a cold-
hearted old skunk, he would at least pout at the thought.

Most normal people would be delighted, or say thank you and
return the sentiment. Indeed, most people would take it calmly,
gratefully, and walk away with the sense that life had just become
a little better. Not Milo Hestler.

She glared at Simon maliciously, her eyeballs growing increasingly more pronounced, and her fingers curling into claws before
she exploded with rage. Gnashing her teeth, she shouted in fury.

"*What do you know about love?!!!* You heartless little minion?
Nothing! You know *nothing* about it!"

She whirled awkwardly in a circle, searching for anything that
would suffice as a weapon. She picked up a mixing spoon and,
limping, began to chase Simon around the kitchen. His smile wiped
clean from his lips, he scooted backwards, keeping her in full view.

"You know *nothing!*" she shrieked. "You . . . ignorant teen! How
could you know? It's not like anything else in the world! You don't
know *me!* You don't know my dreams or *anything!* We can't even
speak the same language! How the heck can you love me if you only
met me five days ago?! You have no right to say that! You can't say
you love me when you don't even know what love is!"

Simon was now thoroughly scared, and dodged repeatedly out of
the path of her mixing spoon. Ajsha was simultaneously translating
Milo's screams into Galo and attempting to calm her down. She
kept trying to grab Milo's arm each time she hobbled by, but Milo
was in a fury hell hath no, and limped fast. Simon would have tried
to restrain her himself, only she kept flailing the spoon, which was
quite hefty and fairly intimidating when brandished. They
scampered around the kitchen for nearly five minutes, Ajsha and
Milo both yelling uncontrollably, and Simon too busy fleeing to say
anything in defense.

Finally, as Ajsha again tried to latch on to Milo's arm, she accidentally knocked the spoon out of her hand. Instantly, Simon grabbed Milo's wrists, dragging her away from where the spoon hand landed on the floor. She struggled, snarling ferociously, but it didn't help. Simon had heard every single translated word and, as he wrestled Milo into a chair, he began to jabber passionately, nodding at Ajsha.

"He said," Ajsha said, somewhat breathless at this point, "'You are wrong. You are wrong, Milo. I know what love is, and I do love you! I don't understand how you can say I don't, but I swear I will show you somehow! You *will* believe me one day.'"

Milo shook her head, glaring daggers at Simon, their faces separated by not even four inches.

"You know nothing of love!" she hissed.

Although she spoke with such conviction, to say that Milo had actually experienced falling in love, therefore making her an authority on the matter, would be untrue. She had never been in love with a boy before, (figuring that, at fourteen, she still had a lot of time to spare) but she was a girl of many thoughts and had spent much time contemplating love.

She had it completely figured out, or at least she thought she did. Nobody really knows love until they're in it, but Milo came very close. She had determined that it must be a sensation you get in the stomach and heart. Yes, the muscle-heart, not just the philosophical one.

"*Sort of an aching,*" she had mused. "*Only you like it.*"

To love, according to Milo, you must notice all the little particulars about your person. The things nobody else sees, or cares to see, and you can't help but love each one, simply because it is a part of your person. It is a little bit of what makes them, them.

For instance, if Simon was really in love with Milo, then he would have noticed, even though she had no highlights, how her hair still shone. And it wasn't just simply brown, but dark chocolate brown. Her eyes were not just green, but deep emerald green, and sparkled just like the gem. Her body was thin, but thin like a neglected child whom he must nurse back to health. Her skin was not just starkly white, but pale and beautiful, like the full moon above the sea. Nobody else, except him, knew this, but these exact thoughts had been running through Simon's head ever since he had first seen Milo drifting unconscious in the ocean.

Ajsha, after prying Simon's fingers off of Milo's wrists, led him into another room. Milo sat rigid and fuming. She wished she could listen to her radio, but of course that was impossible.

Dinner was portioned for three, Milo wanting to avoid getting clobbered again, but tempting fantasies of sprinkling something poisonous onto Simon's food continuously floated through her mind. She was beyond angry with him now. The list for her mutinous attitude seemed to be expanding daily. First, accidentally getting engaged; then getting her assaulted; and now he claimed he loved her! Of course, getting beat upon seemed to be routine for her, wherever she moved. Why shouldn't the cycle break here?

After dinner dishes were washed and dried, Simon left for the darkening outdoors.

"I told him how sad you are about your bedphones," Ajsha said.

During the meal, Milo had decided to hold Simon responsible for the destruction of her beloved item, and had added it to his list of transgressions.

"He's really sorry."

"Sure he is," Milo muttered. "And it's *headphones!*"

At bedtime, Simon still wasn't back yet, which hardly bothered Milo. She hoped he would get lost out there in the dark, forbidding jungle. Ajsha came in to say goodnight and to kiss Milo on the forehead. Milo was beginning to feel truly uncomfortable about that. She felt like the child and Ajsha the parent. It didn't seem fair, since Ajsha had never even had parents, and now she had to act like one. Milo told this to her, and she smiled, assuring Milo that she didn't mind. She padded down to her bedroom, leaving Milo to sleep.

Sometime during the night, Simon returned, waking Milo up. Groaning, she turned on her watch light. It was 3:00 in the morning. She rubbed her eyes then blinked them. Twice. Next to her lay a brand new set of headphones. Milo gasped, hesitated, and then inserted them into her radio. Almost giddy with excitement, she stopped sleeping and listened to some hip-hop.

(Coincidentally, the first song that came on was "Fight the Power".)

9
The Day before the Wedding

THE REST OF the week was, for Milo anyway, spent in pure misery. Each day she would make three meals for three people, not quite trusting that Simon wouldn't report her, but nothing else. She refused to do any other housework.

Not that anyone was asking her to, but she told herself that by refusing to act out any other wife-related labor, she would send Simon a clear message. Of course, Simon didn't receive any messages through that, but by the way she glared at him and ignored all the hopeful conversation starters he sent through Ajsha.

Milo hadn't always been so angry. When she told Ajsha about finding the new headphones, Ajsha, in turn, told her that Simon had gone to the "Crash Site" that night. He had sneaked on to a plane, found a pair of headphones that weren't damaged, and brought them back for her. Milo recalled the headphones that flight attendants distributed for movies, and was rather touched that Simon gone through so much trouble to get her a new pair. At noon, when he came home from work, she was about to swallow her pride and tell him "thank you" when a flamboyant group of women bustled into the house to fit her for the dress.

All of her fury came roaring back as she was pushed on to a stool for measuring and whisked off again for examining of the figure, which earned her many Galo laced clucks of disapproval. Milo might have put up more of a fight, not exactly liking any of the women's remarks Ajsha translated for her, but her legs were far from healed and was reminded every time she took a step.

The next day material was draped, wrapped, and then pinned all over her, before being whipped off, cut, and pinned back on. Milo spent the evening dabbing all the pin pricks on her body with a cold cloth. The next day was flowers, the day after that jewelry and shoes. One evening a person came over and measured Ajsha for her little flower girl dress. People materialized and vanished so quickly that Milo was starting to feel frenzied. She could only afford to do three things during the day, which consisted of cooking, putting up with the preparations, and listening to her radio.

She listened as often as possible, escaping to secluded corners of the house and turning up the volume until all other sounds, including her own thoughts, were blocked out. The music rejuvenated her, and at least for a few short stolen moments she could be happy. She often tried, with no success, to explain to the people doing the preparations that she didn't want to get married. They either couldn't understand her or would suddenly become extremely busy if Ajsha tried to translate. This caused Milo endless amounts of frustration, and as they continued to disregard her opinion, she began to feel more like a prop than the bride.

Two days before the dreaded event, the gaggle of women responsible for Milo's dress dropped by unannounced. Milo had spent the whole day with the boy and the interpreter, surveying a book with pictures of "select locations", and was wrathfully exhausted. But she felt like screaming when the women burst in with a flurry of excited Galo and revealed the dress with a flourish.

It had looked beautiful in the portfolio, but now she saw it for what it meant, and it appeared to her as an ugly, horrid tumble of rags. Oblivious to the way she was cringing, the biddies forced her into another room to try it on. Grudgingly, she slipped out of her clothes and into the dress. It fit perfectly and rode smoothly over her skin, like water to rose petals.

It hung loosely at her feet, rippling at the slightest movement, and the beads on the front glistened in the evening candle light. Its thin straps gave more curve to Milo's angular shoulders, though couldn't hide her protruding collar bones. The veil, woven by hand, was barely see-through, and covered her face just to the chin.

However, Milo was blind to all this beauty as she stood in front of the mirror (which had clearly been confiscated from an airplane bathroom). She gaped, wide-eyed, at herself, as everyone behind her oohed and awed. Simon was ushered in and smiled with delight as soon as he saw her. He went to stand beside her. They both looked into the mirror; Simon in glee, Milo in terror. Simon silently enveloped her hand in his and gave it a squeeze.

Milo didn't try to pull away; her hand, along with the rest of her, had gone limp. The anger that burned inside her was quickly being replaced by harrowing fear. She had often been scared fleetingly, whenever the subject of the wedding was brought up, but this fear was new to her. She was terrified of what she saw in the mirror: A dolled up version of herself, standing next to the stranger who would become her husband.

They were really going to make her do this. She was actually going to get married . . . without her parents . . . without her family . . . without her friends (not that she had any). She was all alone. This wasn't how her wedding was supposed to be, or any wedding for that matter!

Ajsha scampered over, grinning, but stopped when she saw Milo's face. She was apparently the only one in the room who noticed Milo's look of utter despair. Ajsha gently touched her arm, now fully understanding Milo's feelings and her behavior.

"You look lovely," she told her comfortingly.

Milo didn't respond. She didn't say a word as she changed, or as she made dinner, or while they ate, or when they did the dishes.

She didn't talk at all until she was on the floor of the "Big Bedroom", trying to fall asleep. Then she spoke to herself.

"Bob," she said, her inner voice hushed and strained. "I can't do it. I can't go through with it."

"You're going to have to," he sighed. "You don't have a choice."

"That's what I mean," she replied. "I can't marry like this, with all the pressure and threats. I can't. My wedding was supposed to be happy. I'm not exactly happy, Bob! I've come to the conclusion that I must run away."

"Oh! Very clever!" Bob the Conscience said sarcastically. "The run away bride attempt. Well! Too bad I didn't think of that. I could have taken all the credit for it!"

"Please, Bob!" Milo begged.

"Where would you go?" he continued scathingly. "You can't leave; you don't know where you are. Even if you stole a boat, you would just die at sea! And if you hid in the jungle, you would still die, since, let's be honest, you're really more a domestic type. Or they'd find you, and then do who knows what to you. As your conscience, I tell you you're crazy!"

"It was just a suggestion!" she cried, whimpering and digging her knuckles into her forehead.

She inhaled and exhaled shakily, trying to keep all of her churning emotions inside, and not let them out into open air. Unfortunately, it takes noises to contain noises.

Suddenly, Milo heard something other than her own desperate gasps. It sounded like singing; like one of the lullabies that Simon sang to Ajsha every night. Milo paused to listen more closely. Yes, it was singing; clear, melodic words in Galo, coming from above her. She squinted upward, towards the source, and saw a hand silhouetted against the edge of the bed. It was Simon. He was singing to her. She had probably woken him up with all her sniveling.

She hiccuped, but no more. The words, though she couldn't understand them, had a calming, soothing effect on her. Slowly, the knot in her chest eased and she began to feel tired. Just like a lullaby. Heaven only knew what he was saying; he might have been sweetly swearing at her. Nevertheless, his voice was like a spell, and soon, despite her aggrieved state, Milo drifted off to sleep.

The next day, at some point during the afternoon, she and Ajsha were together in the sitting room, when Ajsha quite abruptly said, "You know, you're getting married tomorrow."

Milo, swallowing what felt like a pin cushion, replied, "Yeah? So?"

Ajsha shrugged, picking demurely at one of the couch pillows. "Do you want to talk about it?"

"Do you think I want to talk about it?" Milo mumbled. "If I can help it, I won't be getting married tomorrow."

She spoke with little confidence, though. She had been trying to formulate a plan of escape for several nights, ideas ranging from becoming a hermit to faking her own death. There always seemed to be a hitch, however. Sighing dejectedly, she gazed out one of the sitting room windows, watching sunbeams play on the jagged bark of the palm trees. Ajsha then voiced something she didn't expect.

"I hope you find a way out."

"What!" Milo said, startled. "Why? I thought you wanted –"

"Yes," she admitted softly, tugging at a thread on the pillow. "But it's wrong to force you. It's all just been *wrong*. Usually couples are thrilled the week of their wedding, but it's like we're torturing you. I'm sorry."

Milo, both touched and stunned, was about to respond, when Simon barged in. He had returned from work recently and had just changed. Ignoring Milo's customary menacing glare of greeting, he gibbered to Ajsha. She sprang excitedly from her seat and bounced jubilantly on her toes.

"We're going into town!" she told Milo.

"Joy upon joy," Milo answered flatly, resuming her position for staring out the window.

"Come on!" Ajsha exuberantly, pulling Milo from the chair.

"I think I'll stay behind," she said, flopping back down.

"Why?"

"I don't think the people like me."

"Nonsense!" declared Ajsha, tugging her along.

Of course this wasn't nonsense, but Milo was made to come anyways, Ajsha using a combined method of coaxing and dragging. Once in town, the journey having been anything but cordial, Simon strode away, leaving the females to meander aimlessly. Milo, not having visited the town since her first day on the island, rotated in a circle, taking in all the building and roving inhabitants.

"Crazy," she murmured, again awestruck. She caught sight of the church and shuddered.

She also saw a pack of teenage girls strolling down the street in her direction. They were all chatting gaily to each other, completely oblivious to all the troubles in the world. When Milo entered their view, they stopped talking, halted as one and stared at her. Not wanting to appear impolite, Milo hesitantly waved to them. They simultaneously pierced the air with their noses and stalked past her with an air of indifferent anger. Milo let her hand drop to her side.

"Friendly people you got around here," she said to Ajsha.

The child giggled. "They're jealous of you," she said.

"Jealous of me?" Milo repeated, thunderstruck. "Why in the world would anyone be jealous of me? They're pretty enough, but blondes always seem to be, don't they? They've got nice clothes, a bunch of friends, a nice tan; what do I have that they could possibly want?"

"Simon," Ajsha said simply. "You have Simon."

"Simon?" Milo said incredulously. "Why would they want Simon?"

Ajsha shrugged blithely. "Lots of girls around here do. They all have been trying to attract his attention for years. It got much worse when he became old enough to propose. He used to tell be about how annoying it was. And now they're mad because Simon chose you. They probably wouldn't be so sore, only you aren't acting appreciative."

"You got that right!" Milo retorted, watching the group stop in front of a store and resume their chatter. They now sounded heavily irate, and pointed at forcibly at Milo. Groaning, she suddenly got an idea. She nudged Ajsha.

"Hey," she whispered, "go over there."

"Why?" Ajsha asked.

"I want you to eavesdrop for me."

Ajsha gasped, scandalized, but then slowly grinned. Hooking her hands behind her back, she casually sauntered over to the pack. When she was near enough to listen yet not look suspicious, she stopped and pretended to examine a sign. She listened for about five minutes, her expressions changing from time to time, until she came ambling back.

"So, what's the gossip?" Milo asked out of the corner of her mouth.

"Interesting," Ajsha answered in the same fashion, suppressing a giggle. "Mostly, about how ungrateful you are. How you should be overjoyed to have the 'hottest boy in town'. A couple complained about the husbands they married because they couldn't catch Simon's eye. Then how sorry they felt for Simon for picking a 'stubborn, unattractive . . . bad word'."

Milo let out an offended gasp, but before she could do anything, thunder boomed overhead. Rain appeared so suddenly, it was as if an angel accidentally knocked over a glass, causing water to pour down from the heavens. Ajsha shrieked in surprise and grabbed Milo's hand. Everyone was running to escape the sudden downpour. Ajsha was following a few people into a store, or they were following her. The confusion made it difficult to tell.

Once safely under a roof, Milo, her clothes fairly sodden, exclaimed, "What the heck happened? It was so sunny."

Ajsha was ringing moisture from her long hair. "It's a tropical island, sudden storms are normal," she responded airily, flipping her hair back to place.

"Ah!" said Milo, contemplating this. "Like in a rain forest?"

"No! Never that much rain! We don't have any flooding, thank the Lord. But yes, sudden downpours are also common in rain forests."

Satisfied, Milo took a look at the store they had rushed into. It resembled a hardware store. There was a long counter stretching across the east side of the building, with a door and shelves behind it. The shelves held all sorts of different tools, some genuine, and some forged from various plane parts. There were authentic hammers and screwdrivers, but no nails or screws. In place of nails were thin, pounded out pieces of metal that reminded Milo of her. There didn't seem to be any replacements for screws.

All sorts of other heavy labor nick-knacks were scattered on the shelves and counter, while larger items lay in corners on the floor. The west side of the shop had shelves extending from ceiling to floor. They exhibited electronic do-dads, scraps of metal, rubber, leather, and disassembled control panels.

"They probably ransack those planes," thought Milo as her eyes scanned over the wreckage, like a vulture looking for a delicacy.

The other refugees in the store crowded around the counter, vigorously ringing its bell. The shrill jingling caused a portly gentleman to come hurrying through the door in the eastern wall. He had broad shoulders, bright eyes, and tremendous muscles. His gray hair was bald right in the middle of his head, the rest sticking out like a crown. Hands raised, he shouted above the chaos, silence instantly taking its place. Very calmly, the man then spoke a few sentences in Galo, and several people strayed away from the counter.

"He asked them who came to buy and who came to get out of the rain," Ajsha explained.

"Who is he?" asked Milo, observing the big man with curiosity.

Ajsha shrugged. "I know he owns the store, but I don't know his name."

Before Milo could utter another word, Ajsha walked up to the counter and began to speak politely to the man. He answered with a good-natured chuckle, reaching down to shake her tiny hand with his enormous one. Ajsha turned around, delighted, and motioned for Milo to join them.

As she crossed the shop, Ajsha said, "His name is Gorben Soldier, and guess what? He can speak a little English!"

"You . . . can?" Milo inquired cautiously. He nodded, dipping his prickly chin, and grinned.

"'Fraid it ain't too good yet, but 'o's complainin'? Long as it's English."

Like Ajsha, Gorben Soldier's speech carried a slight lilt.

"How do you know it?" Milo asked, baffled.

"Oh, bin learnin' it ovter ter yers. Harter than ya tink, 'pecially if non' helps yer." He leaned forward, his brows arched knowingly. "Bot, its rewards are wort' it."

Milo nodded briskly, not wanting to disagree with a man with the last name Soldier. He drew back and continued conversationally.

"Anyways, bin hearin' tings 'rom customahs 'bout you. 'Earin' 'bout all ta commotion ya bin causin'. Do't want ta marry, do ya?"

Milo firmly shook her head. Mr. Soldier chuckled, scratched at his scruff, and genially said, "Well, hope ya chenge ya mind. Be a sham' if ya go trew ya weddin' like tat."

Milo simmered. "You agree with them, then?" she demanded hotly. "About this marriage stupidness?"

Mr. Soldier shrugged. "Do't got much choice in ta matta. Wan' ta git married meself ya know."

"Really?" said Ajsha, perking up at once. "To who?"

Mr. Soldier blushed crimson and began fiddling with an object beneath the counter. "Ruby Lanslo," he mumbled quietly.

"Mrs. Lanslo!" Ajsha and Milo both exclaimed at once.

"Shhh!" Mr. Soldier growled, furtively glancing about the store, as if she were lingering nearby. "Do't go yellin' it out. But, yeah. She's bin me crush ever since 'er plane crashed here. Tryin' ta learn English ta impress 'er. Not good enoff yet ta approach 'er, but gettin' tere. But, enough 'bout tat. I've a message fa ya, yang lady," he said, thrusting a beefy finger at Milo. "Tese laws ain't notin' ta mess wit. Tey mean wat tey say, and do't cur if ya do't want ta marry or not. A law es a law, befer a human es a human aroun' here. Git it?"

"Got it," Milo muttered sadly.

She turned away dismally and wandered up to the west wall. Her eyes swept lazily over the merchandise, until they came to rest on one particular item. It was a small speaker, about six inches tall and four inches wide. It had a thin, black wire running out the back, a jack at the end of it. Perfect for inserting into a walk-man or radio. Milo inhaled sharply when she saw it and reverently picked it up. She examined it critically and, finding it beyond her satisfaction, she called out to Mr. Soldier.

"Mr. Soldier?" she said.

"Please!" he insisted. "Jus' cull me Soldier, e'ryone does."

"Well, um, Soldier, how much does this cost?" She held it aloft for him to see. He scrutinized it from where he stood, pursing his lips.

"Abou' a kon, a gen, an' two dlos."

"Seventeen dollars," Ajsha whispered, since Milo wasn't yet familiar with their money system. Milo shook her head and set down the speaker.

"Just wondering," she said.

They stayed in the shop as the rain pelted down outside, drumming rhythmically on the roof. Milo often sent Ajsha to eavesdrop on people who came in. Eavesdropping is, I hope you know, a very rude and imposing sort of activity, but this was of little consequence to the girls. It helped them obtain information, its usefulness therefore outweighing its rudeness. It was also pretty fun. Ajsha would sneak surreptitiously around their target, eventually returning to reveal what she had heard. They heard basically the same thing every time; how Milo was ungrateful, and stubborn and indecent and insulting to their ancestors.

Milo wasn't very concerned by any of that. What worried her was when they talked about sneaking machetes and such into the wedding, in case she tried to pull anything.

It was past noon when the rain finally ceased. Milo and Ajsha bade Soldier goodbye and left the store. Blinking at the light and breathing in the fresh, clean smell of damp earth, they spotted Simon on the other side of the street. He waved to them, and Ajsha waved back, Milo not bothering. The girls started walking toward him, passing the group of females from earlier. They were positively drenched and scowling sourly. Milo chuckled to herself. It was the only good thing about that day, and it wasn't going to get much better. The minute the pack noticed Simon, they flipped their soaked hair back flirtatiously and skipped up to him.

They reached him before Milo and Ajsha did, Ajsha frowning. They circled around him, chatting pathetically and reaching out to grasp arms. Simon smiled pleasantly, wriggling free and joining Milo and Ajsha. They cooed to him in ditzy voices, beckoning him back with doe-eyes. He shook his head, gibbering in Galo, and put his arm around Milo. She gave him the typical shove, sending him flying to the ground, not something she intended. But before she budge, one of the girls darted up to her and smacked her across the face.

Milo gulped in air, her cheek smarting, just as she was slapped the other way. Simon yelled incoherently and wedged himself between the seething girl and Milo, arms spread, shielding her. Not far away, several boys shouted something, whooped, and began to run over.

"What'd they say?" Milo muttered to Ajsha, rubbing her face.

"Cat fight," Ajsha replied nervously.

Milo swallowed hard, but luckily Simon gripped her elbow and quickly led her away, ignoring the disapproving shouts of the boys. Ajsha hurried after them, checking over her shoulder every so often. When they reached the house, Milo collapsed onto a couch, Simon dropped the bag he was carrying, and Ajsha securely shut the front door.

Milo turned to her and said, "It's all nonsense, eh?"

10
The Wedding

THERE ARE FOUR feelings that should never bombard a person all at once: Sadness, fear, anger, and nervousness. When combined into one single feeling, they can cause deadly stress, liable to send one into a depression. But luckily such emotions only mix under rare, extreme circumstances, and such outcomes do not happen every time. Lucky for people like Milo.

After spending the day learning just how much she was resented, she awoke the next morning with a stiff back and pounding in her temples. It had been a restless night of tossing and turning on the compacted dirt floor. She'd had several nightmares about how the wedding would play out the next day. None of them ended the way she wanted: A helicopter dropping out of the sky, landing right in front of the church, and Milo climbing in while throwing her bouquet to Ajsha.

No, none ended like that. She was either brutally bludgeoned to death by Simon's friends, onlookers not doing a thing to help, or when she and Simon kissed, their lips failed to come apart.

She sat slouched at the kitchen table, not eating. For once Simon was there in the morning. He and Ajsha were conversing happily in Galo, not noticing how quiet Milo was. Instead of trying to fall asleep, she had spent precious hours trying to formulate a way to get out of the situation, but nothing came. She had considered the way she had said "Yes" to the proposal, and which finger the ring was placed on the first time. With despair, she realized that there was nothing that could help her escape. A head nod meant "Yes" in any language, and Simon wasn't stupid, he knew what finger that ring had to go on.

And so she sat at the kitchen table, not even bothering to pick at her plate, four feelings swirling around inside her. Sadness, fear, anger, and nervousness. They stabbed and sliced her insides, making her feel sick. As Simon and Ajsha finished eating, she silently stole away to the water-closet and threw-up. She did this twice more, her stomach already empty, yellow bile coming up instead. Ajsha came in and asked her if she was okay. Milo, spitting copiously, lied and said she was.

"Good," Ajsha said, though there was a distinct smell of vomit in the air. "Then come and take a shower."

Milo glanced in the direction of the door, then back at Ajsha. "You're kidding, right?"

"No," she laughed. "What? Did you expect never to wash again?"

"It was a thought," Milo replied, standing up. Truthfully, she had been growing riper by the day.

Ajsha shook her head and said unwaveringly, "It's your wedding day. You don't have to be happy, but you at least have to be clean."

With that, she turned and walked away.

"Traitor!" Milo hissed after her.

The girl stopped for a second, her shoulders drooping, but then straightened up, continuing on and out. Milo heard the door shut. Wiping her mouth with the back of her hand, she went into the bathroom. A chair sat in a corner of the room, laden with a few towels that had embroidered air plane insignias.

Milo scrunched her hair with her fingers. It felt sticky, most likely from the salty ocean water from over a week ago, blended with the vast amount of sweat she secreted daily. With her hair like that, she didn't want to know what her skin felt like. She was surprised she hadn't been asked to wash sooner. Skulking up to the shower, she circled it with her arms crossed. She didn't take her eyes off it, frowning at it as if it had just made some snide remark.

She lightly kicked the basin, it not retaliating in any way. Milo then stepped on the tip of her sock, pulling her foot out. She did this to her other sock, keeping her arms folded. She trailed her hand across the curtain that hung to only one side, contemplating the side that perfectly opened to view. Well, that wouldn't do, would it?

Pushing the towels of the chair, Milo dragged it over to the door. First making sure it was closed securely, she shoved the back of the chair under the knob and pushed it until it was solidly blocking her in.

Satisfied that she was alone, not to be bothered, she returned to the shower. There was only one small window in the bathroom, so that light could come in, and she drew its curtain, sealing herself in dimness. Now quite certain she was protected from anyone nosey, she reached up to the shower funnel and prepared to turn it on.

"One . . . two . . . three!" she said, and repeated three or four times. Mustering up all her inner will power, she finally twisted slowly. Water began to dribble out, growing faster and stronger as she turned it.

With a deep breath, she quickly yanked off the rest of her clothes and stepped into the basin. The water was cool but clean and fresh. There didn't seem to be any soap. She hurriedly cleaned her hair, raking her fingers through the strands, and then rubbed her skin to get rid of any salt, all the while panting in fear. Once her hygiene had returned to normal, she turned off the shower and stepped out, shivering. Grabbing a towel, she dried off, and then wrapped it around her. Another towel was used to bundle up her hair, and then she gathered all her clothes.

Now came the hard part. Clad in nothing but a towel, she had to get to the bedroom unnoticed. Unlocking the door, she crept stealthily down the hall. Finding no one there, she dashed to the bedroom, first checking for Simon, and shut the door behind her. Inhaling hoarsely, she unhooked her dress, which was hanging from the ceiling, and discarded of the first towel.

When she finally emerged from the bedroom, Ajsha was waiting for her in the hallway, dressed in her little flower girl dress. It was sunshine yellow, of all colors, covered in a pattern of tiny, red flowers. A red tropical flower was tucked behind her ear. Milo thought she looked like a dandelion with a ladybug problem. She was carrying a small basket filled with wild flower petals, to match Milo's bouquet. Ajsha positively glowed when she saw Milo.

"You look lovely!" she said euphorically, squirming with excitement.

Milo shrugged, glancing down at her satiny white figure. "You look cute," she returned, though her heart wasn't in it.

Ajsha smiled faintly and smoothed her skirts with a slight grimace of contempt. "Thank you," she murmured. "I know it's not what we picked. Mrs. Kellis said that I 'inspired' her. Hm."

"Where's the boy?" Milo mumbled hopelessly.

"Huh?"

"Simon."

"Oh. He went with a friend over to the church. We should head over there too, the service is supposed to start at eleven."

Milo winced, thinking that it was more like a sentencing than a service. Gulping loudly and not meeting Ajsha's gaze, she gave one sharp nod and headed for the front door.

She walked out of the house, Ajsha hastily catching up and entwining her small hand with Milo's. Outside, it was perfect wedding day conditions, the sun bright and unchallenged by any clouds, with the mildest of breezes wafting in off the sea. Secretly, Milo had been hoping for a monsoon today, but apparently even the weather was against her.

They met no one on their way to town, all the houses they passed dark and quiet. It seemed that everyone was already at the church, waiting for them; waiting to witness the most tumultuous wedding in the island's history. As Milo pictured it, all those unfamiliar faces watching smugly as she got hitched, she trembled violently. Ajsha held on all the firmer.

Milo suddenly faced her, wailing, "I can't do it, Ajsha! I can't! It's unfair! I'm *fourteen*! I'm too young! I don't love him!"

"Shhh!" Ajsha hissed. "Don't yell; there are spies watching us, in case you try to run."

"What?" Milo whispered thickly, glancing around at the surrounding brush. She saw eyes hide themselves and weapons glint among the leaves and twigs.

Breathing unevenly, she confessed to Ajsha, "I . . . I'm so scared."

Ajsha squeezed her hand. "Don't worry, Milo," she said soothingly. "I won't let anything happen to you. We'll get through this."

Milo smiled weakly. "You're some kid, Ajsha," she said.

Ajsha smiled appreciatively. "Come on," she said.

They resumed walking, every so often Milo hearing the crunch of a footstep or swish of a branch, until the town sprang up in the distance. It looked abandoned, the streets eerily empty and all the shops closed. It wasn't until they looked over at the church did they see the crowd. Milo quaked as she took in all the gussied up individuals, all talking enthusiastically in Galo, creating an unintelligible droning hum. Weddings certainly weren't a small affair here.

They walked in that direction, Ajsha not so much accompanying as steering Milo. Milo had a jacket on, making her far less detectable as the bride, but when they reached the church, Ajsha still stowed her behind a nearby tree. People didn't notice at all that she had arrived. They continued their lively chatter, all far more elated than they had reason to be. After all, none of *them* were getting married. But, that's weddings. There's just something irresistible in the air.

Peeking out from behind her tree, Milo could also sense it, but her own four feelings prevented it from affecting her.

She searched the flood of faces, among them Mrs. Lanslo, the Pitts, and Mayor Em-I. The Mayor was speaking to another important looking man, both standing close to where Milo was hidden. Milo poked Ajsha in the shoulder and nodded at the two men.

"Go listen to what they're saying," she told her.

Ajsha seemed a little hesitant about eavesdropping on the Mayor, but did nonetheless. After a while, she returned and shrugged.

"Nothing important," she reported. "The man said, 'Lovely day.' The Mayor said, 'Yes, very. Perfect for a wedding.' 'Why isn't your wife here? Is she still ill?' 'Yes,' the Mayor said, kind of sadly. 'Still not well enough for the outdoors. The doctor said she was getting better, and with all the pills he's giving her, I would expect nothing less. I told her about Master Swallow's wedding, and she was unhappy that she couldn't attend. But even if she could, I doubt she would. Such a quiet creature, she is.'"

"So," Milo mused, after Ajsha finished, "Mayor Em-I has a wife?"

"Of course," Ajsha said. "But we don't really see her much, she's so shy."

"Just like my Milo," Bob the Conscience mockingly piped up.

"Are you here to ridicule or help?" Milo snapped.

"Help," he answered.

"Good!" she said. "Don't go anywhere!"

"I can't," he replied flatly.

The crowd began to move inside the church, ushered inside by several identically dressed teenage boys. One fought his way through the bodies to take Ajsha by the hand to lead her inside. She held back a minute to tell Milo that she was supposed to stay outside the church until the organ played a certain song, then enter and walk down the aisle.

"They'd let me be out here alone?" Milo said doubtfully.

"They're watching you," Ajsha reminded her as she was whisked away.

The large double doors finally shut behind the guests, or spectators, really, leaving the bride completely forlorn. She shrugged her jacket off and laid it on a bench. She noticed a bundle of flower trimmed with lace by the steps. Milo scooped it up and practiced tossing it, effectively bruising most of the petals, until she heard a rustling in the bushes. Hastily, she picked it up, holding it respectfully, and covered her face with the veil.

With nothing else to do but wait, she paced impatiently in front of the doors, wishing she had been allowed to wear her watch along with the jewelry.

"Still thinking of making a break for it?" asked Bob the Conscience.

"What do you think?" she growled.

If he had shoulders, then perhaps Bob the Conscience would have shrugged. He was about to make a witty retort, when the muffled sound of an organ came seeping under the doors. Milo jumped, her heart beginning to hammer painfully. She stared, petrified, at the door handles, not knowing what to do.

"It's okay," she whispered to herself. "It'll be okay."

Her free hand started to float towards a handle, when Bob the Conscience, in an unexpected turn of events, decided to become helpful.

"Wait!" he said.

"Now what?" she inquired crossly.

"This is not your song. The bride must enter during the song 'Here Comes the Bride'. This right now is the bridesmaids and flower girl song. After will be you."

"I wish I could go now and get it over with," Milo grumbled.

"Patience," the conscience stated wisely.

Milo couldn't think of any crisp response, so therefore she took his advice and was patient. Or, at least she waited. The organ continued for several minutes, Milo's pulse thrumming in time to the music, until it abruptly changed.

The next melody was most definitely meant for the bride; even Milo recognized it, and she had gone to only one wedding in her life. She felt like she had been splashed with a bucket of ice water. She stood rigidly, unable to think.

"Milo!" Bob the Conscience hissed. "Milo! Move it!"

Gasping, she jolted into motion. But before she could even touch one of the handles, the doors swung open of their own accord. Bewildered, she peered into the church; it had a small entrance way, with double doors leading into the sanctuary. To the left of the entrance way was a staircase leading down, and to the right was a small room, littered with little wooden chairs and blankets.

But it was the sanctuary that commanded her attention. It was filled with pews, which were filled with people, who were filled with awe. The pews were decorated heavily with colorful flowers and thick glossy ribbons. The aisle between the pews had its coarse wooden floor covered with a long white piece of cloth, stretching all the way to the back. The cloth/rug was already sprinkled with flower petals, courtesy of Ajsha. In the rear of the sanctuary stood an elderly man dressed in his ceremonial best. Behind him were steps, leading up to a platform where a pulpit sat, and behind that was an enormous tub, obviously made from the metal of some unfortunate plane.

To the left of the pastor was Ajsha. She stood in front of a group of teenage girls Milo had never seen before. They each had on a light pink dress and held a handful of flowers. To the right of the pastor stood Simon; tall, proud, and barely containing his pleasure. As the front doors opened, he gazed eagerly down the aisle to see a terrified Milo Hestler (who was about to become Milo Swallow) being urged into the church by people in the entrance way.

Her eyes had gone very wide, and her skin unnaturally pale. The scene in the sanctuary made her tremble uncontrollably, tiny beads of sweat breaking out on her forehead. But nobody could see this, for the thick veil was obscuring her face. The only person who saw that she was trembling was Ajsha, who instantly began to worry.

Milo took a shaky step forward, too afraid to do anything else. She walked stiffly into God's house, faces turning to stare at her. She gripped her bouquet tightly, till her knuckles showed, trying not to look at anybody. She walked slowly, somehow managing to be in time with the organ, which was located behind the bridesmaids. Finally, unable to help herself, she used her eyes to scan the multitude that came to see Simon marry.

Nearly all of the people were strangers to her, aside from the few acquaintances she had made. Though they all stared adoringly, evidently willing to forget their disapproval, Milo was still not comforted. On this day she was supposed to be surrounded by family and friends who loved her. And she was supposed to be walking towards a man she actually wanted to marry, not a boy she couldn't even have a conversation with. Not to mention the fact that her father was supposed to accompany her down the aisle; without him, she felt very scared and alone.

With nobody to hold on to for support, Milo strangled her flowers, wishing that the people would stop staring at her. It wasn't encouraging her any. Her steps got slower and more unsteady, threatening to halt altogether, until she saw a cluster of Simon's beach friends in one of the pews. Apparently they knew she was looking at them, for they snarled and revealed bits of weapons, hidden beneath their shirts. Milo sucked in her breath and forced her legs to continue down the aisle. She longed to see a face that would show pity and support for her plight. But the only face like that was Ajsha's, whose concern was quite visible.

She gave Milo a small smile, but it did nothing to help the poor maiden. The weight of the whole ordeal was making her heart pound and emotions run high. She looked down at her feet, treading on the cloth and petals, and said a short prayer. Not for deliverance from the situation, but for no other girl to have to endure a wedding as horrible as this one. As the "Amen" escaped her lips, a tear fell from her eye and slowly ran down her cheek.

Another followed, and then another. More formed and fell, sobs choking Milo's throat. But she wouldn't let them come out; she refused to let these people see her in a moment of weakness. Nobody saw the tears except Ajsha, who noticed the glistening specks under the veil. Her little brow wrinkled and her belly knotted. She regretted her role in the whole thing.

Simon didn't notice any of Milo's fear or misery. No, he was far too exhilarated. To him, this was the best day of his life: The day of marriage. As Milo neared the pastor, Simon tried to take her hand, but she refused to relinquish any hold on her bouquet. Not wanting to cause trouble, especially with church full of people watching, the boy didn't pursue the matter.

The pastor, smiling warmly, nodded to Ajsha. She came close enough for Milo to hear her.

"Are you ready?" Ajsha whispered.

Milo could only nod, her vocal chords constricted by emotion. Ajsha faced the pastor and gave him the consent to start.

He opened the Bible he was holding and began the ceremony. As his voice boomed and echoed around the vaulted ceiling, Ajsha translated quietly for Milo, who barely paid any attention. The tears had dried up, but she was still hopelessly lost in a vortex of sadness, fear, anger, and nervousness. Everything Ajsha said went in one ear and out the other, leaving no trace of having been there. The pastor's speech was beautiful, but far too surreal and just didn't seem to apply to her.

Milo was starting to feel light-headed, on the verge of hyper-ventilating, and the thought of fainting occurred.

"NO!" she thought vehemently. "No fainting! Pull yourself together, girl!"

She tried to adjust her feelings so that there was only anger, but only succeeded in replacing sadness and fear. Nervousness remained untouched, but Milo figured she had enough anger to see her through. She concentrated so hard that twenty minutes went by without her realizing it. Soon, Ajsha was whispering that the I Do's were coming up.

"Huh?" Milo said, coming out of her trance.

"The I Do's are coming up," Ajsha repeated.

"No vows?" Milo asked, rather hopefully.

"Yes, there are vows, but only the pastor says them, and when you say 'I do' you are agreeing to them. See? He's doing it with Simon."

Milo tilted her head slightly to see the pastor speaking meaningfully to Simon. Once he finished, Simon said something that sounded like, "Ti wa."

The pastor smiled, eyes crinkling at the corners. He then turned to Milo and repeated the vows, Ajsha interpreting.

"'Do you promise to be with this man through sickness and health, through riches and poverty, through peace and trouble?'"

"He's not a man," Milo muttered into her veil, noticing that these were not the vows she usually heard. "And he can vomit to death for all I care."

"'Never to love anyone else . . .'"

"I never loved him in the first place."

"'To stand up for him, to help him raise the child, to never leave him for another man, and to obey the law.'"

"What was that last part there?" Milo whispered.

"He's waiting for you to say 'I do'," said Ajsha.

Milo, who had been staring at a crack in the floor, lifted her head to see the pastor looking at her expectantly.

"What's the point of saying 'I do'?" the bride muttered bitterly. "They're going to make you do it anyway, whether you agree or not."

"Are you going to say it?"

"Do I have a choice?"

"Is that a yes?" Ajsha inquired hesitantly.

"No, it's not a yes. But I don't have a choice, so . . . (sigh) . . . I do."

Ajsha repeated it to the pastor, who announced it to the congregation. He then addressed both the bride and groom. Simon, beaming, turned towards Milo, Ajsha tensing up.

"Milo," she said hurriedly. "I know this is the last thing you want to hear, but the pastor said that Simon may kiss you now."

"What?" Milo squeaked, though she had reckoned it was coming.

Simon slowly lifted the veil from her face. Milo didn't look at him; the last thing on earth she wanted to do at that moment was kiss him. What she would like to have done was stick a knife through him. She felt his hands going about her wait, and glared at him, her eyes narrowed dangerously. The resounding clink of chains from somewhere behind her made her stop. Remembering her legs, she allowed Simon to move towards her mouth, loathing him inch by inch.

His lips slowly embraced hers. This was not how she had intended her first kiss to go; it was one of those milestone events that she had been looking forward to, and she hated Simon for spoiling it.

An idea suddenly flew to her mind. Carefully, making sure to disguise her teeth with her lips, she bit down on Simon's upper lip, feeling exceptionally better as Simon winced. She knew he wouldn't dare scream or wrench away, though he probably felt like doing both.

When their heads separated, Milo smirked nastily at Simon while the audience applauded. Simon ran his tongue over his lip and stared incredulously at Milo, as if to ask, "*Why?*" She gave him a look that clearly said, "You deserved it, you forcer of marriage!"

They turned around, the church thundering with claps, whistles, and exultant yelling. Milo let Simon slip his arm around hers, and together they headed back down the aisle. She felt wonderfully lighter and nigh unto blissful now that she bit him. Simon was sucking on his injured lip, simultaneously nodding to certain friends and casting Milo bemused glances. Ajsha followed close behind, while the organ played the wedding march and everyone in the pews arose to watch them depart. Bob the Conscience was laughing himself silly.

"You wicked, wicked thing!" he chortled. "I've got to admit, Milo, sometimes you can be very clever."

"I have a brainstorm every few years!" she joked.

The three of them, or four if you count the conscience, entered the little room with the tiny chairs upon reaching the entrance hall. Simon, his arm still entwined with Milo's, had to tug her inside. She might not have gone in at all if Ajsha hadn't assured her it was where they were supposed to go. While the wedding audience streamed past the room and out the church doors, Simon bent down to hug Ajsha. As he stood up, he mumbled something to her, her jaw dropping in surprise. She rounded on Milo.

"You bit him?!" Ajsha exclaimed.

"That's right!" Milo said proudly, twirling her bouquet like a baton.

"W-w . . . w-w," Ajsha stammered.

Milo didn't know if she was trying to say, "Why?" or, "Well!"

Getting a hold of herself, Ajsha cleared her throat and said, "He wants to know why you did it."

Milo crossed her arms and faced Simon. "You deserved it, you forcer of marriage!" she snapped.

Ajsha, after regarding Milo blankly for a second translated. Simon rolled his eyes, but then smiled, as if cheered by this unintentional reminder that he was now married. When every single guest had gone by, Simon again slipped his arm around Milo's and led her out. As they exited the church, the crowd parted for them and performed a tradition similar to rice throwing; only they threw gifts.

Simon and Milo quickly sprang apart, in order to have the use of their arms. Milo had to stop and catch things, so as not to be hit by them. She caught a set of wooden kitchen utensils, a pillow, two tablecloths, a pair of sandals, a glass pitcher, (which, instead of being thrown, was handed to her) and a dish rag.

Simon caught a new blanket, new china (also handed to him), new towels, a machete (when Milo saw this she nearly fainted), and a medium sized box.

Ajsha caught a trowel, an enormous paintbrush, three new hairbrushes, and a larger box.

As they separated from the cheering mob, looking more like they had just come from a rummage sale than a wedding, they met the pastor. Simon carefully put his presents on the ground, and Milo gladly copied him. She had red marks on her bare arms where she had caught many of the gifts. Wondering why they had stopped, Milo rested her hands on her hips, peering back at Ajsha.

The little girl in the bright, yellow dress did not see her quizzical look. She was staring past Milo, at the pastor, looking troubled. The pastor, Milo quickly realized, was holding several papers with writing on them, and a beat-up looking pen.

Simon, without any hesitation, accepted the pen and signed the papers. The pen was then handed to Milo. She stood motionless, staring at the papers, the lightness in her body being replaced by lead. She knew what those papers were. Those were marriage certificates. If she signed them, she would officially be married. She stood, not knowing what to do.

Suddenly a knife whizzed past her ear. Nobody noticed, even she wouldn't have, but it came so close that she heard it. She turned her head in the direction she thought it came from, and saw one of Simon's friends from the beach. He was standing behind a tree, shooting her an angry, sinister look.

Eyes wide, her lungs frozen, Milo quickly wrote her name down in all the places that the pastor pointed to. When she had made the last "r", for Hestler, a name that no longer applied to her, she was panting so hard she didn't even notice Simon hugging her. He was so happy he didn't see the expression of horror on her face. Sadness, fear, anger, and nervousness had given way to horror.

11
The Select Location

SOMETIMES PEOPLE COMMIT certain things known as "Desperate Acts". Usually, they are forced to take such rash measures because of sheer stress and lack of better options. However, later on, when all the hubbub has died down and they have a chance to reflect, they realize their actions weren't all that "desperate".

After signing the certificate, Milo and Simon were scheduled to go home, pick up luggage, and head over to the "select location". However, after getting over her shock of now being a legally married fourteen year old, Milo was less keen than ever to follow the agenda. Somehow she managed to convey to Simon that he should go on ahead of her. As reluctant as he was to leave her right then, Simon apparently could tell from her drawn face and fiery glare that she needed some alone time. Once he was well on his way, the island inhabitants waving and yelling goodbye to him, Milo snuck off and hid in some brush. As the people headed back into the church, Milo sprang out, seized Ajsha, and pulled into the bushes.

"Hey!" the child objected, before seeing it was Milo.

"Shhh!" Milo shushed. They squatted amid the leaves and branches, unseen by those passing by.

"What's wrong? What do you want?" Ajsha asked, more quietly.

"You're coming with us!" Milo hissed. "I am not doing this trip alone! Who knows what that creep will try to do if we're alone? Besides, someone has to translate all my insults. Now come!"

"But I'm not supposed to," Ajsha insisted. "You two are meant to be alone. Kids never go. It's a time of relaxation and togetherness for just you and Simon."

"Sure it is," Milo said, latching on to one of her wrists. "But you're coming with us."

"Simon won't allow it," Ajsha warned, reluctantly letting Milo tug her along.

"I had a feeling he wouldn't," Milo admitted, checking their surroundings before emerging out into the open, "but he doesn't have a say in the matter."

"Why not?" asked Ajsha, trailing behind her, casting looks of longing back at the crowd. "He'll send me back to the church the moment he sees me."

"He won't," Milo said assuredly. "I've planned it all out. I'm going to smuggle you in with our luggage."

"That seems like a rather desperate act," observed Ajsha, taking a minute to think about it.

Milo halted abruptly and turned to her. "Honey," she said wearily, "I am a fourteen year old who has crashed on an island. I can't leave, no one knows I'm here, my parents probably think I'm dead, the mayor wouldn't mind if I were dead, and I have just been forced to marry a guy I can't talk to or stand the sight of. I ain't clinging to a whole lot."

With that, she resumed walking, hiking her dress up to her knees with one hand, the other arm still loaded with the projectile presents. Ajsha sighed, but kept pace. As they traveled, Milo relayed the smuggling scheme. Once they reached the hut, Ajsha would sneak in through a window, change, grab a few clothes, and hide in Milo's suitcase.

"You're small enough," Milo informed her, "and I didn't pack much."

"Won't Simon notice the extra weight?"

"Nope," she said. "He's not gonna carry it. And it's got wheels, so it's not a problem. Besides, it's only for the trip there. When we arrive, I'll let you out. Simon will see you, but won't be able to do anything about it!"

"Okay," Ajsha murmured uncertainly.

"What's up? Don't you want to help me?"

"Of course!" she amended hastily. "I'm sorry. You're right. You need emotional support right now. Honestly, I think you handled the wedding very well, considering how unfairly you've been treated."

"Thank you," Milo replied, touched. "So you'll help me?"

"I'll do anything I can."

When they finally reached the house, Ajsha crept around to the back, attempting to be inconspicuous, which is a challenge if you're the color of a lemon. Without any glass in the windows, it was easy for her to hoist herself up and tumble inside. Milo tarried out front, waiting until Ajsha was in, and then trudged up to the door.

Simon was in the kitchen, already changed and sorting the gifts that were thrown to him; he had Ajsha's as well. He looked up to see Milo standing at the threshold, shining with perspiration, her wedding dress clinging to her wiry body. She regarded him with a look of cold abhorrence. Simon grinned, either not recognizing nonverbal hatred or choosing to ignore it. Milo dropped her gifts in an unruly pile, and disappeared into the sitting room. She returned with a pillow, took aim, and launched it at him.

He caught it easily and threw it back. Remembering last time, she swiftly dodged out of the way. She put it back in the sitting room, shooting Simon a look that would not only hurt but scar, and then tramped down the hall to her bedroom. Much to her surprise, she found Ajsha there, a neat bundle under one arm.

"You changed already?" Milo asked in astonishment, quickly shutting the door behind her.

"I am a very efficient child," she replied. She hardly sounded calm, her little six year old voice more pitchy than usual.

"I'll say," Milo muttered. "Alright."

Her suitcase lay opened on the floor. Being the suitcase Milo had used all her life to move, it was on the large side anyway. Over the years, each time she packed it, it always occurred to her that a small person could stowaway in it if need be. Of course, that's a pretty rare need, but nowadays, for Milo anyway, the theme seemed to be rare and ridiculous, so why not?

"Hop in," Milo told Ajsha. "I made sure there was plenty of room for you."

Ajsha carefully sat down in the suitcase, and then curled up on her side, making herself small as possible. She had never been smuggled before, and even though she was defying Simon, the idea starting to excite her. Milo zipped it up, leaving a portion open for air to flow in. Then she peeled off her wedding dress, removed all the jewelry, and dressed in her customary T-shirt and loose jeans. After tying her shoes, she grabbed her backpack and gently lifted one end of the suitcase.

"You all right?" she whispered to Ajsha, who was at the bottom where the wheels met the floor.

"Yes," Ajsha whispered back. "I'm actually quite comfortable."

Milo carefully rolled her precious cargo to the kitchen, where Simon was now sifting her presents. The different objects lay on the floor, sat on the chairs, and were strewn atop the table. He smiled broadly when Milo appeared. They stood silently for a moment, a just married couple with no way to express their individual feelings about what had happened. Whatever bond marriage was supposed to create between two people, Milo didn't feel it towards Simon. Staring at him narrowly from across the kitchen, she knew he was her husband on paper, but that was it.

He spread his arms wide, inviting her to join him in an affectionate embrace. Milo slowly, meticulously, shook her head, more so in disgusted disbelief than turning him down. Simon waited, arms still outstretched, proving he wasn't a quitter. However, when Milo continued to shake her head in tiny, furious jerks, his grin melted off his face and his arms fell.

Sighing resignedly, he approached and tried to take the suitcase from her. She firmly held on to the handle, and he soon gave up. He went to gather his luggage, muttering in Galo and occasionally glancing back at Milo. She was almost tempted to release Ajsha right then and there, just to find out what he was saying.

They finally left the house, only to find a man waiting expectantly by the door. Simon greeted him pleasantly, shaking his hand, and promptly handed him his traveling bag. Milo cautiously bent down to address her suitcase, pretending she was checking her shoes.

"Ajsha," she whispered urgently, "there's a guy here who took Simon's stuff. Who is he?"

"Oh," came the muffled reply, "I forgot! Someone is going to take your things ahead of you, so you two can walk alone."

"Wonderful!" Milo hissed. "That's all I need!"

"What if you refuse to give it to him?" Ajsha asked.

"I can't," Milo whispered apologetically. "That'll look way too suspicious. It's not like they trust me a whole bunch anyway. Sorry. Do you think you'll be okay?"

"Uh," she said, obviously not thrilled with the idea, but still dedicated to the mission. "I – well, yes. I think so. He should be using a cart."

Milo checked the area and saw a square, wooden contraption on round, wooden wheels.

"He is!" she told the stowaway. "I'm going to give you to him, alright? Try not to make any noise. I'll see you when we get there."

"Okay. Goodbye. Please be nice to Simon?"

"No."

Milo straightened up and rolled her suitcase over to the man. He had already tucked Simon's into the cart. With one fluid motion, he took Milo's, swung it through the air, and landed it in the cart. As he swung, a faint scream issued from the suitcase. Simon and the man both looked around for the source. Milo gave a half-hearted scream, which she attributed to a rather gargantuan spider crawling nearby.

The man rolled his eyes and jabbered contemptuously to Simon. He gibbered something back, and Milo could only assume he was defending her, for a second later he tried to pat her back. Gliding away from him, she stored her backpack in the cart herself, now that she knew the man's method of loading, giving a lump in her suitcase a reassuring pat.

The man began to push the cart into the jungle. Simon followed, immediately getting swallowed by the broad, green foliage. The forest surrounded the clearing and the town, but Milo had never dared to explore it. She didn't know what sort of minute or burly creatures resided in there. Eyeing the trees warily, she reluctantly trudged after Simon. What with Ajsha in a suitcase, Milo very well couldn't make a break for it now.

The little group stumbled over unearthed roots and stones for a several minutes, Milo watching as the cart jostled and bumped, till they came to a narrow, winding path. Thankfully it was much smoother than the natural jungle terrain. They had not gone far when the man suddenly broke into a sprint, noisily trundling the cart down the path and leaving the two teens behind.

"Hey!" Milo protested, watching furiously as he became nothing more than a dot in the distance.

A comforting hand rested on her shoulder.

Simon was at her side, smiling at her. Milo fumed, baffled at how he had managed to get so close without her noticing, and slapped his hand. He drew back, angered, and probably more than a little exasperated, and gave her a shove. Since she was Milo, with a barely substantial frame, the push nearly sent her into a tree. She balanced herself before she collided with the scraggly bark, and whirled around to face him, livid. They stood glaring menacingly at each other for a few minutes, not able to communicate, both braced for an attack.

Suddenly Milo began to walk again, trotting past Simon with her head held high. In her opinion, she had nothing to be ashamed of. She was in the right, and had no reason to fight. Furthermore, the odds were not in her favor.

Her actions puzzled Simon, but he was happy that there would be no fight. He resumed walking behind Milo, keeping a healthy distance, and he didn't try to contact her until he felt sure she had calmed down.

About a half an hour later he sensed that she had fully regained her composure, because she was raptly observing the scenery. Jungle flourished on all sides of them, and (in case you haven't visited one) the jungle, just to let you know, is one of the most gorgeous and fascinating places on earth.

It is comprised of interesting trees, flowers, animals, and sounds. It is also filled with interesting bugs, insects, arachnids, and a variety of poisonous critters, but those are of the more unpleasant category. And since Simon and Milo didn't run into any of them on their travels, we will not discuss them any further.

Eventually, Milo stopped by a petite, purplish flower and leaned down to smell it. She inhaled deeply, then "Mmmm!"ed in approval. She stood up, grinning, and continued on. During the half-hour that she had remained quiet, mulling over her few options, she had decided that, if at all possible, she would enjoy herself on this trip. After the petite flower, she halted in front of a large, elegant flower that was taller than she was. Gently, she hooked a finger around its stem and pulled its head down to her nose. She took a whiff, let out a "Blech!", and quickly released the plant.

Simon chuckled behind her, making her jump. She had successfully forgotten he was there. He reached into the tangled brush and extracted a flower. It had blue, stubby petals. He held it out to her, and Milo, not wanting to accept it, leaned forward and sniffed it. It smelled wonderful, and, strangely, it also cleared out her nose and sinuses. She nodded, figuring it was a flower that the island folk used to treat allergies, though the notion was rather ironic.

It went on like this for the rest of the journey through the forest. Milo would pause to examine different flora, and the occasional fauna, and then Simon would show her something else. There wasn't much speech involved, but they managed to make their messages clear. To say that Milo wasn't enjoying herself would be a black lie. When it's warm and you're surrounded by greenery, sampling fragrant plants, it really doesn't matter who your companion is. The whole time, though Milo barely noticed, they were gradually climbing upward.

She finally began to pay attention to this when they were practically on a slant. They were slowly progressing up a mountain-side, as she soon found out once she looked skyward. What she saw made her want to turn and run back.

You see, at times people make mistakes without even realizing it. Milo had made plenty of them in her lifetime. From choosing Bernie Coughindale to be her reading buddy in fourth grade, a disaster she still shuddered to remember; to entering a garden filled with lice, and boarding a plane that was destined to crash. Milo's life was full of mistakes she had made without even realizing it, and two days ago she had committed another one.

I recall telling you how she had spent an entire day browsing through a book with pictures and information about select locations, when they were interrupted by the women with the dress. The couple had still not decided on a location, and at that point Milo was so frustrated that she wanted to scream. Before she was wrangled into the other room, Ajsha and Simon had called out to her, asking her which location they should go to. She was so angry and disgusted that she had yelled at them,

"Surprise me!"

That right there was her mistake, though she wasn't aware of it. But she was now. As she stared up at the mountain, her mind reeled back to the moment she had said that, and sorely wished she hadn't.

The mountain wasn't exactly enormous, but large enough to have about twenty plateaus and ledges projecting off of it. On one of the bigger ledges was a lodge, where they obviously would be staying, but all the other ledges contained natural hot springs. An entrepreneurial spirit had improved the springs by adding jungle foliage around their edges. Brilliant blooming flowers, small banana trees, and different types of moss sat dispersed on the mountainside in crown shaped tufts, surrounding bubbling mineral water that Milo could hear from where she stood.

"The little git!" Milo thought angrily, mouth agape in astonishment. It all was a thousand times more impressive in real life. *"This is the one he chose?! I would never step foot in one of those things with him!"*

She turned to Simon, pointing at the . . . place . . . and giving him a look that said, "Just what is that?!"

He peered in the direction of her finger and grinned. Without even trying to explain, he bolted up a path to the lodge. Not wanting to lose track of him, since the sun was setting and she preferred not to be alone in the jungle in the dark, she ran after him, outraged. She kept trying to catch up to him, but he wouldn't let her. Periodically, he would slow down, allow her to come close enough to gain fresh vigor, and then he would race away. This made Milo angrier and angrier. She followed him with a jump in her step. This system, however infuriating, allowed Simon to get her up the mountain without a fight.

When they at last reached the lodge, both panting and sweating,

Milo realized that he had tricked her. She was about to murder him, when a man came out to welcome them. He uttered a prepared speech in Galo, which was completely wasted on Milo, who was sending Simon threatening gestures with her hands. He stoically ignored her, listening to the man with great interest.

As soon as the man was finished, he ushered the two of them inside, but Simon held up a hand and insisted something in Galo. Milo didn't know what until he pointed to the sky. It was streaked with crimson and gold, setting the ocean ablaze and bathing the tree tops in a scarlet glow. There's no view of a sunset like on a mountain. It made Milo temporarily forget where she was and why; that is, until Simon tried to sidle up to her. Glowering, she pretended to shove someone off the edge on the ledge and then jabbed a finger at him. He backed away, sighing. They stayed outside until the sun had vanished into the horizon. Their host then led them inside, Milo grudgingly following.

The "Lodge on the Ledge" was decorated with a large desk and interesting chairs crafted from whittled palm wood and vines. Unlike the houses by the beach, the whole lodge was made out of palm wood, polished so that it shone warmly. The man, first lighting a lamp, showed them down a long hallway lined with doors. Stopping at one, he opened it and gestured for them to enter, and Simon didn't hesitate.

Milo looked in first, squinting in the dim light, and saw a bed by a window, a door leading to a water-closet, a table with a couple of chairs, and a braided rug on the stone floor. Their luggage was on the bed. Milo sighed, her shoulders slumping, and turned to the man.

"Do you have any arsenic?" she asked him politely.

The man did not respond, his brow knitting perplexedly. Milo reluctantly went into the room. The door closed behind her, making her heart sink. Her hands had just gone to her hips, when she heard a muffled sound issuing from her suitcase. She suddenly remembered that she had packed a little person.

She hastily went over and unzipped the suitcase, throwing off the top. Ajsha sat up gasping and clutching her stomach. Simon let out a cry of surprise. He stared at them, dumbstruck, eyes popping. Milo paid him no mind, helping Ajsha off the bed. Once her feet touched the floor, the child ran to the water-closet, where came the sounds of vomiting.

Simon was still gawking unabashedly; he went up to Milo and spluttered in Galo. She gazed steadily at him, not comprehending. He repeated himself several times, his arms rising and falling pathetically. Milo walked up to him and said sweetly, "You know what?" then thundered, "I CAN'T UNDERSTAND WHAT YOU'RE SAYING!!!"

With that, she whirled around and flounced to the water-closet to see about Ajsha.

"You okay?" she asked her.

Ajsha was kneeling, her head by the rim of the bowl. She nodded. "The rattling . . . the bumping," she breathed and threw up again.

Milo knelt beside her, gently rubbing her back. "Dang," she murmured. "I'm sorry for making you do this," she told the regurgitating victim.

Ajsha shook her head and smiled bravely. "This is nothing," she replied, wiping her mouth. "One time, a pet boar ate a bracelet that belonged to my teacher. I volunteered to search through its turd to find it. You wouldn't believe how much I threw up that day!"

"That's pleasant," said Milo, gagging. "You poor child."

When Ajsha felt stable enough, they went back into the bedroom. Simon was perched on the edge of the bed, looking quite melancholy. Ajsha walked over to him, gibbering timidly. He stared passively up at Milo, and she gave him a triumphant look. Ajsha began to explain things to him, her voice ashamed. His expression changed over the next few minutes, going from betrayed and defeated, to serious, to curious, to amused, and finally he smiled. They hugged, muttering to each other. He then jabbered in Galo, nodding in Milo's direction.

"He says," Ajsha translated happily, "that he understands. He would have preferred if you had mentioned it, but he understands. In fact, he thinks it was quite clever of you."

"Oh, yeah?" she said, then, "Oh, yeah!" grinning.

"Yes," said Ajsha. "And he says that you'll have a better time here if you can talk to one another."

"Ya think!" Milo snapped at him.

Before Ajsha could translate, she yawned deeply. Simon smiled and spoke softly to her. She nodded and said to Milo, "It's time to sleep."

"No, way!" Milo cried, dramatically glancing out the window. "And I thought we were just having an eclipse!"

"Good night," Ajsha said, fetching her clothes bundle from Milo's suitcase and heading towards the door.

"Hey!" Milo said, alarmed. "Where are you going?"

"Simon says there are couches in the hall," she replied, leaving the room.

"Wait!" Milo called out, following her out into the hallway.

"What's wrong?" Ajsha asked, suppressing another yawn.

Milo winced. "Do I have to sleep in the bed with him?" she mumbled, studying her shoes.

Ajsha, catching on, grimaced, but nodded. "Yes," she sighed. "I'm afraid so. Don't worry. I used to have to share a bed in the orphanage. It's just like sleeping alone, only you can't roll around too much. I'll be there in the morning to see how you are. Good luck."

"Thanks," Milo muttered, shuffling back into the room.

After changing into pajamas in the water-closet, she came out to find Simon reclining on the bed, his hands behind his head. He had been staring blissfully at the ceiling, but looked over at Milo when she entered.

Oh, he knew. She knew he knew. A grin played on his lips, and she rolled her eyes. Miserably, she went and sat down on the edge of the tick, hunched forward. Simon sat up, wanting to comfort her. He tried to lay a hand on her shoulder, but she wouldn't allow it. He tried to touch her arched back, but she shook him off. Frustrated, he leaned back for a second, contemplating, then committed a desperate act.

Lunging forward, he wrapped his arms around her, pulling her onto the bed. She struggled fiercely, grunting and trying to break free, but Simon wouldn't be stopped. He was completely out of ideas for going about it gently, and he was down to the last resort. He laid her down in a crumpled, writhing sort of position, then quickly snuffed out the candle. Darkness immediately enshrouded them, leaving Milo no choice but to stay still.

Shifting until her head hit a pillow, she at once became aware of the fact that she was lying next to a different gender. A *boy*. She lay stiff as a board, not daring to move a centimeter. It was such an awkward situation, one that she never even considered before. She became wide awake and frightened, and if you think it childish, girls, just try to imagine yourself being forced to sleep in the same bed with a boy. Particularly one you intensely dislike. Now I'm sure you understand the queasiness in Milo's gut. It grew worse when she thought about how it would continue; that is, until an odd twist of fate occurred and she'd be rescued. But until then, every night would be like this.

Nearly ten million indescribable thoughts besieged Milo's mind. Sleep was surely not possible, not when an enemy lay so close at hand. She couldn't sleep even if she tried, even if she wanted to; she was wide awake, never to slumber again. For a split second, she wished she was back in her own bed, but hastily righted herself. Anything was better than 711 Shady Ally!

For countless minutes, which felt like hours, Milo listened to Simon twitch and fidget restlessly. When he finally stopped, she wished he hadn't, for without the noise it was completely silent. Nothing can be more unsettling than silence. Nothing.

Eventually, Milo began to feel rather tired, the stress and exertion of the day taking its toll, but she didn't let herself drift off. Her stomach wailed for something to digest, and Milo realized that she hadn't eaten anything all day.

Suddenly, she felt something soft touch her forehead, then disappear. It returned on the side of her nose, and then her cheek. It felt familiar, like . . . a kiss!!

"Araaaraghh!!!" she cried out, shooting her hands straight up into the air, slamming into a figure leaning over her.

Simon yelped and fell back.

"You imbecile!!" she shouted. She grabbed her pillow and began to scour her face.

Once finished, she stretched out her hand, and it came to rest on what was clearly the curve of a head. She patted it gently before slamming the pillow over it.

After harassing Simon's skull as long as he would permit, she laid back down. A few minutes later, she felt a small poke on her shoulder, then on the side of her stomach. She shrieked and shouted for him to cut it out. Simon apparently wasn't very tired. He was excited about finally being a married boy. It was slightly normal for him to act in such a way, but took the loud hint and stopped.

Milo was boiling mad, but managed to fall asleep in the next half hour. Again and again she was awoken by nightmares, and continuously faced the problem of falling asleep under the awkward circumstance. When morning finally crawled over the rim of the window, she was exhausted and sufficiently stressed out. Simon had arisen from bed first and was elsewhere when Ajsha came in. She found Milo still in bed, limbs strewn listlessly and staring at the ceiling, an empty expression on her face. Grimly, Ajsha walked over to her.

"Hey," she said, "how are you doing?"

Milo twisted her head towards her, lifted up a pillow, and handed it to her.

"Could you smother me with this?" she asked in a desperate whisper.

Ajsha frowned. "Not so good, huh?"

"What do you think?" Milo groaned, straining to sit up. "How long are we going to be here?"

Ajsha shrugged. "A week."

"A week!" Milo repeated distressfully. "What are we supposed to do for a week?"

"I don't know. Enjoy yourself?"

"Forget it!" Milo retorted. She stiffly got out of the bed and went to the window. She looked out at all the hot springs that were steaming and bubbling.

"The last thing I want to do here is enjoy myself."

Once they were dressed, they left the room to find breakfast. It seemed that Simon had already taken the liberty of getting food, and waved them over to a wide ledge scattered with tables and long benches. They each devoured an enormous mango that had been hallowed out and filled with blackberries and raspberries. Milo, in an effort to ignore Simon's giddy glances, took in the view, scanning the ocean for another speck of land. There wasn't any.

When they finished, wiping their fingers on their clothes, Simon gibbered to Milo. She looked wearily to Ajsha.

"He wants to know if you would like to go into one of the hot springs with him," the child interpreted helpfully.

"No!" Milo answered then spat at his feet.

Ajsha, her nose wrinkling, told Simon this. He shrugged and grinned slyly. He jabbered nonchalantly to Ajsha.

"He asks, 'What else are you going to do?'"

Milo folded her arms, not liking Simon's lack of retaliation. "I'll just stay in the room and listen to my radio."

"The whole time?" Ajsha asked.

"Yes!" Milo replied stubbornly. "I'm not getting anywhere near those springs!"

After a few translations, Simon, who was still grinning, gibbered in Galo.

"He says that you can't listen to your radio, so you'll have to go in a spring."

"No, I won't," Milo insisted. "There's no 'law' saying that I have to sit in a hot spring with my husband."

"No, there aren't. But he says that you won't be able to listen to your radio, because he hid it."

"WHAT?!" Milo bellowed, enraged.

She jumped up and gripped Simon by the neck of his shirt. "If you do anything to harm it," she seethed, "I *swear!* I will torture you till you beg – no, scream! – for mercy! If anything – *anything* – happens to it, you will pay very dearly, boi!!"

Ajsha, thoroughly startled, relayed all this to Simon. He chuckled, making Milo clench tighter and her cheeks flush maroon. He forced another chuckle, though it sounded much less confident. He addressed the interpreter, who spoke to the infuriated one.

"He says that he will do nothing to damage it, but if you want it back you must go in the hot springs with him for the rest of the week."

Milo's nostrils flared, and she pulled him up so they were eye to eye. If it had been any other condition, Simon might have tried to kiss her, since she was so close.

Blackmail, a very desperate act.

Milo fumed, trying to decide which was worse: Being in a hot spring with *him*, or never listening to her radio again. She pondered for a moment, staring lethally into Simon's brown eyes, and had to admit that anything was better than losing "Hush".

"For how long?" she inquired, her voice dripping with disgust.

Simon answered with, "'Two hours each day.'"

Milo shuddered. "Will Ajsha be with us?" she demanded.

"I believe Ajsha can tell you that," Ajsha interjected.

Milo shot her a deadly look, and she quickly conferred with Simon, who was still in Milo's grasp. With some difficulty, he managed to shrug.

"He says that I can be there if I want to."

"And I'm sure you do," Milo remarked sweetly.

Before Ajsha could reply, Milo said hurriedly, "Well, I'm glad that's settled. Ask the lack-wit when we should do this torturous event."

She released him with a push, and Ajsha asked the lack-wit. Smoothing down his shirt, he smiled mischievously, and Ajsha had to speak again.

"He says, 'How 'bout now?'"

Milo's eyes narrowed. "Which one?"

"'That one up there.'"

Simon pointed to a ledge overlooking the jungle, its spring encircled with plenty of pink and orange flowers and springy, green moss.

"Fine!" she hissed. She turned to leave, then whirled around and thrust a finger in Simon's face. "You are a very, very, very evil boy!" With that, she stormed off.

As she was walking into the "Lodge on the Ledge" she noticed for the first time a sign about the springs, written both in Galo and English. She read the English one:

"Welcome to Taren Mountains! Home of the incredible natural hot springs! Besides being a lovely vacation spot, hot springs are known for calming nervous tension, relieving aching muscles, solving romantic problems, and attracting money . . ."

Milo couldn't read anymore. She was happy that no one was around, for she had a strong desire to hit something.

"Why! That little . . . !" she hissed. "That's why he brought me here? Well, to bad for him! Those springs won't be solving any of our 'romantic problems'!!!"

She muttered angrily all the way to their room, where she began to rummage through her clothes. Soon she realized she had made another mistake without knowing it. She hadn't packed a bathing-suit.

Desperately, she searched for something else to wear, pitching her clothes this way and that. She could always put on a T-shirt, but she didn't have a single thing that resembled shorts. This is odd if you think about it, considering she was originally heading to Australia. But Milo really never wore shorts, thinking her toothpick legs looked ridiculous in them. Now panicking, she roused Bob the Conscience.

"What should I do?!" she cried.

"You could cut the legs off one of your jeans," he suggested.

For a minute that sounded like a great idea, until it dawned upon Milo: No scissors.

"Do you really think they would let me have any sharp objects?" she said.

"Probably not," he admitted.

Milo was now close to tears; she had to get back her precious radio. She fretted over her suitcase until she realized something. She couldn't find anything to wear! Surely this was a legitimate reason to call off the whole thing. Simon would have to understand, and return the radio without any hot spring visit. But then again, it was Simon.

She heard a noise at the door. Simon was standing at the threshold. He had been watching her. He was holding the same bag he had brought home the day before the wedding. He tossed it to Milo and winked at her. Right then, Milo really did wish she had a sharp object.

As he left, she peeked into the bag and saw a purple and turquoise bathing-suit. But when she pulled it out she discovered it was a two-piece. She gasped and threw it to the floor, as if it had burned her. She wanted to slaughter Simon . . . slowly. She circled the two-piece, as if expecting it to attack her, and thought hard. True, her radio was depending on her; it was probably scared, wondering where she was or what it had done wrong. Steeling herself, she decided to just wear a T-shirt over the bikini.

She changed, almost painfully, and made sure Simon hadn't lied. Not seeing it in her backpack, she went outside.

There were paths all over the place, leading up, down, and sideways, and it took her a few tries to find the right one. When she arrived at the right spring, she found Simon submerged up to his neck and Ajsha sitting on the side, sticking her feet in. The moss covered all the edges, making everything quite luxurious. They both looked up at her.

"Hello," Ajsha greeted brightly.

"Hi," said Milo, dark as the other side of the moon. "Why aren't you in?"

"I can't swim," she replied simply.

"I don't think that's what you do in these."

"I'm still too small," Ajsha insisted. "Why don't you go in?"

"What an awful idea," Milo said pleasantly, but was gestured to enter by Simon.

For a moment, it seemed as if she wouldn't, but then she reluctantly stepped in, letting the warm, relaxing water engulf her feet. Simon pointed to her T-shirt and gibbered something.

"He wants to know if you're going to take your shirt off," Ajsha translated faithfully.

Milo glared at the boy, wanting to send him a message with a certain one of her fingers, but instead disregarded the question. She sat down, her bony tush meeting a rim of rock half way down the wall of the spring. The water was very deep, only her head sticking out. She inched her way to the wall opposite Simon.

He grinned, following impishly. Greatly annoyed, Milo scooted on, Simon closing in behind her. Seeing that retreat was futile, Milo came to a wobbly halt and sat, crossing her arms and legs. Simon floated to a stop and sat down beside her.

She glared at him, all sorts of nasty images racing through her mind, until she flat out refused to look at him. Now and then, he tried to stroke her arm or touch her chin, which caused her to splash water at him. He playfully splashed back at her, making her splash him, but before it could escalate into a full blown battle, Milo resumed her silent stillness. She refused to get caught up in fun of any sort. Simon attempted to draw her back into a water war, but only succeeded in drenching her.

The only time Ajsha's services were needed was when Simon said anything to Milo, who never answered. This routine carried on through the entire week. Milo had to endure awful nights, then a detestable dip, followed by her zealously complaining about her life to her diary and Bob the Conscience. It was the same pattern every day, lasting until right before they went home.

Breakfast was done, and the daily dip was in progress. Usually Milo would sit in one place and do her best to pretend Simon didn't exist, but that day he was being an extreme nuisance. Perhaps it was because it was their last day, and he was trying to make up for what had been an overall disappointing and uneventful week. He sat as close to her as possible, his legs often brushing hers, slid his fingers along her shoulders, tugged her hair, tried to kiss her, splashed her, nudged her, and anything else he could think of.

Milo, not far from violence, had gone back to running away from him. As usual, he followed, but now with a new determined speed. Milo was heavily irate and kept shouting at him to back off, Ajsha translating. He didn't bother responding, and kept after her like a shark on the prowl, his face slicing cleanly through the water, his eyes focused on her. She splashed at him, but he only splashed back.

Usually Milo stayed near the wall and didn't dare go near the middle, for she had no idea how deep it was. But on that day, she now and then would cross over to evade Simon. During one of these crossings, Simon vanished underwater. Just when she reached the middle of the spring, "something" suddenly grabbed her ankle and pulled her under.

She kicked it away and swam to the surface, the hot water searing her eyelids. She gasped for breath, only to be wrenched under again. This time, she had exhaled before the plunge, and she was out of air as she went down. She tried to kick, but couldn't create enough force to make herself go anywhere. Slowly, she began to sink, and the more she flailed the more oxygen she used up. Not that she had any to begin with. Her lungs screamed for air, her legs desperately searched for something to kick against, and her whole body was unbearably hot, the temperature only getting worse the farther down she went.

Her vision, already dim, began to turn black. She panicked immediately, thinking feverishly to herself, "Not here! Not now! My life stinks, but not that badly!"

Her thoughts slowly began to vaporize, and white was replacing the black. Her limbs quieted, and she hung suspended in the water, languidly falling deeper, like a forgotten marionette. She didn't even notice when someone dragged her up by her shirt, or when her skin felt air. There was beginning to be a green tinge around the white, when an explosive pain brought her back to her senses. Sky appeared before her eyes, dazzlingly blue, and another punch to her stomach caused her to suck air in at a record breaking speed. Water spewed from her throat, dribbling down her cheeks, onto the rocks below. She coughed water and drank air.

She coughed and coughed, and breathed and breathed. Air! How she loved air! The more air the better! She would never take it for granted again! God bless air!

Panting hoarsely, she looked to one side of her to see the blurry outline of Simon. He was shaking uncontrollably and crying. Milo blinked and squinted, Simon coming into focus. His face was contorted with fear and fat tears gushed out of his eyes. Milo had never seen Simon cry before.

Ajsha was on her other side, doing the same, only she wasn't quiet about her crying. She sobbed, hiccupping and sniveling. She ran her arm under her oozing nose and pressed her trembling lips to Milo's forehead.

Simon slipped his arms under Milo's legs and shoulders, and began to carry her. She would have fought if she had any strength, but she was completely limp. He carried to the "Lodge on the Ledge", hastily passing and blubbering something to the maître d', and rushed to their room. Ajsha hurried in his wake, still red faced and sobbing.

She shoved away the covers of the bed for Simon, and he tenderly lay Milo down, nestling her head in a pillow. They spread all manner of cozy blankets over her, because she was shivering. She wasn't sure why she was shivering, but it wasn't because she was cold. It was stifling under the many layers, but Milo didn't even have the strength to croak in protest. Simon stayed by her side the whole night, tucking her in and then loosening the blankets around her. He brushed her hair away from eyes, and held and stroked her hands. Every so often he began to cry.

Milo wished he would stop. It was nauseating her, and keeping her awake.

By the time morning came, Simon had fallen asleep and Milo could sit up. Ajsha wandered in, her eyes red from weeping. When she saw Milo sitting up, she rushed over and hugged her.

"Oh, Milo!" she sobbed. "When Simon . . . and you didn't come up . . . Oh, ho, ho!"

Milo didn't do much to comfort her. She was too tired. Every cell in her body hurt. Through the murkiness, it was becoming clearer that she was lucky to be alive. She looked down at the child clutching her about the waist, and thought dazedly that, compared to almost drowning, smuggling Ajsha didn't seem all that "desperate".

12
When it comes to being a Wife

THE DAY THE three came home, Milo went straight to bed, her head throbbing. The trip back had been stressful, what with Simon rushing to her side every time she exhaled too hard, and Ajsha insisting every twenty minutes that she take a rest. Simon had tried to talk to her, but each time he did, she gave him a weary, betrayed look. The boy was obviously very sorry for what he had done, but Milo was nonetheless furious with him. She just couldn't express it yet because she had no energy.

She spent the entire day in bed, which allowed her to rejuvenate herself. The next morning, right before breakfast, she dragged Ajsha up to Simon and began to yell at him. Milo yelled, releasing all the accumulated bitterness and accusations of the past few days. Ajsha translated, wincing now and then, and Simon took it, his face lined with shame. Milo ended it with,

"You untrustworthy blob of spit!!! Why can't you face the facts?!! We're married, and I don't like it at all!! And never will!!! Thank you for ruining my life, Simon Swallow!"

She then stormed away, slightly surprised at his lack of retaliation. She had called him almost every unpleasant noun she could think of, and had used every over exaggerated adjective and verb she had ever learned. This selection was vast because she was a good scholar. Yet, he acted as if he deserved it. He did, of course, but usually when Milo degraded him, he tried to defend his honor.

The yelling would have been more satisfying if Milo had shouted down at him, but since he was a good two inches taller than her, she had to yell up at him. She considered this for a minute or two before hauling Ajsha back over to Simon. This time she brought a chair with her. She stood on it, and towered over him, feeling quite empowered, indeed. She began yelling at him all over again, mixing up and exchanging verbs and adjectives from the last time. Again Simon didn't do anything about it, but stared up at her with sad, glassy eyes. She ended this tirade with,

"You vulgar pile of vomit!!! Why can't you admit the obvious?!! We are married, and I hate it!!! And always will!!! Thanks for tainting my existence, Simon Swallow!"

Upon finishing, she put the chair back and walked to the kitchen, leaving Ajsha to console Simon, who most likely was on the verge of depression. As she crossed the threshold, she gasped. The whole room was filled with woven reed containers. All sorts of shapes and sizes littered the table and counters, reminding Milo of a post office. A note lay on a rectangular one. Milo read,

Dear Swallows,
I hope the (Milo growled) went well.
Welcome home! I took the liberty of providing
some food for you, since there must be none in the house.
And, not to worry you or anything, but Ajsha
is missing. But we're on it, and we'll
probably find her soon. Enjoy the food!
Love,
Mrs. Lanslo.

Milo looked under it and saw another note, written in Galo. Milo had no idea what it said, but figured it was the same as the English one. Simon walked in, still looking crestfallen but no longer to the point of suicide. Milo gestured around the room, raising her hands questioningly, and he shrugged. He opened a large reed box on the table, and Milo peered into it. It contained what appeared to be a roasted type of bird that still had its feet attached.

Milo, not overly partial to claws, averted her gaze and handed the Galo note to Simon. He read it, chuckled, and called for Ajsha. She obediently appeared, and he gave her the note. She read it and laughed breezily. Milo didn't know what they thought was so hilarious. She found the situation to be rather disturbing. What was she supposed to do with all this food?

"What am I supposed to do with all this food?" she asked Bob the Conscience.

"Economize it," he replied. "Make it last. Ration it. You won't have to cook if you already have food prepared."

"But I like to cook," Milo whined.

"Then shake it up a little," Bob the Conscience said. "Mix and match. Do whatever you want; you're the chef after all."

"That's right," Milo agreed, "I am."

"And it won't last long, so you'll be cooking again in a week or so. Perhaps two, depending on your strategy."

"Well, thanks, Bob!" Milo said happily. "How do you know so much about food?"

"Oh, I learned from you," he replied modestly.

Grinning appreciatively, Milo took a step back and appraised the situation. After a moment's thought, she began to gather the other containers and stacked them on the table. She started opening them one by one, learning what she had to work with.

One held baked fish of all sorts, all golden and meaty. Baked potatoes cut halfway open, creating a crevasse where a lump of butter was tucked. Plump, little birds, no bigger than Milo's hand, all stuffed with tiny dumplings. There was a container brimming with oyster soup, with boiled cabbage drifting through its rich gravy, its oysters tender and succulent. One container had crusty rolls, another ripe olives, another juicy pears and limes. One housed a garden salad that had crisp greens, runner beans, and delectable tomatoes.

Milo plucked up a tomato and bit into it, letting its divine flavor run through her mouth and down her throat. Then she ate its soft red sides, cherishing the moment dearly.

Now that she knew what was there, she sorted the containers into groups and chose the correct places to put them till their food was needed. Some went into cupboards, some were stowed under the counters, and some had their food put in other storage vessels.

Ajsha watched her with great interest. (Simon had gone elsewhere, possibly to the beach.) She sat in a chair, her little legs swinging, and observed how carefully Milo handled the food and how she treated the kitchen. She noted how Milo roved about as if she'd had a lifetime to grow accustomed to each drawer and utensil.

"I'm glad that you're taking care of the food," Ajsha told her.

"How's that?" Milo said distractedly, looking up.

"I said I'm happy you're doing this without getting upset," Ajsha said.

"Why would I be upset?" Milo asked, poking at an orangey congealed mass at the bottom of a container.

"Because," Ajsha said, meticulously choosing her words, "it is a wife-ish thing to do, and I know you don't like wife-ish things."

Milo immediately froze, in the middle of placing something on a shelf. "Well," she said slowly, searching for a defense, "I'd do this any place. I don't mind things like this. Kitchen stuff. Anywhere I go, if there's a kitchen, I'm there. I don't care if you classify it as a 'wife-ish' thing. If I'm going to be forced to stay here, then I'm taking over this room. Simon can't touch me here, this is my castle."

Ajsha nodded, smiling. "Yes," she said. "I'm sure he won't mind. There is a saying, 'The husband may own the house, but the wife owns the kitchen.'"

"Quite true!" Milo agreed. "And I don't give a dang whether or not he minds."

All the containers now put away, and the empty ones waiting in a neat pile by the door, she wet a rag to wipe down the table. Once it was clean, she rummaged through the drawers till she found the new tablecloths that were tossed to her at the wedding.

One was white, embroidered with a pattern of tiny white flowers. The other was checkered with blue and red squares. She chose the checkered one, deciding to save the white one for when company visited. When it comes to being a wife, you have to know which tablecloths are for everyday use or special occasions. This was pointed out to Milo by Bob the Conscience, but she ignored him.

She spread the cloth out on the table and smoothed it down. Next, she probed the cupboards, looking for a vase. Not finding one, she chose a squat wooden bowl to use instead. She asked Ajsha to run outside and pick a few flowers. Ajsha obeyed obligingly, and when she returned, a bundle of light pink hibiscus clutched in her fist, she put them in the bowl, which now had a puddle of water at the bottom. Milo set it in the center of the checked cloth, and they stood back to admire.

"Oh," Ajsha sighed. "It looks so nice, Mother."

"Yeah, it does," Milo agreed. "It's funny how a little color can per- . . . Did you just call me 'mother'?"

"Uh, y-yes," Ajsha answered nervously.

"*Why?*"

"Because," she explained cautiously, "when you were signing the marriage certificates you also signed my adoption papers. You are now legally my mother, and I have to call you that."

"Are there any 'law' that says so?" Milo demanded harshly.

"No, not exactly," Ajsha admitted, taking a step or two backwards. "But Father, that is, Simon, wants me to, and I want to."

"Well, *I* don't!" Milo snapped. "My name is Milo, not Mother!

It doesn't matter if you're my daughter. You are going to call me
Milo!"

"But –"

"None of those 'buts'!" Milo warned, storming off to the big
bedroom.

Once safe within its walls, she took several deep breaths, her
pulse thrumming. Mother. A six year old had just called her, a
fourteen year old, Mother. Milo didn't even want to do that math.
A sour taste seeped into her mouth.

"It's okay!" she murmured to herself. "It's not as if she's really my
daughter. Those sneaky . . . urgh! No. No. It's gonna be fine. She'll
just be like a friend that I . . . own."

This reassured her slightly, though it didn't fully take away the
sting of surprise. Something on the bed caught her attention. It was
her radio. Gasping, she snatched it up and examined it thoroughly.
Relieved that it was in perfect condition, she slipped the
headphones on and turned up the volume. Her good mood began
to reemerge as she listened. Soon her head began to bob, slowly at
first, but it wasn't long before she was dancing around the room.

A strange side effect of Milo listening to her radio was that, when
she was, she liked to accomplish things with her hands. Writing in
her diary was one of them, cooking was another, and then there
was doing housework. One of the reasons why her mother wasn't in
as much opposition as she could have been to her daughter's
constant listening, was that she got an enormous amount of chores
done. It was practically an involuntary thing; she would tune in and
before long start sweeping the floor.

Unfortunately, it was the same on the island, where she
happened to get unusually good reception. She began to fluff the
pillows on the bed and straightened the knotted rag rug on the floor.
She barely even noticed what she was doing, too caught up in her
music. She bounced over to the window and shook out the curtains,
hips swaying. If she had remembered that these weren't just

curtains, but Simon's curtains, she undoubtedly would have stopped. But she didn't, and once his bedroom was sufficiently tidied, she danced across the hall to Ajsha's room.

Indeed, Milo's mother came to greatly appreciate that little radio, for it gave her a clean home. Whether it was a house or an apartment, she could leave while the place was in perfect ruin and return to it looking spotless. She would then think to herself, "Milo's been listening to her radio again." This added personal benefit was among the reasons Milo gave to convince her parents to let her listen to hip-hop. Like many people, Milo's parents thought it a vile music to be tangled up in when they hadn't even heard it themselves.

They were worried it might change her. From being a quiet kid to a disrespectful loudmouth; from isolating herself to associating with large groups of corner loiterers; and from cooking and getting good grades to failing classes and cooking something much more illegal. But of course it didn't change her. She was still quiet, she still isolated herself, she kept cooking and getting good grades, only she was happier. Her parents noted this, along with all the cleaning, and caved. Milo won the rap battle.

And on that very day, with a southern beat bumping in her ear, she finished organizing her new child's bedroom and moved on to the bathroom. When it comes to being a wife, one has to keep the house clean. Naturally, the wife isn't the only person who can do it, and in fact it is immensely helpful to wives if there is assistance. But wives still have been targeted with the responsibility for keeping homes orderly. It is a very "wife-ish" thing to do, a thing Milo never wanted to do. After a while, she arrived in the sitting room, where Ajsha was curled up on a chair, a book on her lap. She hadn't really been paying attention to the book, but had been mulling over how she could convince Milo to let her call her Mother. She blinked in surprise when she saw Milo's bopping, twirling form enter and start ruffling pillows and pulling at cushions.

Milo jumped onto the couch near Ajsha, and smoothed the curtains. She then hopped off and tackled the granite table, removing any rubbish that had no right to be there. Ajsha watched, baffled, as she took the rubbish to the kitchen, threw it out, and grabbed the wet rag from the sink. She came back and washed down the flat stone slab.

Ajsha's puzzled look increased as she watched the ridiculous sight of Milo, simultaneously mouthing words, jerking her shoulders around, and cleaning. She thought it was completely absurd, and anyone else who saw it for the first time would have thought so, too.

Nobody had ever actually witnessed Milo cleaning, not even her, or else she'd probably never clean again. Although the scene was strange and just the teeniest bit frightening, Ajsha was pleased to see her so willingly fulfilling wife-related labor that didn't involve the kitchen.

After the sitting room was completed, Milo not even noticing Ajsha, she paraded into the kitchen. Ajsha trailed after her, hoping to speak to her. Avoiding flailing limbs, she tapped her arm. Milo instantly snapped out of her trance and shut the radio off.

"What?" she inquired, bouncing on her toes.

Ajsha beamed at her. "Father is going to be very happy," she replied.

"You mean Simon?" Milo said. She rolled her eyes. "Great! Just what did I do to make the weasel happy?"

"Why!" Ajsha exclaimed, confused. "You cleaned the house!"

Milo ceased moving and stared at her blankly. "What?"

"You cleaned the house," Ajsha repeated.

"I did?"

Ajsha nodded.

"Oh. Oh, no!" Milo moaned, wrenching off her headphones. "Ah, crap! This happens all the time! I really gotta take up knitting or something."

"I'm proud of you, Mother," Ajsha offered.

"Milo!"

"It was a very wife-ish thing to do," Ajsha pointed out approvingly.

"I didn't mean to do it!" Milo objected stubbornly. "It's just something that happens when I listen to my radio and there's nothing else for me to do. I don't want to be a wife. Remember?"

Ajsha's face fell. "Oh," she said dejectedly, "yes. I'm sorry. Sorry for forgetting."

Milo began to feel bad. "Hey," she said gently, "it's okay. Don't worry about it. I forget things too, but it's not my fault, and it's not yours either."

Ajsha brightened. "What type of things have you forgotten?" she asked conversationally.

Milo opened her mouth, but realized that she didn't have anything to say. She tried to recall a situation where she had forgotten something important. None came to mind, and she impressed at just how good her memory was, for she tended to remember nearly everything.

She remembered the night she and her parents came home to find their house burning. She remembered wandering through the remains the next day and seeing that all her precious childhood items had become ashes. She remembered how hurt she felt when they drove away to live at a different house, looking out the back window of their car at all her friends and relations, not knowing that would be the last time she would see them.

She remembered every place they lived after that, and how horrible they all had been. She remembered the prolonged loneliness and longing for a friend. It was around this time that she started to argue with Bob the Conscience.

Milo's reminiscent silence discouraged Ajsha. Sighing, she sat down on one of the kitchen chairs. She sighed again, only louder. Milo looked down at her apologetically. Then something sprang to her mind

"Oh!" she exclaimed. "I know what I forgot! And it was extremely important too!"

"What was it?" Ajsha asked.

"You warned me about Simon's friends, and when the punks were right in front of me I forgot your warning and ticked them off!"

"Yes," Ajsha muttered quietly then, "Yes! You did, didn't you?"

"Yeah!" Milo said happily, smiling. "And then they brutally beat me!"

"Yeah!" Ajsha said, getting to her feet. She was grinning now and while she was grinning she said, "I am so sorry!"

"I know!" Milo said, laughing. They laughed for a few minutes, neither one of them feeling very sorry. Then, as Ajsha glanced out the window, her smile disappeared.

"I am so sorry," she said gravely.

"Oh, really!" Milo said. "It was my fault. I just didn't *remember*."

At the sound of that old word, she broke into a fit of giggles. But Ajsha shook her head and continued to stare out the window.

"No," she said. "I am sorry."

"Hey! Come on –"

"Look," Ajsha cut in, her finger aimed at the window. Milo turned around to look out the square hole in the wall. What she saw didn't please her.

A group from Simon's mafia – I mean friends! – was standing outside, peering in. Milo recognized a few to be the ones who beat her. She frowned and laid her hands on her bony hips.

"*Why,*" she wondered scathingly, "*do people always show up when you talk about them?*"

The small group began to head towards the front door, and one of them motioned at her to follow. Milo followed, but more out of wariness than hospitality.

She breathed steadily for a moment and then opened the door. The boys were waiting on the other side and tried to enter, but Milo blocked their path. Her left hand rested on the door and her right was still on her hip. She gave them all a sharp, disapproving look. When it comes to being a wife, one must know which friends of the husband not to let into the house while he isn't there. These were not the right friends. Mrs. Lanslo perhaps, but these ruffians weren't stepping one foot into the foyer if Simon wasn't present.

Ajsha timidly crept up behind Milo and asked if her service was needed.

"Of course," Milo answered curtly. "You may ask them what they want."

Cautiously, Ajsha spoke to the boy in front. He grunted an answer. "He says that they're here to see Fath- I mean Simon."

"Is that so?" Milo remarked calmly, albeit acidly. "Well, I'm sorry, boys, but Simon is out at the moment. You'll just have to track him down outside or try here again later. Now, goodbye."

She waited until Ajsha finished translating before shutting the door. As it was swinging, a boy stuck out his foot, jamming the process. Milo pushed hard, but the nuisance wouldn't relent, and sneered at her. The other boys laughed, and the boy in front again tried to enter the house. Milo immediately smacked her right hand onto the other side of the doorway, her entire body now an obstacle. She shot him an annoyed look, and, still attempting to remain calm, spoke to Ajsha.

"Will you please tell them to leave?"

Ajsha swallowed hard, but did as she was asked. The boys huffed with laughter, and the boy in front jabbered a reply. Ajsha's brow wrinkled as she told Milo what he said.

"He says that you two got off on the wrong foot, and he wants to come in so that you can get better acquainted."

"Wrong foot, eh?" Milo muttered. "More like wrong fists. All right, tell them that since Simon isn't here, there is no reason for them to come in."

Ajsha sighed and the interpreting began.

"He asks, 'Why not?'"

"Because, Simon is the reason that you're here at all, and he isn't home. Therefore you have no reason to remain."

"He says, 'You're Simon's wife, so we should come in and make friends with you.'"

Milo snorted. "Why? Just what good would that do? Besides, I don't want to be friends with you, not after what you did to me."

"He says, 'I see you haven't forgotten that.'"

"No, I haven't."

"'So, no making friends?'"

"Never."

"'Never? Well, that's fine. I've always heard that American girls have hearts of ice. We'll just wait inside for Simon. Come on, fellas!' Uh, Milo!" Ajsha suddenly shrieked.

At that moment the whole posse tried to intrude through the doorway, surging as one looming mass at the skeletal figure of Milo. Milo, gulping hard, held strong and shouted over the chaos.

"No you won't! You've caused me enough trouble already! And I've just cleaned! As Simon Swallow's wife, I order you to go away!"

After Ajsha's translations got through to each pair of ears, they all stared at Milo, with an expression of being slightly impressed but mostly surprise. The lead boy began to nod, and soon all the boys were nodding too. As they backed away from the door, one of the boys in the back gave Milo a rude sign with his hand. She growled and slammed the door. She gave a small sigh of relief and turned to Ajsha, who was near tears.

"What's wrong?" Milo asked, quickly tossing her radio onto a couch in the sitting room. Ajsha shook her head, shrugged, and turned towards the kitchen. She hadn't taken two steps before she let out another shriek. Milo rushed to her side to see what was wrong and gasped.

A boy from the group had jumped through the window and landed on the kitchen floor. He was a skinny little imp, with dirty-blonde hair, more dirty than blonde. He glanced around the room

with an evil grin on his face. Before Milo could overcome her shock
and order him out, he reached into a cupboard that had been left
open, and pulled out a container of food.

He pulled off the tightly fitted cover to reveal mashed sweet
potato. He used his fingers to scoop out a generous amount and
tauntingly pretended to fling it at the wall.

"Nooo!" Milo screamed.

She sprinted into the kitchen to stop him, but before she could
reach him, he darted to the other side of the table.

The boy was taller than Milo and had long, gawky legs that
looked they could snap at any moment, but that didn't mean they
weren't fast. The other boys crowded both the kitchen windows,
shoving each other aside in order to see. They began to get caught
up in the action, and jeered at Milo. They hurled comments at her
and cheered on the boy as Milo chased him round and round the
kitchen. He continued to pretend to throw the sweet potato, and
finally succeeded in doing it. Milo screeched as she watched the
orange lump sail across the room and splat against a cupboard.
When it comes to being a wife (a housewife in particular), one
knows that mushy food splattered against furniture simply isn't
done.

Milo rigidly turned towards the boy, her teeth gritted and eyes
flaring. All of his comrades outside said, "Ooooooh!" mockingly.
The chase resumed, now more for vengeance than anything else,
and more sweet potato mash ended up splattered against various
surfaces. Milo desperately tried to catch the imp, but he dodged
away each time she got close enough. The boy's taunts slowly
turned into a chant: "Ca-leb! Ca-leb! Ca-leb!" Milo assumed Caleb
was the guy she was chasing.

She turned out to be right, for when the chanting picked up he
paused and shook a fist in the air. As he did this, Milo attacked him
with a head-first tackle. They both fell to the dirt-packed floor, but
before Milo could wrap her hands around his throat, he flung some

sweet potato, plastering her face. She howled in rage while the boy scurried away. He unfortunately now had a new idea: Instead of throwing the mush at the kitchen interior, he would simply throw it at her.

The next handful landed on her shoulder, just as she had scraped it out of her eyes. She jumped up, growling, and had to dodge out of the way of another handful. Caleb began to chase her around the kitchen, lobbing sweet potato at her. Most of the lumpy projectiles missed their mark, flying past her ears, but she did get hit quite a few times. The boys' laughter and snarky Galo comments grew louder with each hit. This spectacle lasted for several minutes, until a voice rang out above the anarchy.

"CALEB!!!"

The voice did not belong to any of the boys outside or to the one inside. Caleb halted unflatteringly in his tracks and looked to the kitchen threshold. Milo, also stopping and panting heavily, followed his gaze and saw Simon standing there, positively furious. All the noise had ceased, and the air was filled with dead silence. Ajsha stood beside Simon, looking very upset and twisting the hem of her skirt.

Simon surveyed the scene, his glaring eyes trailing first over Milo, then Caleb, and finally the silent heads just beyond the windows. He walked up to Milo, grimly observed her orange splattered body, and raked some mush out of her ponytail. She grabbed his wrist, jerking her head towards Caleb. Simon looked at him angrily, his jaw clenched. He stalked up to him and yanked the container out of his hands. Caleb began to jabber resentfully in Galo, undoubtedly trying to explain his side of things. Before he could even complete a sentence, Simon snapped at him, and the rest of the boys began to gibber, backing Caleb up.

Simon shouted at them and clamped a hand on Caleb's shoulder, dragging him to the front door. He unceremoniously threw the piece of straw out. The boys, all yelling in objection, clustered around Caleb, who had landed in a heap of angles on the ground. Simon roared back and went outside to have a well vocalized discussion.

Sighing, Milo turned to Ajsha. Milo was fuming with wrath; she thought steam might be coming out of her ears. But Ajsha's little face, all flushed and trembling, forced her to calm down. She smiled faintly at her and wiped some goop off her arm.

"I never did like sweet potato anyway," Milo said dismissively. Ajsha bowed her head.

"I'm sorry," she said solemnly.

"Why?" Milo asked. She examined the now spotty kitchen with a sense of weariness. "It's not your fault."

She went to a drawer she knew held rags.

"Yes, it is," Ajsha said, hastening to help.

"How's that?" Milo asked, withdrawing a few rags. She handed one to her.

"Earlier when I was outside, getting the flowers," Ajsha began woefully, "those boys came over to me and asked about the visit to the select location. They wanted to know how it went and if you two had fun, and so on. Well, just the memory of how you nearly drowned made me forget who they were, and I gushed out the story. They felt really bad and wanted to apologize to you, but they also mentioned something about you now mellowing down some. By accident, I swear by accident, I told them you hadn't. This obviously didn't make them happy, but I never thought they would come here and cause trouble."

Milo, who had been gently washing a cupboard, now began to scrub it with an undeserved hostility. "And?" she said shortly.

"And, I am so sorry," Ajsha said soberly, wiping off things more her height.

Milo took a moment to grind her teeth and swallow a couple of sharp comments, then sighed and grinned weakly. "You should have remembered," she murmured.

They both shared a smile for a moment, then went right back to cleaning.

Once they were done, the kitchen no longer looking like it had contracted some sort of fungal disease, Ajsha scrutinized Milo's appearance and frowned.

"You're going to need a shower," she told her.

"No kidding," Milo said gloomily. "Who was that boy anyway?"

"You mean the boy who messed up the kitchen?" Ajsha said, a trace of distaste in her voice. "His name is Caleb Scumm. He's a creep who's always trying to impress Simon and his friends. Quite a moron, really. I almost feel sorry for him."

"Sorry?" Milo scoffed. "Why?"

Ajsha snorted. "I said *almost*. But I do feel sorry for anyone who has to live with him."

Milo was a bit taken aback by her remark. Usually Ajsha was a sweet child who had compassion for everyone. But like most people, Ajsha had her exception.

Simon returned suddenly, shouting out the door as he came, rather hoarse by now. He banged the door shut, running his fingers tiredly through his hair. As he stepped into the kitchen, he started in surprise to see it restored in such a short time. Setting the empty container on the table, he listlessly slumped into a chair. He was not having a good day. He gibbered something to Ajsha, who translated it to Milo.

"He said that he is sorry for all the trouble. Caleb can be aggravating at times."

"Is that what you call it?" Milo replied, with a crisp edge to her voice.

After Ajsha interpreted this, Simon stood up. He stared Milo right in the eye and didn't talk for a minute. He seemed to be gathering gumption. Finally he started to gibber, slowly and articulately.

"He says that they told him you gave them a problem, too. They wanted to talk things out with you, but you didn't want to."

"That's right," Milo said frigidly. "I have no use for people like that."

"He says, 'But they're my friends!'"

"*Your* friends," Milo said coolly. When it comes to being a wife, you have to be able to control the argument. "I personally do not want friends who beat the crud out of me."

Simon rolled his light brown eyes and gibbered angrily, clearly fed up.

"'I told you they won't do that again!'"

"Maybe not," Milo said calmly, though her blood was turning from frost to lava. "But that doesn't eliminate the fact that they did. Nothing can change that. I don't care if you trust them, I don't."

"'I assure you, they are trustworthy.'"

Milo scoffed emphatically. "They are *not*!" she hissed. "You saw what that creep did in here."

"'So what? Yes, Caleb is a creep, but the rest you should forgive.'"

His words stung Milo, but they also managed to infuriate her even more.

"Those simpletons," she said in a grating voice, "have not earned my forgiveness, and neither have you."

"'What have I done?!'" he said once Ajsha had translated, not even Galo hiding his exasperation.

"Two things, boi!" Milo answered, seething and flinging up her fingers one at a time. "One, you forced me to marry you, and two, you tried to kill me."

Everything about Simon softened as he heard this, and his response was quiet and contrite.

"He said, 'I'm happy that I married you. I'm well aware that you aren't, but I am. And I didn't *try* to kill you, it was an accident. It should never have happened, but I was acting stupid. I'm sorry. Really I am. I wasn't trying to kill you. I love you, why would I try to kill you?'"

If he was attempting to console her by saying this, then Simon either had a faulty memory, or he just wasn't a quick learner. True, telling most people, dare I say normal people, that you love them is an effective sedative; but not Milo.

She fumed, her veins bulging and her nose making tiny clicking sounds. Her complexion changed from specter-like, to jaundice, to lime, and back again. Perhaps it was from instinct, or maybe fear, but both Ajsha and Simon took a step back. At last, just when they thought she was going to explode and the kitchen would need to be cleaned for a third time, she opened her throat to yell.

"There you go again with that whole 'I love you' crap! Why don't you cut it out?"

Simon, upon hearing this translated, seemed stunned that this was what had outraged her, and gibbered, "'Because I do love you. I don't see why you find that so hard to believe – '"

"You don't love me!" Milo spat. She threw her rag to the floor and stomped on it. Ajsha watched in alarm, thinking that the many tantrums she had seen in the orphanage had looked a lot like this.

"You just think you do!" Milo continued, glowering. "You don't know what love *is*! Therefore, you could never recognize it."

"'Milo,'" Ajsha began for Simon, who apparently thought it was wise to continue to put distance between them.

"No!" Milo cut in fiercely. "Face it, boi! *Face it!* I don't love you! You don't love me! But don't worry, you're not alone. You don't love me, I don't love me, my parents don't love me, even my own conscience doesn't love me! Nobody could love me! What makes you different?"

Simon didn't respond. He was silent. He was confused. Not just about her mentioning her conscience like it was a person, but also about her thinking nobody loved her. Ajsha, the child and yet the smartest person in the house, wasn't confused at all. Though no one knew it, except for her teachers, Ajsha had been pursuing a beginner course in psychology. From the little experience she had, she could figure out many things from Milo's words. But she would confront her about those things later. Maybe. She'd try. . . . Maybe.

Simon, marshaling his bravery, approached the shaking Milo and tried to take up her hand.

"Get away from me!" she shrieked, jerking away. After Simon heard what she said, though her tone had been plenty, he sighed and left the house.

Milo stayed where she was for a moment, growling and sniffling in a rather private way, and then abruptly stormed off down the hall.

"Milo!" Ajsha called after her.

"Bite me!" she shouted back.

She was going to take a long, steamy shower. When it comes to being a wife, you have to know how to take advantage of the time when what annoys you most is gone, and relax.

13
Church

THERE ARE TIMES in life when consciences are right, even if you don't listen to them. Bob the Conscience certainly had his moments, though Milo did not always heed him. I'm sure you can recall several instances. One of the things he had been spot on about was that if Milo carefully rationed the food Mrs. Lanslo gave them it would last for nearly two weeks. Bob the Conscience was correct in his calculations. Well, actually, it was a week and five and a half days, but it was still a great accomplishment for Milo.

That Friday, as she came back from returning the containers, she realized that next week was the last week of August. She sighed and wondered how her parents were doing. It had been nearly two months since she left. Word of the lost plane must have reached them by now. At the very least, they must have noticed that it had been over a month and she was still absent.

Morose, she entered the hut and began to think about the weekend. Ever since she had washed up on the island, she had spent almost every weekend under her bed. Saturday, she didn't want Simon or Ajsha or anyone bothering her about different activities or chores. She wanted to be left alone on Saturday, without needing to explain why. And on Sunday, she hid under the bed in the morning to avoid her husband and child. Simon and Ajsha went to church on Sunday, and Milo didn't want to be seen before they left, for fear they might tell her to accompany them.

They usually would search the house for her until they had to leave or risk being late. Once they were gone, Milo would heave a sigh of relief and crawl out from her hiding place. When the two came home, they would find her fixing lunch, seemingly deaf to any questions regarding her earlier disappearance. Her actions, both odd and mysterious, were steadily disturbing Ajsha and Simon.

They had no clue as to why she was hiding on Saturday, but they shared an idea of why she might be hiding on Sunday. It was an idea that they hated, and despised even considering. It was the notion that she was avoiding going to church; that maybe she hadn't peace with God. Naturally, they were troubled by a concept like that. They decided to find out, and if it was true, they would help her.

Ajsha had suggested that she confront her alone, given that Simon's presence only made her mad, and it was preferable that she be in a good mood for such a talk. Besides, Simon's limited language skills wouldn't allow him to contribute much. As Milo entered the house on that Friday afternoon, Ajsha pounced upon the opportunity.

Milo had so far successfully avoided talking about church or any church related topics. She did not feel comfortable explaining things to them. If the subject of church was brought up any time other than the weekend, she might have to join them on Sunday, because they would be expecting her. She had enough trouble without adding church into the mix.

Just as Milo closed the font door, Ajsha somberly walked up to her, hands behind her back and her mouth grim. "Milo," she said, "I think we should sit down."

Milo laughed wearily and said, "Child, I just carried twenty-zillion containers to town and came back. All I'm going to be doing is sitting."

"Um," Ajsha said, "well, please, let's go into the sitting room. We need to talk."

Milo, slumping onto a couch, laughed and said, "Usually when someone says that, they are about to breakup with someone." She suddenly looked Ajsha seriously in the eyes. "You're not breaking up with me, are you?"

Ajsha, who was sitting next to her on the couch, little legs crossed, shook her head. "No. We need to talk about church," she said.

Milo shot straight up, alert.

"What about it?" she asked, trying to stay composed.

"Why haven't you been going with us?"

"You've never asked me to," she replied truthfully.

"Shouldn't you try to invite yourself?" Ajsha pressed.

Milo stared at her. "What?" she asked.

Ajsha shook her head. "Wouldn't you want to come with us anyway?" she restated.

Milo didn't have any crafty retort for that, therefore she remained silent, pursing her lips and picking at a loose thread in the cushion. Ajsha tried to meet her gaze, but Milo pulled away. Ajsha sighed. This was precisely what she had been afraid of.

"Milo," she began gently, in a tone that implied a long lecture, "I understand that when you are not a follower of God, it can hurt to talk about church. But you must understand what a wondrous journey the walk with God is. Please, be willing to repent and come join our church family."

"Whoa!" Milo said, putting her hand out in front of her. "*Whoa!*" she said again. "What are you getting at, girl? That I'm not a Christian?!"

Ajsha opened her mouth and promptly shut it again. "You are?" she inquired, uncertain.

"Yes, I most certainly am!" Milo cried defensively.

"Oh!" Ajsha said, relieved but slightly disappointed. She'd had a whole speech prepared. "Well, if you are," she continued, "then why don't you come to church with us?"

Milo became shy again. "Because," she mumbled, becoming intensely interested in a spot on the ceiling, "it's on Sunday."

Ajsha's little brow creased. "Yes," she confirmed. "It is on Sunday. But why would that make a difference?"

"I don't know," Milo mumbled, shifting nervously. "It's just that . . . I am uncomfortable about going on Sunday."

Ajsha remained puzzled. "What other day would you go on?" she asked, mystified.

Milo continued to fidget. "Saturday," she muttered.

"Saturday!" Ajsha repeated loudly, as if such a thing sounded barbaric.

Milo nodded. "Yeah. My parents brought me up going to church on Saturday. We're Seventh-day Adventists, or at least I still am, and Saturday's our day."

"Well," Ajsha said optimistically, hastily getting over her shock, "there's nothing wrong with that! Your parents are quite right. Not everybody goes to church on Sunday. And that's okay!"

Milo eyed her in surprise. "Yeah?" she said.

"Yes," Ajsha assured her firmly. "Is that why you've been hiding on the weekends? Saturday because you didn't want to tell us about your church, and Sunday because you don't want to be invited to our church?"

Milo nodded, abashed. Ajsha nodded too, giving her a consoling pat on the elbow. She knew that human contact was essential during moments such as this.

"It's okay," she said. "When was the last time you've actually been to a church? For a service I mean, getting married doesn't count."

Milo thought back. The last time she remembered being in a church for worship was when she lived in the town her family had moved to right after her first house burned down. The towns after that one didn't have churches for people who attended on Saturday. Even though she couldn't go to a church building, Milo still tried to keep that day dedicated to God. Since she couldn't get her hands on a Bible, the first two she owned burnt up and misplaced while packing, she mostly spent her Saturdays lying down, trying to remember Bible verses or hymns. The rest of the time she spent in prayer. She would pray for every single prayer-worthy matter she could think of, and when she ran out of ideas, she would repeat all of them over again.

Staring shamefully down at her feet, she murmured, "It has been a while."

"I see," Ajsha said, the tips of her fingers pressed together. "Not a problem. You'll just go tomorrow."

"Uhhh," Milo said quickly. "I'm not so sure about that."

"Why not?" Ajsha inquired and sighed. "You want to go? You don't want to go? Why don't you make up your mind? This is like when you were trying to make the bed."

"Did you really have to bring that up?" Milo moaned.

The very day Simon's friends came over and made a mockery of Milo's kitchen ethics, Milo had emerged from her shower feeling considerably more relaxed. She changed, and took a look at the bed, all made up and neat after her dancing rampage. As she examined it, she came to the conclusion that by making it, she was showing signs of acceptance. Not to mention, Simon didn't deserve for her to make their bed. These facts revolving in her mind, she had grabbed the blanket, wrenching it this way and that, messing it up. Next, she battered the pillows into a disorderly position.

When she was done, she stood back to admire her work, and a queer feeling stole over her stomach. The sight of a messy bed made her feel bad, especially since she had always made her bed each and every morning and was proud of it. Immediately she decided that the bed didn't have to suffer for Simon's actions, and so she remade it. As soon as she finished, she realized that an unruly bed would send her despised hubby a clear message, and she quickly messed it up again.

Right after she did, she just couldn't stand the sight of it. She never did like disorderliness in any form; therefore, she once again made it. But as soon as she put the last newly fluffed pillow in place, she again changed her mind and destroyed her work. But that didn't suit her either, and the bed was dressed again. Only to be mussed and then apologetically fixed again. This unnecessary time waster continued for several minutes, the sheets becoming increasingly wrinkled. She just couldn't make up her mind.

"Just make it and have done with it!" Bob the Conscience had thundered at her. At first he had found it amusing, but after the millionth making and unmaking he couldn't stand it any longer.

But Milo, too focused to even argue with him, didn't stop until she heard a cough. She whirled around to see Simon and Ajsha standing in the doorway, looking rather concerned. Quite embarrassed, when she realized that they had been watching for some time, she quietly made the bed and left it alone. Except that she did flip the pillow on Simon's side to the floor.

Milo still wasn't over this event, mainly because when Ajsha had asked her what she was doing, she knew her reasoning was pretty stupid. Milo therefore vaguely explained that she simply couldn't make up her mind. She had asked Ajsha not to talk about it ever again. *Ever* again. That of course that didn't happen, for Ajsha had just brought it up.

Milo sat, momentarily subdued and silent, before saying, "Okay, fine, I'll go tomorrow, but I don't see how I'll be able to get into the church alone. Nobody in town is exactly eager to unlock doors for me."

"Who said you'll be alone?" said Ajsha, delighted that she agreed.

"You're not going with me?" Milo said, practically astonished.

"Of course I am," she replied, "and Simon, too."

"No," Milo said coldly. "Not him. Never him. I don't know how reverent I can be if he's nearby. Besides, you guys go on Sunday."

Ajsha shrugged indifferently. "We can go on your day, and then you can go on ours. That's fair."

"No, no, no, no, no, no, no," Milo said in one breath. "You guys may be free to hop around and experiment, but that's your religion. Mine? It's stringent. We believe certain things, and one of them is that Saturday is church day. Not Sunday. That's important. It just is."

"Hmm," Ajsha mused. "I'm going to have to talk to Fath- I mean, Simon, about this, Mother."

"Milo!"

"Right. I'll give you our conclusion tomorrow." With that, she abruptly slid to her feet and headed towards the front door.

"Hey. Where are you going?" Milo called after her.

"Outside," she called back. "Unlike you, I can't stand staying indoors all day."

Milo snapped her teeth, but knew Ajsha had a point. She really should go outside more often. It was a tropical island after all, a perfect place to get rid of her ghostly pale skin. That is, instead of looking like a snowflake, she could look like a ripe strawberry. Milo didn't tan.

Standing up, she walked into the kitchen, a fragrant island breeze blowing in through a window. Every Friday evening she prepared three meals for Simon and Ajsha to eat on Saturday, since she would be in hiding. She didn't like to do any work on Saturday if she could help it, and wasn't really supposed to. She generally would fix something for her to eat while encamped under the bed, but that day she made the Saturday meals large enough for three. She also put together supper, which was nearly done by the time Simon and Ajsha appeared, following their noses.

Milo glanced furtively at Simon as she whispered to Ajsha, "Did you tell him yet?"

"Not yet," she said carelessly. "But I will while we're eating."

"Terrific!" Milo muttered as they all sat down.

There certainly was a lot of Galo chatter as they ate. Ajsha didn't bother to relate any of the conversation, forcing Milo to watch their expressions in order to glean information. It wasn't a very efficient tactic, especially since Simon caught her squinting at his face twice. She didn't actually find out anything till morning, during breakfast.

"We have made the decision to switch over to Saturday," Ajsha announced after several mouthfuls of fruit-paste.

"What!" Milo said, her mouth still full making it sound like, "Wwaht!" She swallowed and gasped, "You're going to switch?"

"Yep," Ajsha said happily, bouncing giddily in her seat.

"Just because of me?"

"Yep."

Milo looked down at her bowl and the pink mound of mashed guava. "I don't feel so good," she said.

"Come, come," Ajsha said impatiently. "What's wrong?"

"I don't want you to switch just for me," Milo explained, making swirls in her paste with her spoon. "If you're going to switch, it must be because you feel like it's the correct thing for you spiritually. When it comes to church, it isn't about other people."

Ajsha smiled broadly at her. "Thank you for your concern, Mother."

"Milo."

"Father and I discussed that as well, and we've both realized Saturday might be the correct day for worship. Though we both love the Lord very much, we've been feeling strangely detached from the services lately. It's probably because we have been going on Sunday. Now that we've switched, we each can continue to build our spiritual relationship."

"Well, alright, if you're sure. What about the rest of the islanders?" Milo asked. "Will they like you two 'switching'?"

"They'll have to!" Ajsha proclaimed, undaunted. "They all can go on Sunday if they want to. There's nothing wrong with that, and there's nothing wrong with Saturday!"

This stern statement apparently ended the discussion, Ajsha now wearing a curious expression of resoluteness and defiance. Milo, suddenly not keen to disturb her, chewed her food as softly as she could. Just then, they saw Simon walk past and exit through the front door. Evidently, he had already eaten.

"Where's he going?" Milo asked.

"To tell his boss he wants Saturdays off instead of Sundays," Ajsha said. "He's supposed to have at least one day off a week, and most boys use it for church. Those who go to church, I mean."

"You're really taking this in full stride, aren't you?" Milo said, impressed.

"Yep!" Ajsha squeaked delightedly, bringing her empty bowl to the marble sink. On her tip-toes, she reached up and was about to pump water when Milo stopped her.

"Not today," she said. "No work today. This is a day of rest. That's why I made the meals yesterday."

"Oh," said the little girl. "Okay, we can go dress then."

"Yeah, about that!" Milo called after her, as she skipped merrily away. "The only clothes I have are jeans and T-shirts!"

"What?"

Milo went after her, meeting her half way down the hall, and repeated her dilemma.

"Oh," Ajsha said, her voice hushed, fully grasping the severity of the situation. "That's it? Really? You're sure you don't have anything nice enough to wear?"

"No," Milo replied sourly. "I wasn't expecting to attend a church while I was in Australia, so I didn't pack anything fancy. Do you have something to wear?"

"Oh, yes! I have two special Sunday dresses . . . which are now my Saturday dresses! Why don't you wear your wedding dress?"

"In your dreams!" Milo replied in a growly tone. "I've already worn that thing in that church once, and I ain't ever going to do it again!"

"Right," Ajsha whispered. She changed course, heading to the bedroom Milo shared with Simon. Milo followed her, sulking.

"Let's see what you have," she said, going over to one of the bureaus made from the strange wood. She opened a drawer to find it empty. She tried the other drawers close to her height and also found them barren.

"You haven't unpacked yet?" she said in surprise.

Milo winced. "No," she answered grudgingly.

"Why not?"

Milo remained silent.

"Oh," Ajsha murmured, suddenly understanding. "You should."

Milo shrugged and pulled her suitcase and backpack out from beneath the bed. She dropped them onto the bed and unzipped them, making a sweeping gesture for Ajsha to examine their contents. Ajsha padded over and picked through the articles in the suitcase. Finding nothing but cargo pants and different colored T-shirts, she knew Milo wasn't lying. She bit her lower lip.

"What's in there?" she said, pointing to the backpack.

"Clothes wise?" Milo replied. "My pajamas. I like to separate my pajamas from the rest of my clothes. They know what they did."

"Hmm," Ajsha said, not catching the joke. She tipped the bag upside down and satin pajamas came spilling out in a shiny, shimmery cascade. They were all two pieces, except one red nightgown, and all were satin with a lovely glossy texture. There were red pajamas and white pajamas, a few black, and one blue.

"Very nice," Ajsha commented, rubbing the fabric between her fingers, as if she were assessing a gold coin.

"Thanks," Milo said. "I mostly just use the pants and wear a T-shirt with them."

"Uh-huh," Ajsha said, having seen Milo dressed like this plenty of times. "But what do you do with the tops?"

"Usually I don't wear them. I never wear nightgowns, but my mother threw that one in there anyway."

Ajsha sifted through the sleep-wear. Satin can be folded quite small, so Milo's backpack had been crammed full. There were two pairs of red, minus the nightgown, one with long sleeves and one with short sleeves. There were three white pairs: two long sleeves, one short sleeve. Four black ones: two long sleeves, two short. And the blue pair had long sleeves that could easily be shortened.

Ajsha contemplated the various choices for a moment, gauging her quarry with a practiced eye, and before long an idea came to her. She tossed Milo the nightgown and the red short-sleeved top.

"Wear that," she said triumphantly.

Milo stared at her, clutching a dangling garment in each hand. "Ajsha," she said, "these are pajamas. I can't wear pajamas to church."

"Trust me. Just put the nightgown on. I'll be back shortly."

She left the room before Milo could protest further. Milo felt clueless and more than a little skeptical, but put the nightgown on anyway. It had a V shaped neckline and fettuccine straps. Feeling ridiculous, she patiently waited for Ajsha to come back. When she did, she was wearing a little white sundress with a straw hat. Milo grinned at her.

"I wish you had worn that to the wedding," she told her.

"I would have," she answered indignantly. "But that silly woman was determined to put me in that other, awful dress. I didn't want to seem rude. But anyway, I see you put the gown on, now just put the shirt on over it."

Milo did so. Though the shirt was a button down, as were all the pajama shirts, it easily slipped over her head. Its collar came around the neck and to the buttons, and lay pressed down. As it shimmied down the gown, it made the appearance of a nice shirt and skirt outfit. Milo looked into the mirror that hung down beside the bed and was quite pleased. Even if it was sleep-wear.

"Oh, Ajsha. This isn't bad! Not bad at all!"

"You look lovely!" Ajsha agreed. "Since you only have sneakers, you can use the sandals that were given to you at the wedding. No one's worn them yet."

"More like thrown to us," Milo muttered as Ajsha ran off to get them.

When Simon returned he found two dressed and lovely females waiting for him. Ajsha had Milo brush her hair and insisted that she wear it down. When Milo had described her "hair in the face problem", Ajsha devised an alternative. She scrounged up a wide ribbon and showed her how to use it as a headband. With her hair out of her face, yet down, and in her gorgeous new pajama outfit, Milo was simply glowing with beauty. Ajsha didn't look that that bad either, present and perky as ever. But Simon only had eyes for Milo and stared in awe.

He came out of his trance only when he caught sight of Milo's threatening glare, and he hurriedly gibbered to Ajsha before disappearing down the hall.

"He's changing," Ajsha explained.

"Ah!" Milo replied, folding her arms. "So, he is coming with us?"

"Yep," Ajsha confirmed lightly, ignoring the hint of scorn in Milo's voice.

When he reappeared, he was wearing a black button-down T-shirt with khaki pants and sneakers (all undoubtedly from the luggage of an unfortunate plane passenger). If it had been any other situation, Milo might have muttered something like "Wow," or "Dang." But, even when caught off guard, she did no such thing.

They started for town, the sun a glowing button in the azure sky, making all the greenery particularly vibrant. A breeze rolled in off the sea, tousling their hair. It would have been a wholly pleasant trip, if Simon hadn't constantly been attempting to mesh his hand with Milo's. Every few yards she had to shake him off or push him away. She didn't want to be too rude, for it was Saturday, but he wasn't being very tolerable. She finally told Ajsha to politely ask him to back off. When they arrived in town, people stopped and stared as they walked up to the church. Finding the doors unlocked, which made sense because there was no lock, they entered.

The church hadn't changed much since Milo had last been there. All the decorations for the wedding had, of course, been removed, but everything else was untouched. The sanctuary was clean and empty, with its great windows letting sunshine pour in, making long rectangular pools of light on the floor and pews. Milo left Simon and Ajsha by the doors and walked slowly into the sanctuary. The first time she had done that, she had felt afraid and hateful, but now she felt at peace and something resembling happy.

She retraced her steps back to Ajsha and Simon. Simon was giving the interior of the church a peculiar look, as if he couldn't quite believe it still existed on a Saturday. When he saw Milo, he gave her a faint smile, as if to say, "See, I'm making an effort, right?" Milo briefly wondered if Ajsha hadn't stretched the truth a bit about how comfortable Simon really was about switching.

"Wanna give me a tour?" she asked Ajsha.

"Um," she said, watching Simon, not having received a smile of acknowledgement, head into the sanctuary, looking downcast.

"All right," she conceded. She gestured to the little room with the blankets and tiny chairs. "That's the nursery. Mothers bring babies and toddlers in there if they get fussy during the sermon."

"Oh," Milo commented, checking inside. She definitely remembered visits to the Mother's Room when she was a youngster. Grinning, she could also remember Quiet Bags, filled with a delightful assortment of coloring books, crayons, and Bible felts.

Ajsha tugged on the back of her shirt, beckoning for her to follow. They went over to the stairs, which went down a few steps then changed directions, veering to the right before straightening out.

At the bottom, underneath a ceiling of laboriously and lovingly hewn planks, there extended a hallway. A total of five doors were set into the walls, and at the end was room with three calvens and a long, high table. Ajsha indicated to two of the doors.

"Men's bathroom, Women's bathroom," she said, pointing to each in turn, then to the other three doors. "Lamb's room, Sheep's room, Ram's room. They are divided by age."

"Yeah?" Milo murmured. She liked the names of the rooms. "The last time I was here, you know, for worship, I think I was about ready to be transferred into the 'Sheep's room'."

"My!" Ajsha exclaimed, Milo quickly turning a snort of laughter into an indiscreet clearing of the throat. She couldn't help it; Ajsha sounded too much like a nineteen forties socialite. "It has been a while since you've gone to church."

"Yeah?" Milo repeated curiously.

"Yes," Ajsha said. "You are fourteen? You should be in the Ram's room. The Lamb's room has ages one through eight, the Sheep's room has ages eight through twelve, and the Ram's room has twelve through seventeen. The adults use the sanctuary as a classroom. We call it the Shepherd's room."

"Cool," Milo said, grinning.

"The room at the end is used to prepare special dinners," Ajsha finished.

"I see," said Milo. They had been traveling down the hall, and now stepped into the church kitchen.

When the two girls had finished exploring the downstairs, they headed back up. They wandered into the sanctuary, where Simon was sitting in a front pew, his head bowed, clearly praying. Milo wanted to spend some time praying as well, but something else was lingering on her mind.

"Do you have any hymns?" she asked Ajsha.

"Of course," she replied, heading for a pew.

"In English?" Milo added. Ajsha stopped at once and frowned.

"I don't know. We might," she said and pointed to a door behind the organ. "That's the clergyman's study. It has some hymns that were on the first ship to maroon here. But they won't do you any good because they're so old and frail. No, let's see . . . Oh! There is also a box of hymns that we found on Mrs. Lanslo's plane. They will probably suit you better. We don't use them since they are all in English. See if you can find them."

"Thanks," Milo said happily, starting up the aisle.

As she passed Simon, his legs sticking out on the floor, she did a very disrespectful thing and kicked one of his feet. That alone isn't a testament of good manners, but it should never be done to a praying person. Simon gave a start, but didn't break his concentration. Milo realized her mistake afterwards and actually felt sorry. She decided to apologize to him later; after all, it was God's house, a place to let go of any ill spirits or temper.

Passing the hollow-reed organ, she opened the door to the clergyman's study. From there she had no trouble locating the crate with the hymns, tucked away in the corner of a shelf, propping up a line of heavily bound books. Carefully extracting the crate without knocking over any of the books, Milo dropped it on a neatly arranged desk. Having pried off the top and fished out a hymnal, she retreated to a back row in the sanctuary. Reverently flipping through the pages, she found a few of her long-forgotten favorites. Softly, she began singing. As she sang, Milo couldn't help to look about the church. Ajsha had joined Simon in the front, neither of them visibly concerned with her whereabouts.

Guessing she wouldn't be disturbed for a while, Milo let her eyes rove along the many pews and then up to the pulpit. She remembered standing up there, on her wretched wedding day. Details threatened to overwhelm her, and she vigorously shook her head, trying to clear it. She knew what was coming, and was far from enthusiastic. Memories began to flow like a river, and as much as she tried to prevent it, her entire life up until then unfolded in her mind.

As she started a new song, she could see her burnt house, its timbers charred and collapsed. She saw all the friends and relations she left behind, never to meet with again, their faces sad but hopeful, ignorant of the future. Each terrible place she ever lived in blossomed in her mind, along with every brutal beating she had ever endured. The loneliness that had clung to her for years bit and scratched at her now, and all the tears she fought back day after day clawed at the edges of her eyelids.

She gulped, coming to the present and all of her recent injustices. Milo didn't know how much more she could suffer before she snapped. Even if she managed to get off this isle undoubtedly more horrible things would follow her. It seemed, at least according to the evidence, that she was destined to live an anguished life, though she had no idea why. Every single memory remained vivid in her mind, tormenting her. Why? Why her? What had she done to deserve this?

Milo's mouth wobbled and her voice quavered as she past the pulpit at the far wall of the church. It was adorned with an enormous piece of drift wood, which an artist had chiseled to resemble Jesus dying on the cross. Hot tears burned Milo's eyes, her throat tightening.

"*Why have You let this happen to me?*" she thought at the image. "*Can't You see that I'm suffering? I know it's barely anything, compared to droughts and tyrants and stuff, but if You see every sparrow that falls, why can't You see me?*"

She didn't know if it was a prayer or an accusation. Looking down at the hymnal, she flicked a few random pages. Her eyes fell upon a song called "Does Jesus Care?"

She gasped, instinctively checking over both shoulders and up at the slanted ceiling. Slowly, not quite certain of the melody, she began to sing it. It described exactly how she felt, saying that of course He cares. That she needn't ever wonder, He knew all and saw all. It told her exactly what she needed to hear. Tears clouded her eyes, and silently she prayed for forgiveness for doubting. Sniffling, she smiled and sang the song again. It made her feel good, starting on the inside and spreading outward.

She turned to another song and sang it joyfully, yet she still kept her voice low, so as not to alert Ajsha and Simon. Once through with that song, she skimmed back over her life, realizing how minor it all was compared to other issues of mankind. All the suffering and atrocities in the world, and she had the nerve to complain about a few bullies and an early marriage.

Sighing, she decided to keep her mouth shut and just deal with her "horrible life". She felt ashamed about claiming God had forgotten her, when He hadn't. Everything He had to look over and He still cared about her odd but livable life. Milo felt incredibly selfish for thinking in such a way, but she was still comforted by that fact. "His heart is touched by my grief," as the chorus of the song went.

Grinning, her heart elevated, she flipped to a song of praise and let her voice gush out full and strong, if not a little off key. Both Simon and Ajsha jumped, their heads whipping around, quite startled. Apologizing to Ajsha, Milo dropped her voice, even though her soul was filled with sunshine.

After a while, she grew tired of singing and walked to the front of the pews, where Simon and Ajsha were having a hushed Galo conversation. She sat down beside Ajsha, who looked up at her.

"How are you doing?" Ajsha inquired.

"Very well," Milo replied, then added, "you adorable kind child!"

Ajsha's eyebrows rose in surprise, but then she blushed modestly. Simon softly gibbered something to her, making her go from mildly pleased, to shocked. She gaped reprovingly at Milo.

"You kicked him?!" she said.

"Oh," Milo said contritely. "Yeah, tell him I'm sorry about that. Truly sorry. Very truly sorry."

This satisfied Ajsha, mostly because Milo never apologized for anything involving Simon, so therefore she must have meant it. As she relayed Milo's words, Simon look of discontent melted away and he leaned forward to look at Milo.

"Tattle Tale!" she mouthed to him.

They spent the next hour either praying or reading passages from Simon's Galo translation of the Bible. Though she had apologized and did want to be polite, Milo avoided conversing with Simon as much as possible.

"That will send him a clear message," she thought, returning to her previous train of reasoning.

"Of course it will," Bob the Conscience groaned.

At eleven thirty, they got a visit from an unexpected guest. The pastor of the church entered the sanctuary to find the three of them hunched over the Bible, Simon reading and Ajsha interpreting for Milo. The pastor stared in astonishment for a moment, not comprehending why two teenagers and a little kid were here alone. Drawing closer, he noisily cleared his throat. The Swallows all jumped in surprise, their heads twisting around to see who it was. Simon was the first to recover and stood up to greet him. As they shook hands, the pastor spoke, stuttering slightly.

"What're they saying?" Milo whispered to Ajsha.

"He says several villagers told him that we went into the church," she whispered back. "So he has come to see if it was true. He now wants to know why we've come on Saturday."

Simon began to explain their situation.

"He is explaining our situation," said Ajsha.

The pastor and Simon had a very lengthy conversation, most of which Ajsha refused to reveal, forcing Milo to believe it was about her. By the time they were done, the pastor's attitude had improved a good deal. He cheerfully said goodbye, then left.

"He said that we're welcome to come here every Saturday," Ajsha said excitedly.

"Awesome!" Milo said. "He doesn't care that you two switched?"

"Um," Ajsha paused. "I wouldn't say he doesn't care. Let's just go with he doesn't mind."

"Gotcha," Milo muttered, checking her watch. "Why don't we leave? We've been here since nine thirty."

She nosed around the pews and window sills before finding a secret nook behind the organ to stash the hymnal. Overall, she thought things had gone nicely. As they walked back through town, receiving only a scant amount of looks from villagers, those who seemed convinced that they committed some sort of vandalism in the church, a couple of Simon's buddies ran up to him. They both gibbered and gestured wildly, Simon's jaw dropping.

"Their saying that they've trapped a hammerhead shark by the cliffs, and they want him to come and help," Ajsha told Milo.

Milo looked at Simon and saw a spark of excitement flicker in his eyes. But it vanished and he shook his head, turning down the offer. The boys erupted in protest, and Simon had to yell to be heard.

"He's saying that it's because he wants to be as respectful to your day as Sunday," Ajsha translated. Milo shrugged.

"I don't care what he does," she replied stiffly.

They continued through town with the boys trailing after them, calling beseechingly to Simon. After he dismissed them for the fifth time, they gave up and ran off. Milo wasn't sure whether or not Simon was disappointed, but he didn't try to hold her hand the entire journey. He barely even looked at her, preferring to gaze off into the trees. Once home, they changed their clothes and ate the lunch Milo had prepared the day before.

"What now?" Ajsha asked, as they sat in the sitting room. Simon hadn't said much while they ate, and was now staring at the giant stone coffee table. When Ajsha repeated her question in Galo, he merely shrugged. Milo mulled the question over for a moment, trying to recall what her family had done on Saturday afternoons.

"We could go for a walk," she suggested.

"Okay," Ajsha agreed, interpreting the idea for Simon. He didn't respond for a second, his unwavering attention on the granite chunk in front of him. Milo had to admit, taking a walk sounded exceptionally lame compared to herding a shark. Ajsha leaned in close to him, softly repeating the suggestion. This time he nodded.

Simon led them to a pretty, well-trodden path by the beach. The stroll was quiet, none of them feeling very talkative. Simon stopped at a patch of blue sea holly and plucked two of the big flowers. He handed one to each of his ladies. Ajsha giggled and thanked him, but Milo simply stared at hers. It was nearly too big for her to hold, but she felt too guilty to tear it up.

They kept walking, Milo frequently gazing off at the sea, her thoughts rambling away from her. Simon eventually picked up Ajsha, carrying her loosely in his arms. Ajsha laid her head on his shoulder, her lovely eyes fixed intently upon his face. Milo couldn't stand to look at them, all happy and loving. When they came home, Milo crammed the flowers into the squat bowl she used as a vase, and they ended the day with a late supper.

When it came time for bed, Milo took a moment to confront her suitcase and backpack. They both lay on the bed, plump and tinged white from ocean water. She sighed, not ready to admit defeat, but then shut her mouth and dealt with it. When Ajsha came in to kiss her good night, she noticed an empty suitcase in a corner of the room. It was partially unzipped and crumpled, as if it had been flung there. She turned to Milo, who was sitting, slumped, on the edge of the bed.

"I unpacked," she said glumly.

14

The Art of Clothes Washing and Wood Chopping

"Good morning, Mother!"

"Miiiloo!" Milo replied in a pleasant yet annoyed tone.

"Right," Ajsha muttered. She climbed onto a kitchen chair. Milo was by the counter, starting breakfast.

"Has Father gone to work?" asked Ajsha.

"Yes, Simon left for his job," Milo answered somewhat testily. Hearing Simon being referred to as "Father" always put a bad taste in her mouth.

It was the first of September, a day that was about to become very important for Milo. It started out at breakfast. As they sat at the table, munching on nuts and banana slices, Ajsha made an announcement.

"Yesterday I accidentally stepped in clay and smudged my skirt," she told Milo.

Milo stared blankly at her.

"How unfortunate," she offered, not sure if Ajsha was confessing or wanted sympathy.

"Yes, it is," Ajsha acknowledged lightly. "The reason I brought it up was so I could show you the plant that takes out all sorts of stains, including clay. You can use it when you do the laundry."

Milo, about to eat a cashew, paused with her hand in midair and cocked an eyebrow at her.

"Come again," she said.

Ajsha swallowed her mouthful of breakfast and repeated, "You can use it when you do the laundry."

Milo blinked several times before speaking. "Laundry?" she repeated.

"Yes," Ajsha said, torn between giggling and frowning. "You know, washing clothes? Putting them out to dry? Any of that sound familiar?"

"Laundry?" was all Milo could utter.

"You haven't washed any clothes yet!" Ajsha cried, clearly shocked.

Milo shook her head.

"Why not?"

Milo shrugged. "It never came to mind," she answered innocently.

"Well," Ajsha said, "why don't you start today?"

"All right," Milo agreed. "After all, my clothes supply is dwindling. And getting smelly."

"Mine too," Ajsha said, which wasn't entirely true. Simon, in an effort not to rile his wife, had been washing his and Ajsha's clothes all summer. He would have done Milo's as well, but after her reaction to him taking her radio, he didn't dare touch any more of her belongings. Ajsha, without really taking the time to consider it, had assumed that it was Milo doing the laundry. She now realized that this was hardly logical.

"Do you know anything about clothes washing?" she asked her.

"Everything about doing it in a machine," Milo said tartly, thinking longingly of the mainland where all the electricity resided. The glamor of going to bed with the sun was wearing thin on her.

"I'm a cook, not a washer woman."

"I understand," Ajsha assured her gravely.

"But I'm willing to learn," Milo said brightly.

"Great!" Ajsha said, but then thought of a kink in the plan. "What about not doing wife-ish things?"

"Oh, yeah," Milo said, and took a minute to contemplate this ever present issue. "Hmm . . . I don't want us to get sick because of dirty clothes, not to mention I'm rather fond of clean clothes, so . . . why don't I just wash them with a bad attitude whenever Simon is around?"

"Uh," Ajsha mumbled skeptically. "Okay. But couldn't you just —"

"No," Milo interrupted curtly. "I could not."

For a second, Ajsha looked poised to argue, but then seemed to think better of it.

"All right!" she said, putting on a cheerful face. "Very good. We will begin after breakfast."

Once their bellies were full and the dishes stored, the lesson commenced.

First, you had to dress appropriately. Ajsha explained to Milo that when washing clothes you want to wear the oldest, grungiest apparel you have. Since most of Milo's clothes were new, it fell to which ones she disliked the most. A blue T-shirt and pair of jeans that were overly baggy became her designated washing uniform. Ajsha went on to tell her that when clothes washing one must be barefoot at all times. Milo obediently ditched her shoes and socks, which she was glad to be rid of, for they were corroded by sand and no longer comfortable. Then Ajsha told her to put her hair in braids. Ajsha had already woven her highlight streaked hair into two long plaits. Milo followed in suit, noticing with a stab of envy how flat and dull her own hair was.

Next she followed Ajsha outside and together they trooped to the back of the house. Hidden by the hut and squatting by the forest was a shed, rather small, but sturdily built. Ajsha strode with purpose up to its door, opening it to reveal the interior of the shed. The three walls were pierced helter-skelter with nails, driven only halfway into the wood to act as holders for different objects. The west wall held all sorts of hammers, from sledge to normal. The north wall had knives and machetes. The east housed axes and hatchets. There were other items suspended on the walls, but I am not going to bother describing them to you right now. All I will say is, some were used for gardening and some were used for digging.

But for the girls the most important thing in the shed was lying in the middle of its floor. It was a wide wooden tub only about a foot tall, a scrub brush resting forlornly on its bottom. Ajsha tried to heave it out by one of its handles and beckoned for Milo to help her. Once they had carried it to the front of the house, Milo asked where she could find some buckets.

"What for?" Ajsha asked.

"To pump water into, so I can fill the tub."

"Oh, you won't have to pump any water. There's a spring in that," (she pointed across the clearing) "section of the forest. It has a little waterfall, and you put the tub underneath it until you have enough water. It's much, much faster than the pump."

Milo squinted into the trees, as if she could see it from where she stood. "Do all the women go there for water to wash clothes?"

"All women who live around here," Ajsha replied. "The women who live in town have one that's closer. The people who live on the farms have one of their own. It would take forever if everyone had to travel to one place on the island to wash clothes. Everything works better if people have their own spring."

"I'm surprised Simon has all this equipment," remarked Milo, giving the tub a gentle kick. "When a boy moves into his own house, is he required to stockpile all the major work items that wives need?"

"No," Ajsha said evasively, hearing the resentment in her voice.

"He usually gets them out of pure common sense. How else would he get his clothes clean? He can't ask his mother to do it."

"The boys clean their own clothes?" Milo said, suppressing laughter.

"Of course," replied Ajsha, as if this was the most absurd question in the world. "Until they get a wife, they have to do everything themselves. It sort of humbles them."

"Interesting," Milo muttered, not actually ever having noticed whether or not Simon was humble. "Why don't you show me to the spring?" she suggested, lifting the washtub, which was oddly light for its size. Milo figured the wood was hollow.

Ajsha led her through the forest, following a lightly worn pathway, until they reached a grove with an ample dip in the ground. The dip was brimming with crystal clear water, which was trickling over the sides and into the jungle, heading towards the sea. Next to the tiny pond was a wall of earth, from which a flow of water burbled out and fell with a melodic tinkling sound. Rocks had been strategically built up around the spring to keep any dirt from falling in, or eroding during harsh storm.

"There you go," Ajsha said grandly. She showed Milo two broad slabs of stone, one on each side of the waterfall, where the women stood to get water. Milo stepped onto one, positioning herself as closely to the spring as possible without toppling in, and held the tub up under the stream of sparkling liquid.

Once it had enough to do the job, Ajsha told her to just follow the trail back, and abruptly ran ahead and out of sight.

"Darling child," Milo said through clenched teeth, lugging the heavy tub back to the clearing all by her lonesome.

She didn't have much trouble wending her way back, although she quickly learned not to jostle the tub. When she arrived, only partly drenched, she found her adoptive daughter sitting on a stump, waiting for her.

"Good job!" Ajsha called when she saw her.

"Thank you, precious," Milo mumbled. She dragged her burden as far as the middle of the clearing, relinquished her grip, and declared that was where she wanted to work.

"Good!" Ajsha praised, hopping to her feet. "Now come with me."

Reluctantly, Milo followed her into the house, where she made a beeline for the kitchen.

"Now, where would he put it?" Ajsha muttered to herself as she poked around the counter drawers and cupboards.

"And you are looking for . . . ?" asked Milo.

"Soap," said Ajsha shortly, pulling over a chair so she could reach the higher cupboards.

"What does it look like?" Milo inquired, joining the search.

"Like . . . like a gray cake."

"You mean this?" Milo said, removing a tacky lump from a drawer. Several chunks had been sliced off.

"That's it!" Ajsha confirmed. She handed her a knife. "Now cut off a corner."

Milo scrutinized the soap cake. It had been mutilated to the point that it now resembled an octagon. She chose a handsome corner, or at least what she supposed was a corner, and hacked it off.

"Is this all we need?" she asked in amazement, jiggling the soap fragment on her palm.

"That's all."

Milo put the cake and knife away, and then wanted to know what to do with the bit of soap.

"Go drop it in the wash tub, then come back to collect clothes," Ajsha instructed.

Milo obeyed, ambling outside and letting the shard plop into the water with a muted splash, and then returned to gather garments.

"Even Simon's?" Milo asked disgustedly, using her fingernails to pick up pair of swimming trunks.

"Yes," Ajsha replied, grinning. She went rummaging about in

each room, until she found what she was looking for beneath her own bed. "Must have put it there and forgot about it," she muttered, withdrawing a large basket crafted out of palm bark.

"Put the clothes in here," she told Milo, holding it up for her.

"Thanks," Milo said, dumping in her load.

Once she had amassed all the clothes deemed filthy enough to wash (which included her entire wardrobe), she and Ajsha went out to the washtub. The soap she had put in earlier had turned into a frothy lather. Milo plunged a hand into the foam and pulled out the dripping scrub brush.

"I'll be right back," Ajsha announced. "I'm going to find certain plants that can help with clothes washing. Once I show them to you, you should be able to find them on your own."

"Okay," Milo said complacently, determinedly not letting herself reminisce about the ease of a front load washing machine.

As Ajsha wandered off, her sight trained on the ground, Milo tipped the clothes into the tub. They floated in a multicolored heap for a second, before becoming saturated and sinking with a noise that resembled a burp. Milo knelt down, flipped both braids over her shoulders, and pulled out the first garment. It was the shirt she had worn the day Simon's friends had visited, which they hadn't done since. Faded splotches of sweet potato were still visible on the fabric. Grimly, not enjoying the memories, Milo wielded the scrub brush. It had two sides, one covered with bristles, and the other ribbed like a washboard. After several attempts in different positions, she found she could wash properly if she pinned the shirt up against the sides of the tub while rubbing it with the brush. Once she had scoured long enough to feel satisfied, she tossed the soaking wet shirt back into the basket.

"WHAT – ARE – YOU – DOING?!!" screamed a high, young voice.

Milo, lifting her head in alarm, saw Ajsha standing at the edge of the clearing, a look of trauma on her face and a spray of green in her hand. Milo wasn't sure what she did wrong, and froze in the fear she would do it again.

"What's the matter?" she called out.

"What's the matter?!!" Ajsha repeated indignantly, hurrying over to her. "You just threw something wet into the basket!"

"Yeah," Milo said coolly, relaxing. "I didn't know it was a crime."

Ajsha looked ready to explode again, but then drew a deep breath and composed herself.

"Mother –"

"Milo!"

"– you can't just throw a soaking wet shirt, or any other type of clothing, into a basket –"

"Why not?" Milo cut in bluntly.

"That's not the way it's done."

"Why can't it be?" Milo asked crossly.

"You take it so carelessly," Ajsha exclaimed, shaking her head, her pigtails whipping about her shoulders. "You have to understand, clothes washing is an art."

"Since when?" Milo demanded.

"Anything can be an art if you sincerely care about it and create a system for doing it," she said significantly. "You said you wanted to learn, right?"

Milo sighed. "Right."

"So first you must let me show you how to do it properly."

"Fine," Milo mumbled, flinging the shirt back into the tub with a loud slapping sound. "Let the art lesson begin."

"It already has," Ajsha said, kneeling down beside her. She opened her fist. "Now take a look at these plants. Before you start, you have to make sure you have all the plants you need. See this one?"

She held up a spiny, green herb with broad leaves. All the plants still had their roots attached, and the ones that had broad leaves had spiny stems. And the ones that had broad stems had spiny leaves.

"This plant," Ajsha continued, "is used to preserve color. The soap we are using is very strong. Some say, if you wash yourself with it, it could take off a layer of skin."

"Crap!" Milo said, thinking about how her hands had just been submerged in it. "What's it made of?"

"Many things," Ajsha replied, poking at the lather. "Mostly lard."

"First time I've heard that one," Milo muttered to herself, eyeing the floating icebergs of foam with distrust. "Where does the lard come from?"

"Boars. Anyway, the reason for this plant," Ajsha said, resuming her lecture. "When you tear the leaves off and mix them with the water, it helps the clothes keep their color. This plant is plentiful around here, but not so much by the farms. That's why the farmers' clothes always look faded."

Milo accepted the plant from her and ripped off its leaves. Liquid came spilling out from the inner flesh, and she quickly dropped them into the water.

"This one helps the clothes stay soft," Ajsha said, showing her a spiny leafed, broad stemmed plant. That also went in, torn up, its fluid spreading.

"And this one's for a bit of scent," Ajsha finished, giving the leaves an appreciative sniff.

After these plants had been added, she showed Milo the last two. She explained that if you tore off the leaves or stem, depending, and rubbed it on a stain, the stain would wash out. She wrapped up by explaining which plant went to which stain, and Milo was allowed to continue. A few minutes later, Ajsha, not able to help herself, demonstrated a few scrubbing techniques. Once Milo had finally successfully washed an article of clothing, Ajsha told her how to proceed.

"You don't just toss it in the basket all wet," she explained. "First you wring the water out. No, not like that. Watch."

Her little hands grasped the sodden fabric and began to twist. As she did this, water seeped out at an enormous rate. She twisted it until it was a near perfect rope, then she tightly wound the rope into a ball. Unable to squeeze any harder, she let it unwind, now water-free, and pitched it into the laundry basket.

"All right," Milo said, and tried to mimic her as accurately as possible. "How's that?" she asked thickly, holding up her wad of coiled shirt.

"Very good," Ajsha decided with a nod.

This art kept them occupied in a pleasant, sociable fashion right up until Simon came home from work and spotted them. Then things turned ugly, or should I say, very moist. Seeing him walk over, Milo turned on her rotten attitude. She put on a hard, angry face and began to thrash at the water as she finished the last two pieces of clothing. Simon came to a stop a couple of feet away, observed how she was working, and spoke to Ajsha.

"He says that he is glad you are doing the laundry."

"Oh, does he?" Milo said, artfully exasperated. "Well, tell him that I'm not enjoying it!"

Ajsha forced herself not to grin and relayed this to Simon. He answered with,

"'I can see that. You might like it more if you took pride in how you do it.'"

Milo began to scrub the last garment with aggravated vigor. "I always take pride in whatever I do!" she snarled, not looking at him. "The mere fact that you're also benefiting from it is what sickens me!"

She flung the last garment, thoroughly and aggressively wrung dry, onto the mound protruding from the basket, just as Ajsha came back with Simon's reply, which she seemed reluctant to say. "'Come on! It never hurt anyone to get their hands in a little soapy water.'"

Milo, now standing, picked up the tub and, very angrily, snapped, "You want soapy water?! Here's soapy water!"

With that, she hurled the dirty laundry water at him.

He yelped, completely drenched and a shade darker. Ajsha fell back in gales of laughter. Simon, spluttering and spitting, narrowed his eyes at Milo. She shot him a look of triumph, one hand on her hip. He began to tramp off in the direction of the house, leaving a wet trail in his wake. Milo called after him, "Don't drip all over! You drip!"

Ajsha caught her breath from laughing, and Milo asked her what the next step was in the art of washing clothes.

"Drying," she answered through leftover giggles.

She led the way to the front door, Milo carrying the basket by perching it on one hip. By the door fame, a wooden peg jutted out of a slat. Hanging on the peg was a long rope that was knotted at both ends, with excess rope on the other side of the knots for tying. The middle of the rope had been unraveled, but remained held together by the knots. Ajsha took it off the peg with some effort, hoisted it onto her shoulder, and ordered Milo to follow her.

"All right," Milo grumbled, "but you'd better not run off!"

They didn't travel very far, only to a couple of trees. Ajsha gave the rope to Milo and told her to tie one end to a tree. She did so, and Ajsha then pointed to the other tree. Milo walked over to secure the other end, unwinding the rope as she went.

"Make sure the rope it is very tight when you tie it!" Ajsha instructed. "Tight enough for someone to walk across it!"

Milo obeyed, wiping sweat out of her eyes. The rope now suspended in the air and taunt, she slapped a hand across it to test. It made a quiet brioioinggg sound. Pleased with what she heard, Ajsha commenced showing her how to hang the clothes. The method was rather simple, yet quite clever.

Extracting a garment from the pile, she stretched up on her toes and pushed a bit of it through the slit in the rope. She adjusted it so that it was straight and let some of the material hang over one side of the rope. Milo caught on immediately, and soon the entire load was fluttering gently in the breeze.

Surveying her accomplishment, arms folded, Milo licked her teeth in satisfaction.

"Not bad for the first time," Ajsha concluded, also folding her arms. "You're a fast learner and, I must say, a hard worker."

"Thanks, child," Milo said, gratefully accepting the complement.

"Once they are dry all you need to do is fold and put them away. I can help you with that."

"You've been helping me with all of it."

"Yes, but only to teach you how. Children aren't supposed to help wash clothes."

"Not privileged enough?" Milo muttered sardonically.

Ajsha pretended she hadn't heard her. "But we can help with the rest. Now that you've done laundry once, you can do it by yourself from now on."

"Well, only if you really trust me. Why don't we go inside? The sun's high. I've got to prepare the weasel's lunch."

They started towards the house, and Ajsha silently slipped her hand into Milo's. This didn't surprise as much as frighten Milo; she wasn't sure how comfortable she was with such a motherly action. Still only a friend to children, she pulled her hand away. Ajsha turned away from her, worried she had done something wrong.

Then her training kicked in and she was able to deduce a bit about Milo's feelings. She didn't pull away immediately; if she had, then she would be classified as a cold person. But she had to think about pulling away, classifying her as a person uncomfortable with getting too close to people, for fear of becoming vulnerable.

"Ah-ha!" Ajsha said aloud as she mused.

"'Ah-ha' what?" Milo asked.

"Nothing," Ajsha murmured, it dawning on her how much work Milo was going to be.

"Sure," Milo said, unconvinced. "No offense, girl, but you're kinda strange."

Entering their abode, they found Simon, his hair lank as though he just showered, talking to one of his buddies. The boy, not a member of beach gang, had come over to give Simon a sack of mussels, which had been propped up against the kitchen table, and they were now inspecting the house. They took turns gesturing to certain things and discussing them. Milo and Ajsha had slipped in unnoticed, and Milo asked what they were currently talking about. Simon had nodded at the woodpile and was gibbering conversationally.

"He is saying that he needs to chop more wood," Ajsha said in a bored tone. "Why do you like eavesdropping so much?"

"I get information," Milo said slyly. "Ajsha, don't wives have to chop wood?"

"No," she said absently. "That's something the husbands do. Why?"

"Is there a law that states only the husbands can chop wood?" Milo pressed.

"No, it's just something that the husbands do. Why?"

"So, wives can do it without being arrested?"

"Yes, but it's really the husband's responsibility. Why?!"

"Would it be a shocking thing for a wife to do?"

"I suppose so. It would be a rather rebellious thing to do, since it's never done. So, yes, it would be shocking. Why??"

Milo didn't answer any of the why?'s, but spun around and headed out the door.

"Where are you going? What about lunch?!" Ajsha shouted after her.

"Skip it!" Milo called back. "Let the leech starve! Come with me, I need you for something."

Completely mystified, Ajsha obediently followed. They trekked around the hut, back to the shed. This was partly because Milo needed to return the tub, and partly because of the scheme she was incubating in her head. Opening the shed door, she let the tub fall in with a crash, and pointed to the wall sporting the axes and hatchets.

"Ajsha," she said resolutely, "I want you to show me the art of wood chopping!"

The little girl stared at her in disbelief. "What?!" she managed to choke out. "Why do you want to chop wood?"

"To send Mr. Simon a clear message," Bob the Conscience remarked, quite possibly with a smirk.

"Shut up, Bob!" Milo retorted, unfortunately not in her head.

"Who's Bob?" Ajsha asked curiously.

"Never you mind," Milo said hurriedly, berating herself. "Just show me how to chop wood."

"But *why?*" Ajsha asked again. "Does this have anything to do with Simon?"

Milo's face twitched. "Maybe," she squeaked. "Please, Ajsha, show me the art of wood chopping."

"Chopping wood isn't an art!" Ajsha said contemptuously.

"You said that anything can be an art," Milo countered. Ajsha smashed her lips together, regretting her own words. Milo stared her down until finally she relented.

"Where do we start?" Ajsha breathed, her vision roving across the ax wall. She personally hadn't actually ever chopped anything, but she had seen it done many times.

Choosing carefully, she stepped over to the wall and unhooked an ax. She groaned and swayed outside, where the weight of the ax knocked her over, trapping her on the ground.

"Help!" she squealed, thrashing her legs. Milo hastily reached down and yanked the ax off of her. As she scrambled to her feet, Milo dropped the ax and attempted to pick it up again.

"Oh!" she groaned. "Crap! This thing's heavy!"

By calling upon her vicious emergency-strength, Milo was able to keep the ax aloft without being flattened by it.

"Where's the wood?!" Milo said bravely, her arms quivering.

"This way," Ajsha replied nervously, motioning to a copse of short, slender trees several feet away from the tool shed. A few were already felled, a small stack of logs heaped neatly to one side.

They marched over, or at least Milo did. Any other walk besides staggering was impossible. She approached a tree that was lying on the ground. It was the perfect size for the calven, as long as Milo chopped it the appropriate length.

"Okay," Milo wheezed, starting to feel lightheaded. "What do I do?"

Ajsha's mind raced through all of the wood chopping scenes she had witnessed. Remembering how the choppers handled the ax, she instructed Milo.

"Put your right – or left. Which are you?"

"Right," Milo rasped.

"Put your right hand near the ax head. But not so close! Good, now your left hand should be just a little farther back from the middle."

"How's this?" Milo asked, rearranging her hands the best she could.

"Um," Ajsha said, and shifted Milo's left hand backwards. "There. Make sure you are in a good position over the wood. Keep yourself balanced. Good, now as you bring the ax down, move your right hand back towards your left."

Milo teetered for a moment, thinking about how the action should play out. Once she felt she knew what she was supposed to do, she carefully lifted the ax over her shoulder and brought it down, sliding her right hand back as she did. It was a nice swing, but she missed the wood.

"Dang it!" she hissed. She tried doing it again, only to encounter more failure.

Ajsha took a couple of paces backwards as the blows became more violent. Milo paused for a moment, panting heavily. She deliberated for a second and came to the conclusion that her right hand was supposed to aim the ax. That in mind, she once again attempted to chop. This time the ax finally came in contact with the wood. The blow was so strong, and so full of frustration, that the sharp edge went right through, making a clean cut. It was a pretty thin tree, therefore Ajsha wasn't very surprised, but Milo was ecstatic.

"Yeah!!" she howled when it happened. "Oh, yeah! Yeah! I showed that wood! Showed that wood! Didn't I?"

"Oh, yes!" Ajsha said encouragingly, hoping perhaps just one would be enough. "You certainly did!"

"Yeah," Milo agreed, grinning. "That wood knows better than to mess with me! That's right, wood! No one messes with Milo Hestler!"

"*Swallow!*" Ajsha coughed.

But Milo didn't hear. She was now busily hacking the rest of the tree into little pieces. She was thoroughly excited and swinging away at a dangerous rate. More clean chops came and some that had to have repeated strokes to break through. But she didn't care. She was having fun. And she was beginning to feel exceedingly good, her problems evaporating. This was mostly because after a few successful chops, she began to imagine the slim tree trunk as Simon's neck. After that, each blow felt so wonderful that she quickened her pace to get in as many necks as possible.

If anyone had been watching, and someone was, they would have thought she was a maniac. (What with her frantically splitting away, a ridiculous smile on her face and an evil laugh echoing up from her lungs.) Even Ajsha was beginning to get a little afraid. She kept her distance, watching spittle sail from Milo's mouth and her eyes expand. Ajsha wrinkled her brow, wishing she had stayed in the house. A shout brought her attention to the shed. Simon was standing there, rigid with shock, fright, and fury. Ajsha ran over to him, and before he could demand an explanation, she begged him in Galo to make Milo stop.

Simon nodded and began to stride over, though he wasn't entirely sure if he was up for the task. Although Milo was panting hard amid her laughter, she didn't look tired. Her eyes had gone wide and shiny, making her look completely mad. Cautiously, Simon sidled up to her, and when she lifted the ax (every time she did she trembled with effort) he seized the handle and wrenched it out of her clutches. That wasn't an easy thing to do, for Milo was gripping it with determination, and when he tried, her head snapped around at him. At first an evil Don't-mess-with-me-I'm-crazy!-look crowded her face, then, seeing who it was, she came out of her trance.

Her strength gave way, and Simon was able to take hold of the ax as she collapsed on the ground. Ajsha rushed over and helped her sit up. Exhausted, Milo's breath came in short puffs, mingled with the gurgle of phlegm. Simon and Ajsha loomed over her, very concerned, but Bob the Conscience was laughing his head, that wasn't there, off.

"What do you find so funny?" demanded Milo, this time in her mind.

"Told you! Told you shouldn't have chopped the wood!" he said gleefully.

"What?" Milo said. "No you didn't."

"Sure I did," Bob the Conscience insisted. "Or at least something that amounted to that." "Whatever," Milo mentally muttered. "What happened to me?"

"You were envisioning murdering Simon."

Milo squinted up at Simon, her view good from where she sat. She saw his neck and her mouth began to water. The boy was jabbering angrily at Ajsha, who was answering meekly. Dispirited, she turned to Milo.

"Father wants to know why you were chopping the wood."

"For the sake of chopped wood," Milo lied, her chest still heaving.

This answer didn't console Simon any. He shouted at her, through Ajsha, that it was a very stupid and dangerous thing to do. Milo rolled her eyes, bobbing her head and mimicking his words. This incensed Simon even more and he continued to shout, gesticulating wildly for emphasis.

"He said that he was very worried when he saw you," Ajsha translated.

"Sure he was," Milo chuckled, standing up. She couldn't help but feel envious that Simon held the ax with the greatest of ease; its weight didn't seem to bother him a bit.

"He said that you are too weak to use an ax."

"Oh, yeah?!" Milo snapped, rather wobbly on her feet. She jabbed a finger at the chunks she had hewn off. "What does that tell you?!"

Her whole body was shaking like crepe paper, her indifference replaced by outrage. "Don't ever, EVER call me weak!" she spat at him.

Before he could make an equally venomous reply and launch one of their periodic quarrels, his buddy ran up to him, gibbering in Galo. Whatever he said seemed to nab Simon's attention. He looked torn between staying to rebuke Milo and leaving. The island boy began to tug Simon along, giving him a few slaps on the back. Simon murmured something to Ajsha and ran off, first stopping to put away the ax.

"Where's he going?" Milo demanded.

"To town," Ajsha said enthusiastically, all woes forgotten. "He said that we will continue this later."

"Sure we will," Milo muttered. "What's happening in town?"

"The men have come back from your plane," Ajsha said. "Whenever they do, there is always a street sale for all the undamaged goods they found. Whatever is leftover is sent to the stores tomorrow."

"Hmmm," Milo said. "That sounds exciting. Why don't we go see? I don't have any money, but it couldn't hurt to take a look."

"Sure," Ajsha agreed. They dashed off in the direction of the town, still dressed to do laundry.

They arrived a while later, and saw that long tables had been set up in the middle of the town square, each strewn with different items. Many tables had clothing; a couple displayed travel items found in carry-ons, along with stuff you find available on many planes. One table exhibited cages filled with the few surviving pets, separated from their owners. People were bustling everywhere, greeting, shouting, and buying things.

The girls observed the spectacle at a safe distance, not able to see much past people's heads, until they suddenly heard Ajsha's name being called.

"Ajsha! Ajsha! Ajsha, dear!"

Bewildered, they looked in the direction from which it came. They saw a woman about fifty feet away, dressed in a flowing light blue outfit and tottering rapidly towards them. She had on a ridiculously huge straw hat, adorned with tiny artificial birds, people on both sides of her ducking to avoid hitting the rim. Jewelry decorated her neck and wrists in layers, and fluffy black hair framed her face. She was delighted that they had noticed her, waved a bejeweled hand.

"Oh, no," Ajsha moaned, sagging.

"What's the matter?" Milo asked. "Who is that?"

"Hattie Knocker," she said bleakly.

"What's wrong with her?"

Ajsha sighed. "The poor soul. You see, she's slightly out of her mind."

"Really?" Milo said with interest, tilting her head as she watched Hattie approach.

"Yes. But she just barely misses the requirements to be hauled off. Every time she crosses the line, she always finds a way to be normal enough to stay."

"Where would she be 'hauled off ' to?" asked Milo, fighting the urge to laugh. "This place doesn't have an insane asylum, does it?"

"Yes, actually. It's called Fool's Sanctuary. Every now and then, someone will go crazy and that's where we send them. It's way out in the forest, out of the way."

She couldn't say anything else because Hattie Knocker had reached them, her face aglow with exertion and joy.

"Ajsha, darling!" she said, leaning down and kissing her cheek. "How's Granny's favorite girl?"

"I'm okay, Hattie," she replied politely and a bit helplessly.

"Wonderful!" She advanced on Milo. "And this is your new mummy, isn't it? Hello, darling! I'm Ajsha's grandmother."

Milo looked her over. She didn't appear old enough to be a grandmother. Milo placed her at about forty-two.

"Hattie Knocker," Ajsha said, placing a palm on Milo's elbow, "this is Milo."

"Hi," Milo said.

"Hi, hi!" Hattie replied sunnily, and reached into one of the many bags she was carrying. She withdrew a short scarf entwined around a nice bracelet. "This is for you."

She handed it to Ajsha.

"Happy birthday, darling!" Hattie trilled. "I know that it was two days ago, sorry I couldn't make the party."

"No, it's alright. Thank you," Ajsha said weakly.

"You're absolutely welcome! Now, I also have something for you," Hattie told Milo.

"Actually, we have to be going," Ajsha said quickly, shooting Milo a pleading glance.

"Come, come," Hattie said, flapping a hand. "Just let me find it."

"Did you hear that?" Milo asked Ajsha, taking pity on her. "It sounds like Mrs. Lanslo."

"Yeah," she exclaimed, catching on. "Yeah. It does. We should go see what she wants."

"Mrs. Lanslo?" Hattie said, turning around.

With her back to them, the two sane ones swiftly scuttled away and then broke into a run. When Hattie turned back they were gone.

As they jogged, Milo asked Ajsha, "It was your birthday?"

"Yeah," she gasped. "In June."

"Ooooh," Milo said. "How old did you turn?"

"Six," she answered, exasperated.

"Oh, right. Right. So, she thinks she's your grandmother?"

"Yeah." Ajsha puffed along for a moment before saying, "She thinks she's my aunt, she thinks she's my mom, she thinks she's my sister . . . last time I saw her she thought she was my niece."

"How do you know her?"

"She cleans the orphanage. *And* she does a good job, too. See what I mean? Something normal, so she can't be carted off."

Milo suppressed a snigger.

They arrived home and, having skipped lunch, started an early dinner. When Simon reappeared, he had with him several bags and a tattered cardboard box, dotted with holes. He handed the box to Ajsha, while muttering something under his breath. He cast a rueful glance at Milo, and disappeared down the hall.

"Here," she said, handing it to Milo. "He said that Mrs. Lanslo gave it to him. She said that Hattie told her it was for you. He also said he's sorry for yelling at you. He was just really upset."

Milo set the box on the granite table in the sitting room, and untied the twine wrapped around it. She lifted the top and peeked inside. Shrieking with delight, she scooped out a fluffy nine week old kitten. It was completely black with red patches, and mewing with wild abandon.

15
When it comes to being a Mother

MILO WAS ENTHRALLED with the kitten, her heart softening greatly for Hattie Knocker. She had no idea how the woman knew she had a fondness for felines, but she wasn't about to go ask. The truth was that cats were the only animals Milo liked. She found them to be the most intelligent, or only intelligent, animal existing on planet earth. Sure, you say, "But you can teach other animals to do tricks." Milo found that to be sheer stupidity. She wondered how low on self-esteem an animal had to be to allow another creature to rearrange its brain-waves so that it rolled over when a command was heard.

She considered dogs to be one of the most unintelligent species there was. So stupid that it could do practically nothing by itself, and performed idiotic acts for treats while humans laughed. She hated parrots, what with them repeating everything like a moron. Chimps and monkeys were despised by her; forced to take orders from a guy offering a banana. She thought that any animal capable of being lured into the thankless world of performing arts was a dolt.

Cats were, to her anyway, different. They were their own person. They could take care of themselves, they knew the importance of hygiene, and out of all the animal faces in the world theirs were the most expressive. They could show surprise, adoration, contentment, boredom, amusement, and anger. They were smart enough not to fall under the control of another. Unlike other four-legged creatures, cats had their pride. Milo loved them dearly, though she harbored contempt for all other species. She had wanted one for years, but had never been in a good position.

She named the kitten Chaos, for all it had been through. They rapidly became fast friends. At meals, Milo fed her water and raw fish in little chipped saucers. At night, Milo settled her on one of the cushioned chairs in the sitting room, though she only slept there if she felt like it. Most nights she would come waddling down the hall, searching for Milo and announcing her presence in shrill tones. Upon finding her, Chaos would claw her way up onto the bed and curl into a tiny, furry ball inside Milo's elbow, purring daintily through her nose. Milo never reprimanded the kitten. For one thing, she knew it would do as much good as scolding a rock, and two, she loved to turn her back on Simon at night and murmur to Chaos, which annoyed Simon to no end.

Since Milo didn't have a litter box, she let Chaos wander around outside at her leisure, picking her own bathroom in sandy areas. If Milo had had a garden, she might have coaxed the kitten to use that, but she didn't. Yet.

Simon had kept his promise and talked to Ajsha, who in turn talked to Milo, about the wood chopping. Milo readily agreed not to do it anymore and let Simon handle it. She was now so preoccupied with her cat that she didn't care about contriving ways to vex Simon. In fact, Milo was spending so much time with Chaos, and showering her with so much affection, that Simon and Ajsha were beginning to feel jealous. Simon was envious that the cat, the *cat*, was getting more attention than he was. Milo didn't even bother to growl at him nowadays.

Ajsha felt jealous because Milo was now confiding Chaos instead of her. Of course, these were minor jealousies, for Milo did continue to talk to Ajsha enough to keep her satisfied, though she was sure Chaos got to hear details she didn't. As for Simon, Milo made sure that she gave him at least two dirty looks during the day and three piercing stares at night. That kept him satisfied. Dejected, yes, but he didn't complain. It was better than being treated like thin air.

They weren't the only ones flushing green with envy. Bob the Conscience was also feeling the snap, perhaps even more acutely. One day during the second week of September, Milo tried to engage him in conversation, but he wouldn't answer. And if he did, his manner was very tart. Milo finally confronted him about it, right after she asked him if he thought she was getting a tan and he answered, "Like snow . . . stupid head."

"Bob," Milo said, suppressing laughter at such a pathetic insult, "what's wrong? You've been acting really weird lately."

"Me or you?" he asked in a hurt voice.

"What do you mean?" she inquired.

"You know," he mumbled. "Always hanging around your new friend."

Milo pondered for a moment. "Ajsha?" she said.

"No," he grumbled. "That cat."

"Chaos?"

"Yeah. Her."

"Oh, Bob! Is that why you're acting this way?"

"Maybe," he mumbled. He might have averted his gaze, if he'd had any eyes.

"Why, Bob!" Milo chided. "I'm surprised at you. Don't you know that you have always been my one and only true friend? Always?"

"What about Cusser?" he said hatefully.

Milo clamped her mouth shut and thought back to Cusser. Cusser had been one of her greatest friends. He was a stapler that Milo discovered one afternoon on her father's desk. She was seven, and not adjusting well to her new domicile. In her defense, it happened to be a particularly snooty neighborhood that her parents had chosen. She had no friends, was alone most of the time, and longed for company. She picked up that stapler, moved the two parts up and down, and thought it looked exactly like a mouth. Inspired, she instantly proclaimed it a friend, decided it was a boy, and named him Cusser. Milo and Cusser became inseparable at once, not that he had much choice in the matter, possessing only a jaw and no legs. Milo took him everywhere she went, and told him all her secrets. She pretended he was talking back to her by moving the two parts up and down.

She and Cusser became so chummy that her parents felt obligated to worry about her, but only after a neighbor asked them if they were concerned their daughter was friends with an office object. Truthfully, they hadn't noticed. They then thought she should have "real", human friends. However, finding companions for her wasn't easy, for all the surrounding kids didn't want to play with the girl who talked to a stapler. Their parents supported them in this aspect. This didn't bother Milo one bit, even though she was constantly picked on. She was blithely content with her paper-biting buddy.

Cusser lasted until a few months after Milo turned eight. One day, one horrible day, she was playing on the sidewalk, when several known bullies approached and started to tease her and the stapler. One of the boys snatched Cusser out of her hands and tossed him to the others. As they all chucked it to one another, Milo frantically darted about, trying to catch him. One idiot accidentally threw him into the street, and a car ran over Cusser the Stapler, demolishing him. Milo wailed, "Murder!" and rushed to gather the pieces.

She buried him by the gate in the local cemetery, the keeper having gruffly told her that they didn't allow the burial land to be used for inanimate objects, even if they were friends. Milo had to move from that town a couple of months later, and she had tried to take the good memories of Cusser with her and leave the bad ones behind.

Remembering her grand times with him, Milo couldn't help but sigh, and murmur, "Ah, yes! Cusser!"

"Yeah," Bob the Conscience sneered. "Cusser."

"Sorry!" Milo apologized quickly. "I know you always feel like you're competing with him, but, Bob, don't. He was a stapler. A good friend, but a stapler. You are my conscience, and even though you're kind of unreliable, you will always be the best friend I have. I don't have to be polite to you!"

Bob the Conscience sniffed and said emotionally, "Oh, Milo! That's the nicest thing anyone has ever said to me!"

Milo was about to ask him who else could be talking to him, but decided not to pursue the topic.

On the fifteenth of September, which appropriately was a Monday, Milo awoke to muffled scraping sounds. Sticking a knuckle into her eyes, she walked into the kitchen to find Ajsha, already dressed and sitting expectantly at the table.

"Good morning," she said.

"Mornin'," Milo answered drowsily. "Girl, you know it's only seven o'clock?"

"Yes," Ajsha replied, "I know."

"Then why are you up right now?" Milo asked, automatically starting breakfast. When it comes to being a mother, one must not keep a ready child waiting for food. But Milo only considered it keeping her fed, and therefore alive.

"I need to be up early," Ajsha said, swinging her legs. "I start school today."

Milo nearly dropped the bowls she was carrying. "School?" she repeated in amazement. "You have school?"

"Um, yes," Ajsha said, startled. "I have to learn, don't I?"

"But you can already read and write and speak two languages," protested Milo, which, as far as she was concerned, made Ajsha smart enough. If she learned anymore, Milo was really going to start feeling like an idiot.

"Yes," Ajsha admitted, "but I don't know a particle of arithmetic, or science, or civics. Don't look so surprised! We interpreters have extensive educations."

"But, you're too young for things like science," Milo said, sitting down with their food.

"Maybe, but I'm a fast learner, so they let me into more advanced classes," Ajsha said as she took a bowl of what appeared to be a homemade cereal. She spooned some into her mouth, chewed, and grinned. After swallowing she said, "It's good. What is it?"

"I made it yesterday," Milo said. "I'm going to have to go food shopping soon, our supplies is dwindling. This is raspberries in bread. I wrapped dough around each berry and baked them. Made a whole box full. Just shake into a bowl, add milk, and you've got yumminess."

"Mmmm," Ajsha said in approval, scooping more into her mouth. "Clever."

But since the word had a wad of cereal to get past, it sounded like, "Cwevlar."

Milo shook her head. "Don't talk with your mouth full," she admonished.

When it comes to being a mother, the list is so extensive and respectable that one simply can't write it all down. But I have faithfully recorded all that they encountered, and one that is most definitely on the list is reminding children of manners. But to Milo it was a polite request, asking for a better view of the person.

Ajsha obeyed, like the good child she was, and wasn't needed to be reminded for the rest of the meal. Chaos padded into the room, marking her entrance with a rolling purr, and Milo arose to fill her water dish. As she stood pumping at the sink, she happened to look out the window and saw a pile of ropes, their ends tied in loops and difficult knots. Milo got the water and returned to the table.

"What's the rope out there for?" she asked Ajsha, setting the dish on the floor. Chaos scampered over happily and started to lap up the water with a bright pink tongue.

"What rope?" Ajsha said, draining her bowl.

"The rope out there," Milo said, making her lower it.

"There's rope out there?" Ajsha said, wiping her mouth with the back of her hand.

"Yes!" Milo sighed, handing her a cloth napkin. "What's it for?"

Ajsha thought for a moment, dabbing at her lips, and suddenly became excited. "It's fall, isn't it?"

"In most countries," Milo confirmed, remembering with a pang all the maple and birch trees changing color right then in America.

"Then it's boar hunting season!" Ajsha announced gleefully, bouncing in her chair.

"There's a specific season for hunting boar?" Milo said. "Aren't they hunted all year long?"

"Nope, just in the fall. We let the boar babies that are born in the spring grow up before we hunt them. Or more like trap them. That's what the rope is for. Father helps trap them. If I were you, I'd stay out of the forest. The boars live on another part of the island during the spring and summer, but during the winter and fall they come to find food. They don't like us, so they usually keep away and stay in the forests. That's why you shouldn't go in. You never know when you'll step on a trap, then, vvwooooop, up you'll go."

"Then how am I supposed to get my papayas?" Milo inquired huffily. "All we have left is raspberries. I've never tried raspberry butter before."

"Is that what you added to the butter yesterday? Oh, it was good."

"Thank you, it certainly was. But what am I going to do now? Do they forbid people to go into the forest during 'boar hunting season'?"

"No, in fact the experts say to continue every day life as normal. They say that if the boars see we are acting abnormally then they'll know something's up and will be more cautious. Of course, it all sounds like nonsense, but we still abide. The experts are very sensitive," she explained after seeing Milo's skeptical expression.

"What time is it?" she suddenly asked, bringing her bowl to the sink.

Milo squinted at her watch. "Seven-thirty", she said.

"Oh, dear!" Ajsha said, at once flustered. "I'd better get going. School starts at eight. Bye, Mother."

"It's Milo," Milo said, rising, "and I think I'd better go with you. I don't want you walking around alone with boars on the loose."

"Okay," Ajsha agreed, smiling.

She waited while Milo quickly got dressed. Remerging jeans-clad and donning a turquoise T-shirt, Milo led her outside. Together, Ajsha yearning to hold hands, they started towards town. When it comes to being a mother, one brings her children to school herself to protect them from traffic, potential maniacs, getting lost, boars, and any other imaginable evil they could bump into on the way to school. Milo did know this. Though her mother never walked her to school when she was young, she had often seen other kids and their mothers approaching the school hand in hand. Milo normally wouldn't have bothered walking Ajsha, but she didn't feel good about letting her travel unaccompanied with boars lurking about.

They entered the town and saw children hurrying to the school house while calling over their shoulders to their mothers, most of whom were waving forgotten items in the air.

"I can make it from here," Ajsha said.

"Hadn't I better go with you? I mean, don't I have school?" Milo said. Years of mistreatment hadn't made her very fond of school, but it just felt wrong for it to be September and not be going.

"Of course not! Married couples don't go to school."

"Ah," Milo murmured. "So, that's why the boys are so eager to marry. Well farewell, little one!"

As she turned to leave, Ajsha said to her, "Don't think that's why Father married you! He loves you!"

Milo winced, but controlled herself. When it comes to being a mother, one mustn't drag their children into parental arguments. In her case, not unless translations were needed. Therefore Milo merely said, rather sarcastically, "Of course he does. Dear. Darling dear. Bye-bye. Oh! By the way, math is murder. See ya!"

She scuttled away, Ajsha skipping off to gain an education that would make any American six year old dissolve into tears. Once she was on the other side of town, Milo checked her watch. It was precisely 8:12. She wondered if Soldier's shop was open yet. Every so often she would go in there and take a look at that little speaker. She wished she had some island money to buy it; she would have loved to use it for her radio. Sauntering by the shop, she saw that the blinds were lifted. Usually that meant it was opened. She bounded up the stairs and crossed the threshold.

Soldier was rearranging objects on the counter as she entered.

"Milo!" he greeted. "Ho' ya doin'?"

"Good, thanks," she replied, relieved to see that the speaker was still there.

"Good, good," he said genially. "Eh, um, which is it? 'These bunch o' flowers *is* a token o' my affection', or 'These bunch o' flowers *are* a token o' my affection'?"

"This bunch of flowers is a token of my affection," she rattled off, striding over to the wall of shelves.

"Oh. Right. Thanks. Lookin' fer somethin'?"

"No," she said, running her hand over the smooth top of the speaker.

"I see ya've bin fancyin' that contraption t'ere."

"Yeah," Milo sighed, fingering the wire. "But, heck. It's not like I can buy it."

"I see," Soldier said, licking the corner of his mouth. "Say, what are ya doin' up and out so early, anyha?"

"I had to walk Ajsha to school," she replied, lifting the speaker up to her nose to sniff it. It smelled like 1990's west coast hip-hop. "Ahhhh," Milo moaned.

"Oh, yeh!" Soldier said, nodding. He pulled a rag from his apron string and started to polish the counter. "Starts tehday, don't it? So, what are ya goin' ta do fer the rest o' the day?"

"I dunno. Do some writing maybe. I've been neglecting it." She let her lingering hand slip from the shelf and then headed for the door.

"Have a nice day!" Soldier called after her.

"You too!" she called back, though she was beginning to think it was an oxymoron.

She did go home, but before she tackled her diary, she washed the breakfast dishes, even Ajsha's. When it comes to being a mother, one must understand when a child is in a hurry and can't do their own dishes. After that she went to her and Simon's room, splayed herself across the bed, and fell to writing. She informed her diary of all the interesting events of the past few weeks, from her point of view, of course, making Simon sound like an escaped lunatic and her a timorous nun.

She then spent some time listening to her radio, imagining herself far away and dancing with a large group of friends she had yet to meet. She didn't have a clear idea *where* they were dancing, since Milo hadn't yet decided where she might like to live one day. All she knew was that it was somewhere not on this island. Therefore, her daydreaming consisted of bits of places, the dancing location a combination of Pennsylvania hills and Miami sidewalks.

At 11:30 she began to wonder when Ajsha was supposed to come home. Surely they wouldn't keep her past lunchtime; she was way too young to stay there all day. But in case they did, she wondered if she should go to wait for her. Then she thought about lunch, and how hungry Ajsha would be after her first day of school, and thought maybe she should take it with her.

She thought about how nice it would be to surprise Ajsha with a picnic, to thank her for being so nice. When it comes to being a mother, one sometimes likes to surprise their children with special treats. Then Milo thought about Simon, and how unpleasant he would make the outing if he joined them. And *of course* Ajsha would insist he come along. Milo rolled her eyes as she padded bare foot down the hall. She just couldn't understand what their bond was, and Ajsha had yet to bring it up. Speaking of Ajsha, if they did let her out at noon, what if a boar attacked her on her way home? What if a boar intruded on their picnic? Or a whole horde of boars?

Milo needn't have worried, for when she looked out the kitchen window she saw Ajsha skipping through the trees to the house, showing no signs of a boar tussle. Milo was about to sigh with relief when she saw Simon trudging up from the beach. He met Ajsha in the clearing and scooped her up in his arms. They hugged and began to gibber lovingly to each other in Galo, their foreheads pressed together.

Milo snorted, turned scornfully away, and began to look for something to make for lunch. She searched the cupboards and stumbled upon a container of already cooked tuna steaks. She grinned evilly to herself and nosed through the rest of the cupboards until she found the vegetable oil and an egg. The egg had been a gift from Simon; he had given it to her a few days ago, hoping to soften Milo's opinion of him. He did this every so often, to meager results. Since it was only one egg, Milo had very little use for it, and was therefore thoroughly unimpressed with it as a gift. But the tuna had caused her to remember a certain recipe where only one egg was needed.

She pulled out some bread, a lime, and two bowls, and laid out everything on the counter. She dumped the tuna into one of the bowls and flaked it apart with a fork. Slicing the lime in two, she squeezed one half onto the tuna and fluffed it with the fork. She heard Simon and Ajsha come into the house, still jabbering expressively, and she went to greet them. Seeing her, Ajsha scrambled out of Simon's arms and ran up to her.

"Hello, Mother!" she chirped, her face radiant.

"Milo! And, Hi! How was school?"

"It was great!" Ajsha proclaimed, bouncing on her toes. "I have so much to tell you!"

"Awesome!" Milo said, giving Simon a malevolent look out of the corner of her eye. "Why don't you tell me at lunch? You and Simon go freshen up and then you can come in."

"All right," she agreed, and jabbered to Simon.

He nodded and smiled at Milo, who, much to his surprise, smiled back. Not in the most reassuring way, but it was still a smile. The reason why Milo was smiling was because she was very pleased with herself. She returned to the kitchen and cracked the egg into the second bowl. Without bothering to wash her hands, she reached in and, with some difficulty, extricated the whites. Chuckling menacingly, she threw away any unwanted egg parts, and poured a certain amount of oil into the bowl with the egg yolk. She added a squeeze of lime juice, and then used a fork to beat the ingredients together. She beat until the mixture was very smooth and much lighter in color, almost white.

She was making was mayonnaise. Whenever she would make tuna sandwiches, which was what she was making now, in America she would stir mayonnaise into the tuna, along with other flavor enhancers. Since there was no jarred mayonnaise on the island, she rarely made anything nowadays that called for it. Seeing the tuna had reminded her that she couldn't use it, which reminded her of the recipe, and in turn reminded her of the egg. The reason she hadn't made any before now was because the recipe required raw egg yolk, and it it's possible to get sick from eating raw egg anything, especially if where you live the average temperature is eighty-nine degrees and you don't have a fridge.

Mashing down some lime infused tuna on two pieces of bread, she made two separate sandwiches. The tuna remaining in the bowl received her homemade mayo. After adding a generous amount, she mixed it all together, creating an unctuous spread, and mashed it down on another slice of bread. Having used all the fish, she slopped on the leftover mayonnaise, topping it all with a piece of bread and smashing it down so that it looked the same size as the other two. She discarded her prep utensils in the sink and put each sandwich on a plate. She garnished with a few raspberries, for class.

Carefully, Milo arranged the plates on the table so that Simon would end up with the sandwich with the mayonnaise. Her forced family came in just as she remembered water. She gestured, more insistently than usual, for each to sit at a certain place at the table. She went to get glasses, and had her back turned when an unfortunate mistake happened. Giving a glass of water to both of them, she smiled kindly at Simon, who eagerly grinned back. Grace was administered in two languages, and the meal began.

Milo nibbled at her sandwich, watching intently as Simon took a bite of his. His face showed signs of liking, and when he swallowed he spoke to Ajsha, while smiling at Milo.

"He says that he likes the sandwich."

"Does he now?" Milo asked nonchalantly, popping a raspberry into her mouth. "What about you?"

"Oh, yes!" she replied. "No matter what you make, it's always delicious!"

Milo tried to stop herself from blushing, but couldn't. Never before had she received a compliment like that. She shook her head and concentrated on watching Simon eat, searching for signs of intestinal disagreement. After several minutes, she noticed something very wrong. Instead of Simon's sandwich oozing white stuff, Ajsha's was.

Milo gasped, and in a stuttering voice asked Ajsha, "Um, um, um. H-hey, girl. You sure that sandwich tastes okay?"

"Yes," Ajsha said, taking another bite. Two more would finish it. She chewed thoughtfully, then swallowed and said, "Actually, now that you mention it, it does taste a little funny. Not bad, just not like anything I've ever tasted. But, I suppose it's just a part of the recipe."

With those words released, Milo sprang her seat, and just as Ajsha was about to take another bite, she snatched the sandwich away from her.

"Hey!" Ajsha protested in alarm. "What's wrong?"

Milo peeled off the top piece of bread to reveal her homemade mayo.

"Oh, CRAP!" she bellowed, starting to shake. "Oh, Ajsha! I'm so sorry! You weren't supposed to eat this!"

"Why not?" Ajsha whispered, growing frightened.

Simon gibbered to her, wanting to know what was going on. She jabbered back to him an anxious voice, and he addressed Milo.

"He wants to know what's wrong."

"This!" she shrieked frantically, thrusting the bread at his face.

"He wants to know what's wrong with it," Ajsha translated, as Simon ducked to avoid being hit by tuna. "What's that white stuff?"

"Mayonnaise," Milo said, near tears. She was feeling Ajsha's forehead and cheeks. When it comes to being a mother, one doesn't want to purposely make their child ill.

"What's that?" Ajsha asked, having never heard the word before.

"A type of food that you mix with things like tuna and spread on things like bread," Milo rambled off vaguely. "This isn't real mayonnaise but homemade."

"What's the difference?"

"It's made with raw egg yolk! People get sick from eating raw egg parts!" Milo explained angrily, not understanding how Ajsha had ended up with that sandwich. "You know, salmonella and all that great stuff! It's not like I can pasteurize it here or anything."

Ajsha's eyes widened and her hand went to her throat. "Why would you use something like that if you knew it would make me sick?!"

"Well, you weren't supposed to eat it!"

"Who was?"

"HIM!" she roared, jabbing a finger at Simon. "He was supposed to eat it. I don't want you to get sick, but he's another story! . . . No! Don't!"

But it was too late. Ajsha had translated, and Simon had stood up, not pleased. Far from it. He said something in Galo, his voice low and severe.

"He wants to know why you would do something like this," Ajsha interpreted, her own voice cracking.

"You were supposed to eat it, you bum!" Milo shouted. "I wanted *you* to get sick! Ajsha, I'm so sorry. I never – I swear . . . How are you feeling?"

Ajsha thought for a moment and said, "You know, I do feel a little strange." She repeated this to a now worried Simon, and he murmured something in return.

"Father suggests that I go lie down."

"Yeah," whispered Milo, her mind racing. "Yeah, maybe you should."

Before she could move to help, Simon stepped between her and the child, giving Milo a furious glare. Milo threw up her hands and began to clear the table, scraping the remainders of the sandwiches into the trash.

After she was done, she silently scurried down the hall and peeked into Ajsha's room. She was lying rigidly on top of the covers, looking quite scared, as if she expected to explode any second. Simon was sitting beside her, stroking her hand and saying soft, reassuring words. Milo felt terrible, her stomach plummeting down to her dusty feet. Crossing her arms, she rocked side to side, trying to think of a way to help Ajsha. An idea blossomed in her brain, and she hurried off to make it happen.

Simon sat with Ajsha for a while, occasionally rubbing her belly. When she asked, he told her that he doubted that they would need to get the doctor. She asked him not to be angry with "mother" for what happened, or what she had tried to do. The lad reluctantly agreed, only because he couldn't resist the plaintive, little voice, and left her to rest. Quietly, he shut the door behind him and looked down the hall, where came the sound of clattering. He pushed a strand of dirty-blonde hair back behind his ear, where it belonged, exhaled deeply, and headed for the kitchen.

When he arrived, he found his lovely wife rushing around, poking her nose into every cupboard and drawer, in the counters and above. Milo barely noticed him; she was darting about so swiftly, absorbed in her mission. She was taking food items out, sniffing them, and sometimes tasting them. If she made a rotten face, she would place it on the table. Simon had absolutely no idea what she was up to. He tried to get her to tell him, but she merely pushed him away, too much in a hurry to stop and chat, or to stop and gesture inarticulately.

When she had accumulated enough things on the table to meet her satisfaction, she took out a large glass, and began to pour and plop everything into it. Simon sat down at the table and watched as the disgusting foods and fluids were woven together with a large spoon. After a minute, the glass began to give off an atrocious odor.

Simon fidgeted nervously as the revolting stench reached his nose. He wasn't sure why she wanted to make such a concoction, unless, of course, she wanted to suffocate him. Milo vigilantly stirred her ingredients until they became smooth and viscous, and then dipped out a small mouthful with the spoon to try it. She licked a portion of the brew, and immediately dashed over to the trash/barrel to spit it out. She spat several times, and had to gargle a bit with water before her mouth felt close to normal.

Curious of her odd behavior, Simon also spooned out a taste, but instead of licking it he foolishly put it all in his mouth. He gagged violently, the spoon falling to the table with a clack. He followed in suit by high-tailing it to the trash/barrel and spewing out the ghastly beverage. He looked up at Milo and raised his eyebrows, panting.

Strangely, she looked pleased with the result, which Simon now knew well boded no good. She got out a medium sized glass, and poured in the drink until it was full. She took the glass out of the kitchen, but before she moved down the hall, she noticed Chaos in the sitting room, kneading a section of the couch. Milo walked over to her, dipped a finger into her brew, and held it out to Chaos. The feline sniffed at it, as all cats do before eating something, and jumped back, her fluffy kitten fur standing on end. She hissed at the mixture, showing her tiny white teeth and making Milo grin. She said thank you and made a kissy sound.

Milo transported the glass to Ajsha's door. Knocking softly, careful not to spill a drop, she asked for permission to enter. She received a feeble reply of consent. Upon entering, she found Ajsha lying flat down on her bed, eyes wide and looking pale, the afternoon sun bathing her in a warm glow.

"Hey, there," Milo crooned, concerned. "How you feeling?"

"I'm not sure," Ajsha answered wanly, her nose twitching. "What's that smell?"

"This," Milo said, holding up the cup, while shutting the door half way.

"What is it?" Ajsha inquired, her curiosity spurring her into sitting up.

Milo sank onto the bed and handed her the potion. "Something you have to drink," she told her.

Ajsha smelled it and made a face. "You're kidding!" she declared.

"Nope!" Milo said stoutly. "It will help you. The best medicine in the world always smells like a cesspool. Come now. Bottoms up!"

Ajsha stared at her in dismay, then at the drink. She pondered for a moment and finally took a small sip. Her eyes nearly jumped out of her head. She was about to spit it out, but Milo gave her the *Look*. When it comes to being a mother, one must be a master at the *Look*. Groaning and whimpering, Ajsha forced herself to swallow. She began to cough, her tongue stretching out of her mouth. Milo thumped her on the back, and when she was able to breathe again she wheezed,

"What is this made of?"

"Every disgusting, sickening, nauseating, loathsome, repulsive bit of food and liquid I could find!" said Milo, her lip curling at the sight of the muddy, greyish fluid. "And believe me! I found some revolting stuff! Now don't talk, just drink. Don't give me that face! I know it tastes horrible, but it really will help. You need to drink all of it, so come on."

Ajsha looked like she had just received the news that she was scheduled to be executed. She stared at the detestable "medicine" and gave a shuddery sigh. Not wanting to be a disobedient child, she took a deep breath and began to down it. As she gulped the brew, her eyes snapped shut and her brow narrowed in torture. How she managed to swallow all of it at once is unknown, even to her, but she did it. That poor, brave moppet was able to force that terrible stuff down her throat. When the last straggling bit was out of the glass and in her stomach, she lowered the cup with a gasp.

"Atta girl!" Milo praised. She patted her on the back and congratulated her extensively.

"Mother –"

"Milo!"

"How was that . . . STUFF supposed to help me?" Ajsha panted, breaking out in a sweat.

"Well, it's going to work with the stomach. If the body has enough sense to spit that stuff out when it's in your mouth, then it's got to know what to do if it's in your stomach. I felt so bad about what happened that I just had to do something to help you. So I fixed up some 'medicine'."

Milo was quite right in doing this, though it wasn't the nicest of remedies. When it comes to being a mother, one likes to help their child heal if they are ill. Especially if you are the reason they are ill. Ajsha was holding her stomach and wheezing harshly.

"Yes, indeed," Milo said, studying her. "It should be coming up any moment. Bringing with it, all of your lunch, including raw egg yolk."

Just as she predicted, in a couple of minutes Ajsha fell forward, and then jumped off her bed, hand to her mouth. She scrambled out of her bedroom, and rushed into the bathroom as fast as her short legs would take her, then to the water-closet. Milo wandered out into the hallway and heard the unmistakable sounds of vomiting. Simon walked over to her and also heard the regurgitating. His eyes widened and he pointed questioningly at the bathroom.

Milo chuckled and said, "Trust me!"

Not able to understand her, Simon made to move towards the bathroom door, but Milo held out her arm, halting him. She shook her head.

After several minutes of retching, Ajsha staggered out of the bathroom, looking like she had just come back from a battle. Simon gasped and ran over to her. He arrived in time catch her as she fainted. Milo inhaled sharply and hurried over. Simon stood up, carrying the little one in his arms, and gave Milo the meanest, dirtiest look he could manage to give to the one he loved. As he carried Ajsha back to her room, Milo stayed rooted to the spot, feeling like a filthy piece of scum. Eventually, she plodded back to the kitchen and found a bottle to store the potion in. She decided to keep it around in case they ever needed it again.

She felt worse than she had felt in a long time. In fact, she had never felt like this before. She felt so incredibly guilty and miserable, that she wished she was dead. She had known, of course, that Ajsha was going to throw up – that was the point, but she hadn't known she would faint. All this time she had figured that she was the victim of this little adventure, but it was already twice her fault that Ajsha had vomited copiously, and now she was unconscious. She didn't mean for all this to happen. Why couldn't things sort out instead of getting worse? Her insides began to twist up, and her female emotion, that she had been so good at fighting, gnawed at her chest.

She walked by Ajsha's room, just as Simon was exiting it. Choosing not to look at his face, she tried to enter, but he blocked her way, glowering at her warningly. He stomped off and out of the house. Milo's mouth began to twitch and her shoulders began to shake. For once she didn't rebel against Simon, instead going into their room and collapsing onto the bed. She curled into an abstract spiral, and cried her little black heart out, welcoming the pain in her throat.

Chaos padded in and, using a combination of jumping and clawing, got onto the bed. She began to rub against Milo's head, telling her that she loved her. Milo drew her close and stroked her fluffy fur, her tears falling heavily.

"Oh, hoooh!" she mumbled. "Oh, my pretty kitty. Have you ever seen a six year old faint? I have. It's awful. You should have seen her eyes! They rolled back! It's my fault! All my fault! Why the heck did I want to make Simon sick in the first place? What's wrong with me?!"

Chaos snuggled up to her, purring comfortingly. After a minute, Milo resumed crying into a pillow, and Chaos lay down next to her to keep her company. Milo wasn't quiet about her crying, the pillow barely muffling her indulgent wails and sobs, and after about fifteen minutes she heard a noise at the door. She lifted her tear stained face to see Ajsha standing in the doorway, swaying slightly.

"Are you okay?" she asked the sobbing one.

"Am I okay?!" Milo repeated, hastily rolling over. "Are *you* okay?! I'm *so* sorry! I should have never given you that stuff! I had no idea that would happen. Please forgive me!"

Ajsha stared at her with an adoring, albeit bleary, look on her face. "Actually," she said, "I'm feeling very good. I guess I did throw up that egg whatever. Thank you."

"For what?!" Milo bawled, swiping at the thread of snot trailing from her nose. "Making you faint?"

"Come, come," Ajsha said, going over and patting her back.

"There, there."

Milo took a deep breath and let it out shakily. "Right," she said, getting a hold of herself. She sighed and rubbed her sore eyes. "Sorry, I'm being overdramatic. I've kept . . . a lot stored up."

Ajsha nodded, then smiled and told her to wait there. She hurried away and was back in a moment. She had something clasped in her hand.

"Here," she said kindly, handing it to Milo.

Milo looked in her hand and saw an extraordinary necklace. It was a long silver chain and at the end was a flat shell. It was about two inches in diameter, rough and grey on one side and a shimmering, iridescent blue on the other. Amid the blue were swirls of green and purple. It was an abalone shell. Milo had seen abalone jewelry before, but never anything so big, natural, and beautiful. She stared at it in awe before turning to Ajsha.

"It's so beautiful," she whispered.

"I know," Ajsha said fondly. "It's for you."

"What!" Milo gasped. "Ajsha, thank you, but you can't give me this!"

"Why not?" Ajsha demanded. "You deserve it. Please take it! Think of it as a gift from daughter to mother. I want to help you feel better."

Milo thought for a moment, staring at the necklace. She didn't feel right about taking it, or about that daughter-mother remark. But Ajsha wanted her to have it, and she was gazing at her so imploringly. When it comes to being a mother, one must be able to distinguish between the right times to turn down gifts and the right times to accept them. Milo decided that this was the right time to accept.

"Thank you," she whispered.

16
To Market, to Market!

"FOOD WAS MEANT to fill, not to kill," is a saying my Granny often said to my Poppa when he was a kiddie. These are some of the wisest words you will ever hear, and people should feed themselves by it. It is very unfortunate that Milo never heard these words. Sure, she ate healthy and in appropriate amounts, but Milo, of late, had developed a nasty little habit of using food as a weapon. The entire situation with Ajsha and the egg yolk could have been avoided if only Milo had heard the saying,

"Food was meant to fill, not to kill."

Even so, Milo felt exceedingly bad about the incident and tried to make it up to her. She walked her to school in the morning almost every day, and put extra of the scent herb in Ajsha's laundry. Simon had been talked to by Ajsha, and apologized to by Milo, which was her attempt to please Ajsha. In the end, he had fully forgiven Milo, on the condition that she would never do again. Something else unfortunate was that when Ajsha talked to Simon, she forgot to mention a key detail, but this would only matter later.

On the 23rd of September, sometime in the evening, Milo was shuffling around the kitchen, a candle lit on the table. She was looking in every cupboard, drawer, container, and box. Nearly every storage vessel for food was empty.

"I knew it," she muttered to herself. "I knew this day would come."

Simon and Ajsha were in the sitting room, looking over Ajsha's homework, and Milo strode over to them. Well, actually just over to Ajsha.

"It's happened," she announced to her.

Ajsha looked up. "What has?" she asked distractedly, her young mind on fractions.

"We have officially run out of food," Milo stated. She nodded at Simon. "Tell the weasel that I need to go shopping for more."

"Okay," Ajsha said. She began to gibber to Simon, and he looked unbelievably pleased. He jabbered something back, Ajsha translating.

"He said, 'That's fine. We can go tomorrow.'"

"Good. . . . I'm sorry. Did you say 'we'?"

"Yeah," Ajsha said. "We're going with you."

"You can, but he can't."

Simon wasn't happy to hear this. He leaned back on the couch and folded his arms across his chest. He muttered in Galo.

"He wants to know why," Ajsha said.

"I'm sure he does," Milo muttered. "Look, boi, I'll admit you've been good about not ticking me off lately, but I don't think I could stand a shopping trip with you. . . . 'We'! There's no 'we'. There never was. There's only me and you. And her," she quickly added.

Ajsha smiled gratefully, interpreted, and came back with an answer.

"He said that he's coming anyway."

Milo groaned and slumped into a chair. "Lovely!" she hissed.

They all sat enveloped silence for a moment, before Ajsha sudden remembered something. She smacked her forehead with her palm.

"Oh! Wait!" she cried. "I can't go with you tomorrow!"

"Why ever not?" Milo asked angrily.

"I forgot, my class is having an outing tomorrow. We are supposed to be back around four o'clock. The shops will be closed by then."

"And you were planning on telling me this, when?" Milo demanded, standing up.

"I'm sorry!" Ajsha said sincerely. "I forgot, Mother."

"Milo! And an 'outing', eh? You guys have lived here for over one hundred years; surely you have changed it to 'field trip' by now."

"Field trip," Ajsha repeated thoughtfully. "I've heard of those. I'm not sure why we don't say that, but in our defense, we are not visiting a field."

"No," Milo moaned. "You don't have to be going to a – . . . you know what? Never mind. Let's concentrate on what we're going to do about shopping. Maybe you could pretend to be sick and stay home."

"Sick!" Ajsha said, appalled. "During the second week of school?"

"So what?" said Milo. "You're having an 'outing' during the second week of school. Whoever heard of that? When I was living in that wretched apartment building, I *never* went on a field trip. Or an outing."

"Where would you go?"

"I have no idea. But forget it. What are we supposed to do? We can't wait another day. We need food now."

"I don't see what you are so worried about," Ajsha said, returning her attention to the homework on her lap. "You can go without me."

"Uh, no we can't," Milo told her.

"Sure you can."

"Noooo, we can't."

"Why not?"

"Two things, child," Milo said, counting off her fingers. "One: I can't speak Galo. And two: He can't speak English. There are your reasons."

Ajsha mulled this over for a moment before talking to Simon, who had very little idea of what was going on. After a short story, Ajsha brought up their problem. He shrugged and spoke in Galo.

"He says that you two can still go. And that he is sure that you'll both find a way to communicate," Ajsha translated in a That-ends-the-discussion tone.

Milo gaped at her. "Are – you – nuts?" she cried. "There is no way in my will power that I'm going to the market with him alone."

"I assure you his shopping skills are decent," Ajsha said. "Besides, he has the money."

Milo considered this for a second. "That's true," she said. "And Heaven knows I don't have any. Oh! Dang it! I don't know, Ajsha. How are we going to talk to each other?"

Ajsha shrugged. "Gestures, expressions, other people," she suggested. "You know, Mrs. Lanslo works in a food store. She could help you. And (for the sake of being said) you really should try to learn Galo."

"Well, you can forget about that," Milo said firmly. "The only language I know, and will ever know, is English. Oh, believe me, I've tried to learn others, but I've no talent there. Trust me!"

She shuddered, the memory flashing through her mind of the time she had practiced French so that her parents would take her to a very renowned restaurant. Needless to say, they were kicked out after Milo, attempting to order a dish, badly insulted the waiter and his grandfather.

"Very well," Ajsha sighed. "You two can go when Father comes home from work. Don't look so dismayed! Many married couples go shopping together."

"Well! Goodie for them!" Milo said through clenched teeth.

She walked up to Simon, who stood up. Growling, Milo put a hand on his shoulder and pushed him back down. She wanted to tower over him. She ushered Ajsha over for translating.

"Look, boi," Milo began, Ajsha gibbering evenly beside her. "Before we do this, I want to lay down a few rules. Number one: No playing any little tricks on me. Number two: Do *not* try to hold my hand. Number three: If anyone I know, not that there's many, sees us, we are not shopping together. You are merely stalking me. Got that? Number four: Running off to play with your pals is completely optional."

As Ajsha finished, Simon chuckled. He began his long reply.

"He says, 'That's fine. I guess. Whatever you want. I've got a few rules myself. One: Don't try to hit me with any food. Two: Don't get rotten food on purpose. Three: Don't try to sneak off and leave me behind anywhere. Four: Don't get jealous if any girls are eyeing me. Remember, darlin', I'm all yours!'"

He didn't have a chance to say much after that, for Milo had grabbed a pillow and was trying to kill him with it.

"You idiot!" she snapped as she chased him around the room. "What a stupid thing to say! How insulting! You ain't mine! And I ain't yours! Like I would want you! Really!"

He was laughing madly, dodging around the granite table, and hopping on and off the furniture, all the while still talking through Ajsha, who was taking it all as great sport.

"And he says," she called, giggling, "'It is completely optional for you to slap a girl if she comes up and kisses me!'"

Milo snorted. "She can have you for all I care!" she huffed, lunging at Simon with the pillow.

Once this reached Simon, he threw back his head and laughed. In once swift motion, he suddenly whirled around and caught Milo up in his arms. He was about to kiss her, when, out of pure fury, she kicked him in a spot that males find quite painful. No eloquent words can accurately describe the scene that happened next.

First of all, Simon was in a lot of pain, and Ajsha was frozen in shock. But Milo was brimming satisfaction, though she didn't show it. She also didn't show any remorse, and just let the poor lad sink to the floor, groaning and making another funny little sound that was so extraordinary, I haven't bothered to try to describe it.

Ajsha hurried over to him, gibbering comfortingly. Milo leaned over him with a smirk on her face. Now, Milo had never been a mean child, but what she had done, any boy would admit, was exceptionally mean. As Simon looked up at her through wide eyes, he looked at her with new respect, and also with slight fear. It took a while, but eventually Simon unraveled himself and got to his feet. He avoided eye contact with Milo as he limped by her. They all changed and went to bed, Milo giggling for half the night, and Simon not daring to do anything to make her stop.

In the morning Milo ventured outside and picked an island fruit for Ajsha's breakfast. After peeling it, she chopped it into uniform cubes and scraped it into a bowl.

"I'm sorry that I don't have anything for you for lunch," Milo said, as she set it down in front of Ajsha.

"Don't worry about it," Ajsha replied. "I'll just share with someone. Now, are you ready for the day? Do you have our money system down?"

"Oh, yeah!" said Milo, flourishing a piece of paper, on which the Galo currency was converted into dollars and cents. She stuffed it into her pocket. "As long as the boy has the dough, we'll be fine."

She dropped the child off at school, briefly stopped in at Soldier's to ogle at the little speaker, and then trekked back to the house to care for the vacant kitchen. Once it was as spotless and organized as possible, she proceeded with the daily routine of listening to her radio and writing in her diary. After a while she got bored and squirmy, and checked the tiny letters in the corner of her watch to see if it was washing day. It wasn't, for today wasn't Thursday, so she went meandering through the hut, half-heartedly searching for anything that needed to be tidied. In a serious blow to her rebellion, she had recently been doing housework willingly just to avoid boredom.

The house being as scrupulously clean as dirt floors and eclectic furniture allow for, she sat outside by the door to wait for Simon.

Chaos toddled by, and Milo picked her up. She stroked Chaos, lamenting difficult day she had ahead of her, until she saw her hubby come into view. Milo kissed the cat on her fluffy head and put her down, much to her displeasure.

As Milo stood up, Simon approached her, but stopped at a healthy distance. Milo chuckled. Simon cocked his head and stepped a little bit closer. This quelled Milo's mirth. They stood awkwardly for a minute, not used to it being just the two of them. Without an interpreter there to translate, they each began to think of different ways to communicate. Simon was the first to attempt it. He said her name, still with a lilt, and pointed towards the path to town. Milo caught on at once and rubbed her thumb and first two fingers together to indicate money.

Apparently, this is a universally recognized gesture, for Simon nodded and disappeared into the house. Curious, Milo followed. She tailed him to their bedroom, where he went to his bureau. He fished around in its top drawer, and pulled out a leather pouch. Shutting the drawer, he left the room. As he walked past Milo, he shook the pouch in front of her face. It made little clinking, clanging sounds.

They headed for the path through the trees, not quite side by side and the silence was as thick as cold gravy. Other than passing a few people on the path, they went undisturbed for a while, until a boy came running out of a house in the distance. He ran up to Simon, a coil of rope in hand, gave his shoulder a friendly bump, and started yammering away in Galo.

Milo waited impatiently as Simon replied, pointing at her and swinging his money pouch. The boy, who was even tanner than Simon and had shaggy, black tresses, nodded, and waved at Milo. She gave him a half wave, stopping her hand in midair. The boy ended the conversation by making a remark that made Simon laugh, waving vaguely at the forest and then running off. Simon turned back to Milo, who was squinting suspiciously at him, and gestured to move on. Milo resumed walking, but wished she knew what that boy had said.

At last they arrived in town, vibrantly garbed people bustling about at usual, the air filled with the indistinct buzz of Galo. Milo tried to think of a way ask Simon which store they should visit first. She needn't have wasted her imagination; Simon was already heading for a rectangular building on the right side of the road. Milo hastened to catch up. They entered the store to find long, raft-like tables lining the walls, with two end to end in the middle. Sitting on the tables were boxes similar to crates, and each one was filled with fruit. By the east wall were bananas, mangos, guava, oranges, and kiwis. The north wall exhibited limes, star fruit, lemons, papayas, and a type of fruit that looked like a combination of a plum and pear. The west wall belonged to the manager, though he was not in a crate. He was reclining in a chair behind a table that held, instead of fruit, various devices for counting money. The tables in the middle were covered with different kinds of berries.

For a minute, Milo stood in the threshold and admired the quaint, orderly place. The only windows were set high in the walls and were the size of grapefruits, letting in concentrated sunbeams. A lantern hung from the ceiling to help with the lighting. A stack of woven reed shopping baskets sat by the entrance, different sized bowls for berries in all of them.

Milo reached down to grab the handle of one of the baskets, but just as Simon did, too. They both pulled it into the air, and immediately tried to wrench it out of each other's grasp. Milo glared threateningly at him; he made no expression at all, but clung tightly. Neither one was willing to relinquish their grip, though they were probably going to need two baskets anyway. Simon motioned to the rest in the pile and gave a tug. Milo shook her head sharply and tugged back. This went on for another minute, the yanks getting increasingly more aggressive, before Milo picked up another basket and thrust it at him. Realizing that he wasn't going to get the one they were fighting over, Simon grudgingly accepted the other basket.

Milo whirled away with her trophy and ambled into the room. Since the windows were so few and miniscule, letting in only a small amount of the humid outside air, it was rather cool inside the store. Not to mention, when Milo took another look at the ceiling, she noticed an enormous, rotating fan, the blades made out of a blend of banana leaves and palm fronds. Milo was fascinated and had no idea how it was even functioning, until she looked over at the manager and saw he was idly cranking a lever on the wall. The lever was attached to a plethora of ropes and cogs that snaked up the wall, leading to the fan. There were so many of them, all reducing in size and length as they wound down from the ceiling, that turning the lever looked amazingly easy.

"Of course it has to be cool inside here," Milo mused. *"They're storing fruit."*

She began at the north wall, selecting a small bunch of yellow, sickle shaped bananas. She didn't get too many, because she knew bananas don't last long. After picking out a few oranges, she realized that she couldn't read the little price signs because they were in Galo. There also didn't seem to be any written in English. She looked around for Simon and spied him sifting through the raspberries, which were the only thing, besides fish, that they weren't out of. Apparently, Simon liked raspberries and bought them often.

"Hey!" she snapped at him. He didn't look up, for he was unaware what "Hey!" meant. Milo seethed and reluctantly called out, "Simon!"

His head shot up, and, seeing Milo beckoning to him, he joined her. She prodded meaningfully at the little price signs. Simon tapped three bananas one by one, put up two fingers, and said, "Dlos."

"A'ight," Milo said, consulting her slip of paper. "Three bananas equal two dollars."

She indicated to the oranges, and learned that they were one dlo each. The kiwis were one brun, or 50 cents, for two; the limes and lemons were worth the same, while the papayas were one dlo each. She moved on to berries, which were priced by the size of the bowl that the customer put them in. The smallest bowl was one brun, the medium one was one dlo, and the largest was two dlos. Milo got a medium bowl of blackberries, a small bowl of boysenberries, and a small bowl of mulberries. Simon got two large bowls of raspberries.

He had other fruit in his basket that Milo hadn't seen on any of the tables. She pointed to it, sweeping her free hand back and forth inquisitively. He led her to a partially hidden table in the back. It had crates of mangos, litchi, pomegranates, guava, and cantaloupe. After deciphering the prices for all these, and for the odd plum/pear fruit that Milo had dubbed a plar, she continued with her fruit browsing. For a split second, while they were walking in opposite directions down the same aisle, Simon was blocking her way, and she pretended to kick him again. Yelping, he scooted to the side, holding his basket at a particular angle. Milo chuckled merrily and moseyed past him, her head high.

More patrons came into the store before they were ready to check out. During that time, Milo made sure Simon stayed far away from her by intimidating him with her left foot. When they did check out, the manager, or whoever he was, used an abacus to calculate the cost. He tipped the berries into separate cloth bags, and loaded the rest of the fruit into one big sack; the firm fruits on the bottom and the soft ones on top. He added the little bags, and Simon handed him two gens, which were flattened, oval pieces of red metal that had been stamped with the island seal.

Leaving that store, Simon led the way to the next one. As they were walking, they passed a shop that sold meat. Milo knew that they didn't need any, but peeked in through a window anyway. She saw the same elongated, raft-like tables, only laden with slabs and filets of fish, shellfish heaped in buckets of water, a type of meat that looked like beef, and a few boar cuts. She nodded, mentally filing away this information, and ran to keep up with Simon. She figured that boar meat was either very popular, or they hadn't caught many boars yet.

It dawned on Milo that the stores sold goods according to classification, like the sections of a grocery store divided into separate buildings. One had fruit, another had meat, and surely there would be one for baking and dairy products. The shop they entered next offered vegetables.

Milo went straight to work, gathering potatoes, carrots, a radish, onions, cabbage, lettuce, watercress, and several tomatoes. Simon got chicory, sorrel, cardoon, salsify, parsnips, kohlrabi, and a bunch more that I don't know how to pronounce. Once everything was paid for, Milo went outside to wait for Simon, who had gotten sucked into a conversation with the store owner. As she loitered by the side of the building, shifting through her purchases, Milo discovered that she had accidentally bought a rotten tomato. Hearing the thud of footsteps, she looked up to see Simon coming down the stairs. Her mouth twisting maniacally, she hid the tomato behind her back and sauntered up to him.

He eyed her warily, but relaxed when he saw her shake her head. She set her bags down, being careful not to reveal the tomato, and came even closer. As she slowly advanced, he backed up, trying to keep her within his line of vision. When he was almost up against the outer wall of the store, Milo extended an arm towards him, indicating that she wanted a hug.

The poor fool should have realized by then that whenever Milo acted nice, she actually wanted to play a trick. But he was so hopelessly in love with her that he jumped at the chance to show his affection. As he came close, grinning with surprise, Milo quickly put the hand with the tomato behind his head, him not noticing anything. Using her other fingers, she pushed lightly on his sternum. He was somewhat stunned and took stepped backwards, repeatedly looking from his chest to her face, which was coated with a deceptively sweet look. They kept going backwards and just as Simon slammed his back against the wall, Milo dropped the tomato down his shirt.

Milo had heard Simon yelp and even shout before, but she had never heard him scream. However, that's exactly what issued from his throat when he felt rotten tomato guts squish against his back. Truthfully, he thought that he had backed up into a nail and it was his blood that was oozing out all over his skin. Except, it was very cold blood, and it gave off a rather pungent aroma. The smell and the fact that he wasn't in any pain made him realize what had happened, and he never told anyone, excluding one person, what he had thought it was. The juices were seeping through his shirt, undoubtedly staining it, and Milo was consumed by gales of laughter.

Simon stepped forward, the empty tomato carcass falling to the ground, and glared at her with a You-Untrustworthy-Liar!-look. Milo, hardly daunted, noticed a few of his friends nearby and pointed to them, giving Simon a Why-Don't-You-Give-Up-And-Go-Play?-look. Simon glanced in that direction, set his jaw, straightened his back (it had been slightly hunched) and resolutely went on walking, tomato seeds dripping from the back of his shirt.

Milo groaned but followed, first fetching her bags. He led her, in a dignified way that is earned and not bestowed, up to another shop. They entered, Simon holding open the door for Milo though not looking at her, and Mrs. Lanslo jumped up to greet them.

"Why, hello, dears!" she cried, bustling out from behind the counter.

"Hiya, Mrs. Lanslo," Milo answered, holding her breath as she strode past Simon. "How you doing? Still single?"

"W-why yes, dear," she said, startled. "My husband died while I was still living in Ireland. Why do you ask?"

"No reason, no reason," Milo said, glancing around to confirm that the shop they were in sold wheat and dairy products.

She went further into the large, airy room, while Simon paused to speak to Mrs. Lanslo. Milo had an inkling that he was complaining about her. This store contained rotund barrels, instead of tables, brimming with flour and various other grains. Different sized bags hung beside the barrels, half buried scoops sticking out of their contents. The only tables were at the back, neatly laden with crates that held crude glass bottles of milk and makeshift metal tins of butter. One crate, bristling with straw, nestled eggs that Milo had never seen before. They were little, squat, and spotted, unlike the chicken eggs she had used in America. She saw many that resembled the one Simon had given her. There were padded cartons beside these crates, with hollows for the eggs, ranging from a dozen to half a dozen.

Milo edged past a few fellow customers and collected a dozen of the chicks that would never hatch. She was unsure how much butter to get. One tin seemed good, while two seemed better. When it comes to butter, more is always the desired option. She decided on two and moved on to the milk. Simon was already there, and handed her two bottles. Giving him a snide grimace, Milo deliberately got another one. Her basket now uncomfortably heavy, she directed herself towards the flour, the one thing she needed a lot of. Simon seemed to have plenty of experience buying flour, and wanted to get it himself. How did Milo know this? Because when she tried to pick up the scoop, he grabbed it as well.

They glared at each other over the barrel, neither one letting go. Milo jabbed her chin at another barrel, but Simon, his nose burning from his brand new scent, was agitated at the moment and in no mood to be submissive. He pointed to a different barrel, using his own chin. Milo shook her head and tried to jerk the scoop out of his grasp. He pulled back, plunging the tip into the flour, but neither noticed. Milo pulled it back into the air, to shoulder height.

They still didn't realize it was full, and Simon gave a mighty tug in his direction, enveloping him in a cloud of flour.

When the dust settled, his upper body looked a bit like a ghost, the flour granules coating him in a nice, even layer of white. Everyone in the store, after catching the commotion out the corners of their eyes, faced him and began to laugh. Milo was already doubled over, laughing her ever-loving stomach off, and even Mrs. Lanslo gave off a hearty Irish chuckle. Simon was the only one who wasn't laughing. He was staring at Milo, his face slack as if he was going to cry. He was in total possession of the scoop now; Milo had released it. Milo, still giggling, continued on with getting flour, dumping it into a sack. When she was done, she practically had to drag Simon over to the checkout. With his back to her, she saw that the flour was clinging to the tomato juices.

Simon paid for the groceries, sneezing a couple of times, and they left. He refused to pay any attention to Milo, who traipsed along beside him and couldn't stop snickering. Whoever saw them on the street was overcome by hilarity as well. A boy or two called out to Simon, making him snort and wipe vigorously at his face. They had one more stop to make before home.

It was a little shop that sold vegetable oil, coconut shavings, sea salt, honey, and stuff like that. Milo was delighted to see that they had honey, though she was horrified at the price. She was sniffing at an open bottle of oil, when Simon decided to try to talk to her. The trip to the market wasn't going well, and he wanted to get things under control before they got worse. He walked up behind her and tried to get her attention with a few words, but everyone in the shop was speaking Galo and Milo didn't think any of it was directed at her. So when Simon loudly said, "Milo!" she jumped in pure fright and whirled around, oil launching from the bottle onto Simon's face.

It dripped down his hair and mixed with the flour. I'm not sure if you've ever felt any type of oil, though chances are most of you have, but it is unpleasant and slimy to the touch, and must be rubbed off with a dry cloth. It is even more unpleasant when it is on your face, as Simon found out as her tried to rub it out of his eyes. Milo quivered with suppressed giggles, though Simon didn't see a solitary thing funny about the situation. Using his floury arm, he wiped the oil out of his eyes, muttering something in Galo, of which she only registered her name. As he walked away, Milo could have sworn she saw a tear on his cheek, before realizing it was a bead of oil.

They purchased the items and began for home, encumbered by bags and receiving a multitude of hoots and whistles. Simon glared at Milo, and she stuck out her tongue at him. The oil was trickling down his neck, collecting flour and making crumbly wads of dough on his shoulders.

"I guess you do have the dough," Milo told him.

They arrived at the house, arms aching, and had just deposited the groceries on the kitchen table when there was a knock at the door. Milo opened it to reveal the black haired boy Simon had talked to on their way to the market.

"Simon?" he asked politely.

Milo let him in, since he wasn't a member of the beach gang, and when he saw Simon, he inhaled sharply, working to stifle a chuckle. Simon obviously did not want to discuss his current condition and stonily left to change.

"Sorry," Milo told the boy, while unpacking the food. "He's a bit of a grouch today."

Soon Simon was back, his clothes different and by contrast starkly clean, but his face was still a mess. Addressing this issue, he went over to the sink, stuck his head in, and pumped water over his hair and face. As he busily scrubbed off the caked on flour and oil, Milo, still feeling wicked, bumped him "accidentally", and his head collided with the side of the sink. His friend burst out laughing, and Milo raced into the other room. Crouching behind a chair, she heard them shouting and then the creaking and slam of the front door.

She grinned and went back to the kitchen and the awaiting cupboards. At precisely 4:15 Ajsha appeared, sashaying jauntily up to the hut. "Mother!" she called out. "I'm home!"

"No kidding," Milo said. "And, it's Milo! How was your 'outing'?"

"Great!" Ajsha answered, flouncing down at the table. "We went to the Fowl Farm. Where they raise the island birds for eggs," she explained, seeing Milo's alarmed glance.

Milo nodded. "Ohhh. It – well . . . Sounds like fun," she said bracingly.

"It was," Ajsha said. "I can't wait to tell you about it. But, how did the trip to the market go?"

When she heard this question, images sprang up in Milo's mind, and she began to laugh. She zealously related the trip to Ajsha, pausing now and then to chuckle. By the time she finished, Ajsha looked very solemn.

"Poor Father," she whispered.

"What?" Milo cried. "You don't think that's funny?"

"No."

"Not at all?"

"Not a bit."

"Ah! You're lost! By the way, who's that boy?"

"Probably Will Westron. He and Father are best friends and partners in catching boars. They work in the forest outside. He was also best man at the wedding."

"Really?" Milo said, trying to remember if she had seen him up at the altar. His face didn't ring a bell, but honestly, that veil had made her vision fairly hazy. Shrugging, Milo ended the conversation because she had to collect papayas from outside.

"I didn't buy any because I knew I could just go and pick some," she felt the need to explain. Ajsha nodded, still staring at her dolefully. Milo, with great effort, ignored this and dug out a basket from under a counter. She headed outside and was shortly tramping through the forest. After walking for a stretch, she found a papaya tree and picked some ripe ones. She then wandered aimlessly for a bit, until she heard the familiar shouting of the beach, which ran adjacent to the trees. For some reason, just the thought of the water made her shudder.

Hesitating, she tried to estimate how far she was from the beach, and since she could just hear the surf, she figured not far. Taking a few paces forward, she suddenly heard the swishing of ropes and *vvwoooop!* She was flipped upside down, her feet caught in a boar trap, her papayas scattering into the brush.

Milo screamed as she swung back and forth in the air, the blood gushing to her head and her ponytail trailing down like a thick, brown bell rope. Foliage and bark fused into one and swam around her sickeningly, until she started to slow down. The ground was too far away for her to grab hold of any plants, and struggle as she might, she could not break loose. As she stopped swinging, she had to use both hands to keep her shirt up. She stopped screaming and, her lungs heaving, peered up at her feet. They were hopelessly entwined in the difficult knots she had seen before, but she saw a spot where if she pulled hard enough it would all come undone. Taking a couple of deep inhales, she tried reaching up to get to it, but she couldn't quite reach. Her muscles gave out and she went limp, swinging once more. She didn't get an opportunity to try again, for her screaming had alerted someone from the beach, and that someone was now crashing through the forest towards her.

"Oh, good," thought Milo, immensely dizzy. "*They can cut me down.*"

She might have been right, but the person who appeared in front of her was none other than Simon, her husband. He was slightly out of breath and looked highly concerned, but when he saw who it was he looked her up and down, and grinned.

"Hey!" Milo snapped, making sure to keep her shirt up,

concealing all the necessaries. "Simon! Hey! Cut me down!"

Simon, still smirking, leisurely began to circle her, wearing a look that plainly said, "Well, well, *well!* What do we have here?" He turned on heel and walked the other way. He didn't seem in a hurry to assist her in any way.

"Simon!" Milo barked, some desperation creeping in. "Cut me down, right now! Right now! You little weasel! Oh, come on! Please?"

He leaned languidly against a tree and gave her a pleasant, smug smile.

Milo sighed. "You're not going to cut me down, are you?" she muttered.

He tilted his head to one side, still wearing his smile, his eyes roaming up to where her hands gripped the hem of her T-shirt. Milo groaned and tried to figure out what to do.

"What should I do?" she asked Bob the Conscience.

"You shouldn't have been so mean to him at the market," he told her.

"I realize that now, Bob," she said grumpily. "But what should I do *now*, at this very moment? How do I get out of this predicament?"

"I'm a conscience," he said. "I'm supposed to make you feel guilty with the truth. Not solve your problems."

"You're not being very helpful," Milo growled.

"Think hard, Milo," he said waspishly. "If he ain't gonna untie you, you need to do it. Duh!"

"I know that! But, my shirt"

"What about it?"

"It won't stay up! And he's here!"

"Oh hoooo! Right, right, right, right, right, right, right! Well! Looks like you have a problem! Hmmm. Bye!"

"Bob?" Milo cried. "Bob?! Bob!! Bob!!! BOB!!!!" she screamed. "Thanks for nothing."

Fuming, she examined her position. She was caught in a boar

trap by her feet, swinging upside down like a pendulum. She couldn't untie herself, because for that she needed both hands and those were currently holding up her shirt because a boy was present.

"My life is crap," she muttered.

She peered at Simon's upside down form. He was giving her a "Well! Look where you are now! Perhaps you'll be nicer to me the next time we go to the market, eh?" look.

"I know!" Milo cried, slowly revolving in a circle. "I know I deserve this! Okay? I admit it, I was a jerk. Look! I'm sorry! All right? Is that what you want? I'm sorry and I won't do it again, and – and you can't understand me! Aw, crap. Where's an Ajsha when you need one?"

Knowing that he wouldn't be freeing her any time soon, she again attempted to use just one hand to unravel the knots. She reached and reached, but was unsuccessful. Panting, she let her hand drop back then tried again. The fifth effort met failure and she sighed. Just a little bit more and she could be free. She shut her eyes, forcefully breathing in and out. Making up her mind, she whispered,

"Okay. One, two . . . three!!"

She let go of her shirt, stretched up and seized the rope. In one furious tug the rope untangled, sending her crashing to the leafy jungle floor. Moaning, the impact much more painful than she thought it was going to be, she thought she heard laughter. Wincing, Milo lifted her head and saw, through the shrubbery, Simon sink to the ground, laughing uproariously. Enraged, her soreness instantly evaporated and she rapidly stood up. Simon saw her and how angry she was, and, still laughing, scrambled to his feet.

"YOU!" she bellowed.

She ran at him and he had just enough time to sprint away.

"When I catch you, I'll kill you!" she screamed after him.

He didn't know exactly what she was saying, but the implications were clear enough.

They sped through the jungle, dodging tree trunks and leaping over exposed roots, each being whipped in the face by twigs and vines. Simon had taken full advantage of his head start, but Milo wasn't easing up on her gait. Running had been the one thing she was good at in gym, and she had no intention of letting Simon escape. Of course, she was becoming increasingly hoarse, still shouting a good amount of fatal threats at him. They managed to get out of the forest, miraculously, without either one tripping, their zigzagging course leading them out onto the beach. They emerged into a blast of sunlight reflecting off the ocean, and kept running.

Simon ran all the way to their house, where Ajsha was sitting under a tree, chin in hand, reading a book. She saw them swiftly approaching and stood up.

"Ajsha!" Simon called out. He collapsed in front of her and quickly crawled behind her.

"Ajsha!" Milo cried, falling to her knees, coughing dryly.

"What is going on?" Ajsha asked, first in Galo then in English.

Simon started chuckling from behind her legs. Milo smoldered.

"That vile, repulsive, immature idiot –"

Simon cut in, jabbering rapidly in Galo, explaining what happened before he was made to look like a pervert. When he finished, Ajsha, to Milo's horror, began to laugh.

"What are you laughing at?" she demanded, clutching a stitch in her side. "You think that is funny?!"

"Well, you did deserve it," Ajsha said, gaining control of herself.

"Oh, I did, did I?" Milo snarled.

"Well," Ajsha said, flouncing down beside her, "what do you think?"

Milo, still livid, glared at Simon. He was grinning uncontrollably and giving her a look that said, "I'm sorry. I guess we're even now."

Milo sighed, kneading a spot on her forehead. "I think," she began, "I'm going to behave myself at the market."

17
To Dig a Cellar!

THERE ARE PEOPLE in the world who are brilliant. There are people in the world who are smart. There people in the world who are clever, and then there are people in the world who are bright. There are also those who are smart yet clever, and some that are clever yet bright. Then there are people who are semi-bright, but lack smart. Some people are slightly bright, extremely smart, with just a touch of cleverness. Not to mention that there are a rare few who are completely brilliant, not so smart, cleverly bright, and brightly clever.

Milo Hestler (who was really Milo Swallow) so, therefore, Milo Swallow (who was really Milo Hestler), but anyways! *Milo* was one of the non-brilliant, semi-smart, terribly clever, pushing bright people. She was often trying to prove she was, to counterbalance the times when she clearly wasn't, and on occasion accomplished this without even thinking about it.

One of those times occurred near the end of September, particularly the second to last day, on a barbaric island that forced young women to marry atrocious, yet very cute, young men. If any of you are lost at all, I suggest you go back to the beginning of this book and reread the entire thing up until now. That should help jog your memory. For those of you who fully comprehend what's going on, let me continue.

As I said before, it was on the second to last day of September that Milo showed that she was a non-brilliant, semi-smart, terribly clever, pushing bright person. It was the day after another excursion to the market; it had been only a week since the last one, but Simon had insisted on going to see if Milo would really behave herself. She did, forcing herself into a civility that almost hurt, (offering him the first pick of shopping baskets, nodding her head in thanks when he opened a door for her, waiting for him if he stopped to chat with friends . . .)

Bolstered by this new, if not stiff, spurt of manners, Simon felt significantly reassured about market day, and even bought her a tiny bottle of honey, as if rewarding her. (Milo found this rather patronizing, but since she was practicing good manners and actually wanted some honey, she didn't press the matter.) However, Milo had her own reasons for needing to go to the market. Most of her vegetation had wilted from being inside the cupboards, which were inside an incredibly warm house that only got cool when it rained. Milo had to buy fresh ones, and the next day she went pacing back and forth in the kitchen, pondering on how to keep the produce from wilting. She knew that refrigerators were out of the question, and iceboxes were even less likely.

Chaos was on a counter, settled in a content position. The kitten had grown considerably, and all the fish tidbits had helped her pelt to become thick and shiny. She was watching her beloved owner walk to and fro. She didn't offer much help, but purred supportively and listened earnestly whenever Milo addressed her. Bob the Conscience had tried to be of service, but she was still mad about him running out on her when she was in the boar trap and was giving him the silent treatment. Finally, after drilling her brain for ideas, she sagged into a chair. Then out of the blue, without the help of Bob the Conscience, Ajsha, or even Chaos, Milo herself devised a solution.

A cellar!

"A cellar!" Milo said out loud.

"Come again?" Bob the Conscience requested.

"A cellar," Milo repeated, "and I'm not talking to you!"

"Sure, you're not," he said, very happy she had cracked; even a figment of the mind needs someone to talk to. "And a cellar, eh? Not a bad idea. I'm surprised that Simon doesn't have one already."

"So am I," Milo admitted, watching through a window as Ajsha came into the clearing. Milo checked her watch. It was about noon. She got up to greet her.

"Hello, Mother," Ajsha said, coming in through the door.

"It's Milo!" she said. "Please stop calling me that!"

Ajsha didn't reply and brushed past her into the kitchen, where she petted Chaos. She figured it was better to ignore than to lie. Milo followed her and motioned for her to sit. Ajsha willingly obeyed, Milo taking the chair opposite her.

"Ajsha," she began, not wasting any time, "why doesn't Simon have a cellar?"

Ajsha contemplated this query for a moment. "Well," she said reasonably, "no one ever dug him one."

"Why not?"

"Only the wealthy have cellars. Father is a mere fisherboy, and like the rest of the fisherboys, his house is a very simple dwelling. Nothing fancy."

"Well, we should have one!" Milo declared, standing up, as if becoming her own exclamation point.

"We can't afford one." Ajsha sighed. "This type of house is standard for people like Father."

"You're kidding me!" Milo snorted. "All this is way too good for that scuzball. But *I* need a cellar to keep food in. At least . . . until I get rescued."

"Still dreaming about that?" Ajsha asked.

"Yes," Milo said fiercely. "And why can't Simon just dig one himself?"

"Goodness! Father doesn't know how to dig a cellar," said Ajsha.

"Then I'll dig us one!" Milo proclaimed.

"You?"

"I!"

"What do you know about digging a cellar?"

"I'm not an idiot; I know a few things. We had cellars at the first two places I lived. I often went down and examined the architectural structure."

Catching her bemused look, Milo elaborated.

"Before I could read, I was a very bored child. Anyway, I think I can come up with something for us."

"That's wonderful," Ajsha said. "Though, I'm not sure if Father will like the idea."

"Then he won't find out," Milo said, sternly pointing at her. "And you had better not say anything to him!"

"Okay," Ajsha agreed, somewhat thrilled that they were sharing a secret.

Milo, driven by inspiration, immediately began measuring the floor. She chose a large, bare patch of dirt near the back wall and studied it, deliberating how she should dig. She thought and planned for the rest of the day, taking out her diary to scribble ideas on the last pages. After Simon came home, and all through a very subdued supper, she mulled it over. By the next morning, she finally had a decent concept in mind. She described it to Ajsha during breakfast.

"I drew out few designs until I came to an ideal one," she said, showing her a picture, which consisted mainly of stick figures and numbers. "What I'll do is, dig straight down until I'm low enough that the ground won't collapse when I dig outward. Of course, I'll probably reinforce everything with poles or something later on. When I do dig outward, it will be heading outside, under the side of the house. I don't want to risk the house sinking if something goes wrong, though I doubt anything will."

"Sounds good," said Ajsha, handing her back the paper. "I hope it works."

"It will," Milo said, sounding more confident than she felt. "The square I'll be digging," she went on, "will be about three feet each way. That should be big enough for anyone who might want to climb down."

"Still sounds good," Ajsha said, gathering her little book bag. "How are you going to hide it from Father while you're digging?"

Milo paused. "That part I haven't figured out. I thought about just covering the hole with a sheet or something, but you know how Simon can't control his curiosity. So, here's what I figure: He doesn't come home till you do, so while you're gone I'll work as fast as I can, and by the time we explain it all to him, I'll have done so much that he won't be able to stop me! Heh! He, he, he, he!" she cackled, rubbing her palms together.

She saw Ajsha's expression. "Sorry," she said hastily.

Ajsha nodded, taking mental notes. "Do you want me to walk to school by myself today?"

"Sure, why not."

Milo couldn't help but notice that she looked a wee bit disappointed.

"I need the head start," she explained.

Ajsha nodded and smiled faintly. She started for town, checking over her shoulder every so often as if she really did expect to see the house sink. Milo, after waving her off, went to the tool shed behind the hut. Throwing the door wide open, she inspected the walls, choosing a sturdy looking shovel with a short, thick handle. Dragging it into the kitchen, she marked off a square with her big toe, and, glancing repeatedly at her plans, slammed the point of the spade into the dirt.

Though the dirt was packed hard, it wasn't hard enough to withstand the narrow edge of the blade. However, before she could scoop out the shovelful of dirt, she remembered another part of her plan. Hurrying back to the shed, she took out the washtub and brought it back with her. Setting it next to the square on the floor, she dumped the dirt into it.

"I'll just wash it out really well, later," she muttered, hearing Bob the Conscience's affronted reprimands.

"You clean clothes in that!"

"I'LL WASH IT OUT REALLY WELL, LATER!"

She scooped and shoveled, and shoveled and scooped, happy that the dirt was easy to break up. An hour into it, her back and arms began to hurt. She had dug four feet and three inches down, creating a brown, boxy indentation in the floor. Each time the tub got full, Milo struggled to lift it and throw its contents out a window. But now that her vigor was running low, her stringy limbs trembling, she worked slower. Perhaps if the dirt had been more solid and her square a bit larger, she wouldn't have accomplished as much as she did before Simon and Ajsha came home. At about noontime, as father and daughter approached the house they couldn't help but notice a pile of dirt under one of the kitchen windows.

Simon looked at it with interest and Ajsha simply stared at it, hoping it didn't look too suspicious. It looked unbearably suspicious, though, when more dirt suddenly rocketed out of the window and onto the mound. Simon raised his eyebrows, though not exactly in surprise, and walked into the house. Ajsha followed quietly behind, praying that none of this would lead to an angry outburst. They entered the kitchen to find Milo by the far wall, dumping shovelfuls of dirt into the washtub. Milo didn't seem to notice them, until Simon said, in a tone that showed that he was amused and not outraged, "Milo!"

She turned around, panting softly with sweat dribbling down her neck. Simon spoke calmly to her, Ajsha translating his words.

"He said, 'Why are you digging up my kitchen floor?'"

Milo sighed and rammed the spade into the ground. "I," she said proudly, covered in a layer of perspiration and dust as if she had just reemerged from a mine, "am digging a cellar."

Simon was rather surprised when this was interpreted for him. "He said, 'Really?'"

"Yes," Milo replied indignantly. "What did you think I was doing? Do you think I dig holes in kitchen floors for absolutely no reason?"

Simon received this retort and shrugged. He gibbered a reply, gazing at her with a mixture of curiosity and awe. "He said, 'I don't know. You've done so many strange things since I met you. But I suppose you would have a good reason for digging up my floor. But why a cellar?'"

Milo snorted in frustration. "Because we need one, you idiot."

Ajsha translated and came back with, "'Sure, we may need one; everyone does, but we can't afford one. And don't call me an idiot.'"

"So what if we don't have the money?" Milo demanded, thumping the shovel for emphasis. "Just because we are *slightly* poor doesn't mean we have to live that way. Idiot!" she deliberately added. "I am digging us one. I know it's not something for amateurs, but I don't think I'll do too badly. I mean, it's not algebra."

Simon considered this, and the fact that he had never heard of algebra, but she made it sound so nasty that he was pretty glad he hadn't, and finally grinned at her.

"He says, 'If you think you can do it, I'll help with whatever you need. I never did like the idea that I'm at the bottom of the poverty line.'"

"So," Milo said cautiously, "you ain't mad that I'm doing this?"

"'No! Of course not!'"

"Good!" she snapped. "Not that I care, but there's no turning back now, and I don't want to find you sneaking dirt back in the middle of the night!"

Simon threw up his hands, smiling hugely. Through Ajsha, he offered to make lunch and Milo accepted. Defending her plans had renewed her verve and she felt like she could dig to China. Pausing only for short bites, she continued to shovel while Simon and Ajsha sat at the table, chewing fish medley. Simon pumped a glass of water for her and, again through Ajsha, insisted that she drink it. Milo agreed, but only because she was beginning to feel a bit woozy.

Once lunch was over, Ajsha left to play outside, but Simon stayed behind to watch Milo. Maybe he thought she needed the company, or perhaps the notion of a cellar fascinated him and he wanted to witness its creation. Either way, Milo ignored his presence, far too absorbed in her task for such trivialities. He remained at the table, his head propped up sideways on the back of his hand. Milo had her back to him, the hole's depth forcing her to bend over to gather the dirt. She knew that she would eventually have to get *in* the hole in order to burrow further, but not just yet. After a while, Milo occasionally straightening up to crack her back, a realization suddenly hit her. Startled but still unsure, she bent over and pretended to ruffle the dirt with her fingers, while surreptitiously peering past her legs.

Simon, from where he sat watching, had a pleased look on his face; an approving, intrigued look. Some strands of his hair fell in front of his eyes, and he subconsciously brushed them back behind his ear, not taking his eyes off what he was staring at. Milo was horrified. Some of you might think that she was merely jumping to conclusions, as many people do, but Milo had deduced right.

To be fair, Simon's staring wasn't entirely his fault. Sure, he wasn't under hypnotism by some messed up infidel, but Simon *was* attracted to Milo. All of her. Every inch of her. Was it a good thing to do? Absolutely not! It was, in fact, very disrespectful, and rather unwise, especially when he knew that Milo hated him. But, like most boys, he couldn't help but stare at the girl he was attracted to.

White hot anger flared up in Milo. She was so mad she didn't

know what to do, what the etiquette was for these kinds of inci-
dents. Her mind raced pell-mell and stumbled upon her father's last
words to her. Mr. Hestler's last words of wisdom. Flinging away the
shovel, Milo whirled around, stomped up to Simon, and slugged
him. Right across the jaw.

The skin on skin and bone on bone made a sharp smack/crack
noise that echoed throughout the room. Simon gasped, as did Milo:
Her fist hurt; his jaw hurt. He jumped up, clutching his chin and
gaping at her in bewilderment.

"You horrible, disgusting sleaze!" she screamed at him.

She punched him in his stomach. Milo wasn't strong to make
much of an impact, but she had the element of surprise and sharp
fists. Simon made an "oomph!" sound and fell to his knees, clasping
his stomach. Milo pivoted and carried on by kicking him first in
the back and then in the legs. He twisted around and tried to scuttle
away, not getting more than a yard before Milo kicked him in the
oblique. He yelled out, undoubtedly asking her to stop, which she
had no intention of doing.

Now, her father had said to slug him, not to beat him ruthlessly.
But the first hit had felt so good she just had to go on. Simon,
curling up as she again took aim at his abdomen, summoned as
much of his voice as he could, and blared his loudest for Ajsha.
Milo froze in mid-kick when she heard little feet running towards
the house. Making a quick decision, she deserted the boy, leaving
him sprawled on the floor, and hastily resumed digging.

Ajsha barged into the house with a frantic expression and rushed
into the kitchen, where she saw Simon huddled in the dirt. She
yelped and went to lean over to him. She gently touched his
shoulder and he flinched. Peeking out from amid his crossed arms,
he saw it was Ajsha and seemed to sag with relief.

"What happened?" she asked Milo.

She shrugged. "I don't know," she said carelessly, casually tossing
a shower of earth into the washtub. "I was just digging and suddenly

I heard him fall to the floor and start screaming. Has he been doing that for as long as you've known him?"

Ajsha, the polar opposite of a stupid child, didn't buy this one bit. Kneeling down beside him, she softly gibbered to Simon, asking for his version. When he finished, she was frowning. As much as she disliked it, unfortunately she believed this story was the truth.

"Mother," she began sternly.

"Milo!" said Milo under her breath.

"How could you do this?" Ajsha inquired severely, standing up and folding her arms as she had seen so many adults do for serious matters. "After all you've been through with abuse, you now do this to an innocent boy for no good reason?"

"Innocent!" Milo cried, throwing the shovel to the ground and whisking around. "No good reason! Looks like he wasn't telling you the whole story! Don't ever want to be the bad guy, huh, Simon? I don't hurt people for nothing, and let me tell you! He did something!"

"What?" Ajsha inquired.

"He was staring at my butt!" she shouted.

When she had discovered this, she had felt violated, dirty, and betrayed. But after she had throttled him, all three feelings faded away, out of satisfaction; but she was still mutinously mad.

Ajsha was staring blankly at her, wondering whether or not to laugh. This seemed like a Not kind of a situation. Carefully, she chose her next words.

"And . . . that offended you?"

Milo gawked at her. "Yes!" she replied hotly. "Of course it did! The creep! He has no right to be staring at my butt!"

"Why not?" Ajsha asked, controlling herself. "You are married."

"So what?!" Milo projected dubiously.

"So, it's not like he's just some weirdo on the street. And you shouldn't be hurting your husband at all. You don't want to turn into a husband beater."

"Hey! I ain't no husband beater!"

"Maybe not, but you could turn into one. Most husband beaters don't realize they're husband beaters until they are one. Now, please excuse us, Father and I need to talk."

Ajsha helped, or forced, Simon up and together they hobbled into the other room. Milo was left alone with her shovel and dirt. She wasn't certain what had just happened, but kept hearing Bob the Conscience cough something that sounded suspiciously like, "Overreacted!" Glowering, but with nothing else to do, she continued to dig. Hours passed by. Simon went to town, Ajsha went outside, and Milo went down deep. She was at six feet now, and had developed a method to get to the top without a ladder, but she didn't need it just then.

After a while she decided to use it, since the temperature appeared to be dropping. Using the blade of the shovel, she carved out a wide notch in the wall of earth. She dug out many more, making sure they were all approximately one foot apart. When she had enough to reach the top, she stopped, flung the shovel up, and climbed out.

At the top, she lay on her tum and stabbed out the rest of the notches. She estimated that she was down seven feet, four inches, and wondered if it was safe yet to tunnel outward.

"Another foot should do," she decided as Ajsha came in.

She looked Milo over and frowned.

"You need a shower," she told her.

"Don't I know it," she said, emptying the tub out the window. There was quite a heap by now and threatened to spill back into the kitchen. "Great news, I think I'll be able to dig straight ahead tomorrow. I'll need some equipment, but otherwise I'm good."

"Yes," Ajsha said tentatively. "About tomorrow. You and Simon have an appointment."

"For what?" Milo said, washing her hands at the sink.

"A therapy session," Ajsha answered in a nervous tone.

Milo seemed stunned at this news, giving Ajsha a baffled look.

"He made the appointment today," Ajsha explained rapidly. "We are worried about what happened."

"Aw!" Milo said dismissively. "Nothing happened today that therapy can cure!"

"Please!" Ajsha begged. She had foreseen such resistance. "Dr. Dri can help!"

Milo, who was wiping her hands on a dish rag, paused with alarm and stared at her. "Did you just say Dr. Dre?" she demanded breathlessly.

"No," Ajsha said. "Dr. Dri. Iiiiii."

Milo chuckled and said, "Heck, child! If Dr. Dre were my therapist than I'd gladly go."

Ajsha's brow puckered in confusion. "Who's Dr. Dre?" she asked.

Milo got a faraway look in her eyes. "Just a legend," she whispered. She sighed and looked at Ajsha, whose eyes were moist. Milo groaned. "Fine! Fine, all right. Therapy! Woo-hoo! Will you be going with us?"

"Of course," she answered happily, relieved by Milo's willingness. "How else are you going to know what he's saying?"

"How much will this cost Simon?"

"Nothing! It's free! Isn't that wonderful? The Mayor pays Dr. Dri to have sessions with any couple that needs it. Since they can't divorce, he wants to help them if their marriage isn't going well. Sessions are *required* if a partner is beating another."

"Please," Milo said, sinking to her knees, "don't ever use the term *partner* again! And, fine! But I'm not going to get in touch with my inner child. No matter how much he asks! I've been trying for years to break away from my inner child. Now that I have, I ain't going back! She isn't the happiest person, and every time we would get together for tea, she would get all dismal and depressed."

"Oh, really?" Ajsha said, mentally writing down this tidbit. "You would have tea with her?"

"Yeah," Milo said, in a tone that implied she had no idea what she had been thinking.

"I didn't know you drank tea. What type do you like?"

"Mostly chamomile. Yeah, I love chamomile tea. Haven't had it in a while, though. Chamomile tea is something you absolutely need to take your time with and enjoy, but whenever I would have it with my inner child she would go all negative and mopey. I could never concentrate on my tea whenever I was around her, she often brought me down. Me!"

"Is that so?" Ajsha said, mesmerized. "Well, don't worry. I'm sure that Dr. Dri won't be asking you to talk to her."

"Thank heaven," Milo said, beginning supper preparations, clean and pale up to her elbows.

Later, during the meal, Simon, in an effort he apparently thought loving and patient, tried to personally explain to her why they were going to a therapist. Milo, however, had specifically instructed Ajsha not to tell her anything he said. Ajsha apologetically explained this to Simon and dutifully obeyed her mother's orders. While she was eating and ignoring Simon's incoherent noises, Milo mulled over what she would need for the cellar. She figured she would need something to help stabilize its ceiling and walls.

"*Poles should do the trick,*" she thought, munching on creamed peas. "*I'm not sure how Simon will take it if he sees me chopping wood again. But maybe I can get him to do it for me; he's got to be mad at me, but he did say that he'd help me if I needed it. I'll ask him tomorrow, after the Appointment.*"

The next morning she dug down roughly another foot and marked off where she would excavate straight ahead of her. Beaming with satisfaction, she then needed to climb out, shower, and change. She had bathed the night before, always stressful when Simon was at home, but she was just as filthy now. When she walked, swathed in towels, into her and Simon's bedroom, there were a skirt and a cute blouse waiting for her on the bed. She growled darkly at them and shoved them aside.

"Nice try, Simon," she muttered, dressing in her usual uniform.

She met Ajsha and Simon outside at noon, and the three headed for town. Simon didn't seem at all surprised to see her dressed normally, but Ajsha gave her an odd squint. After the typical hike, they arrived in town, and the boy guided them to a small, no-nonsense building. They knocked, Milo scrutinizing the bronze nameplate that had clearly once been the bottom of a bird cage. She couldn't read it. The door was presently opened by a pretty, petite lady with black skin. Smiling at all of them, flashing sparkling white teeth, she ushered them inside.

"She's Dr. Dri's wife," Ajsha whispered to Milo as they stepped into the waiting room. The walls were lined with loveseats. "She's also his secretary."

"What's her name?"

"Marisa Dri," she replied. "Pretty, isn't she?"

"Too good for a therapist," Milo muttered.

Instead of having to wait and take up three loveseats, they were herded farther into the building. Mrs. Dri led them to a room in the rear, where she left them. The room had a desk, two couches and a couple of chairs in it. In one of the chairs sat a black skinned, middle-aged man, dressed impeccably in what had to be the scavenged suit of a traveling businessman and holding a clipboard and pen. To Milo, Dr. Dri could have passed for Dr. Dre, if he just got rid of that well-trimmed beard. Well, she could always pretend.

He stood up to welcome them, grinning blindingly. Murmuring graciously, he gave Simon's hand a hearty shake and Ajsha's a soft one. When he tried to shake Milo's hand, she brushed past him and flopped down on a couch. Dr. Dri regarded her behavior evenly, gibbered to Simon and Ajsha, and then sat back down. Simon moved to sit beside Milo, but she held up her hand and then pointed to a chair. He sighed in agitation, but still sat in the specified chair. Ajsha sat beside Milo.

Dr. Dri cleared his throat began to gibber, directing his words mostly to Simon.

Ajsha said quietly, "He is saying, 'I'm happy to see you, if not happy for the reason. I had figured you, Simon, would be the last person on earth who would need this.'"

Simon gave a noncommittal twitch.

"'So,'" Dr. Dri went on, giving Milo an appraising glance, "'this is her. Not a bad choice, but you say she attacked you yesterday.'"

"I had a reason," Milo muttered, disliking being treated as if she weren't there.

"Be patient," Ajsha whispered. "He'll talk to you in a second. Father's talking to him right now. He's saying, 'Yes, she did. That's why I – we came here. I was so excited about marrying her, but . . . I don't like the fact that our relationship is coming to this.'"

"What relationship?" Milo snapped.

"Dr. Dri is saying, 'I understand. No one does. That's what I'm here for. I heard around town that she wasn't thrilled with our little laws and that she was unhappy about the marriage, but I think she's going a little extreme by turning violent. I think I'll talk to her. Milo –'"

Now he was directing his words at her. She stared back warily.

"'Can you tell me why you attacked your husband?'"

Milo scoffed. "Course I can," she answered, while Ajsha translated. "The little pervert was staring at my butt while I was digging in my kitchen floor. Got to defend my honor, don't I?"

Upon hearing this, Dr. Dri pondered for a moment before answering.

"'You were digging in your kitchen floor?'"

Milo groaned. "Yeah," she said.

"'Why?'"

"To bury him in. Come on! I'm digging us a cellar. Can we focus on why we're here, please?"

"'I'm sorry. So, he was, and I quote, 'Staring at your butt'?'"

"That's right," Milo confirmed, defiantly meeting his calm, brown eyes.

"'And you have a problem with that?'"

"Of course I do!" Milo retorted with dignity.

"'But, he's your husband.'"

"Not by my choice. I didn't, and don't, *want* him as my husband. Everything in this marriage has been forced. We stop at chemistry. He knows that I hate him, yet he deliberately stares at my butt! He was askin' for a smack down."

Dr. Dri considered this for a second, and, like Ajsha the previous day, decided not to laugh. He addressed Simon.

"'Simon,'" Ajsha translated for Milo, "'what do you have to say about this? Did you know that it would offend your wife if you – I *quote* – stared at her butt?'"

Simon shrugged and grinned sheepishly.

"He says, 'I had a feeling, but I couldn't help myself. She's very attractive.'"

When Milo heard this, she tensed in rage and clenched her fists.

"How dare you!" she whispered, her hands automatically searching for a pillow. The therapist instantly held up a hand and jabbered loudly. Ajsha hastily translated.

"Dr. Dri is saying, 'Please, Mrs. Swallow! No violence here!'"

This seemed to stun Milo immobile. Mrs. Swallow. He had called her Mrs. Swallow. She wasn't in detention with a boy she had gotten into a fight with on the soccer field. This was *marriage* counseling. Something inside her was slowly shriveling up and dying.

Inhaling hoarsely, she stared at Dr. Dri imploringly.

"The only reason I was violent was because he was staring at my – well, you know!" she said, upset. "I wouldn't have hurt him if he hadn't. Okay, so I've wanted to hurt him in the past and sometimes still do, but I'm not somebody who hurts people."

Lower lip quivering slightly, she stared at her knees while Ajsha kept up with her flow of speech.

"I've had my fair share of beatings and know it's not pleasant. It's not fun. Whenever I was attacked, I never did anything to deserve it – a couple of times I got punished for being injured! My parents never believed that I was innocent. Well, they did for a while, until it happened so often and wherever we went that they started to think that I caused the fights!"

Her breathing became raspy, and both Simon and Dr. Dri were leaning forward, concerned. Ajsha, though focused on her job, also looked worried. It was the first time any of them had heard this about Milo's past.

"I was always left to heal myself!" she went on. "Maybe it made me bitter, or even tough. I don't know, but, honest, I try to stay away from violence! I hate violence! I can't even believe that I used it! It was some advice my dad gave me! The last thing he said to me before I left! That's the last time I'll listen to him. I mean . . ."

She paused, as if realizing something vital.

"I can't believe I hurt someone for being attracted to me! . . . Some character I'm building for myself, huh?"

Her voice was becoming high pitched and tears were threatening to leak out at any second. She faced Simon, her jaw bulging in determination.

"I'm sorry!" Milo told him. "I'm sorry. You just have no idea what I've been through. I know other people have been through worse, but I have had my troubles, too! No friends! None! Do you know what that's like? No, of course you don't, you ignorant boy!"

She sent him a look that would thaw an ice burg.

"Everyone I've ever met has tried to hurt me! Now I walk around everywhere and think that anyone I see is going to try to hurt me. No trust! Walking around in fear! You have no idea what that's like! Everywhere I go, enemies surround me! Sure, I've fought the feeling for years, but this is how I feel on the inside!"

Tears were now slowly rolling down her cheeks and everyone was staring at them, speechless. Ajsha, who had thought she would never see Milo cry in front of Simon, could barely keep on translating.

"I can't believe I have turned into them!" Milo rasped, truly sounding ashamed. She buried her face in her hands and went on in a garbled voice. "Influenced by bullies! Do you know what people like me turn into?" she said, abruptly fixing Simon with a watery gaze. "Murderers! Murderers! I don't want to turn into a murderer! Do you know what I mean? Huh? No! Of course not! Oh my goodness, how I hate you! I hate you, Simon!"

Simon flinched badly, as if she had slugged him again.

"Yet," she went on, snuffling mightily, "I feel sorry for you. Why? I don't know. Look, I'm sorry! I won't be tomorrow, but right now I am. I'm sorry about attacking you and kicking you, and – that other time I kicked you, and for everything I did to you at the market! But nothing else. Oh, right! I'm sorry I married you! And always will be!"

With that, she retreated into a ball and quietly sobbed. After a moment, she felt strong arms tightly surround her. She lifted her head a fraction, enough to make out Simon's head resting on her neck. He was hugging her, trying to calm her down, and completely disregarding the fact that she had just shared that she hated him, twice. She didn't like it, but she didn't try to pull away. For now, for some inexplicable reason, his embrace was almost comforting.

"I'm sorry," she whispered. "It won't happen again."

Simon heard this from Ajsha and slowly released her. He patted her shoulder, and she patted his arm, in a pushing motion. Leaning forward, he attempted to kiss her temple, but she briskly shook her head in a Too Much motion. He returned to his chair, and the very bemused Dr. Dri took a deep breath to speak to him.

"'I know we haven't been here for that long,'" Ajsha translated as the therapist jabbered, "'but I think that we have made real progress. You can go home, for now. I still highly suggest, however, coming back here for more sessions.'"

"What!" Milo gasped. She was about to furiously exclaim, "I did all that for nothing!" but Bob the Conscience calmly suggested, "Don't."

Milo's mouth clamped shut and she fastened a beady eye upon Dr. Dri. Simon stood up, smiling, and shook the doctor's hand, gibbering emotionally. Ajsha and Milo arose as well and moved forward to shake his hand. When it was Milo's turn, she pulled him towards her so that Ajsha couldn't hear what she was saying.

"Look, man," she hissed rapidly, "I know you can't understand me, but listen. I don't want to come back here. I've got enough crap to deal with without dragging something like this into it! So, what do ya want? Money? Valuables? Revenge? I'll do it. I'll lie or steal or even kill, just don't make me come back here. What's it gonna take? Whatever you want, man, just find a way to tell me, and I'll do it. Don't go to Ajsha, she'll rat. She's that kind of child. Responsible, loving, honest . . . one of *them*. Even though you're a therapist, I know you have a dark side, just like me. Anything to get me out of this! You think about that, doc, and let me know."

This having been rattled off like lightening, she backed away. Dr. Dri gave her an encouraging smile, and Milo had the disheartening feeling that she had just wasted her breath. The Swallows entered the main hallway and headed for the front door. Mrs. Dri looked up from her work and made a remark in Galo.

"She said, 'That was very quick,'" said Ajsha.

"Good job. You little, reliable child," Milo said tetchily.

"Simon!" came suddenly from behind them. They turned to see Dr. Dri positioned in the middle of the hallway, ushering him over. Shrugging, Simon went and they had a hushed conversation. Eventually, Simon nodded and, looking surprised but pleased, rejoined the girls. He told Ajsha what happened.

"How wonderful!" Ajsha said, grasping Milo's hand. "Dr. Dri said that he has changed his mind, and we don't have to come back anymore!"

All of Milo's intestines iced over, and she apprehensively looked back at Dr. Dri as they left. He stood smiling and waving, and, for a split second, Milo thought he winked.

As they trekked home, Ajsha and Simon chatted breezily and though they tried to include Milo, she was consumed by her own thoughts. When they got to the Swallow residence, Milo dove into work. She had Ajsha tell Simon that she needed poles for the cellar. He nodded amicably and they all visited the wood pile. Milo estimated the length of the walls and ceiling, and Simon chopped several very thin trees according to her specifications. Milo had him sever about ten poles for the ceiling, ten for each side wall, and five for the back wall. They stacked them by the wall of the house and trooped inside.

They ate a variety of fruit for a late lunch, then Milo went back to work on the cellar. By now she was down too deep to toss the dirt up into the tub, therefore she showed Ajsha and the other one a system she invented on the spot. She found a long piece of rope in the tool shed and tied a sack at both ends. Arranging a sturdy stick over the opening of the hole and dropping the sacks on both sides, she shoveled dirt into the one that was dangling the bottom. When it was full, Ajsha, or Simon, would hoist it up, letting the other sack drop to the bottom, and empty the dirt into the tub.

Milo was thoroughly delighted with how well it worked, and together, as a forced family, they dug a cellar. Ajsha and Milo yelled their conversation up and down to each other.

"You know," Ajsha called down, her head framed by the golden afternoon sunshine, "most people are buried at just six feet. Eight feet seems a bit much, don't you think?"

"Them gravediggers don't work on a three foot radius," Milo called back up to her.

"True," Ajsha admitted. "Oh, by the way, did I tell you?"

"Apparently not," Milo said, confused. She was scraping at the walls, smoothing them.

"I'm proud of you for opening up at Dr. Dri's," Ajsha said fondly, and loudly.

"You mean all that crap?" Milo said and chuckled. "Child, you believed that?"

"Wasn't it true?" she asked.

"No! And don't tell Simon this. I don't want to go back there."

"So . . . you lied!"

"Yeah," Milo said carelessly, sneezing as a cloud of dust blew up her nose.

"It was all a lie!" Ajsha cried, distressed. "Oh, Milo! How could you?"

"It wasn't *all* a lie."

Ajsha paused for a moment. "No?"

"Naw! The only lie was how I was sorry."

"Oh!" Ajsha exclaimed after a moment. "So, all the rest was the truth?"

"Yeah, that's right."

"Oh!" Ajsha repeated, struggling to reel up the sack. She almost felt happy. "So . . . (huff, huff) you're (huff, huff) not sorry?"

"Heck no!" Milo cried, and then sneezed again, but this time not because of the dust. "This is a great temperature for food. A regular refrigerator down here. Anyway, I still can't figure out how he did it."

"Who? What?"

"Dr. Dri. Before we left, I asked him not to ask us to come back, and then, wham! He says we don't have to. I don't know how he understood me."

"How did you ask him?"

"Very politely!" Milo sniffed "A bit too refined if you ask me!"

"Well, I don't know how he would understand. As far as I know, Dr. Dri doesn't know any English. But, then again, he is a therapist."

Quite true. And therapists are extraordinary people. How they infiltrate other peoples' minds is beyond me! They are semi-brilliant, extremely smart, kind of clever, very bright people. How he managed to comprehend Milo's extreme offer is a shadowed mystery. But some way, somehow, he did, and she never had to have another therapy session again. Though, she really could have used it.

18
Squelch

WHAT MILO HAD revealed at the therapist's rested profoundly on Ajsha's mind, especially the part when she had said that she had no friends. Ajsha, who had grown up in an entire dorm of friends, felt very sorry for her, as did Simon, and for the next couple of days they were unfailingly kind to her. Milo, who didn't catch on that they were expressing their pity, thought they were simply acting strange. There was an overabundance of smiles aimed in her direction, soft replies if she barked at them, sneak attack hugs from Ajsha (Simon figured it would be nicer of him not to), and daily bouquets of island flowers appearing mysteriously on the kitchen table. Milo briefly wondered if they were about to drop some sort of bomb on her, but when a week went by with no tragic announcement, she chalked it up to the heat.

The cellar took them about a week to complete, what with the lack of light and occasional minor cave-in. When every single pole was wedged into place and it had the distinct feel of a narrow catacomb, Simon cut some boards and made shelves for the walls. He had to send Ajsha and Milo into town to buy the nails, which took them a while because Milo stopped to drool over the little speaker in Soldier's shop. Soldier was just the same as ever, except his language was improving at a tremendous rate. Milo's, however, seemed to decrease when she was fawning over the speaker, turning into an ineloquent series of "Uh-huh"s and "Nuh-uh"s.

When the cellar was totally finished, all the last minute additions fulfilled, Simon built a door to cover the hole and Milo moved her vegetation down into the cool depths. To get into the cellar, one would climb down the ladder, (Simon had made one, insisting it was safer than the notches) until they reached the bottom. At the bottom was a doorway, that led into a little room with shelves lining both walls. To transport food up and down, Milo employed her backpack. When it wasn't in use, she hung it on a hook on the inside of the trapdoor. When the door was shut, the pack would hang down in the mouth of the hole.

Now that she was no longer enshrouded with dirt every day, Milo was constantly finding clothes laid out for her on the bed; ones that she would never wear, such as skirts. She would always snort, cast them away, and wear her regular attire. The days wore on, with considerably crisper salads, and near the middle of October, Ajsha confronted Milo about a matter that had been bothering her. It was after lunch and Milo was reclining on a couch in the sitting room, contemplating all forms of napping. Ajsha swiftly walked up to her and declared her complaint.

"Come outside with me," she first requested, wanting to give Milo a chance.

Milo lethargically thought it over for a second and shook her head. "Nah," she said.

"Please," Ajsha whined. "You never go outside. You're always sitting around the house. Father and I think you're plotting a way to escape the island."

"I've been trying for months," Milo mumbled. "Nothing sensible's come."

"So, come play with me! Like I said, you never go outside. You need fresh air."

"I go outside," Milo protested. "And, in case you haven't noticed, we have no glass in our gigantic windows. I've never had so much fresh air in my whole life."

"Fine, but you never *do* anything when you go out," Ajsha persisted. "Come with me to the beach to look for clams."

"No." Milo shuddered. "Not there."

"Why not?"

"Just . . . no, okay?"

How could she tell Ajsha that ever since the disastrous trip to the select location she had been terrified of water?

Milo had never had a fear before and was astounded by how horrible it is. It was like a nightmare that was constantly haunting her, there when she went to sleep and also when she was awake. Whenever she would walk near the beach, she would break out in sweat and shakes upon seeing the waves crashing and frothing. Simply thinking about the sea would cause her to get a twisting sensation in her stomach and tremble all over.

Having a phobia, or fear, or simply being afraid of something, is an unfortunate and uncomfortable situation. Fear is never a pleasant emotion. If someone is truly scared of something, they don't scream and carry on, but are quiet and troubled. Fear is a monster that feeds on your insides and is never satiated. Of course, phobias are nothing to be ashamed of, and people should make sure not to tease but respect people's fears. With that said, let's get back to Milo.

She still didn't want to go to the beach, her reasons her own; therefore, she conjured up an excuse.

"I'm actually going into town today," she told Ajsha, figuring it wouldn't be a lie if she actually went.

Ajsha sighed. "To look at that thing in Soldier's shop?" she asked.

"How many times do I have to tell you, Ajsha?" Milo said, exasperated. "It's called a speaker! And, no. Well, I might stop in for a second to look in on it and talk to Soldier, but for the rest of the time I'm going to stay far away from that shop."

Ajsha seemed mildly surprised and said, "Oh, okay. Do you want company?"

Milo glanced at her nervously. "Do you want to come?"

"Um, not really. I mean, I love spending time with you, but I would really like to go to the beach today."

"Well, that's fine," Milo said, relieved. "Not a problem."

"But I'll be passing through town to meet my friend, so I'll look out for you."

"Ooooh kaaaay," said Milo with false happiness and a pained smile smeared across her face. "What friend, pray tell?"

"Just a friend I made at school."

"Have I met him?" Milo inquired, trying to remember if Ajsha had ever introduced a friend to her. She suddenly realized she wasn't aware that Ajsha had friends outside her and Simon.

"It's not a him," Ajsha replied.

"A her?"

"Yes. And, no you haven't. But she's really nice."

"What about her parents?" Milo asked in an unconscious spurt of responsibility. "Do they know she's going to the beach with you?"

"Yes."

"All right, good. What's her name?"

"Illa Vann Ross. Doesn't she have a lovely name?" Ajsha said wistfully, as if her own name wasn't just as pretty.

"Very," Milo agreed, thinking that her parents probably would never let her be named Illo by accident. "Well, I guess you can leave now."

"You're leaving too, aren't you?"

Milo grinned smartly, rose to her feet, and headed to the door. "Of course I am."

Ajsha followed her and out in the clearing they parted ways. It is very interesting that Milo chose to go to town that day. Some might call if fortuitous; others, destiny. It happened to be the very day that the island farmers delivered their crops and dairy to the awaiting shops. Usually, they would bring their families along, so that they could enjoy a day in society instead of agricultural isolation.

Milo was struck with amazement as she strolled into the village. She had not yet witnessed a delivery day, and, though she knew better, was lazily falling under the impression that the goods in the stores materialized out of nowhere. Wagons hooked up to oxen were parked behind shops and were being unloaded, and people in faded farm clothe were running amok. Siblings herded each other back and forth, gawking in shop windows; couples walked around arm in arm, also gawking in various windows; loners shuffled about with their eyes to the ground, never willing to admit that they really did enjoy the change of scenery. Milo observed this spectacle with great interest, feeling a bit fancy in her bright garments.

After wandering about for a good half-hour, and listening to the babble of the Galo speaking farmers, all of whom were in the process of growing beards, Milo noticed one particular group saun-tering about, with a sibling straggler. The siblings, who were all sisters, seemed to be encouraging this sister to stay behind. They were pushing her away and making shooing gestures with their hands. Milo walked closer for a better view, just as the straggler tripped and collapsed to the ground, igniting laughter among the others. As they hurried away, one of girls called out, "Wislin blecove, Squelch!"

They skipped off laughing, arm in arm, making a mean sister chain, as Milo rushed over to help the girl.

"Are you okay?" Milo asked, helping her up, not caring if she didn't understand.

"Yeah, I'm fine," the girl replied wearily, with an extremely light lilt.

Milo was so shocked that she nearly dropped her.

"Sorry!" Milo cried. "It's just that, how do you know English? I thought that all the farmers only spoke Galo."

"All that don't learn English," the girl muttered, brushing herself off. Seeing Milo's dumbstruck expression, she quickly elaborated. "Sometimes farm life can be slow. Watching plants grow isn't as enthralling as it sounds. I had to pass the time somehow. I don't want to be an interpreter or anything, but knowing English has its benefits."

"Like what?" Milo inquired.

"Well," the girl grinned, "I'm able to talk to you."

Milo grinned back. She liked this girl. She appeared to be about Milo's age. Her skin was light, light dusty brown. She had jet-black hair that hung straight down and was cleanly cut two inches below her ears, and was about an inch and a half shorter than Milo, with large, lively brown eyes. Her face was pretty and had a smile that fit comfortably on it. She looked healthy and strong, unlike Milo who looked sickly and weak, even though she was doing better because of the healthy island food and manual labor.

Milo stuck out her hand and the girl shook it.

"I'm Milo Hestler," Milo said. "Well, actually I'm supposed to be Milo Swallow, so I guess you'd better call me that."

"Hello," said the girl. "I guess you already know my name, since my charming sister screamed it for the whole town to hear."

Milo shook her head. "I can't understand Galo," she said. "The last thing I heard your sister say I think was . . . Squelch? That isn't your name, is it?"

The girl rolled her eyes and stared agitatedly off into the distance. "Yeah," she groaned. "My sister was yelling at me to, 'Stay there, Squelch'. My name is Squelch Welch. And please don't laugh! I've had enough of that."

"How did you get a name like that?" Milo asked, beginning to walk. Squelch fell in beside her.

"It was my mother's fault," she began resentfully. "You see, I have five older sisters, and they all got super beautiful names. Shalane, Julietta, Portia, Marrinette, and Causandra."

"Wow," Milo breathed. "Sorry," she amended quickly, seeing Squelch's face.

Squelch shook her head dismissively. "It's okay. They know it, too. They gloat over it day and night. I'm not exactly a member of their awesome names club. Anyway, after I was born my mother was so fed up with elegant and exquisite names that she didn't want to think up another one. She wanted something 'original' and 'unusual', not lovely and delightful. Out of all the girls she had, she chose me to name Squelch! And out of all original and unusual names: Squelch! Ha! Squelch! Everyone asks me why I have such a stupid name, and I can't even claim abuse because my mother loves it. *I* absolutely hate it!"

"I like it," Milo murmured. "I think it's pretty."

Squelch snorted. "No you don't, you're not deranged, but thanks for trying to make me feel better. Nobody ever tries to anymore. I guess they think I've grown used to it. Ha! Fat chance! Not in fourteen years and not ever! I've been trying to get a nickname forever. Not easy."

Milo had stopped and was staring at her.

"You're fourteen?" she asked.

Squelch also stopped. "Yeah," she said.

"I'm fourteen!" Milo cried, for the first time recognizing the significance of this.

"Get out!" Squelch said, smiling and sounding so modern that Milo laughed. "When's your birthday?"

"March eighteenth," Milo said, smiling.

"Mine's the twentieth!" Squelch exclaimed, excited.

"No way!" Milo said. "That's unbelievable."

They laughed for no reason, and such laughter restores the soul. Milo, in the midst of her mirth, suddenly saw Ajsha walking nearby, looking far too young and small to be by herself, but that's how it is in small communities. Ajsha saw her as well and waved. Milo waved back, rather smugly.

"Oh," Squelch said. "Who ya waving to?"

"My 'daughter'," Milo said fondly and in a way that clearly indicated quotation marks, and pointed her out.

"Ahh!" Squelch said. "Oh, she's cute. I didn't now you're married."

"Yeah," Milo said woefully.

"Then again," Squelch went on, barely noticing the melancholy in her reply, "we only met five minutes ago. I don't know *anything* about you!"

"And I don't know a thing about you," Milo said. An idea slowly formulated in her mind. "But, if you want to, you can come to my house and we can talk."

"Good girl," Bob the Conscience said proudly.

"All right!" Squelch readily agreed. "I don't have anyone to hang out with anyway. You know how people tend to latch on to one thing and ostracize based on it? Well, I'm exhibit A. Who knows? Maybe it'll give us a chance to bond!"

"Bond," Milo murmured dreamily, as she led the way towards the forest path. "I thought I'd never have another chance to do that."

"What about your husband and kid?" Squelch asked.

Milo sneered. "I'd rather die than bond with that love tyrant! And as for Ajsha, that's her name, she loves the love tyrant too much for us to agree on much."

"Don't you love your husband?" Squelch inquired hesitantly.

"Heck no!" Milo declared robustly. "I don't even want to be married to him. Sheesh, I'm only fourteen! I'm way too young to be married or in love."

"Really? Sorry, I guess I just grew up differently. But if that's how you feel, why did you?"

"That's actually an intensely hilarious story," Milo said sardonically. "I'll tell you everything once we get to the house. It's not far, by the beach actually."

Squelch's face lit up. "By the *beach?*" she repeated, awestruck.

"Oh, you're *soooo* lucky! I never get to go to the beach."

Milo shuddered. "I wouldn't call it luck," she muttered. "And, you live on an island for Heaven's sake. What do you mean you never go to the beach?"

"I live in the *middle* of an island," Squelch corrected. "And I rarely go anywhere. The beach is nothing short of mythical to me."

They trudged on, laughing and chatting, until they arrived at the Swallow residence which, embarrassingly, still had a sizable mound of dirt outside one of the kitchen windows. Making a mental note to attend to that as soon as she had a free day, Milo led Squelch inside. In the sitting room, Milo introduced her to Chaos.

"Oh!" Squelch crooned adoringly. "I love kitties." She petted the cat's fluffy head. "She's so pretty."

"I know!" Milo said affectionately, as Chaos squeezed her eyes shut and purred. "A lovely color combination, don't you think?"

"Oh, yes," Squelch agreed. "Beautiful. I like your house too. It's very nice."

"I've heard that it's standardly simple," Milo said, releasing Chaos who lolled on couch cushion, waiting for more attention.

"Well, sort of," Squelch admitted. "But simple is great! You know, dirt floors rock!"

Milo began to laugh.

"No, no!" Squelch insisted. "Really! In this type of climate they stay nice and cool. And, like you say you've done, you can dig cellars in them."

"I've never thought of that," Milo mused, scrunching her toes on the earthen floor. "But that's not why I'm laughing. You sounded just like an American when you said 'rock'. In fact, you *sound* just like an American. Your English is perfect! I mean, Ajsha is fluent and all, but she still has her accent. You! You sound exactly like you were raised in Connecticut."

"Well," Squelch said modestly, sitting down in a chair Milo offered her and not asking where Connecticut was. "I started when

I was eight. I wanted to learn, just for something to do, and one day when we came to town I found a book recently written by an American who came here. I guess he missed home or something. Anyway, in the book he fully explained English, all the metaphors and similes and stuff. It also had a huge English dictionary translated into Galo. That really increased my vocabulary, so much that I impressed my teacher. And it included several pages of American slang, such as 'Rock!' I begged my dad to buy that book for me. *English Vocal-Cords*. By Samuel Murrow. Gotta love that dude. So dad did, and after reading the whole thing through a billion times, I was able to pick up on it. Not that there's a lot of opportunity to use it, what with always being at the farm and most people only speaking Galo. Though, I do like to irritate my sisters with it. They hate it if they think they're being insulted and can't tell for sure. Hee, hee. But, enough about me! You have to tell me the excruciatingly hilarious story about how you ended up married."

Milo sighed. "It's a long one," she warned.

Squelch shrugged. "I've lots of time," she said. "We don't start heading back till nine. Go ahead, start."

"Well," Milo said, leaning back on the couch, "to truly explain it all, and for the full effect, I'd have to tell you the entire story of my tragic life."

Squelch got into a comfortable position, undaunted. Milo began by describing her first home and all the others up to 711 Shady Ally, which was apparently founded by people who couldn't spell. She gloomily recounted 711 Shady Ally's horrors and how when combined, made it the worst habitat so far. She depicted the airplane trip and crash in vivid detail, Squelch cringing with compassion. Milo then told her about the proposal, followed by the forced wedding and mandatory child, sparing no chance to illustrate with colorful words. She talked about the meeting of the parents and Simon's friends, and the nearly fatal visit to the select location; the horrid nights and busy days of wife work; how she had received a cat from a nutcase, and that she had accidentally made her child sick; all about the first trip to the market and her getting caught in a boar trap, and ending with how she had started digging a cellar and ended up going to see a marriage counselor.

Squelch was a first rate listener, gasping, growling, and nodding sympathetically in all the right places. Milo finished it all with, "Then we finished the cellar and I met you, which is where we are now." She wanted to add that meeting her had been the one truly great thing that had happened to her ever since jumping out of that stupid plane, but didn't.

Squelch sat back, mouth agape, and a dazed look on her face.

"Milo," she began, breathless, "what a life you've had! You should write it down. I'm tellin' you, it'll publish and be wicked popular. No one else has been through so much, at least, no one here, and it's twice as impressive because it's based on a true story!"

Milo chuckled in a self-satisfied way. "I am," she revealed. "It's all going into my diary."

"Good," Squelch said. "Hey, are you going to write about me?"

"Of course!" Milo said exuberantly. "Now, tell me all about you."

Squelch, who had been looking pleased and dreamy about possibly being in a book, snapped out of it when she heard Milo ask this.

"Um," she said, then chuckled sheepishly "There's not very much to tell. I haven't had as such an exciting life as you. I mean, come on, I live on a farm. The most exciting thing that ever happens is occasionally we have a hurricane and everyone freaks out about the crops. I help with maintenance, along with my sisters, though none of us are in love with it. I'm the only one in my family that can speak English, which I guess is sort of impressive, though not as impressive as my husband almost drowning me. Not that I have a husband. Every time we visit town, my sisters track down all the eligible boys and flirt their butts off. They want to get married so badly they can taste it, and not to any farmers.

"They're all dying to move away from the farm. Two are very close. Most boys can't resist them, and their seductively delicious names, but whenever I tell a boy my name he tries to put as much ground between us as possible."

"That's terrible!" Milo said, sympathetic. "Idiotic boys! Forget 'em! They don't know nothin'!"

"That's right!" Squelch said with relish. "Their heads is all full of air!"

"Yeah!" Milo said, drawing the word out. "If they ain't intelligent enough to see that Squelch is a beautiful name, or the fact that it don't matter what your name is but who you are, than they don't deserve ya!"

"Mmm hmm," Squelch hummed, lips pursed. She used her hands to point at her face. "They don't deserve all this!"

"That's right, girl!" Milo said, feeling better than she had in roughly eight years.

They both laughed, both full of attitude. Squelch abruptly stopped laughing and met Milo's gaze.

"Who needs boys anyways?" Milo said. "They ain't nothing but trouble, and not worth the hassle."

"Yeah," Squelch said, smiling. "Most, anyway."

"Nearly all," Milo put in. "But a few good ones still exist. None that I've met, though."

They sat quietly for a moment, their sides aching, then Squelch timidly asked, "Milo, um, it's not like I want to burden you or anything, but would you consider wanting to be my friend?"

Milo grinned. "I was about to ask you the same question. In those exact words, too. But I think we already are friends. At least, I hear this is what it feels like."

"Yeah. Yeah, I think so. Wow," murmured Squelch, her face aglow. "So, it's official?"

"Tis' official," Milo confirmed, then, struck by inspiration, asked, "Do you want to stay for dinner?"

"Absolutely," Squelch said. "I'll be able to meet this horrible Simon. And that sweetie pie Ajsha."

"Great," said Milo, leaping up, elated. "Come with me into the kitchen, my fortress against the evils of the world."

Squelch happily obliged, openly admiring how neat it was.

"Thank you," Milo said. "I believe in orderly kitchens."

"So does my mother," Squelch said, then, as if reminded something, added, "I'm thrilled that you want to be friends with me, but I must warn you: I am a very spontaneous and outrageous person sometimes. My mother says I get it from her."

"Marvelous," Milo said, rummaging through the cupboards, balancing on her toes. "I love people like that. They're practically therapy to me! Ah! Hey, baby."

She withdrew a long, squat container and set it on the table. Prying off the top, she revealed long, pale yellow strands of pasta. Squelch was entranced by the sight.

"Where did you get that?" she asked, positively agog.

"I made it," Milo replied. "Yesterday."

"How?" Squelch asked, awestruck at the notion.

"I have the recipe in my cookbook. Flour, eggs, and oil. I made a well in the flour, combined the eggs and oil in it, slowly incorporating everything until it made a ball, and kneaded it a little. Then I let it rest, and afterwards rolled the dough out extremely thin and used a knife to slice it into strands. I let the strands harden in the sun, and now all I have to do is cook them in boiling water and they'll be perfect. Trust me; I've made pasta plenty of times, along with tomato sauce. I prefer things homemade. The sauce is already made, too. For that I diced some tomatoes, an onion, and garlic then simmered everything on the calven."

Squelch gave her a funny look.

"Cauldron slash oven," Milo clarified.

"Ah," Squelch said. Her gaze returned to the container and the unfamiliar food within. "You really like to cook, don't you?"

"Mmm," Milo said, fetching a pot from a cabinet. "Always have. When I was a baby, I would mix different baby foods together and try it. I've been making my own lunch since I was nine. What do you like to do?"

"I like to draw," Squelch answered, getting wood for the chef.

"Thank you," Milo said, accepting the wood and cramming it into the belly of the calven. "And, drawing? Cool. I really can't draw, though sometimes I need to. What do you draw?"

"A *looot* of vegetables. For signs, mostly. I've been perfecting my cabbage for a while now. People who see them say to my mother, 'Mrs. Welch, your daughter has such talent, it's a shame you don't care.'"

Milo was contemplative for a moment. "Your farm doesn't specialize in grapes, does it?"

"No," Squelch replied.

"All right, just checking. . . .Your mom doesn't care about your drawing?"

"Not really," Squelch said, poking distractedly at the linguine. "If I were painting it would be another story. All my sisters paint; they're horrible at it, but as long as it's bright and colorful my mother loves it."

Milo had lit the calven, and was pumping water into the pot.

"I guess she would," she said fairly. "I mean, your clothes aren't very vibrant. That's not your fault, though, since you don't that plant to wash them with."

"No. She keeps trying to transplant it, but there's just too much sun where we live. Eventually someone'll get smart and bottle it. I mean, it must work. You're practically blinding me!"

Milo grinned. "That would be my pale skin."

"No kidding," Squelch remarked. "You look like a ghost. Ohhh, are you?"

"I'm not sure," Milo said in a low, hoarse voice.

They both giggled, thoroughly enjoying themselves as they went about preparing supper. Milo got an idea.

"How about I pick a basketful of that plant for you?"

"Are you sure?" Squelch asked.

"Of course! It's very plentiful around here. Just about popping up all over the place!"

"Okay!" said Squelch. "Thank you, you're awesome. My mother's going to be in total nirvana." Beaming, she glanced out the window and saw a father and a daughter walking hand in hand towards the house.

Milo followed her gaze and said, somewhat critically, "Well, there they are. I can't stand how they are never late, yet never early. I don't understand how they're so prompt. They don't even wear watches. Do you think they can tell time by the sun? 'Cause, I could never do that and – Squelch?"

Squelch was staring bug-eyed at Simon, looking faintly stunned. "*That's* your husband!" she said.

Milo looked from her to the fast approaching Simon. "Yes," she answered in a loathsome tone.

Squelch's jaw dropped. "You didn't tell me he looked like *that*!" she said accusingly.

"What's the difference?" Milo demanded. "He's still a jerk, no matter what he looks like."

"Well . . . yeah," Squelch admitted. "But, I mean, he's *hot*! I'm sorry, but he is! But, no; you're right. Who cares if he's cute as heck? Actually, he looks familiar. I think, in fact I'm almost sure, he's one of the boys my sisters were trying to reel in. Yeah! Yeah, he's *that* one. Oh, they flirted like crazy around him, but he didn't seem that interested. He was very polite and friendly, but was not interested. The other boys were practically crawling all over them, but he didn't think they were that much. He proposed to you after only staring at you for one night?"

"Yes," Milo said stiffly.

"Wow," said Squelch, genuinely impressed. "You must be really something."

Milo blushed but said firmly, "I don't need a boy to make me feel special."

"Good for you!" Squelch congratulated. "I wish I could be like you."

"Why not?" Milo said, laying the last plate. "No one needs another gender to be special or important. A boy liking me shouldn't change my status."

"You're right!" Squelch agreed, seizing the idea. "We don't need the opposite sex to feel complete and powerful! No one does!"

"And yet people lose sight of that."

"Yes, it's very sad."

Simon and Ajsha had entered the house by and were being lured by the aromas from the kitchen. They crossed the threshold to find a stranger conversing with the missus of the dwelling. Milo saw them staring with bald confusion at Squelch, and thought it best to make introductions.

"Ajsha," she began.

"Who is that?" Ajsha interrupted, it coming out a bit more potent than normal.

"I was about to tell you, and don't be so rude," Milo scolded tersely. Slipping an arm around her shoulders, she led Squelch over to them. "This is Squelch Welch. My new friend. No! Sorry, my new *best* friend."

"Hey!" Bob the Conscience rumbled.

"Oh, bite me!" Milo told him in her head. Out loud, she said, "Squelch, this is Ajsha, and the guy standing next to her is Simon. The burglar."

Squelch was shaking hands with Ajsha, who said defensively, "He's not a burglar!"

"Oh, yes he is!" Milo countered.

"What did he rob?" Squelch asked, leering at Simon and pointedly putting her hands on her hips instead of offering him one to shake.

"My marriage-ginity," Milo said firmly.

"Ah, yes!" Squelch said, glaring at Simon. She gibbered to him in Galo and then repeated it in English: "Marriage-ginity robber! How darr yooou!"

The two girls, not including Ajsha, burst into uproarious laughter. It was the first time Simon had ever seen Milo laugh like that, without malice or spite, just purely blissful. It delighted him thoroughly and actually made him smile, despite the fact that he was the joke.

The girls ushered them over to the table, Squelch taking the liberty to explain that she was staying for dinner. After the grateful thanks was given, Milo served the food. Ajsha and Simon seemed just as dumbfounded by the spaghetti as Squelch was. They let it hang from their forks and observed it in wonder. The way they were acting was starting to scare Milo. Surely, they must have seen or at least heard about pasta before. But they looked at it like it was a strange, new specimen someone had just discovered.

Squelch took one bite and instantly began to devour it, saying between bites that it was delicious. But Simon and Ajsha were cautious, remembering the last time Milo cooked something foreign. Milo, mustering up her earnestness, promised them that it wasn't dangerous. After several more reassurances, and a number of "Yes, I'm *sure*!"s, they soon agreed with Squelch. During the meal, Squelch and Milo chatted cordially, not bothering to include Ajsha or Simon. The ending conversation sounded like this –

"No, I can't on Saturday. Remember?"

"Oh, right. How about Monday?"

"Monday sounds good. Are you sure it's close enough?"

"If you follow my directions, than I'm sure you'll have plenty of time and no trouble."

"Great!"

"What's happening on Monday?" Ajsha asked, unable to keep quiet any longer. She wasn't used to not being involved in every aspect of the dinnertime dialogue.

"I'm going to Squelch's house," Milo told her.

"Isn't it far out?"

"Not too far," Squelch said. "It's definitely a walk, but not unbearable. Our farm isn't that big and it's close to town."

"Oh," said Ajsha, and quietly muttered this piece of news to Simon. He nodded, not taking his sights off Milo, who was positively radiant with that new-found-friend afterglow.

Squelch stayed to help clean up, but directly afterwards she had to leave.

"Can you find your way back to town from here?" Milo asked her at the door, it shedding a carpet of light on the dark ground outside.

"Oh, yeah," Squelch answered. "It's pretty straightforward, and everybody's houses are lit up, so I'll see just fine. Goodbye. For now."

"Bye," Milo said.

They gave each other a small hug, which, up to that point, was the best small hug Milo had ever received. Simon watched this small hug from inside the house, feeling envious. He wished he could give Milo a small hug, or a big hug, or even a medium hug. His feelings about Squelch were decidedly mixed. He was overjoyed to see his wife happy, for once, but when a wife lavishes more affection on her friend than her husband, it doesn't inspire confidence.

As Squelch wandered off into the gloom, Milo watched her from the doorway, relishing the warm, euphoric feeling inside. As she shut the door and turned around, Simon sprang from nowhere and tried to hug her.

"Git away!!!" she shrieked, punching his arm.

Jumping back, he yelled, "Dr. Dri!" in hopes that it would quell any further ferocity. As she scowled and stormed away, he slumped in disappointment; he had hoped she was still in a hugging mood.

All Milo could think about over the next few days was her upcoming trip to the Welch farm. She had an abiding love for farms (without them she would have no way to cook) and was eager to see Squelch again. When Monday arrived, she was bursting with excitement. Ajsha sat eating her breakfast and watching her dart around, preparing for the day.

"Uh," Ajsha said, "Mother?"

"Milooo!" Milo sang out shrilly.

"Right, well . . . Can I go with you? You know, to *Squelch's* house?"

Milo froze in mid-movement and faced her, grinning. "*Can* you come with me?" she said slyly. "Sure you *can*. Heck, child, everyone *can* come with me to Squelch's house."

Ajsha smiled. "*May* I go with you to Squelch's house?" she corrected herself.

"Atta good girl," Milo said. "And, no you *may* not."

Ajsha's face fell. "Why not?" she asked.

"Because," Milo said, juggling a loaf of bread, a serrated knife, and a wooden cutting board, "I'm leaving right after I drop you off at school. I can't wait around for you. And besides, I need a vacation away from you and the creep."

Ajsha looked ashamed. "Do I cause you that much trouble?" she whispered, her lashes misting over.

Milo smiled fondly. "No," she said, brushing Ajsha's bangs out of her eyes. "Of course not. If it wasn't for you I'd probably go crazy. Well, crazier. Dang, with all the trouble I've caused you, you probably need a vacation away from *me*."

Ajsha shook her head, dabbing the corners of her eyes with her napkin. "No," she said.

Milo escorted her to school, explaining on the way that Simon would have to make lunch and dinner, though she had laid out a few options for them. They said goodbye at the schoolhouse doors, and Milo departed for the forest at the other end of town.

After passing the last house, she came to the jungle's edge and, just as Squelch had described, there were several rutted roads made by wagon wheels, veering off in a multiple of directions. Recalling their discussion, Milo selected a certain road that swerved to the left. It led her deep into the forest, obscuring the town from behind her.

As she walked, overcome by the exhilaration that accompanies venturing into an unknown area, she passed toad lilies, painted ferns and lady ferns, enormous hydrangeas, and colorful hibiscus. Constantly, Milo forgot that she was in a hurry and kept stopping to examine the flowers that lined the road. She would then try to quicken her pace to make up ground, but would always get distracted by some other new and intriguing sight.

Eventually, she refrained from looking at the side of the road, so as not to get sidetracked by any more flowers. She walked for what, to her at least, seemed like an incredibly long time. To her it felt like hours and hours before she reached Squelch's house, the perpetual furrows of the road and towering, vine ensnared trees becoming monotonous. However, when she did reach it and look at her watch, it was only 10:25.

Squelch's house was more like a large cottage, constructed from coconut tree logs instead of that strange, fibrous wood. Flourishing tropical flower gardens bordered all sides of it and different weathervanes dotted the roof. Flat, grey stones created a winding path to the door, which was beneath a decorated archway that also housed a bell with a rope. Pampas grass grew in neat little clusters under the windows, which were veiled with clear, glinting bead curtains.

With all the elements working together, it looked precisely like a scene from a fairytale, or a design show. Milo could only stare in awe at it for a second. She snapped out of her entrancement when she heard Squelch calling her name.

"Milo! Milo! Milo!"

She came running from behind the house, her sisters following in her wake.

"Hey!" Milo called back, smiling. They met on the flagstone path and had a small hug.

"Here," Milo said, handing her a basket. "I brought you those plants."

"Oh, thanks," Squelch said, accepting it and peering down into the jumble of leaves and stems. "Mother'll do cartwheels. I told her about you. And my sisters and dad. They all want to meet you. Only, for my sake, please don't get too chummy with my sisters. I've lost more friends than I can count that way."

"Have no worries," Milo reassured her. "I have no intentions of becoming overly chummy with anyone but you. Besides, I can't understand what they're saying; so, they can't lure me into their devious little plans."

"I know!" Squelch exclaimed, linking arms with her and heading for the cottage. "They're like human magnets, attracting all potential buddies. It is so mean of them, but I'm not going to let them get you. I'll cling to you if I have to!" she stated, squeezing Milo's arm for emphasis.

"Great," Milo said, forcing back laughter. "A united front should do the trick. By the way, I *love* your house! I live in a hovel compared to it. You never told me it was this gorgeous!"

"Well, thank you. Mother will be floored to hear that. This is all her handiwork. Honestly, it's not really that much. I mean, wood floors, ugh. And you never gave me a chance to talk about it. You were too busy complaining about your life."

"Oh, Squelch!" Milo cried, coloring. "I'm sorry –"

"I'm joking!" Squelch laughed. "Shoot! I've got a lot of work to do on you! Ahhh, yes, but first my sisters."

Her sisters had barred their way to the front door, and were studying Milo with an air of biased curiosity, as if wondering why it was she appealed so much to Squelch. They were all older, taller, and decidedly surly looking, their current environment undoubtedly affecting their mood.

"Milo," Squelch said, "meet Shalane, Julietta, Portia, Marrinette, and Causandra. No need to say which is which; they're usually clumped together, anyways. Girls, this is Milo."

Squelch repeated that last part in Galo, and Milo shook hands with each. She also met Squelch's parents, who were infinitely more cheerful than their first five daughters, and their dog, Rumble. Milo leered at the dog with distaste. Squelch explained that he was a pup that had survived a plane crash.

"He was badly wounded, but we nursed him back to health. He's lived with us ever since," she told her. "We named him Rumble after the first time he chased boars out of the fields. Little guy sounded like a thunderstorm."

Milo gave a tight-lipped smile and tried to ignore the canine for the remainder of her visit, which wasn't easy with him trotting behind everywhere they went. She was shown the rest of the house, which was clean and airy on the inside, with an array of vivid, yet disturbingly distorted paintings taking up most of the wall space. Squelch then showed the farm grounds. She was led past fields of vegetables, herbs, and a modest patch of wheat. They explored the two barns that stored all of the harvested produce, as well as the Welch's steers. Milo had Squelch point out to her the directions of the other farms. Squelch explained all about the two island dairy farms, and how they had increased the population of cows from the first four cows on the first marooned ship.

"Wow," Milo commented at lunch, which was held at the cottage, served by a smiling Mrs. Welch. "That ship had practically everything you would need to survive. It's strange, everything except chickens."

"I know," Squelch agreed, munching on her cucumber sandwich.

"It was supposed to be carrying farm supplies, but no chickens! Honestly! . . . What's a chicken?"

They spent the rest of the afternoon in pure enjoyment, sitting on the porch swing, Squelch showing Milo her drawings (which were quite good), and Mrs. Welch giving Milo a pottery lesson. They used dull red clay dug up from a nearby river bank, and caressed it into bowl shapes. When it came time for Milo to depart, many plans and small hugs were exchanged. Wading in dimness of twilight, Milo headed back to town. On the way, she loaded her arms with flamboyant flowers, presenting one to Mrs. Lanslo when she passed through the village.

By the time she reached what she now thought of as Simon's shack, it was dark. It was past suppertime, and when she entered her miserly abode she found Ajsha and Simon in the sitting room, playing cat's cradle with some yarn. Ajsha squealed upon seeing Milo's flowers and left her game to bound up to her. Milo grinned and stuck a flower in her hair. Ajsha giggled, then took a flower and went up to Simon. Smiling mischievously, she carefully wedged the flower behind his ear.

He laughed and gently fingered it. He spoke softly to her, and, as he did, Ajsha moved her face close up to his. This didn't startle him any; in fact, he was quite used to it, as Milo noticed. Ajsha often did that whenever they talked, and Milo wondered why.

19
Forgiveness can be a Waltz

THINGS WERE EXCEEDINGLY more pleasant for Milo now that Squelch was in her life. The benefits of having a friend that you are completely at ease with are rather staggering. Mainly, Milo's stress levels decreased to an earthly manageable amount, just from voicing all of her complaints to an empathetic ear. In addition to life's mistreatments, they also shared their interests with each other.

Milo exposed Squelch to that urban delight known as rap by turning her radio's volume up to the max, and allowing it to issue through the headphones. This was hardly a terrific system, though.

"If only I had that speaker," Milo would frequently mumble.

Squelch taught her a new repertoire of dance moves and the difficult life lesson that she shouldn't care if people watched her dance. What anybody else thought wasn't important, as long as you were having fun.

"They laugh to hide the fact they're jealous," Squelch told her wisely, demonstrating a wavy arm movement.

Whenever she could, Milo would disappear to the Welch farm, staying there from the early morning until the evening. In turn, Squelch frequently made the journey from her home to the Swallow's bungalow on the beach, and was a regular fixture at dinner. Milo's absences and the continual presence of another

teenage girl around the house had at first unnerved Simon and
Ajsha. However, they couldn't deny that it greatly improved her
attitude. In fact, Milo grew so happy that she almost felt glad that
she was stranded on the island. Almost.

Lulled into a false sense of security and contentment, she didn't
realize that such happiness wouldn't last. It ended precisely on the
eighth of November, which Milo only knew because of the date
setting on her watch. Tropical islands, as all surrounding evidence
pointed to, seemed to only have one season: Warm breeze and
scarlet sunset season. Anyhow, on that day, during the afternoon,
there came a chipper knock on the door, and Ajsha raced down the
hall to answer it.

Milo, who had been changing the sheets on her and Simon's bed,
peeked out the bedroom door to see who it was. Framed by the
doorpost and glaring sun, was a blonde girl. She jabbered cheerfully
to Ajsha, handing her a folded piece of paper. They parted, the girl
giving a fluttery wave, and Ajsha shut the door. Milo trailed after
her into the sitting room and found her studying the scrawl on one
half of the paper.

"What is it?" Milo asked hesitantly, her tone saturated with
suspicion.

"It's for you and Father," said Ajsha, her eyes skimming over the
page again and again.

"I'm sure," Milo said, "but what *is* it?"

Ajsha was quiet a moment before saying, "I think Father should
see it before I tell you."

"Oh," Milo groaned. Only so many things could make Ajsha say
that. "Is it that bad?"

"I can't say," she replied. "Father isn't home yet, and I know he
wasn't going into town, so he must be at the beach with his friends.
Why don't you go get him?"

Milo sighed and said jadedly, "I'll play my English card one more
time."

"Just go!" Ajsha cried unexpectedly. She sounded more anxious than aggravated.

"Okay! Fine!" Milo said, recoiling and throwing up her hands. "If it's that important, why not? I'll be right back," she said, exiting the house and leaving Ajsha still rereading the pleated paper.

Grudgingly, she trudged down to the beach, her feet soon kicking up hot sand. She didn't want to get close to the water, or even look at it; therefore, she decided to summon Simon from afar instead of approaching him. After a short scan, she spotted him with a group of boys by the tide's edge.

"Simon!" she called out. "Hey, *Simon!*"

Whirling around, he saw her rigid form by the tree line. Grinning, he began to stride over, his comrades making taunting remarks in Galo. Simon came up to her, arms outstretched, and she gave him a scathing look that said he really ought to give that up. As his arms fell and she prepared to indicate that he was requested at home, she couldn't help but notice that his shirt was completely unbuttoned.

Quickly, she cast her gaze towards her ankles and couldn't bring herself to look up. The reason for this was not because of any sort of nauseating sight; in fact, when Simon's shirt was completely unbuttoned, normal girls found it quite enticing. The issue was that she had grown such a disliking for the boy as a whole she found it an inappropriate situation for them to be in.

Simon, however, had no shame, nor was aware that he should; he was just a regular guy at the beach. Confused, he tried to ask what was wrong by trying to look her in the face, but she only turned away, keeping his visible torso out of her line of vision. He gave up and merely stood resignedly before her. Milo took several deep, calming breaths, thinking of a way to imply with her hands that she wanted him to close his shirt. She put up her hands, without looking at him, and pushed them together, in a silent clapping motion. After it was evident that he didn't understand, she pointed to his shirt then again made the motion with her hands. Simon looked down at his shirt, comprehending, and looked back up at her with an amused expression on his face.

Milo glimpsed part of this amusement and was greatly annoyed. After several more attempts to get him to close his shirt himself, him looking more tickled by the second, Milo finally had enough. Scowling, she rallied herself, reached out and rapidly began to button a few buttons for him. He stood still, startled. Once she was able to look at his face again, (while she was buttoning, she wasn't watching, so it took a while) she was so angry that she didn't bother trying to gesture, but grabbed his ear and began to tug him along. Yelping, he tried to protest, but in the end decided not to argue.

She dragged him to the house and into the sitting room, where Ajsha sat, worrying at the paper.

"Here you are," Milo told her, pushing Simon into the room, where he stood massaging his ear.

"Took you long enough," Ajsha remarked.

"We'll discuss that later," Milo breathed.

Ajsha looked Simon over and frowned.

"What's wrong?" Milo asked.

"His shirt is buttoned crooked," she said.

Milo looked and saw it was true. Buttons were in wrong buttonholes, some holes had been missed, the collar was distinctly haphazard; all in all, it was a mess.

"Hmm," was Milo's reply.

Ajsha handed the paper to Simon, jabbering matter-of-factly. His eyebrows arching in surprise, he read it through, and when he was finished, his face lit up. Tugging his collar buttons open so he could breathe properly, he began to speak excitedly to Ajsha. She gibbered in a concerned voice, to which Simon answered glibly and told her something to say to Milo, who had been haunting one of the chairs, looking guarded.

"This," Ajsha told her, indicating to the parchment, "is an invitation to a party for one of Simon's friends."

"Really?" Milo said crossly. "Who would be stupid enough to do that? But, I'm getting ahead of myself. First of all, what type of party?"

"Pretty formal," Ajsha said delicately. "Several people on the island can play instruments and they'll be there. So, there will be waltzing and tangoing and stuff like that."

"I knew it!" Milo concluded spitefully. "Whoever this person is, they are quite stupid. I would *never* dance with that creep! I bet he *can't* even dance."

Ajsha made a loud cough that sounded remarkably like a laugh. "Oh, yes he can!" she croaked.

"Pardon?" Milo asked sharply.

"Nothing. And," Ajsha said heavily, "Father said that you're still going. Dancing or not."

"Oh, does he now?" Milo snarled, casting a malevolent glare at Simon, who reclining serenely on a couch. "And why would I do such a thing?"

"Because," Ajsha said, after a brief exchange with Simon, "this friend is expecting him. And that friend knows another one of Father's friends. You've met him. Randolf Fittler."

"Doesn't ring a bell," Milo muttered. "Well, sort of."

"He's the leader of the boys who beat you."

"Oh!" Milo said darkly, sitting up and for some reason checking the window. "Him. Ohhh! So if I don't go, Simon will rat on me. Is that it?"

"No!" Ajsha retorted. "But if you don't show up, Randolf will know, and he'll know why. Then he will come over and –"

"I get it!" Milo cut in miserably. "Man! Dang! This guy's a jerk! Fine! I'll go, but I warn you, I haven't *got* anything formal. And I ain't wearin' my pajamas!"

Ajsha nodded in agreement, relieved now that the worst thing they were discussing was clothes, and told Simon. He didn't seem to believe it, for he responded, through Ajsha:

"'You've got to have something.'"

"Nothing!" Milo shot back, gripping the armrests of the chair.

"He said, '*Sure* you don't! You're not getting out of it that easy. Come on! I bet you have something!'"

He jumped up and started for their bedroom.

"Nothing!" Milo called after him. "I never wear dresses and I wasn't planning to in the outback!"

She and Ajsha scrambled after him, and found him rummaging through Milo's bureau drawers.

"Get out of there!" Milo snapped, outraged.

Before she go shove him away, he suddenly paused and stared down at the drawer he was currently delving into. Milo's irate demands had no effect on him, and he began to shake, clutching the sides of the drawer. Both Milo and Ajsha hushed, bewildered. Reaching in, he brought up the necklace Ajsha had given Milo. Milo had stowed it there, deciding to wear it only on special occasions. It was too beautiful to be seen every day. The problem was that Ajsha had forgotten to tell Simon she had given it to Milo, and discovering it in her drawer not only shocked but infuriated him. He whirled around, teeth gritted, and began to yell at Milo.

She and Ajsha were very startled and only able to discern the subject of his raving when he held up the necklace.

"He is saying," Ajsha said, "'How?! How?!!! How could you?! You've gone to some lengths before, Milo, but I never thought –! Never! Where do you get the nerve?!'"

Milo blinked hard and backed up, very, very perplexed. The chain of the necklace clenched tightly in his fist, Simon stomped up to her and gave her a hard shove.

"Hey!" Milo said, stumbling and bouncing off the edge of the bed. "What's wrong with you?"

Ajsha translated, though it was against her six year old better judgment, and Simon went crazy. He stormed out of the room and down the hall, still yelling at Milo even though he had left her behind.

"He said," Ajsha interpreted, it getting harder to decipher what was spewing out of Simon's mouth, "'What's wrong with *me?!* What's wrong with *you?!* I never knew you could be such a despicable person! I'm just *disgusted* with you!'"

"This isn't the first time," Milo thought huffily, following him, *"that someone has been disgusted with me for no good reason."*

Simon was now pacing back and forth by the front door, going in and out of both thresholds for the kitchen and the sitting room. He saw Milo advancing towards him, Ajsha at her heels, and ground his teeth and resumed shouting. Milo had never seen him so angry. He seemed to be, as the saying goes, beside himself.

Ajsha did her best to keep translating. "'I never *ever* imagined that you would do something like this! So *low.*'"

"Like what?" Milo shouted back, not bothering to wait for a break in the flow.

"'How can you act like this?'" Simon was demanding wildly, pacing feverishly. "'Is this funny to you? Don't you know when to stop, Milo? What type of person would steal something from a child!'"

"What are you talking about?" Milo cried, not daring to come closer. "I've never stolen *anything* from *anyone!* Least of all a child!"

This was the sentence that finally got through.

"'You liar!'" Simon bellowed, though Ajsha said it softly. "'*Liar!* This is going too far! Too far! I just don't know what to do with you! Ajsha has been nothing but nice and kind to you, and you go and do this to her?'"

Banging the door open, he stalked outside.

"Do what?!" Milo screamed, following him out. Ajsha went with her, frantic now that her parents were yelling at each other so fast.

Simon stopped dead, turned, and thrust the necklace in Milo's face.

"'This!'" he hissed, though Ajsha's version was much politer.

"What about it?" Milo snapped, batting it away before it hit her. "I didn't steal it!"

But Simon didn't listen and kept jabbering away wrathfully. Comprehension dawned on Ajsha, but she had no opportunity to say anything. Milo tried to interject with her own words, but Simon kept up a relentless stream of Galo, addressing simultaneously her, thin air, and himself. She got fed up and gave him a tiny nudge to get him to stop. This only succeeded in getting her a powerful shove in return.

"Eln sil, nerii!" Simon shouted at her, red-faced and his spittle flying.

Ajsha gasped, her lungs expanding audibly. "Father!" she shouted reproachfully at him.

"What?" Milo said, rubbing her shoulder. "What'd he say?"

"He – he just called you a curse word," Ajsha said faintly, in shock, "relating mostly to females."

Milo's jaw plummeted. Now *she* was the furious one.

"You, you, you –!" she shrieked, unable to think, her body tensing with rage.

"Vile rat!" Bob the Conscience offered lividly.

"YOU!!!!!!!!" Milo screeched, lunging for his throat.

He grabbed her shoulders just in time to prevent her from achieving her target, but they both fell to the ground. But that wasn't enough to stop Milo. She had been insulted beyond peace. Simon was either going to die or get seriously injured.

They had collided sideways with the ground, and she wrestled to get above him. She tried to punch his face, but he was wriggling so much that she ended up hitting his shoulder. He tried to push her off of him but instead rolled on top of her. They began to grapple violently, Ajsha still translating for them because they were also engaged in loud verbal abuse.

It is nothing short of terrible for a child to have to help her parents insult each other, while watching them try to maim each other. But ever since the wedding plans fiasco, Ajsha was determined to never break down again, no matter how turbulent the argument. And even though she wanted to, she refused to let this brawl get her upset. Despite being scared and flustered, not one tear threatened to escape.

Casting aside the fact that she was smaller and more fragile, Ajsha joined the fray and tried to break them apart, all while continuing to translate. However, the translations only made the feuding couple angrier. The scuffling, clawing, and general slamming into one another grew more ferocious, and then something happened.

Now, they were indeed wrestling, and it wasn't as though they had a referee bellowing rules at them, but, everyone knows, when wrestling, punching is not allowed. But that is what Simon did. He was angrier than he had ever been in his life, which had been wonderfully pleasant and carefree up until a few months ago, and for a minute when it seemed like Milo was winning, he did something to get her off of him.

She had just managed to get on top of him when his fist shot straight up and rammed into her face. There was a sickening thud, and she fell sideways onto the ground. Ajsha gasped and ran around Simon's body to help her. Now, we all know that a boy should never, never *ever* hit a girl. Simon, who had been given the Protector and Provider talk by his father at an early age, was well aware of this, but he did it anyways, and in his opinion she deserved it.

Milo had rolled into a sitting position, Ajsha crouching beside her, gently holding her steady, and they both stated at him, speechless. Blood was dribbling from Milo's nose and leaking into her open mouth.

"You slime," she exclaimed in a shocked voice.

Ajsha translated, her own voice equally stunned.

"Nerii," Simon snarled quietly, his eyes narrowed at Milo, utterly remorseless.

"Father!" Ajsha shouted in protest.

Simon launched into defensive yammering, hoisting himself onto his knees and shaking the necklace, which he had managed to hang on to throughout the brawl.

"I told you!" Milo shouted thickly at him upon learning what he had said. She spat out a glob of bloody saliva. "I didn't steal it! Ajsha gave it to me!"

"'Liar!'" Ajsha translated, Simon sneering. "'Why would she give it to you?'"

Before Milo could answer, Ajsha covered her mouth with a little hand. She had had enough. It was her turn to talk now. She started gibbering firmly to Simon, putting up her other hand when he tried to interrupt. Slowly, his mutinous look began to melt, becoming modified into a sorry and ashamed expression.

"What'd you say to him?" Milo asked, running her fingers under her nose, blood now all over her chin and shirt.

"I told him that I did give it to you and why," Ajsha said, her voice rather raw by now.

At first Simon didn't respond. He seemed frozen on his knees, overwhelmed by shame. Slowly, each word a murmur, Simon spoke, his gaze jumping from Ajsha's face to a spot in midair, as if trying to understand how her story correlated with all visible evidence.

"He is saying," Ajsha whispered, because Simon was whispering,

"'You did? I . . . I . . . I . . . oh.'"

Apparently unable to think of anything to add to this, he stood up. So did Milo, who by now looked like she had just survived a dispute with a bear. They all went into the house, Milo sitting down at the kitchen table while Simon got her a cold, wet cloth. She mutely took it from him, pressing it against her nostrils. Whether she was still in shock, or the punch had knocked the fire out of her, Milo didn't know, but she didn't feel the rage that was supposed follow. Simon sat down in the seat opposite her. Neither one wanted to look at each other, both of them reviewing what had just occurred in their heads. The silence was finally broken by a soft gibber from Simon.

"He said, 'I'm very sorry,'" said Ajsha. She was standing by the doorway, observing her parents.

Something, scarcely anything, yet *something*, deep, *deep* inside Milo, stirred. It wasn't very much, and she chose to ignore it, but it was there.

She shrugged, and then said two sentences she had never thought she would ever say in sequence to Simon. "It's okay," she mumbled. "I'm sorry, too."

They looked up at each other once both these were interpreted. They both wore a pained expression, for two different reasons. Simon dropped the necklace in front of Milo, gibbering under his breath. Ajsha walked up and put her face close to Simon's.

"He said that you don't have to go to the party if you don't want to," Ajsha said, wrapping her arms around his neck. He drew her in, resting his forehead on her little shoulder.

Milo shrugged again, that issue now a million years ago. "I'll go," she sighed. "I don't want Mr. Fittler to come after me. Honestly, though, I have nothing good enough to wear."

They sat mulling this problem over for a moment, Simon not surfacing from his wretchedness and Ajsha patting his back in a steady rhythm. She soon said shyly, "Maybe you don't, but I do."

"Ajsha," Milo chuckled, readjusting her cloth, which was now quite pink, "I may be thin but I'm not that short."

"Oh," Ajsha said, righting Simon and pulling Milo to her feet. "Come on. I'll show you."

She led Milo to her and Simon's bedroom, left her there, and returned with the large box that she had caught at the wedding. Heaving it onto the bed, she dumped out its contents. Skirts, blouses, and tank tops tumbled out in a cascade of colors and textures.

"I remembered it last month," she stated, selecting a few articles and seeing how they paired together.

"So," Milo said, folding her arms. Her nose had dried up, but her face was still gruesome. "*You* were putting those clothes on my bed, not Simon."

"Yes," Ajsha said heavily. "I'm trying to get you to wear something different. I'm surprised you haven't had heatstroke from those jeans you wear."

As she assessed the clothes, Milo left to wash up. When she returned, she sat on the edge of the mattress and asked Ajsha, "Why did Simon go so berserk about the necklace?"

Ajsha didn't look up. "He gave it to me," she said quietly. "He found it in the water one day and made a necklace out of it. It was a birthday present."

Milo was dumbstruck. "Oh, Ajsha," she whispered. "Why didn't you tell me?"

Ajsha shrugged, holding aloft a crinkly blouse. "Would you have taken it?" she asked.

Milo knew that answer. She stayed quiet.

Ajsha eventually had her change into a sarong, a tank top, and a blouse. The sarong was thick, a swirling red and green, and had a special way of tying at the waist, creating a flowing skirt effect. The tank top was turquoise and hugged Milo's thin frame. The blouse was button-up and had excess material at the corners for tying. It was short-sleeved and white, with tiny pockets sewn onto the sleeves. Ajsha had her wear it over the tank top, leaving the buttons undone and the ties knotted into a bow by her navel.

"Perfect," Ajsha said, ruffling the skirt in certain places. "You almost look plumper."

She dashed off to retrieve the sandals.

"Impossible," Milo muttered, looking in the mirror and running her hands down her bony thighs. "Don't lie to me."

The last thing she put on was the necklace, its iridescent blue and green whorls standing out on Milo's stark white chest. She spun in a languid circle, Ajsha contemplating the entire ensemble before nodding in approval. They went into the sitting room, where Simon sat in the chair in the far corner, lost in thought. He looked up upon their entry, focusing his vision on Milo. His lips parted slightly, and he fell into a trance, until Milo lobbed a pillow at him. The impact woke him up and he spoke softly. Ajsha looked very pleased.

"He said that you look very lovely, and once again he is sorry for yelling at you, hurting you, punching you, and . . . well . . . swearing at you. And you do look very nice."

"Really?" Milo said, fidgeting self-consciously. "I feel ridiculous."

Milo had plenty of time to get used to it, for the party wasn't until nighttime. She roamed about the hut, staying away from the kitchen or anywhere with the potential to smudge or stain her outfit. Her nose was a little tender and had a rouge tinge, but hopefully nobody would notice in the dark. Sometime during her wait, Milo's curiosity and boredom got the better of her, and she asked Ajsha, "Why do you get so close to Simon's face when you talk to him?"

Ajsha shrugged and smiled shyly, looking down at her feet. "His breath smells good," she said.

"Oh?" Milo said, feeling somewhat tickled. "Kinda minty fresh?"

Ajsha looked up. "No," she said, frowning thoughtfully. "It smells . . . well, it smells like milk."

"Milk?" Milo repeated, unbelieving.

"Yeah," Ajsha exclaimed softly, it now fully dawning upon her. "Exactly like milk. It always does, except right after he eats. But it always goes back to smelling like milk."

"Why?" Milo asked, her mind racing for any instance when she had seen Simon drinking milk.

"I don't know," Ajsha admitted. "But it smells nice."

Milo was highly skeptical that a person's every day, normal breath could smell like milk. She had heard bad breath be described as sour milk, but just plain milk seemed too out there to be real. Curiosity stabbed at her until she had to either take action or go insane. She stalked up to Simon, who was sitting at the kitchen table. Ignoring his inquisitive look, she thrust her thumb and pointer finger under where his jaw jointed. He gagged and opened his mouth. Before he could swat her hand away, she stuck her nose close and sniffed. To her amazement, his wheezes smelled precisely like milk. Bemused yet satisfied, she released him and walked away, leaving him puzzled and rubbing his throat.

As evening approached, the usual crimson streaks striping the sky, Milo peeked into the bedroom and saw Simon staring malignantly at the bed. He was now dressed in a black, long-sleeved, button-down shirt with a collar, which offset his golden skin gorgeously. He had on khaki pants that were obviously rarely donned, being fairly wrinkle-free, and he was glaring with loathing at a necktie. He didn't seem to know what to do with it. Ajsha walked in, brushing past Milo, and laughed at him. Picking up the tie, she climbed onto the bed and balanced on her knees. Confidently, she wound the tie around his neck and underneath his collar. Ever so professionally, she began to loop and knot it. They murmured to each other, Ajsha small fingers deftly making a triangular lump by his Adam's apple. When she finished, Simon kissed her on the nose. She shrieked in delight and ran out of the room. Milo scrutinized the necktie from a distance.

"Man!" Bob the Conscience muttered. "This kid can do everything!"

"Sure can," Milo whispered.

When it came time for them to depart for the party, they all gathered beyond the front door and Simon tried to slip his arm into Milo's. Jerking away on instinct, she gave him a dirty look. Instead of being annoyed, he merely looked sad. He mumbled instructions and goodbye to Ajsha, who had been deemed worthy to stay by herself, and began to walk, his hands stuffed dejectedly into his pockets.

"Oh, why do you treat him this way?" Ajsha asked Milo, watching his retreating form.

"I don't want him touching me," Milo replied, not wanting to say that it had been a reflex.

"You wrestled with him today," Ajsha reminded her. "And he punched you."

"There you go," Milo said, latching on. "My reason to be angry."

"But I thought you forgave him."

"Well . . . I did," Milo admitted uncomfortably. "But you know how I feel about this. You know why I hate him. He's disregarded my theories and policies on love. Those were important to me. You know, I wouldn't even let myself *date* until I was fifteen? And at *fourteen* I was forced to marry. Forced! It's like saying people's principles mean nothing. I wanted to be in love when I got married, which was supposed to be way in the future. Right now, I'm too young to be in love."

"No one is ever too young to love," Ajsha mumbled and went inside.

Her words, so quiet and few, stung Milo. She stood immobile and silent for a second, realigning her train of thought. Even though she realized that Ajsha was right, she tried to block it out, and ran to catch up with Simon.

They tramped along through the dark jungle, the far off illuminated windows of houses providing just enough light to keep from tripping. After cutting across town, they met up with a group of Simon's friends. Milo kept her distance from them, preferring to give her attention to the hem of her sarong instead of the boisterous chatter. Rather than going to a person's house or a public building, they walked into the forest on the east side of town.

After careful travel, the moon painting all the vines and faces an opalescent hue, they emerged into enormous clearing, carpeted with short grass. At the center of the clearing was a huge, flat granite surface, level with the ground. It was about forty feet in diameter and relatively square. Tables for two were set up all around it, and there was a cluster of instrument playing individuals off to one side. Some had restored orchestra pieces, and others wielded musical devices made from various island bounty. There seemed to be mostly adults milling about and not many teens. And the teens present weren't any Milo would have liked to see. Lanterns sat on every table, sending a soft glow over the field, helping out the moon. Several couples were already dancing.

The boy known as Randolf Fittler was wending his way towards Simon and Milo, a girl almost literally hanging from his beefy arm. He smirked victoriously at Milo, but she didn't react. For some odd reason, she felt slightly sick of employing an attitude. She wasn't always rude and impudent; she actually enjoyed being cheerful and pleasant with people now and then. What depressed her was that there wasn't anybody there worthy of being that way with. Randolf and Simon chatted for a moment, the girl batting her lashes just a bit more than necessary, and Randolf then guided them to a table. They sat down, he and his girl walking off, she scurrying to keep up.

A couple of dishes were set out on the table, should they have an appetite, but Milo wasn't interested. Ever since Ajsha said those words to her, she'd had a churning feeling in her stomach. Milo had a suspicion it was guilt.

As she sat, enduring the guilt, she began to feel decidedly blue and it showed. Looking troubled, she stared silently at the lantern, which was crafted from wire and a scratched champagne flute. Simon watched her, his heart breaking. If there was one thing he wanted to do more than anything at that moment, it was to help her feel better. But he didn't know how he could. For a brief moment, Milo glanced up and he smiled kindly at her. Her face didn't even twitch and she resumed staring at the flickering orange flame. Thinking hard for a way to get past the language barrier, Simon tried using the one word they both understood.

"Milooo."

"What?" she muttered.

"Miiilo."

"What?" she muttered again.

"Milllo."

"What??" she said.

"Mmmilo."

"What!" she snapped.

"Miiilo, Milooo."

"What!!" she shouted, finally looking up and realizing he was singing to the music.

And not necessarily to her, either, but more so to himself. He was softly singing her name to himself. He glanced fleetingly over at her, but then looked towards the granite dance floor, still singing. Milo, wrenched out of her mire of self-pity, was very addled by this. She had no plausible idea as to why he was singing her name. Never having heard her name sung before, Milo started to feel uneasy and vulnerable. She was about to order him to Shut up! when a movement on the dance floor caught her attention.

At the edge of the square stood the hulking figure of Soldier, looking both excited and nervous. Milo followed his gaze and

discovered he was looking at Mrs. Lanslo, who was festooned in a
gown of rich, green silk. Milo almost shrieked as she looked from
her to Soldier. He was taking deep breaths and smoothing out his
lapel. At last, having dredged up as much courage as he could, he
started towards Mrs. Lanslo, striding with purpose. Milo clapped
her hands together in glee.

"He's doing it!" she trilled to Simon. "He's finally approaching
her!"

Though he had no clue what she was saying, Simon could hear
that she was saying it jubilantly, and was happy that she was happy
again. He smiled at the sight of her smile.

"I mean, finally!" Milo went on, seemingly forgetting that her
companion was of the Galo-speaking sort. "His English has been
improving like crazy. You should hear him! All he talks about is her.
Sure, he's still scratchy and gruff, but he talks like a British
gentleman. Hey! D'you know what would be fun? Eavesdropping
on them. I know! It's rude and imposing, but it's *so* much fun! Of
course, it would look stupid and suspicious if we're just standing on
the dance floor doing nothing, so we need to think of a way to
blend in. Let's see, how could we do that?"

She already knew the answer, but she still tried to think of an
alternative method, Simon still grinning blithely at her and being
absolutely no help. Coming up empty, she groaned. But, determined
to eavesdrop, she got up and motioned for Simon to follow. He
ignorantly stood up, and she grabbed his hand, pulling him towards
the dance rock.

The music was playing a brisk waltz, and Milo, even though she
loathed to, motioned for Simon to start dancing with her. He was
hesitant, for he was getting wiser, but seeing how frantic she was, he
decided it was worth the risk. Simon knew the exact position for a
waltz; from Ajsha's cough earlier, he probably was very
knowledgeable about ballroom dancing in general. He cupped one
of her hands in his, and his other hand he wrapped around her and

laid it beneath her shoulder blades. Milo cringed as she felt it through the fabric, but nevertheless she pressed her other hand onto his shoulder.

Now correctly positioned, they sauntered off into the crowd. Even though it was Simon who had the dance know-how, Milo took the lead. She led them in a specific direction, towards where Soldier and Mrs. Lanslo were revolving in a wide circle, Mrs. Lanslo barely reaching Soldier's chest. Simon let her do it; he was happy enough that she was dancing with him, something he thought she would never do. He had actually resigned himself to an evening of repose and dance viewing rather than participating. They finally got close enough to overhear Soldier and Mrs. Lanslo, which was no picnic since there are no straight lines in a waltz. English being what Soldier was trying to impress her with, that was the language they were using. The conversation Milo heard went like this:

Soldier: "My, but don't you look lovely tonight!"

Mrs. Lanslo: (giggle) "Why, thank you, Gorben. You're looking pretty spiffed up, as well."

Soldier: "Thank you. You know, Ruby, I was so very anxious about coming over to talk to you. I was afraid of what I might say. But here I am, feeling comfortable and at easy with you!"

Mrs. Lanslo: "Really, dear? Then why are you shaking like an insect wing?"

Soldier: "Oh, um, I am? Well, ha! I guess I'm still nervous. I . . . I don't know if you're aware, but I have been fancying you for the longest time."

Milo never got to hear if she did or not, for the pair started to drift away.

"C'mon!" she urged Simon, who had been staring at her affectionately while she had been peering over his shoulder. "They're getting away!"

Just then, Milo felt a tap. Releasing Simon, she whirled around, ready to smack someone. There stood a teenage couple, who had been dancing nearby. The girl had politely tapped Milo's shoulder, and now she took Milo's place and started dancing with Simon.

"Hey!" Milo said. "Get your own weasel! I need him right now!"

The girl of course didn't understand and was moving farther away with Simon, who, if he was aggrieved by this, courteously didn't show it. Milo scowled and looked over the boy left behind for her.

"Oh, I guess you'll do," she groaned.

Grabbing him unceremoniously, she started dancing back to Soldier and Mrs. Lanslo. But the boy, much taller than her and apparently stingy about leading, turned them in another direction. Milo snarled and lurched them another way. The boy, possibly wondering what he had gotten himself into, again turned them, and then Milo did and so on until they almost hit a few people. At one point, they got close enough to Soldier for Milo to catch, "Oh yes! Quite!" then she was swept away.

Very frustrated by now, she tried to locate Simon. She spotted him with a few boys, talking. Seeing that he wasn't claimed, she pulled out of the grasp of her current partner and marched off. Advancing on Simon, she indicated that she wanted to dance again. He smiled and eagerly accepted.

"Must be his lucky night," Bob the Conscience remarked.

They waltzed out, Milo in a much better mood now that she was leading again. Avoiding a barrage of elbows, they caught up with Soldier and Mrs. Lanslo just as the music turned slow and sweet. Gauging an appropriate distance, Milo leisurely swayed with Simon while listening.

Mrs. Lanslo: "How very interesting! I never knew. Oh, Gorben! I'm so happy that you came up to me. You should have done it earlier."

Soldier: "Well, I wanted to learn English first. Honestly, Ruby, I wanted to impress you."

Mrs. Lanslo: "Well, don't you think that five years is quite a while? And besides, dear, you don't need to impress me."

Milo listened to and glimpsed this scene with a resounding happiness for the both of them. Involuntarily, she perched her chin on Simon's shoulder as she stared. Instantly, she realized her error and lifted it. But she was still having fun. There's something soothing about a waltz that makes people feel kinder and calmer. It, along with the day's events and Ajsha's proverb, made Milo realize that she had to start to forgive Simon. Not just for all the recent offences, but for everything that she was holding against him.

"*He's really a good guy,*" she mentally admitted as they waltzed, him pressing her as close to him as he dared. "*I still don't like him, but I should forgive him. Just because I hate him doesn't mean God does. He loves this creep. I guess I'll forgive, but I won't forget.*"

"That," Bob the Conscience stated, "is like saying you won't forgive him."

"Fine, my heart will forgive him."

"But your mind won't? That's not forgiveness."

"Sure it is."

"Oh, you stubborn child! Fine! Be contrary! But someday you will have to forgive *and* forget."

It was true, and someday she would, but for now she miraculously let go of the bitterness in her heart, yet not her mind. It was the waltz that brought it on, that motivated her. Forgiveness is like a waltz: Up and down, up and down, sometimes fast, sometimes slow. But always with a partner, and you feel better afterwards.

Milo's heart now felt much lighter, but she still felt a wave of revulsion when she looked at Simon. But, that teensy, tiny something inside Milo that had stirred earlier was still stirring.

Without warning, as Milo was coming out of her reverie about hearts and hatred, Mrs. Lanslo noticed her and Simon dancing together. She waved jovially and started to walk over.

Milo saw this and said, "Oh, crap! We've been spotted! I mean – *I've* been spotted while dancing with you! Ohh. Ooo. Ahhu."

Panicking, she tried to hide behind Simon by making him cross his arms to make him wider and standing behind him. But she wasn't speedy enough.

"Hello, Milo dear!"

Milo jumped and nonchalantly spun around. "Hi, Mrs. Lanslo! Soldier!" she greeted bracingly.

"Hello, Milo," Soldier replied with a wink. "Simon."

Mrs. Lanslo began gibbering to Simon, twirling him to admire how handsome he was. Milo took the opportunity to sidle up next to Soldier.

"Look at you!" she said. "How's it going, player?"

"Pretty good, if I do say so myself," he answered, not knowing what "player" meant.

"Yeah? Awesomeness! Hey, what's she saying right now?" she whispered.

"Um, well, she is wondering why you were letting Simon dance with you. And Si – Why are you looking at me that way?"

"Oh." Milo started, stuttering, "It's just that – Good Heavens, man! Your English has gotten good! How did you do it so quickly?"

"Borrowed a book from someone," he muttered. "See, now Simon is saying that you just suddenly wanted to dance with him. He thinks you are beginning to like him a little bit."

"Oh, does he now?!" Milo barked instantly furious, all mushy inclinations of goodwill vanishing. Both Mrs. Lanslo and Simon jumped at her outburst. Her contorted face leered at Simon's, and he leaned away in confusion.

"Well," she spat, "tell him that only exists in his dreams, and he can forget about me *ever* liking him! EVER! And also tell him that tonight I'm sleeping on the couch!"

Having yelled her piece, she began to stomp away. As she left, she overheard Soldier mutter to himself, "Whew! Simon, I don't know how you survive!"

20
How he's Feeling

AJSHA AWOKE WITH a start sometime during a night. It was quite late out, a crescent moon just visible through her window and a warm, salty breeze stirring her curtains. Blinking hard in the darkness and whimpering softly, she took several deep breaths to calm herself. She had just jolted out of a reoccurring nightmare that she started to have in August. Intermittently, bits of detail would change, but it always consisted of the same topic.

"It was just a dream," she whispered to herself. "Just an image in my mind's eye brought on by stress or harbored anxiety. Common for people with unaddressed issues, secrets, and who eat before sleeping."

She was reciting from one of her psych text books, a habit that normally soothed her, but she still felt uneasy about going back to sleep. Giving her tummy a few meditative pats, she decided that she could use a glass of water. She slid out of bed and wandered into the hall, feeling her way along. There was a faint glow issuing from the kitchen doorway, and when she arrived she found Simon already there, sitting at the table and staring at the glass of water in front of him. Also on the table were a dripping candle and a bowl of raspberries. Looking up, he noticed his daughter.

Now, before we go any farther, I will remind you that up until this chapter, everything that we have heard Simon say has been interpreted by Ajsha. Therefore, we really don't know how he's truly been feeling. So, this chapter will be dedicated to the conversation he and Ajsha had in the kitchen late at night, and everything Simon says will be written down in English, even though he is actually speaking Galo. Now, getting back to Simon . . .

He looked up and saw his daughter.

"Ajsha," he said quietly in surprise. "What are you doing up?"

"I couldn't fall back to sleep," she explained, padding over to him. "So I thought I would get some water."

"Yeah?" Simon said gently, arising to get it for her. "Bad dream?"

Ajsha nodded tiredly, apparently not keen to share.

"Well, here you are, little cutie," he said, handing her a glass full of sloshing clear liquid.

"Thank you," she said, taking a sip and sitting down.

"No problem," he whispered, joining her.

They sipped and nibbled on raspberries for a minute, until Ajsha asked, "Father, why are you up?"

He shrugged sadly, scratching his cup with a fingernail. "I don't know. I couldn't sleep either I guess."

Ajsha leaned forward in concern. "Is anything wrong? Do you feel sick?"

He shook his head, but if he had nodded it wouldn't have been a complete lie.

"It's Mother, isn't it?" she said softly, her gaze intent upon his face.

Simon sighed and looked away. "Yeah," he murmured. He faced Ajsha again and asked, in an almost pained tone, "Is there anything wrong with me?"

"No, Father!" Ajsha exclaimed, surprised. "Why would you even think that?"

"I don't know," he sighed, focusing on the raspberries. "It seems like there is. No matter how hard I try, I can't get her to even *like* me. She won't talk to me – about anything; she glares at me all the time, she never wants to do anything with me. She won't accept my presents. I thought being married was going to be wonderful; your girl always around to hug and kiss and curl up on the couch with after work. I was so excited . . . But, this . . . I just wish I knew what was wrong. Maybe I could make it better. Am I . . . am I coming on too strong for her?"

"Maybe when you first met her," Ajsha said thoughtfully. "But you aren't now. You're giving her plenty of space. Listen, remember what I told you? That she said she has principles about love? She's still angry at you for violating them."

"Still?" Simon said with slight exasperation. "I married her almost five months ago! Why can't she let that go?"

"I don't think five years could help," Ajsha said gently, tenderly patting his elbow. "She's a very stubborn and strong headed girl, and it will be a while before she gets used to living here. But she does want to be loved. I know that."

"She told you?" Simon asked.

"Well, no. But if you read in between the lines, you can definitely tell. A lot has happened to her in a short amount of time, and all of it was against her will. I'm not surprised she's spiteful. Perhaps if you hadn't married her and just dated her, she might have liked you."

"Oh, but, Ajsha," Simon said passionately, trapping her small hand in his, "I *had* to marry her. And, no matter what, I will always be happy I married her. I know nobody gets it. I hear them all the time: pitying me, saying that I deserve better, wondering what drove me to do it. Do you know why I wanted to marry her, Ajsha? Do you know why I fell in love with her instead of one of the other girls? Well, I'll tell you. I haven't told anyone yet; I thought Milo should be the first to hear this story, but I have a feeling that's not going to happen anytime soon, and I want you to know.

"I was out late at that hidden beach, and I saw a plane come soaring through the air, half of it on fire. I was about to follow it to the Crash Site when I saw something floating in the water. Something made me stay and wait for it to come closer. After a while, it neared the shore and I saw that it was a girl. Poor thing, she was knocked out and bleeding and seconds away from falling off her suitcase. Immediately, I went into the water to help her. She needed me. I carried her onto the beach and cleaned her up, bandaging her head and everything. I stayed awake all night, making sure she was okay. She needed me. And, as I took care of her, I began to fall in love with her.

"It was because she needed me, Ajsha. No one else, except you of course, has ever really, *really* needed me. And . . . I don't know. Just looking at her, I felt like something was falling into place; like my life made sense now. I kept telling myself, 'Easy, Simon! Don't get too caught up. Don't get too far ahead of yourself. Use your brain. You know nothing about this girl. You don't know if she'll be nice or nasty.' So, I decided to wait until she woke up to really see if I should marry her. Because I did want to marry her. Maybe it was foolish, but I didn't care who she was, what her name was, where she had come from, what her personality might be, I wanted to *marry* her.

"Well, she woke up the next morning, and even though I couldn't understand her, I could tell she was nice and that was enough for me. I know, I should have waited for an interpreter, but I was impatient from waiting all night. I *really* thought she understood me. I thought finally, it was happening, and everyone would now get off my back about it, and girls that I've known from infancy would stop flocking around me in the street, and, of course, that now I could adopt you. I was so excited, Ajsha. Only after I found out that she hadn't understood did I feel a little stupid, but I guess that's what love does to you. It blinds and deafens you," Simon finished with a dejected sigh.

"Not always," Ajsha said compassionately. She had listened to the tale with mingling feelings of awe and pity. "It can. But it can also make the world clearer to you, and you start to notice and appreciate everything. From the smallest flower that you walked by every day, to a refreshing breeze that you always took for granted. It's like – your mind opens when you're in love. You now see the world differently; everything is more defined and yet beautiful. I've read all about it. And a good way to prevent yourself from becoming a 'fool' in love is to make sure you have reasons for being in love, and to notice all the little things about your person. If you're really in love then all those little things will shine, while other people have to really concentrate to see them."

"Oh, I do see them," Simon said enthusiastically. "Like . . . you said that she doesn't like her hair. Well, I love it. It's so beautiful. So rich and full of color."

"Um, Father," Ajsha said in a tone that implied she didn't wish to contradict him, but facts are facts, "it's not colorful."

"To me it is," Simon said, his eyes misting over as he conjured an image of Milo in his mind. (In his mind, she was always smiling and her jeans actually fit her.) "And her skin's so lovely, so elegant."

"She looks like a piece of marble!" Ajsha exclaimed before she could stop herself.

"Ajsha!" Simon remonstrated. "That's not very nice. Don't you think she's pretty?"

"Of course I do!" Ajsha said earnestly, thinking that at times the truth is mean. "But, I just don't see those things the way you do."

Simon nodded understandingly, and his features became dreamy once more.

"Anyway," he continued, now surveying a laughing imaginary Milo (presumably laughing at something amusing he had said), "her skin's doing better. The sun must have helped, or all that walking she's doing to visit Squelch. Instead of looking sick pale, it looks normal pale. And she's not as thin as she used to be. It must be from eating all that fish. Fish is a good source of protein, you know. You'll learn that in school. She's putting on muscle, which is a relief. I used to watch her move like she would collapse at any moment. It sounds bad, but that's what helped me be attracted to her, her looks. I haven't seen many pale people, or any so scrawny. It's so *interesting*. But, I know looks aren't everything, so I am learning to love everything else about her. For instance, I love the way she cooks."

"Me, too," Ajsha agreed. She paused for a moment. "You know, Father," she went on timidly, "when I go into town, I hear things. People are wondering why you love Mother and keep loving her. I mean, they know that you're stuck with her, but besides that."

Simon looked out the window, where stars were sparkling up in the inky sky. "I've wondered that myself sometimes. I think, 'Look at what she's doing to you! How can you still love her after all this? Are you sure you actually fell in love with her in the first place?' But I know I do, Ajsha. During the night, if there's a moon, I stare at her face. So beautiful, so peaceful. All my anger melts away. I can't stay angry with her. I can barely bring myself to *be* angry at her. She has a strange power over me that she doesn't know about. Even if she did know, I don't think she would care. But, it's weird, because even though she doesn't love me, I still want her to know that I love her. She won't believe it, though. I can't stand it anymore, Ajsha! I don't know what to do."

He broke off, his voice cracking. Ajsha stared at him, stunned and a bit frightened.

"I've never seen you like this," she said. "You are usually so calm. Knowing. Under control."

Simon sniffed into his sleeve and made a sound that was a cross between a scoff and a chuckle.

"I know," he said, grinding the heel of his hand into his forehead. "It's just been very stressful lately. Milo is the most unpredictable girl in the world. She's got me twisting in knots."

"I know," Ajsha whispered, nodding.

They both fell into a grim silence and thought back to a perfect example. About a week ago, at nighttime, Milo had awoken with a thrashing motion from a horrible nightmare, not quite unlike Ajsha. In Milo's nightmare, her parents had somehow found the island, but they didn't want Milo back. They had loudly renounced her as their offspring, and left in their air-craft (which Milo wasn't too sure about, since it appeared almost as if they were floating up and away on nothing.) Anyway, she was hopping up and down on the sand, which was oddly black and red, screaming up at them to come back for her, not to leave her there. They were laughing at her, and rapidly growing things that resembled fangs and talons.

She awoke with a cold sweat seeping from her pores. As the images faded away and the bedroom came into focus, she tried to calm down, reassuring herself that if her parents ever did find her, which she doubted, they would in fact want her and remove her from the island. Assuring as this sounded, Milo felt the need for proof, so she took a careful, long look over her relationship with her parents over the years. As she reminisced, she felt a twinge of worry. She did an examination unlike any other she had done before. Compared to this, all the other times she had looked back on her life seemed like brief glances. It deeply unsettled and upset her. She felt like crying, which she tried to avoid while remembering her life because it made her feel selfish.

She was feeling awful, conflicted with crying and being grateful that it hadn't been worse. Looking beside her, she saw the elongated lump that was Simon under the blanket, slumbering ever so peacefully. Milo was suddenly angry at him, sleeping so undisturbed, in harmony with the world. She now knew how all the wives she had seen on sitcoms felt when they awoke troubled while their husbands slept on carelessly. The more she thought about it, the madder she got.

"He should be suffering with me!" she thought vindictively.

She recalled what the wives on the sitcoms did. They were wise. They woke their husbands by walloping them with a pillow. Milo decided to do that. Raising her pillow above his head, she brought it down with a dull *vvwap*. Simon woke up with drowsy urgency, and Milo smacked him again to help him come to his senses. Now just as awake as her, he settled into a sitting position and looked at her questioningly.

"How can you sleep?" she hissed at him, crossing her arms. "I'm laying here falling to pieces and all you do is *sleep?* I can't understand men like you."

Simon, who had actually been enjoying his time in dreamland, couldn't understand one word; however, she was talking to him, so did details such as the time or comprehension matter?

"Why do you leave me to agony and guiltiness?" Milo continued as Simon leaned back and listened the way you might watch a foreign film (It's all in the tone and gestures.) "Don't you care? Oh, that's right. You LOVE me! Well, heck knows. Maybe you do. . . . I'm not sure if my parents do. I know they do because they have to, but I'm not sure if they actually love me for me. Because of whom I am, not just because I'm their daughter.

"You've got to love people for everything they are, you know. No. I guess you wouldn't. You know nothing about me. I used to try to tell my parents about my traits and interests, but I don't think they were always listening. But, it's not like they didn't *try* to be good parents, and I do love them. I guess no parent is a good parent, no one's perfect and can't be, but sometimes I feel like they weren't trying very *hard*. They had their good spells, thankfully, but there were times when . . . when . . . I was just disgusted with them. Don't look at me like that!"

Simon was wearing a somewhat blank expression, which he had hoped was one of rapt attention.

"It's been hard for me, okay?" Milo said defensively. "I know people have had it far worse, but – I'm sick of not grieving over my troubles. I need to get it out of me. Tears are like trash bags. You put in your garbage like fear, bitterness, clinging to the past, and they get thrown away. I know it sounds sappy, but it's true. You can't keep things bottled up."

So, in an unexpected turn of events, Milo began her pouring out her soul to an increasingly concerned Simon, breaking down as she did. She let it all flow out of her, a thing she should have done a long time ago. Emotional meltdowns are never pleasant and hardly ever convenient, but this was one that was beyond needed. Just about everyone on the planet has experienced one at least once in their life. And, for the duration of the meltdown, they are completely open to consoling and closure. Simon attempted to do this, though he wished he knew what she was saying.

The more she talked, the more upset she became, until she entered the crying phase. She sobbed openly, still trying to talk, there being still so much more to expel. Wanting to comfort her, Simon slowly, tentatively, wrapped his arms around her and hugged her. Milo didn't object, in fact she welcomed it, as is to be expected when in this condition.

As he held her, a skinny, pale mess of tears and snot, she cried and cried, babbling ever onward. Slowly, he began to rock back and forth, his chin on her nearest shoulder, and he began to sing. Milo recognized it as the same song he had sung to her when she had slept on the floor and sung to Ajsha almost every night. It soothed her, though its lyrics were a mystery, and eventually her jumbled, screechy speech came to a halt. It took longer for the tears to stop. But, finally she exhausted her supply, and she wiped her eyes with the back of her hand, snuffling hard to unclog her nose. Leaning away, Simon rubbed her back. Nodding appreciatively, she patted his arm. She smiled and he smiled back.

"Um," she said and cleared her throat. "Um, thank you."

Yes, she was grateful. After all, he had been so nice about it. Still, she laid back down feeling a bit embarrassed. She decided to have

Ajsha repeat the thank you the next day. In the morning, while getting dressed and heading down the hall, she recited what she would say in her head.

"*Hey, Simon, listen. About last night. Thank you. I mean, thanks for being so cool about how I was acting. Sorry, I just really needed to do that, and I want you to know that I'm grateful that you helped me. People need people like you around when things like that happen to them. Thanks for being so understanding. Not that you could understand me or anything, but . . . oh, man.*"

Kneading both her temples, she was about to take the turn into the kitchen, when she saw that Ajsha and Simon in the sitting room, talking excitedly to Will Westron. Milo didn't want to be rude that day and interrupt, but she did ask Ajsha to translate. First, Ajsha gave her a hug, which should have raised Milo's suspicions, and then translated as Simon recounted last night. He described the scene to his friend, boasting (in Milo's opinion) about how he had helped. If that didn't rile Milo enough, Simon, who was so absorbed in his story that he hadn't noticed her yet, went on to say that he thought that by the way she had acted, he had maybe finally got her to like him.

Incensed, her gratitude forgotten, Milo hooked her hand onto Ajsha's arm, marched up to Simon, and proceeded to yell at him. Both he and Will Westron jumped as she raged about how assuming he was, how everything she did around him made him think that she was accepting things, and how she was disappointed that he couldn't be there just once as a fellow human, helping her through something. *Everything* had to point to liking him. And that she was disgusted he had shared this supposition with someone else before presenting it to her. She yelled and spat at him, Ajsha stationing herself between them, just in case, and then stormed away, leaving Simon feeling confused and depressed.

Following this standoff, she caused trouble for him for several days, from refusing to wash his clothes to only partially cooking his food. She had to stop all that when Simon's mafia – I mean friends – started snooping around, but she still gave Simon hard, lethal glares.

Simon hated it when something like this incident happened. It always left him muddled and sad. He just wanted, if anything, to get along with Milo. Usually, she remained mad about such events for a while. He could now shorten it by letting her visit Squelch.

These instances made him feel depressed about how things were going with Milo. He revealed this to Ajsha that night.

"I'm running out of ideas," he said desperately. "I'm not sure what to do anymore. I can't figure this female out. Why she makes things so complicated, I don't know."

"She's been raised differently from you and me," Ajsha said gently. "She's had a hard life, more complicated than ours. She's used to it, so what seems complicated to us is typical to her. And I think she deliberately holds on to her anger to be bitter. But, even so, she has a good heart. You see the way she hugs and kisses her cat, and how fun she is around Squelch. She is always very nice to me; she walks with me to school and always asks what I want for lunch. Yesterday, for the first time, she hugged me. Not just a return hug, but a spontaneous one. I was thrilled. She puts a lot of love into her hugs. I mean, when she gives a hug, she means it. I guess you just need to break down that barrier she's set up for you. Once you do that, I am confident she will love you. Everyone else does; she can't be too different."

"I hope so," Simon said, spontaneous hugs now at the top of his wish list. "And you know I'll do whatever it takes. I'd hate to imagine my life without her. She makes me feel happy, when she's not, you know, making me miserable. When I see her smile, I feel like smiling. When I hear her laugh, I want to laugh, too. I wish we were in a good place, so that I could spend all day with her, just to be with her."

"You wouldn't want to if you saw her in the morning," mumbled

Ajsha, then turned serious. "I know. I love her too. And I've tried, but I can't imagine life without her. She's really changing everything. I would mourn so long if she was ever taken away from us."

Simon finally smiled. "You are much too young to be using words like mourn, or any of those other fancy words you pick up from books."

"I would," Ajsha insisted, standing up. "I keep having nightmares that people are going to find the island and take her away from us. I had the same nightmare tonight. It scares me so much!"

"Oh," Simon said, extending an arm to her. Lips trembling, she went and sat on his lap. He hugged her tightly. "Don't worry, little cutie," he crooned, her head resting against his chest. "No one knows this island exists. No one will ever be able to find us. She will always be here with us. We won't let her escape. Besides, I love her too much to let her go. I would follow her to the ends of the earth, just to let her know I love her. My purpose won't be satisfied until she understands that. Sure, she may bring me down at times, but I'll always bounce back. Somehow, some way, I am *going* to convince her that I adore her thoroughly."

"Why?" Ajsha whispered.

"I'm not entirely sure," Simon chuckled. "She isn't deliberately giving me a lot of reasons. Maybe just to prove that I can be as stubborn as she can be. But, I know that she needs me, and that's what attracts me to her the most. All the other girls may want me, but they don't need me. She does. It's like you said, all I have to do is break down that barrier. I just need to find out how."

"Well," Ajsha said, tilting her head up to look at him. "You could get her something she really, really wants for Christmas."

"Ajsha," Simon said, "you know I can't divorce her."

"No, *no*. Something else."

"Oh. What? I don't know what she wants. Whenever we go to the market, she never strays away from the task. And it's not like we talk a lot."

"You ought to be with her on other trips to town," Ajsha grumbled. "But listen, think about what she likes."

"Well," Simon said slowly, after thinking for a minute. "I know she loves her radio thing."

"Yes, yes, now connect that to a present."

Simon concentrated for a moment and then shook his head. "Nothing's coming."

"Then I'll just show you later," Ajsha said, snuggling against him. "Or, you can follow Milo and find out for yourself."

"All right."

"And, don't forget our little plan."

"Oh," said Simon, grimacing. "Yeah, I'm not so sure about that."

"Why not!" Ajsha demanded, sitting up to look him in the face.

"Sweetie, we've been working on it for months now and can't get anywhere with it."

"Well, we would have, if you hadn't used your time with her radio as blackmail."

Simon grinned sheepishly, but then shuddered and sighed. "Please don't bring that up. And, okay, I'll do it. But even if I hear the melody and the voice, how do I learn the words?"

"Milo told me she wrote the lyrics down in the back of her diary," Ajsha said confidentially. "I'll 'borrow' it from her for a minute. You memorize them, and once you listen to the voice you'll be all set."

"Ajsha!" said Simon, appalled. "I'm not going to look in a girl's diary!"

"You won't," she assured him. "The words are on the very last pages."

Simon wasn't too comforted by this logic, but still said, "Well, all right. But I'd still like to do something extra special for her for Christmas."

"Maybe you could," Ajsha murmured thoughtfully. "We would have to plan it carefully, but I know she would love it." She was cut off by a deep yawn.

Smiling, Simon squeezed her tightly and kissed her forehead. "You need to go back to bed."

Ajsha nodded in assent. "So do you."

"I know," he said and stood up, holding her.

As he exited the kitchen and started for her room, she whispered, "Will you sing to me?"

He grinned, kissing her ear. "Of course I will, little cutie."

A few years ago, Simon had discovered a particular suitcase on board Mrs. Lanslo's crashed plane. It apparently had belonged to a scholar of some kind, for it contained many papers with lullabies written on them. Curious, Simon had had someone translate them onto other papers for him. He memorized all the songs, many written by people far away in both time and distance. Soon, with so much influence, he came up with one himself, but the one he sang to Ajsha that night was some other minstrel's work. He sang it softly to her as he walked down the hall.

When the last words of the song left his lips, Ajsha lay asleep in bed, the blanket tucked around her shoulders. Smiling, he bent down and kissed her forehead.

"Good night, little cutie," he whispered.

Quietly, he breezed out of her room and into his, where he saw Milo sleeping soundly, her mouth parted a millimeter, revealing a gleam of white teeth. Navigating around the bed to his side, he had to grin, and blew her a kiss.

As he lay down, Milo shifted uneasily in her sleep, as if she had felt the kiss land on her. We now must leave Simon to Galo. I hope you have enjoyed and learned something from this chapter. Milo didn't get to. She slept through the whole thing.

21
Christmas

AH, CHRISTMAS! IT is one of the most fantastic times of the year, and one of the most incredible holidays ever to be celebrated. It is that one-of-a-kind holiday that makes people organize and meet at the backs of rooms to mutter to each other. Everyone is sneaking around, eavesdropping, and breaching diaries and journals, seeking information. In turn, people also formulate plots to assist other people in finding out what they fancy for gifts. It can be a rather desperate, greedy time of year, but simultaneously people can stop and focus on the original reason for the celebration: Christ's birth.

So, in short, humans can get themselves all caught up in the festivities, but are still able to halt and realize why it is all so.

It is the same thing on tropical islands, especially those whose governing has only changed marginally from that of the 1800s. Individuals become devious and mischievous at around the start of December, though they all try not to show it. Preparations are made early, for fear of no time later. Plans get made, gifts are sought and bought, and a chance comes along to be perfectly pleasant and cheerful to each other for at least one month.

As you probably guessed, not much Christmas cheer can be found on a tropical island; that is, if you are separated from other human beings. But if you are fortunate to be around others, every-one is so happy and merry that you grow that way too.

On the island populated by Galo-speakers, even though there was no snow, or cold nights by fireplaces, or shorter days and longer nights, people were still in the Christmas spirit, simply because it was the season.

Milo discovered that they still made an effort to make the village look festive, even with the absence of the white fluffy stuff. In the windows of all the shops, a type of garland was strung, or at least a substitute for garland. Palm frond wreaths were tacked to all doors, bows and tiny red flowers speckling the green, spiny leaves. A large tree was hauled to the middle of the village square, palm boughs nailed all over it, facing downward, giving it an appearance of a narrow, tropical Christmas tree. All the palm trees in the area had their trunks decorated with strings of petite white seashells, giving them the deceptive appearance of being wound with lights. All the houses had special tall candles burning brightly in every single window, making the town glow merrily at night. Shops were decorated on the inside and were having sales on their merchandise, many offering gift wrap.

The children in school were organizing a choir of carolers, and Ajsha joined as soon as she heard, claiming that she needed to expand her horizons. They could often be heard practicing inside the schoolhouse. The orphanage was arranging special days to take the children out into town, so they could be filled with Christmas joy and contentment.

Creatures were being hunted to be cooked or sold. People were turning shifty and sly. People such as Simon and Ajsha. Ever since the night of that mournful conversation, they had started stealing away during the day to have short meetings. Milo tried not to bother wondering about what they were up to. She also discovered that her radio and diary were periodically disappearing, only to turn up later in the same exact place she had left them. Eventually she took to hiding them in her bottom drawer and secretly checking on them throughout the day.

The boar hunting wasn't going so well. Apparently the boars were more cunning this year and were taking their time infiltrating the jungle by the village. They had only managed to catch a few loners wandering foolishly about. But the whole herd had yet to appear. Until one night.

It was bedtime, so therefore all the residents of the Swallow house were fast asleep, visions of macaroni and cheese dancing in Milo's head. (She *really* missed it.) Little to their knowledge, the last time the front door had been closed it had not been firmly shut. Soon, a strong nighttime breeze blew it wide open. Milo was sleeping peacefully, drooling slightly, when she suddenly heard a hard grunt. She decided it was a part of her dream, though she had never once in her life made pig-like noises while eating. The sound, muffled at first, quickly became so loud that she was forced out of slumber.

Opening her eyes, all she saw was pitch blackness, helped only by the sickle moon sending a weak gleam through the window. She rubbed her eyes to help them adjust, just as the grunt and a soft squeal came. Milo froze and looked towards the door to see a black figure trot into the bathroom. A ball of fluff suddenly streaked under the bed and delivered a soft, whiny growl. Not sure what just happened, Milo shook her head and lay back down. But before she could close her eyes, the trotting blur ambled into the bedroom. It came up to Milo's side, her laying rigid in fright. It snuffled noisily at her before wandering around the room, then back out into the hall. Milo gasped quietly for air, then, fighting the urge to shout, she shook Simon's shoulder. He stirred, reaching out in his sleep and putting an arm around her. Glowering, Milo gave his bicep a slap and he blearily woke up.

"Simon," Milo hissed. "There's some . . . *thing* in the house!"

He didn't understand, so Milo grabbed his wrist and dragged him across the bed, over to her side, where she led him to the doorway. There, she gestured hysterically out into the hallway. Simon, now alert, peered out to see the bulky creature grunt its way down the hall, nearing Ajsha's bedroom.

Without a moment's hesitation, he rushed back into the bedroom, and pulled a machete out from under his bureau. He dashed out into the hall, and, in a squealing plight, started to drive the boar outside. After a terribly loud and dangerous chase all around the house, he managed to get the beast outdoors, where he kept pursuing it.

Milo, who had been sitting with Ajsha ever since she had awoken from the clamor, felt it was now safe to go to the kitchen and light a candle. Through the window came the sounds of whooping and stampeding, as more boys arrived and helped Simon chase the boar into a trap. With much time and preparation, Milo was serving boar meat at suppertime the next day, of which she ate none. As it turned out, the boar that had infiltrated their hut was the first of many to arrive in the village. The butchery was soon crammed with boar meat, on sale for Christmas.

Eventually, Milo learned that the three of them would be having Christmas dinner at the Pitts' house. This gave her a sinking feeling in the vicinity of her pancreas, since the water between her and Simon's parents hadn't boiled down any. They had only visited twice since the Wedding Plans incident. The first time, Milo got into an interpreted shouting match with Mrs. Pitt over Milo slapping away Simon's hand when he tried to touch her, and the second consisting of Milo stubbornly refusing to come out of her room. For some reason, instead of being relieved, this only made the Pitts surly.

Nonetheless, Milo had to admit that dinner at their place would be better than having it at hers. Quite honestly, when she looked over her, or Simon's, house, she couldn't help feel like one of those people who go around declaring, "Bah! Humbug!" The hut wasn't exactly a good reflection of the Christmas season. It wasn't foul or anything, but it had remained the same while all the other houses had been embellished for the holiday.

Determined to fix this, Milo took a walk through town, looking at the houses and searching for inspiration. Shortly after beginning her stroll, she started to feel like she was being followed and kept checking behind her, but couldn't see anyone. She walked all around town, viewing many spectacular decorations and still feeling followed. Finally, when she whipped her head around, she saw Simon start talking to a villager. Milo didn't know what to think, but she was suddenly distracted by an idea to perk up the hut.

Hurrying home, she went to the toolshed and collected a shovel, the trowel that Ajsha caught at the wedding, and a pronged hoe. She lugged these to the front of the house. Every house on the island had spacious plots of earth on both sides of the front door for gardens. Most of the houses had them, primarily those owned by people with enough thought and energy to put in the work. Simon's was not on this list. Milo had just decided that it should be.

Using the hoe, she proceeded by hacking up the soil and combing it into neat rows. Once the dirt was airy and crumbly, she nodded in satisfaction. Then, to be prepared, she pumped water into a bucket and left it by the door.

Shouldering the shovel, she sauntered off into the forest, taking care not to step in any traps. She found two large clusters of alpinia, whose red flowers were in perfect bloom. Carefully, she jabbed a circle around the roots of a sizable clump until she could lift it all up. She toted it back to the house and planted it under the window. Then she watered it thoroughly, went back to get another one, and did the same on the other side. Scoping for jungle flora, she found and transplanted blue jacaranda, vivid pink anthurium, white and purple spotted toad lilies, lemongrass, white and red amaryllis, orange, scarlet, and yellow dahlias, jasmine, and white and pink pampas grass.

Simon came home in the middle of all this activity. His wife was covered almost totally with dirt, and a half-finished garden was spread out in front of his house. He had arrived when she was planting the amaryllis. She finished watering it, stood up, and saw him. Eyeing the vivid flowers with more interest than shock, he walked over to her and gently smacked her ponytail. Dust flew out, making them both sneeze. Milo gestured around at all the relocated plants and arched her eyebrows, but Simon merely smiled at her, which Milo took as approval. Simon went inside to watch her, (mindfully not staring at anything specific) and Milo gathered the rest of the flowers. The transplanting took all day, but at least she got it done. Encrusted in dirt and blisters, she stood back in the diminishing sunlight and surveyed the results of her toil. It was breathtaking, but she wasn't finished.

Recalling Squelch's house, Milo spent the next day hunting for flat stones. Hauling them one by one to the house, sweat pouring off of her in copious amounts, she dug each a hole and fitted them in. After a long, tiring day, she succeeded in creating a winding path to the house. Now, it was a winding path. Indeed, Milo had it swirling all over the ground; whether she did that on purpose or just was too winded to pay attention is unknown.

When she was done, it was nearing sundown and she thought her back was going to snap. She stood at the end of her path and began to follow it to the house. It took her an extra minute, as opposed to if she had gone straight. But it was fun, nonetheless, and once she reached the last stone she wanted to go back and do it again.

Ajsha and Simon also thought it was fun, for they both walked the whole thing whenever approaching the house. The garden became another thing to keep Milo preoccupied. Remember, she was a lover of well-kept gardens and was determined to keep hers maintained. Often this meant shooing or slapping Simon away from picking any flowers, and she could have murdered Bob the Conscience for all his constant, brusque advice.

Ajsha and Simon continued to have private meetings as the December days droned on, and often gave Milo mysterious looks. One time when Milo went to town, she again was certain she was being watched, but again couldn't detect any evidence. Frustrated and just a little perturbed, she went into Soldier's shop. After chatting with him for a bit, she learned that he was going to spend Christmas with Mrs. Lanslo. Giving him a congratulatory thump on the back, she then moved over to the shelves. While examining her beloved object, she kept glancing at the window, trying to spot a spy. She had been feeling eyes on her in the shop since the beginning of December, but never, to her aggravation, actually saw anyone.

She now had another reason for going into town, however. All the islanders were so full of the Christmas spirit that it had started to infect Milo. Lying in bed on night, she had decided to give a gift to each of her friends: Ajsha, Mrs. Lanslo, Soldier, Squelch, and perhaps even Simon. Why she felt like she wanted to get Simon a present, she couldn't understand, and as much as she tried to disregard the impulse, it wouldn't go away. She figured it was probably a mild form of gratitude, for him being so patient with her and giving her a place to stay. Of course, she would have been content to stay anywhere, without involving marriage. But, it was Christmas, so why not be nice?

Precisely how she was going to obtain these presents, she had very little idea. She thought that maybe she could borrow some island money from Mrs. Lanslo, but she didn't know how she would pay her back.

One day, she sat mulling over this problem in Soldier's shop. She had gone in to look at the speaker, but discovered it gone. Then, fighting off sighs of dismay, she sat on the floor in a far corner and brooded over both her conundrums, the second one now being who else on the island needed a speaker. Soldier noticed her intense expression and occasional quiver of her lower lip.

"What's the matter, Milo?" he asked growing slightly giddy, as he always did whenever he spoke his new language.

"Oh. I have a problem," she answered, sounding pained.

"What is it?" Soldier asked gently.

"Christmas."

He chuckled, his entire body shaking. "Mighty nice problem. Been bit by a shark lately? Now *that's* a problem."

He was referring to a horrific incident that had occurred the previous week. One of the fisherboys had had his foot chomped on by a hammerhead and it had caused quite a stir.

Milo's head snapped up. "I want to buy gifts for a few people," she explained, "but I haven't any money. I considered stealing some money from Simon, but that just doesn't seem Christmas spirity. Though, I probably could pull it off."

"Since when does anything justify stealing from your husband?" Soldier said.

Milo shrugged. "I didn't *say* that it did. I just said I probably *could.* I know where he keeps it and he's always out of the house. Besides, I'd make it up to him by getting him something extra nice."

Soldier was surprised.

"You mean that you were planning on giving him something to begin with?" he asked.

"Yeah," Milo sighed despondently. She shook her head. "I've considered making gifts, but I don't have any materials and I'm not exactly an arts and crafts wiz anyway. So, I have to settle for buying stuff. But I *can't,* because I don't have *money,* and I'm too *proud* to ask Simon for any."

Soldier licked the corner of his mouth. "You know," he said, "I could give you some."

Milo, once overcoming her shock, stared at him all squinty-eyed.

"Ya mean loan, don't you?" she said.

Shrugging his burly shoulders, Soldier said, "Ah, once it's gone, it's gone. And as you won't be able to pay me back without pilfering, let's just call it my gift to you. Besides, it's Christmas time! A time to be kind and generous to everyone. You have seemed to have discovered that. I would be honored to help."

Launching out of her corner, Milo bounded up him, exclaiming, "Oh, Soldier! Thank you! How can I ever repay you? Besides with money – which I can't do."

"Just be nice to Simon for the holiday," he chuckled, patting her arm.

"Oh," Milo grimaced. "I don't think I have the will power. But, I shall try."

"Wonderful," Soldier said. He gave her a supply of island money. "If you need more, come back."

Milo shook her head, pocketing the metal. "Don't worry," she assured him. "I'm a very cheap person. I'll salvage."

Soldier cocked his head. "Don't you mean manage?"

Milo blinked in surprise. "What'd I say?"

She spent the rest of the day roving through all the various stores in town. In one, she found a large Beanie Baby, its tag long gone. It was a doggy with golden fur, made out of a type of silk. One of its ears had been charred a bit, but it was still squishy and adorable. Milo got it for Ajsha because she had noticed that she didn't have any stuffed animals, which she considered unhealthy for a child of her age.

In another store, she bought a glass sphere that was filled with water and different colored glass stones. If you turned the sphere upside down, the stones would slowly fall in a multicolored curtain. It was even more fascinating because the water enlarged their appearance. Milo figured if it entranced her so much, Squelch would love it.

In yet another store she found books. They were cheaper because they were in English. Among the many volumes was *The Adventures of Huckleberry Finn*, which she decided to get for Soldier. Since it was full of complicated dialogue, she thought it might help him develop his English skills.

She bought an hourglass for Mrs. Lanslo, simply because she was a cheap person. Also, the sand in it was multicolored and to watch the grains slowly sift together down into the bottom was truly a magical sight.

Now it was time for the true challenge: Finding a gift for Simon. Milo had to be careful. The last thing she wanted was to get him an item that would lend any kind of double meaning. She just wanted to give him a small, neutral present to express her appreciation. After wandering from shop to shop, her feet starting to ache, and looking through countless miscellaneous objects confiscated from planes or constructed from such, she finally found something that would suffice. It was a wide, silvery ring, engraved with an eye. She bought it and stowed it away without taking a more careful look at it. If she had, she would have discovered that a heart and a U followed the eye.

At home, she put the items in different sized bark boxes (her cheapness hadn't allowed her to indulge in the giftwrap), still not bothering to take a closer look at the ring. She tore paper from her notebook of plagiary, not wanting to waste any from her diary. Scrounging up some string, she wrapped the boxes and drew squiggles on the paper with her pen. She stored the parcels in the cellar on a clean shelf, to wait for the time of opening.

She was far from the only one slinking around buying gifts. Ajsha and Simon were now spending long hours away from the house, and entering through a back window when they came back. Ajsha shut herself in her room for long periods of time, and sometimes even refused to come out for meals. Simon often stole his and Milo's bedroom for his time-spending, answering in blithe, firm Galo whenever the door was knocked upon. Milo was consistently finding herself pacing from the kitchen to the sitting room, neither of which had doors.

On washing days, Milo's mind drifted to what it would be like to freeze-dry wet clothes, as the settlers had done during snowstorms. The conversation in the house, which had been barely anything, dwindled down to nothing. The only communication was that of mysterious looks, mischievous grins, and knowing smiles. Milo played right along. It was as though they all had their own special secrets.

And, though there didn't seem to be any practical reason, the girls in town upped their clinginess to Simon. They had almost no peace at all when they went to the market. The girls, decked out in seasonal finery, crowded exuberantly around Simon, eager to give and receive attention. Milo ignored it the best she could, but they were teasing her last nerve whenever they deliberately pushed her away, most of the time away from what she was trying to buy. Simon acted like he enjoyed the attention, but deep inside he wished it was Milo who was clutching at him, all giggly. To him, these girls were no match for her elfish beauty.

As time passed, the very air began to tremble with the excitement. The breezes seemed to be as jumpy and nervous as the beings they swirled around. Every time Milo caught a glimpse of the Pitts' house her heart seemed to go on strike. Ajsha, who was as determined as ever that Milo should develop some kind of ladylike quality (she herself was always in a skirt), had begun to urge her to wear a dress to the dinner. Of course, Milo had resolutely refused. She had, however, agreed to wear her church ensemble. It was purely out of convenience, since Christmas happened to land on a Saturday that year. But she declined to wear her hair down.

The night before the blessed day, Squelch was over to give her present to Milo, since they wouldn't be seeing each other the next day. They sat in the sitting room, regaling each other with past Christmas experiences and arguing over which one should open their present first.

"No, you should," Squelch informed Milo for the fifth time.

"Oh, please! Don't try to pamper me, girl!" Milo shot back good naturedly.

"No!" Squelch said mulishly. "I refuse to! In fact, I'll storm out of this house right now if you don't open yours first!"

"Oh, fine!" Milo cried, throwing up her hands. "Let me see it, Miss Ungracious!"

Happily, Squelch handed her a small package and bounced excitedly beside her on the couch. Milo tore it open with gusto. She produced from it a clay bead necklace with a shell pendent.

"Oh, Squelch!" Milo exclaimed. "It's beautiful!"

"Really?" she said shyly. "I made it myself. I saw how much you like our curtains, so I took the hint."

"Oh, thank you!" Milo said, draping it around her neck and adjusting the clasp. If it hadn't been for the pendent weighing it down, it would have loosely hugged her throat. "I'll wear it every day," she promised. "Now for yours! Here you are!"

Milo presented her with the squiggly box. Gingerly, Squelch undid the string and unfolded the paper. As she lifted the lid she gasped. She carefully lifted out the sphere.

"O," she said, her lips forming a perfect circle, and turned it upside down. Slowly the stones fell through the water. "Oooo," she said, enchanted. She did it again and then again, the joy on her face growing. "Aww," she whispered. "Oh, I love it!"

"You do?" Milo said, squirming gleefully.

"Mmm!" Squelch confirmed. "Oh. Ah. Oh, yeah! Oh, this thing will keep me entertained for hours!"

"Yeah," Milo agreed. "Same with me. I wonder who had the brilliance to create something like this."

"Someone who is very rich right now," Squelch said, not taking her eyes off the sphere.

"I wouldn't be so sure about that," Milo said, reclining casually on the couch cushions. "I've never seen one anywhere but here before. And I've been all over."

"Then this is probably a prototype that never got to where it was going. Shame. Thanks, girl! So, how are you going to spend tomorrow?"

"Most of it at church," Milo replied, already thinking of Christmas hymns. "Then we're going to have dinner and present swapping at Simon's parent's house. My *word*, am I panicking!"

"Oh, you poor thing," Squelch said sympathetically. "I hope you survive. I'm glad I don't have any in-laws yet. Oh, man! What time is it?"

"Ummm," said Milo, checking the dark sky through the window before consulting her watch. "Eight-ish."

"I need to get going," Squelch said apologetically, gathering her things. "Give Simon a smack for me."

Milo chuckled as she walked her to the door. "Before or after I give him his present?" she asked.

Squelch whirled around. "You're giving him something?!" she exclaimed, agog.

Milo waved her hand flippantly. "Yes, but only out of gratitude."

"Gratitude!" Squelch repeated, disbelieving. "For what? Forcing you to marry him? Getting you beaten? Making your life terrible?!"

Milo suddenly felt the urge to hit him instead of offering him a present. But, resisting, she calmly said, "No. For being patient with me and giving me a place to stay. I've been somewhat of a jerk to him, but he's always been kind to me. He's really a good guy. Sure he's done some stuff, but he's good at heart. I hate him for that!"

Squelch grinned, instantly pacified. "I guess you're right," she admitted. "It is Christmas after all! Just as long as it doesn't tell him anything *unwanted*."

"Don't worry," Milo assured her. "Unless an eye in Galo means 'I'll stop being a pain,' we have nothing to worry about."

"All right. Bye, I love my gift. Merry Christmas!"

"I love my gift, too. Merry Christmas!"

They had a medium hug (they were growing progressively) and Squelch departed.

The next morning, there was an excited tension in the oxygen, as if expecting an explosion at any moment. Everyone was twitching with anticipation as they got ready for church. No one in the village was outside as the Swallows walked through. Everyone was indoors, enjoying tearing wrapping paper apart.

In church, Milo found a place in her hymn book that had a selection of songs in the category of "Birth". She showed Ajsha and soon they were devoutly singing Christ-mass songs. They also looked up the story of Christ's birth in the Bible, reading it aloud in both languages. Milo felt truly peaceful inside, as she always did whenever she was in church.

After, they headed home to wait out the rest of the day, and attempt to relax. They were all gathering their holiday offerings and hiding them in the kitchen. Milo spent a lot of time in her bedroom, getting "tricked out". Chaos watched her from the bed, an amused look on her face. Milo fussed with her hair until she couldn't stand it.

"Chaos," she whined, twisting her head from side to side in the mirror. "I know I've already made the decision, but . . . which way should I leave it? Up or down?"

"Asking the cat for advice now?" Bob the Conscience asked dryly. "I remember a time when you would come crying to me."

"What?" Milo said, letting her dull brown hair tumble down. "I never went to you for advice."

"There was a few times," he sniffed. "Now you don't care what I think about how you look."

"That's right," she said, flexing her spindly arms and frowning at her reflection. Was she getting muscles?

"Oh, really?" spat Bob the Conscience. "I saw it, you know. The present you got for Chaos. Did you get me a present for Christmas?"

"Yeah," Milo snapped. "How would you like two gulps of arsenic?"

"Hey, hey!" Bob the Conscience said sternly. "Calm it! If I go down, you go down."

"Likewise," said Milo menacingly.

"Hey, come on!" he said, his tune changing instantaneously. "You know I was kidding. Why are you so tense? You're like stretched elastic."

"Sorry," she apologized, her angular shoulders sagging. "I'm just on edge because of this dinner."

"Why?"

"Do you really match my intelligence? Do you truly not remember the first time they and I met? And every single time we've seen each other afterwards? They – don't – like – me."

"Oh, I'm sure they've gotten over all that."

"Don't be too sure. And, they're furious with me because their son isn't showing up for church on Sunday mornings. That's got to breed some hostility, and since they are refused my help for the cooking, I have no idea what they're putting in my food."

She fussed with her hair some more, muttering darkly under her breath, until she decided just to leave it up. Taking something out of a drawer, she went over to Chaos.

"Now don't think I've forgotten about you, my pretty kitty," Milo crooned, stretching out next to her on the bed. She showed Chaos a cat-sized collar made from leather and sequins. In an empty space, Milo had etched in the word "Chaos" with a broken shard of glass. The cat purred her thanks while Milo adjusted it around her neck.

Later that evening, laden with parcels, they started out for the Pitts' house. On the way, they stopped at several places in town to give people gifts. Simon knew nearly everybody, so his gift-giving took nigh unto forever, but eventually Milo found herself at Soldier's.

"Why, Milo," he said, accepting the flat package. "You didn't have to –"

"Of course I did," she interrupted jovially. "'Tis the season and crap."

Soldier chuckled. "Too true. Say! Would you look at this? A book."

"Not just a book," Milo corrected. "A *classic*. And I think you will find it engrossing and confusing. But, with practice I think you should be able to distinguish the English."

"Well, thank you very much!" Soldier said, flipping through the pages. "I'd give you your present but Ruby has it. If you want it, you'll need to see her."

"You got me something? How touching. . . . Well, I really need to go now. Merry Christmas. Enjoy your book."

"I will. Merry Christmas," he said, glancing out the door at Simon.

Together, they all went over to see Mrs. Lanslo. She had gifts for all of them, but they would wait to open them with the rest of their presents. However, they did let her open the presents they gave her.

"Why, Ajsha! Thank you, dear! How pretty."

"You're welcome. I made it in school."

She gibbered thanks to Simon after she opened his. They were about to leave when Milo pulled out her parcel with a flourish. They all stared, stunned, at her.

"Milo, dear," Mrs. Lanslo managed to splutter. "You . . . also brought me something?"

"Um, yeah," Milo said, uncomfortable. This wasn't exactly the reaction she had been envisioning. "Of – of course I did. Why wouldn't I?"

"I – I don't know, dear," she murmured, lightly taking the package from her. "I know I haven't been very supportive of your rebellion, or even your feelings. I didn't think you would want to give me anything."

Milo shrugged and jerked her head indifferently. "Maybe you haven't, but who cares? Well, I know I care, but I can't hold a grudge against you for being a law-abiding citizen. Besides, you have been a friend when other people wouldn't want to."

"Thank you," she said, unwrapping the box. She lifted out the hourglass and gasped as she turned it upside down.

"I've never – " she whispered. Simon and Ajsha gawped at it, enchanted.

Milo grinned. "Like it?" she teased.

Mrs. Lanslo looked at her, her eyes shining. "It's beautiful, dear. Thank you."

Feeling like she ought to respond, Milo merrily punched her arm.

"No problem," she choked and made a beeline for the door.

She waited outside in the humid night air until Simon and Ajsha emerged. Beaming at her, Simon attempted to loop his arm through hers, but she snatched it away. Stymied, he led them onward towards the Pitt residence, which rested on the far side of town. As they walked, a lazy wind rustling the various ornaments on trees and dwellings, Ajsha couldn't help but ask, "Why did you punch her?"

"What else was I suppose to do?" Milo replied petulantly.

"Oh my, I don't know. Maybe, hug her?"

Milo began to cackle. "Good one!"

At last they reached their destination, which again made Milo realize she was truly living in a shack, and Simon and Ajsha were greeted warmly by Luna and Lennon Pitt. Milo merely exchanged a look of distaste with them. As they were ushered into the foyer, Milo looked around, understanding just how low class Simon's house was. This place was a palace compared to it.

The floor was made from cut boards, gleaming sleekly in the light of candles lined up on the wall in sconces; two calvens sat adjacent to the wall in the kitchen, food simmering on top of them. The foyer had a coat closet and a hat rack, and rugs that resembled the carpeting in airplanes lay in each room. A clock that had stopped working a long time ago hung on the wall in the living room. There was also an enormous stone fireplace in the living room, lit oil lamps lined up along the mantle. The couches and chairs were plusher than Simon's and designs had been whittled into the legs and arms. An artist had drawn pictures of the family and they were hanging in the hallway. A younger version of Simon, with much shorter hair, was grinning sweetly down at Milo as she wandered through the hall.

At the end of the hallway was the bathroom, which had a polished granite bathtub and wooden racks full of towels. All the curtains in the house had been embroidered with designs, and all the windows had shutters that could be shut when it rained. Peeking into the parent's bedroom, Milo saw a large cannonball bed that was adorned with a quilt. There was also a wardrobe and a huge, ancient looking sea chest next to the bed. Two large mirrors hung on the wall and a potted plant stood on a pedestal.

A loud cough from behind her made Milo nearly jump out of her skin. She whirled around, ready to whack whoever did it. It was Simon. He gave her an accusing look, then smiled and motioned for her to follow him. Perhaps it was because he had caught her snooping, but she trailed after him. He led her around a bend in the hall and stopped at a door. Opening it, he revealed a room containing a single bare bed and small chest. On the bed lay a stuffed toy wolf, looking battered and overly handled. Milo stepped in, looking around. There were no candles in this room, so the only light was what seeped from the hall. Simon followed her and sat on the bed. She looked about, though there wasn't much there to see. It seemed that it had been stripped for parts a while ago.

Milo turned to Simon. "This is your room, isn't it?"

He gazed at her for a moment before smiling faintly. Looking down at the wolf, he petted its head. Milo walked over to the windowsill. Yes, these people had sills. On it were three flat stones with large googly-eyed faces drawn on their grey surfaces. It looked like the work of a four year old. Milo picked one up as Simon looked over at her. She turned to him and pointed at the face. Forcing back a smile, he suppressed a snort of laughter and looked back down. Milo replaced the rock, staring at the crazy pupils and floppy tongue for a second. She bit her lip.

Moving over to the bed, she noticed a picture that might have been a bug unprofessionally carved into the headboard. She sat down and stared at the wolf, then at Simon.

He shrugged and patted the animal's cranium. "Daniel," he said.

"Daniel?" Milo repeated, not sure if it was the wolf's name, or the word for wolf in Galo. She tested. Pointing to herself, she said, "Milo" then pointed to the wolf and said, "Daniel?"

Simon smiled and nodded. Satisfied, she stroked its fur.

"Daniel," she repeated thoughtfully. "What a nice name. Very traditional. The traditional wolf. Do you know what the wolf does, Simon? It goes aaroooooooooooooooo!!!!!"

Shamelessly, unconvincingly, she howled. Simon chuckled, confused. Flushing, Milo turned away, feeling foolish. Sensing that she could do no more good here, she decided to head for the door, first saying goodbye to Daniel the Wolf. As she walked out, she glanced out of the corner of her eye. She saw Simon pick up the wolf and hug it tightly before repositioning it on the mattress. Milo moseyed back down the hall and into the kitchen, where she found Ajsha peering into the grated doors of the calvens.

"Hello," she said. "Where have you been?"

"Around," Milo answered cryptically, scanning a boiling pot. "Hey, girl, did you know that Simon has a toy wolf named Daniel?"

Ajsha's brown eyes widened with surprise. "No," she said.

"Really?" Milo said, stunned. Simon had shown her something he had not even told Ajsha about? "Well, he does."

"He never told me," Ajsha said, her tone a combination of indignation and wonder.

"No?" was all Milo could say. Quickly she changed the subject. "Would you get a load of this house? I wonder what these people do for a living. Run a mob?"

"No, Father's father owns the fishing industry," Ajsha said as casually as if running a mob were mundane employment.

"What?" Milo breathed. "All of it?"

"Yep. The warehouse, the store, the fisherboys and fishermen . . . all of it."

"You mean . . . Simon's dad is his boss?"

"Yes," Ajsha confirmed.

"Oh . . . man!" Milo said in despair. "No wonder they're so mad at me. Wait. They've got to be mad at Simon, too."

"For what? What are you talking about?"

"Saturdays. Church."

Ajsha shrugged. "A little bit. Well, more than a little. Father has always gotten along very well with his parents. But, he likes going to church with you. He's trying to make them understand. You know, his father offered him a higher salary when he came to work for him. Father turned him down, though. He didn't want grandfather to treat him special just because he was his son. He wanted to be treated the same as the other boys."

Milo thought for a moment. "Is it a family business?" she finally inquired.

"Yes, it is."

"Then," Milo whispered, checking over her shoulder, "Simon's going to inherit it?"

"Eventually," Ajsha confirmed slowly, leaning sideways to see what she was looking for.

Milo almost swayed as her thoughts flew. "Then," she said with a type of finality, "he's eligible to gold diggers." Seeing Ajsha's face, she hastily explained. "Girls who pretend to like him for his money."

"That's awful," Ajsha said. "But I guess there are girls out there who would do that."

Milo nodded mutely, images of flirting, hopping girls cycling through her mind. "It's hard on boys who have that option. They can't tell who's real and who isn't. Maybe –" She paused, carefully formulating her thought. "Maybe," she went on, "that's partly why he didn't wait."

"Wait?" Ajsha repeated, puzzled.

"For an interpreter," Milo clarified. "He didn't want me to find out. He wanted to keep things on the down low. He wanted me to get to know him from scratch, unlike all the other girls, who have probably known him all his life. He never – *never* once mentioned any of this."

"I never thought of that," Ajsha said pensively. "He didn't exactly say *why* he didn't wait. All he said was that he couldn't."

"That's all he said?"

"Yes, that's all."

Before Milo could pursue the matter any further, Simon, Luna, and Lennon joined them. It seemed that Simon had had a little chat with his parents concerning manners, for they each gave her a false, strained smile, which she returned. Luna clapped her hands together and motioned for them all into another room. It was a dining room. Yes, a *dining room*. A room set aside strictly for dining. It had a long wooden table in the center, chairs spaced evenly along each side and one at both ends, and another unlit hearth on the back wall. The table was set with fine, non-cracked china, and a tiny jungle shrub decorated with fruit and tassels sat in the middle.

They were guided to chairs. In another effort for hominess, nobody took the ones at the ends; Simon, Milo, and Ajsha on one side, dragging their chairs closer together, and Luna and Lennon on the other. Luna started bringing in plates heaped with steaming, aromatic food. It all looked and smelled good, but it still didn't compare with Milo's plagiaristic food, so I won't betray her by describing it in all the yummy ways I usually do. In fact, I will only describe one thing. The boar. Boar! It was sliced into round medallions on one platter, smothered in oyster gravy.

Milo flinched when she saw it. As Luna proceeded to dole out the bounty, she put a piece of the boar, slathered in gravy, on Milo's plate along with everything else. Milo stared in dismay at the boar, nestled in the dead center of the plate, framed by all the other food. Ajsha was asked to say the blessing, or more like volunteered for Milo's sake, and when it was said in both languages, the devouring commenced.

Simon immediately got pulled into a profound and lengthy conversation with his parents, which Milo was glad of, since she wanted all eyes off her. Spreading her cloth napkin out on her lap, she began to cut the boar into small pieces. Nibbling inconspicuously on the rest of her food, she smoothly removed a boar fragment onto her lap. She tried to do this as unnoticeably as possible; in light of the day, she didn't want Mrs. Pitt to get offended, and she just wasn't prepared to explain that, for her, pig meat is forbidden meat. When eyes did swivel in her direction, the only food on her plate she hadn't finished was the stewed oranges. Don't ask.

Misfortune beheld her when her plate was refilled. Grumbling inwardly that Luna might have taken requests instead of assuming that they wanted a bit of everything, Milo again spirited away her boar helping. Thankfully, they weren't served for a third time.

At long (especially for Milo) last they were finished, Milo's lap as full as her stomach. Arising with the graceful air of a successful hostess, Luna started to clear the table, Simon jumping up to help her. Milo, first removing the boar bundle from her lap, also tried to lend a hand, but Lennon waved her down, gibbering.

"He said that you don't have to help," interpreted Ajsha, "and to go relax in the living room."

"Usually the mother-in-law wants a little help," Milo mumbled sulkily.

The two girls arose, Milo taking her bulging napkin with her, and went to the living room. The wood in the fireplace had been lit, contributing a vast amount of light, though its heat certainly wasn't needed. Tossing her napkin out a window, Milo gathered the two remaining presents she was going to give away. She settled herself in an overly stuffed chair that was *not* a conglomeration of mismatched spare fabric, but one solid pattern, and patiently waited for the others. Ajsha was sitting on a couch, her few gifts piled beside her. Soon the Pitts, one of them a Swallow, filed in.

Simon collected his parcels, and Luna and Lennon disappeared into another room to get theirs. When they returned, Lennon put another log on the flames and the presenting of the presents took place. First, Ajsha went to Luna, and Lennon went to Simon. They gave their present, watched the package get ripped open, and received gracious and thorough thanks. Then it was the receiver's turn to give.

While Simon and his mother were exchanging, Ajsha trotted up to Milo, package in hand.

"Here," she said, smiling. "Merry Christmas!"

"Oh," Milo said, mildly stunned. "Sweetie, you didn't need to get me anything."

"Of course I did," Ajsha said excitedly. "You're my mother. Open it!"

Restraining herself from correcting her, Milo unwrapped the present. A flowing caftan and scarf spilled onto her lap. The caftan was blue with a tropical fish design, the scarf matching, and with them was a pair of white capri pants.

"Do you like it?" Ajsha blurted out, not able to keep quiet any longer. "It was from your plane. I nabbed it before Hattie Knocker could."

382 The Island of Lote

"Ajsha," Milo said, hushed, "it's beautiful. I'm impressed how much you want me out of my regular jeans. But, I'll wear this. I like stuff like this. Thank you."

"You're welcome. The scarf can also work as a belt. I'll show you when we get home."

"Thanks. You're the sweetest. *And* . . . here's your present."

Ajsha stared at the squat, square package she was offering her. "You – you got me a present?"

"Of course, silly," Milo replied, suppressing her exasperation. Why was everyone so flabbergasted that she could be generous? "You've been so kind and helpful and all. Here . . . . Don't keep me in suspense, child! Open it! Open it!"

Recovering from her astonishment, Ajsha rapidly began do so. She got the paper off and extricated the stuffed pup from the box. After closely examining it, she asked, "What is it?"

"It's a Beanie Baby," Milo said, realizing she probably didn't know what that was. "A puppy. Don't you think he's cute?"

Ajsha considered this inquiry for a moment and nodded. "What do I do with it?"

Milo rolled her eyes. "Butcher and grill it. Dang, girl! You . . . I don't know . . . you . . . you cuddle with it, I guess. It's like a friend. It's really soft, great for hugging. 'What do I do with it?' Child! You really need to get in touch with *your* inner child."

Smiling, Ajsha touched the pup's golden head to her cheek. "I love it," she whispered. "I've never had a teddy bear before."

Milo didn't argue, reckoning that she had been given an encyclopedia to sleep with at night. Eventually, while everyone else was preoccupied, Simon ambled up to Milo and perched on an arm of her chair. He handed her a flat, square box. Eyeing him cautiously, she opened it. Inside was a sterling silver bracelet, with dangling silver charms. There was a triangular, holey cheese being sought after by a mouse, which was being chased by a cat. There was three of each, going all around the bracelet. Milo determinedly forced herself not to grin and it showed. Delicately, in awe, she put it on her wrist.

"Thank you," she breathed, focusing on the glinting bracelet and not him.

Remembering his present, she withdrew it and handed it to him. His eyes nearly jumped out. He stared at the parcel, then at Milo, his mouth hanging open. She gave him a dignified, yet impatient, look, and slowly he began to tear off the wrapping. Opening the little box, he lifted out the ring. He was positively delighted with it and, in a flash, hugged Milo's arm. He was still getting wiser.

She was about to give him a routine shove, when she noticed the heart and the U on the ring. Mentally adding the eye, she gasped. Simon sat up and slid the ring onto his ring finger, not noticing the heart and the U, though Milo knew he would later.

"*Oh, well,*" she thought, too tired to care. "*He can't understand it, anyways.*"

Simon moved off to show Ajsha and his parents. When they beamed at it and looked over at Milo, she gave them a shrewd smirk. Ajsha and Milo then showed each other the gifts they had received.

Several minutes later, when Ajsha and her grandparents were babbling happily together about this and that, Simon came back over with another present. Milo scratched her head, because it was itchy, not out of confusion, and accepted it. It was box shaped. She tore the wrapping to reveal, much to her great pleasure, delight, and shock, the speaker from Soldier's shop.

She gasped several times for air before gingerly picking it up. Lifting it high, she turned it over and over in front of her face, and brushed her fingertips all over it to make certain it was real. Face glowing with a radiant smile, she started to choke up.

"Aw, ho," she whispered. "Thank you. Thankyousomuch!!"

She faced Simon and was suddenly speechless. He seemed overjoyed at her reaction. Their eyes met and, for some odd reason she couldn't explain at that moment, Milo had to look away. Instead, she inspected the speaker, near tears. She didn't know how to express her overwhelming thankfulness, except one way. Since it was an epic moment, she consented, slowly leaning forward and hugging Simon. Ever so gently, he embraced her back, for as long as she would permit. It was a quick, blink-and-you-miss-it hug, and she let go with embarrassment.

As she held the speaker in her lap, she lovingly stroked its plastic sides. For a moment she looked back at Simon, and he smiled at her. Milo couldn't bear it, and looked away. When it came time to leave, Milo proudly showed Ajsha the speaker.

"How did he know?" she asked her. "Did you tell him?"

Ajsha shook her head. "Nope," she answered with acute honesty.

Goodbyes and thank yous were thoroughly distributed, and the Swallows left. But the night's surprises weren't over yet. When they were safely back at home, Milo lay on her bed, changed and spending quality time with her new speaker. She heard Simon coming back from Ajsha's room. He stood before her, shivering slightly. They stared at each other, until Milo expectantly said, "Yes?"

Simon gulped and in a raspy, unsure voice said, "I – I lll-. . . I lov-love you."

Milo was thunderstruck. She sat paralyzed, her mouth agape, her sockets bug-eyed. Simon fidgeted nervously in front of her, until she managed to cough out, "Did – di- (ahem). Did you say something?"

Inhaling deeply, Simon repeated, more steadily, "I love you."

Milo began to hyperventilate. Not wanting to go into shock, she took hoarse, calming breaths and said, "You, can speak, English?!"

Pausing for a minute, Simon concentrated hard.

"Little," he said, with a distinct accent. "Now."

Milo gaped at him.

"More later," he assured her.

When she still looked like she might pass out, he said, "Ajsha."

"Ohhh!" she said, her palm striking her heart. "Right, right, right, right! I thought I was hallucinating! So! That's what you two have been sneaking off for. Wanted to surprise me, did ya? Well, ha! Mission accomplished!"

Simon, whose newly conquered English was recent and marginal, didn't bother trying to decipher this, and got onto his side of the bed. He gazed sincerely into Milo's eyes.

"Milo," he said. "I love you."

Shifting uncomfortably, Milo could feel her face burning. He had learned another language just to tell her that. She sighed. She couldn't run from it now. With curiosity, she studied him.

"Well," she murmured, "maybe you do. Dang, boy, that's sad."

Poor Simon was perplexed and said, "No sad. Happy. Happy I love you."

Milo snorted with laughter, which wasn't tactful, but he sounded so funny that she couldn't help it. "Really? I'm not. Good night."

She rolled over, placed the speaker tenderly on the floor, and tried to fall asleep. Simon snuffed the candle and did the same. Despite her reaction, Simon saying that to Milo was the best Christmas present she had ever received. She just wouldn't admit it yet.

22
Love is Friendship Set to Music

THE WEEK PASSED. New Years came and went unnoticed by everyone but Milo. On New Year's night she had gone into a deep depression of despair, refusing to be cheered until the next day. She was upset because it marked just how long she had been on the island. Instead of clinking together glasses of sparkling cider, she was drinking liquid out of half a coconut. But, she got over it quickly and life carried on.

Simon hadn't given up on his English and now openly practiced with Ajsha in front of Milo. They used a technique where Ajsha would say a word in English and then repeat it in Galo. Simon took mountains of notes, many of which Ajsha was having him copy into English. Milo could tell how difficult it was for him by the way he struggled. But, she knew no matter how hard it was for him, it would be even harder for her to learn Galo. He kept at it, endlessly articulating simple, silly sentences concerning fish swimming over, under and around things, and gradually got better.

Milo, thrilled with her speaker, wasted no time inserting it into her radio. The first time she used it she sat in a corner of the sitting room and placed both the radio and speaker on the stone coffee table. She turned on the radio and music flowed out of the speaker like a stereo, filling the whole house with a funky beat. Everyone was able to hear it now, which Simon welcomed.

Milo began to write lyrics down in her diary again, now that she could hear them more clearly. She had recently grown a particular fondness for was a song called "My Boo", which blatantly fell under the label of "romantic". She practically became glued to her radio, waiting for that song to be played so she could be sure of its lyrics. But, it was clearly sung and wasn't too much of a hassle to write down. Before long, Milo could be heard belting it out on wash days.

The speaker also made it easier for Milo to dance to the music, reducing the hazard of sending the little radio flying. Squelch was equally delighted with the services the speaker provided. They often could be found parading throughout the house, the music blasting so hard that, had there been windowpanes, they would have rattled. They tried to get Ajsha interested in the dancing, partially to stop her amused staring. Ajsha, of course, had been raised in a dance-free environment, and therefore tried to set a ladylike example while the two older girls frolicked about her.

Finally, one day she couldn't take it anymore and joined in. It was during a delightful, up-beat song known as "Rich Girl". They, the girls, took advantage of every inch of space in the sitting room, leaping from couch, to table, to the other couch. Jumping to the floor and dancing in circles around the stone chunk. When the end of the song drew near, they all balanced atop the table, using the little space available, which really only allowed for a lot of expressive wiggling.

As misfortune would have it, Simon came home that day with an elderly couple from a few houses over, whom, being both illustrious chefs, wanted to discuss cooking with Milo. Well, you can imagine their surprise and disapproving thoughts when they entered to see three young females dancing wildly on top of a table. Ajsha was the first to notice their wrinkled, frowning expressions. She immediately ceased her spirited squirming and nudged both Milo and

Squelch. Once they too saw the couple and Simon's tightly shut eyes, they froze in bewilderment. Regaining her pride, Milo hastily jumped down the table and shut off the radio. Slowly, Squelch and Ajsha also stepped down, Ajsha swiftly turning a plum color.

The couple thrust their chins in the air, walking past Simon into the kitchen. Milo, who had known that they were coming, but forgot, began to follow them. She was blocked by Simon. He was in a minor state of distress.

"What you doin'?" he asked her.

"You mean, 'What are you doing,'" she corrected automatically, "and I was having fun. It is one of my last joys in life, don't taint it."

Squelch joined her, staring coldly at Simon. "So, he talks now?" she said.

"Yes," Simon said before Milo could reply. "Now."

"Whoa!" Squelch said, backing up, hands in front of her like a shield. "That's scary!"

"Scary?" Simon mumbled, looking to Ajsha for a translation.

"Wrilsta," Ajsha told him.

"Wrilsta!" Simon repeated, looking hurt. Slouching somewhat, he grimly went outside. Milo turned on Squelch.

"You shouldn't have said that," she said sternly.

"Why not?" Squelch inquired innocently. "It's true."

"I know it's true, but it still wasn't very nice."

"What's up with you?" Squelch demanded, putting her hands on her hips.

"Nothing," Milo insisted. "But, Simon's trying very hard to learn English, and for me, so let's not bring him down."

"Why not?" Squelch asked obstinately. "Why does who he's learning it for make a difference?"

"I don't know why. And it doesn't! But . . . can we just cut down on the truth until he understands the language a little better. Okay? It's only fair."

"All right," Squelch relented. "He's your husband."

Scoffing, Milo shook her head. The stubborn girl.

Later that day, once all the company had departed, some in better moods than others, Milo was gardening outside and suddenly heard a soft, musical noise coming from the house. Dropping her trowel, she went inside to find Simon in the sitting room, listening to her radio. Quickly, he saw her and turned it off. Milo found it surprising that she wasn't as furious as she thought she'd be.

"Hey!" she still snapped. "What are you doing?"

Caught in the act, Simon tried to think of an explanation, but couldn't. So he said, "Sorry."

Milo's eyebrows went up. "Why?" she said. "What'd you do?"

Simon edged away as she went to inspect the radio. He concentrated.

"It not broken," he assured her in hesitant, disjointed English. "I not hurt it."

Milo gave him a piercing look, which he stepped back from. "Well," she droned. "All right. But don't let me catch you at it again. Got it?"

After processing what she said, he grinned in relief and nodded. Milo jabbed a nod at him, then took the radio and speaker into their bedroom, stashing it in a secluded corner of a drawer. A couple of days later, Milo went for a stroll around town. It was becoming a habit for her, having finally become bored with the interior of the bungalow. A large crowd of people had congregated in front of Soldier's shop, and were surrounding something. Intrigued, Milo wandered over to investigate. Everyone was crowded around a pyramid of four dozen large cans of paint, each one a different color.

"Where . .?" Milo muttered to herself. She spotted Soldier standing nearby, looking harassed.

The villagers were all arguing with each other and shouting at Soldier. He was trying to calm them down, and evidently failing. After a few more rowdy minutes, he gave up and boomed a firm dismissal. As the people begrudgingly moved away, Milo carefully stepped over to Soldier.

"Where'd all this come from?" she asked, gesturing to the mass of banged-up, tarnished cans.

"Your plane," he answered heavily. "They're still probing it down at the crash site."

"They found these in it?" Milo said skeptically.

"Hidden in the overheads," Soldier said, shaking his own. "Folks will smuggle anything nowadays. There were more, but most of them burned in the fire. Everyone's wondering what I'm going to do with these."

"What do you mean?"

"Well, I can't sell all of them. There are far too many. If I could only get rid of a dozen of them, I might find a use for the rest. I mean, what am I going to do with forty-eight cans of – of – of –"

"Paint," Milo offered.

"Yes! That stuff."

"I don't know. What would you do with thirty-six?"

"Sell them, of course!" he said doggedly. "I can only just manage to find enough people who would want these paint things. Somehow, I'd be able to sell thirty-six, but *forty-eight?* Honestly!"

Milo couldn't really see the problem, having very little experience with inventory, but still wanted to help.

"If you like," she began, "I could take twelve cans. I don't have any money, you know, but –"

"Oh, Milo!" Soldier cut in joyfully. "Would you? That would be simply wonderful! Never mind about money. I just want to get rid of them! Now, go ahead and pick out which ones you want."

Closing her mouth, Milo slowly twisted around to the cans. She had no clue what she was going to do with them, either. As she surveyed her options, she mulled silently until an appealing idea sprang from nowhere. Motivated, she chose a can of red, green, blue, white, black, a can of cream (color), a can of mahogany, aqua, mint, violet, sunshine yellow, and a can of gold.

Once she picked these colors, Soldier went behind his shop and came back with what functioned as a wooden wheelbarrow but was the size of a buggy. Strategically stacking the cans in it, he then escorted Milo home. There, all the cans were unloaded beside the hut, they thanked each other, and Soldier left. However, before Milo could do anything with the paint, she had to make lunch for her approaching housemates. During the meal (seared tilapia with tangy coleslaw) both Ajsha and Simon asked about the paint, but all Milo revealed was that she got it from Soldier. She didn't answer any more until after the last dish was dried and back in its rightful spot.

"What are you paint?" Simon asked her, leaning against the counter.

"'What am I going to paint'?" Milo corrected him. He nodded. She sighed nervously. "Don't get upset or anything, but I thought I would paint the house."

"All of it?" Ajsha gasped.

"No, just the outside," she assured her. "And maybe the kitchen chairs and table? Do you mind, Simon? This is your house."

He looked her over, his expression unfathomable, and said, "You can. I no – don-don't mind."

Milo grinned, despite herself. Later that day, once she had changed into her dingy washing clothes, she stood by the cans, holding the enormous paintbrush that Ajsha had caught at the wedding, and a wet rag and a bucket of water. She was waiting for Ajsha. When Ajsha did come out, Milo was disappointed to see that she wasn't in work clothes at all. She was wearing her best skirt, T-shirt, and little sandals and had her book bag. She looked very grave and important.

"Hillo," Milo greeted shrilly. "Are you going somewhere?"

Ajsha nodded seriously, readjusting the strap on her shoulder.

"Oh," Milo said. "I thought you were going to help me."

"I'd like to," she said, walking up to her. "But today we are having our monthly meeting."

"We?" Milo mumbled, mystified. "Who?"

"The interpreters," Ajsha clarified.

"The interpreters?" Milo repeated, somewhat dubious. "You guys have meetings?"

"Of course. We have one every month. It helps us keep track of things, make plans, and share news."

"News?" Milo said suspiciously.

"Oh, yes. About the people we help. Everyone is very interested in you."

"Huh? Really?" Milo asked, now uneasy. "Great. Now even kids are gossiping about me."

"There are adult interpreters, you know."

"Oh. Well, that doesn't make it any better," she muttered. "I guess you'd better go. Hey, the ladder is there, right?"

"Yes," Ajsha confirmed distractedly, motioning towards the back of the hut. "Right over there."

"And you're sure I can climb it without it breaking?" she pressed.

"Yes, Mother –"

"Milo!"

"Of course," Ajsha said kindly, with a patient smile. "If Father can climb up it safely, then so can you. I dare say, you must weigh less than me."

"Don't be disrespectful," Milo admonished.

"Whoa, ho, ho!" Bob the Conscience said. "Where did that come from?"

"I don't know," she told him, her pulse skipping a beat.

Ajsha reddened. "Yes, you are right, I'm sorry, Mother."

"Milo!"

"Who else?" Ajsha murmured before going off. "Goodbye. I'll see you later."

"Bye," Milo said, waving, then turned to her project.

After a brief analysis, she decided to start with the door. She tried to lower the immense brush into the can of white paint, but it wouldn't fit. Rather irked, she rummaged through the tool shed until she discovered a basin that looked like it was pounded from tin, and poured the paint into it. Sloshing the tip of the brush in the white puddle, she then started to paint the front door.

The brush, being so big, covered a lot of area in a short time. After finishing the door, Milo opened it half way, washed the brush, and painted the door handle gold. Once again washing the brush, she chose the sunshiny yellow to go around the door, around the kitchen windows, and the wall on the other side of the door, where the sitting room was. She had to use the wooden ladder to reach most of it, leaning perilously to the side to paint the framework. Simon emerged from the jungle just as she completed the last swipe of yellow. He looked at the bright paint, eyes glowing, but said nothing and disappeared inside.

At first, Milo felt a little offended. He did know English now, he could say *something*. Then she shrugged, choosing the green to frame the sitting room windows and cover the other wall, where the yellow-framed kitchen windows were. The two colors would meet in a distinct line above the doorway. That would cover the front of the house. It took her a long time and her back was aching when she finished, her body an array of green, yellow, and white splotches. The sun was just starting to set. Not able to wait, she dipped a corner of the brush into the black paint and wrote in small, readable letters next to the door:

Knock as much as you wish,

but if no one answers,

don't bother to come in.

She figured it was a good security system for a place that ran on manners rather than locks. Satisfied with it, she then climbed up the ladder and wrote in large letters above the door:

Houses are built of brick and stone,
but homes are made of love alone.

It was a saying Milo had often heard her mother recite whenever Milo would complain about a new house. She had stepped back to admire it, when suddenly she heard a sound from inside the house. Frowning, Milo gave the brush a hasty wash and set it by the basin. Slowly, she edged through the doorway, being careful not to smudge the paint. She heard the noise again; it was singing. Furthermore, she could understand it. And it wasn't just any old song, either. It was "Hush". And it sounded exactly like the artist who performed it, only there was no music accompanying it so it couldn't be the radio.

"Hello?" Milo hollered as it got louder. "Is L.L. Cool J in the house?"

She couldn't help but be hopeful as she asked.

Though it sounded just like him, L.L. Cool J wasn't the one was singing the song. Simon emerged from their bedroom and started walking towards Milo. His mouth was moving and Mr. Cool J.'s voice was issuing from it, too perfectly synchronize to be dubbed, and with no hint of a lilt. Milo almost fainted. She gaped at Simon as he rapped, unsurely, haltingly, all the lyrics to "Hush". He looked positively clueless as to what he was saying, but he didn't try to understand. It was enough to see that Milo obviously did.

It sounded so perfect, that for a long moment Milo couldn't believe it.

"He must have swallowed my radio!" she thought, horrified.

Simon stopped when he saw the baffled expression plastered on her face. Inhaling deeply, he restarted the song from the beginning. Milo exhaled in a puff and was soon smiling. It *was* her favorite song, and, to be honest, a cute boy rapping it greatly enhanced it. Somehow Simon had managed to memorize every single lyric and duplicate the voice exactly. Seeing her smiling and involuntarily bopping, he grinned too, his voice growing stronger. Coming nearer, he stood in front of Milo and sang it close enough for her to smell his milky breath.

Milo, who felt like she was dreaming, was enchanted. By using the magic that is music, Simon had found a way to knock down Milo's barrier to her heart. It was now open and vulnerable, but Milo didn't care; she barely even noticed. When the song ended, Milo clapped enthusiastically. Simon grinned; Milo already was.

"You like?" he inquired timidly in his regular voice.

Milo struggled to reignite her vocal chords. "Oh! . . . Yes! Very! How? . . . How on Earth did –?"

"Hello? Mother!" Ajsha entering through the door at that second, looking strangely refreshed.

Milo whisked around. "You're home!" she exclaimed, almost accusingly.

Ajsha jumped, startled. "Yes," she said innocently, taking off her book bag.

Milo turned back to Simon. "You won't believe what just happened," she told her, keeping her eyes on him. "Simon just sang, er, rapped 'Hush'."

Ajsha gazed up at Simon. "Oh?" she said.

"Yes," Milo breathed, amazed, Simon abruptly becoming a thing of fascination. "And he sounded exactly, *exactly* like L.L. Cool J.! How on Earth can he do that?"

"How on Earth can he do that?" Simon repeated, his voice sounding precisely like Milo's.

She went inhumanly pale.

Ajsha grinned. "Oh, didn't I tell you? Father's a mimic. He can imitate people's voices and sound one hundred percent like them. We thought it would be a nice surprise if he sang some of your favorite songs for you. You'll have to forgive the way we did it."

But Milo didn't care how they did it. She was still gazing intently at Simon's face, which, bizarrely, seemed new to her. When he smiled at her, she felt blush blooming on her cheeks. Quickly, she

Love is Friendship Set to Music 397

snapped out of it and looked away, then hurried outside, muttering
about putting the paint away for the night.

After a dinner spent lost in blank thought, Milo was sitting on
her bed, pajama clad, as Simon tucked Ajsha in. Feeling more hot
than usual, which was odd, since the temperature hadn't changed,
Milo arose and went to the window, hoping to catch a breeze. She
heard Simon's footsteps, but didn't bother to turn around.

As she slightly leaned her head out into the dark, she heard him
start to sing. Not rap, *sing*. Milo immediately recognized her favorite
"love" song; the song that she had described to Ajsha, admitting
that she had always wanted a boy to sing to her that way.

"That little –" Milo whispered to herself, as Simon sang "Let me
love you."

The song, probably inspire by a similar situation, completely fit
their own. After letting the sweet lyrics flow into her ear for a
moment, Milo turned around and smiled. This sight encouraged
Simon, and he injected more soul into his voice. Walking past him,
Milo went to the bed and crawled under the covers. He lay down
too, propping himself up on his elbow. The song was so beautiful
that Milo's eyes misted over. For a second, she allowed herself to
forget who Simon was, and pretend he was a different boy; one she
had never felt vengeful towards. However, it was hard to
concentrate with his face so close, saying all those words she had
wanted to hear . . .

When he finished, Milo said, "Oh, Simon. That was so beautiful!
I can't believe you learned it."

Shrugging as if it hadn't been as challenging as it was, he smiled
at her. "Please?" he said.

"Please, what?" she asked, still a bit dazed.

"Let me love you," he finished softly.

"Oh!" Milo said, that waking her up.

She looked down at her hands, too flattered to reply. Suddenly,
and with jarring intensity, she realized that she was flattered and

was horrified. Swiftly, she transformed back into steel-girl.

Lifting her considerably colder eyes to Simon's, she firmly said, "No."

It might as well have been a slap; Simon blinked, hurt, sighed at his rejection, and rolled over. At once, a feeling of disappointment and regret swelled up in Milo. She was quite astonished by it, and this time didn't push it away.

"Hey," she said to Simon before fully conscious of what she was doing. "I'm sorry."

He flopped back over and grinned in surprise. "Really?" he inquired, trilling his L's.

Milo nodded.

His smile broadened and he made to hug her, but she shied away. Not pressing it, he snuffed and lay down.

They said good night, which was a new development started shortly after Christmas, and Simon murmured, "I love you."

Milo smirked shyly to herself, her face partially smooshed into her pillow.

"And adore you," he added cautiously.

"Oh!" Milo cried, reflexively elbowing him in the arm. "You evil imp!"

As the complete silence of a house with no whirring electronics fell, Milo stared straight ahead of her, feeling quite addled. What was going on? Was she actually starting to like Simon? She had no idea, for, admittedly, she had never liked a boy that way before, and so she had nothing to compare this to. The idea made her feel weird, though she wasn't entirely sure why. Maybe, after hating him for so long, it seemed impossible that she could like him. If she even did. It appeared as though she did. But she couldn't be sure right then. . . . She would decide in the morning.

No. She couldn't possibly. But . . . perhaps.

The next morning, once Ajsha was dropped off at school, Milo went back to painting the house. She had decided to paint each side two colors. The front was yellow and green, and the back, cut in half, was blue and cream. The east side was mint and violet, and the west side, aqua and red. She worked all day, thankful for Ajsha's help when she came home. By bedtime, they were halfway finished with the second to last wall. Milo was so tired she fell asleep at once, not even hearing Simon whisper that he loved her.

The following day she completed the last two walls, and after supper she painted the kitchen table with the mahogany paint. The chairs then got painted white, with black seats. Everyone had to eat breakfast at the counter in the morning, but they were dry by lunchtime. After a delicious spread of tuna deviled eggs, chive and garlic pasta, and mango coconut salad, Simon headed for the beach while Milo and Ajsha stood outside staring at the house.

"I've never seen anything so colorful," Ajsha remarked dreamily.

"I've seen gardens far more vivid," Milo said, fixing her flowers, which had gotten mussed by the ladder. "There's lots of paint left, so I could do more, only I don't know what."

"I like what you put above the door," Ajsha told her.

"Thanks," Milo said, stretching her overworked limbs. "Whenever I would complain when we moved, my mom would tell me that."

"She sounds wise," Ajsha said.

Milo thought for a moment. "Yeah," she muttered. "Where's Simon?" she asked, changing the subject. "He kinda just took off, didn't he?"

"I don't know. Why do you care?" Ajsha asked slyly.

"I don't!" Milo shot back defensively.

"Liar," Bob the Conscience stated.

"Really???" Milo asked in amazement.

"Look!" Ajsha cried suddenly, pointing towards the beach.

Simon was fast approaching the house, leading a group of his beach friends, most of whom Milo didn't wanted to see. She stared at them wide-eyed, jaw slowly dropping. Never had so many males converged upon her abode at one time. A few nodding to her in acknowledgement, they all began to look over the house. Milo walked up to Simon.

"Wha-what – what are they doing here?" she stammered, gesturing blindly behind her.

"The house," Simon said simply.

"The house?" Milo repeated, dumbfounded.

"Colorful house," Simon explained. "They want to see."

"Oh," was all Milo could breathe. She inhaled for a while and asked, "Do you like it?"

"Yes," Simon answered, grinning. "Only house with rainbow on it. They not believe me, so I tell them to come see."

Milo smiled and turned away, feeling shy. She and Simon walked over to join the throng of boys scrutinizing the house, making varying sounds of approval or incredulity. The cans of paint were stacked neatly by the east wall. Milo's eyes skimmed the faces of the boys until they came to rest on Caleb Scumm. She scowled and decided to keep an eye on him. He was talking with a couple of other boys, and they began to snicker.

"Aw, no," Milo moaned. "Now what?"

Gradually, the boys stared their fill and started to leave. Soon no one was left except Caleb. Warily, Milo watched him as he slunk around looking impish. Suddenly, he darted over to the cans of paint and pried off the top of the red.

"Hey!!" Milo yelled. "Git away from that!"

"Caleb!" Simon shouted. "Fulus dolont shamp!"

But Caleb would listen neither to the English nor the Galo. He rammed his fingers into the paint, grinning maniacally at Milo. Lifting out his fingers, which were now dripping red, he flung the paint at the wall of the house. Milo screamed as it all splattered in droplets all over the mint side. Horrified, Milo stood rooted to the spot, as Simon tackled Caleb to the ground. As they wrestled, he began to yell at him. "Ti fulus pliv ancer Ti gwemp qua, Caleb!"

Milo, recovering from the nausea that was coiling in her gut, drifted up to the wall, feeling thoughtful. The boys were shouting at each other from the ground, and at one point Simon had to punch Caleb to keep him down. Finally, after studying her ruined wall for a minute, Milo had an epiphany.

"Simon," she called out, still staring at the red on the mint. "C'mere."

Puzzled, Simon obeyed. Leaving Caleb flailing on the ground, he came up to her. "So sorry," he said earnestly, pointing to the droplets. "Caleb," he sneered.

Milo nodded, not looking at him. "Yeah, uh-huh. Right. Hey, listen. What do you think these look like?"

Simon looked them over and shrugged. "What you mean?"

Milo tilted her head. "I think they look like bullet holes."

Simon was befuddled for a moment, this being a new word to him. "Bullet?"

"Pwut," Ajsha told him, timidly walking over. When Simon's expression didn't change, she added, "Chulo pwuts."

"Oh!" Simon said, comprehension rearranging his features.

Milo gave Ajsha a funny look. "Chulo?" she inquired.

"Gun," Ajsha explained. "There are a few on the island, but we never use them."

"Good," Milo said, at once feeling nervous. "Let's hope the mayor doesn't have one. But look. Don't the dots look like bullet holes?"

"I suppose so," Ajsha said doubtfully, squinting at the spatters. "I've never seen real bullet holes."

"Good," Milo said again. "But that's what I think it resembles. It looks kinda cool. Like the house has been attacked, by a machine gun or something. Very cool. And it looks more artsy this way. Yes. We should do this to every wall. Mix colors. Dang! Why didn't I think of this before? I should really thank Caleb for this."

"Thank?" repeated Ajsha, aghast.

"Yes, where is he?"

They looked around and saw him trying to skulk away from the scene.

"Thank you for the idea, Caleb!" Milo shouted at him, Ajsha translating for her. He was so surprised that he stumbled over his own bare feet, but didn't stop until he was out of sight.

Milo began to open the paint cans again to bullet-hole all the walls, minus the door, which would be a mite too dramatic. Her husband and daughter offered to help, so Milo explained that they were using their fingers. But when Ajsha objected to this, Milo tore rag strips for all of them. They used them by dipping the ends into the paint and flinging it at the walls. Mint got red, the violet aqua, the blue yellow, the cream got green, the red mint, the aqua violet, the yellow blue, and the green got cream.

When they were done, they had a truly unique looking domicile. They stood back to admire, what was once dull and brown was now completely coated and splattered with paint. Simon and Milo met each other's eyes. Simon smiled, but Milo looked down, chuckling even though there was nothing humorous. Ajsha watched them, feeling very pleased. They all had to take showers that night and when they were ready for bed, feeling clean and sleepy, Milo saw that Simon wasn't around. She wandered into Ajsha's room, where she was lying quietly under the blankets.

"Hey," Milo said casually. "Where's Simon?"

"He went to give Caleb a 'piece of his mind'," Ajsha recited, hugging her plush puppy, whom she had christened Seymour.

Milo pursed her lips and shook her head. "He shouldn't have," she muttered. "Every time someone gives a person a piece of their mind, they make their head a little emptier."

Ajsha giggled and gasped, "Why do you *care* where Father is?"

"I don't," she answered, not meeting her gaze.

"Yes, you do!" Ajsha declared, sitting up. "I saw the way you were looking at him today!"

"Aww, you're seeing things," Milo said hastily.

Sighing impatiently, Ajsha settled back down. "Am not. But, by the way, Father asked if you would sing me to sleep."

Milo froze. "I – I – I don't know any lullabies," she mumbled.

"None?"

"No," she said firmly. "And, why would I sing to you? That's Simon's job."

"But he's not here."

"So?" she argued. "I couldn't possibly sing to you. I mean! That's so motherly and nurturing. I'm not like that. I don't want to be like that."

"I've noticed," Ajsha said. "But do please try. Just for tonight. I'm sure you must know at least one song."

Milo fidgeted. "Well . . . fine, I do. Only it's not really a lullaby. And you'll laugh at me."

"No I won't!" Ajsha insisted pleadingly.

"Are you sure?" Milo pressed.

"Positive!" she reassured her, batting doe-eyes. "Please?"

Milo sighed pitifully. "All right," she conceded. "I'll do my best; try to bear with me."

Delighted, Ajsha nestled down into her pillow, and Milo, not exactly endowed with good pipes, nervously began. She sang "Swing Low, Sweet Chariot", the only song that had ever fully tattooed itself onto her mind. Upon finishing, she heaved an exhale of relief. Much to her surprise, Ajsha was fast asleep. Milo shook her head, marveling at it. She heard a noise at the door and swiveled around in time to see Simon enter the room.

"Back already?" Milo asked, impressed. He stopped beside her.

"Never left," he answered.

"What?" she said, her voice going up an octave.

"Heard you talk 'bout minds fes pieces. So I thought not go," he struggled to get out. He then grinned. "Head too empty already."

Milo giggled, but then frowned. "Fes?" she inquired.

His brow screwed up. "Um . . . con-junction in English."

"And?" she suggested.

"I think."

She nodded and asked him bleakly, "Did you hear me sing?"

"Yep," Simon said. Milo cringed. "Like song. Where you hear it?"

She shrugged, looking down at Ajsha, Seymour clutched possessively to her chest. "Somewhere. Dang! She goes out like a light, doesn't she?"

Simon, guessing this was one of those metaphors he was having so much trouble with, thought hard for a second before nodding. "She sleep plenty," he agreed affectionately.

Milo smirked. "Why don't we leave her to it?"

She turned to leave and had to tug at Simon's sleeve to make him follow. They clambered into bed and Simon extinguished the candle. In the dark he whispered, "Thank you."

"For what?" Milo inquired drowsily, plumping up her pillow. It was getting flat.

"Being nice."

"Oh," she whispered. She paused. "Listen, Simon, um, I want to say I'm sorry. You know, for being unkind to you. I'm not saying you didn't deserve it! But, I've been feeling nicer lately, so you get a break."

"Thank you. I know."

"You know what?"

"I deserve."

"Oh," Milo said, rolling her eyes. "Aren't you just full of surprises?"

"Uh-huh," he said, shifting and making the bed creak. "So you."

"Hey!" she shot.

"Horses!" he countered.

Milo laughed, much louder than she intended, and clamped a hand to her mouth. She was beginning to enjoy herself. After several minutes of silence, which they used to make sure Ajsha hadn't awoken from Milo's boisterous chortle, Simon began to sing

"Let me love you". Milo sunk into her significantly fluffier pillow, and listened tranquilly to his voice and the irresistible lyrics. Music had an impact on her. Perhaps, if Simon had never utilized it, she might have never started to like him so much.

"What!" she thought. *"I like him?! I actually do?* . . . *Oh, well. Why not?"*

Yes, ladies and gentlemen. Why not?

23
Something about my Pretty Gurl

"BE KIND TO unkind people – they need it the most." This is a saying well worthy of some applause. So, if you don't mind. Please. . . . . All right, that's good enough. It is a saying proven quite true and effective. For example . . . Oh! There are just too many. But let's, if you will, take a look at Milo and Simon.

Now, Milo wasn't exactly an unkind person, but, nonetheless, she wasn't being very nice to Simon. Downright malicious, in fact. She had her reasons, of course; although, as these things usually morph into, it eventually became about principle. But, as the above saying goes, Simon, despite this, was still kind to her, and after many long, treacherous months, she came around.

Whether it was on purpose or just a natural progression, she started to spend more time with him. It was so much easier now that he could speak English, and she discovered how much fun he was. Unnoticed by Milo, she started to develop a "caring feeling" for him, which, when she finally realized it, was rather startling for her. But only because it was new; she really had never had one for anyone else before. Indeed, she found that she preferred being with

Simon than with Ajsha. Not that she wasn't terribly fond of Ajsha, but Ajsha, besides being vastly more intellectual than her, took everything so seriously. Simon was different. He liked having fun.

As Milo spent more time with Simon, actually talking and laughing with him, she discovered that she was growing shy when around him. As you may recall, Milo was not a shy person. She never had been, it just wasn't in her chemical makeup, which was why it flummoxed her that she was acting this way. Whenever he smiled at her, she would blush orchid pink and look away, grinning. Mirth would bubble up inside her whenever they talked. It was so bizarre to Milo, that she would feel so high and light whenever she looked at him; that her heart would start pounding whenever he sang to her.

Yet, she would always revert to shyness, and then try to distance herself from him.

Simon noticed these subtle changes blissfully, but was oblivious to how deep they went. This was undoubtedly because of the signals Milo was giving him. For instance, she stilled pulled away if he tried to hold her hand. But, she didn't yank her hand away, she gently withdrew it. It appeared that she was still uncomfortable with touching, though not because she disliked Simon. Milo wanted to be comfortable. In fact, she often caught herself wishing she could hold his hand.

One day while Squelch was visiting, they were tending to the flower garden, or at least using it as a ruse to spy on Simon and his buddies. As she tugged out a weed, her gaze elsewhere, Milo said in a moony voice, "Isn't my husband cute?"

She might as well have punched Squelch. She jumped away, mouth dangling open.

"Are you feeling right?!" she cried, reaching out to palm Milo's hollow cheeks.

"What?" Milo snapped in a friendly way, brushing off her hands.

"Do you *realize* what you just called the burglar?" Squelch asked in a hushed, concerned voice.

"What! I said he was cute."

"Exactly!"

"So? He is cute."

Squelch hurriedly felt her forehead. "I knew it! You're ill. You're burning up."

"Squelch," Milo laughed, again pushing her hand away. "We're out in the blazing sun in humid weather. I bet if you felt your head, you'd also be burning up."

Lips pursing, Squelch immediately did so and shrugged. "Fine," she assented. "But I still demand to know why you called him cute."

"Because he is!" Milo persisted.

"*Buuuut*, since when do you care?"

Milo snorted sharply. "I care!"

"But," Squelch repeated slowly, trying to get all her facts straight. "I thought you hated him."

"I did," Milo acknowledged, this truth now feeling so cruel and pointless. "But I have stopped."

"What?" Squelch asked in amazement, becoming excited. "When did this happen, missy?"

"I'm not really sure," Milo replied, unable to suppress a smile. "I think when he started singing to me. The day I first started to paint the house."

"Which," Squelch interjected, "looks terrific. Super colorful."

"Thank you, ma'am."

"And: Wow!" Squelch exclaimed, bouncing a bit with enthusiasm. "So, you like him now?"

"I think so," Milo said softly, smiling.

"Like him like him, or liiike him like him?" probed Squelch, this distinction crucial.

"I don't know," Milo admitted reflectively. "I think I just like him."

"Well!" Squelch exclaimed firmly, pounding a fist into the soil.

"That settles it. From now on, I will like Simon. Cuz, you know you my gurl and I'll get along with your boy, whoeva he is!"

"Uh, thanks," Milo said, fighting the desire to fall over laughing. "But I don't think he's my 'boy' yet. I mean, I can't even hold his hand."

"Aw, that's okay," Squelch said wisely. "You're getting over a hating spell, and that's to be expected."

"Really?" Milo asked in wonderment.

"Oh, sure."

"Huh!" Milo said, thinking that it did sound logical. "How do you know so much?"

"Ha, well," Squelch admitted with a chuckle. "I don't, really. I'm just presuming."

"Oh," said Milo. "All right! That's fine!"

"Ooh!" Squelch's eyes sparkled and her grin expanded. "Isn't this exciting? Does he know?"

"I think so. Well, I mean, it's possible. I haven't exactly been flirting with him."

Squelch gasped, scandalized. "Why ever not?" she demanded faintly.

"Ummm," Milo said hesitantly, glancing over her shoulders for any nosy passerby's. "I don't know how," she hissed.

"No?" Squelch cried. "Why didn't you say so? I, due to observing my sisters so much, am a flirt-expert. They've evolved their flirting over the years to truly annoying, but I know a few sincere flirts. You are sincere with him, yes?"

"I think I am," Milo said slowly. "I mean, I am his wife."

"True," Squelch agreed. "But still, you never know. Okay, listen. First off, smiling and eye contact. Never hesitate to smile at him, and always have complete, unwavering eye contact."

"Impossible!" Milo interrupted, blurting out her most prevalent issue. "I can't keep eye contact with him! Not even a little, no matter how much I try. I feel so self-conscious when he looks at me.

I feel shy! *Shy!* And I'm not shy! Never have been! But with him it's different. It's so weird."

"Ohh!" Squelch said knowingly. "You are *so* crushin' on him! All right, you need to build up enough confidence to do the eye contact. Until then, try holding hands. Uh, uh! Shush! I know it may be hard at first, but, if you really work at it, I'm sure you can master it."

So Milo, trusting Squelch's flirtation analysis, took her advice and tried to hold his hand. You wouldn't think it to be such a difficult feat, but for Milo it was very perplexing. Apparently, there was an invisible obstruction between her hand and his whenever they were side by side and she tried to make a grab for it. Her fingers just couldn't get within an inch of his. She attempted to at least lay a hand over one of his, but no. Often, she would find herself giggling uncontrollably if she tried this. This puzzled Simon quite a bit. Even when he tried to hold her hand, she couldn't handle it. Muster as she might, she was never able to restrain herself, and usually had to dash away in hilarity. However, she did manage to find a small way to make contact with him.

Whenever she happened to be standing above him, if he was sitting, or crouching, or leaning over to wash his face in the kitchen sink, she would hesitantly flick at his hair. Or gently twist it in between her fingers. But that was it. That was as far as she could go. She wasn't even sure if he knew she was doing it sometimes, but she simply couldn't bring herself to do anything else. Although, she did want to.

But things between them did, miraculously, slowly, progress, and then came the day that Milo felt bored. Dreadfully bored. Seven month itch bored. She wished for something to do other than her usual routine. After perusing her prickly restlessness, she decided that she wanted to read, but what? She didn't have any books with her besides her diary and *Milo's Cookbook of Plagiary*, which she didn't feel like reading, and Simon wasn't exactly a bibliophile, nary a novel to be found in the hut. Suddenly, and with tremendous joy, she remembered that there was a library on the island. Grabbing her shoes, she rushed out the door.

She ran to town, which was a marker of how anxious she was (Milo believed running should only be employed when chasing or being chased), and waited outside Ajsha's school until it let out. This was mostly because she had forgotten which building the library was beneath, and had a hunch she would need an interpreter anyways. Ajsha was certainly surprised to see her there.

"Hello, Mother," she said, walking up to Milo as her fellow pupils flooded past, elated to be free.

"It's Milo!" she shouted furiously, making several children jump. "Milo! Milo! Milo! Milo! How many times must I tell you?! But, never mind; I want you to show me to the library."

Ajsha paused. "Now?" she said.

"Yes, now!"

"Don't we need to go home?"

"No."

"What about lunch?"

"Forget about lunch!" Milo cried. "Show me, gurl! Now!"

Obediently, Ajsha nodded and started walking. "Yes, Mother."

"*MILO!*" Milo screeched through her teeth, stomping along behind her.

Ajsha led her to a small, shack like building, which had nothing inside it but steps descending into the ground. They trod down, down, down and soon found out why the library was established beneath the soil. It stretched for yards and yards, a veritable labyrinth of sleek, wooden shelves that were packed with books. There was a checkout desk by the entrance, and a collection of doors on the left wall, leading to numerous offices, as well as one lone door in the back. Milo at once began to scan the book bindings and found them all in Galo.

"Don't they have any books in English?" she finally asked Ajsha, who was by the reference section.

"They might," she said, leafing through a book with hand drawn pictures. "Usually, once they make Galo copies, they try to sell them. I'll ask the librarian."

After she had gone off, Milo sauntered about in between the shelves, inhaling that papery, inky smell that is books, until she came to an open space clustered with comfy looking chairs and tables, on top of which sat glowing oil lamps. There were oil lamp stands all over the library, mainly in corners and at the ends of shelves, and they all created a dusky light that made everything just visible. Ajsha reappeared shortly with the report.

"She said that some might be in the storage room."

"Great," Milo said, clasping her hands together and looking around. "Where's that?"

"Over there," Ajsha said, motioning towards the lone door.

"Thank you," Milo said, giving her a pat on the cheek and heading for it.

Opening it, she entered a room crammed to the ceiling with boxes. Boxes filled with papers, rags, documents, bottles of polish, rejected drawings, and books. Combing through the books and constantly wiping dust off her hands, Milo found a small collection in English. Selecting a couple, she exited the room and shut the door.

Upon turning around, she almost rammed into a figure dressed imperiously in black and gray robes. Stumbling backwards, she peered up through the dimness and saw the pinched face of Mayor Em-I peeking out amid his impressive beard. Two other men, dressed the same way, were flanking him. They all gave her hard, stern glares.

Milo swallowed with some difficulty, her grip tightening on the books she had just excavated. What little common sense she had left was screaming at her to bow or curtsy or *something*. But she could only manage to wave a bit. All the men exhaled in a deep, gruff way, plainly unimpressed with this miserly greeting. Milo was sure she would have shriveled up and died if Ajsha hadn't materialized the next moment.

"Mother," she said, emerging from nowhere, then saw the Mayor and his assistances. "Mayor Em-I!" she squeaked. She quickly uttered a very formal greeting and looked down at the floor.

The Mayor finally spoke, his voice guttural. Ajsha dutifully translated.

"The mayor said, 'Hello, Mrs. Swallow. Ajsha Swallow. What would you be doing in the library this fine day? Wanting to cause trouble, maybe?'"

Milo, peculiarly, got a thrill out of being called Mrs. Swallow. However, she felt offended that the Mayor had insinuated that she was there to cause trouble.

"No, sir," she replied, as Ajsha translated. "I just wanted to get out some books . . . to read!"

The Mayor's eyes narrowed as he heard this and he spoke again.

"He is saying, 'Good, very good. You see, the library is essentially my second home. My counsel and I are usually here, studying the laws and other books. Our offices are over there.'" He gestured to the line of doors. "'We wouldn't want any problems to occur down here that would distract our work.'"

Milo sincerely shook her head and tried to conceal her quaking. She desperately wanted to edge past him, but his stony glare froze her. Ajsha, who was also plenty intimidated by the mayor, noticed this, and said something to him in Galo. They nodded, in unison believe it or not, and turned to go. Milo waited until each one had closed his door before heaving with relief.

"My word!" Milo blurted out. "That man is scary!"

"Yes," Ajsha agreed, following her to the librarian's desk. "But he is a good mayor."

"As long as he's that," Milo muttered, wiping cold sweat off her brow. "What about husband?"

"Oh, he's a good husband. I heard once that he is very much in love with his wife."

"He had better be," Milo remarked tartly, handing over Ajsha's books first. "Considering the laws he enforces."

"Well, anyway," Ajsha said, moving on swiftly, "she, his wife, is a poor, sickly soul. Always seems to be ill. Though, I've heard she's doing better."

"That's good," Milo said, handing her books over. "Thanks for the info."

The hollow-cheeked librarian, who was indisputably the second palest person on the island, after Milo, due to her subterranean profession, gibbered raspingly to her.

"She wants to know your number," Ajsha told Milo.

"What number?" she said. "I don't have one yet."

"Just say any number," Ajsha said. "Any will do. We don't have the equipment to be very organized here."

Thinking for a moment, Milo suddenly grinned. "Tell her one – one – zero – seven."

Ajsha did so, and the librarian grunted, scribbling in the backs of the books with a pencil. She passed them back, and the girls left.

"What's eleven oh seven?" Ajsha inquired as they climbed the rickety wooden stairs.

"A bit of horror I just gave to someone else," Milo replied stoutly.

At home, Milo splayed out on the couch under the window in the sitting room that faced the clearing, immensely enjoying her books. Only a lengthy series of pleas from Ajsha and Simon were able to wrench her away from them to make dinner.

She couldn't read the next day, for it was washing day. Not for the first time, she considered skipping a week, but her conscience, who went by the name Bob, wouldn't let her. When she went to get water for the tub, several girls were at the miniature waterfall as well, even though Milo had deliberately tried to find a day when no one else washed their clothes. Of course, that was before word had gotten out that she was acting nicer; villagers were actually waving to her lately, instead of shaking their heads in disapproval.

A couple of the girls, balancing their own tubs, waved to her. Milo felt compelled to respond.

"But how?" she asked Bob the Conscience. "They won't be able to understand anything I say."

"Everyone smiles in the same language," he replied brightly.

She shrugged and smiled toothily at them. They looked relieved and grinned back. But the rest of the girls scowled at her. Milo thought she recognized these ones from previous market trips.

An hour and a half later, she was done washing the clothes, so she looped the rope over her shoulder and began to look for a place to hang them where a view of the beach was visible. She wanted to watch Simon. Deciding on two palm trees that were close, but not uncomfortably close, to the beach, she tied the rope. Simon was horsing around with some pals by the water, when saw her and waved. She waved back. As his friends walked off, Simon strolled up to her.

"Hi!" he said, brushing sand off of his shorts.

"Hi," she said shyly, beginning to suspend the moist garments in the rope.

"What you – what *are* you doing?" Simon inquired conversationally.

Milo grinned to herself. "Laundry," she murmured.

"Why here?" he asked.

"Why not?" Milo answered vaguely. "What were you and your fellows talking about?"

Once Simon had deciphered what she meant by "fellows", he said, "You."

"Me!" she uttered, flapping out a T-shirt. "What about me?"

"You beautiful."

Milo laughed, threading the shirt through the rope. "You crazy, boi! I ain't beautiful, I ain't even pretty."

"Yes, you are!" Simon exclaimed.

"Nooo," she insisted, jabbing her head from side to side. "I'm not."

"You are to me," he insisted, stepping closer.

Milo shrugged blissfully, swallowing when she noticed just how close he was. "So, I'm pretty to you? Thanks. I'm the type of gurl that never hears that."

"Gurl?" Simon repeated, confused. "Isn't *girl?*"

"Well, yeah," Milo agreed, reaching down into the basket. "But gurl is just a bit of affectionate slang."

"Oh?" he said, and pondered for a second. "That type of gurl? Well, you my type of gurl. My pretty gurl."

Positively radiating with blush, Milo stared at the ground, a damp skirt clutched in her hands.

"Milo," said Simon softly, tilting his head, "anything wrong?"

"No!" she said, hastily stringing up the skirt. "Why?"

"You never look at me," he said accusingly, then, with a trace of worry, "I am ugly?"

"Oh, no!" Milo said sincerely, looking him full in the face. "Not at all! You're *really* cute! Sorry, I guess I'm feeling sort of shy."

Simon stared at her, eyes round and huge. He was so happy that he looked liable to start crying.

"You think I cute?" he breathed, his tone implying that all his dreams had just come true.

Milo stiffened. "Doesn't everyone?" she said falteringly.

Simon's blithe look vanished. "Yes," he said quietly. "They say so. But I no care they do. Only you."

The burning in face increasing, Milo studied her feet. "Well, I do. You know, on a critical level."

"That all?" he asked sadly, knowing, to her dismay, what "critical" meant.

Milo's hardness at once ordered her to say, "Yes", but she boldly pushed it aside and told the truth. "No," she admitted, gazing straight into his face. "There's more."

Once again Simon looked unbelievably pleased. He held her gaze, savoring the moment, both of them now on the mutual ground of finding one another attractive. It was broken by the boys calling out to Simon, and he turned to leave.

"Bye," Milo said hopefully, watching him go.

"Bye," he returned.

She stood quiet for a moment, staring at them as they attempted to heave a full net across the wet sand, and then shrugged. She finished hanging the clothes and went inside the house to read. After a while, it came time for her to retrieve the clothes. As she walked by the beach, basket on her hip, she noticed that some of the boys by the waves were watching her. Milo glanced around to make sure they were actually lavishing their attention on her and not one of the bikini-clad blondes that were always showing up. (Another reason Milo rarely went to the beach.) Seeing that it was her they were examining, she remembered that Simon had said that they were talking about her being beautiful, and she began to worry.

One particular snot broke away from the group and headed in her direction. He strode over and stood in her path. He stared right at her face, giving her a look that said, "Well. How are you doing? Wanna go play?"

Narrowing her eyes, Milo thrust her chin in the air and walked around him to her clothesline. Either not recognizing the hint or just totally disregarding it, he followed and stood directly behind her. She didn't know who he was, but fervently wished that he would turn around and go someplace far away from her. When she had gone around him, she had glimpsed every boy on the beach, including Simon, stop what they were doing and start watching them.

Then, without warning, as Milo tugged the first shirt off the line, the meathead put his hand on the curve of her shoulder. She froze, enraged, all determination to maintain a haughty dignity being replaced by white-hot fury. It didn't stop there, however. Leisurely, without a smidgen of shame, the boy leaned forward and kissed the side of her neck.

On top of being one of the most disrespectful, inappropriate, roguish things to do, this was also incredibly stupid, especially since it was Milo. Though Milo wasn't many things, one of things she was, was loyal: Loyal to people and to herself. Before the cretin had a chance to do anything else, she whipped around, eyes blazing, and gave him a nerve-cringing smack across the face.

It was such a smack he went sailing to the ground, groaning and spitting sand.

"How dare you!" Milo snarled at him, stomping a foot and whipping the shirt in the air. "I ain't your girl! I am a married woman! Stand up so I can strike you again!"

What Milo did was so absolutely fantastic, unbelievably magnificent, and superb, I could go on about it for quite some time. She stood up for herself, and in a way that many girls avoid. But they shouldn't, for if anyone is being treated in such a way, they have the perfect right to retaliate. Since it was Milo, her retaliation left a sting.

Everyone on the beach was stunned. When Simon saw the kiss, rage had fired up inside him. But now he was simply shocked and delighted, the delivered smack resounding beautifully in his ears. Everyone's mouths were at first hanging low, but they swiftly composed themselves and began to race over to the scene. By that time, the jerk of a boy had stood up, revenge etched in his features, but Milo was faster and punched him in the middle of his face with her sharp fist.

Once more the boy dropped like a stone, and everybody quickened their speed, advancing on the two of them in droves. They all swarmed around them, laughing and hooting, a few good-natured boys giving Milo hearty pats on the back. Milo fell back a bit, coming out of her angry trance and letting her modesty take over. The disgraced boy on the ground was towered over, yelled at, and then picked up and shunted away. He shouted a few nasty sounding sentences over his shoulder, but his voice was soon overridden by all the others. As the last couple of stragglers congratulated Milo (at least she assumed that's what they were saying) and drifted away, Simon came up to her, eyes huge once more. He tried to find the right words to speak as he pointed towards the boy and made vague reenactment motions, but could only stutter.

Milo straightened her back and stood tall. "What?" she demanded, crossing her arms. "I can't defend my honor?"

He shook his head in wonder, a smile flitting across his face. "You say to him you married."

Milo shrank a little. "Yes. But – but – but . . . he – he shouldn't have done it in the first place. A boy should never lay his hands on a girl," she said fiercely.

Simon nodded gravely, showing that he agreed, then grinned and chuckled. "You incredible, Milo," he murmured. "Something about you. . . . Something about my pretty gurl."

Milo, whose complements generally revolved around her cooking, had never received such flattery from this category before. She felt her face becoming red and hastily turned away, grinning. As she tried to pull off another garment, but she got a reminder that her fist hurt.

"Ow," she said, cradling the hand.

"What wrong?" inquired Simon, concerned.

"I don't punch faces much," she replied, indicating to her hand. "It hurts."

"Hurts," Simon repeated, rolling the word around in his mouth. Gently, he took the hand from her and kissed it.

Milo pulled it back from him at once, her face burning, and

continued on with the clothes, but she found she was trembling with suppressed giggles. That night, she relayed the whole story to Ajsha. The little girl was just as shocked as Simon was.

"I don't believe it," she murmured, sitting across from her at the kitchen table, a few lit candles between them.

"I know!" Milo cried sharply. She was soaking her fist in a bowl of cold water. "Can you believe that little pervert?"

"Yes, I can't believe that," Ajsha acknowledged, looking punch-drunk. "I mean, everybody knows you're Simon's wife . . . and all the boys respect Simon so much. But, also the fact that you actually struck him. That's amazing, Mother."

"Amazing," Simon repeated, tasting the word, relishing it. "Yes. She is amazing. Zing. Zing! She is very amazing. Zing."

Milo had to grin, humbly sloshing her hand in the bowl. "Why do you think it's amazing? Wouldn't any other girl on the island do it if it happened to them?"

"No," Ajsha said dryly, rolling her eyes. "They would scream for their boys to come take care of it. So they can test their loyalty to them, and to have the thrill of being rescued. It's the same thing for when other girls are on their boys. They want the boys to push the girls away themselves, instead of them standing up for their guys."

"Some devotion they show," Milo muttered, wincing as she curled her fingers. "I'd think that they would like to stand up for themselves, for their relationships."

"You want to?" Simon asked, staring at her intently.

Milo hesitated. "Yes," she whispered, cautiously, focusing on a groove on the table. "We are married, and no one can just do that. I do have a tiny amount of respect for our vows, though some of them were a little weird. And, I'm not going to let myself to be manhandled by anyone. Find out who that guy is, Simon, and, when you do, give him a whack for me."

Simon snorted derisively. "I will do more," he assured her. "I'd have at beach, only you did first. I need new – new . . . Ajsha, what coceelin betu?"

"Punching bag," Ajsha told him.

"Oh, Simon!" Milo cried, having a sudden, outlandish urge to throw her arms around him, but didn't. Fighting to keep her face straight, she said, "Maybe you shouldn't. Just warn him that you will if he does it again."

"Very well," Simon said, though it was clear he thought the idea was still appetizing.

When they were going to bed, Simon asked, "Your hand okay, Milo?"

Milo smiled happily. "Yes," she said, flexing it for emphasis. "Now. Um . . . thanks for . . . well, just thanks!" With that, before she could blush, she shut her eyes.

"Want me sing?" came Simon's hopeful voice.

"Aren't you tired?" Milo asked, cracking open a lid.

"Little," he admitted, up on his elbow. "But, I want to have time with you. You like when I sing."

"Yeah," Milo sighed to herself. "But not tonight. I'm really bushed. And, we spend plenty of time together."

"Not talking," he muttered, falling on to his back and licking his thumb and finger to douse the candle.

"What?"

"Nothing."

They didn't talk the next day, either, because Milo had to go to Squelch's house. One of Squelch's neighbors wanted to learn English, so Milo and Squelch were giving her lessons. This excited Milo a good deal.

"Maybe we can bring English back and everybody will use it again," she had said to Squelch when she had first asked her to help out.

"No," Squelch had answered. "Many islanders oppose English and encourage others not to use it. They say it binds us to our past life, or something stupid like that. Therefore, it doesn't matter what happens, people here will speak Galo and nothing else. Only the interpreters aren't shunned by those types."

But there was no law decreeing that you couldn't learn English just for the heck of it, so they taught it to the girl. Squelch's neighbor, Veronica "Salsa" Crit, was a brown-eyed twelve year old, with bright red hair in long, bouncy, glossy curls. She was a slim, five foot three bundle of energy and friendliness, and she and Milo rapidly bonded. In return for the English lessons, Salsa was giving Milo and Squelch dance lessons. Salsa got her nickname from being, despite her age, practically an expert salsa dancer.

At first Milo and Squelch felt rather uncomfortable about learning the salsa, considering it's, at times, promiscuous moves, but the rest of it looked like fun, so they agreed. They met in Squelch's yard to study both subjects. It blew the girls away how fast Salsa was learning English. Simon was nothing compared to this girl. And the dance lessons weren't going too badly, either.

That day, they met on Squelch's porch, and Milo told them about what had happened on the beach. The two girls, after just a drop or two of translating, both gasped.

"I can't believe it!" Squelch said, appalled.

"Mmm – mmm, tell me 'bout it," Salsa said, squinting as if she could just visualize it.

"And you slapped him!" Squelch cried.

"And punched him," Milo concluded.

"Oh, my word!" Squelch squeaked, starting to bounce, which she normally did when excited. "You're a wonder, Milo! The eighth wonder of the world."

"You've got to be kidding me!" Milo groaned. "Is this what the world's girls have been reduced to? That every time one stands up for her good self, they all marvel at it? What happened to our pride? But, anyway, enough of that. Yeah, he kissed my neck, it was gross, I punished him physically, and apparently I'm the first female in history to have done so. Moving on to other things."

"Ooooh, yeah, yeah!" Salsa said, hopping from foot to foot. "What the news on Mr. Simon?"

"Yeah, what's up?" Squelch asked eagerly. They moved down to the lawn and sat in a three person circle.

"Well!" Milo began blissfully. "When I told him my hand hurt, he kissed it!"

"Oh?! Ooo! Ha, he," was the reply.

"And, get this," she continued. "He called me his pretty gurl!"

They all laughed in delight, making teasing yet supportive comments. The lessons commenced afterwards and all too soon, Milo needed to go. Before she left, Squelch pulled her aside.

"Do you think you'll teach Simon the salsa and dance with him?" she asked.

"Oh," Milo said, alarmed. "I don't know. That'd be too weird. You know, after all the crap I gave him, I think we should take things, like, slug slow."

"Well," Squelch said, "yeah, that's true. But, I'm talking about when you're really used to things."

"I don't know, it's kind of inappr- . . . you know."

"Yeah," she admitted. "But that's *that* type. Perhaps you can show him the less spicy kind."

"You mean the mild salsa? Oh, sure, I could do that. Considering I wouldn't be caught dead dancing the hot salsa."

"Wise. Besides, you barely know any 'hot' salsa," she reminded her. "Just the mild kind. It's fun; you should definitely show it to him some time."

"I will," Milo said, although the mere idea made her want to keel over giggling. "Someday."

After the customary drawn-out, swaying hugs (progression), she began the journey back. As she was walking through town, the sun a flaming orange behind the palm boughs, she saw the boy she had slapped yesterday stalking in her direction, a small posse of his friends assembled behind him. His eyes were fastened on her and neither he nor his friends looked happy in any way.

Milo quickened her pace and tried to appear fearless. Conflict was something she wanted to avoid at that moment, what with her being greatly outnumbered. But the boy and his supporters stormed right up to her, creating a semi-circle around her. She stopped, the boy glaring at her, his nose and under his eyes a dull puce color. Milo kept her back straight and her eyes set.

"Yes?" she asked in a dramatic voice. "Do you want something?"

Not bothering with preamble, the boy reached out his hand and slapped her across the face. Do you remember how I told you that a boy should never, *ever* hit a girl? Well, the same goes for slapping one. Milo gasped in pain, staggering to keep from toppling over, and a crowd began to form. Milo turned back to the boy, nostrils flaring, and all pretense of dignity gone. He stared back gloatingly, with a teensy sneer that plainly said, "I bet you wish I was kissing you now, huh?" Milo's fingernails dug into the flesh of her palms, and she gritted her teeth. She was sick and tired of being beat up by bullies. It was going to stop right now!

Eyes blazing, body so tense that every single bone and tendon stuck out, and steam just about whistling out of her ears, she let loose a ferocious, frustrated war cry and forcefully grabbed his wrists. The boy, whoever he was, whatever his name was, put up a fight, struggling to break free from Milo's sinewy grip. They yanked each other from side to side, at one point their foreheads almost touching as their enraged irises met. The boy was both bigger and stronger than Milo, but, as it is with most epic battles, purpose is what proves most powerful. Milo, in a burst of adrenaline, threw him sideways into his line of chums.

They all crashed to the ground in a pile of flailing arms and thumping legs. The crowd, who at first had been nervous about the whole scene, now started cheering. It is always an exciting thing to see the small and weak triumph in the end, but Milo hardly heard them, there was so much steam in her ears. Mrs. Lanslo and Soldier hurriedly emerged from the throng.

"Milo!" they called out. "Are you all right?"

"Yeah," she said, rubbing her face. "I can't say the same for him."

"You poor dear!" Mrs. Lanslo cried unhappily, patting her shoulder. "Imagine! A slap right across the face. Oh, it must have hurt!"

"The little dirtbag!" Soldier growled, cracking his knuckles. "Absolutely no respect for the female kind! I'd like to squash him right now, while he's still down."

"Don't worry, Soldier," Milo said in a low voice. "I'll do that."

. . . . . .

"He slapped you!!" Simon shouted in outrage, back at the house. He was feverishly pacing around the sitting room stone coffee table, his fists balled up so tightly that they were turning white.

"Yes," she said sulkily, sitting in one of the chairs, holding her forehead and a cold cloth to her cheek. Just once, she wanted to come home and not need mending. "And it was painful! But don't worry. Afterwards, I threw him into his band of guy thugs."

"Really?" said Ajsha, her face full of surprise. She was sitting on the arm of the chair, holding a glass of chilled fruit juice, which Milo was periodically taking a sip of. Milo nodded.

"You bet I did," she said, wincing as she moved her jaw.

"Milo!" Simon murmured, thrilled. He went to stand beside her. "Are – are you not something else?"

"And," Milo continued, grinning, a bit painfully, and gazing up at him, "after I did that, I stomped on his stomach!"

"Mother!!"

"Milo!"

"Milo!" exclaimed Simon, laughing.

"Exactly!" Milo said, pointing at him. "Very good, Simon!"

"Incredible!" he went on. "Unbelievable! Amazing! Zing. Zing! Wonderful!"

"*Anything for you, cutie,*" Milo thought happily to herself, her face suddenly not smarting so much. "Bob! Can you – Bob!"

"Whaaaat!?" he demanded.

"What are you doing?" she asked curiously.

"I," he said with dignity, "am preparing for a date."

"With who?" Milo asked, though she wanted to ask, what.

"Common Sense," he replied. "We have many interesting conversations and plenty of stories to share. A lovely personality she has."

"No doubt," Milo readily agreed, bewildered. "Well, um, tell her, hi. And . . . can you believe all this!"

"No," he said wryly. "I can't. Never in my whole life have I ever seen anything like this. They will write books and build monuments honoring this very moment in time, and I am just so proud to have been a part of it. May I go now?"

"Yes, yes, go. Enjoy yourself."

"I plan to. Don't wait up. Bye."

Milo nodded, though she wanted to shrug, but was afraid to. Instead, she looked over at Simon. He was staring at her, and shaking his head and grinning like he couldn't stop. Milo heard him murmur, "Just something – something about my pretty gurl."

24

Birthdays are Good Days for Swimming

WHEN IT OCCURRED to Milo that she did not know, she took it calmly and uncaringly. Then when she began to like Simon, she started to get a little bit anxious. She ordered herself to find out, but only got around to it when it occurred to her that it might have already gone by without her knowing it. Therefore, prompted by fear, one day, while it was on her mind, she hurriedly sought out Ajsha and asked her.

"When's Simon's birthday?"

"The twenty-eighth," Ajsha replied without hesitation, not even glancing up from her homework.

"The twenty-eighth of what?" Milo pressed.

"January."

"The twenty-eighth of January," Milo repeated quietly, her brain whizzing. "Wait! That's three days from now."

This remark was what made Ajsha finally lay down her paintbrush and frown in thought.

"Why, yes!" she confirmed after a moment. She saw Milo's distraught expression and added reassuringly, "Don't worry; Father's friends are going to be giving him a party. They do every year. He'll be turning seventeen. Oh. He's growing up so fast!" she added fondly, returning to her half-finished coral reef picture.

"I'm sure," Milo said, trying not to dwell on it too much. Seventeen was an almost inconceivable number for her, but she just kept telling herself that Simon would still be Simon, which kept panic at bay. "But, what should I get for him?" she asked. "It's got to be something really nice."

"How about a kiss?" Ajsha suggested, dipping the tip of her brush into a vivid orange paint.

Milo chuckled forcibly. "In your dreams, sweetheart!"

"Don't you mean his?"

"*And* his. But, other than that, which is not going to happen, what can I get him?"

"I'm sure you'll find something," Ajsha said distractedly, dotting her paper with little gray specks, which she later said was krill, though Milo thought the mere fact that they were visible made them way to big.

And Milo, despite having every intention of getting Simon a nice gift, once again faced the same problem she had at Christmas: She was virtually penniless. This eradicated the shops in town as options, and she couldn't ask anyone for a loan because she couldn't pay it back. Dejected and running out of time, she, out of frantic desperation, started snooping around the different warehouses, searching for any interesting, unwanted objects that might make good birthday presents. In the end, the only thing she found was a leather string, eighteen inches long. She figured that it wasn't much of a gift, but it was all she had and his birthday was tomorrow. Just as planned, his friends were going to throw him a party and it was being held at the Swallows' hut.

That morning, after scrupulously cleaning the house, so that when the boys came in to destroy it they would first notice how neat it was, Milo ventured into the forest to hastily collect some ripe fruit, but couldn't find any. She didn't mind and was eagerly making her way back, when she heard a cough behind her. Pausing, she was about to turn around to see who it was, when something large broke the air and hit her head.

She blacked out at once and never saw the cougher or the hitter. Awaking some time later, her skull throbbing painfully, she tried to move but discovered that her hands and feet were bound together. She tried to cry out and learned she was gagged. It didn't help that she was surrounded by pure darkness and therefore had no clue where she was. Taking a strong whiff, she recognized the pungent smell of an overloaded, under cared for cellar. She also recognized the temperature to be that of a cellar, and the powdery substance by her cheek had to be dirt. She tried to shout for help, but the gag was wedged in too deeply. She tried to wiggle free, but could not, the ropes on her wrists and ankles obviously tied by an expert. For a moment she lay still and tried to focus her furious mind. Whoever had done this was going to be in big trouble if she ever got out.

"I will," she thought determinedly to herself. "I don't know when, but I will. There's no need to worry."

As she began to calm down, her thoughts strayed to Simon and his party. She reckoned he would worry if she didn't show up or, even worse, think that she had stopped liking him and purposefully wasn't attending. With renewed desperation, she returned to squirming and rocking, frantically trying to free herself. She had no luck, and when she had sufficiently worn herself out, she sagged on the dirt, awaiting help.

The hours dragged by. No one came. Milo got deathly bored and attempted screaming several times, which only produced a stifled buzz so quiet that she could barely hear it. As more time slowly crept away, Milo managed to fall asleep. When she woke up, who knows how many hours later, she was still in darkness. Either no one was looking for her, or it hadn't crossed their minds to check any cellars. Whoever had put her there apparently thought she would be fine being tied up all day long, with no food or water. Why bother taking care of your hostage?

Raging mad, Milo once again tried to break free, but to no avail. However, her boiling anger wouldn't allow her to give up, and with a twist of her wrists, her fingers touched what felt like a knot. Gasping, she dug her nails into the lump of rope to untie it. It took her a couple of frustrating minutes, for the knot was very tight, but at last it came undone.

She unraveled the rest with haste and ripped off her gag. Rubbing her wrists and ankles, working the feeling back into them, she let out a mirthless, triumphant laugh. It took a while before she could stand up, being cramped so long. When she could, she groped blindly in the darkness, stumbling over a few things on the way, and finally tripped onto some steps. Climbing them, her head, which was still plenty tender, collided with a door. Making disgruntled moaning sounds, she felt along for the handles and flung it open.

The stars were just becoming visible, night just beginning to hug the sky. A full moon was shining palely on the horizon. Milo inhaled the fresh evening air, a welcome after laying next to what had to be a barrel of long forgotten pickled carrots all day, and at once set off for her house. She had to retrace her steps more than twice before she found it, since she had emerged from the cellar in an area of the jungle she had never been to before. When the hut came into sight, she could have fainted with relief. The lamps were on, giving off a glow and splashing puddles of light on the ground, and Simon was chatting with a few friends outside the door. Milo had never felt happier to see him.

Weak with hunger, thirst, and overexertion, she began to stagger towards him. It took about three seconds for him to notice her.

"Milo!" he called out and rushed to her side. He helped her totter another yard before she had to stop.

"Yo," was all that Milo could utter.

"Where you been?" he cried, bewildered by her ragged

appearance. "You all right?"

"Yeah, yeah," she muttered, stretching her back. "But tomorrow, someone is going to die."

"I was worried!" Simon said, hugging her shoulders and then swiftly letting go when she nearly fell over. "When you didn't come . . . to celebrate. I wanted go search, but they made me go on."

"With the party?" Milo guessed.

"Yes," Simon murmured sadly. "Why didn't you come? Where were you?"

"Lay off, huh?" she snapped quietly. "I was tied up in a cellar all day."

"What?" Simon inquired, stunned instantly. "How you get there?"

"Don't know," she answered. "I was just walking along, not bothering anyone, and someone knocked me out. When I woke up, I was sitting in pitch black, gagged and tied. My head still hurts."

"Oh," Simon said, suddenly looking disgusted. "When Tambry arrive with her friends, she was carrying a club. 'For keeping boars away,' my –"

"Who's Tambry?" Milo interrupted.

"Tambry Ethlins?" Simon said with a low snarl. "Girl who would do this."

"Ah," Milo said, as he shouted something to his friends and they left shouting back what was undoubtedly birthday wishes. She felt like changing the subject. "Well . . . um . . . where's Ajsha?"

Simon turned back to her and looked up at the sky. "Sleep," he muttered. "She tired. Long day. You're filthy," he added, looking her over.

"'Course I am," Milo said crossly, brushing herself off. "Been rolling around in dirt." She bit her lip. "Sorry I couldn't come to your party."

Simon shrugged. "It is all right. I understand."

"You better!" Milo thought viciously, her cranium aching, though

she did truly feel sorry.

"I mean, I'm really, really sorry," she murmured sincerely, forcing herself not to break eye contact. "It is your birthday after all." She paused. "So . . . how does it feel to be seventeen?"

"Like sixteen," he said, not cracking a smile.

Milo chuckled. "I know what you mean."

He sighed. "I wish I could spent my birthday with you," he said softly. "I was looking forward to it."

This made Milo go from feeling bad to terrible. Yes, she had been detained against her will, but she still wanted to make it up to him. Rashly, she decided on an idea.

"Well," she began hesitantly. "Technically, your birthday isn't over yet. Why don't we go do something? Just you and me," she said, pointing from him to herself. "Anything you want."

"Anything?" he repeated, his attention captured.

"That's right. Anything."

He grew excited and contemplated for a moment. "Let's go swimming," he finally said.

Milo almost blacked out again. She thought fast. "You mean . . . you go swimming, and I accompany you?"

Muddled, Simon paused to sort this question out. "Yes," he decided. "Just that."

Milo shrugged helplessly. "Very well," she said, rather shrilly. "Let's . . . go get ready."

They went inside the house, Milo chewing her lip in worry. The interior of the hut bore the unmistakable markings of a party thrown by teenage boys, and when Milo, in an effort to ignore this for the time being, averted her gaze, she saw a slice of pastry sitting on the kitchen table.

"What's that?" Milo asked, changing course.

"Honey cake," Simon answered, following her. "Birthday present. Very sweet. Try it. Taste it."

Not needing a second invitation, her stomach completely empty, Milo broke off a piece to put in her mouth. An unbelievably sweet flavor spread across her tongue. Most cakes sold today in society are much sweeter than that cake. But after eating nothing but meat and fruit and using sugar as sparingly as possible for so long, it was extremely sweet to Milo. She almost started laughing.

"Oh," she said, her thoughts immediately turning to Boston cream pie and profiteroles. "It's good. Ah, very good. Oh, wait! I just remembered, I have a present for you."

"Really?" he said, reaching over to brush a crumb off of her chin with his thumb.

"Mm-hmm," she muttered briefly distracted by his touch. "Well, a poor excuse for one, but one nonetheless. I'll be right back."

Leaving him with the cake, she headed down the hall to their bedroom, inhaling deeply. Once there, she closed the door to change. Though she had no intention of swimming, she thought it best to still put a bathing suit on under her clothes. She withdrew the leather string from her top drawer and went back. Shamefully, she approached Simon and coiled the string in his hand. He pulled it straight and looked it over.

"Thank you," he said unsurely. "What is it?"

Milo opened her mouth slightly and scratched behind an ear.

"Well," she said. "Anything you want. You can tie it around your neck and find a charm to put on it." She brightened at this idea. "The necklace from me, the charm from you."

Simon smiled and tied the string loosely around his throat.

"Thank you," he said again, more warmly, poised to hug her, but didn't. "I'll be right back."

After about five minutes, during which Milo made the rest of the cake disappear, he returned, dressed in swimming shorts, a towel over his shoulder. He led Milo outside and towards the beach. But, instead of heading to the water, he walked along the sand, following the curve of the island. They walked until they arrived at a quiet, sandy cove. The land sloped gently into the water, which was calm and motionless, unlike at the beach where waves continuously pounded the shore. This made the surface of the ocean glasslike, and the black sky, stars, and round moon were reflected with eerie perfection. But what amazed Milo the most was a thirty-foot high, fifty-foot long rectangular boulder sticking from the shore into the water, like a gigantic dock. That was farther up the cove and had several ladders trailing up to the top. Milo peered up at it in the moonlight, then out at the water and shuddered.

Simon tapped her arm. "We swim here," he told her.

Her eyebrows arched and she swallowed hard. "You mean, you will swim and I will be with you?"

Simon contemplated this and said, "Yes. Come on."

He took off his shirt, and waded out into the water. Milo watched helplessly as he dove under and came back up, shattering the night sky's twin. Her spine was prickling painfully and her chest was getting tight. She didn't dare go nearer, not even just to spectate. After splashing about for several minutes, Simon noticed that Milo was still standing rigidly on the shore.

"Come on," he called out, his voice ringing in the air. "The water wonderful. Wonderful water!"

He went under and resurfaced, flaying his wet hair from side to side. He was laughing, but stopped when he saw that Milo hadn't moved.

"Hey," he shouted, beckoning to her with an arm. "Come on!"

Milo stared at him, the whites of her eyes gleaming. She shook her head. Simon frowned.

"What wrong?" he said, doing a backflip. "Come swim."

"N-no," Milo said, feeling like throwing up.

"What?" Simon said, bobbing up and down, his torso making ripples in the water. "No? Why? Come in. Water lovely."

"No," was Milo's single syllable response.

"Why?" he asked imploringly, no longer moving. "Please?"

"No."

After a long, silent moment, Simon swam up to the shore, not taking his eyes off Milo, who remained stiff and upright on the sand. He sat in the shallows and held out his hand. Milo vigorously shook her head.

"Please?" he entreated.

"No."

"Why? Tell me."

"I don't want to," she replied in a short, clipped tone. "You can, but I don't want to."

"Why not?"

"Never mind. You can. Go ahead. Go."

He stared at her, water dripping down his face, the leather string a dark line on his throat.

"I swim every day," he said. "I love it. Love to swim, but tonight I want swim with you. We never go swimming. Don't you like swim?"

Milo wanted to lie. Oh, how she wanted to lie! But she decided it would better if she didn't.

"I used to," she answered truthfully, sounding as if there was an obstruction in her trachea.

"You don't now?" asked Simon upon working this out.

"That's right."

"Oh, come on! Please? For me? Just for tonight?"

Milo shook her head. Being totally immersed in something she was terrified of was not her ideal way of spending any night.

Simon stood up, sloshed out of the water, and walked over to her. He took her hand and insistently tried to pull her towards the water. She stood stiff as a board and didn't budge. After several gentle attempts, he gave a mighty tug, sending her flying forward.

"NO!" Milo screamed at the top of her lungs, flailing wildly. "NO! No! No! Simon! Let me go!"

They were now near the water, and Milo was close to tears. She screamed as she watched the water ebb serenely at her feet, and wrenched out of Simon's grasp. Scrambling madly up the slope, she ran to the trees and buried her face in her hands. Simon stood stunned for a minute, before walking over.

"You're scared," he said softly.

Milo looked up, her face flooded with fear. "Yeah," she said, her tone scalding. "That's it, okay? I'm afraid of the water. I am ridiculously, one hundred percent terrified of it."

"Since when?" he asked.

"Since you almost drowned me," she said bitterly, not meeting his gaze. She ripped a leaf off a nearby bush. "Ever since then, I can't stand it."

Guilt contorted Simon's features and filled his heart. He hated being reminded that he had almost killed his wife, and this made it even worse. He exhaled quietly, pondering how to fix it.

"Come on," he said, pulling her hand again.

"Did you not just hear me?!" Milo shrieked, dropping the leaf and rearing back. "I'm too scared to swim."

"I know," he whispered, not letting go, "but I going to help you."

"Help me?" Milo repeated incredulously, pausing in her attempt to yank her hand free.

"Yep. I help you like swimming again." He hesitated. "I feel awful for what I did. I never – I sorry. Very sorry. Don't worry. Trust me."

Milo peered at him longingly. "I wish I could," she murmured out loud.

"You can," Simon murmured back, entwining his fingers with hers.

A month ago, Milo would have scoffed at this, but things were different now. Now, she actually wanted to believe him and she had just discovered how perfectly her scrawny hand fit into his. Barely aware of what she was doing, she nodded. Simon nodded back.

Still, trusting and being brave are two different things. She was still having issues with the second one.

Simon did finally get her to the water, though he had to drag her most of the way. She kicked her pants off, but left her shirt on over her suit, only because she was very modest. He got her to the water's edge, her breathing hitching, and quickly wound his other arm around her waist. Slowly, very slowly, toes first, then ankles, they stepped into the calm water. Milo began to whimper noisily and was more than ready to run, but had faith in whatever this plan was of Simon's. However, when they were in up to their waists, Milo had enough.

"All right!" she yelled with false cheer. "That's good. Let's go back."

"No," Simon said gently, stroking her waist with his thumb. "Don't worry. Here, feel the water. It's nice, huh?"

Milo had to admit that the water, still rather warm from the sun, was sort of nice, but still petrifying. It didn't help that she couldn't see her feet or if anything was in close proximity to her feet. Or, if her feet were heading towards an underwater ledge that had nothing but open, endless, bottomless ocean on the other side . . .

Milo let out an involuntary gasp. "Shhh," whispered Simon.

He slowly dipped their interlocked hands in the water, swirling them around. Milo began to shiver, though she wasn't cold. Simon shushed her again. Between the shushing and the swirling, her tremors began to subside. Maybe she didn't have a phobia after all. Maybe, it was just a scare and she merely had to get used to the water again. Of course, it helped that Simon's arms were encircling her. Oddly, inconceivably, they made her feel safe. Soon she felt confident enough to let her feet break contact with the muddy bottom, and together they swam a little ways.

"Go under," Simon said once they were up to their chests.

"Forget it, brother," Milo snapped.

"Please?" Simon implored softly, right by her ear. She gulped and suddenly felt herself bending her knees.

With excruciating slowness, they lowered themselves inch by inch until the water tickled their necks. Milo squeezed his hand so hard the whole time that she was half concerned she was hurting him. But the other half didn't really care.

"There," Simon said, the water lapping at their chins. But Milo couldn't stand it any longer. She shot back up.

"Simon, I can't," she yipped distressfully, the fear starting to overwhelm her once more.

"Shhh," he said comfortingly, grasping her hand. "It's okay. I here. I not leaving. Sorry, you'll go under when ready. Come on. Let try strokes."

Her heart thumping like a bass guitar, Milo reluctantly lowered herself again. She tried to lift her arm, but failed. Simon helped her out, lifting it high above her head, and then her other one. Whenever she wanted to run, he would hold her until she felt better. The whole time, they continuously moved farther out in the water. Finally, Milo was motivated enough to go under. Unexpectedly, it made her feel spectacular and she came up laughing.

"Good!" Simon told her, clapping. "Can you swim under?"

"A little," Milo said, wiping her eyes. "But I don't want to right now."

"Of course," he said patiently, nodding. "No rushing. Come on, let go out deeper."

Milo blinked, disconcerted, but agreed, and out they headed. However, the second she took a step and couldn't find the bottom, she screamed. She found herself clinging to Simon for dear life. That was when Simon thought it best to move back. But even when she could walk on the soft, sandy ocean floor again, Milo still clung to Simon. He didn't mind one bit, though. Without her fully realizing it, Milo was putting more trust in Simon than she had ever put in any other human being. Whenever she felt that she was about to lose it, Simon made eye contact with her and assured her that she was fine, that he wouldn't let anything happen to her.

"Really?" Milo asked after the third time.

"Yes," he said. "Always."

"Thank you," she murmured after minute.

As the moon climbed higher, Milo at last decided to swim under the water. This was their primary focus, for it was going underwater that scared Milo the most. She was afraid she might not come back up, since, well . . . it had happened before. Hand in hand, they slipped beneath the surface and started to swim. Several times Milo shot right back up because she was frightened, but Simon was an exceptionally patient boy, always soothing, and waited until she was ready to go back under. They finally managed to swim a few feet before resurfacing.

"This is more terrifying than my wedding!" Milo said as she gasped for air and paddled back to a spot where she could stand. Simon laughed as he swam in circles around her.

"How scary was wedding?" he inquired indulgently.

Milo shrugged, holding her arms close to her, watching him. "I don't know. When I was walking down the aisle, I started to cry."

Simon halted. "You did?" he said in disbelief.

Milo nodded. "Didn't Ajsha tell you?"

"No," Simon said earnestly. "I so sorry. I did not know."

"It's cool." Milo forced herself to smile. "The veil was thick. Besides, I bit you."

He laughed again and went back to swimming, taking dives and graceful plunges.

"Wow," Milo commented. "You're a regular fish, ain't ya? Are you always like this in the water?"

"Yep," he said. "I love to swim. Much swimming when fishing, that's why I have job."

"Not to mention the whole industry is practically yours," Milo put in.

Simon didn't answer. Instead, he dove down and lay on the sandy floor. Milo wondered if he was trying to figure out how she knew that. After about two and a half minutes, he came up for air.

"Whoa," Milo mumbled. She saw a bump on the back of his head. "Uh, Simon," she said, "you've got something in your hair."

"Hmm?" he said, feeling his head. "Oh, it is a sea star. Probably got washed in with tide. Better put it back."

He tried to remove it, but the sea star's five arms held fast, its suction cups fastening to his hair the way it would cling to a rock. Simon and Milo moved to the shallows, where they could sit.

"It won't come off," Simon remarked.

"Want me to try?" Milo asked.

"Please," he replied.

Being careful not to get any of his hair, Milo got a grip on the sea star and gently pulled. When it wouldn't dislodge, she gave a mighty yank.

"Ow!"

"Sorry," Milo said. "But it's all tangled. It has to come out. You don't want me to crop your hair, do you?"

"No!"

"Good, now stay still and bear with me."

Simon set his teeth and ground them as Milo pried off the sea star.

"There," she said cheerfully, throwing it out to sea.

Simon ran his fingers through his tresses. "Good," he said. "Come, let go back."

Releasing a weary sigh, Milo looked out at the ocean. The waves were framed by the silhouettes of palm trees, and the surface was dappled with stars. It all looked like a screensaver, except that she had the option of walking right into it. Milo was momentarily enchanted.

"All right," she agreed. "As long as you're with me."

Grinning, he helped her up. "Why didn't you ever tell me you afraid of water?"

"I didn't want to," Milo replied simply. "I haven't even told Ajsha or Squelch. There're lots of things about me that you don't know."

"I know," he admitted, trailing his fingers through the water. "But I know some things."

"Like what?" she challenged, keeping her elbows high.

"Well, I know you love your cat, and love to cook, and your hop music."

"You mean hip-hop?"

"Yes! That stuff. And that you a hard worker and stand up for what you believe in."

"Is that all?" Milo queried.

"You won't tell me anything else," he accused, splashing her. "Ajsha say that you told her about your life, but she won't tell me any more. All she say is that you had it hard."

The temperature in Milo's body seemed to plummet, and she turned away, shrugging. Worried, Simon glided over to her.

"Hey," he said soothingly, touching her back. "It's okay. You here with me now."

Milo faced him. "It isn't that," she whispered. "It's just –"

That very second, a boisterous noise came from up the beach. A large group of teens emerged from the trail, and headed towards the enormous rock. They all were laughing and joking and dressed for swimming, several hand-holding couples scattered among them. Some noticed Simon and Milo immobile in the water, and started shouting for Simon to come join them.

"Pra!" Simon yelled back at them.

Caleb Scumm stood at the water's edge, yelling and laughing hysterically. Simon fumed.

"Greck mip, Caleb!" he snarled at him.

"What'd you say to him?" Milo asked, noticing that all the girls were in highly revealing two pieces, and instantly felt self-conscious in her sodden, flapping shirt.

"To shut up," Simon answered, glowering.

"Do they want you to go with them?" she whispered.

"Yes. They going diving."

"Diving!" gasped Milo, the notion horrifying. She looked to the boulder and saw the teens shimmying up the rope ladders. At the top, they either jumped or dove off.

Milo shuddered, and Simon put his arm around her. In all honesty, Milo wasn't too keen on having an audience while she relearned how to swim. The teens kept calling to Simon and teasing him. Milo heard her name thrown out a couple of times. He watched them with a look of longing, and Milo knew she was holding him back.

"You can go if you want," she muttered.

"What?" he said leaning down to see her face.

"I said, you can go with them if you want to," she repeated.

His gaze glazed over. "No. I don't want to."

"Yes, you do," she said softly. "It's okay. I don't mind. I'll just go home."

That nearly broke his heart. "No," he said firmly. "Tonight we are going to be together. I not going to leave you. I no jerk."

"Of course you're not," she said reassuringly, "but you can go. I know you want to."

"Not tonight. Tonight it only you and me. You promise me."

Milo stood silent, then nodded. Simon smiled and led her to deeper water, where the black liquid clearly mimicked the night sky.

Once again, the second she couldn't feel solid ground, Milo screamed. She fell over, splashing and flailing, salty water getting in her mouth as she screamed. When she finally found her footing and ceased shrieking, she heard the sound of laughter. Panting, she looked at the top of the rock and saw that all of the teenagers were doubled over in hilarity and pointing at her. Some were even mocking her. They were shouting to Simon, undoubtedly sharing their opinions about Milo.

Tears welled up her eyes, as she hugged herself and glared at them. Simon, yelling angrily in Galo, swam up to her and protectively wrapped his arms around her. The jeering didn't stop, and Milo felt herself being towed to a large, nearby rock that was sticking up out of the water. Once they were standing behind it in shoulder height water, hidden from view, Milo found herself crying on Simon's shoulder, him rubbing her back. Once she became fully aware of this, she hurriedly collected herself.

"Now, *they* are jerks," she sniffed, attempting to remove herself from Simon's arms. But he refused to let her go.

"Forget them," he told her gently.

"Yes, yes, I will," she assured him, still trying to break free. But her meager strength proved no match for his work-strong arms, and he quietly observed her struggle.

"Milo," he said seriously. "You afraid of me?"

"No," she answered, still pushing. "Why?"

"You keep pull away from me. Like now. You no let me hold you. Tell me why."

Not able to avoid such a direct question, she ceased writhing and thought about how best to answer. "*Weeeelllll*," she began. "When I'm around you, I feel shy."

"That it?" he probed, somewhat doubtfully.

"No," she hissed suddenly, becoming feisty. "I am also uncomfortable with it because I haven't been held by anyone since I turned three. Not used to it, see?"

"Oh," Simon exclaimed, appalled. "So, that is it?"

"Yes!" she gasped, spitting water out of her mouth. "And do I need a reason to not want to be held?"

"No," he said firmly. "But I want a reason for me not to hold you. I am your husband."

"Oh!" Milo scoffed sarcastically. "So, therefore you have holding rights? You have a holding warrant? A concealed hugs permit?"

Simon glared down at her, but then sighed and let her go. As he turned away he whispered, "All I want to do is comfort you."

Immediately, Milo felt like she had been stabbed with a knife, and yet she stubbornly believed that she was in the right.

"Hey. I'm sorry," she said. "I truly . . . really am. But you do really need to slow down. Stop moving so fast."

He whirled to face her, spraying drops of water.

"We been married months and months!" he said bitterly. Milo shrank some. "And we barely make eye contact! I can't stand it any longer, Milo! Please stop shoving my affection away!"

Surprisingly, to her at least, that stung, too. Why? She did not know. Well, she had an idea. But something else was currently nagging her.

"Affection?" she repeated quietly.

"Yes," he heaved out. "Every time I try show you I love you, you spit at me."

"Hey!" Milo shot back. "I only did that once! Wait . . . okay, twice."

Simon stared at her, motionless, then began to chuckle. "I know," he sighed. "I guess you right. I must admit, you nicer to me now. What change? One day you loathe me, another you smile at me."

Shrugging, Milo hung her head so he wouldn't see that she was smiling now. "I don't know," she mumbled, digging a foot into the watery, velvety sand. "I just started liking you suddenly. You're so cute and such a nice guy. Then you sang 'Hush' and, well, I'm only human. Please forgive me if I'm still a little skittish."

"It all right," he assured her. "I sorry for being mad."

"I'm cool," she said.

"Yes, you are."

They were quiet for a moment. Milo scratched at her hand, not sure what to say next. She could hear the teens' hyper chatter and the loud splashes made when they dove in. Her skin began to get clammy.

"Um," she said. "Do you wanna go home? I'm kinda cold and it's getting late and . . ."

A shriek of female laughter behind them supplied her last reason. He nodded. "I feeling cold, too. Let's go."

Half swimming, half striding they made it to the shore, where they gathered their things and started to follow the tree line back, the teenagers shouting at them as they left. They walked along in the moonlight, wringing their hair out, until they reached the house. While Milo changed in to dry, cozy pajamas, Simon checked on Ajsha. Once they were both changed and dry, they climbed under the covers.

"Tired?" Simon asked, positioning a pillow behind her back.

"A little," Milo said, not really noticing what he was doing because she was straightening the blanket. "I took a nap in the cellar when I was tied up."

"I'll talk to Tambry about that," he said, an edge to his voice.

"You do that," she said, lying back onto the awaiting pillow. She frowned, then shook her head and asked, "Why do you think Tambry did it? I mean, I've never met her before, so I haven't had an opportunity to insult her personally. Yet."

"Don't," Simon warned. "Tambry taller than me. She a good friend, but she sort of . . . mean. And, she always think she's right. She might have thought you would make a scene at the party. She kept asking me if I was enjoying myself . . ."

"Huh," Milo said, mulling this over. "Well, I guess word hasn't completely gotten around that –"

"That *what?*" Simon asked slyly, leaning towards her.

"That . . . I'm . . . more polite at parties."

Scoffing, Simon lightly hit her with a pillow. Milo laughed.

"So *violent*," she chided. "Hey, don't tell Ajsha that I'm afraid of the water. I don't want to give her another reason to analyze me. That girl is so much smarter than I am, but I'd like to have some respect in her eyes."

"You do," Simon told her compassionately, settling in. "She loves you, you know? She talks about you like proud parent."

"That's what I mean," Milo moaned. "It's like she's the parent and I'm the child. I can't even kiss her good night, but she does it to me."

Simon chuckled.

"It's not funny!" Milo insisted, hurt. "I don't know how to be a mother. Maybe because I didn't have a good model."

"No?"

"He – ck, no."

"Well, maybe you should try do the opposite of her."

Milo laughed. "Simon! I'm not that loving!"

"You sure?" he said, muddled.

"Well," she faltered. "I don't know. We'll see. Oh! Chaos!"

The adolescent cat had jumped onto the bed and was snuggling down in between the two humans. They stroked her fur, and were rewarded with a purr that could put a motorboat to shame. Milo noticed the leather string around Simon's neck and sighed wistfully.

"I wish I could have given you something nicer," she told him.

"I love what you gave me," he said. "And, you gave me a wonderful evening."

"Yeah, but is there anything else you want?" she asked recklessly. "Anything?"

Simon considered this for a moment, scratching Chaos beneath her chin, much to her delight, and suddenly looked bashfully at Milo.

"Can I kiss you?" he asked hopefully.

Rolling her eyes in exasperation, Milo dropped her face into her hands. "No!"

"Please!" Simon begged, all inhibitions vaporizing. "It what I most wanted to do for a long time. Our wedding kiss wasn't so great, and I really want another one. Please, Milo! You don't have to kiss back, just let me kiss you. Please, Milo! Please!"

He tried to peel her hands away from her face, her jerking away with muffled sounds of resistance. Finally, after several minutes of pleading, she lifted her head and stared at him, aloof.

"Fine," she relented crisply. "But just *one* kiss. Got that? One!"

Smiling savagely, Simon nodded with enthusiasm. Slowly, he placed one hand behind her head, and the other on her right shoulder. She didn't move. Encouraged, he slid the hand on her shoulder onto her back. He brought his face close to hers, and she briefly could smell his milky breath. For a moment, he looked into her eyes, unsettling her resolve slightly, and then kissed her lips. Milo had decided ahead of time not to kiss back, but discovered that she really wanted to. She forced herself to focus on not breathing too hard through her nose, instead of the feel of his lips, or how incredibly close his face was to hers, or how strands of his hair were tickling her cheek.

When he did pull away, Milo found that her heart was beating very hard and loud. Simon grinned dopily.

"Thank you so much," he said. "Can I do it again?"

Milo almost nodded, but caught herself and said steadfastly, "No. I said once and I meant *once*."

"Okay," he said, his grin not diminishing. "Thanks anyways."

"Good night, Simon!" she told him firmly, flopping onto her pillow.

"Good night," he said reluctantly. "Did you have fun? Swimming?"

"Yes," she mumbled, determinedly not rolling over to face him. "A little. I don't know if I could go without you, though."

"Oh," Simon murmured, settling into his own pillow. He whispered past a smile, "I see."

It was good that had Milo enjoyed herself. When swimming, that is. Swimming is quite fun and excellent exercise. Although, kissing is pretty fun too, and can indeed be a good cardio workout. It was a lovely that Milo was on her way to recovery, both in the water and otherwise. Besides, birthdays are such nice days for swimming. And other stuff . . .

25
Auntie

HAVE YOU EVER had a crush on someone? I know not everyone has, but for those of you who have, it's nice, isn't it, truly liking someone? How does it feel? Always wanting to be around him or her? Wanting to hug him or her? Or, forgive me, wanting to kiss him or her? It is usually an unfulfilled longing, for you can't just charge up to your crush and kiss them. Even if they knew about your more-than-friendly feelings and even if they returned them, you would always be on the lookout for parents, siblings, close friends, or the typical unannounced neighbor seeking a cup of sugar. Therefore, your chances to kiss become limited and brief, since nobody likes an audience. It all can be exceedingly frustrating, but at least there are specific reasons holding you back.

For Milo, it was even more difficult. She knew, without a shadow of a doubt, that she had a huge crush on Simon. This fact wasn't necessarily a part of her overall escape-the-island plan, but she was well past caring. Only one thought consumed her mind these days, and that was Simon. Ever since he had kissed her on his birthday, she had wanted another one. She yearned to go up to him and give him a smooch, but never did. And, to make matters even more ludicrous, there was nothing holding her back. She was married to him, and therefore had every right to kiss him, or hug him or anything else that might occur to her whenever she felt like it. But she wouldn't. She had too much pride and dignity, supplemented by too much stubbornness. But Simon was getting to her.

So much, in fact, that it would kill her to part with him anywhere. The separation, perhaps, would be less painful, she figured, if she kissed him goodbye. But no, she wouldn't. And Bob the Conscience was getting fed up with hearing her complain about it.

"For Heaven's sake, Milo!" he would explode regularly. "If you want to do it so badly, then do it! Trust me, there's no shame in it."

But she would always respond with, "No, I couldn't. I'm not one of those girls who just goes up to any guy and kisses him."

"He's your husband!" Bob the Conscience would bark.

When he refused to listen anymore, Milo went to Chaos. But even she was getting sick of Milo's pointless griping. Whenever Milo would start to talk about anything involving Simon and his lips, the cat would shoot her a resentful look. Milo kept apologizing, but also kept bringing it up. One day, Chaos got so annoyed that she decided to take action (which is saying something, considering she's a cat).

Milo was in the kitchen, coating a raw fish with a salt, flour, and egg whites mixture, when she heard Simon call out from the sitting room.

"Milo! Milo! Help me!"

Scraping the white gook off her hands, she hurried across the entry way to find Simon lying down on a couch, Chaos perched contentedly, and the teensiest bit smugly, on his chest.

Simon noticed Milo by the threshold and said, "The cat has pinned me down."

Milo restrained herself from laughing. "Just push her off," she said. "I give you permission."

"I've tried," he claimed, "but every time I do, she hurts me."

He demonstrated by trying to sit up. As if on cue, Chaos sunk her claws through his shirt and into his chest. Simon yelped and lay back down. Chaos gave Milo a kitty look that said, rather aggressively, "I will not let this boy up until you kiss him."

Milo twitched her head, which was meant as a discreet "No!" and picked her up. Her claws clung to his skin and then his shirt, but Milo won in the end, fully disconnecting her from Simon, who had winced the entire time, but bravely didn't make a peep. Milo put Chaos outside, both of them shooting glares at each other, and then wet a cloth for Simon. She went back to him and handed it over.

"For her scratches," she explained kindly.

He shrugged. "I'm all right. But thanks," he added gratefully.

Once again Milo got an irresistible urge to kiss him, just because he had suffered pain. But she didn't. She might have imagined it, but she thought she heard Bob the Conscience say, "Oy!"

The following afternoon, when Simon and Ajsha arrived home, Ajsha had some news.

"The Mayor's wife is doing very well. Well enough to be up and around," she reported.

"And," Milo queried, chopping up a bell pepper with lightning speed, "why would we need to know this?"

"Because," Ajsha said good-naturedly, flouncing into a chair. "We should be happy for her. This is the best she's been in a long time."

"Well," Simon joining them. "Good for her. I'm sure that Mayor Em-I was worried."

"Yes, I'm sure," Milo said flatly, scooping the green cubes into the salad bowl. "With all that time he's spending at home."

"Oh, Milo," he whispered. He glanced nervously at the window, as if expecting to see if the mayor's impressively bearded face glaring in at them.

"Where is his house, anyway?" Milo asked Ajsha. It occurred to her that she ought to give it wide berth.

"It's the *big* one on the far side of town," she said.

454   The Island of Lote

"You mean the one that's painted black?"

"That's it."

"Oh-my-word," Milo mumbled. "How can anyone even be near anything black in this heat? They're crazy."

"It's always been black. It's supposed to be imposing."

"Really? Those poor people must be boiling."

After discussing it over lunch, Milo, going against her better judgment, decided that she wanted a close up look at this house. So, two days later, while ambling through town, she went to investigate. She was having a cheerful and pleasant conversation with Bob the Conscience, for once, on the subject of dress coats, when she reached at the front of it.

"Well," Milo observed. "There it is. Two stories and all. Very big. Painted black."

"How obscure," Bob the Conscience commented. "And – hey! That must be Mrs. Em-I."

Milo looked towards the doors of the huge, black house and beheld a stooped woman. She was sweeping the broad, stone steps leading up to the doors with a wild grass broom. She was rather hunched over, as if to hide herself, was about Milo's height, and had pale skin and coarse blonde hair that fell limply down to her waist. Her face bore a sad, ill look that reflected hardship.

As Milo curiously scrutinized her, she muttered, "Interesting looking, no doubt. Definitely looks like she's been sick."

"Oh, most definitely," Bob the Conscience agreed.

As they continued to observe her, and make droll comments, Milo frowned.

"Looks a tad bit familiar, don't she?" she mused aloud.

After a moment, Bob the Conscience said, "Now that you mention it, yes she does."

"Yes," Milo said, twisting an invisible mustache. "But where have I seen her before? Hmmmm."

"I could search your memory banks for you," he offered.

"Don't you dare!" she snapped. "Just because you have access to everything in my brain, doesn't mean I want you snooping through it all."

"Fine!" he said loftily. "But if you ask me, which you wouldn't dream of, would you, she looks like one of your aunts."

Countless memories instantly flashed through Milo's mind like a film reel, and, at last, she agreed with her conscience.

"You're right!" she exclaimed, folding her arms. "She looks exactly like my Aunt Rosario."

"Why! That she does!"

"But that's impossible, isn't it?" she continued quickly. "I mean, what on Earth would Aunt Rosario be doing here, on the same exact island I'm on?"

"Sweeping? Why don't you go ask her?"

Milo considered it, mulling over what might happen if Mayor Em-I ever got wind that she was pestering his wife, then shrugged and walked up to the woman.

"Um," Milo said, unsure if the woman would understand her. "Pardon me."

The woman lifted her face to look at her. Her eyes were filled with grief.

"Um, hello," Milo ventured pleasantly, already half regretting her boldness. "Excuse me, but what is your name? Can . . . can you speak English?"

The woman looked her over with a puzzled and slightly wary expression then said, "Yeah, I can speak English." Her voice was that of grass in the winter: Tired and parched. "And my name is Rosario Em-I. Who are you?"

An icy but not unpleasant feeling blossomed throughout Milo's body, and she stood speechless for a moment, taking small gasps for breaths. She shook her head and began to grin.

"Wh-who were you before you were Rosario Em-I?" she asked tentatively.

The woman known as Rosario Em-I stared at her suspiciously. "I was Rosario Hestler before I married my husband. But, again, who are you and why are you interrogating me?"

"Ohmyword!!!" Milo blurted out, hands flying to her mouth. She hopped up and down for a second, not believing it and yet overjoyed.

"Aunt Rosario!" she cried, flinging her arms wide. "It's me! Milo! Don't you remember me?"

The withered woman stared hard at her, her aggrieved eyes squinting. Then she slowly started to shake her head, her brow furrowing as if she were concentrating.

"Milo Hestler?" she questioned. "She was the only girl I've ever met with that name."

"Yes!" Milo yipped. "Your niece! Don't you remember your brother, Earnest? Recall his little girl? I'm her. Well," she faltered, "I can imagine that you wouldn't. I was only six when you last saw me. Some . . . eight or nine years ago."

The woman inhaled sharply and dropped her broom, which fell onto the stone steps with a clatter. "Milo!" she shouted as loud as her voice would go, making Milo jump, and clutching her wizened face. "My little niece! Yes! I can't believe it. I *can't*! You . . . here. I – I thought I'd never see any of my relatives again."

"Me, neither!" Milo said, her jitters increasing. "Dang, I thought that long before I came here. But . . . you're here, too? What happened?"

"About what?" she exclaimed, straightening up with several audible cracks. "Give me a hug!"

Eagerly, Milo dashed up to her and they embraced, her aunt's grip surprisingly strong for someone who had been bed laden for many months. Aunt Rosario pushed her back, clasping her shoulders, and examined her from head to foot.

"My!" Aunt Rosario whispered, standing, now, perfectly upright. "How you've changed. The last time I saw you, you were this high."

She indicated to her knee. Milo shrugged modestly.

"Well!" she muttered. "Yeah, it was so long ago. What happened to you? The last time I saw *you*, I think you looked a bit healthier."

Aunt Rosario coughed a laugh, pushing her hair back and rubbing one of her eyes.

"Yes, ha, well," she mumbled distractedly, "this heat doesn't agree with me. Oh, where are my manners? Please! Come inside! We can exchange stories."

Milo readily agreed and, completely forgetting whose abode it was, followed her into the large, black house. She almost dropped dead from shock when she saw the inside. The floor was made out of cut boards (adding to Milo's suspicions that there had to be a saw mill as well as a gristmill somewhere on the island) and it was covered with dyed airplane rugs. The kitchen had a huge stone fireplace on the rear wall, with a cooking spit and a cauldron that, from its appearance, looked like it could have come off the first ship. The wooden cabinets were smooth and polished, adorned with flower carvings, and had small, glossy stones for knobs. The table legs had carvings of leafy vines growing up them. The marble sink was pure white, with a shiny metal pump.

Later on, during a tour, Milo would learn that there were exposed rafters by the ceiling in every room and they all had different things hanging from them. In the kitchen, for example, it was dried flowers. The living room had elegant sofas, chairs, and even a loveseat. The living room also has a fireplace, with a mantel. There was a staircase leading up to a second story. The railing on it was also covered with carvings, as was, it seemed, every single wooden object in the house. Years of work. The backs of the chairs were made of wood and not woven fibers, and were engraved with luxurious patterns.

Aunt Rosario was quick to sit Milo down before she fainted. She had instantly become light-headed as soon as she stepped into the house was hit by its stifling temperature. It felt like stepping into a sauna or a pre-heated oven. Aunt Rosario fetched them both a brimming glass of water.

"Forgive me if I don't make tea," she huffed, mopping her face with a wrinkly handkerchief.

"You're forgiven," Milo said, gratefully taking a gulp of water. "How can you live in this place? It's awful in here!"

"I know," Aunt Rosario said quietly, pulling in her chair. "But if you ignore it, it goes away. Well, you get used to it anyway. Right, so, tell me your story. Tell me what's happened to you since your parents carted you away from me."

Milo, flicking water onto her neck, shook her head. "It's a long one," she warned.

It was long, but she told it. Everything. In detail. Right up to the doomed airplane trip to the summer camp that she had never reached, and, honestly, was becoming rather glad she hadn't. She didn't share that particular tidbit, however.

Aunt Rosario didn't bother to set her jaw. She let it droop. She gaped in an astonishment that was beginning to make Milo uncomfortable. Once Milo described how she had crashed, she paused.

"Milo!" Aunt Rosario gasped. She sniffled and took a sip of water. "Excuse me," she said, again extricating the handkerchief from her sleeve. She dabbed her eyes.

"I'm not done," Milo cautioned her, draining her cup.

"No?" she said, arising to refill both their glasses. "Well, haven't you been busy?"

"Yep," Milo agreed, toweling off her drenched face with the inside of her shirt. "I'm married."

"You are!" she exclaimed, whisking around so fast that water slopped from the cups.

Milo nodded, showing Aunt Rosario her engagement ring, which she had just started wearing once more. (It had lain in her bottommost drawer for about six months.)

"Oh, my," her aunt whispered, sitting back down. "My little niece . . . somebody's wife. . . . I did hear, from my husband, that one of the boys had gotten married in July."

"Yeah. Simon Swallow. He married me."

"Really?" Aunt Rosario murmured in wonder. "Oh, I see. Clarence didn't tell me the bride's name. If I had known . . . I might have been able to attend. . . . Though, I was pretty bad in July."

"Clarence?" Milo mumbled to herself. "Clarence Em-I?" She snickered softly.

"Congratulations," Aunt Rosario told her.

"Oh, the wedding's not the half of it. Let me explain."

So, she did. Covering everything from first meeting Simon to up until now, a lot of which Milo was no longer proud of. When she finally ceased talking, Aunt Rosario stared at her, astounded and rather dazed.

"I need to get out more often," she sighed, rubbing one temple. "I'm so sorry about your wedding, Milo. Those laws weren't made to torture people. Only to . . . well, never mind. But, you say that you like him now?"

Milo smiled, glowing from something other than the heat. "Yes, very much," she whispered.

"Good," her aunt said with approval. "He's a fine boy. When he was younger, he would bring me flowers whenever I got sick. But, as I became more ill, I couldn't be seen by anyone but the doctor and Clarence, and I guess I disappeared from everyone's lives."

"Speaking of which," Milo cut in, "you still haven't told me how you got *into* their lives. How the heck did you get here?"

Rotating her glass with the tips of her fingers, Aunt Rosario hummed slightly. "It's like this," she murmured. "A few days after you and your parents left, I left, too. I wanted a change. I went and found work as a flight attendant. A few months after I got that job, my plane crashed here. Not many survived, but I did. I was brought into town to recover, and I met Clarence. Back then, he only worked with the mayor, though he was studying to become one. He was . . . very charming and sweet."

Milo scoffed. "Mayor Em-I?" she said, dubious. "Really?"

Nodding, Aunt Rosario smiled as she reminisced. "Indeed. So kind and sensitive. But, he seemed to be that way only around me. Anyway, he charmed me into marrying him, and a year later he became the mayor. I guess that's what did it. You see, over the years we've been drifting apart; me always so sick, and him always so busy."

"I've heard from people that you're pretty shy," Milo said.

Aunt Rosario hung her head. "Yes," she said listlessly. "I suppose so. But, one can't help but be. It's like living in Hawaii here. Isn't it?"

Milo shook her head. "Naw, I've been to Hawaii. It is not like this. But, similar."

Aunt Rosario shrugged. "Well, anyway, I'm not much of a people person. Being sick all the times doesn't make one feel sociable. I don't know why I bothered to learn Galo. I barely talk to anyone, save my doctor and sometimes my husband. He's not here a lot, though. I remember English by talking to myself. I get so lonely sometimes."

At once, Milo could identify with her aunt. She felt sorry for her.

"I know how you feel," Milo told her. "I was lonely for a long time, too. I started talking to myself as well. Heh, I still do! But, now that I'm here, I'll come and visit you whenever I can."

"You will?" Aunt Rosario said.

"Sure," she said cheerfully. "You know what? Why don't we and our families have dinner together? I really want Ajsha and Simon to meet you. Well, meet you as my aunt."

Aunt Rosario's face lit up, which is quite a good sign for a sickly person. "That would be wonderful! We can all eat here. I don't know if my husband will be able to make it. But I'll be sure to tell him about you."

Milo fell back in her chair, grasping her head. "I've just realized something," she wheezed. "If you're married to the Mayor, then that makes him my uncle!"

Giving her a long look, Aunt Rosario nodded. "Why?" she inquired. "Is that bad?"

"It's not *bad*, but it's not *good*, either." Milo gazed up at the flower festooned rafters, unwilling to reveal this part of her tale. "The Mayor and I aren't exactly on good terms."

"Why not?"

"I told you about my past rebellion. Insurrection, if you think about it. Yeah, he didn't like that much. Once put a dagger to my throat."

"Well," Aunt Rosario replied with unexpected optimism. "Why don't we let sleeping dogs lie?"

"Oh, they're lying," Milo muttered. "They just ain't sleeping."

"I'm sure Clarence will change his tune once he finds out that you're related to him."

"Or," Milo countered with what she thought was much more realistic, "he might be furious and hang me."

"Never!" Aunt Rosario declared aggressively, pounding an emaciated fist on the table, startling Milo. "I won't allow it! I've waited too long for a person to be close with, and I'm not going to let my husband frighten you away. When you go home, tell your family about me and that we're having dinner here tomorrow night."

"I – what? Tomorrow?"

"You heard me, missy. No use prolonging it. If it makes you feel any better, it will probably be a while before I can tell Clarence. It's always uncertain when he'll come home, and I never visit him at the library. So, you won't have to worry about his reaction just yet."

This chancy possibility didn't really alleviate the tightness in Milo's chest (doom was doom, no matter when it happened), but she did her best to smile and nod. She stayed with her aunt for another hour or so, laughing and reminiscing. When she finally did scoot out the door, Aunt Rosario giving her another fierce hug and waving her off, the first thing she noticed as she stepped outside was the drastic change in temperature. It actually gave her goose bumps. It was also turning dark. She ran home, relishing the breeze whipping past her body, and burst through the door to find Simon pacing nervously.

"Where you been?" he asked when he saw her. "I was beginning to think that Tambry tie you up again."

"Oh, I'm sorry," Milo said, hugging Ajsha. "But you wouldn't believe where I've been!"

"Where?" Ajsha asked, pressing her cheek against Milo's side.

Milo recounted the whole story for them as she made dinner (roasted onion and potato soup). They were speechless.

"Can you imagine?" Milo said, adding a splash of cream into the pot to finish the soup. "A relative, right here on the island?"

"I'm so happy for you, Mother," Ajsha said, smiling. "This does rarely happen. In fact, I don't think this had ever happened. Although, when it comes to you, it's mostly things that have never happened. But, she's married to the Mayor so that means –"

"Yes, yes," Milo interrupted with a heavy heart, morosely waving her stirring spoon at her. "I know. He's my uncle. But only by marriage. We don't share blood or anything. Thankfully."

"I still can't believe it," Simon whispered. He looked bit pale and was staring intently at the tabletop. "I am related to the Mayor. And not just any mayor. Mayor Em-I."

Milo suddenly chuckled.

"What?"

"His first name's Clarence."

They all chuckled, though Simon's pallor stayed the same.

"Anyways," Milo said, getting out three bowls. "Tomorrow night we're having dinner over there, so I want the both of you on your best behavior."

Neither Simon nor Ajsha bothered to remind her that generally it wasn't their behavior that needed to be worried over whenever they all went somewhere.

"This is one of my favorite aunts," Milo continued. "She gave me a few cooking lessons when I was young, making cakes and cookies and flans and all."

"Flans?" Ajsha repeated.

"So, please. Behave yourselves."

"We will," they both promised, exchanging a grin.

Actually, they both were very interested in meeting this Aunt Rosario, since they both were very curious about Milo's childhood. Anything to explain the way she was now.

The next evening, they all walked through town till they came upon the looming, black house, which, in the dusky twilight, effectively gave off an imposing air. Before they went inside, Milo warned Simon and Ajsha of just how stifling it was in there. But they didn't wholly believe her until they had actually entered. Once in, they almost ran back out. Luckily, Milo had made them wear light, thin clothes. Despite the heat, Simon and Ajsha were just as enchanted by the exquisite house as Milo was. They gawked like tourists at the Taj Mahal. Aunt Rosario welcomed them with wide open arms, but, to Milo's immense relief, the Mayor wasn't anywhere to be seen.

"Milo!" she greeted jovially, sashaying in from another room, her appearance strikingly different from yesterday. Her long yellow hair was thoroughly combed and piled stylishly atop her head, and she had on a flowery dinner dress, a crisp, white apron on over the skirt. It seems that spunk is derived from looking forward to life.

"Aunt Rosario!" Milo said. They embraced warmly, but not for too long because of how hot it was already. Simon and Ajsha waited patiently, furtively eyeing their surroundings. "These two," Milo finally said, "are my family. Well, my family now, here. This is Ajsha."

"How are you?" Ajsha inquired politely, holding out her hand.

"Better," Aunt Rosario replied, shaking the little hand with her own bony, drawn one.

"That's good. I was happy to hear that your health had improved."

"Well, thank you! Since I found Milo, or she found me, I've been feeling better each minute."

Milo grinned, pleased. "And this is –" she started.

"Don't tell me," Aunt Rosario cut in. "Simon!"

He smiled and nodded graciously.

"How good to see you!" she said, proffering her hand. "It's been a while. I'd be talking to you in Galo, only my Milo tells me you've learned English."

"Yes," he said, gently grasping her hand. "It's nice to see you doing well again."

"Thank you," Aunt Rosario said, taking a step back to inspect him. "Wow, you've just shot straight up. Exactly how old would you be now, Simon?"

"Seventeen," Ajsha said.

"You're not Simon," Milo reminded her.

"Is that right? Seventeen?" Aunt Rosario said in astonishment. "Wow, you look about fifteen!"

Not sure how to answer that, Simon moved on. "I would have never guessed you Milo's aunt."

"No?" she said thoughtfully. "I guess not. She didn't get her looks from her father's side of the family. I'm not sure what we gave her. It's been a long time since we've seen each other."

"But," Milo added as they were led into another room, "we used to live in the same neighborhood. All my relations lived there."

They entered the dining hall – yes, *hall* – to see a long table strewn with dishes. The walls, in strange contrast to the exterior of the manor, were bright sky blue, with clouds sponged on. The floor was painted green, and the table was a squiggly shape, like a path.

The three Swallows gasped with delight when they saw it. Lanterns shaped like birds in flight hung down in a row from the ceiling, casting a bright light over everything. Aunt Rosario motioned for them to sit down. Each chair was carved from a solid piece of wood and excessively whittled to look like bushes and other outdoorsy things.

After the blessing, Simon asked, "Why did you leave the neighborhood?"

Milo shrugged, stroking a fork that looked like pure silver. "Our house burned down. Everything we had was gone. My dad's boss then told him that it would be better if he moved to a different place for work. He's kind of like Dad's mentor or something, plus he pays him. But I don't think we would have moved if the house hadn't burned down."

Aunt Rosario began to concentrate intensely on the food she was doling out (braised brisket with a parsley sauce).

"Perhaps we shouldn't talk about it," she said. "It might be . . . too painful for Milo."

The girl shrugged carelessly. "Not really. I was too young to fully understand what was going on. What happened afterwards is what's painful."

"I so sorry about your house," Simon said earnestly. "Did you ever find out how it happened?"

Aunt Rosario cleared her throat quietly. "Could we please not discuss fires?" she insisted. "Just the thought of such heat makes me feel ill."

But Milo didn't hear her.

"No," she replied conversationally. "We never found out. We weren't there when it caught fire, and the fire department couldn't figure it out, so we really have no idea."

"But however it happened," Ajsha put in helpfully, "it did ruin your life. Didn't it? It started a chain of moving to different houses, and usually wherever you went was bad."

"True," Milo said, taking a spontaneous and pensive bite of beef. "It, you could say, was the starting point of my misery."

"How dramatic," Bob the Conscience said wryly.

"That's awful," said Simon, more sympathetic.

"Yeah, I know," she stated, shocked at how casual she sounded.

"Perhaps," Aunt Rosario said loudly, now distributing sautéed cabbage, "we should change the subject. Why dwell on the past?"

Milo cut a too big piece of cabbage in half. "Well, we can talk about the past, since the past is really where we know each other. We just won't talk about the bad things."

"Then it's good that we're talking about your first home," Ajsha said, swinging her legs from the tall chair. "Cuz the rest of your past is nothing but bad things."

"Oh?" Simon said curiously.

"Maybe," Aunt Rosario cut in once more, sounding flustered. "But let's think about the *good* old times. Shall we?"

"A'ight," Milo said, thinking. Hard. "Well, remember the time when we were cooking together – well, you were cooking and I was 'helping', and I put those yeast pats in the pot."

"What pot?" Ajsha asked, having trouble cutting her brisket since she was trying to keep both pinkies extended. Milo reached over to help her, secretly rolling her eyes.

"I was making soup," Aunt Rosario explained, relaxing. "And I was putting in dumplings, so Milo thought that she was supposed to put these tiny squares of yeast in. I didn't even notice her do it."

"Hey, I didn't know," she said defensively and laughed. "But I wish I had."

"So do I," Aunt Rosario chuckled.

"Why?" Simon asked.

"Because," she went on, "the soup was for a dinner party I was throwing for several important men and women from my work. Well, when they ate the yeast pats, which really did look like little dumplings by that time, it started to rise in their stomachs!"

Simon and Ajsha looked horrified, but Milo and her aunt were laughing uncontrollably. Apparently, yeast is one of the more hilarious aspects of cooking.

"Hoo boy," Milo chuckled, catching her breath and flicking away a tear. "They all had to drink that fizzy stuff instead of the wine."

"But," Aunt Rosario added, trying very hard to be serious for the sake of her other two guests, who were looking scandalized. "We did have other good, and painless, times. I remembered how interested you were in cooking, even after you found out what yeast is."

"She's a great cook," Ajsha piped up, relaxing once more. "We love to eat her food."

Shrugging modestly, Milo took a sip of mango juice.

"It's a little strange, though," Simon remarked, gazing at her musingly. "She talks to the food as she cooks it. And calls it all Bob."

Milo blushed crimson when she heard this, and the laughing inside her head.

"Aunt Rosario," she said, quickly turning to her. "I just *love* your house. I know it's hot and all, but it's still gorgeous. It has to be the finest house on the island."

"It is," she confirmed, rather impassively, gazing about the room. "This is the mayor's house. When a man becomes mayor he and his family moves into here. However, this climate is hardly conducive to black buildings. I understand that it represents authority and somberness, but it tends to just make the mayor hot-tempered and impatient."

"You should paint it white," Ajsha suggested cheerfully, setting down her knife. "It will be much cooler that way."

Aunt Rosario sighed wistfully. "Maybe someday. If Clarence agrees."

"Where is the Mayor?" Simon asked, hoping not to sound too anxious.

"Oh, he couldn't come. Still too busy at the library. So busy, in fact, that I haven't been able to get in touch with him."

"So," Milo said tentatively, "he still doesn't know?"

"I'm afraid not," Aunt Rosario said gently. "I decided not to send a messenger, it will be better if it comes from me. Don't worry, he'll find out soon enough."

"And you're sure he won't be furious?"

"Who said anything about that?" Aunt Rosario asked. "He'll be raging mad."

Milo went gray.

"You should have heard the way he yelled about 'Master Swallow's fiancé'. He was darn angry at you for rejecting the laws. I only just remembered that after you left yesterday."

"Oh, boy," Milo moaned, the food suddenly not agreeing with her.

"But don't worry," she said reassuringly. "He might be mad as senators in a conference room full of babies, but, like I said before, I'll make him get over it. Besides, you're *my* niece, aren't you?"

"That's right," Milo said. "I just don't want to be your deceased niece."

"You won't," Aunt Rosario said forcefully, dolloping a second helping of mashed turnip onto Milo's plate.

The conversation flowed along pleasantly, the guests and the hostess getting to know one another better and sharing stories. However, Milo's aunt resolutely avoided discussing Milo's first house. Until it was time for them to go home, that is. Something drove Aunt Rosario to steal Milo away before they could leave and brought her into another room to talk.

"Milo," she began, wringing her hands nervously. "Um, are you happy that you found me . . . here on the island?"

Milo grinned with delight. "Of course!" she answered. "How could I not? You are family after all, and there's nothing more important than relatives you haven't seen since you were six."

"Yes," Aunt Rosario admitted, still working her hands. "That's true. But –"

She sighed, the evening's glow leaving her complexion.

"Milo," she murmured. "I'm afraid I haven't been completely honest. At least, I mean, I didn't tell you all the . . . secrets."

Milo peered at her, alert. "What do you mean?"

Swallowing hard, Aunt Rosario took a deep breath. "Your first house," she began hesitantly, "it burned down, and you never found out why. Well . . . I did it."

Silence followed this confession, Milo staring at her, not knowing what to say. Not really knowing what to think, or even what to feel. All she knew at that moment was shock.

"I didn't mean to! It was an accident!" Aunt Rosario went on quickly and earnestly. "You and your parents were gone, and I needed something in the house. It was dark, so I lit a match, but I tripped over a rug. The match hit one of those ghastly doilies that your mother had all other the place, and I only just made it outside. I know I should have just turned on the lights or been happy with a non-Teflon pan, but the matches right were there in my pocket and I couldn't see the light switch in the dark, because your parents insisted that they be in the most inconvenient spots . . . and I'm just so sorry! . . . I really am!

"I just *couldn't* tell you guys. That's why I left too. I was so ashamed. But, now I've heard about all the horrible things you've been through, and it's all because of me! I feel so terrible! So awful. If I hadn't burned your poor house down, you probably wouldn't be here right now. We both wouldn't be. I'm so sorry! It's been plaguing me for years. I couldn't keep it in any longer. I had to tell you. Please say something!"

Milo couldn't, for she was in the middle of thinking. Thinking about her life, and how it had been ruined all because her house was destroyed by a fire. It is no exaggeration that one event can change the course of years to come. If she had found out how it had happened earlier, she most likely would have hurt the culprit. But now . . .

She thought about how it barely hurt to think of it now. That if her first house were still standing, she wouldn't be there on the island right then, with no Ajsha, no Squelch, no Simon. No Simon.

"So," she silently prayed. "*You knew.*"

At last Milo looked up at her aunt . . . and smiled. Joy bubbled up within her, and, laughing, she threw her arms around Aunt Rosario.

"Oh, thank you!" she cried joyfully. "Thank you! Thank you! Thank you! Thank you!"

"What?" Aunt Rosario gasped in bewilderment. "But – I . . . your life."

"To heck with my old life!" Milo said firmly, standing back. "Forget my old, sorry, pitiful excuse for a life. My life is wonderful now. I now can finally forget my past, although I always seem to be explaining it. Not anymore, though! I'm done, I'm through, I'm finished! Aunt Rosario, I want to thank you for burning my house down! 'Cause if you didn't, I wouldn't be here . . . and I wouldn't have Simon. And Heaven knows I need him."

Her aunt stood speechless, not able to believe her ears. Her burden was gone. She smiled. Having your burden lifted and taken away, never to bother you again, is simply a marvelous thing. It will no longer torture and strangle you. You feel like you can fly. And it's all called forgiveness.

"Thank you," she whispered, her pale eyes watery. "It's been a weight on my shoulders. The guilt . . . it might have been why, along with the heat, I've been ill for so long. Perhaps I'll get better now." She let out a tinkling laugh. "You really like Simon, don't you?"

Milo nodded, but then stared down at the floor. "Yeah," she said, feeling suddenly that she could confide in her aunt. "And I want to kiss him, but I can't."

"Why, in the name of all palm fronds, not?" she demanded, feisty once more. "You're married."

"I know, but –"

"Please!" Aunt Rosario cut in, taking her by the shoulders. "Listen to me, Milo, and listen well. Simon is a wonderful boy, who loves you very much from what I've seen. Don't let him run away, or drift away, like I did with Clarence. You'll regret it forever. Never hold back your affection. If you want to kiss him, do it! Whenever and wherever you want. You hear me?"

A new fire was kindling in Milo's eyes. "Yes," she whispered.

"Good! Now get out there and do it!" Her aunt motioned sharply to the door.

"Yes, ma'am!"

Back ramrod straight, Milo spun around and marched into the other room. Ajsha and Simon watched her enter, her expression purposeful. But, as she walked close up to Simon, her surge of courage failed her and she began to back away. Suddenly, she glimpsed her aunt's face in the doorway, sending her a fierce look. Milo immediately turned around. She put her arms about Simon and kissed him on his mouth. He almost fell over in surprise, but quickly embraced her back.

Milo's heart was beating a million times per second. She never felt more alive.

"Finally," Bob the Conscience mumbled.

Yes, finally. Finally Milo satisfied that longing. Finally she got a real kiss, with no biting. Finally Simon received back some affection he had so generously given. Finally Ajsha saw her parents kiss properly like real parents should, and she was thrilled. And finally Milo felt her life had been worth it.

26
Dangerously in Love

IT IS AMAZING how, in life, one thing can always lead to another. Sometimes an occurrence sets off a chain of things that eventually leads to a final result. For instance, and I *promise* this is the last time I'll bring it up, when Milo's first house burned down due to the carelessness of an aunt. That set off a whole series of events, ending with happiness.

Another example is when Simon sang "Hush" to Milo. That led to her ceasing to hate him and start liking him, which led to a kiss in the night, which led to her desire to kiss him again, and then finally doing so. And where would that kiss, and all the many kisses after it, lead? This was the question Bob the Conscience was toting around with him. He hadn't exactly approached Milo with it, but instead was waiting to see what would happen.

The night of the dinner at the mayor's house, Milo had walked home with Simon's arm wrapped around her. She was feeling less uncomfortable about human contact lately and was actually starting to enjoy it. She wondered why. When they got home, Milo helped put Ajsha to bed and for once kissed her goodnight. The two teens then retired to their bed, Milo, on impulse, kissing Simon's forehead before she lay down.

"What that for?" Simon asked, privately thinking that her aim had been too high.

"Just because I wanted to," Milo replied, snuggling down under the blanket.

From then on, Milo began to feel excited about sleeping close to Simon, instead of being terrified. She now slept facing towards him as opposed to always keeping her back to him. Whenever she went outside to write, she would sit near the beach to watch him work. Often, she would end up simply gazing contentedly at him, diary forgotten and happiness swirling about inside her. Soon the mere thought of Simon made her feel high and energized.

It didn't take long for her to become aware of how she was acting, and she tried to get a clamp on her emotions and focused them. Once she did, she stopped being so day-dreamy and felt more alert. She had a wiser, older feeling growing in her, yet it also felt like years had been lifted from her. It suddenly didn't matter what age she was, or was going to be. She felt, for some reason, that life now had a meaning, but that it didn't need one. It sounds quite confusing, but to Milo it was rather simple.

Not that she knew or could label what was happening to her. Her only explanation was that she had a crush on Simon. Which had been true at one point, but technically she had out lived the crush phase and had moved to what lay beyond. But how could she possibly know this? How could she tell? Well, she did know how to tell, but still needed to be told.

The change in her was very obvious and one day, during a visit to the Welch farm, Squelch and Salsa were collectively pondering about Milo's new attitude.

"Do you think it's Simon?" Salsa asked Squelch in private and in Galo, to be doubly safe. (They both knew about Milo's affinity for eavesdropping.)

"Maybe," Squelch answered thoughtfully. "That would explain a lot. Have you seen her when she's around him? It's almost like she's in love with him."

"Do you think she is?"

"That would surprise me very much," Squelch chuckled. "But, why not ask her?"

They approached her casually and began to chat, first sitting on the ground.

"You and Simon are sooo cute together," Squelch said, nonchalantly hugging her knees.

"Thanks," Milo replied lightheartedly. "Simon's cute, anyway."

"Not true," said Salsa, giving her a playful tap on the arm. "You are, too. But, you just like him, right? You're not in love with him or anything?"

"Oh, no!" she said confidently. "At least, I don't think so. I highly doubt it."

Squelch and Salsa glanced at each other suspiciously.

"Huh?" Squelch said. "Well, uh, what color's his hair?"

"Dirty-golden," Milo replied at once, carelessly, picking at grass blades.

"How tall is he?" asked Salsa, her eyebrows up.

"Five eight without shoes, five nine with shoes," Milo answered with no trouble.

"Does he smoke leaves?" Squelch questioned.

"What?" Milo said in alarm.

"Some boys do," she informed her gravely.

"Oh," Milo said, shuddering. "Well, he doesn't. His breath always smells milky."

"Milky?" Salsa repeated, exchanging a look with Squelch. "Well, what color are his eyes?"

"Light brown," Milo said, scratching her ear. "And in the light they have golden flecks in them."

"Um," Squelch murmured, thinking frantically. "Does he . . .

chew his nails?"

"Naw!" Milo said, waving the thought into the air. "His nails are very smooth and un-chewed. But when he's nervous he rakes his fingers through his hair."

"What makes his face special?" Salsa demanded, squinting hard at her.

"Huh?" Milo said, leaning away from her. "Um, his nose. It's kinda pointed, but only at the tip."

"I've never noticed that," Squelch remarked.

"I didn't really, either," Milo admitted. "Not till a little while ago. But I also didn't notice that one of his eye teeth is slightly longer than the other."

"Milo!" Salsa squawked suddenly, and Milo fell over. Salsa scrambled to her feet and stood over her. "You're in love!"

"What!?" Milo said, staring up at her, her red curls blazing in the sunlight.

"Have you not heard yourself?" she demanded. "You – you – once said that when people are in love they see the little things in their person that no one else sees. And you are noticing things about Simon that nobody sees but you. You can see without even looking for them."

Lying on her back, Milo stayed quiet, coming to the realization of this. She didn't know what to say. It hadn't occurred to her that she was doing that.

"Trust me," Salsa went on wisely. "I knew it when you said that about his teeth. To us, Simon's teeth are perfectly straight, all of them. He's renowned for it. You don't know how many times I have overheard girls gabbing about it. 'Straight teeth! Straight teeth! Whoo!' Only someone who sees everything about him as special can spot that one little detail. You. *You*, Milo!"

"She's right," Squelch joined in. "You should have heard yourself talk. You're in love."

"Oh, please!" Milo choked out, finally getting up. "You gals are crazy. I assure you I only *like* Simon. Sure, he's my boy, but I don't *love* him. At least," she added softly, "I don't think I do."

"You do," Salsa said, crouching and putting a hand on her arm.

"I don't!" Milo laughed. "Okay, so I happened to notice all kinds of little things about him, but I still haven't felt the achy feeling in my stomach and heart."

"No?" they asked.

"Not that I know of, and I think I'd know," she replied smartly. "Until then, I do not love him."

"Stubborn girl," Squelch muttered.

The next day was one of Milo's favorite types of days. It was very warm outside, but the sky was a solid iron gray and it was rather windy. A slight drizzle played down from the clouds, not enough to dampen, but at least make a thin film of moisture on everything. Milo was absolutely thrilled when she saw the weather. She stuck her head out of a window and inhaled deeply.

"How lovely," she marveled.

The wind carried the irresistible smell of rain and felt good because it was a warm wind. Milo stayed close to the house until after lunch, but then she ventured further, first inviting Ajsha to go with her.

"No thanks," she said, curled up on her bed with a book. "How can you like it out there?"

"It's wonderful outside," Milo insisted, and was off.

Outdoors, she quickly spotted Simon standing under a tree. She eagerly ran up to him.

"Hello, Simon," she said, halting about a foot from him.

"Hello," he answered, pulling her underneath the leaves with him.

"What?" she said, peering out at the landscape. "It's not raining."

"It will later," he said, turning her around and hugging her shoulders. "A day like this is a sign that a cold storm will come." He kissed her cheek. "Why are you outside?"

"I want to go for a walk," she replied, twisting around to see him. "Do you want to go with me?"

"Absolutely," he said gamely. "I'd go anywhere with you."

Milo smirked as she got an urge to kiss him and did so. "You crazy, honey," she accused.

He grinned and grasped her hand. "Only about you," he replied.

Together, they started a slow stroll towards town. Milo felt thoroughly happy. Between her favorite weather and her favorite human, there was little to complain about. She inhaled as much air as her lungs could hold and then let it gush back out.

"It's so nice out," she said dreamily.

"I'd agree," he murmured, squeezing her hand, "only it's dreary out."

"So what?" she said, shrugging. "Dreary's great. I love dreary, dearie."

After a bit they entered the village, and when they passed the Pitt house, a thought came to Milo.

"Why haven't you told Ajsha about Daniel?" she asked Simon.

He mulled for a second. "My wolf?" he said. She nodded and he shrugged. "I don't know. I guess I think it's kind of silly. You know . . . childhood toys."

"Is that why you left him in your room?" she whispered.

"Yeah," he said quietly, his gaze lingering on his old home. "I left behind everything that I didn't want to take to my new house. I showed him to you because . . . well, I really don't know why. I just wanted to. I do love Daniel, you know, but he's still one of my biggest secrets."

"But," Milo said softly, watching their plodding feet. "He's not your biggest. . . How come you never told me that one day you're going to inherit the fishing industry?"

Simon was silent for a minute, also interested in their feet. "Who told you that?" he finally said.

"Ajsha," Milo answered, looking up. He was frowning. "I think

I know why you didn't tell me. You didn't want me to like you just because you were going to be rich someday."

He nodded honestly. "But, I shouldn't have worried," he said with a ghost of a smile. "You didn't even like me. You hated me."

"All in the past," Milo assured him with a laugh, not believing how funny it seemed now."

"Good," he said, kissing her head. "Anyway, a few years ago a couple of girls once pretended to be interested in me because they thought I had money. When they found out I didn't have any personally, they both yelled at me and left. That really scared and hurt me, though I've never told anyone."

Her heart breaking, Milo put an arm around his shoulders. "Don't worry," she told him firmly. "No girl will ever hurt you again. I like you now, and will defend you from gold diggers. Me? I don't really like money. I need it, but don't like it. It causes too many problems."

Grinning, Simon draped an arm over her shoulder, but as he looked ahead, his face went blank. Confused, Milo followed his stare to see Mayor Em-I storming towards them, his impressive beard being blown behind him.

"Oh, no," she squeaked. "He knows."

"Oh, man," Simon said. In one swift motion he grabbed her shoulders and looked into her eyes. "Listen, Milo," he said sharply. "Remember, I love you and Ajsha loves you and we'll have the most darn expensive funeral for you."

"What?" she whispered, eyes wide as saucers.

The Mayor stopped in front of them and towered in all his furious, bushy splendor. Eyes blazing, he glared at the pair of them, Milo feeling like a bug next to a woodpecker. The Mayor began to speak in a terrible, livid voice.

Simon put a protective arm around his stiff wife. "The Mayor said," he translated shakily, "'I've been informed that my wife is your aunt, Mrs. Swallow. How fascinating!'"

Anybody who had braved the outdoors that day started to gather near the scene, exchanging hushed observations in Galo. To answer, all Milo could do was nod and mumble something that sounded like, "Tibish." The Mayor tugged at his beard in frustration.

"He is saying, 'This means, unfortunately, that I'm your uncle. Do you know what that means?'"

Milo swallowed. "Death?" she wheezed.

Simon thought it best not to relay this to the Mayor. Besides, the man was still talking. "'That means, what you do reflects upon me. And my wife. Since there is nothing that can change the marriage, I expect full perfection from you.'"

Perhaps it was the blatant rudeness of this statement, but Milo suddenly got a jolt of courage and said, "Simon, tell him this: You mean the laws? Fine. I'm game with all that. But don't expect me to be perfect."

"'You'll have to be,'" Simon translated.

"But I can't be," Milo argued.

"'Then at least obey the laws,'" Simon interpreted, the mayor snorting in tired exasperation.

"I do," Milo insisted.

"'Since when?'"

She rolled her eyes. "Since now!" she yelled at him.

Without giving him any kind of warning, she grabbed Simon by the shoulders, tipped him low, and kissed him.

A stunned hush fell over the crowd, but eventually they began to cheer and whistle. After kissing for what felt like an appropriately zealous amount, Milo pulled her face away to see Simon's overwhelmed expression. He grinned stupidly up at her as the Mayor stared in shock. She helped Simon stand up, though he still swayed a little, and the Mayor gruffly cleared his throat. The cheering stopped. There was moment of indecision, similar to looking over the edge of a cliff and wondering how much the landing would hurt.

Seconds ticked by. Milo and the Mayor studied each other neither one looking away. The throng had gone from applause to holding its breath. Finally, he stuck out his hand. Milo looked from it to his face and he nodded. She laughed in delight (and a *wee* bit of triumph) and shook the hand. Oh, how sweet is the taste of peace! And oh, how happy Milo was as she danced all the way home on that dreary day.

The beloved dreariness didn't last, however, and by the next day the island was back to its normal sunny. But the day after that it was cloudy out again. Milo the Intrepid still went out into the forest to harvest any ripe fruit. Ajsha watched warily as she marched outside and into the trees. Immediately, Milo noticed that the air was rather cold, but she continued on, undaunted. Confidence spurring her onward, she trod deeper into the jungle. She didn't find much fruit and had to keep searching.

After a while she came to unknown territory. Still needing fruit, she shrugged and entered it. A few minutes later, it started to rain. Just as Simon had predicted, it was icy cold. It pattered all around her on the leaves and flowers, making everything glisten.

"Oh, great," Milo growled. "Precisely what I need. Do you believe this, Bob?"

"Not really," he admitted. "This is a tropical island. One really doesn't expect rain as cold as this. You had better go home."

"Brilliant idea," she said, edging around a large, trickling leaf. "But where would home be?"

"You're lost?" he asked harshly.

"No. I just have no clue where I am."

"Huh," he said sternly. "I wouldn't classify that as good."

"Stop weeping," she snapped. "I'll find my way."

Setting a brisk pace, she set off to do so. After a good while, it became clear that her way was not going to be easy to locate.

"Isn't it terribly funny," she said, twirling slowly, "how everything here looks the same?"

"It's hysterical," Bob the Conscience said scathingly. "You shouldn't have wandered so far."

"I'll remember that next time," she muttered, shivering. "But right now what matters is getting home. If I stay out here much longer, I'll catch a cold."

"Really? The incredible, steel-immune system Milo? Sick?"

"Shut up," she ordered. "It could happen, and probably will if I don't find a way out."

So, onward she went, not finding one. The surroundings did look the same, and it was annoying Milo. All the tall trees and undergrowth that grew up to her hips, the drooping vines and various lichen and moss, the toadstools that grew on the trees, and the many muddy puddles all looked alike. After hours of wandering aimlessly through it all, thoroughly sodden and freezing, Milo decided to sit down. She was exhausted and feeling ill. Her legs burned from walking and her arms ached from holding the basket. She had a headache, felt stiff, and was so cold that her brain was becoming numb.

"Don't sit!" Bob the Conscience cried. "Do *not* sit! You'll fall asleep and then who knows what will happen to you."

"I can't get up," Milo replied lethargically. "I'm too tired."

He kept yelling at her, attempting to get her moving, but to no avail. She sat, leaning back against a gnarled tree trunk and waiting for help, which she hoped would come soon. Darkness flew over her, and she fell into a fitful sleep, the rain pattering in her ear like gunfire. She awoke in the early morning to hearing her name being called. The rain had ceased, weak, watery sunshine filtering down through the leaves. Her forehead was on fire and her throat was tight and sore. She wasn't able to breath through her nose and her head was throbbing. Again, she heard her name and made a feeble attempt to answer. Her heavy, raw eyes searched for the caller. A blurry figure appeared amid the trees and started shouting anxiously. It began to run towards Milo. Suddenly the fog around it vanished, and it was Simon leaning over her.

"Milo!" he whispered, his eyes huge and damp.

"Oh, Simon!" she rasped softly. Her heart started beating and her stomach began to flutter.

"Oh, Milo," Simon said, squatting down to feel her forehead. "You're so sick. You need to go home."

"Simon," she whispered feverishly, his form swimming before her. "I'm so sorry."

Gently, but with a definite sense of urgency, he put an arm behind her back and under her legs. Carefully, he picked her up out of the mud.

"I'm sorry," Milo told him, her head lolling against his shoulder.

"Shhh," he answered, tightening his grip. "It'll be okay. Don't worry. I'll take care of you."

"I'm sorry," she said again, then lost consciousness.

When she reawakened, a cold cloth pressed to her forehead. She was lying in her own bed, covered up to her chin. Her head was still very hot, but it no longer hurt. Blinking the room in to focus, she found that she could actually think and was less tired, but still felt delirious. She also felt boiled, and kicked off her covers. Ajsha materialized from nowhere.

"Oh, Mother!" she said, rushing to her side. "Thank Heaven you're awake. How do you feel?"

"My head –" Milo mumbled, her tongue feeling fuzzy. "It's so hot."

"Yes, you have a fever," Ajsha said, readjusting the cloth. "Father is about to go get the doctor."

"No!" Milo shouted, her voice grating. "No, Ajsha! Don't let him leave. I need him. Go tell him to come here, and you'll go get the doctor. Please go, Ajsha! Please bring him here."

For a moment, the child simply gazed fondly down at her. "Of course," she said and left.

Sighing, Milo lay back. In a moment Simon came in, and Milo's heart began to ache in that wonderful way. Her aching eyes widened. As she looked at Simon, poor, exhausted, haggard looking Simon, she realized at once that it was true.

"So," she whispered in her scratchy voice. "It's true. I don't believe it! But . . . no, I do. It's true. Incredible! Unbelievable. But true. Oh, so true!"

"Oh, hello," Simon said sympathetically, seeing her big, blood-shot eyes staring up at him through her soggy tangle of brown hair.

"Simon!" Milo cried, sitting up and instantly feeling nauseated. "I'm so sorry! You must have been super worried. Please forgive me."

"Hush, baby," Simon said softly, gently pushing her down and fixing the covers.

"Simon!" Milo said, grabbing his wrist with her deathly pale and rather claw-like hand. "I love you!"

Simon stared at her. "Milo, you're not going to die," he said reassuringly, prying off her fingers.

"No! Listen. I love you. I'm in love with you. Don't you understand? Don't you?" Milo asked recklessly. "Don't you believe me?"

Still staring at her, Simon began to inhale fast. He licked his lips and swallowed.

"Milo," he said as calmly as he could. "You're ill and –"

"No!" she cut in, sweat pouring off her face and neck. "It's not the fever talking. It's me! Me! I'm talking! I love you. Please, boy! Tell me you believe me!"

Simon shook his head, fighting back tears. Leaving the bedside, he paced the length of the room before coming back. He smiled. "Are you sure?"

"Yes!" she gasped. "Oh, yes!"

She was letting the tears come down her face, which was bright, cranberry red with fever.

"How much?" Simon asked with some difficulty, not quite sure what he was saying. "How?"

"Dangerously!" Milo cried after a minute. "I'm dangerously in love with you. Do you believe me?"

Simon took a second to breathe, raking his fingers through his hair. At last, he nodded. "Yes!" he said, choking up. "Yes, I do."

Milo began to cry full force, which goes to show that even extremely happy events need a bit of sobbing. Sitting on the edge of the bed, Simon held her close to him. The side of Milo's head was pressed up against his chest, and the side of Simon's face rested on top of her head. Through her crying, Milo suddenly heard a soft thumping sound and realized it was Simon's heartbeat. His heart was beating quite fast, like hers.

Chuckling softly, Milo suddenly felt dizzy and moaned. Simon gently laid her back down on the pillow and smiled lovingly at her.

"When did you start?" he asked, trailing the tips of his fingers along her jaw line.

"Start what?" she asked deliriously, wishing that he would stop flitting around.

"Loving me?"

"Oh," she said. "Well, I suppose I started a while ago, but I just realized it about five minutes ago. Thank you so much for taking care of me. You're always saving my life."

"I couldn't let anyone else do it," he murmured, tracing the outline of her lips. "You're mine to save. You still need me, Milo. And I still need you."

He sat on the end of the bed and waited with her until the doctor arrived. There were several doctors on the island, due to the various people who crashed there. This one was a tall, thin man with white hair and glasses, who looked like he had been hiding out in a cave most of his adult life. He looked Milo over and took her temperature with well-preserved, old timey thermometer. After examining her, he spoke to Simon, who eventually nodded. The doctor gave Milo a pill and Simon paid him a mor. Milo watched him go, wondering if he had a hermit wife.

"The pill costs fifty dollars?" she said.

Nodding, Simon said, "And the visit and all. The pills we have are from the planes that crash here, so we are limited. We have to rely on plants and herbs for the rest. But, don't worry. If it helps you, then it's worth it."

"I had no idea," Milo said dramatically, clutching her fiery brow. "Have no fears, Simon. I won't need any more pills. I can heal myself from here."

"Milo," Simon said reasonably. "You have a serious cold and fever of 100. You'll need more."

"No, I won't!" she insisted stubbornly. "Just to break the fever, but after that no more!"

"But –"

"No! I'll hear no more of it!" she declared, holding up a wobbly hand.

Simon sighed, but then smiled. "But what if something happened and I lost you?" he whispered.

Milo gasped, appalled. "How can you even suggest something like that? What kind of thoughts are going through your mind? Don't upset me with such ideas, Simon."

Still grinning, he went over to her. "Sorry," he apologized and kissed her sweaty forehead. "But please get better."

She confidently smiled and shut her eyes. "I will," she promised.

And she tried. The pills did help to break the fever, and, after some persuading, Simon agreed to let Milo do the rest. She was bed stricken for several days, forcing Simon to sleep elsewhere or else catch her cold and be bed stricken as well. Milo found it harder to sleep at night without her man by her side. He often slipped into her dreams.

One day, while Milo was lying alone in her room, Caleb Scumm's tan, impish face appeared in the window. He jumped through, into the room. Before Milo could yell, he shushed her and produced from behind his back a bouquet of puffy foxtail ferns. Victoriously, he handed them to her. She stared at them.

"I have no clue what to say," she told him honestly. "I suppose I should say, 'It's the thought that counts', only it's obvious that you didn't put a lot of thought into this. Well, I guess this is what constitutes as you trying, so . . . Thank you."

Caleb frowned. That was the second time he had heard her say "Thank You" to him. He knew what it meant from Ajsha. He had not intended on a "Thank You". He didn't want a "Thank You". That's why he had got her ferns. Groaning, he jumped back out the window. Milo stared after him.

"Okay," she muttered. "I'll see you later then."

Caleb wasn't the only one to visit her. Squelch also came by to wish her a speedy recovery. "Here you are," she said cheerfully the following Tuesday, giving her a large spray of flowers.

"Thanks, precious," Milo said thickly, her nose congested. Squelch had brought them in a clay vase, made by her mother, and she placed it on the little bedside table.

"Who gave you the ferns?" she asked, noting the furry bouquet already on the table.

"Oh, Caleb Scumm," Milo muttered, blowing her nose. "He is one strange boy."

"Hmm," Squelch said, eyeing the ferns disdainfully and sitting at the end of the bed. "Speaking of strange boys, have you seen Otto Gauls lately?"

"You mean your senile neighbor? The one Salsa hangs out with?"

"Yeah," she said, smirking. "They are so cute together. A couple of years from now, I'm hearing wedding bells."

"Why would you be hearing those, Squelch?" Milo asked.

"Why do you think? Isn't it obvious?"

"No. We're making it up to amuse ourselves."

"Maybe," Squelch admitted though hardly seemed ashamed. "So what?"

Milo shook her head. "As he said, 'Why does everyone have to be in love with each other? Why can't we all just be friends?'"

After contemplating this quote for a moment, Squelch nodded in agreement. "You're right. Or, he's right. Who said that?"

"I forget. I think his name started with M. But he was quite wise. I think. But, listen, you and Salsa were right."

"About what?" Squelch asked absentmindedly, straightening Milo's sheets.

"Me," Milo said. "I am in love."

Squelch stared open-mouthed at her. "Get out!" she cried, smiling. "No way! Simon? The boy you used to despise?"

Sighing, Milo gazed into the distance, starry-eyed. "Yes," she murmured, "that boy. He changed my mind. I never thought it would happen, but . . . he kind of wore me down. He's kind, sweet, strong . . . and *hot*. And, goodness help me, I love him."

Her friend smiled. "That's so great," she said, patting her leg. "I'm so happy for you. Does he know?"

"Oh, he knows! He's the first one I told. I'd tell Ajsha, only I every time I see her she's either running around the room or telling me not to talk."

"What about her? Do you love her?" Squelch asked.

This inquiry made Milo stop and think for a moment. "I've recently applied a saying to my life," she finally said. "William Shakespeare, I believe. 'Love all, trust few.' So . . . yeah. I guess you could say I love her."

"But don't trust her?"

"Oh, no, I trust her! I trust her very much. Love her very much. I just haven't told her yet."

"Maybe you should," Squelch suggested.

"Maybe I will!" Milo said, liking the idea.

"Great!" Squelch said, leaping to her feet. "I'll go get her."

"No! Wait —"

But she didn't. Milo sagged onto her pillow. She came back momentarily, Ajsha by her side.

"Milo has something to tell you," Squelch informed her, shooting Milo an encouraging look.

"I already know," Ajsha told Milo, beaming.

Milo paled. "I –You do? How?"

"Father," she replied happily. "He's been telling his friends, his parents, family . . . people he sees on the street. 'My wife loves me!' he shouts."

"Ohoo," Milo said, choosing to disregard this. "Great. Well –"

"And I think it's wonderful!" Ajsha continued. "I'm so happy for you! I knew you'd start loving him sooner or later. Simon's so amazing."

"Unreal, but listen," Milo said quickly, "there's something else I need to tell you."

"What?" Ajsha asked, her giddiness diminishing. Milo inhaled deeply.

"It's about you, child," she said softly, extending a hand to her. "At night, when we say goodnight, you tell me that you love me. Well . . . I think I can say it back now."

It took Ajsha a minute to fully digest what had just been said to her. It seemed too good to be true. Had all of her long, hard work really just paid off? Had Milo been cured? Staring at her, so thin and sick on the bed, holding out an imploring hand, it suddenly occurred to Ajsha that curing Milo completely might be impossible. But . . . maybe she could be cured just enough.

With that realization, Ajsha's eyes lit up. "Really? Oh, really, Mother?" she whispered.

"It's Milo," Milo said, clutching her little hand, "and yes."

"Truly?"

"Yes. Dangerously, my dear. I dangerously love you."

"That's what Father said. He said you told him that you are dangerously in love with him."

"I am," Milo confirmed, feeling phlegm in her throat and

coughed. "I'm dangerously in love with him, and I dangerously love you."

"You're not in love with me?" Ajsha inquired.

"Can't say I am. Sorry," Milo said, wondering if you were supposed to fall in love with children.

"That's all right. Father's in love with me," Ajsha said, smiling. "He told me so. He said the moment he laid eyes on me, he fell in love."

"Awww. He's so sweet," Milo said fondly. "Hey, how'd you two meet anyways?"

"Yeah?" Squelch said. She was now sitting on Simon's portion of the bed.

"Well," Ajsha began, hopping onto the bed. "When my plane crashed, he was helping the rescue squad. He was pretty young, but everyone liked him and knew he was trustworthy, so they let him. They were recovering all the orphans, and thought they had found them all. But Father suddenly heard crying inside the wreck. He didn't listen to the men and went in. He followed the crying till he discovered me behind a seat. That's when he fell in love with me. He said that he brought me back to the other infants, only there were so many of us that there weren't enough helpers to take care of us all. So Father volunteered to help take care of me. They even let him name me. He told me he thought of the name Ajsha while he was holding me. We've been friends ever since. He always came to the orphanage after school, and would take me on walks."

"Cool," Milo commented with a smile. "He never told me that story. You were right when you said that you've been friends for a long time."

"Yes," Ajsha said, "and he promised to marry the perfect girl and adopt me. Simon's good at promises. I always knew he wouldn't let me down."

"I ain't perfect," Milo scoffed, feeling far from it at the moment.

"You are to Father," Ajsha pointed out. "Just because you are you,

you are perfect to him. He loves everything about you. He never takes the ring you gave him off."

"I've noticed. Does he know what it means?"

"I do not think so. Does it mean something?"

"Yeah," Milo said. "There are symbols engraved onto the side, an eye, a heart, and a U. The eye means 'I', the heart means 'love', and the U means 'you'. 'I love you'."

"Oh!" said Squelch. "Cool. And you actually mean it now."

"Yeah," Milo had to admit. "Oh, hi!"

Ajsha and Squelch turned their heads to see Simon standing in the doorway.

"Hi," he said, to her and the rest. "Doing better?"

"Much, thank you," Squelch said graciously, patting her hair. Simon stared at her for a moment before pointing wordlessly to Milo, who was laughing.

"Of course," Milo answered, and promptly sneezed. Wiping her streaming eyes, she happened to notice the leather string around his neck. "Have you found a charm for your necklace yet?"

He grinned slyly. "Worry not. I will."

Ajsha scrambled off the bed and ran up to him, hopping excitedly.

"Guess what, Father!" she said, grabbing his hands.

"What?"

"Mother loves me!"

"Actually," Milo said loudly, blowing her nose again. "Milo loves you."

"Really?" Simon inquired, looking over at her.

"Yeah," Milo sighed. "I love her, I love Squelch, here." She winked at her. Squelch made a kissy sound in return. "I love Salsa," Milo went on. "Mrs. Lanslo, Soldier, Chaos, Hattie, the Pitts, though, oh my word, I *hate* them! My aunt, her husband. I even love Randolf Fittler and Tambry Ethlins. I'm a lover that can't be stopped."

"What about Caleb?" Simon asked shrewdly.

She paused. "I'm stopping at him. But, Simon."

She held out her hand. He came and took it, stoking her knuckles with his thumb.

"I'm dangerously in love with you, honey," she whispered, every single word tasting like the gospel truth.

He, and the girls, smiled. "And I'm dangerously in love with you, Milo," he whispered.

"Awwwwww," Squelch and Ajsha sighed in unison.

It was quite a nice little scene in that sick room that day. Don't think that Milo was lying, for she wasn't. She was, in fact, in love with Simon. Or, that is, dangerously in love with him, which seems appropriate, considering that Milo rarely invested in anything that was safe.

She knew it was true because she had all the correct symptoms and because she had tried to deny it at first. That's what love does to you. It creeps up on you and grabs you when you're trying to run away. If you're lucky, it won't let you go. Sometimes, you struggle and fight to break free of love, for sometimes love can hurt, but it doesn't let you go. That's when you know. Like Milo, that's when you know that you are dangerously in love with someone.

27
Courage of the Mad Female

THE WORD "MAD" can mean two things. The first definition is the one everybody is most familiar with: Anger. Mad can indeed mean angry, but it can also mean something else. The word Mad can imply that someone or something is crazy or insane. For example, when they say "Mad cow disease," they do not mean, "Angry cow disease". They mean, "Crazy cow disease."

When a person is mad, or crazy, they are prone to do things that seem out of the question. Dangerous, frightening, intimidating things. Things that rational, sound-minded people don't do. Milo was a mad person, or, to be precise, a mad female. But she wasn't alone. There are plenty of other wonderful, whimsical, wonky mad females in the world. One of them is writing this book, and another one was on the island as well.

As you may recall, Milo had fallen dangerously in love with Simon, and he was positively thrilled about it. All those long months of rejection and gut-grinding misery had miraculously become a thing of the past. The patience and determination that he had put forth, and had questioned more than once, finally rewarded him.

As soon as she had conquered her epic cold, they started spending even more time together. In the morning, Simon would usually get up at five thirty (give or take, considering he didn't have an alarm clock) to go to work. He would kiss Milo's forehead, which she had given him permission to do, grab a bite of breakfast, and leave. When he returned home with Ajsha at lunchtime, Milo would greet him at the door with a hug. She would also hug Ajsha, of course, but she didn't give her the type of kiss that she gave Simon.

At night, Milo slowly agreed to let Simon lovingly wrap his arms around her while he sang to her. She may have been in love, but that didn't erase the fact that she was a complicated teenager and still getting used to the whole holding concept. Simon received a thrill each night when Milo would tell him good night and that she loved him.

Milo was in equal rapture with her recently acknowledged love. Taking her aunt's advice, she kissed Simon any time or place she wanted to: At home, in town, in front of others. The only people she didn't smooch him in front of was his parents. For some reason, she felt afraid to kiss him in front of them. Not that they didn't hear about it from their neighbors and acquaintances. The fact that the Milo girl had gone from a cold-hearted maverick to an ardent kisser didn't escape their notice. However, this proved to be a vital step to healing her relationship with the Pitts. It seemed that Luna and Lennon were willing to forget all the unkind words she had swapped with them in light of her falling in love with their son. At least, Milo could only assume that's what all the mysteriously appearing baskets of muffins meant.

Now that Milo and Simon were finally united in love, they started to unite in parenthood. One night, a horrible thunderstorm hit the island. There hadn't been many thunderstorms since Milo had arrived, mostly just rain showers, but this one made up for them all. The lightning was fantastically bright, vividly illuminating every object under the night sky, and the thunder was loud enough to wake the sleeping dead. It certainly woke the Swallows.

Milo and Simon were awoken both by the thunder and a piercing scream that came from Ajsha. Ajsha wasn't extremely different from other children her age, though that could be debated, and she was dreadfully afraid of thunder and lightning. Out of an inner childhood instinct, she came running into her parent's bedroom.

She halted abruptly beside the bed, her parents peering at her groggily through the darkness. Her instincts now failing her, Ajsha wasn't sure what came next. She was about to tell them "Help!", but thought it might be a little too silly. Nevertheless, she made her point when another thunder clap shook the walls, and she produced a sound that could have shattered glass.

"Child!" Milo cried out, not sure which noise gave her more of a heart attack.

"Come here," Simon said, lifting up the blanket.

Ajsha didn't need a second invitation. She was already scrambling onto the bed, heedless of whomever she might be kicking. She wedged herself in between them, and they tucked the covers in around her.

"Dang, child!" Milo said, rubbing her ears. "I didn't know you were afraid of thunderstorms."

Ajsha was panting hard by then, the blanket up to her nose, her eyes the size of quarters, or bruns. "It's so loud," she whispered.

"Don't worry, little cutie," Simon told her comfortingly, wrapping an arm around her. "You're here with us. I won't let anything harm you."

She didn't look at him, but did nod. The lightning flashed across the sky, lighting up the window, and she whimpered shrilly, huddling closer. Simon smiled compassionately and kissed her head. Milo patted her tightly clenched, tiny fist.

"Don't worry, sweetie," Milo crooned. "If this storm even tries to hurt you, I'll beat it to a twitching lump."

Ajsha looked up at her in awe, her protruding eyes gleaming like orbs in the dark. "You must be mad not to be afraid of such a noise," she said, voice muffled. "Where do you get your courage?"

Milo chuckled, flattered. "Like you said. I'm mad."

Simon reached over and gave her ponytail a tug.

"Try to fall asleep, Ajsha," he said, giving her another kiss.

Nodding slowly, she lay down. Milo and Simon readjusted their pillows to comfort before collapsing onto them.

"Goodnight, Ajsha," Milo said, giving her a vague pat on what turned out to be her face.

"Goodnight," she replied, crinkling her nose as Milo hit it. "I'm sorry that I'm scared of thunder."

"Don't be sorry," Simon said, drawing her close like a teddy bear. "It's okay. Go to sleep."

"Will you sing to me?" she whispered.

"Of course."

"In Galo?" she asked shyly.

Milo grinned. "Go ahead," she told him. "I don't mind."

And so he did, and like magic, in spite of the frequent flashes and crashes, Ajsha fell asleep.

Two days later, Milo went into the kitchen to make the daily breakfast and found a note from Simon on the counter. The scrawl was barely legible, since Simon didn't get to practice writing in English nearly as much as he got to practice speaking it.

Meet me at the beach at ten thirty.

Love, Simon.

Milo's eyebrows went up as soon as she was able to decipher the message. What in the world did he want? She was obedient, as well as curious, and at ten thirty she plodded down to the beach. She spotted Simon unloading a net of fish from his boat, which he had dragged out onto the dark, wet sand. All the fishing boats at the beach looked like wide rowboats made from the strange bamboo-ish wood, and had two tall, narrow poles sticking up on each side. Stretched between the poles was a sail, many of them patched, and each had a rudder in the back to steer. Milo waited until he had loaded the fish into an awaiting cart before approaching him.

"Hey," she said, gamboling up to him. "You wanted me, I'm here. What's up?"

He grinned, grabbed her by the waist, and kissed her. "I have a surprise."

"Your lips are salty," she informed him, tasting her own.

"Thank you. It's called ocean lipstick. Now, come on."

Without further explanation, he took her hand and started to pull her towards the water.

"Wait!" she yelped, prodding at his grasp. "We're not swimming, are we?"

"No," Simon replied, as if that she were being silly. "I'm taking you in the boat with me."

"What?" she gasped, her stomach churning icily. "No way, boy!" she shrieked, writhing in his grip. "What if I fall out?"

"You won't," he said reassuringly, patting her upper arm. "I just want you to be there. You don't have to do anything. You'll be safe. I promise."

It took some persuasion, and some coaxing, and some pleading, but, by some miracle, he did get her into the boat and managed to shove off without her leaping out. The choppy waves pulled them out to the sea, Simon stringing up the sail to catch the wind. Milo clung to the wobbling sides of the little boat and simply refused to look over. Instead, she raptly observed the sky, which was its normal breathtaking blue. After ten minutes had gone by without them capsizing, she decided it was okay to calm down and took deep breaths of briny air.

When they were quite far out, the beach a white line capped by green, Simon dropped his rock and rope anchor and let the net fall over the side.

"I'll be back in a few minutes," he told Milo. She gave him a wordless thumbs-up.

He hopped over the side into the water, shaking the boat a bit. Milo rigidly peered over the edge, down at the exceptionally clear water, and saw his golden form gliding smoothly about, herding fish.

Every now and then he would come up for air, and once in a while get back into the boat to sail to a different spot. Each time, Milo would then watch him twist and twirl under the water like a long-limbed dolphin. She herself had barely moved, preferring to remain stationary at the bottom of the boat. After a one particular shift in location, Milo was watching Simon drive the fish into his net, when something on the surface caught her eye. Squinting, she saw it was a gray triangle, traveling at a very fast rate. Milo knew at once what it was and grew horrified.

"Oh, my word!" she whispered, gripping the edge of the boat. "Simon. Simon!" she screamed. "Simon, there's a shark heading towards you! Simon!! Simon!!"

But he couldn't hear her. Being underwater stifled his hearing, even though they all claim it's such a great conductor of sound. Milo had never been more frightened in all her life. Never. She looked from the shark, to Simon, to the water. The distance between the shark and the boy was rapidly decreasing. She knew that if Simon didn't find out at once he wouldn't make it. He wouldn't come back up for air until he needed it, which could always take a while.

Milo was frozen, too scared to move, terrified that in the next minute she would see her husband be mauled to death in a bloody struggle with the shark. She knew what she had to do if she wanted to save her man, though the mere thought made her heart clang. Saying a quick prayer and squeezing her eyes shut, she jumped into the water.

She swam as fast as she could up to Simon, her mind racing and jeans weighing her down. She couldn't believe that she just jumped into shark infested water of her own free will. But there she was, surrounded by endless, fathomless blue, an oblong gray shape swiftly approaching, and she thought she must be mad. Coming to a stop and hovering underwater, she tapped Simon's arm. Whirling around, he looked surprised to see her. She pointed to the surface and they kicked upward.

"Milo," Simon gasped at the top.

"Simon!" she screeched, bopping down so low that water got in her mouth. "A shark!"

Simon became alert at once and swished around to see the gray triangle heading towards him. He ducked back under, which was the opposite of what Milo thought should be done. He waited, suspended in the water, and just as the shark reached him, he took aim and punched its nose. It got a kind of dazed look, as if it couldn't believe someone had dared. Simon, at the height of impudence, did it three more times. It then turned around and swam away, tail swishing in what might have been shark indignation. If Milo hadn't warned Simon, he certainly wouldn't have noticed the shark until it was too late. He knew that. He went back up to the surface and bobbed, panting with fright.

"Milo," he began, treading at the water, then saw her shivering. Forgetting his own panic, he quickly helped her climb back into the boat. Simon began to shout to the other boats, and they headed for the shark. He sighed and faced Milo, who was trembling in the belly of the boat.

"What happened?" she asked hoarsely, feeling unbearably cold despite the warmth of the water.

"I think you just saved my life," he said soberly, squatting. "I can't believe you did that for me."

"Why not?" she asked, quaking violently.

He shook his head in bafflement. "The water," he whispered. "The shark. To brave two things at once . . . That's so incredible, Milo. Thank you so much."

Sitting up, she hugged him with her stick-like arms, pressing her face into his chest. "I love you," she whispered, her throat clogging.

"I love you, too," he said, enveloping her with his arms, trying to warm her. "I'll never forget this, I promise. Come on. Don't cry."

But she was. Glistening tears were running unabashedly down her cheeks. "I can't help it," she choked. "I was so scared. But . . . you're okay, so everything's fine."

"Yes," he said, wiping her tears away with his thumbs. He kissed her lips then her forehead, drawing her hair behind her ears. "Come. We have to help them."

"With what?" Milo asked, much more composed.

"The shark. We're capturing it."

"You're joking!" Milo said faintly, feeling sick. "For what?"

"Well," he replied reluctantly, stroking her arms. "To kill. We can't have a shark in our fishing waters. We'd let it go if it was by the cliffs, but they have been showing up way too often here. It's not just the fish we're worrying about now. And, there's another reason."

He steered them to the cluster of boats grouped a ways off on the water, Milo staring warily. The other fisherboys had caught the great fish up in their nets and were struggling to control it.

Finally, as Simon reached them, they managed to haul it into one of the larger boats. They all started cheering as the huge thing thrashed around wildly, probably wishing that sharks had the ability to roar. Simon, standing shakily in his own boat, called for quiet and jabbered in Galo, telling them all what Milo had done. Every tanned, damp face stared at her in wonder. Staring back, Milo wondered whether their shock was because she was a girl or she because she had just confirmed how big a nutcase she was.

Once all the boys had recovered, they gathered around the furious shark and wrestled to get him into an upright position. Twenty boys holding him down, ten more opened his massive mouth to reveal rows upon rows of serrated teeth. Everyone started to gibber to Simon and chant his name. He nodded somberly and stepped into the boat with the shark.

"Simon?" Milo said, pulling herself to the bow. "What're you doing?"

"I'm going to pull a tooth out," he said, hoping his calmness would reassure her. It didn't.

"What?!" she shouted. "No, you're not! You'll get your hand bitten off!"

"No. They're holding him tight."

Milo looked at the ten strong boys holding the mouth open, and saw that the shark was losing energy from being out of the water. Even so, she felt extraordinarily nervous about it. She knew that the moment Simon pulled on a tooth the shark would flail, trying to break free so it could bite her husband's arm off. And Milo was so fond of his arms.

But Simon was perfectly confident, and, as Milo shivered with dread, thinking that this was a massive waste of her sacrifice, he picked out a nice large tooth and got a firm hold on it. The shark squirmed a little, but the boys held strong. Slowly, tensing with the effort, Simon started to twist the tooth. It made that stomach-churning sound that a tooth makes when it's being ripped away from flesh. The shark made a desperate attempt to break free, its blank, black eyes not able to see what was going on. Thankfully, he didn't, and Simon was able to yank the tooth out.

He held it up high, and all the boys cheered as he stepped back into his own boat with his prize. The rest of the boys took turns extracting teeth from the shark's mouth, the shark probably wondering why they couldn't just let it die with dignity. The boys who were afraid to declared that they would wait until it was dead. Simon sat in his small vessel, carefully polishing his tooth on his shorts. Milo was staring at him, her eyes narrowed. He saw her.

"What?" he asked innocently.

"What on Earth do you need that tooth so bad for that it was worth risking a body part?"

He grinned and pointed at the leather string around his neck. "A charm," he replied.

Milo's eyes lit up. "Oh," she said, pleased, though from the activity surrounding the shark, she figured it was also an island boy thing.

They finished with the fishing, depositing the catch onto one of the many carts, and went home. While Milo made lunch, Simon wound a length of wire around the crown of the tooth, made a loop at the top, and slid the leather string through. After he retied the necklace about his throat, he grinned at Milo.

"The necklace from you, the charm from me," he said to her. She smiled and reached out to finger it. The edges nicked her skin.

Several days later, they were heading into town to pick up Ajsha from school. Simon had finished work early, and they decided to surprise her. As they drew near the village, they heard a huge commotion. It was similar to that of a few days ago, when the boys had dragged the shark to the butchery, virtually toothless, and a bidding war had started. Today, however, people were yelling wildly, running about, and congregating near the schoolhouse. Milo and Simon broke into a canter, arriving in time to see four men dressed in light gray attempting to get a hold of Hattie Knocker.

"Release me!" she shrieked, her caftan billowing as she flailed her arms. "Let me go, you aliens!"

Milo guiltily restrained herself from laughing, and scanned the scene to see what Hattie had been doing. She spotted a hole in the ground by the wall of the school, an enormous fish inside it. A mangled bush lay next to it, and Hattie had been sticking the branches into the fish. A flint and stone sat by the hole, and Milo figured that Hattie had planned to light the leaves on the branches on fire. But she didn't have any idea why. She turned to Simon, who was talking to a man.

"What happened?" she asked him when he was done.

"Apparently, she stole a fish from the butchery and a bush from someone's garden," he answered.

"What's she using them for?" asked Milo, craning her neck for a better view.

"No one really knows. They can't understand her, so they called in Mrs. Lanslo to talk to her. Hattie told her something about unpleased gods, and that she needed to sacrifice the fish."

Milo rolled her eyes. "Can't she speak Galo?"

"She never learned."

"Go, girl," Milo mumbled.

"She's always doing something like this now and then," Simon continued, almost sounding irritated. "I guess this was the last straw. They want to haul her off."

"To 'Fools' Sanctuary'?"

"Yep," he sighed. "She'll be the life of the party there."

"But they can't do that!" Milo retorted, crossing her arms. "Isn't she normal, too?"

"Not enough. It doesn't help that she did it so close to the school. Unless she breaks free and bakes a casserole in four minutes, they're taking her away."

"Well, that's not fair," Milo said sympathetically. "Do you know what it takes to make a casserole?"

At that moment, Hattie let out a bone-shattering scream.

"Let me go! You are all crazy! I need to go please the gods! Release me, you brutes!" she puffed.

Milo slithered her way through the crowd to get a better view. As soon as she emerged in the front, Hattie saw her.

"Oh, Milo! Milo!" she trilled distressfully, still fighting her captors.

Milo cringed. "Oh, no," she mumbled.

"Cut it out!" Hattie yelled at the men, her fluffy hair whipping their faces. "That's my baby! Milo, tell these idiots that if they don't let me go, the gods will smote them down!"

All eyes turned to Milo, for they knew the name and whom it belonged to. All she could do was shake her head and continuously mouth "No." Simon came and stood beside her, putting his arm around her shoulders.

"Hey!" Hattie screeched when she saw that. "You! Stud muffin!

Quit manhandling my baby!"

"It's okay," Milo quickly assured her, jabbing a thumb in his direction. "I'm married to him!"

"What?" she said in astonishment, absentmindedly elbowing one of the men in the jaw. "But you're nothing but a child."

Milo shrugged. "That doesn't really matter here," she said. "Anyways, I'm happy. Now, these nice fellas are going to take you to a nice, new place to live. You'll like it there. At least I think you will. Will she?" she whispered to Simon.

"She will," he whispered back.

"You will," she told her.

"But I don't want to go with them," she whined, digging her heels into the dirt. "I'm not crazy."

"See! See!" Milo shouted, pointing at her. "That right there is proof that you are! Only people who are truly crazy deny being crazy. They don't think they are, when they really are. So, you are. In fact, you're mad."

"Yes," she agreed hotly, stomping on one of the men's feet. "I am. I'm furious!"

"No, you don't understand. It can –"

"Don't talk to me! Talk to them!"

Milo sighed and glanced at her captors, who were rapidly becoming bruised.

"Hattie," she said earnestly. "They won't understand me. I can't speak Galo. Just like you. We're both lost on this island. I really do feel sorry for you, but you've got to understand the tolerance of people. They have none. It's really, very sad, but what can we do? So, have a good time at the sanctuary and thanks for the cat. Love her."

"No!" Hattie shrieked as the men started to drag her away. "No! No! NO! You can't do this to me! You traitor! You quisling! Rat!!!"

These accusations made Milo feel rather wretched, and she looked down at her feet. Simon steered her away from the Hattie spectacle and kissed her cheek.

"Don't feel bad," he said. "It was bound to happen sooner or later. Forget what she said. You're none of those things. You are very loyal."

Milo gazed up at him, leaning her head on his shoulder. "Really?" she murmured.

"Truly," he said soothingly. "Why, when I saw you punch that boy at the beach, I almost crowed with happiness. I like a loyal girl. Almost as much as I like a girl who's an amazing cook."

Milo grinned. She stopped when she sniffed the air. It smelled like smoke.

"What the –?" she muttered. Following her nose, she looked behind her and gasped.

The entire schoolhouse was on fire. Bright orange flames were eating the walls, shooting out of the windows, and licking the roof. By now everyone had noticed the burning building and had flown into panic mode, screaming and gathering around, trying to put it out. It seemed as though Hattie, in her haste to appease the gods, had set the wrong thing on fire. Everybody gasped and shouted as the teacher emerged from the smoke, guiding a huge group of children of many ages. Parents rushed forward, scooping their precious ones up in their arms, both sobbing.

Milo went with them but couldn't find Ajsha amid the chaos. Two other pairs of parents couldn't find their children either, and were gibbering in despair. Cold fear crept into Milo's stomach as she turned to the schoolhouse.

"No," she whispered. She stalked up to the teacher. "Where is she?" she thundered. The teacher had been coughing, but now gazed at Milo with a wild, puzzled look, her face streaked with soot.

"Ajsha!" Milo yelled.

The teacher began to look around, picking out faces with her eyes, and gasped. Shaking her head hysterically, Milo began to hyperventilate, but couldn't for long because the air was full of smoke. The other parents were a ways off, screaming at the building. Simon walked up to Milo.

"I'm going to help get water," he said, his face set. "Where's Ajsha?"

Milo pointed silently to the building. Simon's eyes expanded. Horrified, he shook his head.

"No," he croaked, staring fearfully at the lashing flames.

Milo nodded angrily, glaring at the whole building. "Yes," she said through gritted teeth.

Clenching her fists, she started to walk forward. No fire was going to consume her baby! Fire had already done too much damage in her life. It would not rob her of the precious little girl who was always been so unfailingly kind to her. Not here, not now. She wasn't going to stand by and let it happen!

"Where are you going?" Simon called out, finally noticing his wife's receding form.

"To get her!" Milo shouted recklessly.

"Milo!" he shouted. "That's suicide! You'll get killed!"

"No I won't!" she insisted, hollering. "I might get injured, or get third degree burns, or lose whatever mental stability I have left, BUT – I –WON'T – DIE!!!"

With that, she mustered all the guts she had and walked into the burning building. People froze to watch her, calling her insane. Just as she had entered, a portion of the roof fell, blocking where she had gone in. Everyone started screaming. Milo felt the same terror, only she didn't scream.

The interior of the schoolhouse was much worse than the exterior. Flames leapt everywhere, but there was no smoke. It all was filtering up through the broken roof and windows. Desks and chairs were littered all over the place, haphazardly overturned and nearly all ablaze.

Bookshelves and tables were here and there, also on fire. School objects, toys, replaceable things were being eaten by the great orange tongues of fire. Milo stepped carefully, her pulse hammering and her conscience yelling at her for being so stupid.

"Do you know nothing?" he cried, frantic. "You're not supposed to go *into* a building that's on fire!! Do you not remember all those instructional animated videos?!"

"Shut up, Bob!" Milo snapped. "My daughter's in here! I'm not going to let her down. I can't lose Ajsha, Bob. I just can't!"

He snorted derisively. "You . . . I ought to leave you to burn."

"I'd like to know where you'd go."

"Good point," he sighed.

So he was stuck, no choice but to go down with her if it came to that. Which, judging from the bleak, cindery scene before them, wasn't an impossibility. Nervously, Milo looked around at all the blazing desks, sweat soaking every garment she had on.

"Ajsha!" she called out. "Ajsha! If you can hear me, answer!"

When no answer came, she swallowed her mounting fears and continued forward. Gingerly, she stepped over blackened, crumbling objects and sniffled, still calling.

"Ajsha!" she screeched. "Ajsha!! Please answer me! It's me! Milo!"

"Mother?" came a tiny voice suddenly from the back. It was the most beautiful noise Milo had ever heard.

"Ajsha!" Milo screamed, peering into the haze. "Where are you?"

"Over here!"

Milo scanned the direction it had issued from, but couldn't see anything except fire. Being extremely careful, she stepped over and ducked under things that were burning. The heat was extraordinary, and occasionally things would collapse with a bang, making her jump. Thankfully, the floor was dirt.

Just as Milo realized she hadn't denounced carbon monoxide poisoning outside, she suddenly saw Ajsha crouched behind a desk that was on fire. It roared and crackled and growled. No, fire is not a quiet thing. The whole place was filled with noise. Milo was drenched with perspiration and when she saw Ajsha, her heart jumped into her throat. Ajsha's little face, streaked with sweat and tears, simply anguished Milo. Her eyes were scrunched tight and she was trembling.

"Hold on, Ajsha!" Milo cried out, desperately looking around.

She spied a pole that wasn't yet ablaze. Snatching it up, Milo pushed the desk out of the way, it falling over and crumbling after sliding a foot. Slowly, unsurely, Ajsha stood up, edged around the wreck, and ran into Milo's arms. Milo squeezed her hard, afraid to let her go.

"Oh, baby!" she sobbed. "You're okay! You poor thing! Come on. We need to get out of here."

She stood up, already searching for an exit, but Ajsha grabbed her hand.

"Wait," she said, coughing a bit. "What about Tony and Shilia?"

"Who?" Milo asked, really wanting to leave.

"My classmates. They're in here, too. I think they are on the other side of the building. We can't leave them!"

With a jolt of recognition, Milo remembered the two parents outside, knowing how they were feeling: Dreading, ill, scared, in disbelief . . . hopeless.

She nodded.

"Where are they exactly?" she inquired over the roar of the flames.

"Tony! Shilia!" Ajsha shouted out, cupping her mouth with her filthy hands.

They heard a terrified response from the other side of the room. Milo picked her way along and peeked through a crisscross of fallen beams to see two small children huddled together in fright. The girl was wailing, while the boy tried to remain calm. He failed when a fiery object crashed to the floor four feet away from them and they both screamed. Milo swallowed hard as she tried to find a way to get to them. The scorched lattice work of beams was obstructive her path. Sighing, she wiped her dripping face.

"I can't reach them," she told Ajsha miserably. "I'm blocked off."

"No!" Ajsha cried, squinting between the logs. "Nooo!"

The other two cried out as well, and Milo longed for something to happen. And something did.

There suddenly came the trill of a war cry from outside, and Hattie Knocker came smashing through the ceiling on the other side of the beams. Milo stood mute and stone-like, in shock. Ajsha's jaw had dropped equally low. Neither knew how Hattie did it, but both, in a turn of events they could never have seen coming, were glad to see her there.

In a hurried, brusque sort of professionalism, Hattie worked her way over to the whimpering kids and hoisted one into each arm. She turned to look at Milo, who had recovered enough to close her mouth.

"Let's get out of here, Milo!" Hattie said, her caftan at serious risk of catching fire.

"Hattie?" Ajsha whispered.

"Good idea," Milo said, picking the girl up. "But how? All the walls are on fire. All of them."

Hattie considered this, no doubt using the type of contemplation available to mad people, and stepped around for a minute. She came upon a charred table close to the back wall. Gathering herself up, she lifted her foot and kicked the table directly into the burning wall.

"No, Hattie!" Milo cried, though it was too late. "It might bring the entire structure down!"

But it didn't. Amazingly, it only left a huge cavity, large enough for a human to duck through. Hattie huffed in satisfaction and climbed out. Milo was slightly impressed, and, because her options were limited, decided to try it. Balancing Ajsha on one hip, she searched along the wall until she found a desk. Giving it a mighty kick, it broke through, but it didn't make as big a hole as Hattie's.

It was narrow and near the floor, but Milo didn't want to take the risk of making it bigger. She exhaled heavily and set Ajsha down. Kneeling in front of her, Milo held her by the arms and looked straight into her eyes.

"Listen, Ajsha," she said seriously and calmly. "I want you to go through this hole. You'll be just fine if you crawl through it. Don't worry. I'll be right behind you."

Ajsha gaped at her in dismay and shook her head.

"I can't leave you behind," she choked out, tears trickling down her cheeks.

"You won't," Milo said reassuringly, but still firm. "I promise. I'll be right behind you. You have my word."

Though she had never actually given her word to anyone before, Milo was certain it was still trustworthy. Ajsha seemed to think so. She threw her little, sooty arms around Milo's neck.

"I love you, Mother!" she wept.

"I love you, too," Milo whispered, hugging her back. She then pulled away and looked into her face. "But don't call me mother. Go on."

The child looked over at the jagged hole and back at her, her eyes large with fright.

"I'll be right behind you," Milo repeated, kissing her forehead. "I promise."

Ajsha snuffled, but got down on her hands and knees. She looked over her shoulder at Milo.

"You'll be fine," she said, another beam crashing down behind her. "It's really nothing. I know you can be brave."

Biting her lip, Ajsha nodded. As she watched her daughter crawl through the blazing wall, Milo's heart raced painfully. As soon as the last of her feet had vanished, Milo heaved a sigh of relief and followed. Carefully, she inched her way outside, feeling the prickle of splintered wood against her back.

When she emerged out into the sunshine, she discovered that

they were behind the schoolhouse. That is, what remained of the schoolhouse. She could hear the hectic sounds of the townspeople as they tried to douse the flames. Ajsha was standing nearby, coughing hard, her shoulders stabbing the air. Milo quickly scooped her up and held her close, just as she heard a low rumbling. She felt a hand touch her arm. It was Hattie. She still had the two children.

"We'd better go," she said, hefting the boy into a high position. "It's collapsing."

And truth be told, it was. Hastily, they stepped away from the building as it started to crumple. They heard the crowd, which now consisted of the whole village, hush. The walls and the roof suddenly caved in and crashed to the ground.

Milo hugged Ajsha tightly, thankful to be alive. Hattie nodded in the direction of the multitude and set off at a brisk trot, the children clinging to her. Milo followed quietly, holding Ajsha close, frequently kissing her on the ear. The crowd was staring at the ruined building, motionless, with buckets of water hanging listlessly in their grip. Then, all at once, someone noticed Hattie and Milo, and the racket started again. This time, it was comprised of relief and vigor. Hattie strode over to the distressed parents, and each pair got back their child. The mothers laughed and cried and shouted all at once as they embraced and kissed their kids. The fathers just laughed and one of laughed and cried simultaneously.

Milo smooched her own little one on the forehead, just as Simon jogged up to them, looking pale and petrified.

"Milo!" he shouted and then saw Ajsha. Tears flooded his swollen eyes.

"Ajsha!" he said breathlessly. "You're all right!"

He took her from Milo and swung her up into the air. She shrieked in delight and laughed. Catching her, he hugged her fiercely and kissed every inch of her face. He spun in a circle, her arms entwined about his neck, then slipped an arm around Milo's waist and drew her in.

"Of course I'm all right," Ajsha said, quite out of breath. "Mother saved me!"

Simon looked down at Milo. "Of course she did!" he muttered. "You crazy female, Milo!"

Smirking, Milo gave one of his ears a tug and kissed his cheek.

"That's *mad* female," she corrected and sighed sadly. "And know it was dangerous, but I just had to do something. I got so scared when I thought about . . . losing . . . Ajsha."

Swallowing hard, he nodded and kissed her, then leaned his forehead against hers.

"I was so scared when I saw you go into that building," he murmured, shivering. "I was afraid I'd never see you again. You and Ajsha. That neither of you were going to come out of that schoolhouse. I ran around it, trying to see you, but couldn't. That . . . that really . . . I went cold all over. But, you did come out, I'll never let either one of you go ever again!"

He hugged the both of them, Milo's face pressed into his chest, as the crowd rumbled all around them. The three Swallows took a moment to breathe, and to absorb the fact that they were all together and safe. Milo grinned, her mouth quivering and a lone tear snaking its way to her chin.

"Looks like Hattie's a hero," she remarked as she saw the bushy haired woman being patted on the back and shaking hands with everyone, looking slightly perplexed.

"Yeah, they're not shipping her anywhere for a while," Simon said, in a tone that implied an eye roll. "This is what I mean. She acts crazy, but then does a thing like this. This is why we can never get rid of her. Of course, she's never done anything like this before. No one has."

People started coming up to Milo, too, seeking to congratulate and express their admiration. They shook hands with her, thumped her on the back, and asked Ajsha to tell her how brave and amazing she was. Milo blushed copiously and massaged her back a lot that day. Blondes came up to her, boys, men and women, non-blondes, even the Mayor's assistants.

"You're a hero now, Mother," Ajsha told her giddily, after a particularly severe assistant actually stuttered when he spoke to her. Milo froze for a second, and then looked down at Ajsha, her expression very stern. Ajsha shrank a bit, sheepishly clasping her hands behind her back.

"Ajsha," Milo began sternly, her tone matching her facial features. "Time after time, I have asked you not to call me mother. And I mean it, dang it. Stop calling me mother!"

Ajsha hung her little head in shame.

"I'd prefer it if you called me Momma," Milo finished.

Gasping, Ajsha looked up in delight and surprise. Simon, who had been in the process of rubbing Milo's lower back, froze, stunned.

"Oh," Ajsha said in wonderment, examining Milo's face for a hint of a lie. "Really?"

"Yep," Milo said, with a conviction she hadn't known until ten minutes ago. "Mother is so formal, it makes me nervous. Momma, well I could like that. It sounds kind of Italian. And you know how much I love my pasta!"

Lashes sparkling with tears, Ajsha hugged Milo's legs.

"I will, Mother!" she squealed happily. "I mean – Momma. I kind of like it, too."

Simon grinned. "So do I," he told Milo, nuzzling her ear. "Momma."

She snorted and nudged him in the ribs. "Don't you dare," she muttered sharply.

"What do you want me to call you?" Ajsha asked Simon.

He shrugged. "Anything you want. Don't worry about me. I'm not picky."

"Shut up," said Milo.

Ajsha pondered for a moment. "Then I think I'll keep calling you Father. Is that all right?"

"Perfect," Simon assured her, stoking back her grimy hair.

"Dandy," Milo agreed, just as Aunt Rosario and Mayor Em-I walked up to them. It was the first time Milo had ever seen them together. It astounded her that they were holding hands.

"You courageous thing!" Aunt Rosario told Milo as she hugged her. "I don't think I could ever have done that. But you," she smiled, cupping her face. "You're special. Very special."

"She's mad," Simon said, grasping Milo's skinny shoulders.

"That I am," Milo had to agree, withering under the strong grip.

"So is Hattie," Ajsha said.

An image flashed through Milo's mind of her and Hattie getting hauled off to Fools' Sanctuary together, fighting every step of the way. She let out an uneasy laugh.

Everybody wanted to talk to Milo, a far cry from them deliberately ignoring her whenever they walked past her. Water and blankets were brought to the ones who had been in the building. Milo described the rescue over and over again, Ajsha dutifully translating and throwing in her own little tidbits. Whatever feuds Milo had had with the people stemming from her past rebellion were gone. They all admired and respected her, which was quite a leap, and forever after Milo was exceedingly popular with them.

It just goes to show what being mad can accomplish. It can provide you with amazing courage, or at least blur your judgment enough for you to choose the unwise option that might possibly work if everything goes just right. It helped Milo during many catastrophic situations. Had she not been a mad female, she undoubtedly wouldn't have had the courage to jump into water to save her husband from a shark. Or run into a burning building to save her child. Or to simply not be afraid of a little lightning and thunder. Yes, it helped Hattie as well, although, *she* was actually insane. Indeed, we can always marvel in awe at the courage of the mad female.

28
Simon's Lullaby

DAYS PASSED SLOWLY, happily . . . safely. The hours were more euphoric than any that Milo had ever felt. Never had she thought that she would feel utterly satisfied with a life consumed by cooking, cleaning, and garden tending, but she was. Of course, like most circumstances in life, it all depends on the company you keep.

One particularly warm, happy, island-breezy afternoon Milo was sitting cross-legged on the bed in her and Simon's bedroom, thinking about what to write next in her diary. She stared at it, its crisp, lined pages staring back. All of her thoughts, feelings, and experiences were recorded in there, and it suddenly occurred to her that this beat-up notebook knew more about her than any human being. Something about this notion struck her as being monumentally Wrong. She decided right then, gazing at the white, awaiting paper and realizing that it could never substitute human ears, to stop writing in it. And she would never publish it; she never really wanted to end up on *Dr. Phil*, anyway. Closing it, she set it on the floor and slid it under the bed.

Languidly, her hand swept over the covers, feeling the enticing softness, and she felt obliged to lie down. It was just an idle sort of day, one where people feel too content to run about busily. Milo lay on her tum, burying her face in the blanket. It was two o'clock, a perfect time to laze.

Her stomach was full from lunch, and Ajsha was playing at a friend's house. Milo kept her eyes shut, inhaling sweet, sun-saturated air, worry free. The silent tranquility was suddenly broken by the sound of footsteps on the dusty dirt floor. They made the quiet, muffled sound footsteps make on dusty dirt floors. They made their way to the bed, where a knee climbed on, making the mattress dip. Milo felt a hand on her back, and in a moment warm breath stirred at her ear.

"Hello?" Simon's voice said softly.

"What up?" Milo mumbled into the blanket.

She heard Simon chuckle. "Good. Then you're awake?"

Moaning, she rolled over and squinted up at him, readjusting to the brightness.

"Yeah, I'm awake," she muttered, struggling to sit up, but Simon pushed her down. "Thank you," she said, rolling onto her face again.

Laughing, he rubbed her back. Chaos padded in from the hall, jumped upon the bed, and snuggled in beside Milo, kitty eyes slanting in glee. Copying her, Simon also cozied up to his wife, lying on the side of his face so that he could look at her. They remained motionless and quiet for moment, until Simon again shattered the serenity.

"You know what?" he asked Milo, tracing her shoulder blade with his finger.

Milo shook her faceless head.

"I know something."

Not really considering this news, Milo shrugged. "Aren't you lucky?" said her stifled voice. "So, what do you know? Dazzle me."

Simon grinned, propped himself up on an elbow, and again brought his mouth within an inch of her ear. Softly, yet with a hint of triumph, he said, "I know when your birthday is."

Hearing this, Milo went rigid. Slowly, mechanically, she lifted her up head and turned it to him.

"Who told you?" she asked sharply.

Simon leaned back down to her level. "Squelch," he answered shortly.

Milo snorted and sat up. "Of course she did," she muttered. "She's the only one I confided in. So, go on, Sherlock. When is it?"

"March," Simon replied, rolling leisurely onto his back. "Eighteenth. Five days from now."

She sagged. "All right, so you know," she said dismally. "What do you want to make of it?"

"A party," he said simply.

"No," Milo said staunchly. "I told you already. No parties for me."

"Why not?" Simon demanded, sitting up. "Why don't you want a birthday party? Everyone has them."

"Not me."

"Not even when you were little?" he persisted.

"Only when I was a whelp," she retorted. "Once we moved, there was no one to invite."

"Well," he countered, "there are people here. People who love and admire you."

"No, Simon," she insisted. "I don't want a birthday party, and you had better not give me one."

"Come on!" Simon said, upset. "Why do you have to act like such a stick in the mud?"

Her eyes narrowed.

"Don't accuse me of such a thing, boi!" she warned. "You know very well that I indulge in many festivities, but birthday parties are not one of them. I never liked them to begin with. Too much singing to me, too much sweet, too much expectancy to be fun and deal with the ridiculousness of it all. I can handle others, but not my own. I might change my mind when I'm older, but for right now, I don't want one. Got it?"

He sighed. "Fine. I don't know why you dislike them, but since you're so sure, I won't. Happy?"

Instantly, Milo felt better, the swelling knot in her stomach unraveling. Smiling, she leaned forward to entwine her arms around him and kiss his head. Simon began to feel pretty good as well. He hugged her back, stealing a kiss, and Chaos, irritated at being ignored, rubbed against them. They released each other, and Milo sat against the pillows, while Simon got to his feet.

"Well," he said robustly. "If you don't want a party, then what *do* you want to do for your birthday?"

She shrugged. "I don't know," she said, unenthusiastic. "Nothing?"

Simon folded his arms. "We have to celebrate somehow," he said stubbornly. "After all, you'll be turning . . . what is it? You're fourteen now, right?"

"Right," Milo confirmed, realizing that she was telling this to a seventeen year old, and abruptly became very happy that it was her birthday soon.

"Right. So, you'll be turning fifteen?"

Milo nodded. "That's it. Fif – teen." She smiled. "Five and ten."

They let this settle in for a moment, both looking and being thoughtful. Simon suddenly started to chuckle.

"What?" Milo asked suspiciously.

"I was just thinking," he said. "You once said that one of your 'principles' was you couldn't date until you were fifteen."

"Yeah," she said. "So?"

"Well. You're going to be fifteen, so . . ."

Milo gave him a long, scrutinizing look. "Are you trying to spit out what I think you're trying to spit out?" she asked.

Grinning, he sat on the bed and grandly took one of her hands in his.

"My dear," he began formally, "would you let me take you on your first date for your birthday?"

His dear sat stunned. When she was again capable of speech, she said, "Oh, my word. That sounds a little weird. Talking about first dates when I'm already married. But, I suppose that's how it was for daughters of sixteenth century fathers, only I doubt they dated at all."

"You haven't been on one already, have you?" he asked, not knowing a quarter of what she was prattling on about.

"Naw!" she said, shaking her head. "And, actually, I'd like to. I want to know what being on a date is like. I think I've earned it. Thus . . . sure. I'd love for you to take me on my first date. After all, I'll be fifteen. All my excuses will be gone. But what would we do?"

"You leave that to me," Simon told her excitedly, brushing his lips against the top of her hand.

Milo, blushing a darling shade of bubblegum, agreed. And though she ordered him to keep the date of her birthday "hush-hush," word got out. First to Ajsha, who could pry anything out of Simon with a bat of her eyelashes, then to Mrs. Lanslo, then to Soldier, and on to anyone else who had been trying to weasel it out of her for months. Of course, they also found out that she was refusing to have a party. But it didn't matter to them. They still tried to find ways to wish her a happy fifteenth.

Simon went into secrecy, preparing for the long-awaited first date. About two days before the upcoming event, friends started wandering out of the woodwork. The third to arrive was Mrs. Lanslo. The first was Soldier, and the second was an excessively giddy twelve year old girl that Milo had met the day the school burned down and hadn't seen since. (She had brought Milo a homemade card which Milo couldn't read, so therefore didn't really know why she was there, and had been reluctant to leave.) Mrs. Lanslo appeared before the front door the day following this awkward visit and, after reading the words painted beside it, knocked.

"Mrs. Lanslo!" Milo said in relief when she opened it. "What are you doing way out here?"

"Just to wish you a happy birthday and give you this, dear," she replied merrily, handing her a covered platter.

"Thanks," Milo said, taking it and letting her in. "How'd you find out when my birthday was?"

"Oh," she said carelessly, meandering into the kitchen. "Ajsha told me."

"Yeah?" Milo said, following her. "How'd she find out?"

"She didn't say," Mrs. Lanslo said evasively. "My! Didn't you perk this place up? It looks lovely, dear. It's a well known fact that a woman's touch is all a man needs to help his house."

"Thanks," Milo said yet again, setting the platter down and lifting the cover. "Honey cake?"

"Yes, it's a special of mine. I make it for Simon, too. You both are so cute together."

"I've heard," Milo said, again figuring this was only because she was camouflaged by Simon's overwhelming glow of attractiveness. "So are you and Soldier."

"Gorben? Oh, shush, dear!" she clucked modestly. "I'm not young enough to be called cute."

"Huh?" Milo said casually. "He was here, you know. Also to wish me a happy birthday."

"Is that so?" Mrs. Lanslo replied nonchalantly, admiring the polished shine of the water pump.

"Oh, yep. He brought me a T.V. screen."

"Did he now?" Mrs. Lanslo said. "Wasn't that nice of him?"

"Certainly was. I'm using it to cover the bathroom window. I never felt safe knowing that anyone could hop in while I'm showering. Anyhow, he said that you told him when my birthday was."

"Oh?" she remarked, picking at her hair. "Is that right? Well, I might have mentioned it to him."

"I'm sure you did."

Squelch was the next to come.

"Happy birthday!" she sang out exuberantly when Milo opened the door.

She gave her a massive hug and pranced inside.

"Now," Milo said, walking after her and letting the door swing shut by itself, "I'm not surprised to see *you* here."

"What do you mean?"

"Oh, nothing. What's that?"

Squelch grinned broadly. "For you," she said, handing her a large bag.

"Thank you," Milo said, putting the bag on the sitting room table and lifting out a large straw hat.

"Oooh," she cooed, trying it on. "Love it! How do I look?" she asked, twirling in a circle.

"Adorable," Squelch answered, flouncing down onto a chair.

"Thank you times fifteen," Milo told her, sitting on a couch, the rim of the hat hitting the wall.

"'Course. You definitely need something to keep you from getting sunburned. Maybe you can go to the beach more often now. So, whatcha doing for your birthday?"

Milo smirked. "You won't believe this," she said, leaning forward conspiratorially, "but Simon is going to take me on my very first date."

Her friend raised her eyebrows. "You haven't been on one yet?" she said in surprise.

"No," Milo snapped, prickly. "I told you already, I was waiting till I was fifteen to start dating. Marriage may have intervened a little, but this will still be my first date. Why? You ever been on one?"

Subdued, Squelch stared down at her feet. "No," she mumbled.

"Well, there you go."

She looked up and grinned. "Yeah, you're right, sorry. I just thought . . . well, you and Simon have been in love and all . . .

maybe you would've done that already. But, never mind. So, you're starting the dating game, eh?"

Milo hesitated. "I'm sorry," she said falteringly. "The 'dating game'?"

"Yeah," Squelch confirmed. "At least, that's what my sisters call it. They say that most of the time dating can be a game, though for them it's more like a hunt. Anyway, you play it and if you win, you either never see the guy again, or have more dates with him."

"Why the various winnings?"

"Depends on the guy."

"Ahh," Milo said sagely. "What about husbands? What's the rule about husbands?"

"They don't know," Squelch said, simpering. "They've never had any."

This didn't comfort Milo all that much, and she began to wonder anxiously about this "dating game". She supposed that on an island where divorce was outlawed, there wasn't too much risk of her losing and never seeing Simon again. Of course, they could remain married even if he vanished into the jungle, never to reappear, ruing the day that he had decided to date his wife. Such farfetched, yet increasingly plausible, possibilities plagued Milo throughout the day, making her forget that the overall point of the Dating Game was to end up with a husband.

"Happy birthday," Ajsha told her one evening in the kitchen, where Milo was using every ounce of her strength to extract a gigantic pot from a cupboard, while wondering who would feed Simon if he became a mountain hermit.

Her stringy muscles trembling, she paused a moment to face to Ajsha. "Thanks, sugar," she panted, taking a small woven box from her. "What is it?"

"A jewelry box," Ajsha said proudly. "I made it in school. You can keep your jewelry in it."

The island educators were currently holding classes in the church, the new schoolhouse still in the process of being built.

"Thank you," Milo said gratefully. "I needed one. All my stuff is lying around everywhere."

"You're welcome, Momma," Ajsha said happily, hugging her before sitting at the table.

Placing the jewelry box by the flour bin, Milo went to fill her gargantuan pot with water.

"What are you going to make?" Ajsha inquired.

"Soup, if I can," Milo huffed, working the pump. "Do we have any birds in the house?"

"I think so. I believe Father brought one home. It might be in the cellar."

"Good man," Milo groaned, lugging the pot to the top of the calven, which she had already lit.

She retrieved the bird and let it sink into the water. Taking out all of the dried herbs, one by one she sprinkled them into the simmering water, creating a savory, steamy facial. She then fetched different vegetables from the cellar and chopped them roughly.

"I'll add them when the bird's cooked," she told Ajsha. "I'll take it out after an hour and take the meat off the bones. Then everything will go in together and cook until the veg is tender."

Ajsha's eyes were shining with admiration. "How clever," she murmured, her chin propped up in her hand. "Is that what you're going to eat on your date with Father?"

"He told you about that?" Milo asked, chopping a stalk of lemon grass into thin rings.

"Mm-hmm."

"Well," Milo said frankly. "Truth be told, I don't know what we're going to eat. Simon's taking care of that. He won't tell me anything he's doing. It makes me jittery."

"Why? Don't you trust Father?"

"'Course I do! But when he gets all secret-agent on me, I start to worry a little bit."

"Oh, trust me," Ajsha said positively. "You have nothing to worry about."

"Why?" Milo asked suspiciously, halting in mid-chop. "Did he tell you something?"

Ajsha smirked to herself. "Maybe," she said airily.

Milo, first deliberately setting down her knife, turned to her. "What? What do you know?"

Shrugging, Ajsha stood up. "I don't know," she said casually.

Milo's eyes narrowed, her hands on her hips, and she started to walk towards the little girl.

"You know something, don't you?" she accused. "What is it? Tell me!"

Slowly, Ajsha smiled and shook her head. Milo ended up chasing her around the house and tickling her within an inch of her life. But still she wouldn't say anything. She laughed, but there were no cryptic messages in it.

The night of the big first date arrived at last. Milo was very excited, since she had come to the conclusion that whether she won or lost the Dating Game, Simon wasn't going anywhere. If he had thought she was obstinate when trying to drive him away, just wait until he saw what she was like when refusing to let go.

Thus consoled, she got dressed in the fish pattern caftan, belt, and white capri pants she had received for Christmas. She used a thin scarf, borrowed from Ajsha, as a hair tie. Checking herself out in her bedroom mirror, she lightly brushed down the material, inhaling deeply.

"All right," she whispered to her chic reflection. "Here we go. Fifteen. I'm fifteen."

"And goin' courtin'!" Bob the Conscience sighed. "So grown up!"

Simon met her in the kitchen fifteen minutes later, wearing a button-down black shirt and khaki pants. Milo grinned with definite approval as she inspected him. When he came closer, she gave him a long kiss.

"Thank you," he said when they finally broke apart. "What was that for?"

"Because I can," she replied blithely, thinking it was better than telling him that she was rewarding him for looking so good. "Now, take me to our romantic evening."

"Can I carry you?" he asked mischievously.

"No!" she gasped. "Don't even think of it, boi! I can walk very well by myself, thank you. *Lead* me there. Don't!" she said severely when he took no heed. "I swear, honey! I will slap you."

Simon backed off, alarmed. Then he frowned and asked seriously, "You wouldn't, would you?"

"I might," she said smoothly. "But it won't be like your face or anything. You know, your arm or something, and gently. A gentle slap. Don't worry; my days of brutality are over."

Relaxing and smiling, Simon proffered his arm. Daintily, Milo hooked her elbow into his, and they sauntered outside, into the bright moonlight. The sky was flawless, not one cloud to obscure the view of glittering stars, and the air was warm with a cool breeze gamboling in from the east. It fluttered the hem of Milo's caftan, as well as her heartstrings. She clutched Simon's arm tighter, not knowing what awaited her, but still rigid with anticipation. He led her along the beach, plucking a flower or two for her here and there.

Eventually they arrived at the sandy cove where they had swum on Simon's birthday. For a moment Milo wondered if he wanted them to swim again. She almost groaned aloud. Not that there weren't many pleasant aspects from the first time that she wouldn't mind revisiting, but she had gotten all dressed up . . . Inwardly, she sighed with relief when he, instead of heading for the water, guided her to the huge, flat stone that was used for diving.

"Wait here," he told her at the bottom. He quickly scrambled up one of the rope ladders and disappeared from sight.

Milo stood patiently at the bottom and waited. Finally, she heard Simon's voice echoing from somewhere up above, telling her to climb up. Groping for the ladder rungs in the dark, Milo carefully made her way up, thankful that even if she did look down, it was too dark to see anything. As her head cleared the edge, she saw the wide, flat expanse of the top of the boulder, in the middle of which sat a candle lit dinner for two. It was set on a small, round table, erected at the center and adorned with their good tablecloth and a clay candelabrum. Simon was standing proudly, perhaps even a little smugly, behind one of the chairs. Milo gasped when she saw it.

"You did all this?" she asked in amazement, tiptoeing over, not wanting to disturb the ambiance.

"Well," he admitted. "You helped."

"I did?" she whispered, gazing at the flickering teardrop shaped flames of the candles.

"Yeah," he said sheepishly, pulling out the chair. "Won't you sit down, madam?"

"Oh," Milo said genially, accepting the offer. "You are so suave."

He grinned, obviously pleased with himself, and took the seat opposite her. They bowed their heads.

"Dear, Lord," Simon prayed reverently. "Thank you for the nice weather. Please bless the food we are about to enjoy. Please bless Milo as she turns fifteen. Thank you for her being born. Please let Ajsha have no more nightmares. And . . . oh! Please help me to face the consequences for breaking a piece of the good china. Amen."

"Amen," Milo echoed. One thing (well, really, one thing on a list of many things) that she liked about Simon and Ajsha was that they didn't care what they prayed about in front of her or anyone. They were very open and shameless. But, even so, she couldn't help herself.

"Which piece?" she said, unfolding her hands.

"The sugar bowl," he said quietly, peeking up at her. "So sorry."

Milo swallowed hard. "That's okay," she managed to say. "What's for dinner? I'm starving."

"There's a first," Simon said. He lifted the covers off the bowls to reveal Milo's soup.

"Ah," Milo said, the aromatic steam caressing her nostrils. "So, that's how I helped, is it?"

Simon grinned imploringly. "It was so good, and you know I can only make fish medley. Do you mind?"

"No," Milo said kindly. "It was one of my better soups. . . . mmm. Still is. Wow. It's so cool up here. I feel like I'm on top of the world. It would be just like you to do a thing like this."

"It would?" he said, amused, dipping his spoon into his golden puddle of soup.

"Sure," she said, peering at him fondly through the candlesticks. "You're such a cool guy. Cool guys come up with cool things. But bringing all this up here must have been some hassle."

"A little," he admitted then glanced coyly over at her. "But it was worth it."

"Really?"

"Absolutely. But, we should be talking date-ish talk, and that does not include how the date came to be. Or, how it got set up."

"Oh?" Milo said. She jauntily leaned her chin on her hand. "Very well. You're the experienced one. So, tell me about yourself, dear Simon. I dare say, I don't very know much."

"No?" he said with a laugh. "We're married."

"Well," she said reasonably, "we didn't have any dates beforehand, so how could I? How could you? And, we didn't grow up together, so we didn't get to slip notes to each other during class or anything. So, we have a lot of catching up to do. What's your favorite color?"

Simon grinned. "I'll answer your questions, but each time I do, you have to answer one of mine."

"Fine, fine," she said cooperatively, shifting in her chair. "Now, what's your favorite color?"

"Blue," he said, settling back and folding his hands on his stomach. "Like the sea. What's yours?"

"Red," she replied promptly. "Like a pomegranate. What's your favorite subject in school?"

"Geography. Yours?"

"Literature," she said, wondering what to ask next. "What's . . . your favorite animal?"

"Porpoise. I love watching them when they're playing in the water. Sometimes, they will let you swim with them. I made friends with one when I was younger. I'm always on the lookout for him when I'm fishing. When did you start writing your diary?"

"The first time we moved." She laughed. "I told my mom what to write. My handwriting was pretty atrocious when I was six. Who is your best friend?"

"Besides you?"

"Sure," she said with an affectionate eye-roll.

"Ajsha. She has always been my very best friend."

"What about Will?"

"Ahhh, Will." His mouth quivered. "He's a close third. It sounds bad to say that, since we've known each other since we were babies, and we spent every second together growing up. I told him everything. Then . . . we both moved out and . . . other things became important. What's it like to fly?"

"Nerve-racking," Milo said with a shudder. "You wouldn't like it. When did you learn how to swim?"

"When I was four. Here, the boys learn to swim at four and the girls at seven. Ajsha will need lessons soon." He turned serious. "Do you miss where you used to live?"

"Heck no!" she laughed. "I'll never miss that place! Whew, okay, moving on." She paused thoughtfully, tapping her spoon against her lips. "Well, have you ever been in love before?"

"Only with Ajsha. No one else has captured my heart." He then asked tentatively, "Do you miss your parents?"

Milo stared at her soup, making swirls in it with her spoon. "I think so," she said softly. "I love them and all, but I can live without them. I wonder if they miss me."

"They probably do. They're probably worried."

Milo scoffed. Simon reached out and took her hand. Flipping it over, he rubbed his thumb in circles on her palm. Simon tended to do that whenever he was about to approach a difficult topic.

"Milo," he said sincerely. "Are you happy here? I know I'm skipping your turn, but are you happy here on the island?"

She smiled at him and meshed her fingers with his. "Of course I am!" she replied, keeping perfect eye contact. "Happier than I've ever been. Ever. Sometimes it's hard to believe, but it's true. Um . . . have you ever wished that someone would find this place and take you to see America?"

Somberly, Simon shook his head and drew his hand back.

"No," he said gravely. "No one can ever find this place, Milo. We'd be ruined if they did. Nobody knows this place exists and they can't. If they did, they would bring in people to gawk at us – at the little civilization on an island. They would flock here and destroy our way of life. They'd cut down the trees and snap with their metal boxes. They'll find this place so amazing, and they'll charge people to come to admire us! People will move here until the island sinks."

Milo sat bewildered at the sting in his voice. "Yeah," she whispered. "People seem to do that. Ruin everything they get their hands on."

"That's why it's so important that no one finds this island."

"But don't some people want to go back? Wouldn't they want the chance?"

"Not that I know of. But, if they did leave, they would have to be sworn to secrecy."

"All right!" Milo said with a light finality, wanting to steer away from such heavy conversation, especially since it felt like Simon had just recited something from a textbook. "So . . . why didn't you guys name the island?"

"Why should we?" he asked, more comfortably. "It's not our island. It's merely letting us stay here. It's God's island, I guess. He can name it. We have no right to. Who's Bob?"

Milo, to be blatantly honest, guffawed. "One of my greatest friends," she said, deciding to tell him. "You won't believe this, but he's my conscience. His full name is Bob the Conscience."

Simon stared at her, a wind ruffling his hair. "Your conscience?" he said doubtfully.

"Uh-huh," she said, not liking the look he was giving her. "You see, at one point I was arguing with it so much, I named it – him. It was around the time I became quite friendless."

Simon's look turned to one of sympathy. "You must have been very, very lonely to start talking to yourself," he whispered.

"I was," she admitted softly, as if the full impact of this had only just hit her. "But I'm not now. Now that I have my boo." She smiled shyly at him "That's you, honey. But don't tell anyone about Bob. I don't want them to think I'm crazy. You're the only one I've ever told."

"Well," he said, after a moment. "Remember when you squished that tomato on me the first time we went to the market?"

She forced herself not to giggle and nodded intently.

"Well, I thought the juices were my blood and you had killed me."

"Oh," she laughed, clamping a hand onto her mouth. "Are you serious? I'm so sorry."

"I never told anyone that. So you'll keep my secret and I'll keep yours."

"Sounds fair," she said guiltily. "Dang, I was mean to you. . . . Um, where'd you learn to dance?"

Blushing profusely, Simon stared at a bead of melting candlewax. "That was my mom's fault.

We have dances a lot here, and I guess she didn't want me to embarrass her. A friend that lived down the street from us taught me. But I enjoy it . . . now. When'd you learn how to dance?"

"Ha! I didn't!"

"What? But you're so good."

"No, I'm not!"

"Sure you are. I've seen you dancing around the house, and you can waltz perfectly. Really? No lessons?"

Milo smirked to herself, an image of her, Squelch, and Salsa tottering all over the place in Squelch's yard flashing through her mind. "Well, I have been having a few lately. I'll show you later. But first I want you to sing."

"All right, madam," Simon agreed, eager to display his odd talent. In truth, even if he wasn't mimicking a singing person but actually singing in his own voice, he still didn't sound too bad, but he preferred to mimic. "What do you want me to sing, baby?"

"'My Boo'," Milo replied without any hesitation. "That way we can both sing, even though I can't sound like Alicia Keys. And it is just unsettling when you do."

Simon grinned. "I like that song. But you still haven't told me what Boo means. I always thought it was a form of jeering."

"Sure," she said. "But it can also mean a person who you have strong relationshipy feelings for. Like a boyfriend or girlfriend, or someone who you visualize as your boyfriend or girlfriend. It's sort of a pet name for a loved one."

"All right," Simon said, still not entirely convinced, but willing to go along with it. He fidgeted into a position conducive for great concentration, as he always had to do when mimicking. But he still managed to stare lovingly at her face.

Gathering a deep breath, he began to sing, crooning the male part of the song to her. When Milo's turn came, she tried to sound the best she could, though singing had never been her strong suit. As they sang the lyrics, their eye contact impeccable, they both began to feel very close to each other. They felt very loving, very happy. Milo felt something else, too, something that she could only describe as perfection; this was indisputably the best birthday she ever had. When they reached the end of the song, they stood up to lean over the table, precariously avoiding the flickering candles, which were now much shorter, and they kissed. They sat back down afterwards, Milo thoughtful.

"That one was very moist," she said at last.

Simon nodded, looking the tiniest bit disgruntled. "Speak for yourself. Ice lips."

"Hey!" she said. "I didn't ask you to slip me any tongue. I don't want that thing in my mouth!"

"Never?" Simon asked, disappointed.

Milo couldn't help but smile. "Well," she said reluctantly. "Not *never*. But definitely no time soon, so keep it in your own trap."

"All right," he conceded. "As you wish. Do you want to dance now?"

"Sounds lovely," she said, relieved that they were moving on. "Even if we don't have any music."

Grinning cunningly, Simon pulled out a small object from underneath the table.

"Forgive me, my love," he said, setting her radio and speaker on the table. "I would have asked permission, but I didn't want to give anything away."

Milo shook her head, her lips pursed. "You little thief," she mumbled, though with obvious amusement. "Let me see it. I know where every type of music is on there."

"I thought you only listened to hip-hop," Simon said as she adjusted it.

"No," she said carelessly, squinting at the miniscule numbers on the dial. "I listen to others. But hip-hop is my favorite, so I listen to it the most. Wonderful music, it is. You have no idea how harshly it's criticized. Really, it's ridiculous. Ah! Classical, found ya. Come on, boo. You can show me how you dance, and then I'll show you the new steps I've learned."

Simon agreed and as the soft, sweet sound of classical music filled the night sky he cupped her hand in his and drew her in to waltz, she actually allowing him to lead this time. They floated their way around the surface of the boulder, keeping a safe distance from the edges and continuously skirting the table. As she bobbed and swayed to the violins and clarinets, Milo felt like she was at a royal ball, only the dance floor was beneath a ceiling of stars and the handsome prince in her arms would inherit a fish business, not a kingdom. She could have gone on dancing in this fashion and with these romantic musings for hours, but Simon wanted her to show him that new dance she kept hinting at.

It took her several minutes of station searching to find the right type of music for a mild salsa, and even longer to feel bold enough to show him. Simon was pleasantly surprised by the dance and rapidly mastered the various steps and the overall attitude of the dance. This particular salsa being quite mild (it was only their first date, after all) it was more fun than anything else, though once or twice they strayed too far to the rock's limits and had to yank each other back before they fell off. Finally, winded from both exertion and laughter, they stopped dancing. It was quite late out by then, the moon already on its nightly descent.

"Now what?" Milo asked sleepily, shivering as she was buffeted by a particularly chilly breeze.

"Now I'm going to walk you home," Simon replied, blowing out the candles, which were nothing more than stubs by now. "I used to always walk my dates home. My mom said that's what a gentleman does. Ha, Ajsha would be cold furious if she saw what time we're getting in."

"I can imagine the sort of words she'd use," Milo muttered. "She talks like she's an English professor. And she's six! How'd that happen?"

"Oh, the usual way. Started reading at four, two books a day. In the last two years she's moved on to higher level books, ones that I can't even understand. She learns the words from them. I can't really like that fact."

"I know what you mean," Milo said, packing up her radio. "Oh. We barely ate anything."

"That proves it was a real date."

They walked home arm in arm, him reassuring her that he would return for the things on the rock tomorrow. Once they got there, they both changed out of their date attire, and Simon went to check on Ajsha. When he got back to their bedroom, Milo was already under the covers.

"Asleep?" she inquired.

"Yes," he replied. "Surprisingly. I didn't even sing to her. She may be the smartest little girl on the planet, but she still needs her lullabies."

Milo chuckled. "Can't escape the inner child," she said. "What kinds of lullabies do you sing?"

"Oh, all sorts. I found some on a plane once. You can find anything on those things."

"So," she murmured, peering at him as he walked around the foot of the bed. "You didn't make them up? Remember when you sang to me? Was that written by someone else?"

"No," Simon said, smiling as he climbed into bed. "That one I made up. I'm not exactly a poet, but I think it came out quite pretty. Of course, we keep these things to ourselves," he added seriously. "I don't need the guys on the beach knowing I wrote a lullaby."

"Will you sing it to me tonight?" Milo asked, nestling in beside him. "It is my birthday, and I promise I won't tell anyone."

He laughed and put his arms around her, kissing her temple.

"If you want me to," he said, and began, the words floating out of his mouth like nectar.

"*The village is gently snoring,*
The night bird sings its lullaby,
The children's' eyes are closed till morning,
Yet you lie there and cry.
The grieves you have my be many,
And perhaps wisdom has grown in your eyes,
But the comforts I give are plenty,
I can help you before your happiness dies.
Think of the heavenly sunshine, softly warming your face,
Marvel at the cool, lush sea we swim in,
Never doubt my loving embrace,
Please go to the world you dream in."
(Then he sang this chorus.)
"*Now let the tears cease,*
Hush for a moment, my love,
May you dream in peace,
With soft blessings from above.
Lay you head down and sleep,
Don't be choked by tears of fright,
No more shall you weep,
I'm here to hold you through the night.
Tonight the lion stays home to eat,
Without him the jungle is quiet,
Yet your tears say you've suffered defeat,
And your sobs aren't denying it.
Forget your sadness, let it drift away,
Your eyes are full of sorrow,
Stars begin to shine as darkness covers day,
Let your soul sleep till tomorrow.
As the moon gently pushes the waves,
Angels are hypnotized by your charms,
Your tired body your slumber saves,
As you fall asleep in my arms."

(He once again repeated the chorus.)
"*Never a beauty so frail,*
Never a doze so light,
Never my protective gaze shall fail,
From your eyes so bright.
My love for you shall never bend,
Though your trials may never halt,
I'm always going to be here to defend,
And remind you it was never your fault.
Please stop your worry and find your peace,
Let the sobs stop from your throat so sore,
Have joy surround you, your smiles never cease,
You're the only lady I adore."
(He then sang the chorus for the final time.)
"*Now let the tears cease,*
Hush for a moment, my love,
May you dream in peace,
With soft blessings from above.
Lay your head down and sleep,
Don't be choked by tears of fright,
No more shall you weep,
I'm here to hold you through the night."

Simon caught his breath as he ended the song. He had to smile. He had always been proud of that song, even though he kept its existence a closely guarded secret. He was impressed that he could come up with something so lovely, what with being someone who tussled with sharks.

"Did you like it?" he asked softly, looking down at Milo. She yawned.

She had loved it, though wasn't immune to its original purpose. "I adore it," she murmured. "So beautiful! You're so smart, Simon. But, it kind of knocked me out. I guess I need to sleep."

"Of course," he whispered, laying her down and kissing her cheek.

"Good night, boo," Milo said, her words slurring a bit. "I love you."

"Good night," Simon said, lying down on his side and draping a protective arm over her. "I love you, too. Hmm. Boo."

The day was done. It was time to sleep. They both had fun, but tomorrow was another one.

29
The Crash Site

DARK CHURNING CLOUDS, evil laughter, someone screaming far off in the distance . . . Ajsha woke up with a start, a cold sweat beading on her neck. Sunshine was spilling through her window, making an abstract puddle of gold on her bed. After staring around at all the everyday, normal objects in her room, she caught her breath and sighed. Milo's head suddenly appeared in the doorway.

"Finally," she said. "It's about time, girl. This is like the longest you've ever slept. Come on, get –are you okay?"

Ajsha sucked in air and accidentally swallowed it. "Yes, Momma," she managed to say. Milo shook her head and clicked her tongue as she came into the room.

"Knew we shouldn't have stayed out so late," she muttered, half to Ajsha, half to herself. "But can you blame us? What a party! I've never danced so much in my life. Did you have fun?"

Ajsha nodded as she got out of bed, determinedly clenching her hands into fists to make them stop quivering. "It was nice of Squelch to invite us. Now both of you are fifteen."

"Sure are," Milo said happily, withdrawing a pair of extremely clean jeans and a T-shirt from Ajsha's bureau.

Ajsha wrinkled her nose. "Jeans?" she said distastefully.

"Yes," Milo replied firmly. "We need rumble clothes for where we're going. No skirts allowed. Don't go complaining, either. Jeans are a wonderful gift and privilege. Remember that."

"Yes, Momma," Ajsha said, though she hardly sounded convinced.

"Good, now change and come get some breakfast."

Milo was very impatient as she waited for Ajsha to come out and eat. She was also unbelievably excited. That day, they were going on a special outing. (Milo tenaciously wanted to call it a trip, or even an excursion, but she was outnumbered by people who couldn't stop calling it an outing, so an Outing it remained. It got on her nerves so badly that it was a marker of how much she wanted to go that she didn't call the whole thing off.) Simon had agreed to take them all to the crash site. Ever since she had first heard about the place, Milo had been very curious about what it was like, and at long last she was going to see it. Squelch was going to go with them, and, much to Milo's exasperation and dismay, she also called it an Outing.

They had celebrated Squelch's fifteenth birthday the night before. There had been much laughter, farm grown food, floating candles in clay pots, and plenty of dancing. Milo grinned as she recalled it. She had brought her radio and speaker with her so that they could have a variety of music. There had been circle dancing, crowd dancing, and even couple dancing, since several families from the neighboring farms attended and brought with them blushing, teenage farm boys. (Squelch's sisters pointedly ignored every single one of them, but Squelch of course wasn't as uppity and danced with many of them.) Salsa had spent most of her time teaching Otto Gauls to dance, though, at least in Milo's opinion, it was time wasted, since all he seemed to want to do was cast wary, shifty looks over everyone present. It wasn't that he couldn't be friendly when he wanted to; he was just strange. Milo had yet to discover what Salsa saw in him.

Ajsha finally emerged from her bedroom and sat down to her

food. Milo was filling a basket with a lunch for four people. Simon entered in, dressed also in jeans and a T-shirt. Milo really had never seen him in jeans. He was usually always dressed for swimming. She *liiiiked* it. Beckoning to him with a finger, she gave him a long, approving kiss.

"Best way to start the day. Yoven fidlo, little cutie," he said, kissing Ajsha on the head.

"Yoven fidlo, Father," she answered groggily, blinking at her bowl of cereal.

"Uh – uh – uh!" Milo snapped, wagging a finger. "No talking – just eating."

Simon turned back to her, smirking. "Aren't you anxious? Don't worry, we'll get there."

Milo nodded emphatically. "Yes. The sooner the better."

They set off at last, everyone donning rarely worn shoes and Milo taking her big, floppy hat. (All of the sunscreen she had packed for Australia had long since been used up.) They met up with dear Squelch in town, and together, as a group, they veered off onto one of the side roads that lead to the west. Milo and Squelch walked side by side, Simon and Ajsha walking ahead.

"So," Milo asked, "have you ever been to the crash site?"

"I don't know," Squelch replied, stepping over something despicable, left by something furry. "I might have when I was really little, but I can't remember it. It's not exactly a favorite outing destination."

Milo kept her comments to herself.

Simon, who had been there numerous times, knew a shortcut through the jungle. It took them off the worn path, through thick overgrowth and over a few streams, heading towards the far side of the island. After an hour of tramping and tripping, they emerged from the trees out onto an enormous sandy beach. What Milo saw made her heart skip a beat.

Airplanes lay crumpled and dilapidated upon the coarse white sand. Parts like wings, engines, and landing gear were strewn about in every direction. The planes had no tires and the good metal had been stripped off, making the air crafts look somewhat skeletal. The windows were gone, the seats, dividing curtains, and carpets were gone, along with the plastic from the overheads and bathrooms. There were about ten airplanes in all, or at least all that remained of airplanes that the islanders couldn't use. The sight of those gigantic dead pieces of machinery, ravaged for their parts, made Milo feel terribly small and powerless. Simon, noticing her frightened expression, put an arm around her shoulders.

"It's awful," she confided in a whisper. "It kinda scares me."

"There's nothing to be afraid of," he told her. "Come on. Let me show you around."

After depositing the picnic basket under a shady tree, they walked about, peering into the different planes, observing the angles they had hit the ground and the scorch marks left by the fires from the explosions. There was a plane dating back to the nineteen-tens, when luxury air travel first started. There seemed to be a plane from each era, all stripped down and rusting badly. Simon even showed Milo her plane. It made her shudder to remember that night, but everyone else wanted to hear the story of her perilous plummet into their lives. So she told it, sharing what details she could remember, and it got them all excited. Secretly, Simon was glad that nobody had woken Milo up when they vacated the plane. However, he felt it would be insensitive to voice this.

Milo was then shown the plane Ajsha had been rescued from, and even walked around inside it. As she was exploring, she saw a charred newspaper clipping on the floor. Picking it up, she read, "Terrifying outbreak in Liverpool hospital. Sixteen infants being moved to America ..."

Biting her lip, she let the clipping flutter back down to the floor. She then took to wandering around alone. One plane didn't have its left side ripped off and she read,

Sweet Mirrelda's Fabric and Thread

Her eyebrows went up, and then her head bobbed up and down. Roaming further on, she came to another plane that still had a patch of siding left. This one said,

TREVOR'S HARDWARE ROOST

She shook her head and decided to rejoin the others. They all were having a great time and played by the waves for a while before eating lunch underneath the trees. It was a delicious picnic (chiefly sandwiches, which are the reigning king of picnic cuisine) and afterwards Milo contentedly stared up at the sky as Squelch and Ajsha ran off to play by the water. Simon lay down next to her, shoulder to shoulder, and held her hand. Milo smiled blithely, soaking up the peace and love, savoring what justly could be deemed a perfect moment, but stopped abruptly when she spotted something in the sky. At that very second, it was nothing more than a speck. But on an island, where the sky is always an endless void of blue, untarnished by anything except the occasional cloud, specks are anything but normal. Within a few seconds, it became more than a speck; it was now a speck with details. Milo blinked once to make sure, but was positive.

An airplane!

"*Simon!!*" Milo screamed at the top of her lungs, a horrifying coldness creeping over her.

"I am right here," he said, rubbing his ear. "There's no need to –"

"Shut up and look up!"

"What? Where?" he asked, peering at the green foliage above them.

"Up there!" she hissed, pointing at the sky, where the detailed speck was enlarging. "Is that –?"

"An airplane!" he shouted, sitting up. "No! I mean, yes it is, but –"

"Ajsha!" Milo cried, also getting up and gesturing wildly. "Squelch! Come here!"

"What's wrong?" they said, sounding worried and rushing over, their pant legs wet from the tide.

"It's an airplane! Up in the sky!"

Their eyes expanded with horror and they threw their heads back. Sure enough, the speck had become a full-fledged aircraft, and it was flying close.

"Oh, good gracious!" Squelch cried, hand sailing to her forehead.

"I don't understand," Ajsha said, trying to succeed as the composed one and failing. "It seems too small to be an airplane."

"Not all airplanes are that size," Milo said, gesturing to the enormous crashed ones. "There are some called private planes that are much tinier. I think that's what that one is."

"It's headed right for the island!" announced Simon, definite anxiety in his voice.

And since the wretched thing was, undeniably, angling straight towards the island, they took a minute to exchange looks of terror and indecision with each other before clumsily throwing on their shoes, fetching the basket, and heading back to town at a run.

The plane was descending languidly, searching for a place to make a landing, having absolutely no intention of passing over this little gem of green in the turquoise ocean. Simon led them through every shortcut he knew, but they couldn't possibly keep up with the speed of the plane. But they still pushed on, crashing and tumbling through the undergrowth as if they were running for their lives. They had to stop briefly once or twice when Ajsha looked like she might collapse, and each time the wait was torturous.

When they finally arrived in town, throats raw and chests aching, people were wandering in droves down to the beach where the fisherboys fished. Apparently, they weren't the only ones who had noticed the plane's appearance. Milo's heart filled with fear as she watched the grave crowds walk towards the only possible runway on the island, besides the Crash Site, which was so littered with airplanes that there was no room. Her stomach lurched as she thought of the threat that had just landed. Private planes were expensive. Only someone quite rich could afford one. And rich people always seem to be concocting silly ideas about how to get even richer.

The four of them followed the throng of villagers, all of them murmuring distraughtly to each other. Milo exchanged a glance with Simon. He looked worried. Wordlessly, he reached out and grasped her hand.

"What's going to happen?" she whispered.

"I don't know," he admitted. "This has only happened once before. Long ago, a ship anchored here and the captain threatened to expose us to the world. So they destroyed his ship, and he and his crew never left. It's up to the Mayor what happens today. Maybe if whoever it is promises to keep us a secret, they can leave. If not . . . well, like I said, that's up to the island council."

Milo nodded grimly, not believing that something that she had once wished so hard for now made her stomach churn with dread.

As the plane came into view through the trees, Milo thought she heard a familiar voice. She shook her head, trying to clear her brain. It was trying to play tricks on her. There was a good sized crowd when they got there. They couldn't see past the multitude of bodies, the people from the plane hidden from view, but as they worked their way to the front, Milo heard,

"Oh, my! They're speaking nonsense!"

"Now, Sherrill-Jean!"

Milo's eyes, already wide from panic, grew even bigger and she almost came to a halt.

"No!" she thought, her intestines no longer twisting but leaping painfully. "Impossible!"

"Is it?" Bob the Conscience said dismally. "Is it really? When it comes to you, Milo dear, impossible doesn't enter the equation."

Milo had to admit he was right, but still mulishly forced herself not to believe it as she wormed her way through the mob. However, once she got to the front, all resolve to be stubborn vaporized, and her jaw fell off and her heart quit.

There, standing in a lavender power suit and hat, was her mother. And standing beside her in pressed dress pants and pilot's jacket and hat was her father. The Hestler parents were now on the island.

All Milo could do was stare, unbelieving, thinking she was dreaming. Positive she was going insane. Certain her lack of sunscreen was causing her to hallucinate. How on Earth? It wasn't possible! It just wasn't possible! Or was it?

Slowly, reluctantly, she coughed, "M-Mom? Dad?"

They didn't hear her. The two parents were unhurriedly gazing at all the faces of the islanders with an expression of bewildered fascination, until their eyes roved over Milo's face. They were about to continue on to the person next to her, but they suddenly stiffened, recognition dawning on their faces and their lips slowly drooping down to make little Os. They turned pale as wax and for minute could only stare, not even daring to blink. Milo, in turn, stared back. They regarded each other with a mixture of shock and disbelief, neither the parents nor the child able to fully grasp what was going on.

"Is it?" they finally choked to each other, not taking their eyes off of Milo. "No. No. It can't be. She's –! Milo?" they called out warily, taking a step forward and then stepping back. "Is that you? Is it actually you?"

The girl tried to collect herself, taking deep breathes and letting them out in a jittery sort of way. Simon was glancing from the Hestlers to her, monstrously confused and growing uneasy.

"It's me," Milo managed to say at last, her eyes stinging. "But is it you?"

"Oh, my!" her mother shrieked, hopping up and down in her high heels, not answering her. "It is Milo! It is! It really is! You're alive?"

"Yes!" Milo cried, rolling her eyes and thinking this should have been obvious. She crossed the strip of sand dividing them from the villagers, since they evidently weren't going to, Simon watching her go with a heavily lined brow. Ajsha whispered something to him in Galo, and he shushed her.

Milo came to a stop about a foot from where her parents were standing, gripping each other's arms. For a silent minute, they simply stood near each other, feeling tears welling up inside them. Milo's tears were half from happiness and half that her parents were there and that was a fact worth crying over. In a sudden instant, all three simultaneously broke into a sobbing, snuffling, wet cascade of tears.

The poor, yet finely dressed, parents hugged their long-lost daughter and went on crying, their tears running down and mingling with her hair. Milo wept as well, her face wedged between their two necks. She couldn't believe they were there. She felt so happy. That was happiness she was feeling, right? Or was it nervousness? She was nervous? Why?

"They're your parents," Bob the Conscience sighed.

Her mother leaned away from Milo and held her face in her hands.

"Milo," she said, sniffing, her mascara making tiny black rivers down her cheeks. "I really can't – When we heard about the plane . . . we were devastated. Just . . ." She swallowed hard. "And everybody got out except you. Isn't that funny?"

"Fate," Milo muttered, not daring to look behind her, feeling the thousands of eyes on her back.

"Oh, hon," her father said, wiping his eyes and clasping her shoulders. "Let me look at you. Well! Say, you look slightly healthier than the last time I saw you. But, changing the subject to a more important question, what are you doing here?"

"What am I doing here?" Milo repeated incredulously, immediately feeling that she had the perfect right to be there and shouldn't be interrogated about it. "What are *you* doing here? And where did that thing come from?" she demanded, thrusting a thumb at the miniature plane, a series of steps leading down from the open door. "Last time we were together, we didn't have enough money to send me to a private school, much less buy something like that!"

"Well," her father said proudly. "It's like this, hon. I got a very large promotion after you left. My good, ol' boss made me vice president. Second in command. Lots of money in that! Bought this rig here and we now live up in the penthouse at 711 Shady Ally."

"You still live there?" Milo said, appalled and taking several steps backwards.

"Absolutely," her mother said primly, opening her purse to find a compact mirror. "It's such a nice place. We were island hopping, but we didn't know that natives live here."

"Mom," Milo groaned, all joyful feelings fading. "They're not natives. They're people."

"Who said they weren't?" she inquired, dabbing at her face. "Natives are people. Of course, when we landed, we didn't expect them to be here. Wait. Um, who's he?"

Milo hesitantly turned around to see Simon standing directly behind her. He had grown too nervous and thought he should go over. After all, she had met *his* parents. Milo bit back a moan, certain, beyond a shadow of a doubt, that things were only going to get worse from here.

"HELLO!" Milo's mother shouted at Simon, enunciating heavily. "HOW ARE YOU?"

Simon gave her a skeptical look. "I'm all right," he said warily. "How are you?"

Both Milo's parents jumped back in surprise. It might have been comical, only it came off more as embarrassing. Milo wondered bleakly who in their right mind thought it would be good for her parents to become wealthy.

"He can speak English?" her father said, ogling Simon like he was the missing link.

"A few can," Milo informed them, silently thinking that he might be a little deaf now.

"Well!" her father exclaimed, in a tone that implied he had money so he could utter such things. Never in her life had Milo wanted to smack her father more. "How about that! Who is he, hon?"

"Well," she said, putting a hand on Simon's arm. "This is Simon Swallow. He is my –"

She stopped short, the words catching in her throat. What in the world was she saying? How could she tell them that she was married? Without warning, all of the aspects of her life on the island seemed to become unsure and unstable, like she didn't know if they were good or not. As if she had been caught doing something bad. She gazed up at Simon, her eyes pleading. His face was expressionless, but his eyes were asking her questions. Questions of loyalty.

"Go on. Tell them," he said to her. "Who am I, Milo?"

Milo deflated somewhat, knowing he was right and feeling ashamed that her parents being there should change that. However, she was right too, because she knew it would. She sighed, raised her eyes to Heaven so that she wouldn't have to look at either of them, and braced herself.

"He's my husband."

Her parents stared at her. The sounds of the ocean lapping at the shore were audible and a bird cawed, but other than that it was unbroken silence. Even the villagers were waiting with bated breath, and they barely knew what was going on.

"What?" her mother finally said.

"I'm her husband," Simon said, standing beside Milo, feeling he should take charge of some sort.

"That's not possible," her father said dismissively. "She's too young to get married."

"Well," Milo said, her heart pounding, knowing that the truth must be tackled before they could move on to other, more pleasant things. "That doesn't really matter here, Dad."

"Do you mean to say that you're already married?" her mother shouted, her calmness gone as if it was a just a mask that was torn off. Milo jumped at the unexpected outburst, Simon putting an arm protectively about her shoulders. The woman glowered at her.

"Now, Sherrill-Jean," her father said sternly, touching her wrist. "I'm sure Milo's kidding."

Sagging, Milo gulped. He had used her name. He was mad at her.

"Actually, Dad, I am. I mean I'm not!" she corrected quickly. "I've been married since July."

"What?!" he roared, also losing all composure. It was actually rather startling. Together, bristling in their swanky attire, the Hestlers seethed at their daughter, who cowered beneath Simon's arm.

"July?" her father fumed. "Do you mean to say that you agreed to get married to a boy you barely knew?"

"Well, no," she said slowly, her blood pounding in her ears. "Not exactly. 'Agree' really isn't the word of choice here. It's actually kind of a funny story. Well, it's funny *now* . . . not so much back then. I think I'll start it with someone reading to you from the law book. Yes, that might be good. Um, AJSHA! Go get it!"

As Ajsha hastened to obey, Milo's mother asked, "Who is Ajsha?"

"That's also funny," Milo said, her head starting to throb. "She's my . . . daughter."

"WHAT?!!!" they both cried at the same time, exceptionally alarmed.

"Adopted!" Milo added hurriedly. "Adopted daughter! She's six!

See, it's all part of the marriage deal – I'll just explain after you hear the laws."

Her parent's shoulders slumped with relief, and they went to stand by the private plane's front tire to await their fabled granddaughter's return. Those in the surrounding mob who could comprehend English were currently bringing the rest up to speed on what was happening. Shocked mutterings permeated the vicinity, though everyone had enough sense not to bother Milo or Simon right then, both of them looking incredibly preoccupied. Soon the tightly packed crowds began to break up, many people, mostly those who could stand only so much excitement for one day, headed back towards town. The more iron-nerved stuck around, leaning against trees and milling in circles, gossiping and wondering when the Mayor would arrive.

As they waited for Ajsha, Simon asked Milo in a whisper, "Why are you afraid of your parents? It's like you're scared of what they'll do."

"Oh, do be quiet, Simon," she whispered back. "You don't know these two. I'm telling you, you don't. Certain things are difficult to tell them, all right? Who knows whose head they'll rip off when they hear the laws. Probably mine . . . or yours."

Simon didn't know how to respond. He wanted to argue, to tell her that she was safe and that she shouldn't worry. However, since Milo looked like she was about to be poisoned, and he figured mere words wouldn't console her. He would have to prove it. Reaching out, he slipped a hand into hers and gave it squeeze. Instead of squeezing back, Milo jumped and checked to see if her parents were watching. Simon suppressed a groan.

Presently, Ajsha came back with Mrs. Lanslo and the massive law book. Nervously, the woman stood between the plane and the islanders and read the marriage laws to the parents. When Mrs. Lanslo finished, they both were outraged in their own way. Milo's father was shaking with fury, and her mother looked liable to faint. It isn't easy for parents to learn that their daughter is ensnared within such unheard of, fiendish laws, even if they are a slightly lower category of parent. Once they had paced a little and muttered angrily a little, to themselves and each other, Milo's parents glared at all the remaining island people.

"Do you mean to say that you enforced these laws on my baby girl?!" her father yelled at them.

By now there were several professional interpreters among the denizens. They stood at the front and explained what was happening. Everyone looked quite insulted.

"Yes," Milo said rashly, hoping this would clear everything up and they could move on.

No such luck. Milo's mother grabbed her by the shoulders and shook her. "Tell me exactly what happened," she commanded. "Tell me!" she snapped when Milo was about to protest.

"Um . . . Wouldn't you want to come inside where we can sit?" Milo suggested, already quite worn out and not exactly eager to have half the town hear her version of the wedding.

"Actually, Sherrill-Jean," her father interjected, sounding interested. "It would be nice if –"

"No! Tell me here! Now!"

Milo sighed and, stomach grinding to mush, told her parents what had occurred following her departure to Australia. From meeting Simon, to the Mayor holding a dagger to her throat when she refused to wear the engagement ring, and step by step through the wedding. As he heard her describing the despair she had felt on that day, Simon began to feel rather bad. Her parents didn't bother with sympathy and immediately grew furious. When Milo came to the end of her story, her father broke. Up. Down. Everywhere.

"This is an outrage!" he shouted at random. "You filthy barbarians! All of you! My poor daughter is lost, stranded, and you put her through hell! The audacity! But, there may be some wiggle room." He said this last part quietly, and to himself.

"Milo," he said, turning to her, "you are underage, too young to marry. Therefore, in order for you to actually be married, your mother or I would have to sign a paper, giving you permission."

Milo felt her heart drop down to somewhere near her ankles. "So," she said under her breath, her voice full of disappointment and dread, "I'm not really married?"

"Not legally," he confirmed unfeelingly. "You weren't born here, so technically the laws don't apply to you. The only way you could be is if we signed the marriage certificate."

Stiffly, Milo looked back at all those faces. They too were just finding all this out. All looked stunned and worried. But the face that looked the worst was Simon's. He had paled and looked like his entire world had just been ripped away from him. Her heart aching, Milo wanted to comfort him, but dared not. Ajsha looked devastated. Milo felt awful too, and utterly helpless.

"Well!" her mother said cheerfully, completely unaware of the terrible sorrow in her daughter's soul. "That's wonderful! We can take Milo home and forget this ever happened!"

Milo looked up in alarm. "Leave?" she whispered hoarsely.

Leave the island? Leave her only friends? Leave Chaos? Leave Market Day and Washing Day? Leave Ajsha?! Leave Simon?!! *Forget?*

"Of course," her mother declared sensibly. "You can't possibly want to stay here."

Milo remembered a time when she would have agreed with this. But now? How could she go? Did she want to leave? Did she?

"No," Simon said, panting and raking his fingers through his hair. He couldn't believe what was happening. How could they do this to him? How could they take away the one he loved? They couldn't. They wouldn't!

"No! You can't!" he insisted with a bit of a tremor, stepping forward to be next to Milo.

"Shut up, you!" Milo's father shouted savagely, spitting some. "We'll take our daughter where we please. You have no say in it!"

Rage boiled up in Simon. "I'm her husband!" he yelled.

"No you're not!" her mother screeched. "You just heard my husband! You and Milo are *not* married! So just stay out of this!"

As Simon winced and shook with repressed wrath, Ajsha timidly approached Milo. "They're not really taking you away?" she whispered, voice warbling. "Are they, Momma?"

"Quiet, kid!" Milo's mother shot defensively. "She is not your mom!"

Admittedly, this might have been overly harsh, but, in all honesty, no mother is ever thrilled to hear her fifteen year old daughter be called "Momma". Tears welled up in Ajsha's eyes as she ran to Simon, who picked her up.

"Don't talk to her like that!" he growled, clutching her to his chest.

"Mr. and Mrs. Hestler," Squelch said, walking up bravely before Milo's mother or father could retaliate. "Please don't take Milo away. I'm her best friend, Squelch Welch."

Milo's parents stared at her, and it was impossible to tell whether they were more surprised at her name or that Milo had a friend. "What kind of idiot names their child 'Squelch'?" her father asked his wife meanly. Apparently, it was the former.

Milo groaned hopelessly, and Squelch fell back, stunned. Her throat started to tighten and her eyes burned. They had hit her where it hurt. She went over to Simon, who patted her back.

"Don't listen to them," he told her in Galo.

"I knew this would happen," Ajsha sobbed in Galo, her tears dampening Simon's T-shirt. "I knew that someday someone would find her and take her away from us!"

"Shh," Simon said soothingly. "It'll be okay. Milo loves us. Or at least, I hope she loves us enough." He glanced at Milo, who looked like she wanted nothing more than to melt away.

"Please," Soldier said, singling himself out from the crowd, his brow lined with purpose. "Milo means so much to us. She really changed this place. She's special."

"Keep your words off us," Milo's father barked, brushing off his suit for emphasis. "Barbarians!"

"Dad!" Milo yelped, putting her hands up as if she could halt the words in midair. "Stop that!"

"Milo!" her mother said strictly, in a familiar tone. "Don't talk to your father that way."

Suddenly back in every kitchen the Hestlers had ever occupied, Milo snorted and crossed her arms. "I see you two haven't changed," she muttered, old emotions arising.

Her father and mother gave each other a long look, and then faced her again. Their expressions were somber, their hands clasped in front of them. Milo froze, wondering what was coming.

"Milo," her mother began sincerely, her voice catching. She shook her head. "Don't. Please. You see, we have. We've changed. When you disappeared, we were horrified and woe-stricken."

"We started to look over our lives as parents," her father said mournfully. "We realize that we haven't – well . . . been the best."

Milo blinked. She thought she'd never hear them say that. Never.

"We decided to change," her father went on. "We felt awful that we weren't able to be good parents to you while you were alive. We turned around, hon. We've changed. Really we have. Now we want to take you away from here. That's what good parents would do. Take their child away from the place where their child suffers. You can't possibly be happy here."

"She is!" barked someone from within the crowd.

There were gasps and murmurs alike as the multitude of bodies parted and Aunt Rosario Em-I marched smartly up to the scene. Even Milo was baffled to see her so far from her home.

She halted before the Hestlers and planted her hands on her

hips. "Well," she said, staring at them critically. "Hello, Earnest. Sherrill-Jean. Don't you remember me? Surely you recognize your own sister, Earnest."

Milo's father stood in shock for a moment, before spluttering back to life.

"Rosario?" he sputtered, staring so hard it was as if he were trying to see through her.

"It can't be," Milo's mother said, paling so that the rouge on her cheeks stood out.

Aunt Rosario nodded. "It is," she said scornfully. "I was here long before Milo. I was a flight attendant when we crashed. I married the mayor of this island. I burned down your first house. I am nearly always sick and alone, but I'm happy and content here, so don't even try to talk me into anything!"

"What was that about a house?"

"Nothing. Don't try to change the subject. The point is, just as I am happy here and you can't make me leave, Milo's happy here and you can't make her leave."

"Nonsense," Milo's father said, regaining a certain sense of pomp, still not quite convinced that he was speaking to his sister. He scratched at his hairline, trying to reorient himself. "How do I know you're even my sister? Here, only my sister knows what my middle name is."

Aunt Rosario kept her hands on her hips and smirked. "Jabez," she said.

Milo's father paled too. Then he smiled. "Rosario!" he cried happily, opening his arms.

"I said don't change the subject," she remonstrated sharply. "The point is, you're inflicting a lot of pain on the good people of this island by saying you'll take Milo away."

Milo's mother's lips curled around her teeth, a quirk Milo had never seen her do before. "They'll just have to find a way to live without her. Rosario. The barbarians."

"They're not barbarians, Mom!" Milo hissed, peering furtively at the crowd, who were getting quite disgruntled. "You've got to stop saying that. They're people. People just like you and me."

"Nonsense!" her father said again, the island heat obviously not helping his already low sense of decorum. He dabbed at the corner of his mouth with a sleeve. "People don't hold daggers to another's throat to force them to say vows. You can't possibly like living among them, Milo."

"She does!" Aunt Rosario snapped, with a glare that dared her brother to snap back. He didn't.

"Please," Mrs. Lanslo chimed in. "She does. She really is happy. She does want to stay here."

"Shut up," Milo's father said, aiming his venom at her, and for good measure added, "Old hag!"

"You shut up!" Soldier spat, striding forward, on the brink of cracking his knuckles.

"Milo," her mother said to her, twisting her away from all this and making her stare into her eyes. "You aren't okay here, are you? You don't want to stay here, do you? Now tell the truth."

Milo looked mutely at her parents and then back at her new people who had no specific name, but were just people. She glanced from her mother to Ajsha. From her father to Simon. They all waited silently. She, gulped, not knowing what to say. All solid ground had been blown away.

"W-well," she began nervously. All eyes were fastened onto her. She felt like they were crushing her. "I don't know. I mean, I guess so. I mean ... I – I – I –"

She searched around for comfort, but couldn't find any. "I suppose so," she said, her not even sure what she was referring to. "But . . . Oh, stop! I don't know what to know. What to think."

"How can you say that?" her father demanded.

"Yes, how?" Aunt Rosario remarked angrily.

Tears pricked the back of Milo's eyeballs. Did she want to stay?

Did she want to leave? If she left, where would she go? Back to 711 Shady Ally, spelled without the e? She quaked.

"She wants to stay," Squelch piped up courageously, noticing Milo's cringing. "We're all just scaring her. This is her home now."

"Hush up!" Milo's mother snapped. "Only Milo can say what's what. Milo, listen. Hear this: You *can* stay. That's right; I said we've changed. We won't force you to do anything. We'll let you stay here, but only if you say that's what you want and why. But if you say you'll go, we'll whisk you away faster than you can blink. Only you can tell us." She leaned closer, plucked eyebrows in a V. "I hope you pick right. I hope you pick us. America. Society. Electricity."

"That's right, hon," her father interjected. "In the penthouse you'll have two double ovens, a grill, and a deep fat fryer. Four refrigerators. You can be what you always wanted. A caterer."

"What?" Milo said, cocking her head to see past her mother's death glare. "You mean cook?"

"Yeah, that. Whatever. Just make the right choice and come home with us. To your *real* home," he articulated severely. "Not this foolishness. Come home with us, your parents. The people who actually love you. We love you so much, hon. Right, Sherrill-Jean?"

"I guess so. I mean –! Of course we do!" she amended hastily. "You're meant to be with us, Milo. Not these horrific jerks. You'll be happy once you're with us."

"Who says that she isn't happy now?" growled Soldier.

"She will," her father replied calmly, slightly cowed by Soldier's girth. "Once she comes to her senses and sees that leaving is the best thing. She's wants to be with those who love her."

"Who says that we don't?" Squelch cried, two fat tears rolling unwelcomingly down her face.

Milo's mother and father looked at each other and exploded with laughter.

"How could you!" they laughed with a lack of inhibition brought on by the oppressive heat and recently acquired money. "She's stubborn, skinny, and a nutcase! How could anyone but parents love that?"

Stunned by her parents' outburst, Milo felt her own prickling tears break free and slide down. Glancing behind her, she saw that nearly everyone was looking in every direction but at her. She couldn't tell if it was out of tact, or shame from partly agreeing. The exception was Simon. He was giving her a hard, determined look. A Fight Back look. She nodded, eyes narrowing.

"I'm more than that!" she yelled at her parents over their chortling. "I'm way more! More than you'll ever know! You don't know crap about me! Therefore, that's what you think of me! Well, Milo Swallow is more than that!"

The Hestlers had ceased their merriment and were now glaring lividly at her. Her father brought his face close to hers to speak. He did not have milky breath.

"Look at yourself," he hissed. "You've forgotten who you are. The one thing I asked of you, Milo, you forgot. I asked you not to forget that you're a Hestler, and you did."

Milo felt herself flush with an undeserved shame. It just came naturally to think of herself as a Swallow. She did forget. She had willingly forgotten. How could she? She began to feel bad. How could her feelings be so mixed up? Why was she feeling for both?

"Ain't my fault," Bob the Conscience told her.

Milo's father straightened up, smoothing down his jacket in what he might have thought was a dignified manner. "We'll give you the rest of today and . . . tomorrow to decide. We'll even let you spend it with them. Then you'll come to us and we'll hear what you've decided. Remember, Milo, we have changed."

"Yes," her mother agreed. "We'll stay on the plane. It has a *bed and bath*," she said pointedly.

Milo stood numb for a moment, before her head inclined minutely in a nod. Rigidly, she turned around and faced the mob of lookers and listeners. As she slunk away from her parents, she didn't bother to say goodbye to them, nor did they offer one. As the island people slowly started to disperse, Squelch and Simon went up to Milo. Simon was still holding Ajsha.

"Well," Squelch said in a forced cheerful tone. "Crazy day, huh? You're not leaving, are you?"

Milo shrugged helplessly. "I don't know," she mumbled reluctantly.

"No!" Ajsha cried, fresh showers falling from her eyes. "You can't leave, Momma! I'll miss you too much! I can't live without you! I love you, Momma. Don't leave."

Milo winced. She couldn't look at Ajsha; she hated seeing a child in hysterics, especially one that was rarely in hysterics. It must be bad if Ajsha couldn't maintain composure.

"But . . . think!" Squelch said insistently. "You said so yourself, you've never had any friends except here. You were miserable where you used to live. Do you really think that going back there is the answer?"

Milo couldn't respond, not that she wanted to, for Mrs. Lanslo appeared suddenly with Soldier.

"You're really not going away, are you, dear?" she inquired unhappily. "I know you didn't like it here at first, but what about now, dear? Don't you like it here now?"

"Of course she does," Soldier replied for her. "And she loves her husband and kid and friends. Heh! That's right, huh, Milo?"

Milo shrugged again, not denying, not confirming. She was having trouble swallowing. Mrs. Lanslo bit her nails, and Soldier frowned dangerously.

"Well," he said curtly, "I hope you think it out thoroughly. We'd miss you, girl. Life is more interesting with you here, Milo. Don't forget all the stuff we do for each other."

"No," Milo whispered. "I won't. I'd never forget any of you. You've all been so good to me. But, this I really need to figure out for myself. By myself. I'm sorry."

She turned away from them and proceeded to walk towards her

house. Squelch shared some words of love and comfort with her before having to go home. Several other people came up to her and tried to persuade her to stay. Even Randolf Fittler and his unruly gang, including Caleb Scumm, approached her to apologize for any past happenings. Even they wanted her to stay, though they didn't say why. Probably for Simon's sake. Simon quietly interpreted, since Ajsha was still collecting herself. Milo merely shrugged each time, wishing they would leave her alone.

Ajsha finally got people to keep their distance, but then even she tried to talk Milo into not going. Simon hushed her as they arrived at the house. Carefully, Milo walked the entire stone pathway and looked her colorful house over. She read the words by the door, then the ones above it. Her gaze lingered painfully on those. She sighed miserably.

"Houses are built of brick and stone, but homes are made of love alone."

She then entered and walked into the sitting room, where she ran her hands over the makeshift furniture and patted the granite table. She then wandered into the kitchen, where she did the same thing. She gently stroked the painted chairs and table and ran her fingertips along the counter tops. She opened cupboards and drawers, only to close them again. She opened the cellar door and fingered her mussed backpack. It was strange. It was as if she had never seen any of it before and yet was trying so hard to savor it. Exhaling heavily, she roamed up the hallway.

She went into her bedroom and limply sat down on the bed. Chaos appeared from nowhere and jumped up, Milo picking her up. Milo held the feline to her face and sniffed her. She smelled like the outside. Salty and fresh and sweet. Milo sniffled, thinking about how she loved that smell. Ajsha and Simon quietly peeked into the room. Ajsha gathered her courage and entered.

"Momma?" she said, failing to keep her voice steady. "You won't go, will you?"

Milo's only response was to mutter something about her needing to stop crying or else she'd get sick. Simon ushered Ajsha back out into the hall. Milo collapsed onto the bed and remained there for the rest of the day. Many locals visited, wanting to talk to her, but Simon always shooed them away. Most didn't even have a connection to her, but right then she was the most exciting thing on the island. Truthfully, she was going down in their history for what was happening. The great Hestler stand-off would be studied years from now in the history class of every grade level.

However, it was far from over yet. Curled up on the sheets, Milo held her head. The island was pulling her one way, her parents were yanking her another, and it was making her head spin. Simon remained the only one who didn't try to influence her in any way. That night, Milo lay wide awake. Simon wasn't sleeping, either, but he didn't try to talk to her. Milo felt rather distant from him, though he lay close. Eventually, her eyes grew heavy with sleep and she sighed.

"What should I do?" she murmured, reaching out to place a wrist on his shoulder.

"It's your choice," Simon said simply, scalding his tongue. "Do whatever you want."

Milo knew she should, but what if the choice she wanted wasn't the right one? What was she going to do? She fell into a fitful sleep festooned with nightmares. In the nightmares, she saw all the people on the island she cared about standing in a group and staring at her. Their faces were expressionless, but it scared her. She woke up numerous times and only by some miracle was able to fall back to sleep.

In the morning she quietly made the bed and made breakfast for the family that wasn't really hers. She uttered not a word and ate nothing. When she was done with the dishes, she drifted back to her bedroom. Ajsha, too flustered to remain pent up all day, went out to seek reassurance from friends, but Simon stayed. When he finally looked into their bedroom, he saw Milo sitting cross-legged on the bed and staring out the window, Chaos loyally coiled on her lap.

"You all right?" he asked quietly after knocking softly on the doorframe.

She shook her head, not looking at him. Sighing, he sat down beside her. He laid his head morosely on her shoulder, and Milo patted his hand comfortingly.

"Would you miss me?" she asked in a whisper, a whisper for only the two of them.

He was silent for a moment, considering his reply. "I don't want to say," he murmured. "I don't want you to stay for me. That's not fair. I forced you to be with me once, Milo; I won't do it again. This is your decision alone. I'm not going to pressure you."

"I know," said Milo, her throat tight with emotion. "And I'm grateful, but I need to know whether you would be happy or not if I left. I've got to know if you'd miss me. Please say you would."

Simon really didn't want to hurt his wife any, but she had asked.

"Of course I would," he choked out. "I'd miss you *soooo* much. I love you so much, Milo. It would wreck me if you left. But, whatever your decision is, I will support it."

"You will?" Milo said, sniffing. "Why?"

Simon sat up and turned her face so she would look at him. "Because I want you to be happy. If you're happy, then I'm happy. Because I love you, and that's all that matters."

He kissed her cheek and stood up to leave. At the doorway, he turned back to her.

"Don't worry about what's right or wrong," he said earnestly. "Just choose what you want. Only what *you* want."

With that, he left, disappearing into the house that had been Milo's reality only yesterday, but now loomed around her strange and surreal. Seeing her parents had partially drawn Milo from the person she had become into the person she had been, and the two were currently colliding with each other.

"I know what I want," Milo told Chaos, stroking her head, "but there was a time when I didn't want it. We're not married . . . I could leave. But should I? I'm only fifteen. What's right? Being with parents or with your family? What should I do? Dang, why am I so confused?"

Have you ever heard the expression, "When in doubt, listen to your heart"?

Well, at that very moment, Milo thought of it. Arising from the bed, she walked all the way to the church to pray, as it is a very good thing to do when consumed by doubt. People paused to stare at her as she did so, thrill-seekers and such. When she finally came home, she decided to take the ageless, timeless, and priceless advice and actually follow her heart. But where did it lead? Well, the good thing about hearts is that they are usually quite blunt and straightforward. And when she took the time to listen to it, Milo had to agree with her heart.

30
I Do

IT WAS VERY early in the morning, the sun barely teasing the horizon, but Milo had woken up anyways. She felt sleep was quite out of the question considering the situation she was in. The only other one up was Simon, who must have felt the same way, though for different reasons. They had dressed and were wandering silently about the hut, feeling tremendously nervous and fidgety. Eventually, Simon walked into their bedroom and found Milo sitting stiffly on the bed, looking drawn in the dim half-light. He smiled weakly at her, and she made a feeble attempt to return it.

"You ready?" he asked her gently.

"Yes," she sighed. "Simon, you don't have to . . . I can do this by myself."

"No," he said firmly. "I am your husband. You're not going alone. I'll either see you off, or take you home. Whichever way, I'll be there."

Milo smiled gratefully at him. Then she exhaled forcefully and fell onto her back. "Oh!" she moaned, pounding her fists on the sheets. "When did things get so confusing?"

"I don't know," Simon admitted, sitting down on the bed. He stroked her forehead. "I remember a time when you would have jumped into that plane before it had even touched down. . . . I even remember when you hated me so much that you were ready to make me sick with a raw egg."

Wincing, Milo sat up and stared into Simon's eyes.

"Hey," she said. "I can't say how sorry I am. Not just about that, but everything. I know I treated you like crap. Please try to forget how I acted. I was different back then. I was so stubborn."

Simon grinned. "There's a saying, 'A stubborn wife makes a bad lover, but a good cook.'"

Milo actually laughed out loud. "So true! But I want to be both. . . . Like I said, I'm sorry."

"I know. It's okay. You had a reason for everything you did. Still, you were better than most. Some people, when they come here, just sit on the beach and stare out at the sea. I'm glad you didn't do that."

"Yeah," Milo murmured. "I guess I adapted better than I thought I did. . . . I mean, I didn't try to build a raft or anything."

"Yeah," Simon laughed. "That's happened too . . . never ends well."

They lapsed into silence, the light-hearted moment passing. Finally Milo said, "Simon, even if I do go, I want you to know that I do love you. I wasn't lying about that. I do love you and Ajsha."

He swallowed hard. "And we love you, Milo," he whispered. "No matter where you are."

Milo leaned to the side and kissed his temple. "Thanks, boo. Ya hungry?"

"Not really," he muttered. "You?"

"No. I guess I'm too nervous. But I didn't eat anything yesterday, so I'd better today. When I don't eat for a long time I start throwing up. I know it makes no sense, but that's what happens."

"Maybe some fruit?" Simon proposed, deciding not to comment on this particular idiosyncrasy.

"Sure," she agreed, somewhat eager to get out of the bedroom. She hadn't seen much else, lately.

Hand in hand, just two teens, the spousal illusion gone, they walked into the kitchen and ate some mangoes and raspberries. Milo felt better after that, one of the sick feelings inside her clearing up, and as she was washing the dishes Simon came up behind her. Gently brushing her hair aside, he kissed her shoulder and put his arms around her. Milo's throat tightened and her nose burned. Oh, but she was not going to cry. Not today. Today, she would be strong. If she could. At the moment, Simon wasn't helping.

Eventually, Ajsha walked in, looking sleep deprived and sullen. She hugged Milo's legs, burying her face in her jeans. Milo patted her head, feeling thoroughly hugged, and fixed her some breakfast. She ate it quietly, too choked with emotion to utter a single syllable, though she continuously cast Milo beseeching glances. Just as Ajsha went to dress, people started to gather in front of the house. Milo's stomach churned as she looked out the window at all of them.

"When should we leave?" she listless asked Simon, turning towards him.

He smiled faintly. "Is there any hurry?" he inquired, reaching out to touch her arm.

"I'd like to get this over with."

His face and hand fell, but he said softly, "I understand."

They headed outside when Ajsha came back, her long hair in a very stiff braid appropriate for funerals. Before they left, Milo picked up Chaos and kissed her fuzzy head. She whispered into her ear, rubbed her human forehead against her kitty one, and then set her down. The feline peered up at Milo with a sort of stunned fascination, as if wondering why the proceedings didn't involve her. Sighing, Milo turned and began to walk away, first blowing a kiss to her flowers. The light morning breeze shifted just enough to bend the stems towards her, and every petal fluttered in such a way that the flowers might have been waving.

The assembled people watched the three of them for a second before following. The crowd included Mrs. Lanslo, Soldier, Randolf

Fittler and his gang, Hattie Knocker, Aunt Rosario with Mayor Em-I, (which might have made Milo anxious at one time, but now she just didn't care) and Salsa and Squelch. The rest, who were more strangers than friends, also supported Milo, while the remaining spectators, mostly youngsters, were only there for the excitement. They all headed towards the beach, Milo in front, her face unreadable.

When the procession arrived, Milo's parents were waiting impatiently for her, dressed in their most imperious wealthy-person attire. They wore strict, I-know-I'm-better-than-you looks. Milo stopped twenty feet from them. Turning on the spot, she hugged Salsa and Squelch, who gasped and mournfully shook their heads. Milo dammed up her tears as she left them and the entire mob, and neared her parents.

"Well?" her father said, not bothering to say good morning.

"Have you made your decision?" her mother said, also not bothering.

"Yes," Milo said quietly, staring straight at them. She felt like telling them good morning, just to spite them, but also felt it would be a lie. "I have. It wasn't easy, but I think it's the right one."

"Good," her mother said, sounding relieved. "Good! I'm proud of you, Milo. I've never really had a reason to be, but I am now. Come on, then! Hop aboard!"

Milo didn't budge. "Do you remember," she went on as if her mother hadn't spoken, "my childhood? Do you?"

"What?" her father said, halting on his way to the plane. "What's that got to do with anything?"

"Do you?" Milo inquired severely, standing rigidly on the sand like a dividing pole.

Interpreters in the crowd began to translate the conversation into Galo. Her father peered at them suspiciously, trudging back over to his wife, who was also squinting at them distrustfully.

"Of course we do," he replied tartly, crossing his arms. Milo's mother nodded in agreement.

"Was I happy at all?"

"What?" they asked, clueless as to what this had to do with their current situation.

"Please just answer my question."

"Of course you were!" her mother answered briskly, checking both her watch and the crowd.

"Oh, think hard," Milo said quietly.

Her parents started at her tone and stared at her, finally ignoring everything around them.

"Was I ever really happy?" Milo asked. "Was I? No. I wasn't. I was an outcast. A sad, scared, hopeless outcast. But mostly I was lonely. Really lonely. So lonely that I made friends with a stapler. And when he was gone, I started talking to my conscience. I was so desperate for a friendship that I started talking to myself! Do you call that happy? Do you? I've *never* really, truly have been happy any place you've taken me. And you guys didn't exactly help."

Her parents fidgeted uneasily and looked down at their feet as a genuine emotion that they didn't recognize suddenly surged through their hearts. Guiltiness was new to them.

"Then I came here," Milo went on, more loudly, her stomach hurting. "Things changed. You know, at first I was miserable and wanted to leave. I *longed* to leave. I wished each night and day that someone would find me and take me away. I wanted to leave so much, no one has any idea. Well, except, of course, my conscience, whom I talk to! And I *hated* Simon! I hated him for forcing me to marry him and all the crap that came with it."

There was some peevish mumbling behind her as this was translated, but she ignored it.

"Could you blame me?" she demanded. "Yes, if you had come then, I would have gone with you without question. You wouldn't even have had to have landed; I would have jumped from a palm tree into the plane as you circled around. But now . . . now things are different. They've been different for a while.

"The difference is that I'm in love. I fell in love with Simon."

There was an awed silence that followed this. The mob smiled and her parents' mouths dropped.

"What?" her father stammered, looking from her to Simon, who stared back defiantly. "But he –"

"I know," she cut in. "But that doesn't matter now. I love him and my daughter. And you know what? I am actually grateful to him for forcing me to marry him. Back then, I hated it, but not now. Crazy, huh?" she laughed softly. She looked them over pityingly. "No. You don't get it. *I'm happy here!* I – Love – It – Here! This is the first home I've ever really had. I have my own family now. I have my own *house* and my own *kitchen* and even a *cat*. I dug us a cellar and planted a flower garden and painted our house. I cook and clean and wash, and I am *happy*. I'm happy when I'm productive. And, I actually have *friends* here. Friends, as in *plural*, as in more than one! Good . . . *great* friends."

Those friends were sucking in their breath with mounting anticipation. Simon stared at her, not daring to blink, or else all hope would be lost and she would vanish.

"I've never been happy anywhere else," Milo plowed on, her volume steadily increasing. "At first, I didn't understand why it was all happening. I even wondered if God had stopped caring and just left me to suffer. The island and the wedding seemed like the last thing I could take. But, you know, I don't think that way anymore. I think that maybe God meant for me to come here; that all this was His answer for my lousy life. Like He was saying, 'I know how you're doing, but I have a plan for you. So just try to trust Me and hang in there. You may not know what's going to happen, but I do, and I'll take care of you. I have a plan for you.'

"And this was his plan," she said. "Okay, yes, it's an island, an unknown, mystery island with its own language and economy and rules that don't make sense. And, no, I don't know why they have people marry at such young ages. Heck, maybe it's a conspiracy or something to make the island population grow faster."

When Mayor Em-I heard this translated, he coughed into his fist. As did his colleagues.

"But," Milo went on, her voice warbling with sincerity. "It doesn't matter. Finally, since we first moved, I am happy. Before, I couldn't forget about my past because I thought it would also be my future, the same friendless, homeless, nomad lifestyle on repeat. But this is my future now, and I can forget. You said that you want to start being good parents, and I'm sure you must think that good parents would take their daughter away from a strange island where, yes, there is no electricity, or health insurance, or glass in the windows. True, but think about it. Good parents also don't want their kids to wallow in misery, and that's what I'll do anywhere else except here. If you really want to be good parents, if you really mean it, then you'd let me stay here? Right?"

"What're you trying to say?" her mother asked, suddenly gentle; the steam pricked out of her.

Milo inhaled deeply, aware of every eye on her and every strained set of lungs holding in oxygen and every pair of ears waiting to hear her final verdict.

"I'm saying that I want to stay."

A moment of silence followed these word, her parents motionless and without retort, and the interpreters struggling past their elation to loosen their tongues. When they finally relayed her answer to the crowd, a roar of delight went up. For the first time in two days, Simon took an easy breath, his chest no longer constricted. But Milo wasn't done.

"I realize that this can't be easy for you," she said quickly, while she had her parent's attention. The interpreters yelled something along the lines of "Shut up! Shut up!" and a hush fell on the people.

"But," Milo implored, her body trembling with apprehension, "please, it seems that our marriage certificates aren't complete. I know I'm really young and maybe it just seems silly, but I want to remain married to Simon. We're not . . . being irresponsible or anything. And I love him more than I thought I could love anyone. And, for some reason I've yet to figure out, he loves me even more. So, Dad, Mom, could you please sign the certificates?"

Once again, all present held their breath, especially Simon, waiting for the answer. Milo waited with a throbbing pulse, feeling as though she was at the brink of an abyss, and that everything that ever mattered or ever would matter was suspended within the two possible replies.

Milo's parents, to an unknowing observer, might have looked defeated, but actually they were touched. Whatever sudden riches had done to alter them, thinking that they had lost their daughter, their only child, had done far more. And it was this remorse, this contrition, which visited them now. When they had finished thinking through all she had said, Mr. and Mrs. Hestler looked at each other, both knowing each others' thoughts: Though this all was exceedingly bizarre, it was time for them to start being good parents.

"Milo," her mother said, smiling at her, "we're going to let you stay and we'll sign the papers."

Milo, overcome by both relief and shock started to gasp, as the crowd started to roar again upon hearing the translation. She felt like keeling over, all of her strength and tension draining away. Unwanted tears threatened to spill, but she managed to keep them at bay and turn herself to see Simon's beaming, breathless form. Suddenly Milo had her strength back, and everyone cheered as she ran into his arms. Or he ran into hers. It was hard to tell. They kissed over and over again, hugging each other tightly, determined never to let go. Stray tears slipped down both their faces, but neither noticed. The shouting died away, and that bubble of separate time and space known to couples sprung up around the two of them.

"You wanted to stay," Simon whispered, smiling, his hands clutching her back.

"Oh, I'll never leave you," Milo whispered back, her eyes shut. "Not even for the world."

Leaning away, yet still holding her close, Simon looked at her face. "You'd give up the world?"

Milo nodded calmly, her lips curling unintentionally into a smile. "I've tried the world. The world sucks. But, even if it didn't, I'd still want you more."

He grinned and kissed her again, as their bubble of privacy dissolved and the surrounding sounds became audible once more. Ajsha was close to bursting with joy, laughs and shouts issuing simultaneously out of her. As the couple broke apart, she rushed up to Milo and jumped to hug her. Milo had just enough time to turn from Simon and stoop down to catch her.

"Momma!" Ajsha cried joyously, entwining her arms about Milo's neck. "You're staying!"

"That's right, sugar!" Milo confirmed, chuckling and kissing her nose. "I ain't going nowhere! You stuck with me for the rest of your life!"

Squelch and Salsa, who had been holding each other fearfully the whole time, were now whooping and wiping away leftover tears. They pranced up to her, Salsa doing a few cartwheels.

"Oh, girl, you scared me!" Squelch laughed thickly as Milo put Ajsha down.

"Sorry," Milo apologized, hugging her fiercely.

"Don't do anything like that again," Salsa ordered, hugging her too.

"Heh," Milo scoffed. "I really don't think I'm capable of doing this again. I so want a nap."

She jumped as a booming laugh resounded from behind her.

Whirling around, she had enough time to register that it was Soldier before she was caught up in a rib-splintering hug.

"Ha-ha!" he thundered jubilantly. "Knew it! Knew it all along! Never doubted ya for second!"

"No?" Milo wheezed, wriggling one hand free enough to pat his elbow.

"Really, now, Gorben," Mrs. Lanslo tutted, coming up beside them. "Let the poor dear breathe."

"Oh, sorry," Soldier apologized bashfully, setting Milo back on her feet, perhaps an inch or so skinnier than when he had picked her up.

"S'all good," she muttered amiably, embracing Mrs. Lanslo, just as Aunt Rosario burst through the throng of bodies, her pallid cheeks quite rosy. Her husband was a couple of paces behind her.

"You've no right to give us all heart attacks like that!" she said as they hugged.

"Sorry," Milo said yet again, glancing up at the Mayor, who returned it with a look that assured her that they didn't need to hug. Milo nodded appreciatively.

As she and her aunt parted, Milo noticed her parents timidly approaching the group. They both looked much more pleasant and rather curious. A thought that, due to the recent controversy, seemed odd, occurred to Milo. She glanced at her island family, then at her biological family, and felt it was time to close the gap.

"Mom, Dad," she said, taking Simon's hand and pulling him over to them, "this is Simon Swallow. My husband. Well, husband once you sign the papers."

They studied each other for a moment, letting all previous biases fade away, and at last smiled at each other. Of course, this also meant overlooking the fact that they all had been very rude.

"Hellooo," Milo's mother said sweetly, going and shaking his hand.

"How are you, son?" her father tried, shaking his hand with a grip fitting of a humbled rich man.

"Terrific, now," Simon answered, somewhat shy, somewhat eager. "It's so nice to meet you two – you know, without the yelling. How are you? Now, I mean?"

"Fine! Fine! Yes, sorry about our first encounter. We're not proud of our behavior. But, we were in shock . . . you've really got to understand."

"I do," he assured them. "It's all right. I don't blame you."

"And," Milo broke in, not liking the mistiness in her father's eyes, "this is Ajsha. My wonderful daughter." She gently pushed Ajsha forward, the little girl hesitant, since these were, in all honesty, the people she had been having nightmares about for months.

"Well, hello, sweetie," Milo's mother said, bending down. "How are you?"

"Fine," Ajsha said, shyly accepting the proffered manicured hand. "Now."

More introductions were made as they started to head into town, Milo intent on getting their signatures on those certificates before they changed their minds. They passed the Swallows' house along the way, and Milo's parents gasped as they saw it. They insisted that they just had to go inside. As they looked around at everything, they thoroughly expressed how proud they were of Milo for keeping such a tidy home and enduring in such a primitive structure. (Milo groaned.)

Then finally they went into town. The Hestlers, who, for the past two days, had been strictly under the impression that the inhabitants lived in tepees, simply marveled at it all and commented on every single detail. They were shown the stores and where the schoolhouse burned down, which, of course, prompted the story of how Milo became a hero. All she could do was stand

and shrug modestly while her parents gasped and stared at her with amazement. The next stop was the library. As they sat down on a tree bench, Mayor Em-I went down to retrieve Simon and Milo's marriage certificates.

"This is so sad," her mother said when she signed them. "I didn't even get to see my own daughter get married. My only little girl."

"I know," her father agreed. "I didn't even get to walk my own daughter down the aisle. You're it for us, Milo. It's so sad. And I was looking forward to passing you off, too."

Milo considered how they were feeling and felt sorry for them. An idea came to her. An enormous, colossal, fantastic thought. She swiveled to look at Simon. He had a quirk in the corner of his lips that indicated he was thinking the very same thing. They smirked at each other. Quietly, they stole away to talk, choosing a prime moment, since Aunt Rosario had finally gotten around to explaining that the mayor was her husband. (The sizing up didn't take long, Mayor Em-I winning.) When they were hidden behind a store, Milo faced Simon, her eyes gleaming.

"Are you thinking what I'm thinking?" she asked.

"We get married again?" he said hopefully.

She grinned at him and gently put a finger to her temple.

"That's right," she said, forcing herself not to cackle. "It's brilliant. My parents will be there and I'll actually enjoy myself. I will *want* to get married. What do ya say?"

"Absolutely!" he replied enthusiastically. "Technically, the last time wasn't even legal, and I'd never object to marrying you twice."

"Shoot!" Milo exclaimed, smiling and reaching up to give him a smooch. "I'm still shocked you wanted to do it the first time!"

They went back, hands entwined, and coughed numerous times for attention. Milo's parents had just finished signing their names, Mayor Em-I and Mr. Hestler shooting one another looks.

"We have made a decision," Milo announced, nodding at Ajsha

to translate. "Or I have, and he liked it. I don't know. But, we are going to have another wedding!"

Everyone, English and Galo speakers alike, gasped in delight and voiced their approval.

"Really?" Milo's father asked.

"Yes," Simon confirmed, draping an arm about Milo's thin shoulders. "The last time didn't really count because the certificates weren't signed, and Milo, to put it mildly, didn't want to. I think it's definitely worth doing over."

"I concur," Milo said. "I know it's only been two days, but I'm so over only having a boyfriend."

"Oh, Milo!" her mother choked out, leaping up from the bench and clasping her hands together. "I'm so excited! My daughter's wedding! My fourteen year old daughter's wedding!"

"Fifteen, Mom," Milo muttered, rubbing one eye in exasperation. "Fifteen."

"Right! Fifteen, sorry," her mother amended. "Fifteen's much better."

"I'll help!" Mrs. Lanslo offered before Milo could make a retort. "Just let me do everything."

"Oh, no you don't!" Milo said, rounding on her sternly. "*I'm* going to be taking care of this wedding. Every bit of it. It's mine, after all."

Both Mrs. Lanslo and Milo's mother started to protest, the first pointing out that it was too big a job for one person, and the second claiming that she had some good ideas. Milo however, in classic Milo fashion, was unyielding. The two women submitted at last, Mrs. Lanslo's condition being that she could assist in some form, and Mrs. Hestler's that the whole thing take place soon because Mr. Hestler was expected back on the mainland not long from now.

"Fine," Milo consented, giving Simon an inquiring look.

"We can start planning tonight," he told her with a grin.

And plan they did. Or, Milo planned and people carried out her orders, just like a real bride. The idea of her own wedding, prepared her way, enthralled her. Sure, last time she got to pick her clothes and jewelry and all the other minor accessories that people would only notice if they weren't there, but this time around she was in charge of *everything*. Everyone was quite willing to help out; therefore, she didn't get to boss and yell at people the way she thought wedding planners should. Nevertheless, it still beat the heck out of the first time, when *nobody* was listening to her.

She began by assigning people their parts. Squelch was going to be her maid of honor, though Bob the Conscience wanted the position and gave Milo a headache for giving it away. Meanwhile, Salsa, Mrs. Lanslo, and Hattie were going to be her bridesmaids. Ajsha, of course, was going to be the flower girl, this time in a dress of her choice. Simon again chose Will Westron to be his best man and several of his beach friends for groomsmen. Milo's father was going to walk her down the aisle, much to his pride and delight, and the Reverend Chouhouse was going to perform the ceremony.

One aspect of this wedding that was going to be different was that it was being held outside instead of in the church. Milo didn't want the old memories to muddy up the new ones. They picked a nice grassy area that was surrounded by leaning coconut trees and had a view of the ocean. All the chairs that were normally used at dances were brought out of storage and set up in rows. Since there wasn't enough for the whole town, plus the many farm families who had heard about the ordeal and wanted to come, the final word became that if you wanted to attend, bring your own seat.

One afternoon Milo had Simon accompany her into their bedroom, once their house was empty of the daily onslaught of company, which ranged from her parents, to his, to anyone involved with the wedding. (Milo had wanted it to be a small wedding from the get-go, but the accumulating list of guests, none of whom she had legal right to refuse, had caused her to need extra help with things such as decorations and food.) Incidentally, Milo had decided that, due to the unexpected amount of guests, the dinner was going to be a pot-luck affair.

"Help me lift the tick," she said, motioning Simon over to the bed.

Shrugging, he complied. Underneath, pressed against the slats, was Milo's wedding dress.

"Ahh," Simon said as she fished it out. "So that's where you put it. Why there?"

She grinned. "Where else? It's not like I wanted to frame it. Besides, it kept it wrinkle-free."

She flapped it out, admiring the way the beads glistened, and then went to check on Ajsha.

"How ya doing, love?" she asked, coming in to her room.

"Fine, Momma," Ajsha answered. She showed her a dress that was hanging up at the end of her bed. "Just like you said: A white sun dress, with a pink bow around the waist."

"Perfect," Milo commented upon examining it. She leaned down and kissed Ajsha's forehead.

Ajsha giggled. "I like this wedding much better than the last one," she said, stroking the folds of her dress's skirt. "So much more elegant. Are you excited, Momma?"

"Oh, you have no idea, babe," Milo said, smiling. "And this time I won't be wearing that ridiculous veil. I want every single person to see my ethereal glow! It's just a shame that my parents have to leave right after. I'm not saying I want them to stay here! That is, I'm only thinking of them. Once you go penthouse, you don't go back! Though, they seem to be having a good time translating with the Pitts. Maybe this wedding will smooth things over between us."

"Maybe," Ajsha said thoughtfully. "Let's just hope Hattie stays sane enough to make it through the whole ceremony, or that Caleb Scumm won't start acting like . . . well . . . like – like a scum!"

Milo smirked to herself. "Don't worry. He won't."

"Why are you so sure?" Ajsha asked suspiciously, all too familiar with that smirk.

"Because," Milo replied confidently, "Tambry Ethlins is quite good at the whole hostage thing, and isn't too moral to be bribed. If Caleb tries *anything*, he'll find himself tied up in her cellar!"

Ajsha nodded, impressed. Milo walked back to her bedroom, where Simon was waiting for her just inside the door.

"Hey, boo," she said as he jumped to hug her. After pacifying him with a kiss, she scratched the top of her head, thinking. "Let me show you something."

Sitting him down, she pointed to each symbol on his ring, decrypting them. "I – Love – You."

Simon concentrated for a moment, processing this new information, and finally grinned. He stopped when he saw her engagement ring hanging loosely on her finger.

"Can I do something?" he inquired softly.

"Sure," she said absently, tucking his hair behind his ears. "What?"

He slipped the ring off her finger and kneeled down on one knee in front of her. Taking hold of her left hand, he held up the ring, its stone glinting in the afternoon sunlight. Milo's eyes widened and she inhaled sharply, a tingling sensation spreading throughout her entire body.

"The proper way," he said quietly. "The way I wanted to do it the first time. Milo, there is no one else in the world like you, and I have loved you ever since I first . . . found you. I always knew that I was missing something, but I didn't know what until I . . . found you. Will you marry me?"

Milo smiled. Though it was her second wedding, it was her first time ever hearing those four words. "Yes," she said. "Yes, yes, yes!"

Grinning, he put the ring back on her finger. He stood up and they embraced, knowing that they were now fully prepared.

"Yes," Milo said again, into his shoulder.

Don't laugh at them. They wouldn't have cared, anyway.

The day of the wedding finally arrived, the early morning rays drying up the dew on the flower petals and chairs at the site. Simon lay contentedly in bed and took his time waking up. When he looked beside him, he saw his lovely bride struggling to wake up. He grinned and, leaning over her, kissed the side of her nose. That woke her. Her eyelids popped open and she stared at him.

"We're getting married today!" she said in a low voice.

"Again," Simon said, propping himself up on an elbow. "In fact, just between us, it makes me nervous to call it getting married. It's like saying we weren't married at all. I know we weren't officially, but that was only because of one little detail. The rest of it was legitimate, at least for here, so why don't we say 'renewal of vows'?"

Milo stared at him, this too big a speech for first thing in the morning. "Yeah," she said slowly. "I like that better, too. Though, the vows they have here are a bit freaky."

Simon said that was true, and that it all revolved around the laws. Milo nodded, rolling her eyes. They got up, roused Ajsha, and the three quickly ate breakfast. Each bathed, Simon going last, since he didn't need as much time to get dressed. Ajsha put on her dress first and then went into Milo's room to help her.

"Thanks, darling. You're such a little fashion bug," Milo told Ajsha as she circled her, smoothing out her skirt. "I saw those drawings in your room. You've got some good ideas, girl."

"Thank you, Momma," Ajsha said, blushing vibrantly at the praise. "I don't think I want to be a psychiatrist anymore; clothes are more fun. Let me see, now . . . both necklaces."

Milo put on the necklaces Squelch and Ajsha had given her, rather than the mother of pearl set she has worn before. She also donned the cat, mouse, cheese bracelet Simon had given to her for Christmas. Embellishments complete, she examined herself in front of the mirror, nodding.

"What do you think, Bob?" she said, not caring that the necklaces didn't match her dress.

"Why!" he cried with surprise. "Are you really asking *me?*"

"Do I know any other Bob the Conscience who lives inside my head?" she inquired.

If he had a face, he would have smiled. "You look lovely," he said earnestly. "And you'd better not know any other! I'm so proud of you. You should wear your hair down for your mother."

"Aren't you just full of useful advice?" she said rudely, but let it fall to her shoulders anyway.

A little while later, when Ajsha was elsewhere, most likely overseeing some last minute wedding prep, Simon came in. He was a bit stiff, since his mother had been kind enough to starch his suit with arrowroot, but was still in an exceptionally good mood.

"You look so beautiful," he sighed, grinning as he looked her over.

"Thanks, Si," she murmured, using a recently adapted nickname. "You look just precious."

He rolled his eyes, but continued to grin. "Anything you need?" he asked. "Or want?"

She pondered for a minute and said, "Yeah. Sing me 'Hush'."

He nodded, happy to comply. The romantic song "Hush" came forth from his throat and Milo smiled. Not only was it her favorite song of all time, it was also the song that knocked down that barrier between Simon and her heart, making it more sacred than ever. It seemed right to kick off such a day with it. She gazed lovingly at Simon as he mimicked it, letting the words speak to her. They slowly came together and danced, letting the anticipation make their hearts beat in loud unison, before a horde of frenzied bride's maids and groom's men barged in on their serenity and whisked them away.

They were escorted to the wedding site in a clustered sort of procession, the bride and groom both being surrounded by their respected parties and only catching glimpses of each other the entire trip. The village was eerily quiet, all the shops closed and houses empty, every citizen having already flocked to the site. Milo could see farm wagons parked off in the outskirts, the oxen waiting placidly for their owners' return. As she was bustled past, Milo wondered if the farmers and villagers ever really came together for any special occasion. Based on the stories she had heard from Squelch, she was guessing they did not, and that this was a singular kind of event.

It was now easy to locate the wedding area, due to its cumulative rows and rows of chairs that stretched into the distance and varied from stuffed to wooden, whatever could be carried. A length of white, glossy fabric lay in the middle of the sea of seats, vivid against the green grass, and led up to the altar. It had been continuously extended throughout the morning to compensate for the growing number of seats, so that it wasn't one solid piece of material, but many overlapping each other. Milo was made to halt at the start of it, where, after some last minute dress tweaking, the bride's maid lined up to be escorted down the aisle by the groom's men. Simon had quickly waved goodbye to Milo before being sent to stand by the reverend.

Milo had enlisted the musicians who played at dances, and they were now grouped far off to the side, waiting for their cue to start. Gripping her bouquet of pampas grass tightly, Milo inhaled deeply and nodded to them. A soft, sweet melody began to float through the air, silencing any excited mutterings. The bridesmaids, dressed in red, went first, splitting with the groom's men upon reaching the alter to stand in their designated spots.

Milo watched them go, briefly scanning the mass of heads. Milo's mother, dressed in violet, was sitting in the front row with Aunt Rosario and Mayor Em-I. Soldier was not far behind them, being a close friend. The Pitts sat in the opposite row, looking bemused yet proud. The Fittler gang was there, this time devoid of threatening weapons, as well as Squelch's family and Otto Gauls, who was obviously trying to keep his cool around so many people by staring raptly at Salsa.

Ajsha went next, scattering red hibiscus petals on the white path. Milo's father came up to her.

"Nervous, hon?" he asked bravely, evidently hoping he wasn't alone.

"Yes," she admitted. "But at least I'm not scared. Or mutinous. How you holding up?"

"Oh. I'll be all right," he squeaked. "I'm excited! You look beautiful. Underage, but beautiful. You're, uh, mom has a camera, so we'll bring you some pictures once we get them developed."

"Yeah," Milo said, latching onto the opportunity. "That's something I need to talk to you about. Later, though. Right now, I'm ready to say I do. Again."

"Right, hon," he said, holding his arm out to her. "Looks like they're ready for us."

Everyone had stood up and was gazing at her. Squelch and Salsa looked like they would explode from suppressing their excitement. Milo took her father's arm and began the walk down the aisle. If you actually want it, walking down the aisle can be quite exhilarating and pleasurable. People are smiling at you, and you are smiling back. At least Milo was. She was grinning without having to think about it, her lips acted of their own accord. What else could she do? She was happy. Yes, getting married was making her happy.

Looking up at the altar, she saw Simon. Simon. He was her goal. Her job was to get to him. He was her future. He was her cure. He was her reason. He was her love.

"He's your Boo," Bob the Conscience sang out, infected by the romantic atmosphere.

They finally reached the altar, after an uncommonly long saunter down the aisle, and Milo's father gave her hand to Simon. They stood in front of the reverend, staring at each other's faces, Milo's mother's camera flashing madly. As the Reverend Chouhouse spoke, Milo gazed at Simon intently. He batted his eyelashes playfully at her. She almost laughed. Ajsha was faithfully translating everything that was said. When they came to the vows, Ajsha translated back what Milo repeated. They were the same vows as before, only this time they held actual meaning.

At last, the reverend turned to Simon and asked him that illustrious question. Simon, aglow with inner bliss, said, "I do," first in English and then in Galo. The reverend then turned to Milo.

"He says," Ajsha whispered by her elbow, "'Do you, Milo Pereta Hestler, take Simon Adam Swallow to be your lawfully wedded husband?'"

Milo grinned proudly and answered, "I do."

Those binding words. Oh, but how Milo loved them! Now.

The reverend smiled when Ajsha relayed this reply and pronounced the two husband and wife, (adding, "again") and then gave Simon permission to kiss her. He smirked and drew her in. As she smelled his milky breath, she got an idea. As their lips collided, she slowly pushed her tongue into his mouth, so that hers come in slimy contact with his. Don't ask me why. It really wasn't appropriate timing, but it certainly pleased Simon, as well as surprised him. As they separated and everyone clapped, he gave her a smug, well – well – well look.

She grinned saucily at him, batting her eyelashes. He smiled and kissed her again, both of them jabbing their tongues back and forth and . . . please don't make me tell you about it anymore! Arm in arm, they walked back down the elongated aisle and past an ocean of faces; thankfully, this time no one threw any gifts. Milo's mother was still snapping pictures, her face tearstained.

When they reached the end, they waited for the rest to arrive. Once Squelch and the other females had gracefully traversed the white path, they gathered around Milo, talking.

"Oh, Milo!" Squelch said, hugging her. "You were so stunning! You were all right, too, Si."

"What are you talking about, dear?" Mrs. Lanslo said. "He was wonderful!"

Simon shrugged merrily, secretly hoping nobody had noticed they were French kissing.

"Yes," agreed Soldier, extracting himself from the flow of guests who were leaving with their chairs. "Well done, Simon. She's worth twice?"

"Ab – so – lute – ly," he said, wrapping his arms around her.

"Are we gonna party to – night!" Salsa sang out, performing a complex salsa move with an invisible partner. Within the crowd, Otto Gauls colored with jealousy for this partner.

"Oh, yes, sur!" Milo confirmed, laughing and reaching up to kiss Simon on the cheek.

Her parents suddenly appeared before them, chests puffed and lips trembling. Milo couldn't remember the last time they had looked that proud. Or proud at all.

"Milo," they began quietly.

They strode forward and kissed her.

"My heart's all swollen," her father croaked, wiping beneath his eyes.

"And I'm overjoyed," her mother said, stroking Milo's long, highlight-free hair, which was actually behaving itself and not obscuring her face. "You're the loveliest bride I've ever seen. But we really need to go. Sorry we can't stay for the party."

"Yeah," her father mumbled, still dabbing at his face. "Since we're such party maniacs."

"Oh," Milo said, rather stunned. She had expected them to at least stay for the reception. Oh, well. "Of course. Um, Simon, Ajsha. Let's go see them off."

A chorus of "Goodbye, Mr. and Mrs. Hestler!" rang out from the English speaking folk, and a symphony of "Deetic sru, Triv fes Trives Hestler!" from the Galo speaking folk. Milo kept them entertained by pitching her bouquet at them before going. The recently married ones and their daughter walked the in-laws down to the beach, where they had yet more things to discuss.

"Mom," Milo said seriously, once they were standing near the plane. "Dad. You need to understand something. You can't tell anyone about the island. No one."

"Why?" her mother asked, tilting her head in a way implied innocence, but was really stupidity.

"Tourists would come and destroy it," Milo told her simply, figuring it was best to be as bare-bones as possible.

"Ah yes!" her father exclaimed empathetically, making the Swallows jump. "Those darn tourists! Always parading around like they're entitled to everything they see! I understand, hon."

"You do?" she said, exchanging a shocked look with Simon and Ajsha.

"Yes, of course."

"Really?" she said in astonishment. She had expected it to be much harder, her parents never having been known for their understanding quality. What she didn't know was that in the past year her father had taken an intense dislike to tourists, another symptom of Penthouse Syndrome.

"So," Simon piped up. "You'll keep the island a secret? From everyone?"

"We won't tell a soul," Milo's mother assured him, patting his cheek. "And we will come back for visits! But, we'll make sure no one follows us. And even if they do, we'll just fly around to confuse them, and then lose them. After all, now that I have a grand-daughter, I want to see her often."

Ajsha smiled up at her. "And I want to see you, too," she said warmly. She had yet to tell anyone, but her nightmares had stopped.

"What a sweetheart!" Milo's father exclaimed. He looked at his watch. "Well, we'd best be leaving now. I have to report in for work at eight o'clock sharp tomorrow morning. It's a shame. I would have enjoyed catching up more with Rosario, if only that husband of hers wasn't such a hoverer. It feels weird leaving you here, hon; just when we found you."

Milo smiled reassuringly at them. "You'll be fine. Besides, after all this, I would absolutely hate living in an apartment building. I like having an ocean breeze blow across my face in the morning, know what I mean? And we'll see each other again, right?"

"For sure!" her mother said, reaching out to grasp her hand. "And not a soul will find out about this place. It will be like a family secret. Of course, we might have to destroy all your baby pictures, so that nobody asks where our daughter is . . ."

"Or," Milo quickly interjected, "you could bring them here."

"True," her mother mused, before sniffling and staring fondly at her daughter. "I'm so proud of you, Milo," she whispered, unable to speak any louder. "We did worry that your unstable childhood and, well . . . unrelenting nature would cause you to have problems when out on your own. But, you've proven yourself to be an amazing young woman. You've overcome adversity to find love and happiness. What more could parents ask for? Is there anything else you need from the mainland? Anything?"

"Well," Milo said thoughtfully. "You could bring over the rest of my clothes. Unless you threw them out?"

"No."

"Oh, good! Well, them, and two packages of triple a batteries. I'm running low on them. Oh! And some cheese. Actually, a lot of cheese. And macaroni. Yeah, if you could bring me copious amounts of both cheese and macaroni, I would be extremely happy. Ooh! And sugar. They really don't have a lot of sugar resources here, so if you could just bring a few ten pound bags, that'd be good. Yeah."

Leaning towards Simon, she muttered out of a corner of her mouth, "I'mma make you caramels."

Before he could respond, either vocally or with a confused glance, Milo's father spoke hastily.

"Very good," he said, still consulting his watch. "As you wish. Goodbye! Goodbye, Simon!"

"Goodbye," Simon said, shaking hands with him and then embracing Milo's mother.

"Goodbye," Ajsha joined in, hugging each in turn. "Fly safely."

They smiled, kissed her cheek, and faced Milo. "Goodbye, hon," her father said, fighting off intruding tears. "You're a Swallow now. Don't forget it, or that we love you."

"Goodbye," her mother said, gazing pleadingly at her for a split second. "We have changed."

"I know you have," Milo said, her throat swelling up. "Love you, too. Goodbye."

She wrapped her arms around the both of them, saying by touch what she couldn't say with words, and then pulled away hurriedly.

That all expressed, the Hestlers climbed into their private plane and turned it on, the roar of the engine filling all their ears. After letting it warm up, they circled around and took off. The Swallows waved as they watched it climb into the air. Then, Simon and Milo in each other's arms, they strolled down the beach, with Ajsha trailing behind. Mom and Dad Hestler watched them from the air, and if you too had been flying in the air that day, over that island, you would have seen them, too.

You would have seen them happily walking, arm in arm, with a dear child following behind. You would have seen them. On that island. That island which was once filled with hate, and was now full of love. The island of hate and love. The island of love and hate. Indeed, you would have seen on the Island of Lote, that day, two young, and one even younger, people walking off into their happily ever after.

CPSIA information can be obtained at www.ICGtesting.com
Printed in the USA
BVOW02s0624131214

378881BV00002B/4/P